'There are all sorts of writers of all sorts of nightmares, but M.R. James wrote the best ghost stories. He may well have created the ghost story in its current form. Nobody can do what he did as well as he could.'
Neil Gaiman

'I have given M.R. James the title of genius, an accolade which should not be lightly bestowed.'
Ruth Rendell

'A writer of great supernatural imagination, a master of style and purity . . . I believe that it is unlikely his ghost stories will ever be surpassed.'
Christopher Lee

'M.R. James is the most influential British writer of supernatural fiction.'
Ramsey Campbell

'His own subtle and oblique way of constructing narrative has been my dictum: less is more.'
Basil Copper

'M.R. James did more for the ghost story than any other writer. He raised the art of writing tales of terror to a new high level.'
Hugh Lamb

'Stylish, beautifully constructed, mountingly sinister and ultimately frightening tales.'
Peter Haining

'I was agreeably sensible of their eeriness . . . There is much invention shown in their construction.'
Thomas Hardy

'The name of Montague Rhodes James at once signifies the very best in ghost fiction.'
Mike Ashley

'The tales of M.R. James remain as entertaining, and as implausibly plausible, as ever.'
Michael Cox

'James is perhaps unsurpassed in originality by any living writer.'
Clark Ashton Smith

'The most frightening, learned and humorous ghost stories.'
Sir John Betjeman

'M.R. James is one of horror fiction's few class acts.'
Geoff Ryman

'A literary weird fictionist of the very first rank.'
H.P. Lovecraft

Also by M.R. James

SHORT STORY COLLECTIONS

Ghost-Stories of an Antiquary (1904)

More Ghost Stories of an Antiquary (1911)

A Thin Ghost and Others (1919)

Ander og Trolddom, translated by Ragnhild Undset (1919)

A Warning to the Curious and Other Ghost Stories (1925)

The Collected Ghost Stories of M.R. James (1931)

The Penguin Complete Ghost Stories of M.R. James (1931)

Thirteen Ghost Stories (1935)

Ghost Stories of an Antiquary (1937)

Best Ghost Stories of M.R. James (1944)

Three Ghosts, with H.G. Wells and Rudyard Kipling (1947)

More Ghost Stories (1959)

Ghost Stories of an Antiquary (1971)

Ghost Stories of M.R. James (1973)

The Complete Ghost Stories of M.R. James (1984)

Collected Ghost Stories (1985)

The Ghost Stories of M.R. James (1986)

'Casting the Runes' and Other Ghost Stories (1987)

A Warning to the Curious: The Ghost Stories of M.R. James (1987)

The Ghost Stories of M.R. James (1991)

Collected Ghost Stories (1992)

Room 13 and Other Ghost Stories: Elementary Level (1992)

Two Ghost Stories: A Centenary (1993)

Ghost Stories (1994)

The Haunted Dolls' House, with Robert Louis Stevenson (1995)

Selected Ghost Stories (1995)

A Warning to the Curious (1998)

Casting the Runes (1998)

The Fenstanton Witch and Others: M.R. James in Ghosts and Scholars (1999)

A Warning to the Curious (1999)

The Haunted Dolls' House and Other Stories (2000)

A Pleasing Terror: The Complete Supernatural Writings of M.R. James (2001)

Collected Ghost Stories (2002)

Count Magnus and Other Ghost Stories: The Complete Ghost Stories of M.R. James Vol.1 (2005)

The House in Picture and Abbott Thomas's Treasure: Beginner, with F.H. Cornish (2005)

The Haunted Dolls' House and Other
  Stories: The Complete Ghost
  Stories of M.R. James Vol.2 (2006)

Ghost Stories of an Antiquary (2006)

Collected Ghost Stories (2007)

Canon Alberic's Scrap-book (2011)

Collected Ghost Stories (2011)

SEPARATE PUBLICATIONS

The Five Jars (1922)

Wailing Well (1928)

The Five Jars (1976)

The Five Jars (1995)

MEMOIR

Eton and King's: Recollections,
  Mostly Trivial 1875–1925 (1926)

Eton and King's: Recollections,
  Mostly Trivial 1875–1925 (2006)

AS EDITOR

Madam Crowl's Ghost and Other
  Tales of Mystery, by Joseph
  Sheridan Le Fanu (1923)

AS TRANSLATOR

Hans Andersen: Forty Stories, by
  Hans Christian Andersen (1930)

The Little Mermaid, by Hans
  Christian Andersen (1935)

Hans Andersen: Forty-Two Stories, by
  Hans Christian Andersen (1953)

NON-FICTION

Some Remarks on Ghost Stories
  (1985)

INTRODUCTIONS

Ghost-Stories of an Antiquary (1904)

The Story of a Troll-Hunt, by James
  McBryde (1904)

More Ghost Stories of an Antiquary
  (1911)

A Thin Ghost and Others (1919)

The Lion's Birthday, by Emily
  Plenderleath Harrison (1920)

Madam Crowl's Ghost and Other
  Tales of Mystery, by Joseph
  Sheridan Le Fanu (1923)

Ghosts and Marvels, edited by V.H.
  Collins (1924)

A Warning to the Curious and Other
  Ghost Stories (1925)

Uncle Silas, by Joseph Sheridan Le
  Fanu (1926)

The Collected Ghost Stories of M.R.
  James (1931)

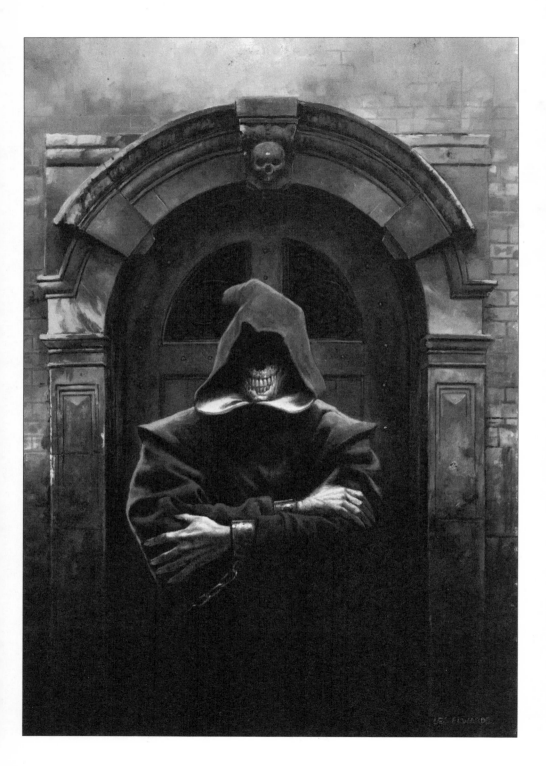

Curious Warnings

The Great Ghost Stories of

M.R. JAMES

150TH ANNIVERSARY EDITION

Edited with an Afterword by

STEPHEN JONES

Illustrated by

LES EDWARDS

Jo Fletcher

BOOKS

First published in Great Britain in 2012 by

Jo Fletcher Books
an imprint of Quercus
55 Baker Street
7th Floor, South Block
London
W1U 8EW

A CIP catalogue reference for this book is available
from the British Library

ISBN 978 0 85738 804 9

10 9 8 7 6 5 4 3 2 1

Text design and typesetting by Lindsay Nash
Printed and bound in Great Britain by Clays Ltd, St Ives plc

For more information about M.R. James and his fiction,
Go to the *Ghosts & Scholars* website:

www.pardoes.info/roanddarroll/GS.html

Contents

Editor's Note	xv
Ghosts – Treat Them Gently!	1
Ghost Stories	5
Canon Alberic's Scrap-book	9
Lost Hearts	22
The Ash-tree	34
Count Magnus	48
The Mezzotint	62
Number 13	74
'Oh, Whistle, and I'll Come to You, My Lad'	90
The Treasure of Abbot Thomas	110
The Stalls of Barchester Cathedral	129
Casting the Runes	147
Martin's Close	170
Mr. Humphreys and His Inheritance	194
The Rose Garden	222
A School Story	235
The Tractate Middoth	243
The Story of a Disappearance and an Appearance	260
An Episode of Cathedral History	275
The Diary of Mr. Poynter	292
The Residence at Whitminster	304
Two Doctors	331
The Uncommon Prayer-book	340
The Five Jars	356
I: The Discovery	356
II: The First Jar	364

III: The Second Jar 368

IV: The Small People 373

V: Danger to the Jars 382

VI: The Cat, Wag, Slim and Others 391

VII: The Bat-Ball 400

VIII: Wag at Home 407

The Haunted Dolls' House 415

A Neighbour's Landmark 427

After Dark in the Playing Fields 440

There Was a Man Dwelt by a Churchyard 445

A View from a Hill 450

A Warning to the Curious 468

An Evening's Entertainment 487

Wailing Well 499

Rats 510

The Experiment: A New Year's Eve Ghost Story 518

The Malice of Inanimate Objects 524

A Vignette 529

The Bulbul and the Cuckoo: An Indian Folk Tale 535

Stories I Have Tried to Write 537

A Night in King's College Chapel 540

The Fenstanton Witch 546

John Humphreys 557

Marcilly-le-Hayer 571

The Game of Bear 575

Speaker Lenthall's Tomb 579

Merfield House 589

Living Night 594

Some Remarks on Ghost Stories 596

Afterword: 'The Stony Grin of Unearthly Malice'
by Stephen Jones 605

Acknowledgements

Special thanks, as always, go to my editor and publisher Jo Fletcher, Val and Les Edwards, Nicola Budd, Lindsay Nash, Peter Gibbs, Colin Murray, Hugh Lamb, Neil Gaiman, Johnny Mains, Robert Lloyd Parry, Reggie Oliver, Jim Bryant, Simon Ball, Nicholas Rhodes James, Richard Dalby, the late Michael Cox and, especially, Rosemary Pardoe, for all their help and support.

'Editor's Note' copyright © Stephen Jones 2012.

'Ghosts – Treat Them Gently!', first published in *The Evening News*, 17 April 1931.

'Ghost Stories', first published in *The Eton Rambler* No. 2, 18 May 1880 and *The Eton Rambler* No. 4, 21 June 1880.

'Canon Alberic's Scrap-book', first published under the title 'The Scrap-book of Canon Alberic' in *National Review* Vol. XXV, No. 145, March 1895.

'Lost Hearts', first published in *Pall Mall Magazine*, Vol. VII, No. 32, December 1895.

'The Ash-tree', first published in *Ghost-Stories of an Antiquary* (1904).

'Count Magnus', first published in *Ghost-Stories of an Antiquary* (1904).

'The Mezzotint', first published in *Ghost-Stories of an Antiquary* (1904).

'Number 13', first published in *Ghost-Stories of an Antiquary* (1904).

'"Oh, Whistle, and I'll Come to You, My Lad"', first published in *Ghost-Stories of an Antiquary* (1904).

'The Treasure of Abbot Thomas', first published in *Ghost-Stories of an Antiquary* (1904).

'The Stalls of Barchester Cathedral', first published under the title 'The Stalls of Barchester Cathedral: Materials for a Ghost Story' in *Contemporary Review* Vol. XCVII, No. 35, 1910.

'Casting the Runes', first published in *More Ghost Stories of an Antiquary* (1911).

'Martin's Close', first published in *More Ghost Stories of an Antiquary* (1911).

'Mr. Humphreys and His Inheritance', first published in *More Ghost Stories of an Antiquary* (1911).

'The Rose Garden', first published in *More Ghost Stories of an Antiquary* (1911).

'A School Story', first published in *More Ghost Stories of an Antiquary* (1911).

'The Tractate Middoth', first published in *More Ghost Stories of an Antiquary* (1911).

'The Story of a Disappearance and an Appearance', first published in *Cambridge Review*, 4 June 1913.

'An Episode of Cathedral History', first published in *Cambridge Review*, 10 June 1914.

'The Diary of Mr. Poynter', first published in *A Thin Ghost and Others* (1919).

'The Residence at Whitminster', first published in *A Thin Ghost and Others* (1919).

'Two Doctors', first published in *A Thin Ghost and Others* (1919).

'The Uncommon Prayer-book', first published in *Atlantic Monthly*, Vol. 127, No. 6, June 1921.

'The Five Jars', first published in 1922.

'The Haunted Dolls' House', first published in *Empire Review*, Vol. XXXVIII, No. 265, February 1923.

'A Neighbour's Landmark', first published in *The Eton Chronic*, 17 March 1924.

'After Dark in the Playing Fields', first published in *College Days*, No. 10, 28 June 1924.

'There Was a Man Dwelt by a Churchyard', first published in *Snapdragon*, 6 December 1924.

'A View from a Hill', first published in *London Mercury*, Vol. XII, No. 67, May 1925.

'A Warning to the Curious', first published in *London Mercury*, Vol. XII, No. 70, August 1925.

'An Evening's Entertainment', first published in *A Warning to the Curious* (1925).

'Wailing Well', first published in 1928.

'Rats', first published in *At Random*, 23 March 1929.

'The Experiment: A New Year's Eve Ghost Story', first published in *Morning Post*, 31 December 1931.

'The Malice of Inanimate Objects', first published in *The Masquerade*, No. 1, June 1933.

'A Vignette', first published in *The London Mercury and Bookman*, No. 35, November 1936.

'The Bulbul and the Cuckoo: An Indian Folk Tale' (aka 'The Story of the

Editor's Note

M.R. JAMES was a wonderful storyteller, but he was not much of a stylist. Well, he *was* a stylist – but he wrote in a unique style that was very much all his own.

The marvellous thing about language is that it is always changing, and the way in which stories were written in James' time – in some cases more than 100 years ago now – is very different to how fiction is presented to today's readers. Not just certain words or phrases which have passed out of popular usage, but with the application of spelling and punctuation as well.

While re-reading the author's classic supernatural stories in preparation for compiling this present collection of his work, the possibility struck me that he had never really been properly edited before. It is more than likely – especially given James' stated resistance initially to having his work collected in print form – that the original publications of his work were mostly set from the 'rough' manuscripts he had prepared for his annual Christmas readings to a select audience.

As anyone who is used to public speaking knows, a script can be very different to a page of prose – the 'beats' and timbre of reading aloud are not always the same as a carefully constructed piece of fiction.

With his run-on paragraphs, multiple viewpoints, sequential dialogue exchanges, narratives within narratives and frankly eccentric use of punctuation and spelling, it became very apparent to me that although these stories were written to be performed aloud, they were not necessarily presented in the best way to be read on the printed page. Yet this is exactly how they have always been published since the late 19th century onwards.

So, after consulting a number of experts in the field, I have elected, for this new edition of M.R. James' work, to re-punctuate his fiction for a modern audience. I realise that this might be an extremely controversial decision amongst enthusiasts, but the avowed intent of these books is to bring classic works to the attention of contemporary readers, and by making the tales herein more accessible – without cutting a single word of the author's original version – I can only hope that these wonderful ghost stories will go on to chill generations of new readers for another century and more.

For those who might accuse me of vandalising the sacred text, I can only say that I do have some experience of editing horror fiction and, in my opinion, these minor changes bring out the true power of James' writing and the often remarkable and disturbing images that he created.

No longer are his wit, erudition or pleasing terrors lost amongst pages and pages of unbroken print, complicated sentences and protracted paragraphs. Letters, manuscripts and inscriptions are now clearly delineated within the body of the narrative and are presented here in a manner that simply clarifies the complex structure and manifold narratives employed within many of these stories.

If anything, these modifications have allowed me to appreciate even more what a fine – and truly influential – writer M.R. James was. It is my hope that the same will be true of the reader.

For those who want the original versions – exactly as they were first published (but not necessarily as the author may have intended them, had he given more thought to the process) – then there are plenty of different editions of his work out there that contain exactly that.

But for those who wish to perhaps rediscover what a remarkable and, I'm delighted to say, *still relevant* author M.R. James is to the modern horror genre, then I trust that you will at least give this present volume a chance.

It goes without saying, of course, that any faults are mine and not the author's.

Stephen Jones
London, England
September, 2011

Ghosts – Treat Them Gently!

THEIR MOST FAMOUS CREATOR EXPLAINS
HOW TO GET THE BEST OUT OF THEM

WHAT FIRST INTERESTED me in ghosts? This I can tell you quite definitely. In my childhood I chanced to see a toy Punch and Judy set, with figures cut out in cardboard. One of these was The Ghost. It was a tall figure habited in white with an unnaturally long and narrow head, also surrounded with white, and a dismal visage.

Upon this my conceptions of a ghost were based, and for years it permeated my dreams.

Other questions – why I like ghost stories, or what are the best, or why they are the best, or a recipe for writing such things – I have never found it easy to be so positive about. Clearly, however, the public likes them. The recrudescence of ghost stories in recent years is notable: it corresponds, of course, with the vogue of the detective tale.

The ghost story can be supremely excellent in its kind, or it may be deplorable. Like other things, it may err by excess or defect. Bram Stoker's *Dracula* is a book with very good ideas in it, but – to be vulgar – the butter is spread far too thick. Excess is the fault here: to give an example of erring by defect is difficult, because the stories that err in that way leave no impression on the memory.

I am speaking of the literary ghost story here. The story that claims to be 'veridical' (in the language of the Society of Psychical Research) is a very different affair. It will probably be quite brief, and will conform to some one of several familiar types. This is but reasonable, for, if there be ghosts – as I am quite prepared to believe – the true ghost story need do no more than illustrate their normal habits (if normal is the right word), and may be as mild as milk.

The literary ghost, on the other hand, has to justify his existence by some startling demonstration, or, short of that, must be furnished with a background that will throw him into full relief and make him the central feature.

Since the things which the ghost can effectively do are very limited in number, ranging about death and madness and the discovery of secrets, the setting seems to me all-important, since in it there is the greatest opportunity for variety.

It is upon this and upon the first glimmer of the appearance of the supernatural that pains must be lavished. But we need not, we should not, use all the colours in the box. In the infancy of the art we needed the haunted castle on a beetling rock to put us in the right frame: the tendency is not yet extinct, for I have but just read a story with a mysterious mansion on a desolate height in Cornwall and a gentleman practising the worst sort of magic. How often, too, have ruinous old houses been described or shown to me as fit scenes for stories!

'Can't you imagine some old monk or friar wandering about this long gallery?' No, I can't.

I know Harrison Ainsworth could: *The Lancashire Witches* teems with Cistercians and what he calls votaresses in mouldering vestments, who glide about passages to very little purpose. But these fail to impress. Not that I have not a soft corner in my heart for *The Lancashire Witches*, which – ridiculous as much of it is – has distinct merits as a story.

It cannot be said too often that the more remote in time the ghost is the harder it is to make him effective, always supposing him to be the ghost of a dead person. Elementals and such-like do not come under this rule.

Roughly speaking, the ghost should be a contemporary of the seer. Such was the elder Hamlet and such Jacob Marley. The latter I cite with confidence and in despite of critics, for, whatever may be urged against some parts of *A Christmas Carol*, it is, I hold, undeniable that the introduction, the advent, of Jacob Marley is tremendously effective.

And be it observed that the setting in both these classic examples is contemporary and even ordinary. The ramparts of the Kronborg and the chambers of Ebenezer Scrooge were, to those who frequented them, features of everyday life.

But there are exceptions to every rule. An ancient haunting can be made terrible and can be invested with actuality, but it will tax your best endeavours to forge the links between past and present in a satisfying way. And in any case there must be ordinary level-headed modern persons – Horatios – on the scene, such as the detective needs his Watson or his Hastings to play the part of the lay observer.

Setting or environment, then, is to me a principal point, and the more readily appreciable the setting is to the ordinary reader the better. The other essential is that our ghost should make himself felt by gradual stirrings diffusing an atmosphere of uneasiness before the final flash or stab of horror.

Must there be horror? you ask. I think so. There are but two really good ghost stories I know in the language wherein the elements of beauty and pity dominate terror. They are Lanoe Falconer's 'Cecilia de Noel' and Mrs. Oliphant's 'The Open Door'. In both there are moments of horror; but in both we end by saying with Hamlet: 'Alas, poor ghost!' Perhaps my limit of two stories is overstrict; but that these two are by very much the best of their kind I do not doubt.

On the whole, then, I say you must have horror and also malevolence. Not less necessary, however, is reticence. There is a series of books I have read, I think American in origin, called *Not at Night* (and with other like titles), which sin glaringly against this law. They have no other aim than that of Mr. Wardle's Fat Boy.

Of course, all writers of ghost stories do desire to make their readers' flesh creep; but these are shameless in their attempts. They are unbelievably crude and sudden, and they wallow in corruption. And if there is a theme that ought to be kept out of the ghost story, it is that of the charnel house. That and sex, wherein I do not say that these *Not at Night* books deal, but certainly other recent writers do, and in so doing spoil the whole business.

To return from the faults of ghost stories to their excellence. Who, do I think, has best realised their possibilities? I have no hesitation in saying that it is Joseph Sheridan Le Fanu. In the volume called *In a Glass Darkly* are four stories of paramount excellence, 'Green Tea', 'The Familiar', 'Mr. Justice Harbottle', and 'Carmilla'. All of these conform to my requirements: the settings are quite different, but all *seen* by the writer; the approaches of the supernatural nicely graduated; the climax adequate. Le Fanu was a scholar and poet, and these tales show him as such. It is true that he died as long ago as 1873, but there is wonderfully little that is obsolete in his manner.

Of living writers I have some hesitation in speaking, but on any list that I was forced to compile the names of E.F. Benson. Blackwood, Burrage, De la Mare and Wakefield would find a place.

But, although the subject has its fascinations, I see no use in being pontifical about it. These stories are meant to please and amuse us. If they do so, well; but, if not, let us relegate them to the top shelf and say no more about it.

M. R. James.

Ghost Stories

I

EVERYONE, I THINK, has an innate love of the supernatural. Everyone can remember a time when he has carefully searched his curtains – and poked in the dark corners of his room before retiring to rest – with a sort of pleasurable uncertainty as to whether there might not be a saucer-eyed skeleton or a skinny-sheeted ghoul in hiding somewhere.

I invariably go through this ceremony myself. Of course we all know there are no such things – but someone might be going to play us a trick, you know; and anyhow it's best to be quite sure.

People do tell such very odd stories. Such is the substance of most people's expressed views about ghosts, as heard either in the course of conversation, or in debating – where the subject is discussed on the average once in two halves – and the opener is credulous, and 'every speaker tells his tale', and one audacious mortal opposes – rarely more. I pity that rash individual when he seeks his couch.

Some classes of ghost stories it is very hard, seriously speaking, not to believe. Omens, Family Tokens and Forewarnings are of this sort.

Here is one, 'never before published', told me by an old man 'who was there at the time'. I suppress names.

In the early part of last century, the wife of the squire of a certain village was driving across her park on the way to a county ball. The evening was grey and misty. [This goes without saying.]

5

Suddenly she looked out of the carriage window and '*saw suffen*'; as to what the something was my old man would not venture a statement. I gathered, however, that it was the lady's 'double'.

One of the horses broke loose, the other turned straight back to the Hall.

The lady never went out of the house again except in her coffin. [Impressive silence.] Of course my informant didn't go to believe no such thing; but still, there was the story.

One really authentic one, which I fear a good many people must know, and I will lay my unquiet pen.

To be short: General Blucher was returning home alone from the wars. On entering the house he saw, sitting at the fire in a peculiar attitude, his parents – long since dead, and his sisters sitting round the room.

On greeting them he received no answer.

One of his sisters rose and touched him. He swooned, and when he came to himself was alone.

He was for some days delirious, but in a lucid interval, feeling himself at the point of death, he sent for his sovereign, told him the facts: said his sister had warned him he was to die that day, and so expired.

The aspect of my furniture is so terrific at this point that I really must stop.

II

I am painfully aware that my last effort on this subject was meagre and abrupt in the extreme. But this, I have no doubt, everyone who took the trouble to read it, perceived for himself.

It strikes me after a perusal of several books of tales of the supernatural, that no really adequate collection of them has yet appeared; including, as it should, the best both of fiction and of real life. Such a book would be almost as hard to produce as a good hymn book.

First, the compiler must be particular in his choice, for the numberless 'well authenticated' ghost stories one meets with in the ordinary collections have a certain sameness about them which tells after awhile.

We all know how, in 18—, Mrs. C—, a respectable lady residing in the small town of D—, was one day sitting by an open window looking out into a small garden in front of the house; and how she saw her nephew – at that moment in India – walking up a gravel path leading to the front door; and how she exclaimed 'That's Johnny', when he instantly disappeared; and how the next mail brought the news of his death, which had occurred at the precise moment at which she had seen the apparition.

So much for the commonest form of story.

It is desirable, too, that the teller of these tales should assume the tone of one who believes in the truth of what he is relating. (I fear, by the way, that I have transgressed my own rule.)

And he should stoop occasionally to the incredible, by which I mean the sort of tale which deals in blood and bones, and sheeted spectres, and other phenomena in the nature of walking undertakers' advertisements, though the term 'incredible' must not be understood to apply to the following story, for which I can produce perfectly unexceptionable evidence, possessing as I do, an intimate acquaintance with the sources and reliability of 'all and sundry the incidents therein contained and expressed as hereinafter followeth':

A 'belated wanderer' arrived at a country village too late to procure a lodging for the night. As the season was summer, and the night fine, he determined to sleep out-of-doors, and actuated by some inexplicable impulse, he pitched his camp in the churchyard.

He laid himself down under a buttress on the north side of the building, and in blissful ignorance of the fact that he was surrounded by the graves of murderers and suicides (who were there, as is often the case, buried on the north side of the church), he fell asleep.

After awhile he awoke with a dim and unpleasant consciousness that something was pulling at his clothes. Rather startled at this, he hastily got up and looked round him.

Above him the moon was shining, through the windows of the tower, and the bells stood out sharply and clearly against it. Beyond the churchyard he could see hills and woods, and in the valley below him a broad still mere on which the moon was shining.

So after admiring the view for some minutes he was just composing himself to sleep again, when the moonlight caught an object nearer to him – almost at his feet in fact.

Nothing less than two glassy eyes belonging to a form that crouched there in the long grass. It was covered with what looked like a stained and tattered shroud, and he could dimly discern its long skinny-clawed hands, eager, as it seemed, to grasp something.

Further particulars did not possess sufficient interest to detain him. The terms 'walked', 'ran', or even 'proceeded' are scarcely adequate to express the pace at which he put distance between himself and the churchyard.

Suffice it to say he left.

I began this paper with the intention of recounting in it several narratives of a thrilling nature, but space forbids. I can only apologise for the deceptive title and incoherent contents of what I have written, and make an end *quam celerrime*.

Canon Alberic's Scrap-book

ST. BERTRAND DE COMMINGES is a decayed town on the spurs of the Pyrenees, not very far from Toulouse, and still nearer to Bagnères-de-Luchon. It was the site of a bishopric until the Revolution, and has a cathedral which is visited by a certain number of tourists.

In the spring of 1883 an Englishman arrived at this old-world place – I can hardly dignify it with the name of city, for there are not a thousand inhabitants. He was a Cambridge man, who had come specially from Toulouse to see St. Bertrand's Church, and had left two friends, who were less keen archaeologists than himself, in their hotel at Toulouse, under promise to join him on the following morning. Half-an-hour at the church would satisfy *them*, and all three could then pursue their journey in the direction of Auch.

But our Englishman had come early on the day in question, and proposed to himself to fill a notebook and to use several dozens of plates in the process of describing and photographing every corner of the wonderful church that dominates the little hill of Comminges.

In order to carry out this design satisfactorily, it was necessary to monopolise the verger of the church for the day. The verger or sacristan (I prefer the latter appellation, inaccurate as it may be) was accordingly sent for by the somewhat brusque lady who keeps the inn of the Chapeau Rouge. And when he came, the Englishman found him an unexpectedly interesting object of study.

It was not in the personal appearance of the little, dry, wizened old man that the interest lay, for he was precisely like dozens of other church-guardians in France, but in a curious furtive, or rather hunted and oppressed, air which he had. He was perpetually half-glancing behind him; the muscles of his back and shoulders seemed to be hunched in a continual nervous contraction, as if he were expecting every moment to find himself in the clutch of an enemy.

The Englishman hardly knew whether to put him down as a man haunted by a fixed delusion, or as one oppressed by a guilty conscience, or as an unbearably henpecked husband.

The probabilities, when reckoned up, certainly pointed to the last idea. But, still, the impression conveyed was that of a more formidable persecutor even than a termagant wife.

However, the Englishman (let us call him Dennistoun) was soon too deep in his notebook and too busy with his camera to give more than an occasional glance to the sacristan.

Whenever he did look at him, he found him at no great distance, either huddling himself back against the wall or crouching in one of the gorgeous stalls.

Dennistoun became rather fidgety after a time. Mingled suspicions that he was keeping the old man from his *déjeuner*, that he was regarded as likely to make away with St. Bertrand's ivory crozier, or with the dusty stuffed crocodile that hangs over the font, began to torment him.

'Won't you go home?' he said at last; 'I'm quite well able to finish my notes alone. You can lock me in if you like. I shall want at least two hours more here, and it must be cold for you, isn't it?'

'Good Heavens!' said the little man, whom the suggestion seemed to throw into a state of unaccountable terror, 'such a thing cannot be thought of for a moment. Leave *monsieur* alone in the church? No, no. Two hours, three hours, all will be the same to me. I have breakfasted, I am not at all cold, with many thanks to *monsieur*.'

'Very well, my little man,' quoth Dennistoun to himself. 'You have been warned, and you must take the consequences.'

Before the expiration of the two hours, the stalls, the enormous dilapidated organ, the choir-screen of Bishop John de Mauléon, the remnants of glass and tapestry, and the objects in the treasure-chamber, had been well and truly examined – the sacristan still keeping at Dennistoun's heels, and every now and then whipping round as if he had been stung, when one or other of the strange noises that trouble a large empty building fell on his ear. Curious noises they were sometimes.

'Once,' Dennistoun said to me, 'I could have sworn I heard a thin metallic voice laughing high up in the tower. I darted an inquiring glance at my sacristan. He was white to the lips.

'"It is he – that is – it is no one. The door is locked," was all he said, and we looked at each other for a full minute.'

Another little incident puzzled Dennistoun a good deal. He was examining a large dark picture that hangs behind the altar, one of a series illustrating the miracles of St. Bertrand. The composition of the picture is well-nigh indecipherable, but there is a Latin legend below, which runs thus:

Qualiter S. Bertrandus liberavit hominem quem
diabolus diu volebat strangulare.
(How St. Bertrand delivered a man whom
the Devil long sought to strangle.)

Dennistoun was turning to the sacristan with a smile and a jocular remark of some sort on his lips, but he was confounded to see the old man on his knees, gazing at the picture with the eye of a suppliant in agony, his hands tightly clasped, and a rain of tears on his cheeks.

Dennistoun naturally pretended to have noticed nothing, but the question would not away from him, 'Why should a daub of this kind affect anyone so strongly?' He seemed to himself to be getting some sort of clue to the reason of the strange look that had been puzzling him all the day. The man must be a monomaniac, but what was his monomania?

It was nearly five o'clock. The short day was drawing in, and the church began to fill with shadows, while the curious noises – the muffled footfalls and distant talking voices that had been perceptible all day – seemed, no doubt because of the fading light and the consequently quickened sense of hearing, to become more frequent and insistent.

The sacristan began for the first time to show signs of hurry and impatience. He heaved a sigh of relief when camera and notebook were finally packed up and stowed away, and hurriedly beckoned Dennistoun to the western door of the church, under the tower.

It was time to ring the Angelus. A few pulls at the reluctant rope, and the great bell Bertrande, high in the tower, began to speak, and swung her voice up among the pines and down to the valleys, loud with mountain-streams, calling the dwellers on those lonely hills to remember and repeat the salutation of the angel to her whom he called Blessed among women.

With that a profound quiet seemed to fall for the first time that day upon the little town, and Dennistoun and the sacristan went out of the church.

On the doorstep they fell into conversation.

'*Monsieur* seemed to interest himself in the old choir-books in the sacristy.'

'Undoubtedly. I was going to ask you if there were a library in the town.'

'No, *monsieur*. Perhaps there used to be one belonging to the Chapter, but it is now such a small place—' Here came a strange pause of irresolution, as it seemed. Then, with a sort of plunge, he went on: 'But if *monsieur* is amateur *des vieux livres*, I have at home something that might interest him. It is not a hundred yards.'

At once all Dennistoun's cherished dreams of finding priceless manuscripts in untrodden corners of France flashed up, to die down again the next moment. It was probably a stupid missal of Plantin's printing, about 1580. Where was the likelihood that a place so near Toulouse would not have been ransacked long ago by collectors?

However, it would be foolish not to go – he would reproach himself for ever after if he refused. So they set off. On the way the curious irresolution and sudden determination of the sacristan recurred to Dennistoun, and he wondered in a shamefaced way whether he was being decoyed into some purlieu to be made away with as a supposed rich Englishman.

He contrived, therefore, to begin talking with his guide, and to drag in, in a rather clumsy fashion, the fact that he expected two friends to join him early the next morning.

To his surprise, the announcement seemed to relieve the sacristan at once of some of the anxiety that oppressed him. 'That is well,' he said quite brightly – 'that is very well. *Monsieur* will travel in company with his friends. They will be always near him. It is a good thing to travel thus in company – sometimes.'

The last word appeared to be added as an afterthought, and to bring with it a relapse into gloom for the poor little man.

They were soon at the house, which was one rather larger than its neighbours, stone-built, with a shield carved over the door, the shield of Alberic de Mauléon, a collateral descendant, Dennistoun tells me, of Bishop John de Mauléon. This Alberic was a Canon of Comminges from 1680 to 1701. The upper windows of the mansion were boarded up, and the whole place bore, as does the rest of Comminges, the aspect of decaying age.

Arrived on his doorstep, the sacristan paused a moment.

'Perhaps,' he said, 'perhaps, after all, *monsieur* has not the time?'

'Not at all – lots of time – nothing to do till tomorrow. Let us see what it is you have got.'

The door was opened at this point, and a face looked out, a face far younger than the sacristan's, but bearing something of the same distressing look – only here it seemed to be the mark, not so much of fear for personal safety as of acute anxiety on behalf of another.

Plainly, the owner of the face was the sacristan's daughter; and, but for the expression I have described, she was a handsome girl enough. She brightened up considerably seeing her father accompanied by an able-bodied stranger.

A few remarks passed between father and daughter, of which Dennistoun only caught these words, said by the sacristan, 'He was laughing in the church,' words which were answered only by a look of terror from the girl.

But in another minute they were in the sitting-room of the house, a small, high chamber with a stone floor, full of moving shadows cast by a wood-fire that flickered on a great hearth.

Something of the character of an oratory was imparted to it by a tall cruci-fix, which reached almost to the ceiling on one side; the figure was painted of the natural colours, the cross was black. Under this stood a chest of some age and solidity, and when a lamp had been brought, and chairs set, the sac-ristan went to this chest, and produced therefrom, with growing excitement and nervousness, as Dennistoun thought, a large book, wrapped in a white cloth, on which cloth a cross was rudely embroidered in red thread.

Even before the wrapping had been removed, Dennistoun began to be interested by the size and shape of the volume. 'Too large for a missal,' he thought, 'and not the shape of an antiphoner; perhaps it may be something good, after all.'

The next moment the book was open, and Dennistoun felt that he had at last lit upon something better than good.

Before him lay a large folio, bound, perhaps, late in the 17th century, with the arms of Canon Alberic de Mauléon stamped in gold on the sides. There may have been a hundred and fifty leaves of paper in the book, and on almost every one of them was fastened a leaf from an illuminated manuscript.

Such a collection Dennistoun had hardly dreamed of in his wildest moments.

Here were ten leaves from a copy of Genesis, illustrated with pictures, which could not be later than A.D. 700. Further on was a complete set of pictures from a Psalter, of English execution, of the very finest kind that the 13th century could produce. And, perhaps best of all, there were twenty leaves of uncial writing in Latin, which, as a few words seen here and there told him at once, must belong to some very early unknown patristic treatise. Could it possibly be a fragment of the copy of Papias 'On the Words of Our Lord', which was known to have existed as late as the 12th century at Nîmes?[†]

In any case, his mind was made up; that book must return to Cambridge with him, even if he had to draw the whole of his balance from the bank and stay at St. Bertrand till the money came.

He glanced up at the sacristan to see if his face yielded any hint that the book was for sale. The sacristan was pale, and his lips were working.

'If *monsieur* will turn on to the end,' he said.

So *monsieur* turned on, meeting new treasures at every rise of a leaf; and at the end of the book he came upon two sheets of paper, of much more recent date than anything he had yet seen, which puzzled him considerably.

They must be contemporary, he decided, with the unprincipled Canon Alberic, who had doubtless plundered the Chapter library of St. Bertrand to form this priceless scrap-book.

---

† We now know that these leaves did contain a considerable fragment of that work, if not of that actual copy of it.

On the first of the paper sheets was a plan, carefully drawn and instantly recognisable by a person who knew the ground, of the south aisle and cloisters of St. Bertrand's. There were curious signs looking like planetary symbols, and a few Hebrew words, in the corners; and in the north-west angle of the cloister was a cross drawn in gold paint. Below the plan were some lines of writing in Latin, which ran thus:

Responsa 12mi Dec. 1694. Interrogatum est: Inveniamne?
Responsum est: Invenies. Fiamne dives? Fies. Vivamne invidendus?
Vives. Moriarne in lecto meo? Ita.
(Answers of the 12th of December, 1694. It was asked: Shall I find
it? Answer: Thou shalt. Shall I become rich? Thou wilt. Shall I live
an object of envy? Thou wilt. Shall I die in my bed? Thou wilt.)

'A good specimen of the treasure-hunter's record – quite reminds one of Mr. Minor-Canon Quatremain in "Old St. Paul's",' was Dennistoun's comment, and he turned the leaf.

What he then saw impressed him, as he has often told me, more than he could have conceived any drawing or picture capable of impressing him. And, though the drawing he saw is no longer in existence, there is a photograph of it (which I possess) which fully bears out that statement.

The picture in question was a sepia drawing at the end of the 17th century, representing, one would say at first sight, a Biblical scene. For the architecture (the picture represented an interior) and the figures had that semi-classical flavour about them which the artists of two hundred years ago thought appropriate to illustrations of the Bible.

On the right was a King on his throne, the throne elevated on twelve steps, a canopy overhead, lions on either side – evidently King Solomon. He was bending forward with outstretched sceptre, in attitude of command. His face expressed horror and disgust, yet there was in it also the mark of imperious will and confident power.

The left half of the picture was the strangest, however. The interest plainly centred there. On the pavement before the throne were grouped four soldiers, surrounding a crouching figure which must be described in a moment. A fifth soldier lay dead on the pavement, his neck distorted, and his eyeballs starting from his head. The four surrounding guards were looking at the King. In their faces the sentiment of horror was intensified. They seemed, in fact, only restrained from flight by their implicit trust in their master. All this terror was plainly excited by the being that crouched in their midst.

I entirely despair of conveying by any words the impression which this figure makes upon anyone who looks at it. I recollect once showing the photograph of the drawing to a lecturer on morphology – a person of, I was going to say, abnormally sane and unimaginative habits of mind. He absolutely refused to be alone for the rest of that evening, and he told me afterwards that for many nights he had not dared to put out his light before going to sleep.

However, the main traits of the figure I can at least indicate. At first you saw only a mass of coarse, matted black hair. Presently it was seen that this covered a body of fearful thinness, almost a skeleton, but with the muscles standing out like wires. The hands were of a dusky pallor, covered, like the body, with long, coarse hairs, and hideously taloned. The eyes, touched in with a burning yellow, had intensely black pupils, and were fixed upon the throned King with a look of beast-like hate. Imagine one of the awful bird-catching spiders of South America translated into human form, and endowed with intelligence just less than human, and you will have some faint conception of the terror inspired by this appalling effigy.

One remark is universally made by those to whom I have shown the picture: 'It was drawn from the life.'

As soon as the first shock of his irresistible fright had subsided, Dennistoun stole a look at his hosts. The sacristan's hands were pressed upon his eyes. His daughter, looking up at the cross on the wall, was telling her beads feverishly.

At last the question was asked, 'Is this book for sale?'

There was the same hesitation, the same plunge of determination that he had noticed before, and then came the welcome answer.

'If *monsieur* pleases.'

'How much do you ask for it?'

'I will take two hundred and fifty francs.'

This was confounding. Even a collector's conscience is sometimes stirred, and Dennistoun's conscience was tenderer than a collector's.

'My good man!' he said again and again, 'your book is worth far more than two hundred and fifty francs, I assure you – far more.'

But the answer did not vary: 'I will take two hundred and fifty francs, not more.'

There was really no possibility of refusing such a chance. The money was paid, the receipt signed, a glass of wine drunk over the transaction, and then the sacristan seemed to become a new man. He stood upright, he ceased to throw those suspicious glances behind him, he actually laughed or tried to laugh.

Dennistoun rose to go.

'I shall have the honour of accompanying *monsieur* to his hotel?' said the sacristan.

'Oh no, thanks! It isn't a hundred yards. I know the way perfectly, and there is a moon.'

The offer was pressed three or four times, and refused as often.

'Then, *monsieur* will summon me if – if he finds occasion. He will keep the middle of the road, the sides are so rough.'

'Certainly, certainly,' said Dennistoun, who was impatient to examine his prize by himself, and he stepped out into the passage with his book under his arm.

Here he was met by the daughter. She, it appeared, was anxious to do a little business on her own account – perhaps, like Gehazi, to 'take somewhat' from the foreigner whom her father had spared.

'A silver crucifix and chain for the neck. *Monsieur* would perhaps be good enough to accept it?'

Well, really, Dennistoun hadn't much use for these things. What did *mademoiselle* want for it?

'Nothing – nothing in the world. *Monsieur* is more than welcome to it.'

The tone in which this and much more was said was unmistakably genuine, so that Dennistoun was reduced to profuse thanks, and submitted to have the chain put round his neck. It really seemed as if he had rendered the father and daughter some service which they hardly knew how to repay.

As he set off with his book they stood at the door looking after him, and they were still looking when he waved them a last good night from the steps of the Chapeau Rouge.

Dinner was over, and Dennistoun was in his bedroom, shut up alone with his acquisition. The landlady had manifested a particular interest in him since he had told her that he had paid a visit to the sacristan and bought an old book from him.

He thought, too, that he had heard a hurried dialogue between her and the said sacristan in the passage outside the *salle à manger*, some words to the effect that 'Pierre and Bertrand would be sleeping in the house' had closed the conversation.

All this time a growing feeling of discomfort had been creeping over him – nervous reaction, perhaps, after the delight of his discovery. Whatever it was, it resulted in a conviction that there was someone behind him, and that he was far more comfortable with his back to the wall.

All this, of course, weighed light in the balance as against the obvious value of the collection he had acquired. And now, as I said, he was alone in his bedroom, taking stock of Canon Alberic's treasures, in which every moment revealed something more charming.

'Bless Canon Alberic!' said Dennistoun, who had an inveterate habit of talking to himself. 'I wonder where he is now? Dear me! I wish that landlady would learn to laugh in a more cheering manner – it makes one feel as if there was someone dead in the house.

'Half a pipe more, did you say? I think perhaps you are right. I wonder what that crucifix is that the young woman insisted on giving me? Last century, I suppose. Yes, probably. It is rather a nuisance of a thing to have round one's neck – just too heavy. Most likely her father had been wearing it for years. I think I might give it a clean up before I put it away.'

He had taken the crucifix off, and laid it on the table, when his attention was caught by an object lying on the red cloth just by his left elbow. Two or three ideas of what it might be flitted through his brain with their own incalculable quickness.

'A penwiper? No, no such thing in the house. A rat? No, too black. A large spider? I trust to goodness not – no. Good God! A hand like the hand in that picture!'

In another infinitesimal flash he had taken it in. Pale, dusky skin, covering nothing but bones and tendons of appalling strength; coarse black hairs, longer than ever grew on a human hand; nails rising from the ends of the fingers and curving sharply down and forward, grey, horny and wrinkled.

He flew out of his chair with deadly, inconceivable terror clutching at his heart. The shape, whose left hand rested on the table, was rising to a standing posture behind his seat, its right hand crooked above his scalp.

There was black and tattered drapery about it; the coarse hair covered it as in the drawing. The lower jaw was thin – what can I call it? – shallow, like a beast's; teeth showed behind the black lips; there was no nose; the eyes, of a fiery yellow, against which the pupils showed black and intense, and the exulting hate and thirst to destroy life which shone there, were the most horrifying features in the whole vision. There was intelligence of a kind in them – intelligence beyond that of a beast, below that of a man.

The feelings which this horror stirred in Dennistoun were the intensest physical fear and the most profound mental loathing.

What did he do? What could he do? He has never been quite certain what words he said, but he knows that he spoke, that he grasped blindly at the silver crucifix, that he was conscious of a movement towards him on the part of the demon, and that he screamed with the voice of an animal in hideous pain.

Pierre and Bertrand, the two sturdy little serving-men, who rushed in, saw nothing, but felt themselves thrust aside by something that passed out between them, and found Dennistoun in a swoon.

They sat up with him that night, and his two friends were at St. Bertrand by nine o'clock next morning. He himself, though still shaken and nervous, was almost himself by that time, and his story found credence with them, though not until they had seen the drawing and talked with the sacristan.

Almost at dawn the little man had come to the inn on some pretence, and had listened with the deepest interest to the story retailed by the land-lady. He showed no surprise.

'It is he – it is he! I have seen him myself,' was his only comment. And to all questionings but one reply was vouchsafed: '*Deux fois je l'ai vu; mille fois je l'ai senti.*' He would tell them nothing of the provenance of the book, nor any details of his experiences. 'I shall soon sleep, and my rest will be sweet. Why should you trouble me?' he said.[†]

[†] He died that summer; his daughter married, and settled at St. Papoul. She never understood the circumstances of her father's 'obsession'.

We shall never know what he or Canon Alberic de Mauléon suffered. At the back of that fateful drawing were some lines of writing which may be supposed to throw light on the situation:

Contradictio Salomonis cum demonio nocturno.
Albericus de Mauleone delineavit.
V. Deus in adiutorium. Ps. Qui habitat.
Sancte Bertrande, demoniorum effugator, intercede pro
me miserrimo.
Primum uidi nocte 12mi Dec. 1694: uidebo mox ultimum. Peccaui et
passus sum, plura adhuc passurus. Dec. 29, 1701.[†]

I have never quite understood what was Dennistoun's view of the events I have narrated. He quoted to me once a text from Ecclesiasticus: 'Some spirits there be that are created for vengeance, and in their fury lay on sore strokes.' On another occasion he said: 'Isaiah was a very sensible man; doesn't he say something about night monsters living in the ruins of Babylon? These things are rather beyond us at present.'

Another confidence of his impressed me rather, and I sympathised with it.

We had been, last year, to Comminges, to see Canon Alberic's tomb. It is a great marble erection with an effigy of the Canon in a large wig and soutane, and an elaborate eulogy of his learning below.

I saw Dennistoun talking for some time with the Vicar of St. Bertrand's, and as we drove away he said to me: 'I hope it isn't wrong. You know I am a Presbyterian – but I – I believe there will be "saying of Mass and singing of dirges" for Alberic de Mauléon's rest.'

---

† The Dispute of Solomon with a demon of the night. Drawn by Alberic de Mauléon. *Versicle.* O Lord, make haste to help me. *Psalm.* Whoso dwelleth (xci.).

Saint Bertrand, who puttest devils to flight, pray for me most unhappy. I saw it first on the night of Dec. 12, 1694: soon I shall see it for the last time. I have sinned and suffered, and have more to suffer yet. Dec. 29, 1701.

The 'Gallia Christiana' gives the date of the Canon's death as December 31, 1701, 'in bed, of a sudden seizure'. Details of this kind are not common in the great work of the Sammarthani.

Then he added, with a touch of the Northern British in his tone, 'I had no notion they came so dear.'

The book is in the Wentworth Collection at Cambridge. The drawing was photographed and then burnt by Dennistoun on the day when he left Comminges on the occasion of his first visit.

Lost Hearts

It was, as far as I can ascertain, in September of the year 1811 that a post-chaise drew up before the door of Aswarby Hall, in the heart of Lincolnshire.

The little boy who jumped out as soon as it had stopped, looked about him with the keenest curiosity during the short interval that elapsed between the ringing of the bell and the opening of the hall door.

He saw a tall, square, red-brick house, built in the reign of Anne. A stone-pillared porch had been added in the purest classical style of 1790; the windows of the house were many, tall and narrow, with small panes and thick white woodwork. A pediment, pierced with a round window, crowned the front.

There were wings to right and left, connected by curious glazed galleries, supported by colonnades, with the central block. These wings plainly contained the stables and offices of the house. Each was surmounted by an ornamental cupola with a gilded vane.

An evening light shone on the building, making the window-panes glow like so many fires.

Away from the Hall in front stretched a flat park studded with oaks and fringed with firs, which stood out against the sky. The clock in the church-tower, buried in trees on the edge of the park, only its golden weather-cock catching the light, was striking six, and the sound came gently beating down the wind.

It was altogether a pleasant impression, though tinged with the sort of melancholy appropriate to an evening in early autumn, that was conveyed to the mind of the boy who was standing in the porch waiting for the door to open to him.

The post-chaise had brought him from Warwickshire, where, some six months before, he had been left an orphan. Now, owing to the generous offer of his elderly cousin, Mr. Abney, he had come to live at Aswarby.

The offer was unexpected, because all who knew anything of Mr. Abney looked upon him as a somewhat austere recluse, into whose steady-going household the advent of a small boy would import a new and, it seemed, incongruous element.

The truth is that very little was known of Mr. Abney's pursuits or temper.

The Professor of Greek at Cambridge had been heard to say that no one knew more of the religious beliefs of the later pagans than did the owner of Aswarby. Certainly his library contained all the then available books bearing on the Mysteries, the Orphic poems, the worship of Mithras, and the Neo-Platonists.

In the marble-paved hall stood a fine group of Mithras slaying a bull, which had been imported from the Levant at great expense by the owner. He had contributed a description of it to the *Gentleman's Magazine*, and he had written a remarkable series of articles in the *Critical Museum* on the superstitions of the Romans of the Lower Empire.

He was looked upon, in fine, as a man wrapped up in his books, and it was a matter of great surprise among his neighbours that he should even have heard of his cousin, Stephen Elliot, much more that he should have volunteered to make him an inmate of Aswarby Hall.

Whatever may have been expected by his neighbours, it is certain that Mr. Abney – the tall, the thin, the austere – seemed inclined to give his young cousin a kindly reception. The moment the front door was opened he darted out of his study, rubbing his hands with delight.

'How are you, my boy? How are you? How old are you?' said he. 'That is, you are not too much tired, I hope, by your journey to eat your supper?'

'No, thank you, sir,' said Master Elliot; 'I am pretty well.'

'That's a good lad,' said Mr. Abney. 'And how old are you, my boy?'

It seemed a little odd that he should have asked the question twice in the first two minutes of their acquaintance.

'I'm twelve years old next birthday, sir,' said Stephen.

'And when is your birthday, my dear boy? Eleventh of September, eh? That's well – that's very well. Nearly a year hence, isn't it? I like – ha, ha! – I like to get these things down in my book. Sure it's twelve? Certain?'

'Yes, quite sure, Sir.'

'Well, well! Take him to Mrs. Bunch's room, Parkes, and let him have his tea – supper – whatever it is.'

'Yes, sir,' answered the staid Mr. Parkes, and conducted Stephen to the lower regions.

Mrs. Bunch was the most comfortable and human person whom Stephen had as yet met in Aswarby. She made him completely at home: they were great friends in a quarter of an hour, and great friends they remained.

Mrs. Bunch had been born in the neighbourhood some fifty-five years before the date of Stephen's arrival, and her residence at the Hall was of twenty years standing. Consequently, if anyone knew the ins and outs of the house and the district, Mrs. Bunch knew them; and she was by no means disinclined to communicate her information.

Certainly there were plenty of things about the Hall and the Hall gardens which Stephen, who was of an adventurous and enquiring turn, was anxious to have explained to him.

'Who built the temple at the end of the laurel walk?

'Who was the old man whose picture hung on the staircase, sitting at a table, with a skull under his hand?'

These and many similar points were cleared up by the resources of Mrs. Bunch's powerful intellect.

There were others, however, of which the explanations furnished were less satisfactory.

One November evening Stephen was sitting by the fire in the housekeeper's room reflecting on his surroundings.

'Is Mr. Abney a good man, and will he go to Heaven?' he suddenly asked, with the peculiar confidence which children possess in the ability of their elders to settle these questions, the decision of which is believed to be reserved for other tribunals.

'Good? – Bless the child!' said Mrs. Bunch. 'Master's as kind a soul as ever I see! Didn't I never tell you of the little boy as he took in out of the

street, as you may say, this seven years back? And the little girl, two years after I first come here?'

'No. Do tell me all about them, Mrs. Bunch – now this minute!'

'Well,' said Mrs. Bunch, 'the little girl I don't seem to recollect so much about. I know master brought her back with him from his walk one day, and give orders to Mrs. Ellis, as was housekeeper then, as she should be took every care with. And the pore child hadn't no one belonging to her – she told me so her own self – and here she lived with us a matter of three weeks it might be.

'And then, whether she were somethink of a gypsy in her blood or what not, but one morning she out of her bed afore any of us had opened a eye, and neither track nor yet trace of her have I set eyes on since.

'Master was wonderful put about, and had all the ponds dragged; but it's my belief she was had away by them gypsies, for there was singing round the house for as much as an hour the night she went, and Parkes, he declares he heard them a-calling in the woods all that afternoon.

'Dear, dear! a hodd child she was, so silent in her ways and all, but I was wonderful taken up with her, so domesticated she was – surprising.'

'And what about the little boy?' said Stephen.

'Ah, that pore boy!' sighed Mrs. Bunch. 'He were a foreigner – Jevanny he called himself – and he come a-tweaking his 'urdy-gurdy round and about the drive one winter day, and master 'ad him in that minute, and ast all about where he came from, and how old he was, and how he made his way, and were was his relatives, and all as kind as heart could wish.

'But it went the same way with him.

'They're a hunruly lot, them foreign nations, I do suppose, and he was off one fine morning just the same as the girl. Why he went and what he done was our question for as much as a year after; for he never took his 'urdy-gurdy, and there it lays on the shelf.'

The remainder of the evening was spent by Stephen in miscellaneous cross-examination of Mrs. Bunch and in efforts to extract a tune from the hurdy-gurdy.

That night he had a curious dream. At the end of the passage at the top of the house, in which his bedroom was situated, there was an old disused bathroom. It was kept locked, but the upper half of the door was glazed, and, since the muslin curtains which used to hang there had long been gone, you could look in and see the lead-lined bath affixed to the wall on the right hand, with its head towards the window.

On the night of which I am speaking, Stephen Elliot found himself, as he thought, looking through the glazed door. The moon was shining through the window, and he was gazing at a figure which lay in the bath.

His description of what he saw reminds me of what I once beheld myself in the famous vaults of St. Michan's Church in Dublin, which possess the horrid property of preserving corpses from decay for centuries.

A figure inexpressibly thin and pathetic, of a dusty leaden colour, enveloped in a shroud-like garment, the thin lips crooked into a faint and dreadful smile, the hands pressed tightly over the region of the heart.

As he looked upon it, a distant, almost inaudible moan seemed to issue from its lips, and the arms began to stir. The terror of the sight forced Stephen backwards, and he awoke to the fact that he was indeed standing on the cold boarded floor of the passage in the full light of the moon.

With a courage which I do not think can be common among boys of his age, he went to the door of the bathroom to ascertain if the figure of his dream were really there. It was not, and he went back to bed.

Mrs. Bunch was much impressed next morning by his story, and went so far as to replace the muslin curtain over the glazed door of the bathroom.

Mr. Abney, moreover, to whom he confided his experiences at breakfast, was greatly interested, and made notes of the matter in what he called 'his book'.

The spring equinox was approaching, as Mr. Abney frequently reminded his cousin, adding that this had been always considered by the ancients to be a critical time for the young: that Stephen would do well to take care of himself, and shut his bedroom window at night; and that Censorinus had some valuable remarks on the subject.

Two incidents that occurred about this time made an impression upon Stephen's mind.

The first was after an unusually uneasy and oppressed night that he had passed – though he could not recall any particular dream that he had had.

The following evening Mrs. Bunch was occupying herself in mending his nightgown.

'Gracious me, Master Stephen!' she broke forth rather irritably, 'how do you manage to tear your nightdress all to flinders this way? Look here, sir, what trouble you do give to poor servants that have to darn and mend after you!'

There was indeed a most destructive and apparently wanton series of slits or scorings in the garment, which would undoubtedly require a skilful needle to make good. They were confined to the left side of the chest – long, parallel slits, about six inches in length, some of them not quite piercing the texture of the linen. Stephen could only express his entire ignorance of their origin: he was sure that they were not there the night before.

'But,' he said, 'Mrs. Bunch, they are just the same as the scratches on the outside of my bedroom door; and I'm sure I never had anything to do with making them.'

Mrs. Bunch gazed at him open-mouthed, then snatched up a candle, departed hastily from the room, and was heard making her way upstairs.

In a few minutes she came down.

'Well,' she said, 'Master Stephen, it's a funny thing to me how them marks and scratches can 'a' come there – too high up for any cat or dog to 'ave made 'em, much less a rat. For all the world like a Chinaman's finger-nails, as my uncle in the tea-trade used to tell us of when we was girls together.

'I wouldn't say nothing to master, not if I was you, Master Stephen, my dear; and just turn the key of your door when you go to your bed.'

'I always do, Mrs. Bunch, as soon as I've said my prayers.'

'Ah, that's a good child: always say your prayers, and then no one can't hurt you.'

Herewith Mrs. Bunch addressed herself to mending the injured nightgown, with intervals of meditation, until bed-time. This was on a Friday night in March, 1812.

On the following evening the usual duet of Stephen and Mrs. Bunch was augmented by the sudden arrival of Mr. Parkes, the butler, who as a rule kept himself rather to himself in his own pantry. He did not see that Stephen was there: he was, moreover, flustered, and less slow of speech than was his wont.

'Master may get up his own wine, if he likes, of an evening,' was his first remark. 'Either I do it in the daytime or not at all, Mrs. Bunch. I don't know what it may be: very like it's the rats, or the wind got into the cellars; but I'm not as young as I was, and I can't go through with it as I have done.'

'Well, Mr. Parkes, you know it is a surprising place for the rats, is the Hall.'

'I'm not denying that, Mrs. Bunch; and to be sure, many a time I've heard the tale from the men in the shipyards about the rat that could speak. I never laid no confidence in that before; but tonight, if I'd demeaned myself to lay my ear to the door of the further bin, I could pretty much have heard what they was saying.'

'Oh, there, Mr. Parkes, I've no patience with your fancies! Rats talking in the wine-cellar indeed!'

'Well, Mrs. Bunch, I've no wish to argue with you: all I say is, if you choose to go to the far bin, and lay your ear to the door, you may prove my words this minute.'

'What nonsense you do talk, Mr. Parkes – not fit for children to listen to! Why, you'll be frightening Master Stephen there out of his wits.'

'What! Master Stephen?' said Parkes, awaking to the consciousness of the boy's presence. 'Master Stephen knows well enough when I'm a-playing a joke with you, Mrs. Bunch.'

In fact, Master Stephen knew much too well to suppose that Mr. Parkes had in the first instance intended a joke. He was interested, not altogether pleasantly, in the situation; but all his questions were unsuccessful in inducing the butler to give any more detailed account of his experiences in the wine-cellar.

We have now arrived at March 24, 1812.

It was a day of curious experiences for Stephen: a windy, noisy day, which filled the house and the gardens with a restless impression.

As Stephen stood by the fence of the grounds, and looked out into the park, he felt as if an endless procession of unseen people were sweeping past him on the wind, borne on restlessly and aimlessly, vainly striving to stop themselves, to catch at something that might arrest their flight and bring them once again into contact with the living world of which they had formed a part.

After luncheon that day Mr. Abney said:

'Stephen, my boy, do you think you could manage to come to me tonight as late as eleven o'clock in my study? I shall be busy until that time, and I wish to show you something connected with your future life which it is most important that you should know. You are not to mention this matter to Mrs. Bunch nor to anyone else in the house; and you had better go to your room at the usual time.'

Here was a new excitement added to life; Stephen eagerly grasped at the opportunity of sitting up till eleven o'clock.

He looked in at the library door on his way upstairs that evening, and saw a brazier, which he had often noticed in the corner of the room, moved out before the fire; an old silver-gilt cup stood on the table, filled with red wine, and some written sheets of paper lay near it. Mr. Abney was sprinkling some incense on the brazier from a round silver box as Stephen passed, but did not seem to notice his step.

The wind had fallen, and there was a still night and a full moon. At about ten o'clock Stephen was standing at the open window of his bedroom, looking out over the country. Still as the night was, the mysterious population of the distant moonlit woods was not yet lulled to rest.

From time to time strange cries as of lost and despairing wanderers sounded from across the mere. They might be the notes of owls or waterbirds, yet they did not quite resemble either sound.

Were not they coming nearer? Now they sounded from the nearer side of the water, and in a few moments they seemed to be floating about among the shrubberies.

Then they ceased. But just as Stephen was thinking of shutting the window and resuming his reading of *Robinson Crusoe*, he caught sight of two figures standing on the gravelled terrace that ran along the garden side of the Hall – the figures of a boy and girl, as it seemed. They stood side by side, looking up at the windows.

Something in the form of the girl recalled irresistibly his dream of the figure in the bath. The boy inspired him with more acute fear.

Whilst the girl stood still, half-smiling, with her hands clasped over her heart, the boy, a thin shape, with black hair and ragged clothing, raised his arms in the air with an appearance of menace and of unappeasable hunger and longing.

The moon shone upon his almost transparent hands, and Stephen saw that the nails were fearfully long and that the light shone through them.

As he stood with his arms thus raised, he disclosed a terrifying spectacle.

On the left side of his chest there opened a black and gaping rent, and there fell upon Stephen's brain, rather than upon his ear, the impression of one of those hungry and desolate cries that he had heard resounding over the woods of Aswarby all that evening.

In another moment this dreadful pair had moved swiftly and noiselessly over the dry grass and he saw them no more.

Inexpressibly frightened as he was, he determined to take his candle and go down to Mr. Abney's study, for the hour appointed for their meeting was near at hand.

The study or library opened out of the front hall on one side, and Stephen, urged on by his terrors, did not take long in getting there.

To effect an entrance was not so easy. The door was not locked, he felt sure, for the key was on the outside of it as usual. His repeated knocks produced no answer. Mr. Abney was engaged: he was speaking. What! Why did he try to cry out? And why was the cry choked in his throat? Had he, too, seen the mysterious children?

But now everything was quiet, and the door yielded to Stephen's terrified and frantic pushing.

On the table in Mr. Abney's study certain papers were found which explained the situation to Stephen Elliot when he was of an age to understand them.

The most important sentences were as follows:

It was a belief very strongly and generally held by the ancients —
of whose wisdom in these matters I have had such experience as
induces me to place confidence in their assertions — that by enacting
certain processes, which to us moderns have something of a barbaric
complexion, a very remarkable enlightenment of the spiritual
faculties in man may be attained: that, for example, by absorbing
the personalities of a certain number of his fellow-creatures, an
individual may gain a complete ascendancy over those orders of
spiritual beings which control the elemental forces of our universe.

It is recorded of Simon Magus that he was able to fly in the air,
to become invisible, or to assume any form he pleased, by the agency
of the soul of a boy whom, to use the libellous phrase employed by

the author of the Clementine Recognitions, *he had 'murdered'. I find it set down, moreover, with considerable detail in the writings of Hermes Trismegistus, that similar happy results may be produced by the absorption of the hearts of not less than three human beings below the age of twenty-one years. To the testing of the truth of this receipt I have devoted the greater part of the last twenty years, selecting as the corpora vilia of my experiment such persons as could conveniently be removed without occasioning a sensible gap in society. The first step I effected by the removal of one Phoebe Stanley, a girl of gypsy extraction, on March 24, 1792. The second, by the removal of a wandering Italian lad, named Giovanni Paoli, on the night of March 23, 1805. The final 'victim' – to employ a word repugnant in the highest degree to my feelings – must be my cousin, Stephen Elliott. His day must be this March 24, 1812.*

The best means of effecting the required absorption is to remove the heart from the living subject, to reduce it to ashes, and to mingle them with about a pint of red wine, preferably port. The remains of the first two subjects, at least, it will be well to conceal: a disused bathroom or wine-cellar will be found convenient for such a purpose. Some annoyance may be experienced from the psychic portion of the subjects, which popular language dignifies with the name of ghosts. But the man of philosophic temperament – to whom alone the experiment is appropriate – will be little prone to attach importance to the feeble efforts of these beings to wreak their vengeance on him. I contemplate with the liveliest satisfaction the enlarged and emancipated existence which the experiment, if successful, will confer on me; not only placing me beyond the reach of human justice (so-called) but eliminating to a great extent the prospect of death itself.

Mr. Abney was found in his chair, his head thrown back, his face stamped with an expression of rage, fright and mortal pain.

In his left side was a terrible lacerated wound, exposing the heart. There was no blood on his hands, and a long knife that lay on the table was perfectly clean. A savage wildcat might have inflicted the injuries.

The window of the study was open, and it was the opinion of the coroner that Mr. Abney had met his death by the agency of some wild creature.

But Stephen Elliot's study of the papers I have quoted led him to a very different conclusion.

The Ash-tree

EVERYONE WHO HAS travelled over Eastern England knows the smaller country-houses with which it is studded – the rather dank little buildings, usually in the Italian style, surrounded with parks of some eighty to a hundred acres.

For me they have always had a very strong attraction: with the grey paling of split oak, the noble trees, the meres with their reed-beds, and the line of distant woods. Then, I like the pillared portico – perhaps stuck on to a red-brick Queen Anne house which has been faced with stucco to bring it into line with the 'Grecian' taste of the end of the 18th century; the hall inside, going up to the roof, which hall ought always to be provided with a gallery and a small organ. I like the library, too, where you may find anything from a Psalter of the 13th century to a Shakespeare quarto.

I like the pictures, of course; and perhaps most of all I like fancying what life in such a house was when it was first built, and in the piping times of landlords' prosperity, and not least now, when, if money is not so plentiful, taste is more varied and life quite as interesting. I wish to have one of these houses, and enough money to keep it together and entertain my friends in it modestly.

But this is a digression. I have to tell you of a curious series of events which happened in such a house as I have tried to describe.

It is Castringham Hall in Suffolk. I think a good deal has been done to the building since the period of my story, but the essential features I have sketched are still there – Italian portico, square block of white house, older

34

inside than out, park with fringe of woods, and mere. The one feature that marked out the house from a score of others is gone.

As you looked at it from the park, you saw on the right a great old ash-tree growing within half-a-dozen yards of the wall, and almost or quite touching the building with its branches.

I suppose it had stood there ever since Castringham ceased to be a fortified place, and since the moat was filled in and the Elizabethan dwelling-house built. At any rate, it had well nigh attained its full dimensions in the year 1690.

In that year the district in which the Hall is situated was the scene of a number of witch-trials. It will be long, I think, before we arrive at a just estimate of the amount of solid reason – if there was any – which lay at the root of the universal fear of witches in old times. Whether the persons accused of this offence really did imagine that they were possessed of unusual powers of any kind; or whether they had the will at least, if not the power, of doing mischief to their neighbours; or whether all the confessions, of which there are so many, were extorted by the mere cruelty of the witch-finders – these are questions which are not, I fancy, yet solved.

And the present narrative gives me pause. I cannot altogether sweep it away as mere invention. The reader must judge for himself.

Castringham contributed a victim to the *auto-da-fé*. Mrs. Mothersole was her name, and she differed from the ordinary run of village witches only in being rather better off and in a more influential position. Efforts were made to save her by several reputable farmers of the parish. They did their best to testify to her character, and showed considerable anxiety as to the verdict of the jury.

But what seems to have been fatal to the woman was the evidence of the then proprietor of Castringham Hall – Sir Matthew Fell. He deposed to having watched her on three different occasions from his window, at the full of the moon, gathering sprigs 'from the ash-tree near my house'.

She had climbed into the branches, clad only in her shift, and was cutting off small twigs with a peculiarly curved knife, and as she did so she seemed to be talking to herself. On each occasion Sir Matthew had done his best to capture the woman, but she had always taken alarm at some accidental noise he had made, and all he could see when he got down to the garden was a hare running across the park in the direction of the village.

On the third night he had been at the pains to follow at his best speed, and had gone straight to Mrs. Mothersole's house. But he had had to wait a quarter of an hour battering at her door, and then she had come out very cross, and apparently very sleepy, as if just out of bed. And he had no good explanation to offer of his visit.

Mainly on this evidence, though there was much more of a less striking and unusual kind from other parishioners, Mrs. Mothersole was found guilty and condemned to die. She was hanged a week after the trial, with five or six more unhappy creatures, at Bury St. Edmunds.

Sir Matthew Fell, then Deputy-Sheriff, was present at the execution.

It was a damp, drizzly March morning when the cart made its way up the rough grass hill outside Northgate, where the gallows stood. The other victims were apathetic or broken down with misery, but Mrs. Mothersole was, as in life so in death, of a very different temper.

Her 'poysonous Rage', as a reporter of the time puts it, 'did so work upon the Bystanders – yea, even upon the Hangman – that it was constantly affirmed of all that saw her that she presented the living Aspect of a mad Divell. Yet she offer'd no Resistance to the Officers of the Law. Onely she looked upon those that laid Hands upon her with so direfull and venomous an Aspect that – as one of them afterwards assured me – the meer Thought of it preyed inwardly upon his Mind for six Months after.'

However, all that she is reported to have said was the seemingly meaningless words: 'There will be guests at the Hall.' Which she repeated more than once in an undertone.

Sir Matthew Fell was not unimpressed by the bearing of the woman. He had some talk upon the matter with the Vicar of his parish, with whom he travelled home after the assize business was over.

His evidence at the trial had not been very willingly given. He was not specially infected with the witch-finding mania, but he declared, then and afterwards, that he could not give any other account of the matter than that he had given, and that he could not possibly have been mistaken as to what he saw.

The whole transaction had been repugnant to him, for he was a man who liked to be on pleasant terms with those about him. But he saw a duty to be done in this business, and he had done it. That seems to have been the gist of his sentiments, and the Vicar applauded it, as any reasonable man must have done.

A few weeks after, when the moon of May was at the full, Vicar and Squire met again in the park, and walked to the Hall together. Lady Fell was with her mother, who was dangerously ill, and Sir Matthew was alone at home; so the Vicar, Mr. Crome, was easily persuaded to take a late supper at the Hall.

Sir Matthew was not very good company this evening. The talk ran chiefly on family and parish matters, and, as luck would have it, Sir Matthew made a memorandum in writing of certain wishes or intentions of his regarding his estates, which afterwards proved exceedingly useful.

When Mr. Crome thought of starting for home, about half-past nine o'clock, Sir Matthew and he took a preliminary turn on the gravelled walk at the back of the house.

The only incident that struck Mr. Crome was this: they were in sight of the ash-tree which I described as growing near the windows of the building, when Sir Matthew stopped and said: 'What is that that runs up and down the stem of the ash? It is never a squirrel? They will all be in their nests by now.'

The Vicar looked and saw the moving creature, but he could make nothing of its colour in the moonlight. The sharp outline, however, seen for an instant, was imprinted on his brain, and he could have sworn, he said, though it sounded foolish, that, squirrel or not, it had more than four legs.

Still, not much was to be made of the momentary vision, and the two men parted. They may have met since then, but it was not for a score of years.

Next day Sir Matthew Fell was not downstairs at six in the morning, as was his custom, nor at seven, nor yet at eight. Hereupon the servants went and knocked at his chamber door. I need not prolong the description of their anxious listenings and renewed batterings on the panels.

The door was opened at last from the outside, and they found their master dead and black. So much you have guessed. That there were any marks of violence did not at the moment appear, but the window was open.

One of the men went to fetch the parson, and then by his directions rode on to give notice to the coroner. Mr. Crome himself went as quick as he might to the Hall, and was shown to the room where the dead man lay.

He has left some notes among his papers which show how genuine a respect and sorrow was felt for Sir Matthew, and there is also this passage, which I transcribe for the sake of the light it throws upon the course of events, and also upon the common beliefs of the time:

There was not any the least Trace of an Entrance having been forc'd to the Chamber. But the Casement stood open, as my poor Friend would always have it in this Season.

He had his Evening Drink of small Ale in a silver vessel of about a pint measure, and tonight had not drunk it out. This Drink was examined by the Physician from Bury, a Mr. Hodgkins, who could not, however, as he afterwards declar'd upon his Oath, before the Coroner's quest, discover that any matter of a venomous kind was present in it.

For, as was natural, in the great Swelling and Blackness of the Corpse, there was talk made among the Neighbours of Poyson. The Body was very much Disorder'd as it laid in the Bed, being twisted after so extream a sort as gave too probable Conjecture that my worthy Friend and Patron had expir'd in great Pain and Agony.

And what is as yet unexplain'd, and to myself the Argument of some Horrid and Artfull Designe in the Perpetrators of this Barbarous Murther, was this, that the Women which were entrusted with the laying-out of the Corpse and washing it, being both sad Persons and very well Respected in their Mournfull Profession, came to me in a great Pain and Distress both of Mind and Body, saying, what was indeed confirmed upon the first View, that they had no sooner touch'd the Breast of the Corpse with their naked Hands than they were sensible of a more than ordinary violent Smart and Acheing in their Palms, which, with their whole Forearms, in no long time swell'd so immoderately, the Pain still continuing, that, as afterwards proved, during many weeks they were forc'd to lay by the exercise of their Calling; and yet no mark seen on the Skin.

Upon hearing this, I sent for the Physician, who was still in the House, and we made as carefull a Proof as we were able by the Help of a small Magnifying Lens of Crystal of the condition of the Skinn on this Part of the Body, but could not detect with the

Instrument we had any Matter of Importance beyond a couple of small Punctures or Pricks, which we then concluded were the Spotts by which the Poyson might be introduced, remembering that Ring of Pope Borgia, *with other known Specimens of the Horrid Art of the Italian Poysoners of the last age.*

So much is to be said of the Symptoms seen on the Corpse. As to what I am to add, it is meerly my own Experiment, and to be left to Posterity to judge whether there be anything of Value therein.

There was on the Table by the Beddside a Bible of the small size, in which my Friend – punctuall as in Matters of less Moment, so in this more weighty one – used nightly, and upon his First Rising, to read a sett Portion.

And I taking it up – not without a Tear duly paid to him which from the Study of this poorer Adumbration was now pass'd to the contemplation of its great Originall – it came into my Thoughts, as at such moments of Helplessness we are prone to catch at any the least Glimmer that makes promise of Light, to make trial of that old and by many accounted Superstitious Practice of drawing the Sortes: *of which a Principall Instance, in the case of his late Sacred Majesty the Blessed Martyr King* Charles *and my Lord* Falkland, *was now much talked of.*

I must needs admit that by my Trial not much Assistance was afforded me. Yet, as the Cause and Origin of these Dreadful Events may hereafter be search'd out, I set down the Results, in the case it may be found that they pointed the true Quarter of the Mischief to a quicker Intelligence than my own.

I made, then, three trials, opening the Book and placing my Finger upon certain Words: which gave in the first these words, from Luke xiii. 7, Cut it down; *in the second, Isaiah xiii. 20,* It shall never be inhabited; *and upon the third Experiment, Job xxxix. 30,* Her young ones also suck up blood.

This is all that need be quoted from Mr. Crome's papers. Sir Matthew Fell was duly coffined and laid into the earth, and his funeral sermon, preached by Mr. Crome on the following Sunday, has been printed under the title of 'The Unsearchable Way; or, England's Danger and the Malicious Dealings of Anti-Christ', it being the Vicar's view, as well as that most commonly held in the neighbourhood, that the Squire was the victim of a recrudescence of the Popish Plot.

His son, Sir Matthew the second, succeeded to the title and estates. And so ends the first act of the Castringham tragedy. It is to be mentioned, though the fact is not surprising, that the new Baronet did not occupy the room in which his father had died. Nor, indeed, was it slept in by anyone but an occasional visitor during the whole of his occupation.

He died in 1735, and I do not find that anything particular marked his reign, save a curiously constant mortality among his cattle and livestock in general, which showed a tendency to increase slightly as time went on.

Those who are interested in the details will find a statistical account in a letter to the *Gentleman's Magazine* of 1772, which draws the facts from the Baronet's own papers. He put an end to it at last by a very simple expedient, that of shutting up all his beasts in sheds at night, and keeping no sheep in his park. For he had noticed that nothing was ever attacked that spent the night indoors.

After that the disorder confined itself to wild birds, and beasts of chase. But as we have no good account of the symptoms, and as all-night watching was quite unproductive of any clue, I do not dwell on what the Suffolk farmers called the 'Castringham sickness'.

The second Sir Matthew died in 1735, as I said, and was duly succeeded by his son, Sir Richard. It was in his time that the great family pew was built out on the north side of the parish church. So large were the Squire's ideas that several of the graves on that unhallowed side of the building had to be disturbed to satisfy his requirements.

Among them was that of Mrs. Mothersole, the position of which was accurately known, thanks to a note on a plan of the church and yard, both made by Mr. Crome.

A certain amount of interest was excited in the village when it was known that the famous witch, who was still remembered by a few, was to be exhumed. And the feeling of surprise, and indeed disquiet, was very strong when it was found that, though her coffin was fairly sound and unbroken, there was no trace whatever inside it of body, bones, or dust.

Indeed, it is a curious phenomenon, for at the time of her burying no such things were dreamt of as resurrection-men, and it is difficult to conceive any rational motive for stealing a body otherwise than for the uses of the dissecting-room.

The incident revived for a time all the stories of witch-trials and of the exploits of the witches, dormant for forty years, and Sir Richard's orders that the coffin should be burnt were thought by a good many to be rather foolhardy, though they were duly carried out.

Sir Richard was a pestilent innovator, it is certain. Before his time the Hall had been a fine block of the mellowest red brick, but Sir Richard had travelled in Italy and become infected with the Italian taste, and, having more money than his predecessors, he determined to leave an Italian palace where he had found an English house.

So stucco and ashlar masked the brick; some indifferent Roman marbles were planted about in the entrance-hall and gardens; a reproduction of the Sibyl's temple at Tivoli was erected on the opposite bank of the mere; and Castringham took on an entirely new, and, I must say, a less engaging, aspect. But it was much admired, and served as a model to a good many of the neighbouring gentry in after-years.

One morning (it was in 1754) Sir Richard woke after a night of discomfort. It had been windy, and his chimney had smoked persistently, and yet it was so cold that he must keep up a fire. Also something had so rattled about the window that no man could get a moment's peace.

Further, there was the prospect of several guests of position arriving in the course of the day, who would expect sport of some kind, and the inroads of the distemper (which continued among his game) had been lately so serious that he was afraid for his reputation as a game-preserver.

But what really touched him most nearly was the other matter of his sleepless night. He could certainly not sleep in that room again.

That was the chief subject of his meditations at breakfast, and after it he began a systematic examination of the rooms to see which would suit his notions best.

It was long before he found one. This had a window with an eastern aspect and that with a northern. This door the servants would be always passing, and he did not like the bedstead in that. No, he must have a room with a western look-out, so that the sun could not wake him early, and it must be out of the way of the business of the house.

The housekeeper was at the end of her resources. 'Well, Sir Richard,' she said, 'you know that there is but one room like that in the house.'

'Which may that be?' said Sir Richard.

'And that is Sir Matthew's – the West Chamber.'

'Well, put me in there, for there I'll lie tonight,' said her master. 'Which way is it? Here, to be sure'; and he hurried off.

'Oh, Sir Richard, but no one has slept there these forty years. The air has hardly been changed since Sir Matthew died there.' Thus she spoke, and rustled after him.

'Come, open the door, Mrs. Chiddock. I'll see the chamber, at least.'

So it was opened, and, indeed, the smell was very close and earthy. Sir Richard crossed to the window, and, impatiently, as was his wont, threw the shutters back, and flung open the casement. For this end of the house was one which the alterations had barely touched, grown up as it was with the great ash-tree, and being otherwise concealed from view.

'Air it, Mrs. Chiddock, all today, and move my bed-furniture in in the afternoon. Put the Bishop of Kilmore in my old room.'

'Pray, Sir Richard,' said a new voice, breaking in on this speech, 'might I have the favour of a moment's interview?'

Sir Richard turned round and saw a man in black in the doorway, who bowed.

'I must ask your indulgence for this intrusion, Sir Richard. You will, perhaps, hardly remember me. My name is William Crome, and my grandfather was Vicar here in your grandfather's time.'

'Well, sir,' said Sir Richard, 'the name of Crome is always a passport to Castringham. I am glad to renew a friendship of two generations' standing. In what can I serve you? For your hour of calling – and, if I do not mistake you, your bearing – shows you to be in some haste.'

'That is no more than the truth, sir. I am riding from Norwich to Bury St. Edmunds with what haste I can make, and I have called in on my way to leave with you some papers which we have but just come upon in looking over what my grandfather left at his death. It is thought you may find some matters of family interest in them.'

'You are mighty obliging, Mr. Crome, and, if you will be so good as to follow me to the parlour, and drink a glass of wine, we will take a first look at these same papers together.

'And you, Mrs. Chiddock, as I said, be about airing this chamber . . . Yes, it is here my grandfather died . . . Yes, the tree, perhaps, does make the place a little dampish . . . No, I do not wish to listen to any more. Make no difficulties, I beg. You have your orders – go.

'Will you follow me, sir?'

They went to the study. The packet which young Mr. Crome had brought – he was then just become a Fellow of Clare Hall in Cambridge, I may say, and subsequently brought out a respectable edition of Polyaenus – contained among other things the notes which the old Vicar had made upon the occasion of Sir Matthew Fell's death.

And for the first time Sir Richard was confronted with the enigmatical *Sortes Biblicæ* which you have heard. They amused him a good deal.

'Well,' he said, 'my grandfather's Bible gave one prudent piece of advice – *Cut it down*. If that stands for the ash-tree, he may rest assured I shall not neglect it. Such a nest of catarrhs and agues was never seen.'

The parlour contained the family books, which, pending the arrival of a collection which Sir Richard had made in Italy, and the building of a proper room to receive them, were not many in number.

Sir Richard looked up from the paper to the bookcase. 'I wonder,' says he, 'whether the old prophet is there yet? I fancy I see him.'

Crossing the room, he took out a dumpy Bible, which, sure enough, bore on the flyleaf the inscription: *To Matthew Fell, from his Loving Godmother, Anne Aldous, 2 September, 1659.*

'It would be no bad plan to test him again, Mr. Crome. I will wager we get a couple of names in the Chronicles. Hm! What have we here? "Thou shalt seek me in the morning, and I shall not be." Well, well! Your grandfather would have made a fine omen of that, hey? No more prophets for me! They are all in a tale.

'And now, Mr. Crome, I am infinitely obliged to you for your packet. You will, I fear, be impatient to get on. Pray allow me – another glass.'

So with offers of hospitality, which were genuinely meant (for Sir Richard thought well of the young man's address and manner), they parted.

In the afternoon came the guests – the Bishop of Kilmore, Lady Mary Hervey, Sir William Kentfield, etc. Dinner at five, wine, cards, supper, and dispersal to bed.

Next morning Sir Richard is disinclined to take his gun with the rest. He talks with the Bishop of Kilmore. This prelate, unlike a good many of the Irish Bishops of his day, had visited his see, and, indeed, resided there for some considerable time.

This morning, as the two were walking along the terrace and talking over the alterations and improvements in the house, the Bishop said, pointing to the window of the West Room: 'You could never get one of my Irish flock to occupy that room, Sir Richard.'

'Why is that, my lord? It is, in fact, my own.'

'Well, our Irish peasantry will always have it that it brings the worst of luck to sleep near an ash-tree, and you have a fine growth of ash not two yards from your chamber window.'

'Perhaps,' the Bishop went on, with a smile, 'it has given you a touch of its quality already, for you do not seem, if I may say it, so much the fresher for your night's rest as your friends would like to see you.'

'That, or something else, it is true, cost me my sleep from twelve to four, my lord. But the tree is to come down tomorrow, so I shall not hear much more from it.'

'I applaud your determination. It can hardly be wholesome to have the air you breathe strained, as it were, through all that leafage.'

'Your lordship is right there, I think. But I had not my window open last night. It was rather the noise that went on – no doubt from the twigs sweeping the glass – that kept me open-eyed.'

'I think that can hardly be, Sir Richard. Here – you see it from this point. None of these nearest branches even can touch your casement unless there were a gale, and there was none of that last night. They miss the panes by a foot.'

'No, sir, true. What, then, will it be, I wonder, that scratched and rustled so – ay, and covered the dust on my sill with lines and marks?'

At last they agreed that the rats must have come up through the ivy.

That was the Bishop's idea, and Sir Richard jumped at it.

So the day passed quietly, and night came, and the party dispersed to their rooms, and wished Sir Richard a better night.

And now we are in his bedroom, with the light out and the Squire in bed. The room is over the kitchen, and the night outside still and warm, so the window stands open.

There is very little light about the bedstead, but there is a strange movement there. It seems as if Sir Richard were moving his head rapidly to and fro with only the slightest possible sound.

And now you would guess, so deceptive is the half-darkness, that he had several heads, round and brownish, which move back and forward, even as low as his chest.

It is a horrible illusion. Is it nothing more? There! Something drops off the bed with a soft plump, like a kitten, and is out of the window in a flash. Another – four – and after that there is quiet again.

Thou shalt seek me in the morning, and I shall not be.

As with Sir Matthew, so with Sir Richard – dead and black in his bed! A pale and silent party of guests and servants gathered under the window when the news was known. Italian poisoners, Popish emissaries, infected air – all these and more guesses were hazarded, and the Bishop of Kilmore looked at the tree, in the fork of whose lower boughs a white tom-cat was crouching, looking down the hollow which years had gnawed in the trunk. It was watching something inside the tree with great interest.

Suddenly it got up and craned over the hole. Then a bit of the edge on which it stood gave way, and it went slithering in. Everyone looked up at the noise of the fall.

It is known to most of us that a cat can cry, but few of us have heard, I hope, such a yell as came out of the trunk of the great ash. Two or three screams there were – the witnesses are not sure which – and then a slight and muffled noise of some commotion or struggling was all that came. But Lady Mary Hervey fainted outright, and the housekeeper stopped her ears and fled till she fell on the terrace.

The Bishop of Kilmore and Sir William Kentfield stayed. Yet even they were daunted, though it was only at the cry of a cat, and Sir William swallowed once or twice before he could say: 'There is something more than we know of in that tree, my lord. I am for an instant search.'

And this was agreed upon. A ladder was brought, and one of the gardeners went up, and, looking down the hollow, could detect nothing but a few dim indications of something moving. They got a lantern, and let it down by a rope.

'We must get at the bottom of this. My life upon it, my lord, but the secret of these terrible deaths is there.'

Up went the gardener again with the lantern, and let it down the hole cautiously. They saw the yellow light upon his face as he bent over, and saw his face struck with an incredulous terror and loathing before he cried out in a dreadful voice and fell back from the ladder – where, happily, he was caught by two of the men – letting the lantern fall inside the tree.

He was in a dead faint, and it was some time before any word could be got from him.

By then they had something else to look at. The lantern must have broken at the bottom, and the light in it caught upon dry leaves and rubbish that lay there, for in a few minutes a dense smoke began to come up, and then flame; and, to be short, the tree was in a blaze.

The bystanders made a ring at some yards' distance, and Sir William and the Bishop sent men to get what weapons and tools they could. For, clearly, whatever might be using the tree as its lair would be forced out by the fire.

So it was. First, at the fork, they saw a round body covered with fire – the size of a man's head – appear very suddenly, then seem to collapse and fall back. This, five or six times. Then a similar ball leapt into the air and fell on the grass, where after a moment it lay still.

The Bishop went as near as he dared to it, and saw – what but the remains of an enormous spider, veinous and seared! And, as the fire burned lower down, more terrible bodies like this began to break out from the trunk, and it was seen that these were covered with greyish hair.

All that day the ash burned, and until it fell to pieces the men stood about it, and from time to time killed the brutes as they darted out. At last there was a long interval when none appeared, and they cautiously closed in and examined the roots of the tree.

'They found,' says the Bishop of Kilmore, 'below it a rounded hollow place in the earth, wherein were two or three bodies of these creatures that had plainly been smothered by the smoke.

'And, what is to me more curious, at the side of this den, against the wall, was crouching the anatomy or skeleton of a human being, with the skin dried upon the bones, having some remains of black hair, which was pronounced by those that examined it to be undoubtedly the body of a woman, and clearly dead for a period of fifty years.'

Count Magnus

BY WHAT MEANS the papers out of which I have made a connected story came into my hands is the last point which the reader will learn from these pages. But it is necessary to prefix to my extracts from them a statement of the form in which I possess them.

They consist, then, partly of a series of collections for a book of travels, such a volume as was a common product of the forties and fifties. Horace Marryat's *Journal of a Residence in Jutland and the Danish Isles* is a fair specimen of the class to which I allude. These books usually treated of some unfamiliar district on the Continent. They were illustrated with woodcuts or steel plates. They gave details of hotel accommodation, and of means of communication, such as we now expect to find in any well-regulated guide-book, and they dealt largely in reported conversations with intelligent foreigners, racy innkeepers and garrulous peasants. In a word, they were chatty.

Begun with the idea of furnishing material for such a book, my papers as they progressed assumed the character of a record of one single personal experience, and this record was continued up to the very eve, almost, of its termination.

The writer was a Mr. Wraxall. For my knowledge of him I have to depend entirely on the evidence his writings afford, and from these I deduce that he was a man past middle age, possessed of some private means, and very much alone in the world. He had, it seems, no settled abode in England, but was a denizen of hotels and boarding-houses. It is probable that he entertained the idea of settling down at some future time which never came, and

I think it also likely that the Pantechnicon fire in the early seventies must have destroyed a great deal that would have thrown light on his antecedents, for he refers once or twice to property of his that was warehoused at that establishment.

It is further apparent that Mr. Wraxall had published a book, and that it treated of a holiday he had once taken in Brittany. More than this I cannot say about his work, because a diligent search in bibliographical works has convinced me that it must have appeared either anonymously or under a pseudonym.

As to his character, it is not difficult to form some superficial opinion. He must have been an intelligent and cultivated man. It seems he was near being a Fellow of his college at Oxford – Brasenose, as I judge from the Calendar. His besetting fault was pretty clearly that of over-inquisitiveness, possibly a good fault in a traveller, certainly a fault for which this traveller paid dearly enough in the end.

On what proved to be his last expedition, he was plotting another book. Scandinavia, a region not widely known to Englishmen forty years ago, had struck him as an interesting field. He must have lighted on some old books of Swedish history, or memoirs, and the idea had struck him that there was room for a book descriptive of travel in Sweden, interspersed with episodes from the history of some of the great Swedish families. He procured letters of introduction, therefore, to some persons of quality in Sweden, and set out thither in the early summer of 1863.

Of his travels in the North there is no need to speak, nor of his residence of some weeks in Stockholm. I need only mention that some *savant* resident there put him on the track of an important collection of family papers belonging to the proprietors of an ancient manor-house in Vestergothland, and obtained for him permission to examine them.

The manor-house, or *herrgård*, in question is to be called Råbäck (pronounced something like Roebeck) though that is not its name. It is one of the best buildings of its kind in all the country, and the picture of it in Dahlenberg's *Suecia antiqua et moderna*, engraved in 1694, shows it very much as the tourist may see it today. It was built soon after 1600, and is, roughly speaking, very much like an English house of that period in respect of material – red-brick with stone facings – and style. The man who built it was a scion of the great house of De la Gardie, and his descendants possess it still. De la Gardie is the name by which I will designate them when mention of them becomes necessary.

They received Mr. Wraxall with great kindness and courtesy, and pressed him to stay in the house as long as his researches lasted. But, preferring to be independent, and mistrusting his powers of conversing in Swedish, he settled himself at the village inn, which turned out quite sufficiently comfortable, at any rate during the summer months.

This arrangement would entail a short walk daily to and from the manor-house of something under a mile. The house itself stood in a park, and was protected – we should say grown up – with large old timber. Near it you found the walled garden, and then entered a close wood fringing one of the small lakes with which the whole country is pitted. Then came the wall of the demesne, and you climbed a steep knoll – a knob of rock lightly covered with soil – and on the top of this stood the church, fenced in with tall dark trees.

It was a curious building to English eyes. The nave and aisles were low, and filled with pews and galleries. In the western gallery stood the handsome old organ, gaily painted, and with silver pipes. The ceiling was flat, and had been adorned by a 17th-century artist with a strange and hideous 'Last Judgement', full of lurid flames, falling cities, burning ships, crying souls, and brown and smiling demons. Handsome brass coronæ hung from the roof; the pulpit was like a dolls' house covered with little painted cherubs and saints; a stand with three hour-glasses was hinged to the preacher's desk.

Such sights as these may be seen in many a church in Sweden now, but what distinguished this one was an addition to the original building. At the eastern end of the north aisle the builder of the manor-house had erected a mausoleum for himself and his family. It was a largish eight-sided building, lighted by a series of oval windows, and it had a domed roof, topped by a kind of pumpkin-shaped object rising into a spire, a form in which Swedish architects greatly delighted. The roof was of copper externally, and was painted black, while the walls, in common with those of the church, were staringly white. To this mausoleum there was no access from the church. It had a portal and steps of its own on the northern side.

Past the churchyard the path to the village goes, and not more than three or four minutes bring you to the inn door.

On the first day of his stay at Råbäck Mr. Wraxall found the church door open, and made these notes of the interior which I have epitomised. Into the mausoleum, however, he could not make his way. He could, by looking through the keyhole, just descry that there were fine marble effigies and sarcophagi of copper, and a wealth of armorial ornament, which made him very anxious to spend some time in investigation.

The papers he had come to examine at the manor-house proved to be just the kind of thing he wanted for his book. There were family correspondence, journals, and account-books of the earliest owners of the estate, very carefully kept and clearly written, full of amusing and picturesque detail.

The first De la Gardie appeared in them as a strong and capable man. Shortly after the building of the mansion there had been a period of distress in the district, and the peasants had risen and attacked several châteaux and done some damage. The owner of Råbäck took a leading part in suppressing the trouble, and there was reference to executions of ringleaders and severe punishments inflicted with no sparing hand.

The portrait of this Magnus de la Gardie was one of the best in the house, and Mr. Wraxall studied it with no little interest after his day's work. He gives no detailed description of it, but I gather that the face impressed him rather by its power than by its beauty or goodness. In fact, he writes that Count Magnus was an almost phenomenally ugly man.

On this day Mr. Wraxall took his supper with the family, and walked back in the late but still bright evening.

I must remember, he writes, *to ask the sexton if he can let me into the mausoleum at the church. He evidently has access to it himself, for I saw him tonight standing in the steps, and, as I thought, either locking or unlocking the door.*

I find that early on the following day Mr. Wraxall had some conversation with his landlord. His setting it down at such length as he does surprised me at first; but I soon realised that the papers I was reading here were, at least in their beginning, the materials for the book he was meditating, and that it was to have been one of those quasi-journalistic productions which admit of the introduction of an admixture of conversational matter.

His object, he says, was to find out whether any traditions of Count Magnus de la Gardie lingered on in the scenes of that gentleman's activity, and whether the popular estimate of him were favourable or not. He found that the Count was decidedly not a favourite.

If his tenants came late to their work on the days which they owed to him as Lord of the Manor, they were set on the wooden horse, or flogged and branded in the manor-house yard. One or two cases there were of men who had occupied lands which encroached on the lord's domain, and whose houses had been mysteriously burnt on a winter's night, with the whole family inside. But what seemed to dwell on the innkeeper's mind most – for he returned to the subject more than once – was that the Count had been on the Black Pilgrimage, and had brought something or someone back with him.

You will naturally inquire, as Mr. Wraxall did, what the Black Pilgrimage may have been. But your curiosity on the point must remain unsatisfied for the time being, just as his did. The landlord was evidently unwilling to give a full answer, or indeed any answer, on the point; and being called out for the moment, trotted out with obvious alacrity, only putting his head in at the door to say that he was called away to Skara, and should not be back until evening.

So Mr. Wraxall had to go unsatisfied to his day's work at the manor-house. The papers on which he was just then engaged soon put his thoughts into another channel, for he had to occupy himself with glancing over the correspondence between Sophia Albertina in Stockholm and her married cousin Ulrica Leonora at Råbäck in the years 1705–1710. The letters were of exceptional interest for the light they threw upon the culture of that period in Sweden, as anyone can testify who has read the full edition of them in the publications of the Swedish Historical Manuscripts Commission.

In the afternoon he had done with these, and after returning the boxes in which they were kept to their places on the shelf, he proceeded, very naturally, to take down some of the volumes nearest to them, in order to determine which of them had best be his principal subject of investigation next day.

The shelf he had hit upon was occupied mostly by a collection of account-books in the writing of the first Count Magnus. But one among them was not an account-book, but a book of alchemical and other tracts in another 16th-century hand. Not being very familiar with alchemical literature, Mr. Wraxall spends much space which he might have spared in setting out the names and beginnings of the various treatises: The book of the Phœnix, book of the Thirty Words, book of the Toad, book of Miriam, Turba Philosophorum, and so forth.

And then he announces with a good deal of circumstance his delight at finding, on a leaf originally left blank near the middle of the book, some writing of Count Magnus himself headed 'Liber nigræ peregrinationis'.

It is true that only a few lines were written, but there was quite enough to show that the landlord had that morning been referring to a belief at least as old as the time of Count Magnus, and probably shared by him. This is the English of what was written:

If any man desires to obtain a long life, if he would obtain a faithful messenger and see the blood of his enemies, it is necessary that he should first go into the city of Chorazin and there salute the prince . . .

Here there was an erasure of one word, not very thoroughly done, so that Mr. Wraxall felt pretty sure that he was right in reading it as aëris ('of the air'). But there was no more of the text copied, only a line in Latin: *Quære reliqua hujus materiei inter secretiora* (See the rest of this matter among the more private things).

It could not be denied that this threw a rather lurid light on the tastes and beliefs of the Count. But to Mr. Wraxall, separated from him by nearly three centuries, the thought that he might have added to his general force-fulness alchemy, and to alchemy something like magic, only made him a more picturesque figure. And when, after a rather prolonged contemplation of his picture in the hall, Mr. Wraxall set out on his homeward way, his mind was full of the thought of Count Magnus.

He had no eyes for his surroundings, no perceptions of the evening scents of the woods or the evening light on the lake. And when all of a sudden he pulled up short, he was astonished to find himself already at the gate of the churchyard, and within a few minutes of his dinner. His eyes fell on the mausoleum.

'Ah,' he said, 'Count Magnus, there you are. I should dearly like to see you.'

Like many solitary men, he writes, *I have a habit of talking to myself aloud; and, unlike some of the Greek and Latin particles, I do not expect an answer. Certainly and perhaps fortunately in this case, there was neither voice nor any that regarded – only the woman who, I suppose, was cleaning up the church, dropped some metallic object on the floor, whose clang startled me. Count Magnus, I think, sleeps sound enough.*

That same evening the landlord of the inn, who had heard Mr. Wraxall say that he wished to see the clerk or deacon (as he would be called in Sweden) of the parish, introduced him to that official in the inn parlour. A visit to the De la Gardie tomb-house was soon arranged for the next day, and a little general conversation ensued.

Mr. Wraxall, remembering that one function of Scandinavian deacons is to teach candidates for Confirmation, thought he would refresh his own memory on a Biblical point.

'Can you tell me,' he said, 'anything about Chorazin?'

The deacon seemed startled, but readily reminded him how that village had once been denounced.

'To be sure,' said Mr. Wraxall, 'it is, I suppose, quite a ruin now?'

'So I expect,' replied the deacon. 'I have heard some of our old priests say that Antichrist is to be born there. And there are tales—'

'Ah! What tales are those?' Mr. Wraxall put in.

'Tales, I was going to say, which I have forgotten,' said the deacon. And soon after that he said good night.

The landlord was now alone, and at Mr. Wraxall's mercy; and that inquirer was not inclined to spare him.

'Herr Nielsen,' he said, 'I have found out something about the Black Pilgrimage. You may as well tell me what you know. What did the Count bring back with him?'

Swedes are habitually slow, perhaps, in answering, or perhaps the landlord was an exception. I am not sure. But Mr. Wraxall notes that the landlord spent at least one minute in looking at him before he said anything at all. Then he came close up to his guest, and with a good deal of effort he spoke:

'Mr. Wraxall, I can tell you this one little tale, and no more – not any more. You must not ask anything when I have done.

'In my grandfather's time – that is, ninety-two years ago – there were two men who said: "The Count is dead; we do not care for him. We will go tonight and have a free hunt in his wood" – the long wood on the hill that you have seen behind Råbäck.

'Well, those that heard them say this, they said: "No, do not go. We are sure you will meet with persons walking who should not be walking. They should be resting, not walking."

'These men laughed. There were no forest-men to keep the wood, because no one wished to live there. The family were not here at the house. These men could do what they wished.

'Very well, they go to the wood that night. My grandfather was sitting here in this room. It was the summer, and a light night. With the window open, he could see out to the wood, and hear.

'So he sat there, and two or three men with him, and they listened. At first they hear nothing at all. Then they hear someone – you know how far away it is – they hear someone scream, just as if the most inside part of his soul was twisted out of him. All of them in the room caught hold of each other, and they sat so for three-quarters of an hour. Then they hear someone else, only about three hundred ells off. They hear him laugh out loud. It was not one of those two men who laughed, and indeed, they have all of them said that it was not any man at all. After that they hear a great door shut.

'Then, when it was just light with the sun, they all went to the priest. They said to him: "Father, put on your gown and your ruff, and come to bury these men, Anders Bjornsen and Hans Thorbjorn."

'You understand that they were sure these men were dead. So they went to the wood – my grandfather never forgot this. He said they were all like so many dead men themselves. The priest, too, he was in a white fear. He said when they came to him: "I heard one cry in the night, and I heard one laugh afterwards. If I cannot forget that, I shall not be able to sleep again."

'So they went to the wood, and they found these men on the edge of the wood. Hans Thorbjorn was standing with his back against a tree, and all the time he was pushing with his hands – pushing something away from him which was not there. So he was not dead. And they led him away, and took him to the house at Nykjoping and he died before the winter. But he went on pushing with his hands.

'Also Anders Bjornsen was there – but he was dead. And I tell you this about Anders Bjornsen: that he was once a beautiful man, but now his face was not there, because the flesh of it was sucked away off the bones.

'You understand that? My grandfather did not forget that. And they laid him on the bier which they had brought, and they put a cloth over his head, and the priest walked before. And they began to sing the psalm for the dead as well as they could.

'So, as they were singing the end of the first verse, one fell down, who was carrying the head of the bier, and the others looked back, and they saw that the cloth had fallen off, and the eyes of Anders Bjornsen were looking up, because there was nothing to close over them. And this they could not bear. Therefore the priest laid the cloth upon him, and sent for a spade, and they buried him in that place.'

The next day Mr. Wraxall records that the deacon called for him soon after his breakfast, and took him to the church and mausoleum. He noticed that the key of the latter was hung on a nail just by the pulpit, and it occurred to him that, as the church door seemed to be left unlocked as a rule, it would not be difficult for him to pay a second and more private visit to the monuments if there proved to be more of interest among them than could be digested at first.

The building, when he entered it, he found not unimposing. The monuments, mostly large erections of the 17th and 18th centuries, were dignified if luxuriant, and the epitaphs and heraldry were copious. The central space of the domed room was occupied by three copper sarcophagi, covered with finely engraved ornament. Two of them had, as is commonly the case in Denmark and Sweden, a large metal crucifix on the lid. The third, that of Count Magnus, as it appeared, had, instead of that, a full-length effigy engraved upon it, and round the edge were several bands of similar ornament representing various scenes.

One was a battle, with cannon belching out smoke, and walled towns, and troops of pikemen. Another showed an execution. In a third, among trees, was a man running at full speed, with flying hair and outstretched hands. After him followed a strange form. It would be hard to say whether the artist had intended it for a man, and was unable to give it the requisite similitude, or whether it was intentionally made as monstrous as it looked. In view of the skill with which the rest of the drawing was done, Mr. Wraxall felt inclined to adopt the latter idea.

The figure was unduly short, and was for the most part muffled in a hooded garment which swept the ground. The only part of the form which projected from that shelter was not shaped like any hand or arm. Mr. Wraxall compares it to the tentacle of a devil-fish, and continues: *On seeing this, I said to myself, 'This, then which is evidently an allegorical representation of some kind – a fiend pursuing a hunted soul – may be the origin of the story of Count Magnus and his mysterious companion. Let us see how the huntsman is pictured: doubtless it will be a demon blowing his horn.'*

But, as it turned out, there was no such sensational figure, only the semblance of a cloaked man on a hillock, who stood leaning on a stick, and watching the hunt with an interest which the engraver had tried to express in his attitude.

Mr. Wraxall noted the finely worked and massive steel padlocks – three in number – which secured the sarcophagus. One of them, he saw, was detached, and lay upon the pavement. And then, unwilling to delay the deacon longer or waste his own working-time, he made his way onward to the manor-house.

It is curious, he notes, *how, on retracing a familiar path, one's thoughts engross one to the absolute exclusion of surrounding objects. Tonight, for the second time, I had entirely failed to notice where I was going (I had planned a private visit to the tomb-house to copy the epitaphs), when I suddenly, as it were, awoke to consciousness, and found myself (as before) turning in at the churchyard gate, and, as I believe, singing or chanting some such words as, 'Are you awake, Count Magnus? Are you asleep, Count Magnus?' and then something more which I have failed to recollect. It seemed to me that I must have been behaving in this nonsensical way for some time.*

He found the key of the mausoleum where he had expected to find it, and copied the greater part of what he wanted. In fact, he stayed until the light began to fail him.

I must have been wrong, he writes, *in saying that one of the locks of the Count's sarcophagus was unfastened; I see tonight that two are loose. I picked both up, and laid them carefully on the window-ledge, after trying unsuccessfully to close them. The remaining one is still firm, and, though I take it to be a spring lock, I cannot guess how it is opened. Had I succeeded in undoing it, I am almost afraid I should have taken the liberty of opening the sarcophagus.*

It is strange, the interest I feel in the personality of this, I fear, somewhat ferocious and grim old noble.

The day following was, as it turned out, the last of Mr. Wraxall's stay at Råbäck. He received letters connected with certain investments which made it desirable that he should return to England. His work among the papers was practically done, and travelling was slow. He decided, therefore, to make his farewells, put some finishing touches to his notes, and be off.

These finishing touches and farewells, as it turned out, took more time than he had expected. The hospitable family insisted on his staying to dine with them – they dined at three – and it was verging on half-past six before he was outside the iron gates of Råbäck.

He dwelt on every step of his walk by the lake, determined to saturate himself, now that he trod it for the last time, in the sentiment of the place and hour.

And when he reached the summit of the churchyard knoll, he lingered for many minutes, gazing at the limitless prospect of woods near and distant, all dark beneath a sky of liquid green.

When at last he turned to go, the thought struck him that surely he must bid farewell to Count Magnus as well as the rest of the De la Gardies. The church was but twenty yards away, and he knew where the key of the mauso-leum hung.

It was not long before he was standing over the great copper coffin, and as usual, talking to himself aloud: 'You may have been a bit of a rascal in your time, Magnus,' he was saying, 'but for all that I should like to see you, or rather—'

Just at that instant, he says, *I felt a blow on my foot. Hastily enough I drew it back, and something fell on the pavement with a clash. It was the third, the last of the three padlocks which had fastened the sarcophagus. I stooped to pick it up, and – Heaven is my witness that I am writing only the bare truth – before I had raised myself there was a sound of metal hinges creaking, and I distinctly saw the lid shifting upwards.*

I may have behaved like a coward, but I could not for my life stay for one moment. I was outside that dreadful building in less time than I can write – almost as quickly as I could have said – the words. And what frightens me yet more, I could not turn the key in the lock.

As I sit here in my room noting these facts, I ask myself (it was not twenty minutes ago) whether that noise of creaking metal continued, and I cannot tell whether it did or not. I only know that there was something more than I have written that alarmed me, but whether it was sound or sight I am not able to remember. What is this that I have done?

Poor Mr. Wraxall! He set out on his journey to England on the next day, as he had planned, and he reached England in safety. And yet, as I judge from his changed hand and inconsequent jottings, a broken man. One of the several small notebooks that have come to me with his papers gives, not a key to, but a kind of inkling of, his experiences.

Much of his journey was by canal-boat, and I find not less than six painful attempts to enumerate and describe his fellow-passengers. The entries are of this kind:

24. Pastor of village in Skåne. Usual black coat and soft black hat.
25. Commercial traveller from Stockholm going to Trollhättan.
Black cloak, brown hat. 26. Man in long black cloak, broad-leafed hat, very old-fashioned.

This entry is lined out, and a note added: *Perhaps identical with No. 13. Have not yet seen his face.* On referring to No. 13, I find that he is a Roman priest in a cassock.

The net result of the reckoning is always the same. Twenty-eight people appear in the enumeration, one being always a man in a long black cloak and broad hat, and the other a 'short figure in dark cloak and hood'. On the other hand, it is always noted that only twenty-six passengers appear at meals, and that the man in the cloak is perhaps absent, and the short figure is certainly absent.

On reaching England, it appears that Mr. Wraxall landed at Harwich, and that he resolved at once to put himself out of the reach of some person or persons whom he never specifies, but whom he had evidently come to regard as his pursuers.

Accordingly he took a vehicle – it was a closed fly – not trusting the railway, and drove across country to the village of Belchamp St. Paul.

It was about nine o'clock on a moonlit August night when he neared the place. He was sitting forward, and looking out of the window at the fields and thickets – there was little else to be seen – racing past him.

Suddenly he came to a cross-road. At the corner two figures were standing motionless. Both were in dark cloaks; the taller one wore a hat, the shorter a hood. He had no time to see their faces, nor did they make any motion that he could discern. Yet the horse shied violently and broke into a gallop, and Mr. Wraxall sank back into his seat in something like desperation. He had seen them before.

Arrived at Belchamp St. Paul, he was fortunate enough to find a decent furnished lodging, and for the next twenty-four hours he lived, comparatively speaking, in peace.

His last notes were written on this day. They are too disjointed and ejaculatory to be given here in full, but the substance of them is clear enough. He is expecting a visit from his pursuers – how or when he knows not – and his constant cry is 'What has he done?' and 'Is there no hope?' Doctors, he knows, would call him mad, policemen would laugh at him. The parson is away. What can he do but lock his door and cry to God?

People still remember last year at Belchamp St. Paul how a strange gentleman came one evening in August years back, and how the next morning but one he was found dead, and there was an inquest; and the jury that viewed the body fainted, seven of 'em did, and none of 'em wouldn't speak to what they see, and the verdict was visitation of God; and how the people as kep' the 'ouse moved out that same week, and went away from that part.

But they do not, I think, know that any glimmer of light has been thrown, or could be thrown, on the mystery.

It so happened that last year the little house came into my hands as part of a legacy. It had stood empty since 1863, and there seemed no prospect of letting it. So I had it pulled down, and the papers of which I have given you an abstract were found in a forgotten cupboard under the window in the best bedroom.

The Mezzotint

SOME TIME AGO I believe I had the pleasure of telling you the story of an adventure which happened to a friend of mine by the name of Dennistoun, during his pursuit of objects of art for the museum at Cambridge.

He did not publish his experiences very widely upon his return to England, but they could not fail to become known to a good many of his friends, and among others to the gentleman who at that time presided over an art museum at another University.

It was to be expected that the story should make a considerable impression on the mind of a man whose vocation lay in lines similar to Dennistoun's, and that he should be eager to catch at any explanation of the matter which tended to make it seem improbable that he should ever be called upon to deal with so agitating an emergency.

It was, indeed, somewhat consoling to him to reflect that he was not expected to acquire ancient MSS. for his institution; that was the business of the Shelburnian Library. The authorities of that might, if they pleased, ransack obscure corners of the Continent for such matters.

He was glad to be obliged at the moment to confine his attention to enlarging the already unsurpassed collection of English topographical drawings and engravings possessed by his museum.

Yet, as it turned out, even a department so homely and familiar as this may have its dark corners, and to one of these Mr. Williams was unexpectedly introduced.

Those who have taken even the most limited interest in the acquisition of topographical pictures are aware that there is one London dealer whose aid is indispensable to their researches. Mr. J.W. Britnell publishes at short intervals very admirable catalogues of a large and constantly changing stock of engravings, plans, and old sketches of mansions, churches, and towns in England and Wales.

These catalogues were, of course, the ABC of his subject to Mr. Williams: but as his museum already contained an enormous accumulation of topographical pictures, he was a regular, rather than a copious, buyer; and he rather looked to Mr. Britnell to fill up gaps in the rank and file of his collection than to supply him with rarities.

Now, in February of last year there appeared upon Mr. Williams' desk at the museum a catalogue from Mr. Britnell's emporium, and accompanying it was a typewritten communication from the dealer himself. This latter ran as follows:

DEAR SIR——

   We beg to call your attention to No. 978 in our accompanying catalogue, which we shall be glad to send on approval.

                    Yours faithfully,
                    J.W. BRITNELL

To turn to No. 978 in the accompanying catalogue was with Mr. Williams (as he observed to himself) the work of a moment, and in the place indicated he found the following entry:

978. — *Unknown*. Interesting mezzotint: View of a manor-house, early part of the century. 15 by 10 inches; black frame. £2 2s.

It was not specially exciting, and the price seemed high. However, as Mr. Britnell, who knew his business and his customer, seemed to set store by it, Mr. Williams wrote a postcard asking for the article to be sent on approval, along with some other engravings and sketches which appeared in the same catalogue.

And so he passed without much excitement of anticipation to the ordinary labours of the day.

A parcel of any kind always arrives a day later than you expect it, and that of Mr. Britnell proved, as I believe the right phrase goes, no exception to the rule.

It was delivered at the museum by the afternoon post of Saturday, after Mr. Williams had left his work, and it was accordingly brought round to his rooms in college by the attendant, in order that he might not have to wait over Sunday before looking through it and returning such of the contents as he did not propose to keep.

And here he found it when he came in to tea, with a friend.

The only item with which I am concerned was the rather large, black-framed mezzotint of which I have already quoted the short description given in Mr. Britnell's catalogue. Some more details of it will have to be given, though I cannot hope to put before you the look of the picture as clearly as it is present to my own eye.

Very nearly the exact duplicate of it may be seen in a good many old inn parlours, or in the passages of undisturbed country mansions at the present moment. It was a rather indifferent mezzotint, and an indifferent mezzotint is, perhaps, the worst form of engraving known.

It presented a full-face view of a not very large manor-house of the last century, with three rows of plain sashed windows with rusticated masonry about them, a parapet with balls or vases at the angles, and a small portico in the centre. On either side were trees, and in front considerable expanse of lawn.

The legend *A.W.F. sculpsit* was engraved on the narrow margin, and there was no further inscription.

The whole thing gave the impression that it was the work of an amateur. What in the world Mr. Britnell could mean by affixing the price of £2 2s. to such an object was more than Mr. Williams could imagine.

He turned it over with a good deal of contempt. Upon the back was a paper label, the left-hand half of which had been torn off. All that remained were the ends of two lines of writing: the first had the letters *—ngley Hall*; the second, *—ssex.*

It would, perhaps, be just worthwhile to identify the place represented, which he could easily do with the help of a gazetteer, and then he would send it back to Mr. Britnell, with some remarks reflecting upon the judgement of that gentleman.

He lighted the candles, for it was now dark, made the tea, and supplied the friend with whom he had been playing golf (for I believe the authorities of the University I write of indulge in that pursuit by way of relaxation). And tea was taken to the accompaniment of a discussion which golfing persons can imagine for themselves, but which the conscientious writer has no right to inflict upon any non-golfing persons.

The conclusion arrived at was that certain strokes might have been better, and that in certain emergencies neither player had experienced that amount of luck which a human being has a right to expect.

It was now that the friend – let us call him Professor Binks – took up the framed engraving, and said:

'What's this place, Williams?'

'Just what I am going to try to find out,' said Williams, going to the shelf for a gazetteer. 'Look at the back. Somethingley Hall, either in Sussex or Essex. Half the name's gone, you see. You don't happen to know it, I suppose?'

'It's from that man Britnell, I suppose, isn't it?' said Binks. 'Is it for the museum?'

'Well, I think I should buy it if the price was five shillings,' said Williams; 'but for some unearthly reason he wants two guineas for it. I can't conceive why. It's a wretched engraving, and there aren't even any figures to give it life.'

'It's not worth two guineas, I should think,' said Binks. 'But I don't think it's so badly done. The moonlight seems rather good to me. And I should have thought there *were* figures, or at least a figure just on the edge in front.'

'Let's look,' said Williams. 'Well, it's true the light is rather cleverly given. Where's your figure? Oh yes! Just the head, in the very front of the picture.'

And indeed there was – hardly more than a black blot on the extreme edge of the engraving – the head of a man or woman, a good deal muffled up, the back turned to the spectator, and looking towards the house.

Williams had not noticed it before.

'Still,' he said, 'though it's a cleverer thing than I thought, I can't spend two guineas of museum money on a picture of a place I don't know.'

Professor Binks had his work to do, and soon went. And very nearly up to Hall time Williams was engaged in a vain attempt to identify the subject of his picture.

'If the vowel before the *ng* had only been left, it would have been easy enough,' he thought. 'But as it is, the name may be anything from Guestingley to Langley, and there are many more names ending like this than I thought. And this rotten book has no index of terminations.'

Hall in Mr. Williams's college was at seven. It need not be dwelt upon. The less so as he met there colleagues who had been playing golf during the afternoon, and words with which we have no concern were freely bandied across the table – merely golfing words, I would hasten to explain.

I suppose an hour or more to have been spent in what is called common-room after dinner. Later in the evening some few retired to Williams's rooms, and I have little doubt that whist was played and tobacco smoked.

During a lull in these operations Williams picked up the mezzotint from the table without looking at it, and handed it to a person mildly interested in art, telling him where it had come from, and the other particulars which we already know.

The gentleman took it carelessly, looked at it, then said, in a tone of some interest:

'It's really a very good piece of work, Williams. It has quite a feeling of the romantic period. The light is admirably managed, it seems to me, and the figure, though it's rather too grotesque, is somehow very impressive.'

'Yes, isn't it?' said Williams, who was just then busy giving whisky-and-soda to others of the company, and was unable to come across the room to look at the view again.

It was by this time rather late in the evening, and the visitors were on the move. After they went Williams was obliged to write a letter or two and clear up some odd bits of work. At last, some time past midnight, he was disposed to turn in, and he put out his lamp after lighting his bedroom candle.

The picture lay face upwards on the table where the last man who looked at it had put it, and it caught his eye as he turned the lamp down. What he saw made him very nearly drop the candle on the floor, and he declares now that if he had been left in the dark at that moment he would have had a fit. But, as that did not happen he was able to put down the light on the table and take a good look at the picture.

It was indubitable – rankly impossible, no doubt, but absolutely certain. In the middle of the lawn in front of the unknown house there was a figure where no figure had been at five o'clock that afternoon.

It was crawling on all-fours towards the house, and it was muffled in a strange black garment with a white cross on the back.

I do not know what is the ideal course to pursue in a situation of this kind. I can only tell you what Mr. Williams did.

He took the picture by one corner and carried it across the passage to a second set of rooms which he possessed. There he locked it up in a drawer, sported the doors of both sets of rooms, and retired to bed. But first he wrote out and signed an account of the extraordinary change which the picture had undergone since it had come into his possession.

Sleep visited him rather late, but it was consoling to reflect that the behaviour of the picture did not depend upon his own unsupported testimony. Evidently the man who had looked at it the night before had seen something of the same kind as he had, otherwise he might have been tempted to think that something gravely wrong was happening either to his eyes or his mind.

This possibility being fortunately precluded, two matters awaited him on the morrow. He must take stock of the picture very carefully, and call in a witness for the purpose, and he must make a determined effort to ascertain what house it was that was represented.

He would therefore ask his neighbour Nisbet to breakfast with him, and he would subsequently spend a morning over the gazetteer.

Nisbet was disengaged, and arrived about 9:30. His host was not quite dressed, I am sorry to say, even at this late hour.

During breakfast nothing was said about the mezzotint by Williams, save that he had a picture on which he wished for Nisbet's opinion. But those who are familiar with University life can picture for themselves the wide and delightful range of subjects over which the conversation of two Fellows of Canterbury College is likely to extend during a Sunday morning breakfast. Hardly a topic was left unchallenged, from golf to lawn-tennis.

Yet I am bound to say that Williams was rather distraught. For his interest naturally centred in that very strange picture which was now reposing, face downwards, in the drawer in the room opposite.

The morning pipe was at last lighted, and the moment had arrived for which he looked. With very considerable – almost tremulous – excitement, he ran across, unlocked the drawer, and, extracting the picture – still face downwards – ran back, and put it into Nisbet's hands.

'Now,' he said, 'Nisbet, I want you to tell me exactly what you see in that picture. Describe it, if you don't mind, rather minutely. I'll tell you why afterwards.'

'Well,' said Nisbet, 'I have here a view of a country-house – English, I presume – by moonlight.'

'Moonlight? You're sure of that?'

'Certainly. The moon appears to be on the wane, if you wish for details, and there are clouds in the sky.'

'All right. Go on. I'll swear,' added Williams in an aside, 'there was no moon when I saw it first.'

'Well, there's not much more to be said,' Nisbet continued. 'The house has one – two – three rows of windows, five in each row, except at the bottom, where there's a porch instead of the middle one, and—'

'But what about figures?' said Williams, with marked interest.

'There aren't any,' said Nisbet. 'But—'

'What! No figure on the grass in front?'

'Not a thing.'

'You'll swear to that?'

'Certainly I will. But there's just one other thing.'

'What?'

'Why, one of the windows on the ground-floor – left of the door – is open.'

'Is it really? My goodness! He must have got in,' said Williams, with great excitement; and he hurried to the back of the sofa on which Nisbet was sitting, and, catching the picture from him, verified the matter for himself.

It was quite true. There was no figure, and there was the open window.

Williams, after a moment of speechless surprise, went to the writing-table and scribbled for a short time. Then he brought two papers to Nisbet, and asked him first to sign one – it was his own description of the picture, which you have just heard – and then to read the other which was Williams's statement written the night before.

'What can it all mean?' said Nisbet.

'Exactly,' said Williams. 'Well, one thing I must do – or three things, now I think of it. I must find out from Garwood' – this was his last night's visitor – 'what he saw, and then I must get the thing photographed before it goes further, and then I must find out what the place is.'

'I can do the photographing myself,' said Nisbet, 'and I will. But, you know, it looks very much as if we were assisting at the working out of a tragedy somewhere. The question is – has it happened already, or is it going to come off? You must find out what the place is.

'Yes,' he said, looking at the picture again, 'I expect you're right: he has got in. And if I don't mistake there'll be the devil to pay in one of the rooms upstairs.'

'I'll tell you what,' said Williams. 'I'll take the picture across to old Green' (this was the senior Fellow of the College, who had been Bursar for many years). 'It's quite likely he'll know it. We have property in Essex and Sussex, and he must have been over the two counties a lot in his time.'

'Quite likely he will,' said Nisbet. 'But just let me take my photograph first. But look here, I rather think Green isn't up today. He wasn't in Hall last night, and I think I heard him say he was going down for the Sunday.'

'That's true, too,' said Williams; 'I know he's gone to Brighton. Well, if you'll photograph it now, I'll go across to Garwood and get his statement, and you keep an eye on it while I'm gone. I'm beginning to think two guineas is not a very exorbitant price for it now.'

In a short time he had returned, and brought Mr. Garwood with him. Garwood's statement was to the effect that the figure, when he had seen it, was clear of the edge of the picture, but had not got far across the lawn. He remembered a white mark on the back of its drapery, but could not have been sure it was a cross. A document to this effect was then drawn up and signed, and Nisbet proceeded to photograph the picture.

'Now what do you mean to do?' he said. 'Are you going to sit and watch it all day?'

'Well, no, I think not,' said Williams. 'I rather imagine we're meant to see the whole thing. You see, between the time I saw it last night and this morning there was time for lots of things to happen, but the creature only got into the house. It could easily have got through its business in the time and gone to its own place again; but the fact of the window being open, I think, must mean that it's in there now.

'So I feel quite easy about leaving it. And, besides, I have a kind of idea that it wouldn't change much, if at all, in the daytime. We might go out for a walk this afternoon, and come in to tea, or whenever it gets dark.

'I shall leave it out on the table here, and sport the door. My skip can get in, but no one else.'

The three agreed that this would be a good plan. And, further, that if they spent the afternoon together they would be less likely to talk about the business to other people – for any rumour of such a transaction as was going on would bring the whole of the Phasmatological Society about their ears.

We may give them a respite until five o'clock.

At or near that hour the three were entering Williams's staircase. They were at first slightly annoyed to see that the door of his rooms was unsported, but in a moment it was remembered that on Sunday the skips came for orders an hour or so earlier than on weekdays.

However, a surprise was awaiting them.

The first thing they saw was the picture leaning up against a pile of books on the table, as it had been left, and the next thing was Williams's skip, seated on a chair opposite, gazing at it with undisguised horror.

How was this? Mr. Filcher (the name is not my own invention) was a servant of considerable standing, and set the standard of etiquette to all his own college and to several neighbouring ones, and nothing could be more alien to his practice than to be found sitting on his master's chair, or appearing to take any particular notice of his master's furniture or pictures.

Indeed, he seemed to feel this himself. He started violently when the three men came into the room, and got up with a marked effort. Then he said:

'I ask your pardon, sir, for taking such a freedom as to set down.'

'Not at all, Robert,' interposed Mr. Williams. 'I was meaning to ask you some time what you thought of that picture.'

'Well, sir, of course I don't set up my opinion again yours, but it ain't the pictur I should 'ang where my little girl could see it, sir.'

'Wouldn't you, Robert? Why not?'

'No, sir. Why, the pore child, I recollect once she see a Door Bible, with pictures not 'alf what that is, and we 'ad to set up with her three or four nights afterwards, if you'll believe me. And if she was to ketch a sight of this skelinton here, or whatever it is, carrying off the pore baby, she would be in a taking.

'You know 'ow it is with children: 'ow nervish they git with a little thing and all. But what I should say, it don't seem a right pictur to be laying about, sir, not where anyone that's liable to be startled could come on it.

'Should you be wanting anything this evening sir? Thank you, sir.'

With these words the excellent man went to continue the round of his masters, and you may be sure the gentlemen whom he left lost no time in gathering round the engraving.

There was the house, as before, under the waning moon and the drifting clouds. The window that had been open was shut, and the figure was once more on the lawn: but not this time crawling cautiously on hands and knees. Now it was erect and stepping swiftly, with long strides, towards the front of the picture. The moon was behind it, and the black drapery hung down over its face so that only hints of that could be seen, and what was visible made the spectators profoundly thankful that they could see no more than a white dome-like forehead and a few straggling hairs.

The head was bent down, and the arms were tightly clasped over an object which could be dimly seen and identified as a child, whether dead or living it was not possible to say. The legs of the appearance alone could be plainly discerned, and they were horribly thin.

From five to seven the three companions sat and watched the picture by turns. But it never changed. They agreed at last that it would be safe to leave it, and that they would return after Hall and await further developments.

When they assembled again, at the earliest possible moment, the engraving was there, but the figure was gone, and the house was quiet under the moonbeams.

There was nothing for it but to spend the evening over gazetteers and guide-books.

Williams was the lucky one at last, and perhaps he deserved it. At 11:30 p.m. he read from Murray's *Guide to Essex* the following lines:

'16½ miles, *Anningley*. The church has been an interesting building of

Norman date, but was extensively classicised in the last century. It contains the tombs of the family of Francis, whose mansion, Anningley Hall, a solid Queen Anne house, stands immediately beyond the churchyard in a park of about 80 acres.

'The family is now extinct, the last heir having disappeared mysteriously in infancy in the year 1802. The father, Mr. Arthur Francis, was locally known as a talented amateur engraver in mezzotint. After his son's disappearance he lived in complete retirement at the Hall, and was found dead in his studio on the third anniversary of the disaster, having just completed an engraving of the house, impressions of which are of considerable rarity.'

This looked like business, and, indeed, Mr. Green on his return at once identified the house as Anningley Hall.

'Is there any kind of explanation of the figure, Green?' was the question which Williams naturally asked.

'I don't know, I'm sure, Williams. What used to be said in the place when I first knew it, which was before I came up here, was just this: old Francis was always very much down on these poaching fellows, and whenever he got a chance he used to get a man whom he suspected of it turned off the estate, and by degrees he got rid of them all but one.

'Squires could do a lot of things then that they daren't think of now. Well, this man that was left was what you find pretty often in that country – the last remains of a very old family. I believe they were Lords of the Manor at one time. I recollect just the same thing in my own parish.'

'What, like the man in *Tess of the D'Urbervilles*?' Williams put in.

'Yes, I dare say; it's not a book I could ever read myself. But this fellow could show a row of tombs in the church there that belonged to his ancestors, and all that went to sour him a bit.

'But Francis, they said, could never get at him – he always kept just on the right side of the law – until one night the keepers found him at it in a wood right at the end of the estate. I could show you the place now; it marches with some land that used to belong to an uncle of mine.

'And you can imagine there was a row; and this man Gawdy (that was the name, to be sure – Gawdy; I thought I should get it – Gawdy), he was unlucky enough – poor chap! – to shoot a keeper.

'Well, that was what Francis wanted, and grand juries – you know what they would have been then – and poor Gawdy was strung up in double-quick time. And I've been shown the place he was buried in, on the north side of the church – you know the way in that part of the world: anyone that's been hanged or made away with themselves, they bury them that side.

'And the idea was that some friend of Gawdy's – not a relation, because he had none – poor devil! – he was the last of his line: kind of *spes ultima gentis* – must have planned to get hold of Francis' boy and put an end to his line, too.

'I don't know – it's rather an out-of-the-way thing for an Essex poacher to think of – but, you know, I should say now it looks more as if old Gawdy had managed the job himself. Boo! I hate to think of it! Have some whisky, Williams!'

The facts were communicated by Williams to Dennistoun, and by him to a mixed company, of which I was one, and the Sadducean Professor of Ophiology another.

I am sorry to say that the latter, when asked what he thought of it, only remarked: 'Oh, those Bridgeford people will say anything' – a sentiment which met with the reception it deserved.

I have only to add that the picture is now in the Ashleian Museum. That it has been treated with a view to discovering whether sympathetic ink has been used in it, but without effect; that Mr. Britnell knew nothing of it save that he was sure it was uncommon; and that, though carefully watched, it has never been known to change again.

Number 13

AMONG THE TOWNS OF JUTLAND, Viborg justly holds a high place. It is the seat of a bishopric; it has a handsome but almost entirely new cathedral, a charming garden, a lake of great beauty, and many storks.

Near it is Hald, accounted one of the prettiest things in Denmark. And hard by is Finderup, where Marsk Stig murdered King Erik Glipping on St. Cecilia's Day, in the year 1286. Fifty-six blows of square-headed iron maces were traced on Erik's skull when his tomb was opened in the 17th century.

But I am not writing a guide-book.

There are good hotels in Viborg – Preisler's and the Phœnix are all that can be desired. But my cousin, whose experiences I have to tell you now, went to the Golden Lion the first time that he visited Viborg. He has not been there since, and the following pages will perhaps explain the reason of his abstention.

The Golden Lion is one of the very few houses in the town that were not destroyed in the great fire of 1726, which practically demolished the cathedral, the Sognekirke, the Raadhuus, and so much else that was old and interesting.

It is a great red-brick house – that is, the front is of brick, with corbie steps on the gables and a text over the door. But the courtyard into which the omnibus drives is of black and white 'cage-work' in wood and plaster.

The sun was declining in the heavens when my cousin walked up to the door, and the light smote full upon the imposing façade of the house. He was delighted with the old-fashioned aspect of the place, and promised himself a thoroughly satisfactory and amusing stay in an inn so typical of old Jutland.

It was not business in the ordinary sense of the word that had brought Mr. Anderson to Viborg. He was engaged upon some researches into the Church history of Denmark, and it had come to his knowledge that in the Rigsarkiv of Viborg there were papers, saved from the fire, relating to the last days of Roman Catholicism in the country.

He proposed, therefore, to spend a considerable time – perhaps as much as a fortnight or three weeks – in examining and copying these, and he hoped that the Golden Lion would be able to give him a room of sufficient size to serve alike as a bedroom and a study.

His wishes were explained to the landlord, and, after a certain amount of thought, the latter suggested that perhaps it might be the best way for the gentleman to look at one or two of the larger rooms and pick one for himself.

It seemed a good idea.

The top floor was soon rejected as entailing too much getting upstairs after the day's work. The second floor contained no room of exactly the dimensions required. But on the first floor there was a choice of two or three rooms which would, so far as size went, suit admirably.

The landlord was strongly in favour of Number 17, but Mr. Anderson pointed out that its windows commanded only the blank wall of the next house, and that it would be very dark in the afternoon. Either Number 12 or Number 14 would be better, for both of them looked on the street, and the bright evening light and the pretty view would more than compensate him for the additional amount of noise.

Eventually Number 12 was selected. Like its neighbours, it had three windows, all on one side of the room; it was fairly high and unusually long. There was, of course, no fireplace, but the stove was handsome and rather old – a cast-iron erection, on the side of which was a representation of Abraham sacrificing Isaac, and the inscription, *I Bog Mose, Cap. 22*, above. Nothing else in the room was remarkable; the only interesting picture was an old coloured print of the town, date about 1820.

Supper-time was approaching, but when Anderson, refreshed by the ordinary ablutions, descended the staircase, there were still a few minutes before the bell rang. He devoted them to examining the list of his fellow-lodgers.

As is usual in Denmark, their names were displayed on a large blackboard, divided into columns and lines, the numbers of the rooms being painted in at the beginning of each line. The list was not exciting.

There was an advocate, or Sagförer, a German, and some bagmen from Copenhagen. The one and only point which suggested any food for thought was the absence of any Number 13 from the tale of the rooms, and even this was a thing which Anderson had already noticed half-a-dozen times in his experience of Danish hotels.

He could not help wondering whether the objection to that particular number, common as it is, was so widespread and so strong as to make it difficult to let a room so ticketed, and he resolved to ask the landlord if he and his colleagues in the profession had actually met with many clients who refused to be accommodated in the thirteenth room.

He had nothing to tell me (I am giving the story as I heard it from him) about what passed at supper, and the evening, which was spent in unpacking and arranging his clothes, books and papers, was not more eventful.

Towards eleven o'clock he resolved to go to bed, but with him, as with a good many other people nowadays, an almost necessary preliminary to bed, if he meant to sleep, was the reading of a few pages of print, and he now remembered that the particular book which he had been reading in the train, and which alone would satisfy him at that present moment, was in the pocket of his greatcoat, then hanging on a peg outside the dining-room.

To run down and secure it was the work of a moment, and, as the passages were by no means dark, it was not difficult for him to find his way back to his own door.

So, at least, he thought. But when he arrived there, and turned the handle, the door entirely refused to open, and he caught the sound of a hasty movement towards it from within.

He had tried the wrong door, of course. Was his own room to the right or to the left? He glanced at the number: it was 13. His room would be on the left, and so it was.

And not before he had been in bed for some minutes, had read his wonted three or four pages of his book, blown out his light, and turned over to go to sleep, did it occur to him that, whereas on the blackboard of the hotel there had been no Number 13, there was undoubtedly a room numbered 13 in the hotel.

He felt rather sorry he had not chosen it for his own. Perhaps he might have done the landlord a little service by occupying it, and given him the chance of saying that a well-born English gentleman had lived in it for three weeks and liked it very much. But probably it was used as a servant's room or something of the kind. After all, it was most likely not so large or good a room as his own.

And he looked drowsily about the room, which was fairly perceptible in the half-light from the street-lamp. It was a curious effect, he thought. Rooms usually look larger in a dim light than a full one, but this seemed to have contracted in length and grown proportionately higher. Well, well! Sleep was more important than these vague ruminations – and to sleep he went.

On the day after his arrival Anderson attacked the Rigsarkiv of Viborg. He was, as one might expect in Denmark, kindly received, and access to all that he wished to see was made as easy for him as possible.

The documents laid before him were far more numerous and interesting than he had at all anticipated. Besides official papers, there was a large bundle of correspondence relating to Bishop Jörgen Friis, the last Roman Catholic who held the see, and in these there cropped up many amusing and what are called 'intimate' details of private life and individual character.

There was much talk of a house owned by the Bishop, but not inhabited by him, in the town. Its tenant was apparently somewhat of a scandal and a stumbling-block to the reforming party. He was a disgrace, they wrote, to the city; he practised secret and wicked arts, and had sold his soul to the enemy. It was of a piece with the gross corruption and superstition of the Babylonish Church that such a viper and blood-sucking *Troldmand* should be patronised and harboured by the Bishop.

The Bishop met these reproaches boldly. He protested his own abhorrence of all such things as secret arts, and required his antagonists to bring the matter before the proper court – of course, the spiritual court – and sift it to the bottom. No one could be more ready and willing than himself to condemn Mag. Nicolas Francken if the evidence showed him to have been guilty of any of the crimes informally alleged against him.

Anderson had not time to do more than glance at the next letter of the Protestant leader, Rasmus Nielsen, before the record office was closed for the day, but he gathered its general tenor, which was to the effect that Christian men were now no longer bound by the decisions of Bishops of Rome, and that the Bishop's Court was not, and could not be, a fit or competent tribunal to judge so grave and weighty a cause.

On leaving the office, Mr. Anderson was accompanied by the old gentleman who presided over it, and, as they walked, the conversation very naturally turned to the papers of which I have just been speaking.

Herr Scavenius, the Archivist of Viborg, though very well informed as to the general run of the documents under his charge, was not a specialist in those of the Reformation period. He was much interested in what Anderson had to tell him about them. He looked forward with great pleasure, he said, to seeing the publication in which Mr. Anderson spoke of embodying their contents.

'This house of the Bishop Friis,' he added, 'it is a great puzzle to me where it can have stood. I have studied carefully the topography of old Viborg, but it is most unlucky – of the old terrier of the Bishop's property which was made in 1560, and of which we have the greater part in the Arkiv, just the piece which had the list of the town property is missing.

'Never mind. Perhaps I shall some day succeed to find him.'

After taking some exercise – I forget exactly how or where – Anderson went back to the Golden Lion, his supper, his game of patience, and his bed.

On the way to his room it occurred to him that he had forgotten to talk to the landlord about the omission of Number 13 from the hotel, and also that he might as well make sure that Number 13 did actually exist before he made any reference to the matter.

The decision was not difficult to arrive at. There was the door with its number as plain as could be, and work of some kind was evidently going on inside it, for as he neared the door he could hear footsteps and voices, or a voice, within.

During the few seconds in which he halted to make sure of the number, the footsteps ceased, seemingly very near the door, and he was a little startled at hearing a quick hissing breathing as of a person in strong excitement.

He went on to his own room, and again he was surprised to find how much smaller it seemed now than it had when he selected it. It was a slight disappointment, but only slight. If he found it really not large enough, he could very easily shift to another.

In the meantime he wanted something – as far as I remember it was a pocket-handkerchief – out of his portmanteau, which had been placed by the porter on a very inadequate trestle or stool against the wall at the farthest end of the room from his bed.

Here was a very curious thing: the portmanteau was not to be seen. It had been moved by officious servants – doubtless the contents had been put in the wardrobe.

No, none of them were there.

This was vexatious.

The idea of a theft he dismissed at once. Such things rarely happen in Denmark, but some piece of stupidity had certainly been performed (which is not so uncommon), and the *stuepige* must be severely spoken to.

Whatever it was that he wanted, it was not so necessary to his comfort that he could not wait till the morning for it, and he therefore settled not to ring the bell and disturb the servants.

He went to the window – the right-hand window it was – and looked out on the quiet street. There was a tall building opposite, with large spaces of dead wall; no passers-by; a dark night; and very little to be seen of any kind.

The light was behind him, and he could see his own shadow clearly cast on the wall opposite. Also the shadow of the bearded man in Number 11 on the left, who passed to and fro in shirtsleeves once or twice, and was seen first brushing his hair, and later on in a nightgown.

Also the shadow of the occupant of Number 13 on the right.

This might be more interesting. Number 13 was, like himself, leaning on his elbows on the window-sill looking out into the street. He seemed to be a tall thin man – or was it by any chance a woman? – at least, it was someone who covered his or her head with some kind of drapery before going to bed, and, he thought, must be possessed of a red lamp-shade – and the lamp must be flickering very much.

There was a distinct playing up and down of a dull red light on the opposite wall. He craned out a little to see if he could make any more of the figure, but beyond a fold of some light, perhaps white, material on the window-sill he could see nothing.

Now came a distant step in the street, and its approach seemed to recall Number 13 to a sense of his exposed position, for very swiftly and suddenly he swept aside from the window, and his red light went out.

Anderson, who had been smoking a cigarette, laid the end of it on the window-sill and went to bed.

Next morning he was woke by the *stuepige* with hot water, etc. He roused himself, and after thinking out the correct Danish words, said as distinctly as he could:

'You must not move my portmanteau. Where is it?'

As is not uncommon, the maid laughed, and went away without making any distinct answer.

Anderson, rather irritated, sat up in bed, intending to call her back, but he remained sitting up, staring straight in front of him. There was his portmanteau on its trestle, exactly where he had seen the porter put it when he first arrived.

This was a rude shock for a man who prided himself on his accuracy of observation. How it could possibly have escaped him the night before he did not pretend to understand; at any rate, there it was now.

The daylight showed more than the portmanteau: it let the true proportions of the room with its three windows appear, and satisfied its tenant that his choice after all had not been a bad one.

When he was almost dressed he walked to the middle one of the three windows to look out at the weather. Another shock awaited him.

Strangely unobservant he must have been last night. He could have sworn ten times over that he had been smoking at the right-hand window the last thing before he went to bed, and here was his cigarette-end on the sill of the middle window.

He started to go down to breakfast. Rather late, but Number 13 was later: here were his boots still outside his door – a gentleman's boots. So then Number 13 was a man, not a woman.

Just then he caught sight of the number on the door. It was 14. He thought he must have passed Number 13 without noticing it. Three stupid mistakes in twelve hours were too much for a methodical, accurate-minded man, so he turned back to make sure.

The next number to 14 was number 12, his own room. There was no Number 13 at all.

After some minutes devoted to a careful consideration of everything he had had to eat and drink during the last twenty-four hours, Anderson decided to give the question up. If his sight or his brain were giving way he would have plenty of opportunities for ascertaining that fact; if not, then he was evidently being treated to a very interesting experience. In either case the development of events would certainly be worth watching.

During the day he continued his examination of the episcopal correspondence which I have already summarised. To his disappointment, it was incomplete. Only one other letter could be found which referred to the affair of Mag. Nicolas Francken. It was from the Bishop Jörgen Friis to Rasmus Nielsen. He said:

'Although we are not in the least degree inclined to assent to your judgement concerning our court, and shall be prepared if need be to withstand you to the uttermost in that behalf, yet forasmuch as our trusty and well-beloved Mag. Nicolas Francken, against whom you have dared to allege certain false and malicious charges, hath been suddenly removed from among us, it is apparent that the question for this time falls.

'But forasmuch as you further allege that the Apostle and Evangelist St. John in his heavenly Apocalypse describes the Holy Roman Church under the guise and symbol of the Scarlet Woman, be it known to you,' etc.

Search as he might, Anderson could find no sequel to this letter nor any clue to the cause or manner of the 'removal' of the *casus belli*. He could only suppose that Francken had died suddenly. And as there were only two days between the date of Nielsen's last letter – when Francken was evidently still in being – and that of the Bishop's letter, the death must have been completely unexpected.

In the afternoon he paid a short visit to Hald, and took his tea at Baekkelund. Nor could he notice, though he was in a somewhat nervous frame of mind, that there was any indication of such a failure of eye or brain as his experiences of the morning had led him to fear.

At supper he found himself next to the landlord.

'What,' he asked him, after some indifferent conversation, 'is the reason why in most of the hotels one visits in this country the number thirteen is left out of the list of rooms? I see you have none here.'

The landlord seemed amused.

'To think that you should have noticed a thing like that! I've thought about it once or twice myself, to tell the truth. An educated man, I've said, has no business with these superstitious notions. I was brought up myself here in the High School of Viborg, and our old master was always a man to set his face against anything of that kind. He's been dead now this many years – a fine upstanding man he was, and ready with his hands as well as his head. I recollect us boys, one snowy day—'

Here he plunged into reminiscence.

'Then you don't think there is any particular objection to having a Number 13?' said Anderson.

'Ah! To be sure. Well, you understand, I was brought up to the business by my poor old father. He kept a hotel in Aarhuus first, and then, when we were born, he moved to Viborg here, which was his native place, and had the Phoenix here until he died. That was in 1876. Then I started business in Silkeborg, and only the year before last I moved into this house.'

Then followed more details as to the state of the house and business when first taken over.

'And when you came here, was there a Number 13?'

'No, no. I was going to tell you about that. You see, in a place like this, the commercial class – the travellers – are what we have to provide for in general. And put them in Number 13? Why, they'd as soon sleep in the street, or sooner.

'As far as I'm concerned myself, it wouldn't make a penny difference to me what the number of my room was, and so I've often said to them. But they stick to it that it brings them bad luck.

'Quantities of stories they have among them of men that have slept in a Number 13 and never been the same again, or lost their best customers, or – one thing and another,' said the landlord, after searching for a more graphic phrase.

'Then, what do you use your Number 13 for?' said Anderson, conscious as he said the words of a curious anxiety quite disproportionate to the importance of the question.

'My Number 13? Why, don't I tell you that there isn't such a thing in the house? I thought you might have noticed that. If there was it would be next door to your own room.'

'Well, yes. Only I happened to think – that is, I fancied last night that I had seen a door numbered thirteen in that passage. And, really, I am almost certain I must have been right, for I saw it the night before as well.'

Of course, Herr Kristensen laughed this notion to scorn, as Anderson had expected, and emphasised with much iteration the fact that no Number 13 existed or had existed before him in that hotel.

Anderson was in some ways relieved by his certainty but still puzzled, and he began to think that the best way to make sure whether he had indeed been subject to an illusion or not was to invite the landlord to his room to smoke a cigar later on in the evening. Some photographs of English towns which he had with him formed a sufficiently good excuse.

Herr Kristensen was flattered by the invitation, and most willingly accepted it. At about ten o'clock he was to make his appearance, but before that Anderson had some letters to write, and retired for the purpose of writing them.

He almost blushed to himself at confessing it, but he could not deny that it was the fact that he was becoming quite nervous about the question of the existence of Number 13 – so much so that he approached his room by way of Number 11, in order that he might not be obliged to pass the door, or the place where the door ought to be.

He looked quickly and suspiciously about the room when he entered it, but there was nothing, beyond that indefinable air of being smaller than usual, to warrant any misgivings.

There was no question of the presence or absence of his portmanteau tonight. He had himself emptied it of its contents and lodged it under his bed.

With a certain effort he dismissed the thought of Number 13 from his mind, and sat down to his writing.

His neighbours were quiet enough. Occasionally a door opened in the passage and a pair of boots was thrown out, or a bagman walked past humming to himself, and outside, from time to time a cart thundered over the atrocious cobble-stones, or a quick step hurried along the flags.

Anderson finished his letters, ordered in whisky and soda, and then went to the window and studied the dead wall opposite and the shadows upon it.

As far as he could remember, Number 14 had been occupied by the lawyer, a staid man, who said little at meals, being generally engaged in studying a small bundle of papers beside his plate.

Apparently, however, he was in the habit of giving vent to his animal spirits when alone. Why else should he be dancing? The shadow from the next room evidently showed that he was. Again and again his thin form crossed the window, his arms waved, and a gaunt leg was kicked up with surprising agility. He seemed to be barefooted, and the floor must be well laid, for no sound betrayed his movements.

Sagförer Herr Anders Jensen, dancing at ten o'clock at night in a hotel bedroom, seemed a fitting subject for a historical painting in the grand style; and Anderson's thoughts, like those of Emily in the *Mysteries of Udolpho*, began to 'arrange themselves in the following lines':

'When I return to my hotel,
  At ten o'clock p.m.,
The waiters think I am unwell;
  I do not care for them.
But when I've locked my chamber door,
  And put my boots outside,
I dance all night upon the floor.
And even if my neighbours swore,
I'd go on dancing all the more,
For I'm acquainted with the law,
And in despite of all their jaw,
Their protests I deride.'

Had not the landlord at this moment knocked at the door, it is probable that quite a long poem might have been laid before the reader.

To judge from his look of surprise when he found himself in the room,

Herr Kristensen was struck, as Anderson had been, by something unusual in its aspect. But he made no remark.

Anderson's photographs interested him mightily, and formed the text of many autobiographical discourses. Nor is it quite clear how the conversation could have been diverted into the desired channel of Number 13, had not the lawyer at this moment begun to sing, and to sing in a manner which could leave no doubt in anyone's mind that he was either exceedingly drunk or raving mad.

It was a high, thin voice that they heard, and it seemed dry, as if from long disuse. Of words or tune there was no question. It went sailing up to a surprising height, and was carried down with a despairing moan as of a winter wind in a hollow chimney, or an organ whose wind fails suddenly.

It was a really horrible sound, and Anderson felt that if he had been alone he must have fled for refuge and society to some neighbour bagman's room.

The landlord sat open-mouthed.

'I don't understand it,' he said at last, wiping his forehead. 'It is dreadful. I have heard it once before, but I made sure it was a cat.'

'Is he mad?' said Anderson.

'He must be; and what a sad thing! Such a good customer, too, and so successful in his business, by what I hear, and a young family to bring up.'

Just then came an impatient knock at the door, and the knocker entered, without waiting to be asked. It was the lawyer, in déshabillé and very rough-haired. And very angry he looked.

'I beg pardon, sir,' he said, 'but I should be much obliged if you would kindly desist—'

Here he stopped, for it was evident that neither of the persons before him was responsible for the disturbance. And after a moment's lull it swelled forth again more wildly than before.

'But what in the name of Heaven does it mean?' broke out the lawyer. 'Where is it? Who is it? Am I going out of my mind?'

'Surely, Herr Jensen, it comes from your room next door? Isn't there a cat or something stuck in the chimney?'

This was the best that occurred to Anderson to say, and he realised its futility as he spoke. But anything was better than to stand and listen to that horrible voice, and look at the broad, white face of the landlord, all perspiring and quivering as he clutched the arms of his chair.

'Impossible,' said the lawyer, 'impossible. There is no chimney. I came here because I was convinced the noise was going on here. It was certainly in the next room to mine.'

'Was there no door between yours and mine?' said Anderson eagerly.

'No, sir,' said Herr Jensen, rather sharply. 'At least, not this morning.'

'Ah!' said Anderson. 'Nor tonight?'

'I am not sure,' said the lawyer with some hesitation.

Suddenly the crying or singing voice in the next room died away, and the singer was heard seemingly to laugh to himself in a crooning manner.

The three men actually shivered at the sound.

Then there was a silence.

'Come,' said the lawyer, 'what have you to say, Herr Kristensen? What does this mean?'

'Good Heaven!' said Kristensen. 'How should I tell! I know no more than you, gentlemen. I pray I may never hear such a noise again.'

'So do I,' said Herr Jensen, and he added something under his breath. Anderson thought it sounded like the last words of the Psalter, '*omnis spiritus laudet Dominum*', but he could not be sure.

'But we must do something,' said Anderson, 'the three of us. Shall we go and investigate in the next room?'

'But that is Herr Jensen's room,' wailed the landlord. 'It is no use – he has come from there himself.'

'I am not so sure,' said Jensen. 'I think this gentleman is right: we must go and see.'

The only weapons of defence that could be mustered on the spot were a stick and umbrella.

The expedition went out into the passage, not without quakings. There was a deadly quiet outside, but a light shone from under the next door. Anderson and Jensen approached it. The latter turned the handle, and gave a sudden vigorous push. No use. The door stood fast.

'Herr Kristensen,' said Jensen, 'will you go and fetch the strongest servant you have in the place? We must see this through.'

The landlord nodded, and hurried off, glad to be away from the scene of action. Jensen and Anderson remained outside looking at the door.

'It is Number 13, you see,' said the latter.

'Yes; there is your door, and there is mine,' said Jensen.

'My room has three windows in the daytime,' said Anderson, with difficulty suppressing a nervous laugh.

'By George, so has mine!' said the lawyer, turning and looking at Anderson. His back was now to the door. In that moment the door opened, and an arm came out and clawed at his shoulder. It was clad in ragged, yellowish linen, and the bare skin, where it could be seen, had long grey hair upon it.

Anderson was just in time to pull Jensen out of its reach with a cry of disgust and fright, when the door shut again, and a low laugh was heard.

Jensen had seen nothing, but when Anderson hurriedly told him what a risk he had run, he fell into a great state of agitation, and suggested that they should retire from the enterprise and lock themselves up in one or other of their rooms.

However, while he was developing this plan, the landlord and two able-bodied men arrived on the scene, all looking rather serious and alarmed. Jensen met them with a torrent of description and explanation, which did not at all tend to encourage them for the fray.

The men dropped the crowbars they had brought, and said flatly that they were not going to risk their throats in that devil's den. The landlord was miserably nervous and undecided, conscious that if the danger were not faced his hotel was ruined, and very loath to face it himself.

Luckily Anderson hit upon a way of rallying the demoralised force. 'Is this,' he said, 'the Danish courage I have heard so much of? It isn't a German in there, and if it was, we are five to one.'

The two servants and Jensen were stung into action by this, and made a dash at the door.

'Stop!' said Anderson. 'Don't lose your heads. You stay out here with the light, landlord, and one of you two men break in the door, and don't go in when it gives way.'

The men nodded, and the younger stepped forward, raised his crowbar, and dealt a tremendous blow on the upper panel. The result was not in the least what any of them anticipated.

There was no cracking or rending of wood – only a dull sound, as if the solid wall had been struck. The man dropped his tool with a shout, and began rubbing his elbow. His cry drew their eyes upon him for a moment, then Anderson looked at the door again.

It was gone. The plaster wall of the passage stared him in the face, with a considerable gash in it where the crowbar had struck it.

Number 13 had passed out of existence.

For a brief space they stood perfectly still, gazing at the blank wall. An early cock in the yard beneath was heard to crow; and as Anderson glanced in the direction of the sound, he saw through the window at the end of the long passage that the eastern sky was paling to the dawn.

'Perhaps,' said the landlord, with hesitation, 'you gentlemen would like another room for tonight – a double-bedded one?'

Neither Jensen nor Anderson was averse to the suggestion. They felt inclined to hunt in couples after their late experience.

It was found convenient, when each of them went to his room to collect the articles he wanted for the night, that the other should go with him and hold the candle.

They noticed that both Number 12 and Number 14 had *three* windows.

Next morning the same party reassembled in Number 12.

The landlord was naturally anxious to avoid engaging outside help, and yet it was imperative that the mystery attaching to that part of the house should be cleared up.

Accordingly the two servants had been induced to take upon them the function of carpenters. The furniture was cleared away, and, at the cost of a good many irretrievably damaged planks, that portion of the floor was taken up which lay nearest to Number 14.

You will naturally suppose that a skeleton – say that of Mag. Nicolas Francken – was discovered. That was not so.

What they did find lying between the beams which supported the flooring was a small copper box. In it was a neatly folded vellum document, with about twenty lines of writing.

Both Anderson and Jensen (who proved to be something of a palæographer) were much excited by this discovery, which promised to afford the key to these extraordinary phenomena.

I possess a copy of an astrological work which I have never read. It has, by way of frontispiece, a woodcut by Hans Sebald Beham, representing a number of sages seated round a table. This detail may enable connoisseurs to identify the book.

I cannot myself recollect its title, and it is not at this moment within reach. But the fly-leaves of it are covered with writing, and, during the ten years in which I have owned the volume, I have not been able to determine which way up this writing ought to be read, much less in what language it is.

Not dissimilar was the position of Anderson and Jensen after the protracted examination to which they submitted the document in the copper box.

After two days' contemplation of it, Jensen, who was the bolder spirit of the two, hazarded the conjecture that the language was either Latin or Old Danish.

Anderson ventured upon no surmises, and was very willing to surrender the box and the parchment to the Historical Society of Viborg to be placed in their museum.

I had the whole story from him a few months later, as we sat in a wood near Upsala, after a visit to the library there, where we – or, rather, I – had laughed over the contract by which Daniel Salthenius (in later life Professor of Hebrew at Königsberg) sold himself to Satan.

Anderson was not really amused.

'Young idiot!' he said, meaning Salthenius, who was only an undergraduate when he committed that indiscretion, 'how did he know what company he was courting?'

And when I suggested the usual considerations he only grunted.

That same afternoon he told me what you have read. But he refused to draw any inferences from it, and to assent to any that I drew for him.

'Oh, Whistle, and I'll Come to You, My Lad'

'I SUPPOSE YOU will be getting away pretty soon, now. Full term is over, Professor,' said a person not in the story to the Professor of Ontography, soon after they had sat down next to each other at a feast in the hospitable hall of St. James's College.

The Professor was young, neat, and precise in speech.

'Yes,' he said. 'My friends have been making me take up golf this term, and I mean to go to the East Coast – in point of fact to Burnstow – (I dare say you know it) for a week or ten days, to improve my game. I hope to get off tomorrow.'

'Oh, Parkins,' said his neighbour on the other side, 'if you are going to Burnstow, I wish you would look at the site of the Templars' preceptory, and let me know if you think it would be any good to have a dig there in the summer.'

It was, as you might suppose, a person of antiquarian pursuits who said this, but, since he merely appears in this prologue, there is no need to give his entitlements.

'Certainly,' said Parkins, the Professor. 'If you will describe to me whereabouts the site is, I will do my best to give you an idea of the lie of the land when I get back. Or I could write to you about it, if you would tell me where you are likely to be.'

'Don't trouble to do that, thanks. It's only that I'm thinking of taking my family in that direction in the Long, and it occurred to me that, as very few of the English preceptories have ever been properly planned, I might have an opportunity of doing something useful on off-days.'

The Professor rather sniffed at the idea that planning out a preceptory could be described as useful. His neighbour continued:

'The site – I doubt if there is anything showing above ground – must be down quite close to the beach now. The sea has encroached tremendously, as you know, all along that bit of coast. I should think, from the map, that it must be about three-quarters of a mile from the Globe Inn, at the north end of the town.

'Where are you going to stay?'

'Well, *at* the Globe Inn, as a matter of fact,' said Parkins. 'I have engaged a room there. I couldn't get in anywhere else. Most of the lodging-houses are shut up in winter, it seems; and, as it is, they tell me that the only room of any size I can have is really a double-bedded one, and that they haven't a corner in which to store the other bed, and so on.

'But I must have a fairly large room, for I am taking some books down, and mean to do a bit of work. And though I don't quite fancy having an empty bed – not to speak of two – in what I may call for the time being my study, I suppose I can manage to rough it for the short time I shall be there.'

'Do you call having an extra bed in your room roughing it, Parkins?' said a bluff person opposite. 'Look here, I shall come down and occupy it for a bit; it'll be company for you.'

The Professor quivered, but managed to laugh in a courteous manner.

'By all means, Rogers; there's nothing I should like better. But I'm afraid you would find it rather dull. You don't play golf, do you?'

'No, thank Heaven!' said rude Mr. Rogers.

'Well, you see, when I'm not writing I shall most likely be out on the links, and that, as I say, would be rather dull for you, I'm afraid.'

'Oh, I don't know! There's certain to be somebody I know in the place. But, of course, if you don't want me, speak the word, Parkins. I shan't be offended. Truth, as you always tell us, is never offensive.'

Parkins was, indeed, scrupulously polite and strictly truthful. It is to be feared that Mr. Rogers sometimes practised upon his knowledge of these characteristics.

In Parkins' breast there was a conflict now raging, which for a moment or two did not allow him to answer. That interval being over, he said:

'Well, if you want the exact truth, Rogers, I was considering whether the room I speak of would really be large enough to accommodate us both comfortably. And also whether (mind, I shouldn't have said this if you hadn't pressed me) you would not constitute something in the nature of a hindrance to my work.'

Rogers laughed loudly.

'Well done, Parkins!' he said. 'It's all right. I promise not to interrupt your work; don't you disturb yourself about that. No, I won't come if you don't want me, but I thought I should do so nicely to keep the ghosts off.'

Here he might have been seen to wink and to nudge his next neighbour.

Parkins might also have been seen to become pink.

'I beg pardon, Parkins,' Rogers continued; 'I oughtn't to have said that. I forgot you didn't like levity on these topics.'

'Well,' Parkins said, 'as you have mentioned the matter, I freely own that I do *not* like careless talk about what you call ghosts. A man in my position,' he went on, raising his voice a little, 'cannot, I find, be too careful about appearing to sanction the current beliefs on such subjects.

'As you know, Rogers – or as you ought to know – for I think I have never concealed my views—'

'No, you certainly have not, old man,' put in Rogers *sotto voce*.

'—I hold that any semblance, any appearance of concession to the view that such things might exist is equivalent to a renunciation of all that I hold most sacred. But I'm afraid I have not succeeded in securing your attention.'

'Your *undivided* attention, was what Dr. Blimber actually *said*,[†] Rogers interrupted, with every appearance of an earnest desire for accuracy. 'But I beg your pardon, Parkins: I'm stopping you.'

'No, not at all,' said Parkins. 'I don't remember Blimber; perhaps he was before my time. But I needn't go on. I'm sure you know what I mean.'

'Yes, yes,' said Rogers, rather hastily, 'just so. We'll go into it fully at Burnstow, or somewhere.'

---

† Mr. Rogers was wrong, *vide Dombey and Son*, chapter xii.

In repeating the above dialogue I have tried to give the impression which it made on me, that Parkins was something of an old woman – rather hen-like, perhaps, in his little ways; totally destitute – alas! – of the sense of humour, but at the same time dauntless and sincere in his convictions, and a man deserving of the greatest respect.

Whether or not the reader has gathered so much, that was the character which Parkins had.

On the following day Parkins did, as he had hoped, succeed in getting away from his college, and in arriving at Burnstow.

He was made welcome at the Globe Inn, was safely installed in the large double-bedded room of which we have heard, and was able before retiring to rest to arrange his materials for work in apple-pie order upon a commodious table which occupied the outer end of the room, and was sur-rounded on three sides by windows looking out seaward. That is to say, the central window looked straight out to sea, and those on the left and right commanded prospects along the shore to the north and south respectively.

On the south you saw the village of Burnstow. On the north no houses were to be seen, but only the beach and the low cliff backing it. Immediately in front was a strip – not considerable – of rough grass, dotted with old anchors, capstans, and so forth; then a broad path; then the beach.

Whatever may have been the original distance between the Globe Inn and the sea, not more than sixty yards now separated them.

The rest of the population of the inn was, of course, a golfing one, and included few elements that call for a special description. The most conspicu-ous figure was, perhaps, that of an *ancien militaire*, secretary of a London club, and possessed of a voice of incredible strength, and of views of a pronouncedly Protestant type.

These were apt to find utterance after his attendance upon the ministra-tions of the Vicar, an estimable man with inclinations towards a picturesque ritual, which he gallantly kept down as far as he could out of deference to East Anglian tradition.

Professor Parkins, one of whose principal characteristics was pluck, spent the greater part of the day following his arrival at Burnstow in what he had called improving his game, in company with this Colonel Wilson.

And during the afternoon – whether the process of improvement were to blame or not, I am not sure – the Colonel's demeanour assumed a colouring so lurid that even Parkins jibbed at the thought of walking home with him from the links.

He determined, after a short and furtive look at that bristling moustache and those incarnadined, features, that it would be wiser to allow the influences of tea and tobacco to do what they could with the Colonel before the dinner-hour should render a meeting inevitable.

'I might walk home tonight along the beach,' he reflected. 'Yes, and take a look – there will be light enough for that – at the ruins of which Disney was talking. I don't exactly know where they are, by the way; but I expect I can hardly help stumbling on them.'

This he accomplished, I may say, in the most literal sense, for in picking his way from the links to the shingle beach his foot caught, partly in a gorse-root and partly in a biggish stone, and over he went.

When he got up and surveyed his surroundings, he found himself in a patch of somewhat broken ground covered with small depressions and mounds. These latter, when he came to examine them, proved to be simply masses of flints embedded in mortar and grown over with turf. He must, he quite rightly concluded, be on the site of the preceptory he had promised to look at.

It seemed not unlikely to reward the spade of the explorer: enough of the foundations was probably left at no great depth to throw a good deal of light on the general plan. He remembered vaguely that the Templars, to whom this site had belonged, were in the habit of building round churches, and he thought a particular series of the humps or mounds near him did appear to be arranged in something of a circular form.

Few people can resist the temptation to try a little amateur research in a department quite outside their own, if only for the satisfaction of showing how successful they would have been had they only taken it up seriously.

Our Professor, however, if he felt something of this mean desire, was also truly anxious to oblige Mr. Disney. So he paced with care the circular area he had noticed, and wrote down its rough dimensions in his pocket-book. Then he proceeded to examine an oblong eminence which lay east of the centre of the circle, and seemed to his thinking likely to be the base of a platform or altar.

At one end of it, the northern, a patch of the turf was gone – removed by some boy or other creature *feræ naturæ*. It might, he thought, be as well to probe the soil here for evidences of masonry, and he took out his knife and began scraping away the earth.

And now followed another little discovery: a portion of soil fell inward as he scraped, and disclosed a small cavity. He lighted one match after another to help him to see of what nature the hole was, but the wind was too strong for them all.

By tapping and scratching the sides with his knife, however, he was able to make out that it must be an artificial hole in masonry. It was rectangular, and the sides, top, and bottom, if not actually plastered, were smooth and regular. Of course it was empty.

No! As he withdrew the knife he heard a metallic clink, and when he introduced his hand it met with a cylindrical object lying on the floor of the hole. Naturally enough, he picked it up, and when he brought it into the light, now fast fading, he could see that it, too, was of man's making – a metal tube about four inches long, and evidently of some considerable age.

By the time Parkins had made sure that there was nothing else in this odd receptacle, it was too late and too dark for him to think of undertaking any further search. What he had done had proved so unexpectedly interesting that he determined to sacrifice a little more of the daylight on the morrow to archæology. The object which he now had safe in his pocket was bound to be of some slight value at least, he felt sure.

Bleak and solemn was the view on which he took a last look before starting homeward. A faint yellow light in the west showed the links, on which a few figures moving towards the club-house were still visible, the squat Martello tower, the lights of Aldsey village, the pale ribbon of sands intersected at intervals by black wooden groynes, the dim and murmuring sea. The wind was bitter from the north, but was at his back when he set out for the Globe.

He quickly rattled and clashed through the shingle and gained the sand, upon which, but for the groynes which had to be got over every few yards, the going was both good and quiet. One last look behind, to measure the distance he had made since leaving the ruined Templars' church, showed him a prospect of company on his walk, in the shape of a rather indistinct personage, who seemed to be making great efforts to catch up with him, but made little, if any, progress.

I mean that there was an appearance of running about his movements, but that the distance between him and Parkins did not seem materially to lessen. So, at least, Parkins thought, and decided that he almost certainly did not know him, and that it would be absurd to wait until he came up.

For all that, company, he began to think, would really be very welcome on that lonely shore, if only you could choose your companion. In his unenlightened days he had read of meetings in such places which even now would hardly bear thinking of.

He went on thinking of them, however, until he reached home, and particularly of one which catches most people's fancy at some time of their childhood. 'Now I saw in my dream that Christian had gone but a very little way when he saw a foul fiend coming over the field to meet him.'

'What should I do now,' he thought, 'if I looked back and caught sight of a black figure sharply defined against the yellow sky, and saw that it had horns and wings? I wonder whether I should stand or run for it. Luckily, the gentleman behind is not of that kind, and he seems to be about as far off now as when I saw him first.'

'Well, at this rate he won't get his dinner as soon as I shall; and, dear me! it's within a quarter of an hour of the time now. I must run!'

Parkins had, in fact, very little time for dressing.

When he met the Colonel at dinner, Peace – or as much of her as that gentleman could manage – reigned once more in the military bosom. Nor was she put to flight in the hours of bridge that followed dinner, for Parkins was a more than respectable player.

When, therefore, he retired towards twelve o'clock, he felt that he had spent his evening in quite a satisfactory way, and that, even for so long as a fortnight or three weeks, life at the Globe would be supportable under similar conditions – 'especially,' thought he, 'if I go on improving my game.'

As he went along the passages he met the boots of the Globe, who stopped and said:

'Beg your pardon, sir, but as I was a-brushing your coat just now there was somethink fell out of the pocket. I put it on your chest of drawers, sir in your room, sir – a piece of a pipe or somethink of that, sir. Thank you, sir.

You'll find it on your chest of drawers, sir – yes, sir. Good night, sir.'

The speech served to remind Parkins of his little discovery of that afternoon.

It was with some considerable curiosity that he turned it over by the light of his candles. It was of bronze, he now saw, and was shaped very much after the manner of the modern dog-whistle. In fact it was – yes, certainly it was – actually no more nor less than a whistle.

He put it to his lips, but it was quite full of a fine, caked-up sand or earth, which would not yield to knocking, but must be loosened with a knife. Tidy as ever in his habits, Parkins cleared out the earth on to a piece of paper, and took the latter to the window to empty it out.

The night was clear and bright, as he saw when he had opened the casement, and he stopped for an instant to look at the sea and note a belated wanderer stationed on the shore in front of the inn.

Then he shut the window, a little surprised at the late hours people kept at Burnstow, and took his whistle to the light again.

Why, surely there were marks on it, not merely marks, but letters! A very little rubbing rendered the deeply-cut inscription quite legible, but the Professor had to confess, after some earnest thought, that the meaning of it was as obscure to him as the writing on the wall to Belshazzar.

There were legends both on the front and on the back of the whistle. The one read thus:

FLA

FUR   BIS

FLE

The other:

⌗ QUIS EST ISTE QUI UENIT ⌗

'I ought to be able to make it out,' he thought, 'but I suppose I am a little rusty in my Latin. When I come to think of it, I don't believe I even know the word for a whistle.

97

'The long one does seem simple enough. It ought to mean, "Who is this who is coming?" Well, the best way to find out is evidently to whistle for him.'

He blew tentatively and stopped suddenly, startled and yet pleased at the note he had elicited. It had a quality of infinite distance in it, and, soft as it was, he somehow felt it must be audible for miles round. It was a sound, too, that seemed to have the power (which many scents possess) of forming pictures in the brain.

He saw quite clearly for a moment a vision of a wide, dark expanse at night, with a fresh wind blowing, and in the midst a lonely figure – how employed, he could not tell. Perhaps he would have seen more had not the picture been broken by the sudden surge of a gust of wind against his casement, so sudden that it made him look up, just in time to see the white glint of a sea-bird's wing somewhere outside the dark panes.

The sound of the whistle had so fascinated him that he could not help trying it once more, this time more boldly.

The note was little, if at all, louder than before, and repetition broke the illusion – no picture followed, as he had half-hoped it might.

'But what is this? Goodness! What force the wind can get up in a few minutes! What a tremendous gust! There! I knew that window-fastening was no use! Ah! I thought so – both candles out. It's enough to tear the room to pieces.'

The first thing was to get the window shut. While you might count twenty Parkins was struggling with the small casement, and felt almost as if he were pushing back a sturdy burglar, so strong was the pressure.

It slackened all at once and the window banged to and latched itself.

Now to relight the candles and see what damage, if any, had been done.

No, nothing seemed amiss; no glass even was broken in the casement. But the noise had evidently roused at least one member of the household: the Colonel was to be heard stumping in his stockinged feet on the floor above, and growling.

Quickly as it had risen, the wind did not fall at once. On it went, moaning and rushing past the house, at times rising to a cry so desolate that, as Parkins disinterestedly said, it might have made fanciful people feel quite uncomfortable. Even the unimaginative, he thought after a quarter of an hour, might be happier without it.

Whether it was the wind, or the excitement of golf, or of the researches in the preceptory that kept Parkins awake, he was not sure.

Awake he remained, in any case, long enough to fancy (as I am afraid I often do myself under such conditions) that he was the victim of all manner of fatal disorders. He would lie counting the beats of his heart, convinced that it was going to stop work every moment, and would entertain grave suspicions of his lungs, brain, liver, etc. – suspicions which he was sure would be dispelled by the return of daylight, but which until then refused to be put aside.

He found a little vicarious comfort in the idea that someone else was in the same boat. A near neighbour (in the darkness it was not easy to tell his direction) was tossing and rustling in his bed, too.

The next stage was that Parkins shut his eyes and determined to give sleep every chance. Here again over-excitement asserted itself in another form – that of making pictures. *Experto crede*, pictures do come to the closed eyes of one trying to sleep, and are often so little to his taste that he must open his eyes and disperse them.

Parkins' experience on this occasion was a very distressing one. He found that the picture which presented itself to him was continuous. When he opened his eyes, of course, it went; but when he shut them once more it framed itself afresh, and acted itself out again, neither quicker nor slower than before. What he saw was this:

A long stretch of shore – shingle edged by sand, and intersected at short intervals with black groynes running down to the water – a scene, in fact, so like that of his afternoon's walk that, in the absence of any landmark, it could not be distinguished therefrom.

The light was obscure, conveying an impression of gathering storm, late winter evening, and slight cold rain. On this bleak stage at first no actor was visible. When, in the distance, a bobbing black object appeared. A moment more, and it was a man running, jumping, clambering over the groynes, and every few seconds looking eagerly back.

The nearer he came the more obvious it was that he was not only anxious, but even terribly frightened, though his face was not to be distinguished. He was, moreover, almost at the end of his strength. On he came, each successive obstacle seemed to cause him more difficulty than the last.

'Will he get over this next one?' thought Parkins. 'It seems a little higher than the others.'

Yes: half-climbing, half-throwing himself, he did get over, and fell all in a heap on the other side (the side nearest to the spectator). There, as if really unable to get up again, he remained crouching under the groyne, looking up in attitude of painful anxiety.

So far no cause whatever for the fear of the runner had been shown. But now there began to be seen, far up the shore, a little flicker of something light-coloured moving to and fro with great swiftness and irregularity. Rapidly growing larger, it, too, declared itself as a figure in pale, fluttering draperies, ill-defined. There was something about its motion which made Parkins very unwilling to see it at close quarters.

It would stop, raise arms, bow itself toward the sand, then run stooping across the beach to the water-edge and back again; and then, rising upright, once more continue its course forward at a speed that was startling and terrifying.

The moment came when the pursuer was hovering about from left to right only a few yards beyond the groyne where the runner lay in hiding. After two or three ineffectual castings hither and thither it came to a stop, stood upright, with arms raised high, and then darted straight forward towards the groyne.

It was at this point that Parkins always failed in his resolution to keep his eyes shut.

With many misgivings as to incipient failure of eyesight, overworked brain, excessive smoking, and so on, he finally resigned himself to light his candle, get out a book, and pass the night waking, rather than be tormented by this persistent panorama, which he saw clearly enough could only be a morbid reflection of his walk and his thoughts on that very day.

The scraping of match on box and the glare of light must have startled some creatures of the night – rats or what not – which he heard scurry across the floor from the side of his bed with much rustling.

Dear, dear! The match is out! Fool that it is!

But the second one burnt better, and a candle and book were duly procured, over which Parkins pored till sleep of a wholesome kind came upon him, and that in no long space.

For about the first time in his orderly and prudent life he forgot to blow out the candle, and when he was called next morning at eight there was still a flicker in the socket and a sad mess of guttered grease on the top of the little table.

After breakfast he was in his room, putting the finishing touches to his golfing costume – fortune had again allotted the Colonel to him for a partner – when one of the maids came in.

'Oh, if you please,' she said, 'would you like any extra blankets on your bed, sir?'

'Ah! Thank you,' said Parkins. 'Yes, I think I should like one. It seems likely to turn rather colder.'

In a very short time the maid was back with the blanket.

'Which bed should I put it on, sir?' she asked.

'What? Why, that one – the one I slept in last night,' he said, pointing to it.

'Oh yes! I beg your pardon, sir, but you seemed to have tried both of 'em; leastways, we had to make 'em both up this morning.'

'Really? How very absurd!' said Parkins. 'I certainly never touched the other, except to lay some things on it. Did it actually seem to have been slept in?'

'Oh yes, sir!' said the maid. 'Why, all the things was crumpled and throwed about all ways, if you'll excuse me, sir, quite as if anyone 'adn't passed but a very poor night, sir.'

'Dear me,' said Parkins. 'Well, I may have disordered it more than I thought when I unpacked my things. I'm very sorry to have given you the trouble, I'm sure. I expect a friend of mine soon, by the way – a gentleman from Cambridge – to come and occupy it for a night or two. That will be all right, I suppose, won't it?'

'Oh yes, to be sure, sir. Thank you, sir. It's no trouble, I'm sure,' said the maid, and departed to giggle with her colleagues.

Parkins set forth, with a stern determination to improve his game.

I am glad to be able to report that he succeeded so far in this enterprise that the Colonel, who had been rather repining at the prospect of a second day's play in his company, became quite chatty as the morning advanced; and his voice boomed out over the flats, as certain also of our own minor poets have said, 'like some great bourdon in a minster tower'.

'Extraordinary wind, that, we had last night,' he said. 'In my old home we should have said someone had been whistling for it.'

'Should you, indeed!' said Parkins. 'Is there a superstition of that kind still current in your part of the country?'

'I don't know about superstition,' said the Colonel. 'They believe in it all over Denmark and Norway, as well as on the Yorkshire coast. And my experience is, mind you, that there's generally something at the bottom of what these country-folk hold to, and have held to for generations. But it's your drive' (or whatever it might have been: the golfing reader will have to imagine appropriate digressions at the proper intervals).

When conversation was resumed, Parkins said, with a slight hesitancy:

'Apropos of what you were saying just now, Colonel, I think I ought to tell you that my own views on such subjects are very strong. I am, in fact, a convinced disbeliever in what is called the "supernatural".'

'What!' said the Colonel, 'do you mean to tell me you don't believe in second-sight, or ghosts, or anything of that kind?'

'In nothing whatever of that kind,' returned Parkins firmly.

'Well,' said the Colonel, 'but it appears to me at that rate, sir, that you must be little better than a Sadducee.'

Parkins was on the point of answering that, in his opinion, the Sadducees were the most sensible sons he had ever read of in the Old Testament. But, feeling some doubt as to whether much mention of them was to be found in that work, he preferred to laugh the accusation off.

'Perhaps I am,' he said, 'but— Here, give me my cleek, boy! Excuse me one moment, Colonel.' A short interval. 'Now, as to whistling for the wind, let me give you my theory about it.

'The laws which govern winds are really not at all perfectly known – to fisher-folk and such, of course, not known at all. A man or woman of eccentric habits, perhaps, or a stranger, is seen repeatedly on the beach at some unusual hour, and is heard whistling.

'Soon afterwards a violent wind rises. A man who could read the sky perfectly or who possessed a barometer could have foretold that it would. The simple people of a fishing-village have no barometers, and only a few rough rules for prophesying weather. What more natural than that the eccentric personage I postulated should be regarded as having raised the wind, or that he or she should clutch eagerly at the reputation of being able to do so?

'Now, take last night's wind: as it happens, I myself was whistling. I blew a whistle twice, and the wind seemed to come absolutely in answer to my call. If anyone had seen me—'

The audience had been a little restive under this harangue, and Parkins had, I fear, fallen somewhat into the tone of a lecturer. But at the last sentence the Colonel stopped.

'Whistling, were you?' he said. 'And what sort of whistle did you use? Play this stroke first.' Interval.

'About that whistle you were asking, Colonel. It's rather a curious one. I have it in my— No; I see I've left it in my room. As a matter of fact, I found it yesterday.'

And then Parkins narrated the manner of his discovery of the whistle, upon hearing which the Colonel grunted, and opined that, in Parkins's place, he should himself be careful about using a thing that had belonged to a set of Papists, of whom, speaking generally, it might be affirmed that you never knew what they might not have been up to.

From this topic he diverged to the enormities of the Vicar, who had given notice on the previous Sunday that Friday would be the Feast of St. Thomas the Apostle, and that there would be service at eleven o'clock in the church. This and other similar proceedings constituted in the Colonel's view a strong presumption that the Vicar was a concealed Papist, if not a Jesuit; and Parkins, who could not very readily follow the Colonel in this region, did not disagree with him.

In fact, they got on so well together in the morning that there was no talk on either side of their separating after lunch.

Both continued to play well during the afternoon, or, at least, well enough to make them forget everything else until the light began to fail them. Not until then did Parkins remember that he had meant to do some more investigating at the preceptory; but it was of no great importance, he reflected. One day was as good as another. He might as well go home with the Colonel.

As they turned the corner of the house, the Colonel was almost knocked down by a boy who rushed into him at the very top of his speed, and then, instead of running away, remained hanging on to him and panting.

The first words of the warrior were naturally those of reproof and objurgation, but he quickly discerned that the boy was almost speechless with fright. Inquiries were useless at first. When the boy got his breath he began to howl, and still clung to the Colonel's legs. He was at last detached, but continued to howl.

'What in the world *is* the matter with you? What have you been up to? What have you seen?' said the two men.

'Ow, I seen it wive at me out of the winder,' wailed the boy, 'and I don't like it.'

'What window?' said the irritated Colonel. 'Come, pull yourself together, my boy.'

'The front winder it was, at the 'otel,' said the boy.

At this point Parkins was in favour of sending the boy home, but the Colonel refused; he wanted to get to the bottom of it, he said. It was most dangerous to give a boy such a fright as this one had had, and if it turned out that people had been playing jokes, they should suffer for it in some way.

And by a series of questions he made out this story: The boy had been playing about on the grass in front of the Globe with some others. Then they had gone home to their teas, and he was just going, when he happened to look up at the front winder and see it a-wiving at him.

It seemed to be a figure of some sort, in white as far as he knew – couldn't see its face; but it wived at him, and it warn't a right thing – not to say not a right person.

Was there a light in the room? No, he didn't think to look if there was a light. Which was the window? Was it the top one or the second one? The seckind one it was – the big winder what got two little uns at the sides.

'Very well, my boy,' said the Colonel, after a few more questions. 'You run away home now. I expect it was some person trying to give you a start. Another time, like a brave English boy, you just throw a stone – well, no, not that exactly, but you go and speak to the waiter, or to Mr. Simpson, the landlord, and – yes – and say that I advised you to do so.'

The boy's face expressed some of the doubt he felt as to the likelihood of Mr. Simpson's lending a favourable ear to his complaint, but the Colonel did not appear to perceive this, and went on:

'And here's a sixpence – no, I see it's a shilling – and you be off home, and don't think any more about it.'

The youth hurried off with agitated thanks, and the Colonel and Parkins went round to the front of the Globe and reconnoitred. There was only one window answering to the description they had been hearing.

'Well, that's curious,' said Parkins. 'It's evidently my window the lad was talking about. Will you come up for a moment, Colonel Wilson? We ought to be able to see if anyone has been taking liberties in my room.'

They were soon in the passage, and Parkins made as if to open the door. Then he stopped and felt in his pockets.

'This is more serious than I thought,' was his next remark. 'I remember now that before I started this morning I locked the door. It is locked now, and, what is more, here is the key.' And he held it up. 'Now,' he went on, 'if the servants are in the habit of going into one's room during the day when one is away, I can only say that – well, that I don't approve of it at all.'

Conscious of a somewhat weak climax, he busied himself in opening the door (which was indeed locked) and in lighting candles. 'No,' he said, 'nothing seems disturbed.'

'Except your bed,' put in the Colonel.

'Excuse me, that isn't my bed,' said Parkins. 'I don't use that one. But it does look as if someone had been playing tricks with it.'

It certainly did: the clothes were bundled up and twisted together in a most tortuous confusion. Parkins pondered.

'That must be it,' he said at last: 'I disordered the clothes last night in unpacking, and they haven't made it since. Perhaps they came in to make it, and that boy saw them through the window; and then they were called away and locked the door after them. Yes, I think that must be it.'

'Well, ring and ask,' said the Colonel, and this appealed to Parkins as practical.

The maid appeared, and, to make a long story short, deposed that she had made the bed in the morning when the gentleman was in the room, and hadn't been there since. No, she hadn't no other key. Mr. Simpson he kep' the keys; he'd be able to tell the gentleman if anyone had been up.

This was a puzzle.

Investigation showed that nothing of value had been taken, and Parkins remembered the disposition of the small objects on tables and so forth well enough to be pretty sure that no pranks had been played with them. Mr. and Mrs. Simpson furthermore agreed that neither of them had given the duplicate key of the room to any person whatever during the day.

Nor could Parkins, fair-minded man as he was, detect anything in the demeanour of master, mistress or maid that indicated guilt. He was much more inclined to think that the boy had been imposing on the Colonel.

The latter was unwontedly silent and pensive at dinner and throughout the evening. When he bade good night to Parkins, he murmured in a gruff undertone:

'You know where I am if you want me during the night.'

'Why, yes, thank you, Colonel Wilson, I think I do. But there isn't much prospect of my disturbing you, I hope. By the way,' he added, 'did I show you that old whistle I spoke of? I think not. Well, here it is.'

The Colonel turned it over gingerly in the light of the candle.

'Can you make anything of the inscription?' asked Parkins, as he took it back.

'No, not in this light. What do you mean to do with it?'

'Oh, well, when I get back to Cambridge I shall submit it to some of the archæologists there, and see what they think of it. And very likely, if they consider it worth having, I may present it to one of the museums.'

''M!' said the Colonel. 'Well, you may be right. All I know is that, if it were mine, I should chuck it straight into the sea. It's no use talking, I'm well aware, but I expect that with you it's a case of live and learn. I hope so, I'm sure, and I wish you a good night.'

He turned away, leaving Parkins in act to speak at the bottom of the stair, and soon each was in his own bedroom.

By some unfortunate accident, there were neither blinds nor curtains to the windows of the Professor's room. The previous night he had thought little of this, but tonight there seemed every prospect of a bright moon rising to shine directly on his bed, and probably wake him later on.

When he noticed this he was a good deal annoyed, but, with an ingenuity which I can only envy, he succeeded in rigging up, with the help of a railway-rug, some safety-pins and a stick and umbrella, a screen which, if it only held together, would completely keep the moonlight off his bed.

And shortly afterwards he was comfortably in that bed.

When he had read a somewhat solid work long enough to produce a decided wish for sleep, he cast a drowsy glance round the room, blew out the candle, and fell back upon the pillow.

He must have slept soundly for an hour or more, when a sudden clatter shook him up in a most unwelcome manner. In a moment he realised what had happened: his carefully-constructed screen had given way, and a very bright frosty moon was shining directly on his face. This was highly annoying. Could he possibly get up and reconstruct the screen? Or could he manage to sleep if he did not?

For some minutes he lay and pondered over the possibilities; then he turned over sharply, and with all his eyes open lay breathlessly listening.

There had been a movement, he was sure, in the empty bed on the opposite side of the room. Tomorrow he would have it moved, for there must be rats or something playing about in it.

It was quiet now. No! The commotion began again. There was a rustling and shaking: surely more than any rat could cause.

I can figure to myself something of the Professor's bewilderment and horror, for I have in a dream thirty years back seen the same thing happen. But the reader will hardly, perhaps, imagine how dreadful it was to him to see a figure suddenly sit up in what he had known was an empty bed.

He was out of his own bed in one bound, and made a dash towards the window, where lay his only weapon, the stick with which he had propped his screen.

This was, as it turned out, the worst thing he could have done, because the personage in the empty bed, with a sudden motion, slipped from the bed and took up a position, with outspread arms, between the two beds, and in front of the door.

Parkins watched it in a horrid perplexity. Somehow, the idea of getting past it and escaping through the door was intolerable to him. He could not have borne – he didn't know why – to touch it; and as for its touching him, he would sooner dash himself through the window than have that happen.

It stood for the moment in a band of dark shadow, and he had not seen what its face was like. Now it began to move, in a stooping posture, and all at once the spectator realised, with some horror and some relief, that it must be blind, for it seemed to feel about it with its muffled arms in a groping and random fashion.

Turning half-away from him, it became suddenly conscious of the bed he had just left, and darted towards it, and bent over and felt the pillows in a way which made Parkins shudder as he had never in his life thought it possible.

In a very few moments it seemed to know that the bed was empty, and then, moving forward into the area of light and facing the window, it showed for the first time what manner of thing it was.

Parkins, who very much dislikes being questioned about it, did once describe something of it in my hearing, and I gathered that what he chiefly remembers about it is a horrible, an intensely horrible, face *of crumpled linen.* What expression he read upon it he could not or would not tell, but that the fear of it went nigh to maddening him is certain.

But he was not at leisure to watch it for long. With formidable quickness it moved into the middle of the room, and, as it groped and waved, one corner of its draperies swept across Parkins's face. He could not – though he knew how perilous a sound was – he could not keep back a cry of disgust, and this gave the searcher an instant clue.

It leapt towards him upon the instant, and the next moment he was half-way through the window backwards, uttering cry upon cry at the utmost pitch of his voice, and the linen face was thrust close into his own.

At this, almost the last possible second, deliverance came, as you will have guessed: the Colonel burst the door open, and was just in time to see the dreadful group at the window.

When he reached the figures only one was left. Parkins sank forward into the room in a faint, and before him on the floor lay a tumbled heap of bedclothes.

Colonel Wilson asked no questions, but busied himself in keeping everyone else out of the room and in getting Parkins back to his bed; and himself, wrapped in a rug, occupied the other bed for the rest of the night.

Early on the next day Rogers arrived, more welcome than he would have been a day before, and the three of them held a very long consultation in the Professor's room. At the end of it the Colonel left the hotel door carrying a small object between his finger and thumb, which he cast as far into the sea as a very brawny arm could send it. Later on the smoke of a burning ascended from the back premises of the Globe.

Exactly what explanation was patched up for the staff and visitors at the hotel I must confess I do not recollect. The Professor was somehow cleared of the ready suspicion of delirium tremens, and the hotel of the reputation of a troubled house.

There is not much question as to what would have happened to Parkins if the Colonel had not intervened when he did. He would either have fallen out of the window or else lost his wits. But it is not so evident what more the creature that came in answer to the whistle could have done than frighten.

There seemed to be absolutely nothing material about it save the bed-clothes of which it had made itself a body. The Colonel, who remembered a not very dissimilar occurrence in India, was of opinion that if Parkins had closed with it it could really have done very little, and that its one power was that of frightening. The whole thing, he said, served to confirm his opinion of the Church of Rome.

There is really nothing more to tell, but, as you may imagine, the Professor's views on certain points are less clear-cut than they used to be.

His nerves, too, have suffered: he cannot even now see a surplice hanging on a door quite unmoved, and the spectacle of a scarecrow in a field late on a winter afternoon has cost him more than one sleepless night.

The Treasure of Abbot Thomas

I

Verum usque in præsentem diem multa garriunt inter se Canonici de abscondito quodam istius Abbatis Thomæ thesauro, quem sæpe, quanquam adhuc incassum, quæsiverunt Steinfeldenses. Ipsum enim Thomam adhuc florida in ætate existentem ingentem auri massam circa monasterium defodisse perhibent; de quo multoties interrogatus ubi esset, cum risu respondere solitus erat: 'Job, Johannes, et Zacharias vel vobis vel posteris indicabunt'; idemque aliquando adiicere se inventuris minime invisurum. Inter alia huius Abbatis opera, hoc memoria præcipue dignum iudico quod fenestram magnam in orientali parte alæ australis in ecclesia sua imaginibus optime in vitro depictis impleverit: id quod et ipsius effigies et insignia ibidem posita demonstrant. Domum quoque Abbatialem fere totam restauravit: puteo in atrio ipsius effosso et lapidibus marmoreis pulchre cælatis exornato. Decessit autem, morte aliquantulum subitanea perculsus, ætatis suæ anno lxxiido, incarnationis vero Dominic mdxxixo.

'I SUPPOSE I SHALL have to translate this,' said the antiquary to himself, as he finished copying the above lines from that rather rare and exceedingly diffuse book, the *Sertum Steinfeldense Norbertinum.*[†] 'Well, it may as well be done first as last,' and accordingly the following rendering was very quickly produced:

Up to the present day there is much gossip among the Canons about a certain hidden treasure of this Abbot Thomas, for which those of Steinfeld have often made search, though hitherto in vain. The story is that Thomas, while yet in the vigour of life, concealed a very large quantity of gold somewhere in the monastery. He was often asked where it was, and always answered, with a laugh: 'Job, John, and Zechariah will tell either you or your successors.' He sometimes added that he should feel no grudge against those who might find it. Among other works carried out by this Abbot I may specially mention his filling the great window at the east end of the south aisle of the church with figures admirably painted on glass, as his effigy and arms in the window attest. He also restored almost the whole of the Abbot's lodging, and dug a well in the court of it, which he adorned with beautiful carvings in marble. He died rather suddenly in the seventy-second year of his age, AD 1529.

The object which the antiquary had before him at the moment was that of tracing the whereabouts of the painted windows of the Abbey Church of Steinfeld. Shortly after the Revolution, a very large quantity of painted glass made its way from the dissolved abbeys of Germany and Belgium to this country, and may now be seen adorning various of our parish churches, cathedrals, and private chapels.

Steinfeld Abbey was among the most considerable of these involuntary contributors to our artistic possessions (I am quoting the somewhat ponderous preamble of the book which the antiquary wrote), and the greater part of the glass from that institution can be identified without much difficulty by the help, either of the numerous inscriptions in which the place is

---

† An account of the Premonstratensian abbey of Steinfeld, in the Eiffel, with lives of the Abbots, published at Cologne in 1712 by Christian Albert Erhard, a resident in the district. The epithet *Norbertinum* is due to the fact that St. Norbert was founder of the Premonstratensian Order.

mentioned, or of the subjects of the windows, in which several well-defined cycles or narratives were represented.

The passage with which I began my story had set the antiquary on the track of another identification.

In a private chapel – no matter where – he had seen three large figures, each occupying a whole light in a window, and evidently the work of one artist. Their style made it plain that the artist had been a German of the 16th century; but hitherto the more exact localising of them had been a puzzle. They represented – will you be surprised to hear it? – JOB PATRIARCHA, JOHANNES EVANGELISTA, ZACHARIAS PROPHETA, and each of them held a book or scroll, inscribed with a sentence from his writings.

These, as a matter of course, the antiquary had noted, and had been struck by the curious way in which they differed from any text of the Vulgate that he had been able to examine. Thus the scroll in Job's hand was inscribed: *Auro est locus in quo absconditur* (for *conflatur*);[†] on the book of John was: *Habent in vestimentis suis scripturam quam nemo novit* (for *in vestimento scriptum*, the following words being taken from another verse);[††] and Zacharias had: *Super lapidem unum septem oculi sunt* (which alone of the three presents an unaltered text).[†††]

A sad perplexity it had been to our investigator to think why these three personages should have been placed together in one window. There was no bond of connection between them – either historic, symbolic, or doctrinal – and he could only suppose that they must have formed part of a very large series of Prophets and Apostles, which might have filled, say, all the clerestory windows of some capacious church.

But the passage from the *Sertum* had altered the situation by showing that the names of the actual personages represented in the glass now in Lord D——'s chapel had been constantly on the lips of Abbot Thomas von Eschenhausen of Steinfeld, and that this Abbot had put up a painted window, probably about the year 1520, in the south aisle of his abbey church.

---

† There is a place for gold where it is hidden.

†† They have on their raiment a writing which no man knoweth.

††† Upon one stone are seven eyes.

It was no very wild conjecture that the three figures might have formed part of Abbot Thomas' offering; it was one which, moreover, could probably be confirmed or set aside by another careful examination of the glass. And, as Mr. Somerton was a man of leisure, he set out on pilgrimage to the private chapel with very little delay.

His conjecture was confirmed to the full. Not only did the style and technique of the glass suit perfectly with the date and place required, but in another window of the chapel he found some glass, known to have been bought along with the figures, which contained the arms of Abbot Thomas von Eschenhausen.

At intervals during his researches Mr. Somerton had been haunted by the recollection of the gossip about the hidden treasure, and, as he thought the matter over, it became more and more obvious to him that if the Abbot meant anything by the enigmatical answer which he gave to his question-ers, he must have meant that the secret was to be found somewhere in the window he had placed in the abbey church.

It was undeniable, furthermore, that the first of the curiously-selected texts on the scrolls in the window might be taken to have a reference to hidden treasure.

Every feature, therefore, or mark which could possibly assist in elucidating the riddle which, he felt sure, the Abbot had set to posterity he noted with scrupulous care, and, returning to his Berkshire manor-house, consumed many a pint of the midnight oil over his tracings and sketches.

After two or three weeks, a day came when Mr. Somerton announced to his man that he must pack his own and his master's things for a short journey abroad, whither for the moment we will not follow him.

II

Mr. Gregory, the Rector of Parsbury, had strolled out before breakfast, it being a fine autumn morning, as far as the gate of his carriage-drive, with intent to meet the postman and sniff the cool air. Nor was he disappointed of either purpose.

Before he had had time to answer more than ten or eleven of the miscellaneous questions propounded to him in the lightness of their hearts by his young offspring, who had accompanied him, the postman was seen approaching; and among the morning's budget was one letter bearing a foreign postmark and stamp (which became at once the objects of an eager competition among the youthful Gregorys), and was addressed in an uneducated, but plainly an English hand.

When the Rector opened it, and turned to the signature, he realised that it came from the confidential valet of his friend and squire, Mr. Somerton. Thus it ran:

HONOURD SIR,

Has I am in a great anxeity about Master I write at is Wish to Beg you Sir if you could be so good as Step over. Master Has add a Nastey Shock and keeps His Bedd. I never Have known Him like this but No wonder and Nothing will serve but you Sir. Master says would I mintion the Short Way Here is Drive to Cobblince and take a Trap. Hopeing I Have maid all Plain, but am much Confused in Myself what with Anxiatey and Weakfulness at Night. If I might be so Bold Sir it will be a Pleasure to see a Honnest Brish Face among all These Forig ones.

I am Sir
Your obedt Servt
WILLIAM BROWN.

P.S. – The Villiage for Town I will not Turm It is name Steenfeld.

The reader must be left to picture to himself in detail the surprise, confusion, and hurry of preparation into which the receipt of such a letter would be likely to plunge a quiet Berkshire parsonage in the year of grace 1859. It is enough for me to say that a train to town was caught in the course of the day, and that Mr. Gregory was able to secure a cabin in the Antwerp boat and a place in the Coblentz train. Nor was it difficult to manage the transit from that centre to Steinfeld.

I labour under a grave disadvantage as narrator of this story in that I have never visited Steinfeld myself, and that neither of the principal actors in the episode (from whom I derive my information) was able to give me anything but a vague and rather dismal idea of its appearance.

I gather that it is a small place, with a large church despoiled of its ancient fittings; a number of rather ruinous great buildings, mostly of the 17th century, surround this church; for the abbey, in common with most of those on the Continent, was rebuilt in a luxurious fashion by its inhabitants at that period.

It has not seemed to me worthwhile to lavish money on a visit to the place, for though it is probably far more attractive than either Mr. Somerton or Mr. Gregory thought it, there is evidently little, if anything, of first-rate interest to be seen – except, perhaps, one thing, which I should not care to see.

The inn where the English gentleman and his servant were lodged is, or was, the only 'possible' one in the village. Mr. Gregory was taken to it at once by his driver, and found Mr. Brown waiting at the door. Mr. Brown, a model when in his Berkshire home of the impassive whiskered race who are known as confidential valets, was now egregiously out of his element, in a light tweed suit, anxious, almost irritable, and plainly anything but master of the situation.

His relief at the sight of the 'honest British face' of his Rector was unmeasured, but words to describe it were denied him. He could only say:

'Well, I ham pleased, I'm sure, sir, to see you. And so I'm sure, sir, will master.'

'How *is* your master, Brown?' Mr. Gregory eagerly put in.

'I think he's better, sir, thank you; but he's had a dreadful time of it. I 'ope he's gettin' some sleep now, but—'

'What has been the matter – I couldn't make out from your letter? Was it an accident of any kind?'

'Well, sir, I 'ardly know whether I'd better speak about it. Master was very partickler he should be the one to tell you. But there's no bones broke – that's one thing I'm sure we ought to be thankful—'

'What does the doctor say?' asked Mr. Gregory.

They were by this time outside Mr. Somerton's bedroom door, and speaking in low tones. Mr. Gregory, who happened to be in front, was feeling for the handle, and chanced to run his fingers over the panels. Before Brown could answer, there was a terrible cry from within the room.

'In God's name, who is that?' were the first words they heard. 'Brown, is it?'

'Yes, sir – me, sir, and Mr. Gregory,' Brown hastened to answer, and there was an audible groan of relief in reply.

They entered the room, which was darkened against the afternoon sun, and Mr. Gregory saw, with a shock of pity, how drawn, how damp with drops of fear, was the usually calm face of his friend, who, sitting up in the curtained bed, stretched out a shaking hand to welcome him.

'Better for seeing you, my dear Gregory,' was the reply to the Rector's first question, and it was palpably true.

After five minutes of conversation Mr. Somerton was more his own man, Brown afterwards reported, than he had been for days. He was able to eat a more than respectable dinner, and talked confidently of being fit to stand a journey to Coblentz within twenty-four hours.

'But there's one thing,' he said, with a return of agitation which Mr. Gregory did not like to see, 'which I must beg you to do for me, my dear Gregory. Don't,' he went on, laying his hand on Gregory's to forestall any interruption, 'don't ask me what it is, or why I want it done. I'm not up to explaining it yet; it would throw me back – undo all the good you have done me by coming.

'The only word I will say about it is that you run no risk whatever by doing it, and that Brown can and will show you tomorrow what it is. It's merely to put back – to keep – something— No. I can't speak of it yet. Do you mind calling Brown?'

'Well, Somerton,' said Mr. Gregory, as he crossed the room to the door, 'I won't ask for any explanations till you see fit to give them. And if this bit of business is as easy as you represent it to be, I will very gladly undertake it for you the first thing in the morning.'

'Ah, I was sure you would, my dear Gregory; I was certain I could rely on you. I shall owe you more thanks than I can tell. Now, here is Brown. Brown, one word with you.'

'Shall I go?' interjected Mr. Gregory.

'Not at all. Dear me, no. Brown, the first thing tomorrow morning – (you don't mind early hours, I know, Gregory) – you must take the Rector to – *there*, you know' (a nod from Brown, who looked grave and anxious), 'and he and you will put that back. You needn't be in the least alarmed; it's *perfectly* safe in the daytime. You know what I mean. It lies on the step, you know, where – where we put it.' (Brown swallowed dryly once or twice, and, failing to speak, bowed.) 'And – yes, that's all.

'Only this one other word, my dear Gregory. If you *can* manage to keep from questioning Brown about this matter, I shall be still more bound to you. Tomorrow evening, at latest, if all goes well, I shall be able, I believe, to tell you the whole story from start to finish.

'And now I'll wish you good night. Brown will be with me – he sleeps here – and if I were you, I should lock my door. Yes, be particular to do that. They – they like it, the people here, and it's better. Good night, good night.'

They parted upon this, and if Mr. Gregory woke once or twice in the small hours and fancied he heard a fumbling about the lower part of his locked door, it was, perhaps, no more than what a quiet man, suddenly plunged into a strange bed and the heart of a mystery, might reasonably expect. Certainly he thought, to the end of his days, that he had heard such a sound twice or three times between midnight and dawn.

He was up with the sun, and out in company with Brown soon after. Perplexing as was the service he had been asked to perform for Mr. Somerton, it was not a difficult or an alarming one, and within half-an-hour from his leaving the inn it was over. What it was I shall not as yet divulge.

Later in the morning Mr. Somerton, now almost himself again, was able to make a start from Steinfeld. And that same evening, whether at Coblentz or at some intermediate stage on the journey I am not certain, he settled down to the promised explanation.

Brown was present, but how much of the matter was ever really made plain to his comprehension he would never say, and I am unable to conjecture.

III

This was Mr. Somerton's story:

'You know roughly, both of you, that this expedition of mine was undertaken with the object of tracing something in connection with some old painted glass in Lord D——'s private chapel. Well, the starting-point of the whole matter lies in this passage from an old printed book, to which I will ask your attention.'

And at this point Mr. Somerton went carefully over some ground with which we are already familiar.

'On my second visit to the chapel,' he went on, 'my purpose was to take every note I could of figures, lettering, diamond-scratchings on the glass, and even apparently accidental markings.

'The first point which I tackled was that of the inscribed scrolls. I could not doubt that the first of these, that of Job – "There is a place for the gold where it is hidden" – with its intentional alteration, must refer to the treasure. So I applied myself with some confidence to the next, that of St. John – "They have on their vestures a writing which no man knoweth".

'The natural question will have occurred to you: was there an inscription on the robes of the figures? I could see none. Each of the three had a broad black border to his mantle, which made a conspicuous and rather ugly feature in the window. I was nonplussed, I will own, and but for a curious bit of luck I think I should have left the search where the Canons of Steinfeld had left it before me.

'But it so happened that there was a good deal of dust on the surface of the glass, and Lord D——, happening to come in, noticed my black-ened hands, and kindly insisted on sending for a Turk's-head broom to clean down the window. There must, I suppose, have been a rough piece in the broom. Anyhow, as it passed over the border of one of the mantles, I noticed that it left a long scratch, and that some yellow stain instantly showed up.

'I asked the man to stop his work for a moment, and ran up the ladder to examine the place. The yellow stain was there, sure enough, and what had come away was a thick black pigment, which had evidently been laid on with the brush after the glass had been burnt, and could therefore be easily scraped off without doing any harm.

'I scraped, accordingly, and you will hardly believe – no, I do you an injustice; you will have guessed already – that I found under this black pig-ment two or three clearly-formed capital letters in yellow stain on a clear ground. Of course, I could hardly contain my delight.

'I told Lord D—— that I had detected an inscription which I thought might be very interesting, and begged to be allowed to uncover the whole of it. He made no difficulty about it whatever, told me to do exactly as I pleased, and then, having an engagement, was obliged – rather to my relief, I must say – to leave me. I set to work at once, and found the task a fairly easy one.

'The pigment, disintegrated, of course, by time, came off almost at a touch, and I don't think that it took me a couple of hours, all told, to clean the whole of the black borders in all three lights. Each of the figures had, as the inscription said, "a writing on their vestures which nobody knew".

'This discovery, of course, made it absolutely certain to my mind that I was on the right track. And, now, what was the inscription? While I was cleaning the glass I almost took pains not to read the lettering, saving up the treat until I had got the whole thing clear. And when that was done, my dear Gregory, I assure you I could almost have cried from sheer disappointment. What I read was only the most hopeless jumble of letters that was ever shaken up in a hat. Here it is:

JOB: REVICIOPEDMOOMSMVIVLISLCAVIBASBATAOVT

ST. JOHN: RDIIEAMRLESIPVSPODSEEIRSETTAAESGIAVNNR

ZECHARIAH: FTEEAILNQDPVAIVMTLEEATTOHIOONVMCA
AT.H.Q.E

'Blank as I felt and must have looked for the first few minutes, my disappointment didn't last long. I realised almost at once that I was dealing with a cipher or cryptogram, and I reflected that it was likely to be of a pretty simple kind, considering its early date. So I copied the letters with the most anxious care.

'Another little point, I may tell you, turned up in the process which confirmed my belief in the cipher. After copying the letters on Job's robe I counted them, to make sure that I had them right. There were thirty-eight. And, just as I finished going through them, my eye fell on a scratching made with a sharp point on the edge of the border. It was simply the number xxxviii in Roman numerals.

'To cut the matter short, there was a similar note, as I may call it, in each of the other lights. And that made it plain to me that the glass-painter had had very strict orders from Abbot Thomas about the inscription, and had taken pains to get it correct.

'Well, after that discovery you may imagine how minutely I went over the whole surface of the glass in search of further light. Of course, I did not neglect the inscription on the scroll of Zechariah ("Upon one stone are seven eyes"), but I very quickly concluded that this must refer to some mark on a stone which could only be found *in situ*, where the treasure was concealed. To be short, I made all possible notes and sketches and tracings, and then came back to Parsbury to work out the cipher at leisure.

'Oh, the agonies I went through! I thought myself very clever at first, for I made sure that the key would be found in some of the old books on secret writing. The *Steganographia* of Joachim Trithemius, who was an earlier contemporary of Abbot Thomas, seemed particularly promising; so I got that, and Selenius' *Cryptographia* and Bacon's *de Augmentis Scientiarum*, and some more. But I could hit upon nothing.

'Then I tried the principle of the "most frequent letter", taking first Latin and then German as a basis. That didn't help, either. Whether it ought to have done so, I am not clear. And then I came back to the window itself, and read over my notes, hoping almost against hope that the Abbot might himself have somewhat supplied the key I wanted. I could make nothing out of the colour or pattern of the robes. There were no landscape backgrounds with subsidiary objects; there was nothing in the canopies. The only resource possible seemed to be in the attitudes of the figures.

'"Job," I read: "scroll in left hand, forefinger of right hand extended upwards. John: holds inscribed book in left hand; with right hand blesses, with two fingers. Zechariah: scroll in left hand; right hand extended upwards, as Job, but with three fingers pointing up."

'In other words, I reflected, Job has *one* finger extended, John has *two*, Zechariah has *three*. May not there be a numeral key concealed in that?

'My dear Gregory,' said Mr. Somerton, laying his hand on his friend's knee, 'that was the key. I didn't get it to fit at first, but after two or three trials I saw what was meant. After the first letter of the inscription you skip one letter, after the next you skip two, and after that skip three. Now look at the result I got. I've underlined the letters which form words:

DREVICIOPEDMOOMSMVIVLISLCAVIBASBATAOVT

RDIIEAMRLESIPVSPODSEEIRSETTAAESGIAVNNR

FTEEAILNQDPVAIVMTLEEATTOHIOONVMCAAT.H.Q.E.

'Do you see it? *Decem millia auri reposita sunt in puteo in at . . .* (Ten thousand [pieces] of gold are laid up in a well in . . .), followed by an incomplete word beginning *at*. So far so good. I tried the same plan with the remaining letters; but it wouldn't work, and I fancied that perhaps the placing of dots after the three last letters might indicate some difference of procedure.

'Then I thought to myself, "Wasn't there some allusion to a well in the account of Abbot Thomas in that book the *Sertum*?" Yes, there was: he built a *puteus in atrio* (a well in the court). There, of course, was my word *atrio*. The next step was to copy out the remaining letters of the inscription, omitting those I had already used. That gave what you will see on this slip:

RVIIOPDOOSMVVISCAVBSBTAOTDIEAMLSIVSPDEERS
ETAEGIANRFEEALQDVAIMLEATTHOOVMCA.H.Q.E.

'Now, I knew what the first three letters I wanted were – namely, *rio* – to complete the word *atrio*; and, as you will see, these are all to be found in the first five letters. I was a little confused at first by the occurrence of two *i*s, but very soon I saw that every alternate letter must be taken in the remainder of the inscription. You can work it out for yourself; the result, continuing where the first "round" left off, is this:

> *rio domus abbatialis de Steinfeld a me, Thoma, qui posui custodem super ea. Gare à qui la touche.*

'So the whole secret was out: ·

> *Ten thousand pieces of gold are laid up in the well in the court of the Abbot's house of Steinfeld by me, Thomas, who have set a guardian over them.* Gare à qui la touche.

'The last words, I ought to say, are a device which Abbot Thomas had adopted. I found it with his arms in another piece of glass at Lord D——'s, and he drafted it bodily into his cipher, though it doesn't quite fit in point of grammar.

'Well, what would any human being have been tempted to do, my dear Gregory, in my place? Could he have helped setting off, as I did, to Steinfeld, and tracing the secret literally to the fountain-head? I don't believe he could.

'Anyhow, I couldn't, and, as I needn't tell you, I found myself at Steinfeld as soon as the resources of civilisation could put me there, and installed myself in the inn you saw. I must tell you that I was not altogether free from forebodings – on one hand of disappointment, on the other of danger.

'There was always the possibility that Abbot Thomas' well might have been wholly obliterated, or else that someone, ignorant of cryptograms, and guided only by luck, might have stumbled on the treasure before me. And then' – there was a very perceptible shaking of the voice here – 'I was not entirely easy, I need not mind confessing, as to the meaning of the words about the guardian of the treasure. But, if you don't mind, I'll say no more about that until – until it becomes necessary.

'At the first possible opportunity Brown and I began exploring the place. I had naturally represented myself as being interested in the remains of the abbey, and we could not avoid paying a visit to the church, impatient as I was to be elsewhere. Still, it did interest me to see the windows where the glass had been, and especially that at the east end of the south aisle.

'In the tracery lights of that I was startled to see some fragments and coats-of-arms remaining – Abbot Thomas' shield was there, and a small figure with a scroll inscribed *Oculos habent, et non videbunt* (They have eyes, and shall not see), which, I take it, was a hit of the Abbot at his Canons.

'But, of course, the principal object was to find the Abbot's house. There is no prescribed place for this, so far as I know, in the plan of a monastery. You can't predict of it, as you can of the chapter-house, that it will be on the eastern side of the cloister, or, as of the dormitory, that it will communicate with a transept of the church. I felt that if I asked many questions I might awaken lingering memories of the treasure, and I thought it best to try first to discover it for myself. It was not a very long or difficult search.

'That three-sided court south-east of the church, with deserted piles of building round it, and grass-grown pavement, which you saw this morning, was the place. And glad enough I was to see that it was put to no use, and was neither very far from our inn nor overlooked by any inhabited building; there were only orchards and paddocks on the slopes east of the church. I can tell you that fine stone glowed wonderfully in the rather watery yellow sunset that we had on the Tuesday afternoon.

'Next, what about the well? There was not much doubt about that, as you can testify. It is really a very remarkable thing. That curb is, I think, of Italian marble, and the carving I thought must be Italian also. There were reliefs, you will perhaps remember, of Eliezer and Rebekah, and of Jacob opening the well for Rachel, and similar subjects. But, by way of disarming suspicion, I suppose, the Abbot had carefully abstained from any of his cynical and allusive inscriptions.

'I examined the whole structure with the keenest interest, of course – a square well-head with an opening in one side; an arch over it, with a wheel for the rope to pass over, evidently in very good condition still, for it had been used within sixty years, or perhaps even later, though not quite recently.

'Then there was the question of depth and access to the interior. I suppose the depth was about sixty to seventy feet; and as to the other point, it really seemed as if the Abbot had wished to lead searchers up to the very door of his treasure-house, for, as you tested for yourself, there were big blocks of stone bonded into the masonry, and leading down in a regular staircase round and round the inside of the well.

'It seemed almost too good to be true. I wondered if there was a trap – if the stones were so contrived as to tip over when a weight was placed on them. But I tried a good many with my own weight and with my stick, and all seemed, and actually were, perfectly firm. Of course, I resolved that Brown and I would make an experiment that very night.

'I was well prepared. Knowing the sort of place I should have to explore, I had brought a sufficiency of good rope and bands of webbing to surround my body, and crossbars to hold to, as well as lanterns and candles and crow-bars, all of which would go into a single carpet-bag and excite no suspicion. I satisfied myself that my rope would be long enough, and that the wheel for the bucket was in good working order, and then we went home to dinner.

'I had a little cautious conversation with the landlord, and made out that he would not be overmuch surprised if I went out for a stroll with my man about nine o'clock, to make (Heaven forgive me!) a sketch of the abbey by moonlight. I asked no questions about the well, and am not likely to do so now. I fancy I know as much about it as anyone in Steinfeld. At least' – with a strong shudder – 'I don't want to know any more.

'Now we come to the crisis, and, though I hate to think of it, I feel sure, Gregory, that it will be better for me in all ways to recall it just as it happened.

'We started, Brown and I, at about nine with our bag, and attracted no attention; for we managed to slip out at the hinder end of the inn-yard into an alley which brought us quite to the edge of the village. In five minutes we were at the well, and for some little time we sat on the edge of the well-head to make sure that no one was stirring or spying on us. All we heard was some horses cropping grass out of sight farther down the eastern slope. We were perfectly unobserved, and had plenty of light from the gorgeous full moon to allow us to get the rope properly fitted over the wheel.

'Then I secured the band round my body beneath the arms. We attached the end of the rope very securely to a ring in the stonework. Brown took the lighted lantern and followed me. I had a crowbar.

'And so we began to descend cautiously, feeling every step before we set foot on it, and scanning the walls in search of any marked stone.

'Half-aloud I counted the steps as we went down, and we got as far as the thirty-eighth before I noted anything at all irregular in the surface of the masonry. Even here there was no mark, and I began to feel very blank, and to wonder if the Abbot's cryptogram could possibly be an elaborate hoax. At the forty-ninth step the staircase ceased. It was with a very sinking heart that I began retracing my steps, and when I was back on the thirty-eighth – Brown, with the lantern, being a step or two above me – I scrutinised the little bit of irregularity in the stonework with all my might. But there was no vestige of a mark.

'Then it struck me that the texture of the surface looked just a little smoother than the rest, or, at least, in some way different. It might possibly be cement and not stone. I gave it a good blow with my iron bar. There was a decidedly hollow sound, though that might be the result of our being in a well. But there was more. A great flake of cement dropped on to my feet, and I saw marks on the stone underneath. I had tracked the Abbot down, my dear Gregory. Even now I think of it with a certain pride.

'It took but a very few more taps to clear the whole of the cement away, and I saw a slab of stone about two feet square, upon which was engraven a cross. Disappointment again, but only for a moment. It was you, Brown, who reassured me by a casual remark. You said, if I remember right:

'"It's a funny cross. Looks like a lot of eyes."

'I snatched the lantern out of your hand, and saw with inexpressible pleasure that the cross was composed of seven eyes, four in a vertical line, three horizontal. The last of the scrolls in the window was explained in the way I had anticipated. Here was my "stone with the seven eyes".

'So far the Abbot's data had been exact, and, as I thought of this, the anxiety about the "guardian" returned upon me with increased force. Still, I wasn't going to retreat now.

'Without giving myself time to think, I knocked away the cement all round the marked stone, and then gave it a prise on the right side with my crowbar. It moved at once, and I saw that it was but a thin light slab, such as I could easily lift out myself, and that it stopped the entrance to a cavity. I did lift it out unbroken, and set it on the step, for it might be very important to us to be able to replace it.

'Then I waited for several minutes on the step just above. I don't know why, but I think to see if any dreadful thing would rush out. Nothing happened.

'Next I lit a candle, and very cautiously I placed it inside the cavity, with some idea of seeing whether there were foul air, and of getting a glimpse of what was inside. There *was* some foulness of air which nearly extinguished the flame, but in no long time it burned quite steadily.

'The hole went some little way back, and also on the right and left of the entrance, and I could see some rounded light-coloured objects within which might be bags. There was no use in waiting. I faced the cavity, and looked in. There was nothing immediately in the front of the hole. I put my arm in and felt to the right, very gingerly . . .

'Just give me a glass of cognac, Brown. I'll go on in a moment, Gregory . . .

'Well, I felt to the right, and my fingers touched something curved, that felt – yes – more or less like leather. Dampish it was, and evidently part of a heavy, full thing. There was nothing, I must say, to alarm one. I grew bolder, and putting both hands in as well as I could, I pulled it to me, and it came. It was heavy, but moved more easily than I expected. As I pulled it towards the entrance, my left elbow knocked over and extinguished the candle. I got the thing fairly in front of the mouth and began drawing it out.

'Just then Brown gave a sharp ejaculation and ran quickly up the steps with the lantern. He will tell you why in a moment.

'Startled as I was, I looked round after him, and saw him stand for a minute at the top and then walk away a few yards. Then I heard him call softly, "All right, sir", and went on pulling out the great bag, in complete darkness. It hung for an instant on the edge of the hole, then slipped forward on to my chest, and *put its arms round my neck*.

'My dear Gregory, I am telling you the exact truth. I believe I am now acquainted with the extremity of terror and repulsion which a man can endure without losing his mind. I can only just manage to tell you now the bare outline of the experience.

'I was conscious of a most horrible smell of mould, and of a cold kind of face pressed against my own, and moving slowly over it, and of several – I don't know how many – legs or arms or tentacles or something clinging to my body. I screamed out, Brown says, like a beast, and fell away backward from the step on which I stood, and the creature slipped downwards, I suppose, on to that same step. Providentially the band round me held firm.

'Brown did not lose his head, and was strong enough to pull me up to the top and get me over the edge quite promptly. How he managed it exactly I don't know, and I think he would find it hard to tell you. I believe he contrived to hide our implements in the deserted building near by, and with very great difficulty he got me back to the inn.

'I was in no state to make explanations, and Brown knows no German. But next morning I told the people some tale of having had a bad fall in the abbey ruins, which, I suppose, they believed.

'And now, before I go further, I should just like you to hear what Brown's experiences during those few minutes were. Tell the Rector, Brown, what you told me.'

'Well, sir,' said Brown, speaking low and nervously, 'it was just this way. Master was busy down in front of the 'ole, and I was 'olding the lantern and looking on, when I 'eard somethink drop in the water from the top, as I thought. So I looked up, and I see someone's 'ead lookin' over at us.

'I s'pose I must ha' said somethink, and I 'eld the light up and run up the steps, and my light shone right on the face. That was a bad un, sir, if ever I see one! A holdish man, and the face very much fell in, and larfin, as I thought.

'And I got up the steps as quick pretty nigh as I'm tellin' you, and when I was out on the ground there warn't a sign of any person. There 'adn't been the time for anyone to get away, let alone a hold chap, and I made sure he warn't crouching down by the well, nor nothink.

'Next thing I hear master cry out somethink 'orrible, and hall I see was him hanging out by the rope, and, as master says, 'owever I got him up I couldn't tell you.'

'You hear that, Gregory?' said Mr. Somerton. 'Now, does any explanation of that incident strike you?'

'The whole thing is so ghastly and abnormal that I must own it puts me quite off my balance. But the thought did occur to me that possibly the – well, the person who set the trap might have come to see the success of his plan.'

'Just so, Gregory, just so. I can think of nothing else so – *likely*, I should say, if such a word had a place anywhere in my story. I think it must have been the Abbot . . .

'Well, I haven't much more to tell you. I spent a miserable night, Brown sitting up with me. Next day I was no better: unable to get up; no doctor to be had; and, if one had been available, I doubt if he could have done much for me. I made Brown write off to you, and spent a second terrible night. And, Gregory, of this I am sure, and I think it affected me more than the first shock, for it lasted longer: there was someone or something on the watch outside my door the whole night. I almost fancy there were two.

'It wasn't only the faint noises I heard from time to time all through the dark hours, but there was the smell – the hideous smell of mould. Every rag I had had on me on that first evening I had stripped off and made Brown take it away. I believe he stuffed the things into the stove in his room. And yet the smell was there, as intense as it had been in the well; and, what is more, it came from outside the door.

'But with the first glimmer of dawn it faded out, and the sounds ceased, too. And that convinced me that the thing or things were creatures of darkness, and could not stand the daylight. And so I was sure that if anyone could put back the stone, it or they would be powerless until someone else took it away again.

'I had to wait until you came to get that done. Of course, I couldn't send Brown to do it by himself, and still less could I tell anyone who belonged to the place.

'Well, there is my story. And if you don't believe it, I can't help it. But I think you do.'

'Indeed,' said Mr. Gregory, 'I can find no alternative. I *must* believe it! I saw the well and the stone myself, and had a glimpse, I thought, of the bags or something else in the hole.

'And, to be plain with you, Somerton, I believe my door was watched last night, too.'

'I dare say it was, Gregory. But, thank goodness, that is over. Have you, by the way, anything to tell about your visit to that dreadful place?'

'Very little,' was the answer. 'Brown and I managed easily enough to get the slab into its place, and he fixed it very firmly with the irons and wedges you had desired him to get, and we contrived to smear the surface with mud so that it looks just like the rest of the wall.

'One thing I did notice in the carving on the well-head, which I think must have escaped you. It was a horrid, grotesque shape perhaps more like a toad than anything else, and there was a label by it inscribed with the two words, *Depositum custodi.*[†]

[†]   Keep that which is committed to thee.

The Stalls of Barchester Cathedral

THIS MATTER BEGAN, as far as I am concerned, with the reading of a notice in the obituary section of the *Gentleman's Magazine* for an early year in the 19th century:

> On February 26th, at his residence in the Cathedral Close of Barchester, the Venerable John Benwell Haynes, D.D., aged 57, Archdeacon of Sowerbridge and Rector of Pickhill and Candley.
>
> He was of —— College, Cambridge, and where, by talent and assiduity, he commanded the esteem of his seniors; when, at the usual time, he took his first degree, his name stood high in the list of *wranglers*. These academical honours procured for him within a short time a Fellowship of his College.
>
> In the year 1783 he received Holy Orders, and was shortly afterwards presented to the perpetual Curacy of Ranxton-sub-Ashe by his friend and patron the late truly venerable Bishop of Lichfield ... His speedy preferments, first to a Prebend, and subsequently to the dignity of Precentor in the Cathedral of Barchester, form an eloquent testimony to the respect in which he was held and to his eminent qualifications. He succeeded to the Archdeaconry upon the sudden decease of Archdeacon Pulteney in 1810.

His sermons, ever conformable to the principles of the religion and Church which he adorned, displayed in no ordinary degree, without the least trace of enthusiasm, the refinement of the scholar united with the graces of the Christian. Free from sectarian violence, and informed by the spirit of the truest charity, they will long dwell in the memories of his hearers. [Here a further omission.]

The productions of his pen include an able defence of Episcopacy, which, though often perused by the author of this tribute to his memory, afford but one additional instance of the want of liberality and enterprise which is a too common characteristic of the publishers of our generation.

His published works are, indeed, confined to a spirited and elegant version of the *Argonautica* of Valerius Flaccus, a volume of *Discourses Upon the Several Events in the Life of Joshua*, delivered in his Cathedral, and a number of the charges which he pronounced at various visitations, to the clergy of his Archdeaconry. These are distinguished by etc., etc. The urbanity and hospitality of the subject of these lines will not readily be forgotten by those who enjoyed his acquaintance.

His interest in the venerable and awful pile under whose hoary vault he was so punctual an attendant, and particularly in the musical portion of its rites, might be termed filial, and formed a strong and delightful contrast to the polite indifference displayed by too many of our Cathedral dignitaries at the present time

The final paragraph, after informing us that Dr. Haynes died a bachelor, says:

It might have been augured that an existence so placid and benevolent would have been terminated in a ripe old age by a dissolution equally gradual and calm. But how unsearchable are the workings of Providence!

The peaceful and retired seclusion amid which the

honoured evening of Dr. Haynes's life was mellowing to its close was destined to be disturbed, nay, shattered, by a tragedy as appalling as it was unexpected. The morning of the 26th of February—

But perhaps I shall do better to keep back the remainder of the narrative until I have told the circumstances which led up to it. These, as far as they are now accessible, I have derived from another source.

I had read the obituary notice which I have been quoting, quite by chance, along with a great many others of the same period. It had excited some little speculation in my mind, but, beyond thinking that, if I ever had an opportunity of examining the local records of the period indicated, I would try to remember Dr. Haynes, I made no effort to pursue his case.

Quite lately I was cataloguing the manuscripts in the library of the college to which he belonged. I had reached the end of the numbered volumes on the shelves, and I proceeded to ask the librarian whether there were any more books which he thought I ought to include in my description.

'I don't think there are,' he said, 'but we had better come and look at the manuscript class and make sure. Have you time to do that now?'

I had time. We went to the library, checked off the manuscripts, and, at the end of our survey, arrived at a shelf of which I had seen nothing.

Its contents consisted for the most part of sermons, bundles of fragmentary papers, college exercises, *Cyrus*, an epic poem in several cantos, the product of a country clergyman's leisure, mathematical tracts by a deceased professor, and other similar material of a kind with which I am only too familiar. I took brief notes of these.

Lastly, there was a tin box, which was pulled out and dusted. Its label, much faded, was thus inscribed: *Papers of the Ven. Archdeacon Haynes. Bequeathed in 1834 by his sister, Miss Letitia Haynes.*

I knew at once that the name was one which I had somewhere encountered, and could very soon locate it.

'That must be the Archdeacon Haynes who came to a very odd end at Barchester. I've read his obituary in the *Gentleman's Magazine*. May I take the box home? Do you know if there is anything interesting in it?'

The librarian was very willing that I should take the box and examine it at leisure. 'I never looked inside it myself,' he said, 'but I've always been meaning to. I am pretty sure that is the box which our old Master once said ought never to have been accepted by the college.

'He said that to Martin years ago; and he said also that as long as he had control over the library it should never be opened. Martin told me about it, and said that he wanted terribly to know what was in it. But the Master was librarian, and always kept the box in the lodge, so there was no getting at it in his time, and when he died it was taken away by mistake by his heirs, and only returned a few years ago.

'I can't think why I haven't opened it. But, as I have to go away from Cambridge this afternoon, you had better have first go at it. I think I can trust you not to publish anything undesirable in our catalogue.'

I took the box home and examined its contents, and thereafter consulted the librarian as to what should be done about publication, and, since I have his leave to make a story out of it, provided I disguise the identity of the people concerned, I will try what can be done.

The materials are, of course, mainly journals and letters. How much I shall quote and how much epitomise must be determined by considerations of space. The proper understanding of the situation has necessitated a little – not very arduous – research, which has been greatly facilitated by the excellent illustrations and text of the Barchester volume in Bell's *Cathedral Series*.

When you enter the choir of Barchester Cathedral now, you pass through a screen of metal and coloured marbles, designed by Sir Gilbert Scott, and find yourself in what I must call a very bare and odiously furnished place.

The stalls are modern, without canopies. The places of the dignitaries and the names of the prebends have fortunately been allowed to survive, and are inscribed on small brass plates affixed to the stalls. The organ is in the triforium, and what is seen of the case is Gothic. The reredos and its surroundings are like every other.

Careful engravings of a hundred years ago show a very different state of things. The organ is on a massive classical screen. The stalls are also classical and very massive. There is a baldacchino of wood over the altar, with urns upon its corners. Farther east is a solid altar screen, classical in design, of wood, with a pediment, in which is a triangle surrounded by rays, enclosing certain Hebrew letters in gold. Cherubs contemplate these. There is a pulpit with a great sounding-board at the eastern end of the stalls on the north side, and there is a black and white marble pavement. Two ladies and a gentleman are admiring the general effect.

From other sources I gather that the archdeacon's stall then, as now, was next to the bishop's throne at the south-eastern end of the stalls. His house almost faces the west front of the church, and is a fine red-brick building of William the Third's time.

Here Dr. Haynes, already a mature man, took up his abode with his sister in the year 1810. The dignity had long been the object of his wishes, but his predecessor refused to depart until he had attained the age of ninety-two.

About a week after he had held a modest festival in celebration of that ninety-second birthday, there came a morning, late in the year, when Dr. Haynes, hurrying cheerfully into his breakfast-room, rubbing his hands and humming a tune, was greeted, and checked in his genial flow of spirits, by the sight of his sister, seated, indeed, in her usual place behind the tea-urn, but bowed forward and sobbing unrestrainedly into her handkerchief.

'What – what is the matter? What bad news?' he began.

'Oh, Johnny, you've not heard? The poor dear archdeacon!'

'The archdeacon, yes? What is it – ill, is he?'

'No, no; they found him on the staircase this morning; it is so shocking.'

'Is it possible! Dear, dear, poor Pulteney! Had there been any seizure?'

'They don't think so, and that is almost the worst thing about it. It seems to have been all the fault of that stupid maid of theirs, Jane.'

Dr. Haynes paused. 'I don't quite understand, Letitia. How was the maid at fault?'

'Why, as far as I can make out, there was a stair-rod missing, and she never mentioned it, and the poor archdeacon set his foot quite on the edge of the step – you know how slippery that oak is – and it seems he must have fallen almost the whole flight and broken his neck.

'It *is* so sad for poor Miss Pulteney. Of course, they will get rid of the girl at once. I never liked her.'

Miss Haynes's grief resumed its sway, but eventually relaxed so far as to permit of her taking some breakfast.

Not so her brother, who, after standing in silence before the window for some minutes, left the room, and did not appear again that morning.

I need only add that the careless maid-servant was dismissed forthwith, but that the missing stair-rod was very shortly afterwards found *under* the stair-carpet – an additional proof, if any were needed, of extreme stupidity and carelessness on her part.

For a good many years Dr. Haynes had been marked out by his ability, which seems to have been really considerable, as the likely successor of Archdeacon Pulteney, and no disappointment was in store for him. He was duly installed, and entered with zeal upon the discharge of those functions which are appropriate to one in his position.

A considerable space in his journals is occupied with exclamations upon the confusion in which Archdeacon Pulteney had left the business of his office and the documents appertaining to it. Dues upon Wringham and Barnswood have been uncollected for something like twelve years, and are largely irrecoverable; no visitation has been held for seven years; four chancels are almost past mending. The persons deputised by the archdeacon have been nearly as incapable as himself.

It was almost a matter for thankfulness that this state of things had not been permitted to continue, and a letter from a friend confirms this view:

ὁ κατέχων, it says (in rather cruel allusion to the Second Epistle to the Thessalonians), *is removed at last. My poor friend! Upon what a scene of confusion will you be entering! I give you my word that, on the last occasion of my crossing his threshold, there was no single paper that he could lay hands upon, no syllable of mine that he could hear, and no fact in connection with my business that he could remember. But now, thanks to a negligent maid and a loose stair-carpet, there is some prospect that necessary business will be transacted without a complete loss alike of voice and temper.*

This letter was tucked into a pocket in the cover of one of the diaries. There can be no doubt of the new archdeacon's zeal and enthusiasm:
'Give me but time to reduce to some semblance of order the innumerable errors and complications with which I am confronted, and I shall gladly and sincerely join with the aged Israelite in the canticle which too many, I fear, pronounce but with their lips.'

This reflection I find, not in a diary, but a letter. The doctor's friends seem to have returned his correspondence to his surviving sister.

He does not confine himself, however, to reflections. His investigation of the rights and duties of his office are very searching and business-like, and there is a calculation in one place that a period of three years will just suffice to set the business of the Archdeaconry upon a proper footing. The estimate appears to have been an exact one.

For just three years he is occupied in reforms. But I look in vain at the end of that time for the promised *Nunc dimittis*.

He has now found a new sphere of activity. Hitherto his duties have precluded him from more than an occasional attendance at the Cathedral services. Now he begins to take an interest in the fabric and the music.

Upon his struggles with the organist, an old gentleman who had been in office since 1786, I have no time to dwell; they were not attended with any marked success. More to the purpose is his sudden growth of enthusiasm for the Cathedral itself and its furniture. There is a draft of a letter to Sylvanus Urban (which I do not think was ever sent) describing the stalls in the choir. As I have said, these were of fairly late date – of about the year 1700, in fact.

The archdeacon's stall, situated at the south-east end, west of the episcopal throne (now so worthily occupied by the truly excellent prelate who adorns the See of Barchester), is distinguished by some curious ornamentation. In addition to the arms of Dean West, by whose efforts the whole of the internal furniture of the choir was completed, the prayer-desk is terminated at the eastern extremity by three small but remarkable statuettes in the grotesque manner.

One is an exquisitely modelled figure of a cat, whose crouching posture suggests with admirable spirit the suppleness, vigilance, and craft of the redoubted adversary of the genus Mus. Opposite to this is a figure seated upon a throne and invested with the attributes of royalty; but it is no earthly monarch whom the carver has sought to portray. His feet are studiously concealed by the long robe in which he is draped: but neither the crown nor the cap which he wears suffice to hide the prick-ears and curving horns which betray his Tartarean origin; and the hand which rests upon his knee is armed with talons of horrifying length and sharpness.

Between these two figures stands a shape muffled in a long mantle. This might at first sight be mistaken for a monk or 'friar of orders grey', for the head is cowled and a knotted cord depends from somewhere about the waist. A slight inspection, however, will lead to a very different conclusion.

The knotted cord is quickly seen to be a halter, held by a hand all but concealed within the draperies; while the sunken features and, horrid to relate, the rent flesh upon the cheek-bones, proclaim the King of Terrors.

These figures are evidently the production of no unskilled chisel; and should it chance that any of your correspondents are able to throw light upon their origin and significance, my obligations to your valuable miscellany will be largely increased.

There is more description in the paper, and, seeing that the woodwork in question has now disappeared, it has a considerable interest. A paragraph at the end is worth quoting:

Some late researches among the Chapter accounts have shown me that the carving of the stalls was not, as was very usually reported, the work of Dutch artists, but was executed by a native of this city or district named Austin. The timber was procured from an oak copse in the vicinity, the property of the Dean and Chapter, known as Holywood. Upon a recent visit to the parish within whose boundaries it is situated, I learned from the aged and truly respectable incumbent that traditions still lingered amongst the inhabitants of the great size and age of the oaks employed to furnish the materials of the stately structure which has been, however imperfectly, described in the above lines. Of one in particular, which stood near the centre of the grove, it is remembered that it was known as the Hanging Oak. The propriety of that title is confirmed by the fact that a quantity of human bones was found in the soil about its roots, and that at certain times of the year it was the custom for those who wished to secure a successful issue to their affairs, whether of love or the ordinary business of life, to suspend from its boughs small images or puppets rudely fashioned of straw, twigs, or the like rustic materials.

So much for the archdeacon's archæological investigations. To return to his career as it is to be gathered from his diaries.

Those of his first three years of hard and careful work show him throughout in high spirits, and, doubtless, during this time, that reputation for hospitality and urbanity which is mentioned in his obituary notice was well deserved. After that, as time goes on, I see a shadow coming over him – destined to develop into utter blackness – which I cannot but think must have been reflected in his outward demeanour.

He commits a good deal of his fears and troubles to his diary; there was no other outlet for them, He was unmarried, and his sister was not always with him. But I am much mistaken if he has told all that he might have told. A series of extracts shall be given:

AUG. 30, 1816 – *The days begin to draw in more perceptibly than ever. Now that the Archdeaconry papers are reduced to order, I must find some further employment for the evening hours of autumn and winter. It is a great blow that Letitia's health will not allow her to stay through these months. Why not go on with my* Defence of Episcopacy? *It may be useful.*

SEPT. 15 – *Letitia has left me for Brighton.*

OCT. 11 – *Candles lit in the choir for the first time at evening prayers. It came as a shock: I find that I absolutely shrink from the dark season.*

NOV. 17 – *Much struck by the character of the carving on my desk: I do not know that I had ever carefully noticed it before. My attention was called to it by an accident. During the* Magnificat *I was, I regret to say, almost overcome with sleep. My hand was resting on the back of the carved figure of a cat which is the nearest to me of the three figures on the end of my stall. I was not aware of this, for I was not looking in that direction, until I was startled by* what seemed a softness, a feeling as of rather rough and coarse fur, and a sudden movement, as if the creature were twisting round its head to bite me. I regained complete consciousness in an instant, and I have some idea that I must have uttered a suppressed exclamation, for I noticed that Mr. Treasurer turned his head quickly in my direction. The impression of the unpleasant feeling was so strong that I found myself rubbing my hand upon my surplice. This accident led me to examine the figures after prayers more carefully than I had done before, and I realised for the first time with what skill they are executed.

DEC. 6 – I do indeed miss Letitia's company. The evenings, after I have worked as long as I can at my Defence, are very trying. The house is too large for a lonely man, and visitors of any kind are too rare. I get an uncomfortable impression when going to my room that there is company of some kind. The fact is (I may as well formulate it to myself) that I hear voices. This, I am well aware, is a common symptom of incipient decay of the brain – and I believe that I should be less disquieted than I am if I had any suspicion that this was the cause. I have none – none whatever, nor is there anything in my family history to give colour to such an idea. Work, diligent work, and a punctual attention to the duties which fall to me is my best remedy, and I have little doubt that it will prove efficacious.

JAN. 1 – My trouble is, I must confess it, increasing upon me. Last night, upon my return after midnight from the Deanery, I lit my candle to go upstairs. I was nearly at the top when something whispered to me, 'Let me wish you a happy New Year.' I could not be mistaken: it spoke distinctly and with a peculiar emphasis. Had I dropped my candle, as I all but did, I tremble to think what the consequences must have been. As it was, I managed to get up the last flight, and was quickly in my room with the door locked, and experienced no other disturbance.

JAN. 15 – I had occasion to come downstairs last night to my workroom for my watch, which I had inadvertently left on my table when I went up to bed. I think I was at the top of the last flight when I had a sudden impression of a sharp whisper in my ear

'Take care.' I clutched the balusters and naturally looked round at once. Of course, there was nothing. After a moment I went on — it was no good turning back — but I had as nearly as possible fallen: a cat — a large one by the feel of it — slipped between my feet, but again, of course, I saw nothing. It may have been the kitchen cat, but I do not think it was.

FEB. 27 — A curious thing last night, which I should like to forget. Perhaps if I put it down here I may see it in its true proportion. I worked in the library from about 9 to 10. The hall and staircase seemed to be unusually full of what I can only call movement without sound: by this I mean that there seemed to be continuous going and coming, and that whenever I ceased writing to listen, or looked out into the hall, the stillness was absolutely unbroken. Nor, in going to my room at an earlier hour than usual — about half-past ten — was I conscious of anything that I could call a noise. It so happened that I had told John to come to my room for the letter to the bishop which I wished to have delivered early in the morning at the Palace. He was to sit up, therefore, and come for it when he heard me retire. This I had for the moment forgotten, though I had remembered to carry the letter with me to my room. But when, as I was winding up my watch, I heard a light tap at the door, and a low voice saying, 'May I come in?' (which I most undoubtedly did hear), I recollected the fact, and took up the letter from my dressing-table, saying, 'Certainly: come in.' No one, however, answered my summons, and it was now that, as I strongly suspect, I committed an error: for I opened the door and held the letter out. There was certainly no one at that moment in the passage, but, in the instant of my standing there, the door at the end opened and John appeared carrying a candle. I asked him whether he had come to the door earlier; but am satisfied that he had not. I do not like the situation; but although my senses were very much on the alert, and though it was some time before I could sleep, I must allow that I perceived nothing further of an untoward character.

With the return of spring, when his sister came to live with him for some months, Dr. Haynes's entries become more cheerful, and, indeed, no symptom of depression is discernible until the early part of September, when he was again left alone.

And now, indeed, there is evidence that he was incommoded again, and that more pressingly. To this matter I will return in a moment, but I digress to put in a document which, rightly or wrongly, I believe to have a bearing on the thread of the story.

The account-books of Dr. Haynes, preserved along with his other papers, show, from a date but little later than that of his institution as archdeacon, a quarterly payment of £25 to J.L. Nothing could have been made of this, had it stood by itself. But I connect with it a very dirty and ill-written letter, which, like another that I have quoted, was in a pocket in the cover of a diary. Of date or postmark there is no vestige, and the decipherment was not easy. It appears to run:

> *Dr. Sr.*
> *I have bin expetin to her off you theis last wicks, and not Having done so must supose you have not got mine witch was saying how me and my man had met in with bad times this season all seems to go cross with us on the farm and which way to look for the rent we have no knowledge of it this been the sad case with us if you would have the great liberality* [probably, but the exact spelling defies reproduction] *to send fourty pounds otherwise steps will have to be took which I should not wish. Has you was the Means of me losing my place with Dr. Pulteney I think it is only just what I am asking and you know best what I could say if I was Put to it but I do not wish anything of that unpleasant Nature being one that always wish to have everything Pleasant about me.*
> *Your obedt Servt,*
> *JANE LEE*

About the time at which I suppose this letter to have been written there is, in fact, a payment of £40 to J.L.

We return to the diary:

OCT. 22 – *At evening prayers, during the Psalms, I had that same experience which I recollect from last year. I was resting my hand on one of the carved figures, as before (I usually avoid that of the cat now), and – I was going to have said – a change came over it, but that seems attributing too much importance to what must after all, be due to some physical affection in myself: at any rate, the wood seemed to become chilly and soft as if made of wet linen. I can assign the moment at which I became sensible of this. The choir were singing the words* (Set thou an ungodly man to be ruler over him and) let Satan stand at his right hand.

The whispering in my house was more persistent tonight. I seemed not to be rid of it in my room. I have not noticed this before. A nervous man, which I am not, and hope I am not becoming, would have been much annoyed, if not alarmed, by it. The cat was on the stairs tonight. I think it sits there always. There is no kitchen cat.

NOV. 15 – *Here again I must note a matter I do not understand. I am much troubled in sleep. No definite image presented itself, but I was pursued by the very vivid impression that wet lips were whispering into my ear with great rapidity and emphasis for some time together. After this, I suppose, I fell asleep, but was awakened with a start by a feeling as if a hand were laid on my shoulder. To my intense alarm I found myself standing at the top of the lowest flight of the first staircase. The moon was shining brightly enough through the large window to let me see that there was a large cat on the second or third step. I can make no comment. I crept up to bed again, I do not know how. Yea, mine is a heavy burden.* [Then follows a line or two which has been scratched out. I fancy I read something like 'acted for the best'.]

Not long after this it is evident to me that the archdeacon's firmness began to give way under the pressure of these phenomena. I omit as unnecessarily painful and distressing the ejaculations and prayers which, in the months of December and January, appear for the first time and become increasingly frequent.

Throughout this time, however, he is obstinate in clinging to his post. Why he did not plead ill-health and take refuge at Bath or Brighton I cannot tell. My impression is that it would have done him no good; that he was a man who, if he had confessed himself beaten by the annoyances, would have succumbed at once, and that he was conscious of this.

He did seek to palliate them by inviting visitors to his house. The result he has noted in this fashion:

JAN. 7 — *I have prevailed on my cousin Allen to give me a few days, and he is to occupy the chamber next to mine.*
JAN. 8 — *A still night. Allen slept well, but complained of the wind. My own experiences were as before: still whispering and whispering. What is it that he wants to say?*
JAN. 9 — *Allen thinks this a very noisy house. He thinks, too, that my cat is an unusually large and fine specimen, but very wild.*
JAN. 10 — *Allen and I in the library until 11. He left me twice to see what the maids were doing in the hall: returning the second time he told me he had seen one of them passing through the door at the end of the passage, and said if his wife were here she would soon get them into better order. I asked him what coloured dress the maid wore; he said grey or white. I supposed it would be so.*
JAN. 11 — *Allen left me today. I must be firm.*

These words, *I must be firm,* occur again and again on subsequent days; sometimes they are the only entry. In these cases they are in an unusually large hand, and dug into the paper in a way which must have broken the pen that wrote them.

Apparently the archdeacon's friends did not remark any change in his behaviour, and this gives me a high idea of his courage and determination. The diary tells us nothing more than I have indicated of the last days of his life. The end of it all must be told in the polished language of the obituary notice:

The morning of the 26th of February was cold and tempestuous. At an early hour the servants had occasion to go into the front hall of the residence occupied by the lamented subject of these lines. What was their horror upon observing the form of their beloved and respected master lying upon the landing of the principal staircase in an attitude which inspired the gravest fears. Assistance was procured, and an universal consternation was experienced upon the discovery that he had been the object of a brutal and a murderous attack. The vertebral column was fractured in more than one place. This might have been the result of a fall: it appeared that the stair-carpet was loosened at one point. But, in addition to this, there were injuries inflicted upon the eyes, nose and mouth, as if by the agency of some savage animal, which, dreadful to relate, rendered those features unrecognisable. The vital spark was, it is needless to add, completely extinct, and had been so, upon the testimony of respectable medical authorities, for several hours. The author or authors of this mysterious outrage are alike buried in mystery, and the most active conjecture has hitherto failed to suggest a solution of the melancholy problem afforded by this appalling occurrence.

The writer goes on to reflect upon the probability that the writings of Mr. Shelley, Lord Byron, and M. Voltaire may have been instrumental in bringing about the disaster, and concludes by hoping, somewhat vaguely, that this event may 'operate as an example to the rising generation'; but this portion of his remarks need not be quoted in full.

I had already formed the conclusion that Dr. Haynes was responsible for the death of Dr. Pulteney. But the incident connected with the carved figure of death upon the archdeacon's stall was a very perplexing feature. The conjecture that it had been cut out of the wood of the Hanging Oak was not difficult, but seemed impossible to substantiate. However, I paid a visit to Barchester, partly with the view of finding out whether there were any relics of the woodwork to be heard of.

I was introduced by one of the canons to the curator of the local museum, who was, my friend said, more likely to be able to give me information on the point than anyone else.

I told this gentleman of the description of certain carved figures and arms formerly on the stalls, and asked whether any had survived. He was able to show me the arms of Dean West and some other fragments. These, he said, had been got from an old resident, who had also once owned a figure – perhaps one of those which I was inquiring for. There was a very odd thing about that figure, he said.

'The old man who had it told me that he picked it up in a wood-yard, whence he had obtained the still extant pieces, and had taken it home for his children. On the way home he was fiddling about with it and it came in two in his hands, and a bit of paper dropped out. This he picked up and, just noticing that there was writing on it, put it into his pocket, and subsequently into a vase on his mantelpiece.

'I was at his house not very long ago, and happened to pick up the vase and turn it over to see whether there were any marks on it, and the paper fell into my hand. The old man, on my handing it to him, told me the story I have told you, and said I might keep the paper.

'It was crumpled and rather torn, so I have mounted it on a card, which I have here. If you can tell me what it means I shall be very glad, and also, I may say, a good deal surprised.'

He gave me the card. The paper was quite legibly inscribed in an old hand, and this is what was on it:

> *When I grew in the Wood*
> *I was water'd wth Blood*
> *Now in the Church I stand*
> *Who that touches me with his Hand*
> *If a Bloody hand he bear*
> *I councell him to be ware*
> *Lest he be fetcht away*
> *Whether by night or day,*
> *But chiefly when the wind blows high*
> *In a night of February.*

> *This I drempt, 26 Febr. A° 1699. JOHN AUSTIN.*

'I suppose it is a charm or a spell: wouldn't you call it something of that kind?' said the curator.

'Yes,' I said, 'I suppose one might. What became of the figure in which it was concealed?'

'Oh, I forgot,' said he. 'The old man told me it was so ugly and frightened his children so much that he burnt it.'

Casting the Runes

April 15th, 190——.

DEAR SIR,

I am requested by the Council of the —— Association
to return to you the draft of a paper on 'The Truth of
Alchemy', which you have been good enough to offer to
read at our forthcoming meeting, and to inform you that
the Council do not see their way to including it in the
programme.

I am,

Yours faithfully,

—— Secretary.

April 18th

Dear Sir,

I am sorry to say that my engagements do not permit
of my affording you an interview on the subject of
your proposed paper. Nor do our laws allow of your
discussing the matter with a Committee of our Council,
as you suggest. Please allow me to assure you that the
fullest consideration was given to the draft which you
submitted, and that it was not declined without having

```
been referred to the judgement of a most competent
authority. No personal question (it hardly be necessary
for me to add) can have had the slightest influence on
the decision of the Council.
```

Believe me (ut supra).

April 20th.

```
The Secretary of the —— Association begs respectfully
to inform Mr. Karswell that it is impossible for him
to communicate the name of any person or persons to
whom the draft of Mr. Karswell's paper may have been
submitted, and further desires to intimate that he
cannot undertake to reply to any further letters on
this subject.
```

'And who *is* Mr. Karswell?' inquired the Secretary's wife. She had called at his office, and (perhaps unwarrantably) had picked up the last of these three letters, which the typist had just brought in.

'Why, my dear, just at present Mr. Karswell is a very angry man. But I don't know much about him otherwise, except that he is a person of wealth, his address is Lufford Abbey, Warwickshire, and he's an alchemist, apparently, and wants to tell us all about it. And that's about all – except that I don't want to meet him for the next week or two. Now, if you're ready to leave this place, I am.'

'What have you been doing to make him angry?' asked Mrs. Secretary.

'The usual thing, my dear, the usual thing. He sent in a draft of a paper he wanted to read at the next meeting, and we referred it to Edward Dunning – almost the only man in England who knows about these things – and he said it was perfectly hopeless, so we declined it.

'So Karswell has been pelting me with letters ever since. The last thing he wanted was the name of the man we referred his nonsense to – you saw my answer to that. But don't you say anything about it, for goodness' sake'

'I should think not, indeed. Did I ever do such a thing? I do hope, though, he won't get to know that it was poor Mr. Dunning.'

'Poor Mr. Dunning? I don't know why you call him that. He's a very happy man, is Dunning. Lots of hobbies and a comfortable home, and all his time to himself.'

'I only meant I should be sorry for him if this man got hold of his name, and came and bothered him.'

'Oh, ah! Yes. I dare say he would be poor Mr. Dunning then.'

The Secretary and his wife were lunching out, and the friends to whose house they were bound were Warwickshire people. So Mrs. Secretary had already settled it in her own mind that she would question them judiciously about Mr. Karswell.

But she was saved the trouble of leading up to the subject, for the hostess said to the host, before many minutes had passed, 'I saw the Abbot of Lufford this morning.'

The host whistled. '*Did* you? What in the world brings him up to town?'

'Goodness knows. He was coming out of the British Museum gate as I drove past.'

It was not unnatural that Mrs. Secretary should inquire whether this was a real Abbot who was being spoken of.

'Oh no, my dear. Only a neighbour of ours in the country who bought Lufford Abbey a few years ago. His real name is Karswell.'

'Is he a friend of yours?' asked Mr. Secretary, with a private wink to his wife.

The question let loose a torrent of declamation. There was really nothing to be said for Mr. Karswell. Nobody knew what he did with himself. His servants were a horrible set of people; he had invented a new religion for himself, and practised no one could tell what appalling rites; he was very easily offended, and never forgave anybody. He had a dreadful face (so the lady insisted, her husband somewhat demurring); he never did a kind action, and whatever influence he did exert was mischievous.

'Do the poor man justice, dear,' the husband interrupted. 'You forget the treat he gave the school children.'

'Forget it, indeed! But I'm glad you mentioned it, because it gives an idea of the man. Now, Florence, listen to this.

'The first winter he was at Lufford this delightful neighbour of ours wrote to the clergyman of his parish (he's not ours, but we know him very well) and offered to show the school children some magic-lantern slides. He said he had some new kinds which he thought would interest them.

'Well, the clergyman was rather surprised, because Mr. Karswell had shown himself inclined to be unpleasant to the children – complaining of their trespassing, or something of the sort; but of course he accepted, and the evening was fixed and our friend went himself to see that everything went right.

'He said he never had been so thankful for anything as that his own children were all prevented from being there – they were at a children's party at our house, as a matter of fact. Because this Mr. Karswell had evidently set out with the intention of frightening these poor village children out of their wits, and I do believe, if he had been allowed to go on, he would actually have done so.

'He began with some comparatively mild things. Red Riding Hood was one, and even then, Mr. Farrer said, the wolf was so dreadful that several of the smaller children had to be taken out. And he said Mr. Karswell began the story by producing a noise like a wolf howling in the distance, which was the most gruesome thing he had ever heard.

'All the slides he showed, Mr. Farrer said, were most clever. They were absolutely realistic, and where he had got them or how he worked them he could not imagine.

'Well, the show went on, and the stories kept on becoming a little more terrifying each time, and the children were mesmerised into complete silence.

'At last he produced a series which represented a little boy passing through his own park – Lufford, I mean – in the evening. Every child in the room could recognise the place from the pictures. And this poor boy was followed, and at last pursued and overtaken, and either torn to pieces or somehow made away with, by a horrible hopping creature in white, which you saw first dodging about among the trees, and gradually it appeared more and more plainly.

'Mr. Farrer said it gave him one of the worst nightmares he ever remembered and what it must have meant to the children doesn't bear thinking of.

'Of course this was too much, and he spoke very sharply indeed to Mr. Karswell, and said it couldn't go on. All *he* said was: "Oh, you think it's time to bring our little show to an end and send them home to their beds? *Very well!*" And then, if you please, he switched on another slide, which showed a great mass of snakes, centipedes, and disgusting creatures with wings, and somehow or other he made it seem as if they were climbing out of the picture and getting in amongst the audience. And this was accompanied by a sort of dry rustling noise which sent the children nearly mad, and of course they stampeded. A good many of them were rather hurt in getting out of the room and I don't suppose one of them closed an eye that night.

'There was the most dreadful trouble in the village afterwards. Of course the mothers threw a good part of the blame on poor Mr. Farrer, and, if they could have got past the gates, I believe the fathers would have broken every window in the Abbey.

'Well, now, that's Mr. Karswell – that's the Abbot of Lufford, my dear, and you can imagine how we covet *his* society.'

'Yes, I think he has all the possibilities of a distinguished criminal, has Karswell,' said the host. 'I should be sorry for anyone who got into his bad books.'

'Is he the man, or am I mixing him up with someone else?' asked the Secretary (who for some minutes had been wearing the frown of the man who is trying to recollect something). 'Is he the man who brought out a *History of Witchcraft* some time back – ten years or more?'

'That's the man, do you remember the reviews of it?'

'Certainly I do. And what's equally to the point, I knew the author of the most incisive of the lot. So did you – you must remember John Harrington; he was at John's in our time.'

'Oh, very well indeed, though I don't think I saw anything of him between the time I went down and the day I read the account of the inquest on him.'

'Inquest?' said one of the ladies. 'What has happened to him?'

'Why, what happened was that he fell out of a tree and broke his neck. But the puzzle was, what could have induced him to get up there. It was a mysterious business, I must say.

'Here was this man – not an athletic fellow, was he? And with no eccentric twist about him that was ever noticed – walking home along a country lane late in the evening – no tramps about – and he suddenly begins to run like mad, loses his hat and stick, and finally shins up a tree – quite a difficult tree – growing in the hedgerow. A dead branch gives way, and he comes down with it and breaks his neck, and there he's found next morning with the most dreadful face of fear on him that could be imagined.

'It was pretty evident, of course, that he had been chased by something, and people talked of savage dogs, and beasts escaped out of menageries. But there was nothing to be made of that.

'That was in '89, and I believe his brother Henry (whom I remember well at Cambridge, but *you* probably don't) has been trying to get on the track of an explanation ever since. He, of course, insists there was malice in it, but I don't know. It's difficult to see how it could have come in.'

After a time the talk reverted to the *History of Witchcraft*. 'Did you ever look into it?' asked the host.

'Yes, I did,' said the Secretary. 'I went so far as to read it.'

'Was it as bad as it was made out to be?'

'Oh, in point of style and form, quite hopeless. It deserved all the pulverising it got. But, besides that, it was an evil book. The man believed every word of what he was saying, and I'm very much mistaken if he hadn't tried the greater part of his receipts.'

'Well, I only remember Harrington's review of it, and I must say if I'd been the author it would have quenched my literary ambition for good. I should never have held up my head again.'

'It hasn't had that effect in the present case. But come, it's half-past three. I must be off.'

On the way home the Secretary's wife said, 'I do hope that horrible man won't find out that Mr. Dunning had anything to do with the rejection of his paper.'

'I don't think there's much chance of that,' said the Secretary. 'Dunning won't mention it himself, for these matters are confidential, and none of us will for the same reason.

'Karswell won't know his name, for Dunning hasn't published anything on the same subject yet. The only danger is that Karswell might find out, if he was to ask the British Museum people who was in the habit of consulting alchemical manuscripts. I can't very well tell them not to mention Dunning, can I? It would set them talking at once.

'Let's hope it won't occur to him.'

However, Mr. Karswell was an astute man.

This much is in the way of prologue.

On an evening rather later in the same week, Mr. Edward Dunning was returning from the British Museum, where he had been engaged in research, to the comfortable house in a suburb where he lived alone, tended by two excellent women who had been long with him.

There is nothing to be added by way of description of him to what we have heard already. Let us follow him as he takes his sober course homewards.

A train took him to within a mile or two of his house, and an electric tram a stage farther. The line ended at a point some three hundred yards from his front door.

He had had enough of reading when he got into the car, and indeed the light was not such as to allow him to do more than study the advertisements on the panes of glass that faced him as he sat. As was not unnatural, the advertisements in this particular line of cars were objects of his frequent contemplation, and, with the possible exception of the brilliant and convincing dialogue between Mr. Lamplough and an eminent K.C. on the subject of Pyretic Saline, none of them afforded much scope to his imagination.

I am wrong: there was one at the corner of the car farthest from him which did not seem familiar. It was in blue letters on a yellow ground, and all that he could read of it was a name – *John Harrington* – and something like a date.

It could be of no interest to him to know more, but for all that, as the car emptied, he was just curious enough to move along the seat until he could read it well. He felt to a slight extent repaid for his trouble. The advertisement was *not* of the usual type. It ran thus:

In memory of John Harrington, F.S.A., of The Laurels
Ashbrooke. Died Sept. 18th, 1889. Three months were allowed.

The car stopped. Mr. Dunning, still contemplating the blue letters on the yellow ground, had to be stimulated to rise by a word from the conductor.

'I beg your pardon,' he said, 'I was looking at that advertisement – it's a very odd one, isn't it?'

The conductor read it slowly. 'Well, my word,' he said, 'I never see that one before. Well, that is a cure, ain't it? Someone bin up to their jokes 'ere, I should think.'

He got out a duster and applied it, not without saliva, to the pane and then to the outside. 'No,' he said, returning, 'that ain't no transfer. Seems to me as if it was reg'lar *in* the glass, what I mean in the substance, as you may say. Don't you think so, sir?'

Mr. Dunning examined it and rubbed it with his glove, and agreed. 'Who looks after these advertisements, and gives leave for them to be put up? I wish you would inquire. I will just take a note of the words.'

At this moment there came a call from the driver: 'Look alive, George, time's up.'

'All right, all right; there's somethink else what's up at this end. You come and look at this 'ere glass.'

'What's gorn with the glass?' said the driver, approaching. 'Well, and oo's 'Arrington? What's it all about?'

'I was just asking who was responsible for putting the advertisements up in your cars, and saying it would be as well to make some inquiry about this one.'

'Well, sir, that's all done at the Company's office, that work is. It's our Mr. Timms, I believe, looks into that. When we put up tonight I'll leave word, and per'aps I'll be able to tell you tomorrer if you 'appen to be coming this way.'

This was all that passed that evening. Mr. Dunning did just go to the trouble of looking up Ashbrooke, and found that it was in Warwickshire.

Next day he went to town again. The car (it was the same car) was too full in the morning to allow of his getting a word with the conductor. He could only be sure that the curious advertisement had been made away with.

The close of the day brought a further element of mystery into the transaction. He had missed the tram, or else preferred walking home, but at a rather late hour, while he was at work in his study, one of the maids came to say that two men from the tramways was very anxious to speak to him.

This was a reminder of the advertisement, which he had, he says, nearly forgotten. He had the men in – they were the conductor and driver of the car – and when the matter of refreshment had been attended to, asked what Mr. Timms had had to say about the advertisement.

'Well, sir, that's what we took the liberty to step round about,' said the conductor. 'Mr Timms 'e give William 'ere the rough side of his tongue about that. 'Cordin' to 'im there warn't no advertisement of that description sent in, nor ordered, nor paid for, nor put up, nor nothink, let alone not bein' there, and we was playing the fool takin' up his time.

'"Well," I says, "if that's the case, all I ask of you, Mr. Timms," I says, "is to take and look at it for yourself," I says. "Of course if it ain't there," I says, you may take and call me what you like. "Right," he says, "I will," and we went straight off.

'Now, I leave it to you, sir, if that ad, as we term 'em, with 'Aarrington on it warn't as plain as ever you see anythink – blue letters on yeller glass, and as I says at the time, and you borne me out, reg'lar *in* the glass, because, if you remember, you recollect of me swabbing it with my duster.'

'To be sure I do, quite clearly – well?'

'You may say well, I don't think. Mr. Timms he gets in that car with a light – no, he told William to 'old the light outside. "Now," he says, "where's your precious ad what we've 'eard so much about?"

'"'Ere it is," I says, "Mr. Timms" and I laid my 'and on it.' The conductor paused.

'Well,' said Dunning, 'it was gone, I suppose. Broken?'

'Broke! – Not it. There warn't, if you'll believe me, no more trace of them letters – blue letters they was – on that piece o' glass, than – well, it's no good *me* talkin'. *I* never see such a thing. I leave it to William here if – but there, as I says, where's the benefit in me going on about it?'

'And what did Mr. Timms say?'

'Why 'e did what I give 'im leave to – called us pretty much anythink he liked, and I don't know as I blame him so much neither.

'But what we thought, William and me did, was as we seen you take down a bit of a note about that – well, that letterin'—'

'I certainly did that, and I have it now. Did you wish me to speak to Mr. Timms myself, and show it to him? Was that what you came in about?'

'There, didn't I say as much?' said William. 'Deal with a gent if you can get on the track of one, that's my word. Now perhaps, George, you'll allow as I ain't took you very far wrong tonight.'

'Very well, William, very well. No need for you to go on as if you'd 'ad to frog's-march me 'ere. I come quiet, didn't I? All the same for that, we 'adn't ought to take up your time this way, sir. But if it so 'appened you could find time to step round to the Company's orfice in the morning and tell Mr. Timms what you seen for yourself, we should lay under a very 'igh obligation to you for the trouble.

'You see it ain't bein' called – well, one thing and another, as we mind, but if they got it into their 'ead at the orfice as we seen things as warn't there, why, one thing leads to another, and where we should be a twelvemunce 'ence – well, you can understand what I mean.'

Amid further elucidations of the proposition, George, conducted by William, left the room.

The incredulity of Mr. Timms (who had a nodding acquaintance with Mr. Dunning) was greatly modified on the following day by what the latter could tell and show him, and any bad mark that might have been attached to the names of William and George was not suffered to remain on the Company's books. But explanation there was none.

Mr. Dunning's interest in the matter was kept alive by an incident of the following afternoon. He was walking from his club to the train, and he noticed some way ahead a man with a handful of leaflets such as are distributed to passers-by by agents of enterprising firms.

This agent had not chosen a very crowded street for his operations – in fact, Mr. Dunning did not see him get rid of a single leaflet before he himself reached the spot.

One was thrust into his hand as he passed. The hand that gave it touched his, and he experienced a sort of little shock as it did so. It seemed unnaturally rough and hot. He looked in passing at the giver but the impression he got was so unclear that, however much he tried to reckon it up subsequently, nothing would come.

He was walking quickly, and as he went on glanced at the paper. It was a blue one. The name of HARRINGTON in large capitals caught his eye. He stopped, startled, and felt for his glasses.

The next instant the leaflet was twitched out of his hand by a man who hurried past and was irrecoverably gone.

He ran back a few paces, but where was the passer-by? And where the distributor?

It was in a somewhat pensive frame of mind that Mr. Dunning passed on the following day into the Select Manuscript Room of the British Museum, and filled up tickets for Harley 3586, and some other volumes.

After a few minutes they were brought to him, and he was settling the one he wanted first upon the desk, when he thought he heard his own name whispered behind him.

He turned round hastily, and in doing so, brushed his little portfolio of loose papers on to the floor. He saw no one he recognised except one of the staff in charge of the room, who nodded to him, and he proceeded to pick up his papers.

He thought he had them all, and was turning to begin work, when a stout gentleman at the table behind him, who was just rising to leave, and had collected his own belongings, touched him on the shoulder, saying, 'May I give you this? I think it should be yours,' and handed him a missing quire.

'It is mine, thank you,' said Mr. Dunning.

In another moment the man had left the room.

Upon finishing his work for the afternoon, Mr. Dunning had some conversation with the assistant in charge, and took occasion to ask who the stout gentleman was.

'Oh, he's a man named Karswell,' said the assistant. 'He was asking me a week ago who were the great authorities on alchemy, and of course I told him you were the only one in the country. I'll see if I can catch him – he'd like to meet you, I'm sure.'

'For heaven's sake don't dream of it!' said Mr. Dunning. 'I'm particularly anxious to avoid him.'

'Oh! Very well,' said the assistant. 'He doesn't come here often. I dare say you won't meet him.'

More than once on the way home that day Mr. Dunning confessed to himself that he did not look forward with his usual cheerfulness to a solitary evening. It seemed to him that something ill-defined and impalpable had stepped in between him and his fellow-men – had taken him in charge, as it were.

He wanted to sit close-up to his neighbours in the train and in the tram, but as luck would have it both train and car were markedly empty. The conductor George was thoughtful, and appeared to be absorbed in calculations as to the number of passengers.

On arriving at his house he found Dr. Watson, his medical man, on his doorstep. 'I've had to upset your household arrangements, I'm sorry to say, Dunning. Both your servants *hors de combat*. In fact, I've had to send them to the Nursing Home.'

'Good heavens! What's the matter?'

'It's something like ptomaine poisoning, I should think. You've not suffered yourself, I can see, or you wouldn't be walking about. I think they'll pull through all right.'

'Dear, dear. Have you any idea what brought it on?'

'Well, they tell me they bought some shell-fish from a hawker at their dinner-time. It's odd. I've made inquiries, but I can't find that any hawker has been to other houses in the street.

'I couldn't send word to you. They won't be back for a bit yet. You come and dine with me tonight, anyhow, and we can make arrangements for going on. Eight o'clock. Don't be too anxious.'

The solitary evening was thus obviated, at the expense of some distress and inconvenience it is true. Mr. Dunning spent the time pleasantly enough with the doctor (a rather recent settler), and returned to his lonely home at about 11:30.

The night he passed is not one on which he looks back with any satisfaction. He was in bed and the light was out. He was wondering if the charwoman would come early enough to get him hot water next morning, when he heard the unmistakable sound of his study door opening.

No step followed it on the passage floor, but the sound must mean mischief, for he knew that he had shut the door that evening after putting his papers away in his desk. It was rather shame than courage that induced him to slip out into the passage and lean over the banisters in his nightgown, listening.

No light was visible; no further sound came; only a gust of warm, or even hot air played for an instant round his shins. He went back and decided to lock himself into his room.

There was more unpleasantness, however.

Either an economical suburban company had decided that their light would not be required in the small hours, and had stopped working, or else something was wrong with the meter. The effect was in any case that the electric light was off. The obvious course was to find a match, and also to consult his watch. He might as well know how many hours of discomfort awaited him.

So he put his hand into the well-known nook under the pillow. Only, it did not get so far. What he touched was, according to his account, a mouth, with teeth, and with hair about it, and, he declares, not the mouth of a human being.

I do not think it is any use to guess what he said or did. But he was in a spare room with the door locked and his ear to it before he was clearly conscious again. And there he spent the rest of a most miserable night, looking every moment for some fumbling at the door. But nothing came.

The venturing back to his own room in the morning was attended with many listenings and quiverings.

The door stood open, fortunately, and the blinds were up (the servants had been out of the house before the hour of drawing them down). There was, to be short, no trace of an inhabitant. The watch, too, was in its usual place. Nothing was disturbed, only the wardrobe door had swung open, in accordance with its confirmed habit.

A ring at the back door now announced the charwoman, who had been ordered the night before, and nerved Mr. Dunning, after letting her in, to continue his search in other parts of the house.

It was equally fruitless.

The day thus begun went on dismally enough. He dared not go to the Museum – in spite of what the assistant had said, Karswell might turn up there, and Dunning felt he could not cope with a probably hostile stranger. His own house was odious; he hated sponging on the doctor. He spent some little time in a call at the Nursing Home, where he was slightly cheered by a good report of his housekeeper and maid.

Towards lunchtime he betook himself to his club, again experiencing a gleam of satisfaction at seeing the Secretary of the Association. At luncheon Dunning told his friend the more material of his woes, but could not bring himself to speak of those that weighed most heavily on his spirits.

'My poor dear man,' said the Secretary, 'what an upset! Look here: we're alone at home, absolutely. You must put up with us. Yes! No excuse. Send your things in this afternoon.'

Dunning was unable to stand out. He was, in truth, becoming acutely anxious, as the hours went on, as to what that night might have waiting for him.

He was almost happy as he hurried home to pack up.

His friends, when they had time to take stock of him, were rather shocked at his lorn appearance, and did their best to keep him up to the mark. Not altogether without success.

But, when the two men were smoking alone later, Dunning became dull again. Suddenly he said, 'Gayton, I believe that alchemist man knows it was I who got his paper rejected.'

Gayton whistled. 'What makes you think that?' he said.

Dunning told of his conversation with the Museum assistant, and Gayton could only agree that the guess seemed likely to be correct.

'Not that I care much,' Dunning went on, 'only it might be a nuisance if we were to meet. He's a bad-tempered party, I imagine.'

Conversation dropped again. Gayton became more and more strongly impressed with the desolateness that came over Dunning's face and bearing and finally – though with a considerable effort – he asked him point-blank whether something serious was not bothering him.

Dunning gave an exclamation of relief. 'I was perishing to get it off my mind,' he said. 'Do you know anything about a man named John Harrington?'

Gayton was thoroughly startled, and at the moment could only ask why.

Then the complete story of Dunning's experiences came out – what had happened in the tramcar, in his own house, and in the street, the troubling of spirit that had crept over him, and still held him. And he ended with the question he had begun with.

Gayton was at a loss how to answer him. To tell the story of Harrington's end would perhaps be right. Only, Dunning was in a nervous state, the story was a grim one, and he could not help asking himself whether there were not a connecting link between these two cases, in the person of Karswell.

It was a difficult concession for a scientific man, but it could be eased by the phrase 'hypnotic suggestion'. In the end he decided that his answer tonight should he guarded. He would talk the situation over with his wife.

So he said that he had known Harrington at Cambridge, and believed he had died suddenly in 1889, adding a few details about the man and his published work.

He did talk over the matter with Mrs. Gayton, and, as he had anticipated, she leapt at once to the conclusion which had been hovering before him. It was she who reminded him of the surviving brother, Henry Harrington, and she also who suggested that he might be got hold of by means of their hosts of the day before.

'He might be a hopeless crank,' objected Gayton.

'That could be ascertained from the Bennetts, who knew him,' Mrs. Gayton retorted and she undertook to see the Bennetts the very next day.

It is not necessary to tell in further detail the steps by which Henry Harrington and Dunning were brought together.

The next scene that does require to be narrated is a conversation that took place between the two.

Dunning had told Harrington of the strange ways in which the dead man's name had been brought before him, and had said something, besides, of his own subsequent experiences. Then he had asked if Harrington was disposed, in return, to recall any of the circumstances connected with his brother's death.

Harrington's surprise at what he heard can be imagined, but his reply was readily given.

'John,' he said, 'was in a very odd state, undeniably, from time to time during some weeks before, though not immediately before, the catastrophe. There were several things: the principal notion he had was that he thought he was being followed.

'No doubt he was an impressionable man, but he never had had such fancies as this before. I cannot get it out of my mind that there was ill-will at work, and what you tell me about yourself reminds me very much of my brother.'

'Can you think of any possible connecting link?'

'There is just one that has been taking shape vaguely in my mind. I've been told that your brother reviewed a book very severely not long before he died, and just lately I have happened to cross the path of the man who wrote that book in a way he would resent.'

'Don't tell me the man was called Karswell.'

'Why not? That is exactly his name.'

Henry Harrington leant back. 'That is final to my mind. Now I must explain further. From something he said, I feel sure that my brother John was beginning to believe – very much against his will – that Karswell was at the bottom of his trouble.

'I want to tell you what seems to me to have a bearing on the situation. My brother was a great musician, and used to run up to concerts in town. He came back, three months before he died, from one of these, and gave me his programme to look at – an analytical programme: he always kept them.

'"I nearly missed this one," he said. "I suppose I must have dropped it. Anyhow, I was looking for it under my seat and in my pockets and so on, and my neighbour offered me his, said 'might he give it me, he had no further use for it,' and he went away just afterwards. I don't know who he was – a stout, clean-shaven man. I should have been sorry to miss it. Of course I could have bought another, but this cost me nothing."

'At another time he told me that he had been very uncomfortable both on the way to his hotel and during the night. I piece things together now in thinking it over.

'Then, not very long after, he was going over these programmes, putting them in order to have them bound up, and in this particular one (which by the way I had hardly glanced at), he found quite near the beginning a strip of paper with some very odd writing on it in red and black – most carefully done – it looked to me more like Runic letters than anything else.

'"Why," he said, "this must belong to my fat neighbour. It looks as if it might be worth returning to him – it may be a copy of something. Evidently someone has taken trouble over it. How can I find his address?"

'We talked it over for a little and agreed that it wasn't worth advertising about, and that my brother had better look out for the man at the next concert to which he was going very soon.

'The paper was lying on the book and we were both by the fire. It was a cold, windy summer evening. I suppose the door blew open, though I didn't notice it. At any rate a gust – a warm gust it was – came quite suddenly between us, took the paper and blew it straight into the fire. It was light, thin paper, and flared and went up the chimney in a single ash.

'"Well," I said, "you can't give it back now."

'He said nothing for a minute. Then rather crossly, "No, I can't. But why you should keep on saying so I don't know."

'I remarked that I didn't say it more than once. "Not more than four times, you mean," was all he said. I remember all that very clearly, without any good reason. And now to come to the point.

'I don't know if you looked at that book of Karswell's which my unfortunate brother reviewed. It's not likely that you should. But I did, both before his death and after it.

'The first time we made game of it together. It was written in no style at all – split infinitives and every sort of thing that makes an Oxford gorge rise.

'Then there was nothing that the man didn't swallow: mixing up classical myths, and stories out of the *Golden Legend* with reports of savage customs of today – all very proper, no doubt, if you know how to use them, but he didn't. He seemed to put the *Golden Legend* and the *Golden Bough* exactly on a par, and to believe both. A pitiable exhibition, in short.

'Well, after the misfortune, I looked over the book again. It was no better than before, but the impression which it left this time on my mind was different.

'I suspected – as I told you – that Karswell had borne ill-will to my brother, even that he was in some way responsible for what had happened. And now his book seemed to me to be a very sinister performance indeed.

'One chapter in particular struck me, in which he spoke of "casting the Runes" on people, either for the purpose of gaining their affection or of getting them out of the way – perhaps more especially the latter. He spoke of all this in a way that really seemed to me to imply actual knowledge.

'I've not time to go into details, but the upshot is that I am pretty sure from information received that the civil man at the concert was Karswell. I suspect – I more than suspect – that the paper was of importance, and I do believe that if my brother had been able to give it back, he might have been alive now.

'Therefore, it occurs to me to ask you whether you have anything to put beside what I have told you.'

By way of answer, Dunning had the episode in the Manuscript Room at the British Museum to relate.

'Then he did actually hand you some papers. Have you examined them? No? Because we must, if you'll allow it, look at them at once, and very carefully.'

They went to the still-empty house – empty, for the two servants were not yet able to return to work. Dunning's portfolio of papers was gathering dust on the writing-table. In it were the quires of small-sized scribbling paper which he used for his transcripts, and from one of these as he took it up, there slipped and fluttered out into the room with uncanny quickness, a strip of thin light paper.

The window was open, but Harrington slammed it to, just in time to intercept the paper, which he caught.

'I thought so,' he said. 'It might be the identical thing that was given to my brother. You'll have to look out, Dunning. This may mean something quite serious for you.'

A long consultation took place. The paper was narrowly examined. As Harrington had said, the characters on it were more like Runes than anything else, but not decipherable by either man, and both hesitated to copy them, for fear, as they confessed, of perpetuating whatever evil purpose they might conceal.

So it has remained impossible (if I may anticipate a little) to ascertain what was conveyed in this curious message or commission. Both Dunning and Harrington are firmly convinced that it had the effect of bringing its possessors into very undesirable company.

That it must be returned to the source whence it came they were agreed, and further, that the only safe and certain way was that of personal service. And here contrivance would be necessary, for Dunning was known by sight to Karswell. He must, for one thing, alter his appearance by shaving his beard. But then might not the blow fall first?

Harrington thought they could time it. He knew the date of the concert at which the 'black spot' had been put on his brother: it was June 18th. The death had followed on September 18th.

Dunning reminded him that three months had been mentioned on the inscription on the car-window. 'Perhaps,' he added with a cheerless laugh, 'mine may be a bill at three months too. I believe I can fix it by my diary.

'Yes, April 23rd was the day at the Museum. That brings us to July 23rd. Now, you know, it becomes extremely important to me to know anything you will tell me about the progress of your brother's trouble, if it is possible for you to speak of it.'

'Of course. Well, the sense of being watched whenever he was alone was the most distressing thing to him. After a time I took to sleeping in his room, and he was the better for that. Still, he talked a great deal in his sleep.

'What about? Is it wise to dwell on that, at least before things are straightened out? I think not, but I can tell you this: two things came for him by post during those weeks, both with a London postmark, and addressed in a commercial hand. One was a woodcut of Bewick's, roughly torn out of the page: one which shows a moonlit road and a man walking along it, followed by an awful demon creature. Under it were written the lines out of the 'Ancient Mariner' (which I suppose the cut illustrates) about one who, having once looked round—

> walks on,
> And turns no more his head,
> Because he knows a frightful fiend
> Doth close behind him tread.

The other was a calendar, such as tradesmen often send. My brother paid no attention to this, but I looked at it after his death, and found that everything after September 18th had been torn out.

'You may be surprised at his having gone out alone the evening he was killed, but the fact is that during the last ten days or so of his life he had been quite free from the sense of being followed or watched.'

The end of the consultation was this. Harrington, who knew a neighbour of Karswell's, thought he saw a way of keeping a watch on his movements. It would be Dunning's part to be in readiness to try to cross Karswell's path at any moment, to keep the paper safe and in a place of ready access.

They parted.

The next weeks were no doubt a severe strain upon Dunning's nerves. The intangible barrier which had seemed to rise about him on the day when he received the paper, gradually developed into a brooding blackness that cut him off from the means of escape to which one might have thought he might resort.

No one was at hand who was likely to suggest them to him, and he seemed robbed of all initiative. He waited with inexpressible anxiety as May, June and early July passed on, for a mandate from Harrington. But all this time Karswell remained immovable at Lufford.

At last, in less than a week before the date he had come to look upon as the end of his earthly activities, came a telegram:

> Leaves Victoria by boat train Thursday night. Do not
> miss. I come to you tonight. Harrington.

He arrived accordingly, and they concocted plans. The train left Victoria at nine and its last stop before Dover was Croydon West.

Harrington would mark down Karswell at Victoria, and look out for Dunning at Croydon, calling to him if need were by a name agreed upon. Dunning, disguised as far as might be, was to have no label or initials on any hand luggage, and must at all costs have the paper with him.

Dunning's suspense as he waited on the Croydon platform I need not attempt to describe. His sense of danger during the last days had only been sharpened by the fact that the cloud about him had perceptibly been lighter. But relief was an ominous symptom, and, if Karswell eluded him now, hope was gone. And there were so many chances of that. The rumour of the journey might be itself a device.

The twenty minutes which he paced the platform and persecuted every porter with inquiries as to the boat train were as bitter as any he had spent. Still, the train came, and Harrington was at the window. It was important, of course, that there should be no recognition, so Dunning got in at the farther end of the corridor carriage, and only gradually made his way to the compartment where Harrington and Karswell were. He was pleased, on the whole, to see that the train was far from full.

Karswell was on the alert, but gave no sign of recognition.

Dunning took the seat not immediately facing him and attempted, vainly at first, then with increasing command of his faculties, to reckon the possibilities of making the desired transfer.

Opposite to Karswell, and next to Dunning, was a heap of Karswell's coats on the seat. It would be of no use to slip the paper into these – he would not be safe, or would not feel so, unless in some way it could be proffered by him and accepted by the other.

There was a handbag, open, and with papers in it. Could he manage to conceal this (so that perhaps Karswell might leave the carriage without it), and then find and give it to him? This was the plan that suggested itself. If he could only have counselled with Harrington! But that could not be.

The minutes went on. More than once Karswell rose and went out into the corridor. The second time Dunning was on the point of attempting to make the bag fall off the seat, but he caught Harrington's eye, and read in it a warning. Karswell, from the corridor, was watching: probably to see if the two men recognised each other.

He returned, but was evidently restive, and, when he rose the third time, hope dawned, for something did slip off his seat and fall with hardly a sound to the floor.

Karswell went out once more, and passed out of range of the corridor window. Dunning picked up what had fallen, and saw that the key was in his hands in the form of one of Cook's ticket-cases, with tickets in it. These cases have a pocket in the cover, and within very few seconds the paper of which we have heard was in the pocket of this one.

To make the operation more secure, Harrington stood in the doorway of the compartment and fiddled with the blind. It was done, and done at the right time, for the train was now slowing down towards Dover.

In a moment more Karswell re-entered the compartment. As he did so,

Dunning, managing, he knew not how, to suppress the tremble in his voice, handed him the ticket-case, saying, 'May I give you this, sir? I believe it is yours.'

After a brief glance at the ticket inside, Karswell uttered the hoped-for response, 'Yes, it is. Much obliged to you, sir,' and he placed it in his breast pocket.

Even in the few moments that remained – moments of tense anxiety, for they knew not to what a premature finding of the paper might lead – both men noticed that the carriage seemed to darken about them and to grow warmer; that Karswell was fidgety and oppressed; that he drew the heap of loose coats near to him and cast it back as if it repelled him and that he then sat upright and glanced anxiously at both.

They, with sickening anxiety, busied themselves in collecting their belongings, but they both thought that Karswell was on the point of speaking when the train stopped at Dover Town. It was natural that in the short space between town and pier they should both go into the corridor.

At the pier they got out, but so empty was the train that they were forced to linger on the platform until Karswell should have passed ahead of them with his porter on the way to the boat, and only then was it safe for them to exchange a pressure of the hand and a word of concentrated congratulation.

The effect upon Dunning was to make him almost faint. Harrington made him lean up against the wall, while he himself went forward a few yards within sight of the gangway to the boat at which Karswell had now arrived.

The man at the head of it examined his ticket, and, laden with coats he passed down into the boat.

Suddenly the official called after him, 'You, sir, beg pardon, did the other gentleman show his ticket?'

'What the devil do you mean by the other gentleman?' Karswell's snarling voice called back from the deck.

The man bent over and looked at him. 'The devil? Well, I don't know, I'm sure,' Harrington heard him say to himself, and then aloud, 'My mistake, sir. Must have been your rugs! Ask your pardon.'

And then, to a subordinate near him, ''ad he got a dog with him, or what?

Funny thing: I could 'a' swore 'e wasn't alone. Well, whatever it was, they'll 'ave to see to it aboard. She's off now. Another week and we shall be gettin' the 'oliday customers.'

In five minutes more there was nothing but the lessening lights of the boat, the long line of the Dover lamps, the night breeze, and the moon.

Long and long the two sat in their room at the 'Lord Warden'. In spite of the removal of their greatest anxiety, they were oppressed with a doubt, not of the lightest. Had they been justified in sending a man to his death, as they believed they had? Ought they not to warn him, at least?

'No,' said Harrington. 'If he is the murderer I think him, we have done no more than is just. Still, if you think it better – but how and where can you warn him?'

'He was booked to Abbeville only,' said Dunning. 'I saw that. If I wired to the hotels here in Joanne's Guide, "Examine your ticket-case, Dunning," I should feel happier. This is the 21st: he will have a day. But I am afraid he has gone into the dark.'

So telegrams were left at the hotel office.

It is not clear whether these reached their destination or whether, if they did, they were understood.

All that is known is that on the afternoon of the 23rd, an English travel-ler, examining the front of St. Wulfram's Church at Abbeville, then under extensive repair, was struck on the head and instantly killed by a stone falling from the scaffold erected round the north-western tower, there being, as was clearly proved, no workman on the scaffold at that moment. And the travel-ler's papers identified him as Mr. Karswell.

Only one detail shall be added. At Karswell's sale a set of Bewick, sold with all faults, was acquired by Harrington. The page with the woodcut of the traveller and the demon was, as he had expected, mutilated.

Also, after a judicious interval, Harrington repeated to Dunning some-thing of what he had heard his brother say in his sleep. But it was not long before Dunning stopped him.

Martin's Close

SOME FEW YEARS BACK I was staying with the rector of a parish in the West, where the society to which I belong owns property. I was to go over some of this land. And, on the first morning of my visit, soon after breakfast, the estate carpenter and general handy man, John Hill, was announced as in readiness to accompany us.

The rector asked which part of the parish we were to visit that morning. The estate map was produced, and when we had showed him our round, he put his finger on a particular spot.

'Don't forget,' he said, 'to ask John Hill about Martin's Close when you get there. I should like to hear what he tells you.'

'What ought he to tell us?' I said.

'I haven't the slightest idea,' said the rector, 'or, if that is not exactly true, it will do till lunch-time.' And here he was called away.

We set out. John Hill is not a man to withhold such information as he possesses on any point, and you may gather from him much that is of interest about the people of the place and their talk.

An unfamiliar word, or one that he thinks ought to be unfamiliar to you, he will usually spell – as c-o-b cob, and the like. It is not, however, relevant to any purpose to record his conversation before the moment when we reached Martin's Close.

The bit of land is noticeable, for it is one of the smallest enclosures you are likely to see – a very few square yards, hedged in with quickset on all sides, and without any gate or gap leading into it. You might take it for a small cottage garden long-deserted, but that it lies away from the village and bears no trace of cultivation.

It is at no great distance from the road, and is part of what is there called a moor – in other words, a rough upland pasture cut up into largish fields.

'Why is this little bit hedged off so?' I asked, and John Hill (whose answer I cannot represent as perfectly as I should like) was not at fault.

'That's what we call Martin's Close, sir. 'Tes a curious thing 'bout that bit of land, sir. Goes by the name of Martin's Close, sir. M-a-r-t-i-n Martin. Beg pardon, sir, did Rector tell you to make inquiry of me 'bout that, sir?'

'Yes, he did.'

'Ah, I thought so much, sir. I was tell'n Rector 'bout that last week, and he was very much interested. It 'pears there's a murderer buried there, sir, by the name of Martin.

'Old Samuel Saunders, that formerly lived yurr at what we call South-town, sir, he had a long tale 'bout that, sir: terrible murder done 'pon a young woman, sir. Cut her throat and cast her in the water down yurr.'

'Was he hung for it?'

'Yes, sir, he was hung just up yurr on the roadway, by what I've 'eard, on the Holy Innocents' Day, many hundred years ago, by the man that went by the name of the bloody judge: terrible red and bloody, I've 'eard.'

'Was his name Jeffreys, do you think?'

'Might be possible 'twas – Jeffreys – J-e-f – Jeffreys. I reckon 'twas, and the tale I've 'eard many times from Mr. Saunders – how this young man Martin – George Martin – was troubled before his crule action come to light by the young woman's sperit.'

'How was that, do you know?'

'No, sir, I don't exactly know how 'twas with it. But by what I've 'eard he was fairly tormented – and rightly tu. Old Mr. Saunders, he told a history regarding a cupboard down yurr in the New Inn. According to what he related, this young woman's sperit come out of this cupboard: but I don't racollect the matter.'

This was the sum of John Hill's information. We passed on, and in due time I reported what I had heard to the Rector.

He was able to show me from the parish account-books that a gibbet had been paid for in 1684, and a grave dug in the following year, both for the benefit of George Martin. But he was unable to suggest anyone in the parish, Saunders being now gone, who was likely to throw any further light on the story.

Naturally, upon my return to the neighbourhood of libraries, I made search in the more obvious places.

The trial seemed to be nowhere reported. A newspaper of the time, and one or more newsletters, however, had some short notices, from which I learnt that, on the ground of local prejudice against the prisoner (he was described as a young gentleman of a good estate), the venue had been moved from Exeter to London; that Jeffreys had been the judge, and death the sentence, and that there had been some 'singular passages' in the evidence.

Nothing further transpired till September of this year.

A friend who knew me to be interested in Jeffreys then sent me a leaf torn out of a second-hand bookseller's catalogue with the entry: JEFFREYS, JUDGE: *Interesting old MS. trial for murder*, and so forth, from which I gathered, to my delight, that I could become possessed, for a very few shillings, of what seemed to be a verbatim report, in shorthand, of the Martin trial.

I telegraphed for the manuscript and got it.

It was a thin bound volume, provided with a title written in longhand by someone in the 18th century, who had also added this note:

> *My father, who took these notes in court, told me that the prisoner's friends had made interest with Judge Jeffreys that no report should be put out: he had intended doing this himself when times were better, and had shew'd it to the Revd. Mr. Glanvil, who incourag'd his design very warmly, but death surpriz'd them both before it could be brought to an accomplishment.*

The initials *W.G.* are appended. I am advised that the original reporter may have been T. Gurney, who appears in that capacity in more than one State trial.

This was all that I could read for myself. After no long delay I heard of someone who was capable of deciphering the shorthand of the 17th century, and a little time ago the typewritten copy of the whole manuscript was laid before me.

The portions which I shall communicate here help to fill in the very imperfect outline which subsists in the memories of John Hill and, I suppose, one or two others who live on the scene of the events.

The report begins with a species of preface, the general effect of which is that the copy is not that actually taken in court, though it is a true copy in regard to the notes of what was said; but that the writer has added to it some 'remarkable passages' that took place during the trial, and has made this present fair copy of the whole, intending at some favourable time to publish it; but has not put it into longhand, lest it should fall into the possession of unauthorised persons, and he or his family be deprived of the profit.

The report then begins:

This case came on to be tried on Wednesday, the 19th
of November, between our sovereign lord the King, and
George Martin Esquire, of (I take leave to omit some of
the place-names), at a sessions of oyer and terminer and
gaol delivery, at the Old Bailey, and the prisoner, being
in Newgate, was brought to the bar.

Clerk of the Crown: George Martin, hold up thy hand
(which he did).
    Then the indictment was read, which set forth that the
prisoner: 'not having the fear of God before his eyes,
but being moved and seduced by the instigation of the
devil, upon the 15th day of May, in the 36th year of our
sovereign lord King Charles the Second, with force and
arms in the parish aforesaid, in and upon Ann Clark,
spinster, of the same place, in the peace of God and of
our said sovereign lord the King then and there being,
feloniously, wilfully, and of your malice aforethought
did make an assault and with a certain knife value a
penny the throat of the said Ann Clark then and there
did cut, of the which wound the said Ann Clark then and

there did die, and the body of the said Ann Clark did cast into a certain pond of water situate in the same parish (with more that is not material to our purpose) against the peace of our sovereign lord the King, his crown and dignity'.

Then the prisoner prayed a copy of the indictment.

L.C.J. (Sir George Jeffreys): What is this? Sure you know that is never allowed. Besides, here is a plain indictment as ever I heard; you have nothing to do but to plead to it.

Pris.: My lord, I apprehend there may be matter of law arising out of the indictment, and I would humbly beg the court to assign me counsel to consider of it. Besides, my lord, I believe it was done in another case: copy of the indictment was allowed.

L.C.J.: What case was that?

Pris.: Truly, my lord, I have been kept close prisoner ever since I came up from Exeter Castle, and no one allowed to come at me and no one to advise with.

L.C.J.: But I say, what was that case you allege?

Pris.: My lord, I cannot tell your lordship precisely the name of the case, but it is in my mind that there was such an one, and I would humbly desire——

L.C.J.: All this is nothing. Name your case, and we will tell you whether there be any matter for you in it. God forbid but you should have anything that may be allowed you by law: but this is against law, and we must keep the course of the court.

Att.-Gen. (Sir Robert Sawyer): My lord, we pray for the King that he may he asked to plead.

Cl. of Ct.: Are you guilty of the murder whereof you stand indicted, or not guilty?

Pris.: My lord, I would humbly offer this to the court. If I plead now, shall I have an opportunity after to except against the indictment?

L.C.J.: Yes, yes, that comes after verdict: that will be saved to you, and counsel assigned if there be matter of law: but that which you have now to do is to plead.

Then after some little parleying with the court (which seemed strange upon such a plain indictment) the prisoner pleaded <u>Not Guilty</u>.

Cl. of Ct.: Culprit. How wilt thou be tried?
Pris.: By God and my country.
Cl. of Ct.: God send thee a good deliverance.
L.C.J.: Why, how is this? Here has been a great to-do that you should not be tried at Exeter by your country, but be brought here to London, and now you ask to be tried by your country. Must we send you to Exeter again?
Pris.: My lord, I understood it was the form.
L.C.J.: So it is, man: we spoke only in the way of pleasantness. Well, go on and swear the jury.

So they were sworn. I omit the names. There was no challenging on the prisoner's part, for, as he said, he did not know any of the persons called.

Thereupon the prisoner asked for the use of pen, ink, and paper, to which the L.C.J. replied: 'Ay, ay, in God's name let him have it.'

Then the usual charge was delivered to the jury, and the case opened by the junior counsel for the King, Mr. Dolben.

The Attorney-General followed:

May it please your lordship, and you gentlemen of the jury, I am of counsel for the King against the prisoner at the bar.

You have heard that he stands indicted for a murder done upon the person of a young girl. Such crimes as this

175

you may perhaps reckon to be not uncommon, and, indeed, in these times, I am sorry to say it, there is scarce any act so barbarous and unnatural but what we may hear almost daily instances of it.

But I must confess that in this murder that is charged upon the prisoner there are some particular features that mark it out to be such as I hope has but seldom if ever been perpetrated upon English ground.

For as we shall make it appear, the person murdered was a poor country girl (whereas the prisoner is a gentleman of a proper estate) and, besides that, was one to whom Providence had not given the full use of her intellects, but was what is termed among us commonly an innocent or natural: such an one therefore, as one would have supposed a gentleman of the prisoner's quality more likely to overlook, or, if he did notice her, to be moved to compassion for her unhappy condition, than to lift up his hand against her in the very horrid and barbarous manner which we shall show you he used.

Now to begin at the beginning and open the matter to you orderly: About Christmas of last year, that is the year 1683, this gentleman, Mr. Martin, having newly come back into his own country from the University of Cambridge, some of his neighbours, to show him what civility they could (for his family is one that stands in very good repute all over that country), entertained him here and there at their Christmas merrymakings, so that he was constantly riding to and fro, from one house to another, and sometimes, when the place of his destination was distant, or for other reason, as the unsafeness of the roads, he would be constrained to lie the night at an inn.

In this way it happened that he came, a day or two after the Christmas, to the place where this young girl lived with her parents, and put up at the inn there,

called the New Inn, which is, as I am informed, a house
of good repute.

Here was some dancing going on among the people of the
place, and Ann Clark had been brought in, it seems, by
her elder sister to look on; but being, as I have said, of
weak understanding, and, besides that, very uncomely in
her appearance, it was not likely she should take much
part in the merriment; and accordingly was but standing
by in a corner of the room.

The prisoner at the bar, seeing her, one must suppose
by way of a jest, asked her would she dance with him.
And in spite of what her sister and others could say to
prevent it and to dissuade her——

L.C.J.: Come, Mr. Attorney, we are not set here to listen
to tales of Christmas parties in taverns. I would not
interrupt you, but sure you have more weighty matters
than this. You will be telling us next what tune they
danced to.

Att-Gen.: My lord, I would not take up the time of the
court with what is not material: but we reckon it to be
material to show how this unlikely acquaintance begun.
And as for the tune, I believe, indeed, our evidence will
show that even that hath a bearing on the matter in hand.

L.C.J.: Go on, go on, in God's name: but give us nothing
that is impertinent.

Att-Gen.: Indeed, my lord, I will keep to my matter.
But, gentlemen, having now shown you, as I think, enough
of this first meeting between the murdered person and
the prisoner, I will shorten my tale so far as to say
that from then on there were frequent meetings of the
two: for the young woman was greatly tickled with having
got hold (as she conceived it) of so likely a sweetheart,
and he being once a week at least in the habit of passing
through the street where she lived, she would be always
on the watch for him.

And it seems they had a signal arranged: he should
whistle the tune that was played at the tavern. It is a
tune, as I am informed, well known in that country, and
has a burden, 'Madam, will you walk, will you talk with
me?'

L.C.J.: Ay, I remember it in my own country, in
Shropshire. It runs somehow thus, doth it not? (Here
his lordship whistled a part of a tune, which was very
observable, and seemed below the dignity of the court.
And it appears he felt it so himself for he said:) But this
is by the mark, and I doubt it is the first time we have
had dance-tunes in this court.

The most part of the dancing we give occasion for is
done at Tyburn. (Looking at the prisoner, who appeared
very much disordered.) You said the tune was material
to your case, Mr. Attorney, and upon my life I think Mr.
Martin agrees with you.

What ails you, man? Staring like a player that sees a
ghost.

Pris.: My lord, I was amazed at hearing such trivial,
foolish things as they bring against me.

L.C.J.: Well, well, it lies upon Mr. Attorney to show
whether they be trivial or not. But I must say, if he has
nothing worse than this he has said, you have no great
cause to be in amaze. Doth it not lie something deeper?
But go on, Mr. Attorney.

Att-Gen.: My lord and gentlemen — all that I have said so
far you may indeed very reasonably reckon as having an
appearance of triviality. And, to be sure, had the matter
gone no further than the humouring of a poor silly girl
by a young gentleman of quality, it had been very well.

But to proceed.

We shall make it appear that after three or four
weeks the prisoner became contracted to a young
gentlewoman of that country, one suitable every way

to his own condition, and such an arrangement was on foot that seemed to promise him a happy and a reputable living.

But within no very long time it seems that this young gentlewoman, hearing of the jest that was going about that countryside with regard to the prisoner and Ann Clark, conceived that it was not only an unworthy carriage on the part of her lover, but a derogation to herself that he should suffer his name to be sport for tavern company: and so without more ado she, with the consent of her parents, signified to the prisoner that the match between them was at an end.

We shall show you that upon the receipt of this intelligence the prisoner was greatly enraged against Ann Clark as being the cause of his misfortune (though indeed there was nobody answerable for it but himself), and that he made use of many outrageous expressions and threatenings against her, and subsequently upon meeting with her both abused her and struck at her with his whip. But she, being but a poor innocent, could not be persuaded to desist from her attachment to him, but would often run after him testifying with gestures and broken words the affection she had to him; until she was become, as he said, the very plague of his life. Yet, being that affairs in which he was now engaged necessarily took him by the house in which she lived, he could not (as I am willing to believe he would otherwise have done) avoid meeting with her from time to time.

We shall further show you that this was the posture of things up to the 15th day of May in this present year.

Upon that day the prisoner comes riding through the village, as of custom, and met with the young woman. But in place of passing her by, as he had lately done, he stopped, and said some words to her with which she appeared wonderfully pleased, and so left her; and after that day she was nowhere to be found, notwithstanding a strict search was made for her.

The next time of the prisoner's passing through the place, her relations inquired of him whether he should know anything of her whereabouts, which he totally denied.

They expressed to him their fears lest her weak intellects should have been upset by the attention he had showed her, and so she might have committed some rash act against her own life, calling him to witness the same time how often they had beseeched him to desist from taking notice of her, as fearing trouble might come of it. But this, too, he easily laughed away.

But in spite of this light behaviour, it was noticeable in him that about this time his carriage and demeanour changed, and it was said of him that he seemed a troubled man.

And here I come to a passage to which I should not dare to ask your attention, but that it appears to me to be founded in truth, and is supported by testimony deserving of credit. And, gentlemen, to my judgement it doth afford a great instance of God's revenge against murder, and that He will require the blood of the innocent.

(Here Mr. Attorney made a pause, and shifted with his papers. And it was thought remarkable by me and others, because he was a man not easily dashed.)

L.C.J.: Well, Mr. Attorney, what is your instance?
Att-Gen.: My lord, it is a strange one, and the truth is that, of all the cases I have been concerned in, I cannot call to mind the like of it.

But to be short, gentlemen, we shall bring you testimony that Ann Clark was seen after this 15th of

May, and that, at such time as she was so seen, it was
impossible she could have been a living person.

(Here the people made a hum, and a good deal of laughter,
and the Court called for silence, and when it was made——)

L.C.J.: Why, Mr. Attorney, you might save up this tale
for a week; it will be Christmas by that time, and you
can frighten your cook-maids with it (at which the people
laughed again, and the prisoner also, as it seemed).

God, man, what are you prating of — ghosts and
Christmas jigs and tavern company and here is a man's
life at stake. (To the prisoner): And you, sir, I would
have you know there is not so much occasion for you to
make merry neither. You were not brought here for that,
and if I know Mr. Attorney he has more in his brief than
he has shown yet.

Go on, Mr. Attorney. I need not, mayhap, have
spoken so sharply, but you must confess your course is
something unusual.

Att-Gen.: Nobody knows it better than I, my lord: but I
shall bring it to an end with a round turn.

I shall show you, gentlemen, that Ann Clark's body was
found in the month of June, in a pond of water, with the
throat cut; that a knife belonging to the prisoner was
found in the same water; that he made efforts to recover
the said knife from the water; that the coroner's quest
brought in a verdict against the prisoner at the bar,
and that therefore he should by course have been tried
at Exeter.

But that, suit being made on his behalf, on account
that an impartial jury could not be found to try him in
his own country, he hath had that singular favour shown
him that he should he tried here in London.

And so we will proceed to call our evidence.

* * *

Then the facts of the acquaintance between the prisoner
and Ann Clark were proved, and also the coroner's
inquest. I pass over this portion of the trial, for it
offers nothing of special interest.

Sarah Arscott was next called and sworn.

Att-Gen.: What is your occupation?

S.: I keep the New Inn at——

Att-Gen.: Do you know the prisoner at the bar?

S.: Yes: he was often at our house since he come first at
Christmas of last year.

Att-Gen.: Did you know Ann Clark?

S.: Yes, very well.

Att-Gen.: Pray, what manner of person was she in her
appearance?

S.: She was a very short thick-made woman: I do not know
what else you would have me say.

Att-Gen.: Was she comely?

S.: No, not by no manner of means: she was very uncomely,
poor child! She had a great face and hanging chops and a
very bad colour like a puddock.

L.C.J.: What is that, mistress? What say you she was like?

S.: My lord, I ask pardon. I heard Esquire Martin say she
looked like a puddock in the face; and so she did.

L.C.J.: Did you that? Can you interpret her, Mr. Attorney?

Att-Gen.: My lord, I apprehend it is the country word for
a toad.

L.C.J.: Oh, a hop-toad! Ay, go on.

Att-Gen.: Will you give an account to the jury of what
passed between you and the prisoner at the bar in May last?

S.: Sir, it was this. It was about nine o'clock the
evening after that Ann did not come home, and I was about
my work in the house. There was no company there only
Thomas Snell, and it was foul weather.

Esquire Martin came in and called for some drink, and I, by way of pleasantry, I said to him, 'Squire, have you been looking after your sweetheart?' and he flew out at me in a passion and desired I would not use such expressions. I was amazed at that, because we were accustomed to joke with him about her.

L.C.J.: Who, her?

S.: Ann Clark, my lord. And we had not heard the news of his being contracted to a young gentlewoman elsewhere, or I am sure I should have used better manners.

So I said nothing, but being I was a little put out, I begun singing, to myself as it were, the song they danced to the first time they met, for I thought it would prick him: It was the same that he was used to sing when he came down the street. I have heard it very often: 'Madam, will you walk, will you talk with me?' And it fell out that I needed something that was in the kitchen.

So I went out to get it, and all the time I went on singing, something louder and more hold-like. And as I was there all of a sudden I thought I heard someone answering outside the house, but I could not be sure because of the wind blowing so high.

So then I stopped singing, and now I heard it plain, saying, 'Yes, sir, I will walk, I will talk with you,' and I knew the voice for Ann Clark's voice.

Att-Gen.: How did you know it to be her voice?

S.: It was impossible I could be mistaken. She had a dreadful voice, a kind of a squalling voice, in particular if she tried to sing. And there was nobody in the village that could counterfeit it, for they often tried.

So, hearing that, I was glad, because we were all in anxiety to know what was gone with her: for though she was a natural, she had a good disposition and was very tractable. And says I to myself, 'What, child! Are you returned, then?' and I ran into the front room, and said to Squire Martin as I passed by, 'Squire, here is your sweetheart back again: shall I call her in?' and with that I went to open the door.

But Squire Martin he caught hold of me, and it seemed to me he was out of his wits, or near upon. 'Hold, woman, says he, 'in God's name!' and I know not what else. He was all of a-shake.

Then I was angry, and said I, 'What! Are you not glad that poor child is found?' And I called to Thomas Snell and said, 'If the Squire will not let me, do you open the door and call her in.'

So Thomas Snell went and opened the door, and the wind setting that way blew in and overset the two candles that was all we had lighted. And Esquire Martin fell away from holding me. I think he fell down on the floor, but we were wholly in the dark, and it was a minute or two before I got a light again.

And while I was feeling for the fire-box, I am not certain but I heard someone step 'cross the floor, and I am sure I heard the door of the great cupboard that stands in the room open and shut to.

Then, when I had a light again, I see Esquire Martin on the settle, all white and sweaty as if he had swounded away, and his arms hanging down. And I was going to help him; but just then it caught my eye that there was something like a bit of a dress shut into the cupboard door, and it came to my mind I had heard that door shut. So I thought it might be some person had run in when the light was quenched, and was hiding in the cupboard.

So I went up closer and looked: and there was a bit of a black stuff cloak, and just below it an edge of a brown stuff dress, both sticking out of the shut of the door. And both of them was low down, as if the person that had them on might be crouched down inside.

Att-Gen.: What did you take it to be?

S.: I took it to be a woman's dress.

Att-Gen.: Could you make any guess whom it belonged to? Did you know anyone who wore such a dress?

S.: It was a common stuff, by what I could see. I have seen many women wearing such a stuff in our parish.

Att-Gen.: Was it like Ann Clark's dress?

S.: She used to wear just such a dress: but I could not say on my oath it was hers.

Att-Gen.: Did you observe anything else about it?

S.: I did notice that it looked very wet: but it was foul weather outside.

L.C.J.: Did you feel of it, mistress?

S.: No, my lord, I did not like to touch it.

L.C.J.: Not like? Why that? Are you so nice that you scruple to feel of a wet dress?

S.: Indeed, my lord, I cannot very well tell why: only it had a nasty ugly look about it.

L.C.J.: Well, go on.

S.: Then I called again to Thomas Snell, and bid him come to me and catch anyone that come out when I should open the cupboard door. 'For,' says I, 'there is someone hiding within, and I would know what she wants.'

And with that Squire Martin gave a sort of a cry or a shout and ran out of the house into the dark, and I felt the cupboard door pushed out against me while I held it, and Thomas Snell helped me: but for all we pressed to keep it shut as hard as we could, it was forced out against us, and we had to fall back.

L.C.J.: And pray what came out — a mouse?

S.: No, my lord, it was greater than a mouse, but I could not see what it was: it fleeted very swift over the floor and out at the door.

L.C.J.: But come; what did it look like? Was it a person?

S.: My lord, I cannot tell what it was, but it ran very low, and it was of a dark colour. We were both daunted by it, Thomas Snell and I, but we made all the haste we could after it to the door that stood open. And we looked out, but it was dark and we could see nothing.

L.C.J.: Was there no tracks of it on the floor? What floor have you there?

S.: It is a flagged floor and sanded, my lord, and there was an appearance of a wet track on the floor, but we could make nothing of it, neither Thomas Snell nor me, and besides, as I said, it was a foul night.

L.C.J.: Well, for my part, I see not — though to be sure it is an odd tale she tells — what you would do with this evidence.

Att-Gen.: My lord, we bring it to show the suspicious carriage of the prisoner immediately after the disappearance of the murdered person: and we ask the jury's consideration of that; and also to the matter of the voice heard without the house.

Then the prisoner asked some questions not very material, and Thomas Snell was next called, who gave evidence to the same effect as Mrs. Arscott, and added the following:

Att-Gen.: Did anything pass between you and the prisoner during the time Mrs. Arscott was out of the room?

Th.: I had a piece of twist in my pocket.

Att-Gen.: Twist of what?

Th.: Twist of tobacco, sir, and I felt a disposition to take a pipe of tobacco. So I found a pipe on the chimney-piece, and being it was twist, and in regard of me having by an oversight left my knife at my house, and me not having over many teeth to pluck at it, as your lordship or anyone else may have a view by their own eyesight——

L.C.J.: What is the man talking about? Come to the matter, fellow! Do you think we sit here to look at your teeth?

Th.: No, my lord, nor I would not you should do, God forbid! I know your honours have better employment, and better teeth, I would not wonder.

L.C.J.: Good God, what a man is this! Yes, I have better teeth, and that you shall find if you keep not to the purpose.

Th.: I humbly ask pardon, my lord, but so it was. And I took upon me, thinking no harm, to ask Squire Martin to lend me his knife to cut my tobacco.

And he felt first of one pocket and then of another and it was not there at all. And says I, 'What! Have you lost your knife, Squire?' And up he gets and feels again and he sat down, and such a groan as he gave. 'Good God!' he says, 'I must have left it there.' 'But,' says I, 'Squire, by all appearance it is not there. Did you set a value on it,' says I, 'you might have it cried.'

But he sat there and put his head between his hands and seemed to take no notice to what I said. And then it was Mistress Arscott come tracking back out of the kitchen place.

Asked if he heard the voice singing outside the house, he said 'No,' but the door into the kitchen was shut, and there was a high wind: but says that no one could mistake Ann Clark's voice.

Then a boy, William Reddaway, about thirteen years of age, was called, and by the usual questions, put by the Lord Chief Justice, it was ascertained that he knew the nature of an oath. And so he was sworn. His evidence referred to a time about a week later.

Att-Gen.: Now, child, don't be frighted: there is no one here will hurt you if you speak the truth.

L.C.J.: Ay, if he speak the truth. But remember, child,

thou art in the presence of the great God of Heaven and
Earth, that hath the keys of Hell, and of us that are
the king's officers, and have the keys of Newgate; and
remember, too, there is a man's life in question. And if
thou tellest a lie, and by that means he comes to an ill
end, thou art no better than his murderer. And so speak
the truth.

Att-Gen.: Tell the jury what you know, and speak out.
Where were you on the evening of the 23rd of May last?

L.C.J.: Why, what does such a boy as this know of days.
Can you mark the day, boy?

W.: Yes, my lord, it was the day before our feast, and
I was to spend sixpence there, and that falls a month
before Midsummer Day.

One of the Jury: My lord, we cannot hear what he says.

L.C.J.: He says he remembers the day because it was the
day before the feast they had there, and he had sixpence
to lay out. Set him upon the table there. Well, child, and
where wast thou then?

W.: Keeping cows on the moor, my lord.

But, the boy using the country speech, my lord could not
well apprehend him, and so asked if there was anyone that
could interpret him, and it was answered the parson of
the parish was there, and he was accordingly sworn and
so the evidence given. The boy said:

'I was on the moor about six o'clock, and sitting behind a
bush of furze near a pond of water: and the prisoner came
very cautiously and looking about him, having something
like a long pole in his hand, and stopped a good while
as if he would be listening, and then began to feel in
the water with the pole: and I being very near the water
— not above five yards — heard as if the pole struck
up against something that made a wallowing sound, and
the prisoner dropped the pole and threw himself on the

ground, and rolled himself about very strangely with his hands to his ears, and so after a while got up and went creeping away.'

Asked if he had had any communication with the prisoner: 'Yes, a day or two before, the prisoner, hearing I was used to be on the moor, he asked me if I had seen a knife laying about, and said he would give sixpence to find it. And I said I had not seen any such thing, but I would ask about. Then he said he would give me sixpence to say nothing, and so he did.'

L.C.J.: And was that the sixpence you were to lay out at the feast?
W.: Yes, if you please, my lord.

Asked if he had observed anything particular as to the pond of water, he said, 'No, except that it begun to have a very ill smell and the cows would not drink of it for some days before.'

Asked if he had ever seen the prisoner and Ann Clark in company together, he began to cry very much, and it was a long time before they could get him to speak intelligibly.

At last the parson of the parish, Mr. Matthews, got him to be quiet, and the question being put to him again, he said he had seen Ann Clark waiting on the moor for the prisoner at some way off, several times since last Christmas.

Att-Gen.: Did you see her close, so as to be sure it was she?
W.: Yes, quite sure.
L.C.J.: How quite sure, child?
W.: Because she would stand and jump up and down and clap her arms like a goose (which he called by some country name: but the parson explained it to be a goose).

And then she was of such a shape that it could not be no
one else.

Att-Gen.: What was the last time that you so saw her?

Then the witness began to cry again and clung very much
to Mr. Matthews, who bid him not be frightened.

And so at last he told this story: that on the day
before their feast (being the same evening that he had
before spoken of) after the prisoner had gone away, it
being then twilight and he very desirous to get home,
but afraid for the present to stir from where he was lest
the prisoner should see him, remained some few minutes
behind the bush, looking on the pond, and saw something
dark come up out of the water at the edge of the pond
farthest away from him, and so up the bank.

And when it got to the top where he could see it plain
against the sky, it stood up and flapped the arms up
and down, and then run off very swiftly in the same
direction the prisoner had taken. And being asked very
strictly who he took it to be, he said upon his oath that
it could be nobody but Ann Clark.

Thereafter his master was called, and gave evidence
that the boy had come home very late that evening and
been chided for it, and that he seemed very much amazed,
but could give no account of the reason.

Att-Gen.: My lord, we have done with our evidence for
the King.

Then the Lord Chief Justice called upon the prisoner
to make his defence; which he did, though at no great
length, and in a very halting way, saying that he
hoped the jury would not go about to take his life on
the evidence of a parcel of country people and children
that would believe any idle tale, and that he had been

very much prejudiced in his trial; at which the L.C.J.
interrupted him, saying that he had had singular favour
shown to him in having his trial removed from Exeter,
which the prisoner acknowledging, said that he meant
rather that since he was brought to London there had not
been care taken to keep him secured from interruption
and disturbance.

Upon which the L.C.J. ordered the Marshal to be
called, and questioned him about the safe-keeping of
the prisoner, but could find nothing: except the Marshal
said that he had been informed by the underkeeper that
they had seen a person outside his door or going up the
stairs to it: but there was no possibility the person
should have got in.

And it being inquired further what sort of person
this might be, the Marshal could not speak to it save by
hearsay, which was not allowed.

And the prisoner, being asked if this was what he
meant, said no, he knew nothing of that, but it was very
hard that a man should not be suffered to be at quiet
when his life stood on it.

But it was observed he was very hasty in his denial.
And so he said no more, and called no witnesses.

Whereupon the Attorney-General spoke to the jury.

[A full report of what he said is given, and, if time allowed, I would extract
that portion in which he dwells on the alleged appearance of the murdered
person: he quotes some authorities of ancient date, as St. Augustine *de cura
pro mortuis gerenda* (a favourite book of reference with the old writers on
the supernatural) and also cites some cases which may be seen in Glanvil's,
but more conveniently in Mr. Lang's books. He does not, however, tell us
more of those cases than is to he found in print.]

The Lord Chief Justice then summed up the evidence for
the jury.

His speech, again, contains nothing that I find worth copying out: but he was naturally impressed with the singular character of the evidence, saying that he had never heard such given in his experience; but that there was nothing in law to set it aside, and that the jury must consider whether they believed these witnesses or not.

And the jury after a very short consultation brought the prisoner in Guilty.

So he was asked whether he had anything to say in arrest of judgement, and pleaded that his name was spelt wrong in the indictment, being Martin with an I, whereas it should be with a Y.

But this was overruled as not material, Mr. Attorney saying, moreover, that he could bring evidence to show that the prisoner by times wrote it as it was laid in the indictment.

And, the prisoner having nothing further to offer, sentence of death was passed upon him, and that he should be hanged in chains upon a gibbet near the place where the fact was committed, and that execution should take place upon the 28th December next ensuing, being Innocents' Day.

Thereafter the prisoner being to all appearance in a state of desperation, made shift to ask the L.C.J. that his relations might be allowed to come to him during the short time he had to live.

L.C.J.: Ay, with all my heart, so it be in the presence of the keeper; and Ann Clark may come to you as well, for what I care.

At which the prisoner broke out and cried to his lordship not to use such words to him, and his lordship very angrily told him he deserved no tenderness at any man's hands for a cowardly butcherly murderer that had not

the stomach to take the reward of his deeds: 'And I hope
to God,' said he, 'that she will be with you by day and by
night till an end is made of you.'

Then the prisoner was removed, and, so far as I saw,
he was in a swound, and the Court broke up.

I cannot refrain from observing that the prisoner
during all the time of the trial seemed to be more uneasy
than is commonly the case even in capital causes: that,
for example, he was looking narrowly among the people
and often turning round very sharply, as if some person
might be at his ear.

It was also very noticeable at this trial what a
silence the people kept, and further (though this might
not be otherwise than natural in that season of the
year), what a darkness and obscurity there was in the
court room, lights being brought in not long after two
o'clock in the day, and yet no fog in the town.

It was not without interest that I heard lately from some young men who
had been giving a concert in the village I speak of, that a very cold reception was accorded to the song which has been mentioned in this narrative:
'Madam, Will You Walk?'

It came out in some talk they had next morning with some of the local
people that that song was regarded with an invincible repugnance; it was not
so, they believed, at North Tawton, but here it was reckoned to be unlucky.

However, why that view was taken no one had the shadow of an idea.

Mr. Humphreys and His Inheritance

ABOUT FIFTEEN YEARS AGO, on a date late in August or early in September, a train drew up at Wilsthorpe, a country station in Eastern England.

Out of it stepped (with other passengers) a rather tall and reasonably good-looking young man, carrying a handbag and some papers tied up in a packet. He was expecting to be met, one would say, from the way in which he looked about him: and he was, as obviously, expected.

The stationmaster ran forward a step or two, and then, seeming to recollect himself, turned and beckoned to a stout and consequential person with a short round beard who was scanning the train with some appearance of bewilderment.

'Mr. Cooper,' he called out. 'Mr. Cooper, I think this is your gentleman.' And then to the passenger who had just alighted: 'Mr. Humphreys, sir? Glad to bid you welcome to Wilsthorpe. There's a cart from the Hall for your luggage, and here's Mr. Cooper, what I think you know.'

Mr. Cooper had hurried up, and now raised his hat and shook hands. 'Very pleased, I'm sure,' he said, 'to give the echo to Mr. Palmer's kind words. I should have been the first to render expression to them but for the face not being familiar to me, Mr. Humphreys. May your residence among us be marked as a red-letter day, sir.'

'Thank you very much, Mr. Cooper,' said Humphreys, 'for your good wishes, and Mr. Palmer also. I do hope very much that this change of – er – tenancy – which you must all regret, I am sure – will not be to the detriment of those with whom I shall be brought in contact.'

He stopped, feeling that the words were not fitting themselves together in the happiest way, and Mr. Cooper cut in, 'Oh, you may rest satisfied of that, Mr. Humphreys. I'll take it upon myself to assure you, sir, that a warm welcome awaits you on all sides. And as to any change of propriety turning out detrimental to the neighbourhood, well, your late uncle—'

And here Mr. Cooper also stopped, possibly in obedience to an inner monitor, possibly because Mr. Palmer, clearing his throat loudly, asked Humphreys for his ticket.

The two men left the little station, and – at Humphreys' suggestion – decided to walk to Mr. Cooper's house, where luncheon was awaiting them.

The relation in which these personages stood to each other can be explained in a very few lines.

Humphreys had inherited – quite unexpectedly – a property from an uncle: neither the property nor the uncle had he ever seen. He was alone in the world – a man of good ability and kindly nature, whose employment in a Government office for the last four or five years had not gone far to fit him for the life of a country gentleman. He was studious and rather diffident, and had few out-of-door pursuits except golf and gardening.

Today he had come down for the first time to visit Wilsthorpe and confer with Mr. Cooper, the bailiff, as to the matters which needed immediate attention.

It may be asked how this came to be his first visit? Ought he not in decency to have attended his uncle's funeral? The answer is not far to seek: he had been abroad at the time of the death, and his address had not been at once procurable. So he had put off coming to Wilsthorpe till he heard that all things were ready for him.

And now we find him arrived at Mr. Cooper's comfortable house, facing the parsonage, and having just shaken hands with the smiling Mrs. and Miss Cooper.

During the minutes that preceded the announcement of luncheon the party settled themselves on elaborate chairs in the drawing-room,

Humphreys, for his part, perspiring quietly in the consciousness that stock was being taken of him.

'I was just saying to Mr. Humphreys, my dear,' said Mr. Cooper, 'that I hope and trust that his residence among us here in Wilsthorpe will be marked as a red-letter day.'

'Yes, indeed, I'm sure,' said Mrs. Cooper heartily, 'and many, many of them.'

Miss Cooper murmured words to the same effect, and Humphreys attempted a pleasantry about painting the whole calendar red, which, though greeted with shrill laughter, was evidently not fully understood. At this point they proceeded to luncheon.

'Do you know this part of the country at all, Mr. Humphreys?' said Mrs. Cooper, after a short interval. This was a better opening.

'No, I'm sorry to say I do *not*,' said Humphreys. 'It seems very pleasant, what I could see of it coming down in the train.'

'Oh, it *is* a pleasant part. Really, I sometimes say I don't know a nicer district, for the country; and the people round, too: such a quantity always going on. But I'm afraid you've come a little late for some of the better garden parties, Mr. Humphreys.'

'I suppose I have. Dear me, what a pity!' said Humphreys, with a gleam of relief. And then, feeling that something more could be got out of this topic, 'But after all, you see, Mrs. Cooper, even if I could have been here earlier, I should have been cut off from them, should I not? My poor uncle's recent death, you know—'

'Oh dear, Mr. Humphreys, to be sure; what a dreadful thing of me to say!' (And Mr. and Miss Cooper seconded the proposition inarticulately.) 'What must you have thought? I *am* so sorry: you must really forgive me.'

'Not at all, Mrs. Cooper, I assure you. I can't honestly assert that my uncle's death was a great grief to me, for I had never seen him. All I meant was that I supposed I shouldn't be expected to take part for some little time in festivities of that kind.'

'Now, really it's very kind of you to take it in that way, Mr. Humphreys, isn't it, George? And you *do* forgive me? But only fancy! You never saw poor old Mr. Wilson!'

'Never in my life; nor did I ever have a letter from him. But, by the way, you have something to forgive *me* for. I've never thanked you, except by letter, for all the trouble you've taken to find people to look after me at the Hall.'

'Oh, I'm sure that was nothing, Mr. Humphreys; but I really do think that you'll find they give satisfaction. The man and his wife whom we've got for the butler and housekeeper we've known for a number of years: such a nice respectable couple, and Mr. Cooper, I'm sure, can answer for the men in the stables and gardens.'

'Yes, Mr. Humphreys, they're a good lot. The head gardener's the only one who's stopped on from Mr. Wilson's time. The major part of the employees, as you no doubt saw by the will, received legacies from the old gentleman and retired from their posts, and as the wife says, your house-keeper and butler are calculated to render you every satisfaction.'

'So everything, Mr. Humphreys, is ready for you to step in this very day, according to what I understood you to wish,' said Mrs. Cooper. 'Everything, that is, except company, and there I'm afraid you'll find yourself quite at a standstill. Only we did understand it was your intention to move in at once. If not, I'm sure you know we should have been only too pleased for you to stay here.'

'I'm quite sure you would, Mrs. Cooper, and I'm very grateful to you. But I thought I had really better make the plunge at once. I'm accustomed to living alone, and there will be quite enough to occupy my evenings – looking over papers and books and so on – for some time to come. I thought if Mr. Cooper could spare the time this afternoon to go over the house and grounds with me—'

'Certainly, certainly, Mr. Humphreys. My time is your own, up to any hour you please.'

'Till dinner-time, Father, you mean,' said Miss Cooper. 'Don't forget we're going over to the Brasnetts. And have you got all the garden keys?'

'Are you a great gardener, Miss Cooper?' said Mr. Humphreys. 'I wish you would tell me what I'm to expect at the Hall.'

'Oh, I don't know about a *great* gardener, Mr. Humphreys: I'm very fond of flowers – but the Hall garden might be made quite lovely, I often say. It's very old-fashioned as it is: and a great deal of shrubbery. There's an old temple, besides, and a maze.'

'Really? Have you explored it ever?'

'No-o,' said Miss Cooper, drawing in her lips and shaking her head. 'I've often longed to try, but old Mr. Wilson always kept it locked. He wouldn't even let Lady Wardrop into it. (She lives near here, at Bentley, you know, and she's a *great* gardener, if you like.) That's why I asked Father if he had all the keys.'

'I see. Well, I must evidently look into that, and show you over it when I've learnt the way.'

'Oh, thank you so much, Mr. Humphreys! Now I shall have the laugh of Miss Foster (that's our rector's daughter, you know; they're away on their holiday now – such nice people). We always had a joke between us which should be the first to get into the maze.'

'I think the garden keys must be up at the house,' said Mr. Cooper, who had been looking over a large bunch. 'There are a number there in the library.

'Now, Mr. Humphreys, if you're prepared, we might bid goodbye to these ladies and set forward on our little tour of exploration.'

As they came out of Mr. Cooper's front gate, Humphreys had to run the gauntlet – not of an organised demonstration, but of a good deal of touching of hats and careful contemplation from the men and women who had gathered in somewhat unusual numbers in the village street.

He had, further, to exchange some remarks with the wife of the lodge-keeper as they passed the park gates, and with the lodge-keeper himself, who was attending to the park road.

I cannot, however, spare the time to report the progress fully. As they traversed the half-mile or so between the lodge and the house, Humphreys took occasion to ask his companion some question which brought up the topic of his late uncle, and it did not take long before Mr. Cooper was embarked upon a disquisition.

'It is singular to think, as the wife was saying just now, that you should never have seen the old gentleman. And yet – you won't misunderstand me, Mr. Humphreys, I feel confident, when I say that in my opinion there would have been but little congeniality betwixt yourself and him. Not that I have a word to say in deprecation – not a single word.

'I can tell you what he was,' said Mr. Cooper, pulling up suddenly and fixing Humphreys with his eye. 'Can tell you what he was in a nutshell, as the saying goes. He was a complete, thorough valentudinarian. That describes him to a T. That's what he was, sir, a complete valentudinarian. No participation in what went on around him.

'I did venture, I think, to send you a few words of cutting from our local paper, which I took the occasion to contribute on his decease. If I recollect myself aright, such is very much the gist of them. But don't, Mr. Humphreys,' continued Cooper, tapping him impressively on the chest – 'don't you run away with the impression that I wish to say aught but what is most creditable – *most* creditable – of your respected uncle and my late employer.

'Upright, Mr. Humphreys – open as the day; liberal to all in his dealings. He had the heart to feel and the hand to accommodate. But there it was: there was the stumbling-block – his unfortunate health – or, as I might more truly phrase it, his *want* of health.'

'Yes, poor man. Did he suffer from any special disorder before his last illness – which, I take it, was little more than old age?'

'Just that, Mr. Humphreys – just that. The flash flickering slowly away in the pan,' said Cooper, with what he considered an appropriate gesture, 'the golden bowl gradually ceasing to vibrate.

'But as to your other question I should return a negative answer. General absence of vitality? Yes. Special complaint? No, unless you reckon a nasty cough he had with him.

'Why, here we are pretty much at the house. A handsome mansion, Mr. Humphreys, don't you consider?'

It deserved the epithet, on the whole: but it was oddly proportioned – a very tall red-brick house, with a plain parapet concealing the roof almost entirely. It gave the impression of a town house set down in the country. There was a basement, and a rather imposing flight of steps leading up to the front door. It seemed also, owing to its height, to desiderate wings, but there were none. The stables and other offices were concealed by trees. Humphreys guessed its probable date as 1770 or thereabouts.

The mature couple who had been engaged to act as butler and cook-housekeeper were waiting inside the front door, and opened it as their new master approached. Their name, Humphreys already knew, was Calton. Of their appearance and manner he formed a favourable impression in the few minutes' talk he had with them.

It was agreed that he should go through the plate and the cellar next day with Mr. Calton, and that Mrs. C. should have a talk with him about linen, bedding, and so on – what there was, and what there ought to be.

Then he and Cooper, dismissing the Caltons for the present, began their view of the house.

Its topography is not of importance to this story. The large rooms on the ground floor were satisfactory, especially the library, which was as large as the dining-room, and had three tall windows facing east. The bedroom prepared for Humphreys was immediately above it. There were many pleasant, and a few really interesting, old pictures. None of the furniture was new, and hardly any of the books were later than the seventies.

After hearing of and seeing the few changes his uncle had made in the house, and contemplating a shiny portrait of him which adorned the drawing-room, Humphreys was forced to agree with Cooper that in all probability there would have been little to attract him in his predecessor.

It made him rather sad that he could not be sorry – *dolebat se dolere non posse* – for the man who, whether with or without some feeling of kindliness towards his unknown nephew, had contributed so much to his well-being; for he felt that Wilsthorpe was a place in which he could be happy, and especially happy, it might be, in its library.

And now it was time to go over the garden: the empty stables could wait, and so could the laundry. So to the garden they addressed themselves, and it was soon evident that Miss Cooper had been right in thinking that there were possibilities. Also that Mr. Cooper had done well in keeping on the gardener.

The deceased Mr. Wilson might not have, indeed plainly had not, been imbued with the latest views on gardening, but whatever had been done here had been done under the eye of a knowledgeable man, and the equipment and stock were excellent.

Cooper was delighted with the pleasure Humphreys showed, and with the suggestions he let fall from time to time. 'I can see,' he said, 'that you've found your meatear here, Mr. Humphreys: you'll make this place a regular signosier before very many seasons have passed over our heads.

'I wish Clutterham had been here – that's the head gardener – and here he would have been of course, as I told you, but for his son's being horse doover with a fever, poor fellow! I should like him to have heard how the place strikes you.'

'Yes, you told me he couldn't be here today, and I was very sorry to hear the reason, but it will be time enough tomorrow.

'What is that white building on the mound at the end of the grass ride? Is it the temple Miss Cooper mentioned?'

'That it is, Mr. Humphreys – the Temple of Friendship. Constructed of marble brought out of Italy for the purpose, by your late uncle's grandfather. Would it interest you perhaps to take a turn there? You get a very sweet prospect of the park.'

The general lines of the temple were those of the Sibyl's Temple at Tivoli, helped out by a dome, only the whole was a good deal smaller. Some ancient sepulchral reliefs were built into the wall, and about it all was a pleasant flavour of the grand tour.

Cooper produced the key, and with some difficulty opened the heavy door. Inside there was a handsome ceiling, but little furniture. Most of the floor was occupied by a pile of thick circular blocks of stone, each of which had a single letter deeply cut on its slightly convex upper surface.

'What is the meaning of these?' Humphreys inquired.

'Meaning? Well, all things, we're told, have their purpose, Mr. Humphreys, and I suppose these blocks have had theirs as well as another. But what that purpose is or was (Mr Cooper assumed a didactic attitude here), I, for one, should be at a loss to point out to you, sir.

'All I know of them – and it's summed up in a very few words – is just this: that they're stated to have been removed by your late uncle, at a period before I entered on the scene, from the maze. That, Mr. Humphreys, is—'

'Oh, the maze!' exclaimed Humphreys. 'I'd forgotten that: we must have a look at it. Where is it?'

Cooper drew him to the door of the temple, and pointed with his stick. 'Guide your eye,' he said (somewhat in the manner of the Second Elder in Handel's *Susanna*—

> Far to the west direct your straining eyes
> Where yon tall holm-tree rises to the skies).

'Guide your eye by my stick here, and follow out the line directly opposite to the spot where we're standing now, and I'll engage, Mr. Humphreys,
that you'll catch the archway over the entrance. You'll see it just at the end of
the walk answering to the one that leads up to this very building.

'Did you think of going there at once? Because if that be the case, I must
go to the house and procure the key. If you would walk on there, I'll rejoin
you in a few moments' time.'

Accordingly Humphreys strolled down the ride leading to the temple,
past the garden-front of the house, and up the turfy approach to the archway
which Cooper had pointed out to him.

He was surprised to find that the whole maze was surrounded by a high
wall, and that the archway was provided with a padlocked iron gate. But
then he remembered that Miss Cooper had spoken of his uncle's objection
to letting anyone enter this part of the garden.

He was now at the gate, and still Cooper came not. For a few minutes
he occupied himself in reading the motto cut over the entrance, 'Secretum
meum mihi et filiis domus meae', and in trying to recollect the source of it.

Then he became impatient and considered the possibility of scaling
the wall. This was clearly not worthwhile. It might have been done if he
had been wearing an older suit. Or could the padlock – a very old one – be
forced? No, apparently not. And yet, as he gave a final irritated kick at the
gate, something gave way, and the lock fell at his feet.

He pushed the gate open, inconveniencing a number of nettles as he did
so, and stepped into the enclosure.

It was a yew maze, of circular form, and the hedges, long untrimmed,
had grown out and upwards to a most unorthodox breadth and height.
The walks, too, were next door to impassable. Only by entirely disregard-
ing scratches, nettle-stings, and wet, could Humphreys force his way along
them. But at any rate this condition of things, he reflected, would make it
easier for him to find his way out again, for he left a very visible track.

So far as he could remember, he had never been in a maze before, nor did
it seem to him now that he had missed much. The dankness and darkness,
and smell of crushed goosegrass and nettles were anything but cheerful. Still,
it did not seem to be a very intricate specimen of its kind.

Here he was (by the way, was that Cooper arrived at last? No!) very nearly at the heart of it, without having taken much thought as to what path he was following. Ah! There at last was the centre, easily gained. And there was something to reward him.

His first impression was that the central ornament was a sundial; but when he had switched away some portion of the thick growth of brambles and bindweed that had formed over it, he saw that it was a less ordinary decoration.

A stone column about four feet high, and on the top of it a metal globe – copper, to judge by the green patina – engraved, and finely engraved too, with figures in outline, and letters.

That was what Humphreys saw, and a brief glance at the figures convinced him that it was one of those mysterious things called celestial globes, from which, one would suppose, no one ever yet derived any information about the heavens.

However, it was too dark – at least in the maze – for him to examine this curiosity at all closely, and besides, he now heard Cooper's voice, and sounds as of an elephant in the jungle. Humphreys called to him to follow the track he had beaten out, and soon Cooper emerged panting into the central circle.

He was full of apologies for his delay; he had not been able, after all, to find the key. 'But there!' he said, 'you've penetrated into the heart of the mystery unaided and unannealed, as the saying goes.

'Well! I suppose it's a matter of thirty to forty years since any human foot has trod these precincts. Certain it is that I've never set foot in them before. Well, well! What's the old proverb about angels fearing to tread? It's proved true once again in this case.'

Humphreys' acquaintance with Cooper, though it had been short, was sufficient to assure him that there was no guile in this allusion, and he forbore the obvious remark, merely suggesting that it was fully time to get back to the house for a late cup of tea, and to release Cooper for his evening engagement.

They left the maze accordingly, experiencing well-nigh the same ease in retracing their path as they had in coming in.

'Have you any idea,' Humphreys asked, as they went towards the house, 'why my uncle kept that place so carefully locked?'

Cooper pulled up, and Humphreys felt that he must be on the brink of a revelation.

'I should merely be deceiving you, Mr. Humphreys, and that to no good purpose, if I laid claim to possess any information whatsoever on that topic. When I first entered upon my duties here, some eighteen years back, that maze was word for word in the condition you see it now, and the one and only occasion on which the question ever arose within my knowledge was that of which my girl made mention in your hearing.

'Lady Wardrop – I've not a word to say against her – wrote applying for admission to the maze. Your uncle showed me the note – a most civil note – everything that could be expected from such a quarter.

'"Cooper," he said, "I wish you'd reply to that note on my behalf."

'"Certainly, Mr. Wilson," I said, for I was quite inured to acting as his secretary, "what answer shall I return to it?"

'"Well," he said, "give Lady Wardrop my compliments, and tell her that if ever that portion of the grounds is taken in hand I shall be happy to give her the first opportunity of viewing it, but that it has been shut up now for a number of years, and I shall be grateful to her if she kindly won't press the matter."

'That, Mr. Humphreys, was your good uncle's last word on the subject, and I don't think I can add anything to it. Unless,' added Cooper, after a pause, 'it might be just this: that, so far as I could form a judgement, he had a dislike (as people often will for one reason or another) to the memory of his grandfather, who, as I mentioned to you, had that maze laid out.

'A man of peculiar tenets, Mr. Humphreys, and a great traveller. You'll have the opportunity, on the coming Sabbath, of seeing the tablet to him in our little parish church – put up it was some long time after his death.'

'Oh! I should have expected a man who had such a taste for building to have designed a mausoleum for himself.'

'Well, I've never noticed anything of the kind you mention. And, in fact, come to think of it, I'm not at all sure that his resting-place is within our boundaries at all: that he lays in the vault I'm pretty confident is not the case. Curious now that I shouldn't be in a position to inform you on that heading. Still, after all, we can't say, can we, Mr. Humphreys, that it's a point of crucial importance where the pore mortal coils are bestowed?'

At this point they entered the house, and Cooper's speculations were interrupted.

Tea was laid in the library, where Mr. Cooper fell upon subjects appropriate to the scene. 'A fine collection of books! One of the finest, I've understood from connoisseurs, in this part of the country; splendid plates, too, in some of these works.

'I recollect your uncle showing me one with views of foreign towns – most absorbing it was: got up in first-rate style. And another all done by hand, with the ink as fresh as if it had been laid on yesterday, and yet, he told me, it was the work of some old monk hundreds of years back.

'I've always taken a keen interest in literature myself. Hardly anything to my mind can compare with a good hour's reading after a hard day's work; far better than wasting the whole evening at a friend's house – and that reminds me, to be sure. I shall be getting into trouble with the wife if I don't make the best of my way home and get ready to squander away one of these same evenings! I must be off, Mr. Humphreys.'

'And that reminds *me*,' said Humphreys, 'if I'm to show Miss Cooper the maze tomorrow we must have it cleared out a bit. Could you say a word about that to the proper person?'

'Why, to be sure. A couple of men with scythes could cut out a track tomorrow morning. I'll leave word as I pass the lodge, and I'll tell them, what'll save you the trouble, perhaps, Mr. Humphreys, of having to go up and extract them yourself: that they'd better have some sticks or a tape to mark out their way with as they go on.'

'A very good idea! Yes, do that; and I'll expect Mrs. and Miss Cooper in the afternoon, and yourself about half-past ten in the morning.'

'It'll be a pleasure, I'm sure, both to them and to myself, Mr. Humphreys. Good night!'

Humphreys dined at eight. But for the fact that it was his first evening, and that Calton was evidently inclined for occasional conversation, he would have finished the novel he had bought for his journey.

As it was, he had to listen and reply to some of Calton's impressions of the neighbourhood and the season: the latter, it appeared, was seasonable, and the former had changed considerably – and not altogether for the worse – since Calton's boyhood (which had been spent there).

The village shop in particular had greatly improved since the year 1870. It was now possible to procure there pretty much anything you liked in reason: which was a conveniency, because suppose anythink was required of a suddent (and he had known such things before now), he (Calton) could step down there (supposing the shop to be still open), and order it in, without he borrered it of the Rectory, whereas in earlier days it would have been useless to pursue such a course in respect of anything but candles, or soap, or treacle, or perhaps a penny child's picture-book, and nine times out of ten it'd be something more in the nature of a bottle of whisky you'd be requiring; leastways—

On the whole Humphreys thought he would be prepared with a book in future.

The library was the obvious place for the after-dinner hours. Candle in hand and pipe in mouth, he moved round the room for some time, taking stock of the titles of the books. He had all the predisposition to take interest in an old library, and there was every opportunity for him here to make systematic acquaintance with one, for he had learned from Cooper that there was no catalogue save the very superficial one made for purposes of probate.

The drawing up of a *catalogue raisonné* would be a delicious occupation for winter. There were probably treasures to be found, too: even manuscripts, if Cooper might be trusted.

As he pursued his round the sense came upon him (as it does upon most of us in similar places) of the extreme unreadableness of a great portion of the collection. 'Editions of Classics and Fathers, and Picart's *Religious Ceremonies*, and the *Harleian Miscellany*, I suppose are all very well, but who is ever going to read Tostatus Abulensis, or Pineda on Job, or a book like this?'

He picked out a small quarto, loose in the binding, and from which the lettered label had fallen off; and observing that coffee was waiting for him, retired to a chair.

Eventually he opened the book. It will be observed that his condemnation of it rested wholly on external grounds. For all he knew it might have been a collection of unique plays, but undeniably the outside was blank and forbidding.

As a matter of fact, it was a collection of sermons or meditations, and mutilated at that, for the first sheet was gone. It seemed to belong to the latter end of the 17th century.

He turned over the pages till his eye was caught by a marginal note: '*A Parable of this Unhappy Condition*', and he thought he would see what aptitudes the author might have for imaginative composition.

I have heard or read, *so ran the passage*, whether in the way of *Parable* or true *Relation* I leave my Reader to judge, of a Man who, like *Theseus*, in the *Attick Tale*, should adventure himself, into a *Labyrinth* or *Maze*: and such an one indeed as was not laid out in the Fashion of our *Topiary* artists of this Age, but of a wide compass, in which, moreover, such unknown Pitfalls and Snares, nay, such ill-omened Inhabitants were commonly thought to lurk as could only be encountered at the Hazard of one's very life.

Now you may be sure that in such a Case the Disswasions of Friends were not wanting. 'Consider of such-an-one' says a Brother 'how he went the way you wot of, and was never seen more.'

'Or of such another' says the Mother 'that adventured himself but a little way in, and from that day forth is so troubled in his Wits that he cannot tell what he saw, nor hath passed one good Night.'

'And have you never heard' cries a Neighbour 'of what Faces have been seen to look out over the *Palisadoes* and betwixt the Bars of the Gate?'

But all would not do: the Man was set upon his Purpose. For it seems it was the common fireside Talk of that Country that at the Heart and Centre of this *Labyrinth* there was a jewel of such Price and Rarity that would enrich the Finder thereof for his life: and this should be his by right that could persever to come at it.

What then? *Quid multa?* The Adventurer pass'd the Gates, and for a whole day's space his Friends without had no news of him, except it might be by some indistinct Cries heard afar off in the Night, such as made them turn in their restless Beds and sweat for very Fear, not doubting but that their Son and Brother had put one more to the *Catalogue* of those unfortunates that had suffer'd shipwreck on that Voyage.

So the next day they went with weeping Tears to the Clark of the Parish to order the Bell to be toll'd. And their Way took them hard by the gate of the *Labyrinth*: which they would have hastened by, from the Horrour they had of it, but that they caught sight of a sudden of a Man's Body lying in the Roadway, and going up to it (with what Anticipations may be easily figured) found it to be him whom they reckoned as lost: and not dead, though he were in a Swound most like Death.

They then, who had gone forth as Mourners came back rejoycing, and set to by all means to revive their Prodigal. Who, being come to himself and hearing of their Anxieties and their Errand of that Morning, 'Ay' says he 'you may as well finish what you were about: for, for all I have brought back the Jewel (which he shew'd them, and 'twas indeed a rare Piece) I have brought back that with it that will leave me neither Rest at Night nor Pleasure by Day.' Whereupon they were instant with him to learn his Meaning, and where his Company should be that went so sore against his Stomach.

'O' says he ''tis here in my Breast: I cannot flee from it, do what I may.'

So it needed no Wizard to help them to a guess that it was the Recollection of what he had seen that troubled him so wonderfully. But they could get no more of him for a long Time but by Fits and Starts.

However at long and at last they made shift to collect somewhat of this kind: that at first, while the Sun was bright, he went merrily on, and without any Difficulty reached the Heart of the *Labyrinth* and got the Jewel, and so set out on his way back rejoycing. But as the Night fell, *wherein all the Beasts of the Forest do move*, he begun to be sensible of some Creature keeping Pace with him and, as he thought, *peering and looking upon him* from the next Alley to that he was in. And that when he should stop, this Companion should stop also, which put him in some Disorder of his Spirits.

And, indeed, as the Darkness increas'd, it seemed to him that there was more than one, and, it might be, even a whole Band of such Followers: at least so he judg'd by the Rustling and Cracking that they kept among the Thickets. Besides that there would be at a Time a Sound of Whispering, which seem'd to import a Conference among them. But in regard of who they were or what Form they were of, he would not be persuaded to say what he thought.

Upon his Hearers asking him what the Cries were which they heard in the Night (as was observ'd above) he gave them this Account: That about Midnight (so far as he could judge) he heard his Name call'd from a long way off; and he would have been sworn it was his Brother that so call'd him. So he stood still and hilloo'd at the Pitch of his Voice, and he suppos'd that the Echo, or the Noyse of his Shouting, disguis'd for the Moment any lesser sound; because, when there fell a Stillness again, he distinguish'd a Trampling (not loud) of running Feet coming very close behind him, wherewith he was so daunted that himself set off to run, and that he continued till the Dawn broke.

Sometimes when his Breath fail'd him, he would cast himself flat on his Face, and hope that his Pursuers might over-run him in the Darkness, but at such a Time they would regularly make a Pause, and he could hear them pant and snuff as it had been a Hound at Fault: which wrought in him so extream an Horrour of mind, that he would be forc'd to betake himself again to turning and doubling, if by any Means he might throw them off the Scent.

And, as if this Exertion was in itself not terrible enough, he had before him the constant Fear of falling into some Pit or Trap, of which he had heard, and indeed seen with his own Eyes that there were several, some at the sides and other in the Midst of the Alleys. So that in fine (he said) a more dreadful Night was never spent by Mortal Creature than that he had endur'd in that *Labyrinth*; and not that jewel which he had in his Wallet, nor the richest that was ever brought out of the *Indies*, could be a sufficient Recompence to him for the Pains he had suffered.

I will spare to set down the further Recital of this Man's Troubles, inasmuch as I am confident my Reader's Intelligence will

hit the *Parallel* I desire to draw. For is not this Jewel a just Emblem
of the Satisfaction which a Man may bring back with him from a
Course of this World's Pleasures? And will not the Labyrinth serve
for an Image of the World itself wherein such a Treasure (if we may
believe the common Voice) is stored up?

At about this point Humphreys thought that a little Patience would
be an agreeable change, and that the writer's 'improvement' of his Parable
might be left to itself.

So he put the book back in its former place, wondering as he did so
whether his uncle had ever stumbled across that passage; and if so, whether
it had worked on his fancy so much as to make him dislike the idea of a
maze, and determine to shut up the one in the garden.

Not long afterwards he went to bed.

The next day brought a morning's hard work with Mr. Cooper, who, if
exuberant in language, had the business of the estate at his fingers' ends.

He was very breezy this morning, Mr. Cooper was: had not forgotten
the order to clear out the maze – the work was going on at that moment
– his girl was on the tentacles of expectation about it. He also hoped that
Humphreys had slept the sleep of the just, and that we should be favoured
with a continuance of this congenial weather.

At luncheon he enlarged on the pictures in the dining-room, and pointed
out the portrait of the constructor of the temple and the maze. Humphreys
examined this with considerable interest.

It was the work of an Italian, and had been painted when old Mr.
Wilson was visiting Rome as a young man. (There was, indeed, a view of
the Colosseum in the background.) A pale thin face and large eyes were the
characteristic features. In the hand was a partially unfolded roll of paper, on
which could be distinguished the plan of a circular building, very probably
the temple, and also part of that of a labyrinth.

Humphreys got up on a chair to examine it, but it was not painted with
sufficient clearness to be worth copying. It suggested to him, however, that
he might as well make a plan of his own maze and hang it in the hall for the
use of visitors.

This determination of his was confirmed that same afternoon. For when Mrs. and Miss Cooper arrived, eager to be inducted into the maze, he found that he was wholly unable to lead them to the centre.

The gardeners had removed the guide-marks they had been using, and even Clutterham, when summoned to assist, was as helpless as the rest.

'The point is, you see, Mr. Wilson – I should say 'Umphreys – these mazes is purposely constructed so much alike, with a view to mislead. Still, if you'll foller me, I think I can put you right. I'll just put my 'at down 'ere as a starting-point.'

He stumped off, and after five minutes brought the party safe to the hat again.

'Now that's a very peculiar thing,' he said, with a sheepish laugh. 'I made sure I'd left that 'at just over against a bramble-bush, and you can see for yourself there ain't no bramble-bush not in this walk at all. If you'll allow me, Mr. Humphreys – that's the name, ain't it, sir? – I'll just call one of the men in to mark the place like.'

William Crack arrived, in answer to repeated shouts. He had some difficulty in making his way to the party. First he was seen or heard in an inside alley, then, almost at the same moment, in an outer one. However, he joined them at last, and was first consulted without effect and then stationed by the hat, which Clutterham still considered it necessary to leave on the ground.

In spite of this strategy, they spent the best part of three-quarters of an hour in quite fruitless wanderings, and Humphreys was obliged at last, seeing how tired Mrs. Cooper was becoming, to suggest a retreat to tea, with profuse apologies to Miss Cooper. 'At any rate you've won your bet with Miss Foster,' he said; 'you have been inside the maze. And I promise you the first thing I do shall be to make a proper plan of it with the lines marked out for you to go by.'

'That's what's wanted, sir,' said Clutterham, 'someone to draw out a plan and keep it by them. It might be very awkward, you see, anyone getting into that place and a shower of rain come on, and them not able to find their way out again.

'It might be hours before they could be got out, without you'd permit of me makin' a short cut to the middle: what my meanin' is, takin' down a couple of trees in each 'edge in a straight line so as you could git a clear view right through. Of course that'd do away with it as a maze, but I don't know as you'd approve of that.'

'No, I won't have that done yet. I'll make a plan first, and let you have a copy. Later on, if we find occasion, I'll think of what you say.'

Humphreys was vexed and ashamed at the fiasco of the afternoon, and could not be satisfied without making another effort that evening to reach the centre of the maze.

His irritation was increased by finding it without a single false step.

He had thoughts of beginning his plan at once, but the light was fading, and he felt that by the time he had got the necessary materials together, work would be impossible.

Next morning accordingly, carrying a drawing-board, pencils, compasses, cartridge paper, and so forth (some of which had been borrowed from the Coopers and some found in the library cupboards), he went to the middle of the maze (again without any hesitation), and set out his materials. He was, however, delayed in making a start.

The brambles and weeds that had obscured the column and globe were now all cleared away, and it was for the first time possible to see clearly what these were like.

The column was featureless, resembling those on which sundials are usually placed. Not so the globe. I have said that it was finely engraved with figures and inscriptions, and that on a first glance Humphreys had taken it for a celestial globe. But he soon found that it did not answer to his recollection of such things.

One feature seemed familiar: a winged serpent – *Draco* – encircled it about the place which, on a terrestrial globe, is occupied by the equator. But on the other hand, a good part of the upper hemisphere was covered by the outspread wings of a large figure whose head was concealed by a ring at the pole or summit of the whole.

Around the place of the head the words *princeps tenebrarum* could be deciphered. In the lower hemisphere there was a space hatched all over with cross-lines and marked as *umbra mortis*. Near it was a range of mountains, and among them a valley with flames rising from it. This was lettered (will you be surprised to learn it?) *vallis filiorum Hinnom*.

Above and below *Draco* were outlined various figures not unlike the pictures of the ordinary constellations, but not the same. Thus, a nude man with a raised club was described, not as *Hercules* but as *Cain*. Another, plunged up to his middle in earth and stretching out despairing arms, was *Chore*, not *Ophiuchus*, and a third, hung by his hair to a snaky tree, was *Absolon*. Near the last, a man in long robes and high cap, standing in a circle and addressing two shaggy demons who hovered outside, was described as *Hostanes magus* (a character unfamiliar to Humphreys).

The scheme of the whole, indeed, seemed to be an assemblage of the patriarchs of evil, perhaps not uninfluenced by a study of Dante.

Humphreys thought it an unusual exhibition of his great-grandfather's taste, but reflected that he had probably picked it up in Italy and had never taken the trouble to examine it closely. Certainly, had he set much store by it, he would not have exposed it to wind and weather.

He tapped the metal – it seemed hollow and not very thick – and, turning from it, addressed himself to his plan.

After half-an-hour's work he found it was impossible to get on without using a clue. So he procured a roll of twine from Clutterham, and laid it out along the alleys from the entrance to the centre, tying the end to the ring at the top of the globe.

This expedient helped him to set out a rough plan before luncheon, and in the afternoon he was able to draw it in more neatly.

Towards tea-time Mr. Cooper joined him, and was much interested in his progress. 'Now this—' said Mr. Cooper, laying his hand on the globe, and then drawing it away hastily. 'Whew! Holds the heat, doesn't it, to a surprising degree, Mr. Humphreys.

'I suppose this metal – copper, isn't it? – would be an insulator or conductor, or whatever they call it.'

'The sun has been pretty strong this afternoon,' said Humphreys, evading the scientific point, 'but I didn't notice the globe had got hot.

'No – it doesn't seem very hot to me,' he added.

'Odd!' said Mr. Cooper. 'Now I can't hardly bear my hand on it. Something in the difference of temperament between us, I suppose. I dare say you're a chilly subject, Mr. Humphreys. I'm not: and there's where the distinction lies.

'All this summer I've slept, if you'll believe me, practically *in statu quo*, and had my morning tub as cold as I could get it. Day out and day in – let me assist you with that string.'

'It's all right, thanks. But if you'll collect some of these pencils and things that are lying about I shall be much obliged.

'Now I think we've got everything, and we might get back to the house.'

They left the maze, Humphreys rolling up the clue as they went.

The night was rainy.

Most unfortunately it turned out that, whether by Cooper's fault or not, the plan had been the one thing forgotten the evening before. As was to be expected, it was ruined by the wet. There was nothing for it but to begin again (the job would not be a long one this time).

The clue therefore was put in place once more and a fresh start made.

But Humphreys had not done much before an interruption came in the shape of Calton with a telegram. His late chief in London wanted to consult him. Only a brief interview was wanted, but the summons was urgent. This was annoying, yet it was not really upsetting.

There was a train available in half-an-hour, and, unless things went very cross, he could be back, possibly by five o'clock, certainly by eight.

He gave the plan to Calton to take to the house, but it was not worth-while to remove the clue.

All went as he had hoped. He spent a rather exciting evening in the library, for he lighted tonight upon a cupboard where some of the rarer books were kept.

When he went up to bed he was glad to find that the servant had remembered to leave his curtains undrawn and his windows open. He put down his light, and went to the window which commanded a view of the garden and the park.

It was a brilliant moonlight night. In a few weeks' time the sonorous winds of autumn would break up all this calm. But now the distant woods were in a deep stillness: the slopes of the lawns were shining with dew; the colours of some of the flowers could almost be guessed.

The light of the moon just caught the cornice of the temple and the curve of its leaden dome, and Humphreys had to own that, so seen, these conceits of a past age have a real beauty.

In short, the light, the perfume of the woods, and the absolute quiet called up such kind old associations in his mind that he went on ruminating them for a long, long time.

As he turned from the window he felt he had never seen anything more complete of its sort. The one feature that struck him with a sense of incongruity was a small Irish yew, thin and black, which stood out like an outpost of the shrubbery, through which the maze was approached. That, he thought, might as well be away: the wonder was that anyone should have thought it would look well in that position.

However, next morning, in the press of answering letters and going over books with Mr. Cooper, the Irish yew was forgotten.

One letter, by the way, arrived this day which has to be mentioned. It was from that Lady Wardrop whom Miss Cooper had mentioned, and it renewed the application which she had addressed to Mr. Wilson.

She pleaded, in the first place, that she was about to publish a *Book of Mazes*, and earnestly desired to include the plan of the Wilsthorpe Maze, and also that it would be a great kindness if Mr. Humphreys could let her see it (if at all) at an early date, since she would soon have to go abroad for the winter months.

Her house at Bentley was not far distant, so Humphreys was able to send a note by hand to her suggesting the very next day or the day after for her visit. It may be said at once that the messenger brought back a most grateful answer, to the effect that the morrow would suit her admirably.

The only other event of the day was that the plan of the maze was successfully finished.

This night again was fair and brilliant and calm, and Humphreys lingered almost as long at his window. The Irish yew came to his mind again as he was on the point of drawing his curtains, but either he had been misled by a shadow the night before, or else the shrub was not really so obtrusive as he had fancied. Anyhow, he saw no reason for interfering with it.

What he *would* do away with, however, was a clump of dark growth which had usurped a place against the house wall, and was threatening to obscure one of the lower range of windows.

It did not look as if it could possibly be worth keeping. He fancied it dank and unhealthy, little as he could see of it.

Next day (it was a Friday – he had arrived at Wilsthorpe on a Monday) Lady Wardrop came over in her car soon after luncheon. She was a stolid elderly person, very full of talk of all sorts and particularly inclined to make herself agreeable to Humphreys, who had gratified her very much by his ready granting of her request.

They made a thorough exploration of the place together, and Lady Wardrop's opinion of her host obviously rose sky-high when she found that he really knew something of gardening. She entered enthusiastically into all his plans for improvement, but agreed that it would be a vandalism to interfere with the characteristic laying-out of the ground near the house.

With the temple she was particularly delighted, and, said she, 'Do you know, Mr. Humphreys, I think your bailiff must be right about those lettered blocks of stone. One of my mazes – I'm sorry to say the stupid people have destroyed it now – it was at a place in Hampshire – had the track marked out in that way.

'They were tiles there, but lettered just like yours, and the letters, taken in the right order, formed an inscription – what it was I forget – something about Theseus and Ariadne. I have a copy of it, as well as the plan of the maze where it was. How people can do such things!

'I shall never forgive you if you injure *your* maze. Do you know, they're becoming very uncommon? Almost every year I hear of one being grubbed up.

'Now, do let's get straight to it. Or, if you're too busy, I know my way there perfectly, and I'm not afraid of getting lost in it – I know too much about mazes for that. Though I remember missing my lunch – not so very long ago either – through getting entangled in the one at Busbury.

'Well, of course, if you *can* manage to come with me, that will be all the nicer.'

After this confident prelude justice would seem to require that Lady Wardrop should have been hopelessly muddled by the Wilsthorpe maze. Nothing of that kind happened: yet it is to be doubted whether she got all the enjoyment from her new specimen that she expected.

She was interested – keenly interested – to be sure, and pointed out to Humphreys a series of little depressions in the ground which, she thought, marked the places of the lettered blocks. She told him, too, what other mazes resembled his most closely in arrangement, and explained how it was usually possible to date a maze to within twenty years by means of its plan. This one, she already knew, must be about as old as 1780, and its features were just what might be expected.

The globe, furthermore, completely absorbed her. It was unique in her experience, and she pored over it for long.

'I should like a rubbing of that,' she said, 'if it could possibly be made. Yes, I am sure you would be most kind about it, Mr. Humphreys, but I trust you won't attempt it on my account, I do indeed. I shouldn't like to take any liberties here. I have the feeling that it might be resented.

'Now, confess,' she went on, turning and facing Humphreys, 'don't you feel – haven't you felt ever since you came in here – that a watch is being kept on us, and that if we overstepped the mark in any way there would be a – well, a pounce?

'No? *I* do; and I don't care how soon we are outside the gate.

'After all,' she said, when they were once more on their way to the house, 'it may have been only the airlessness and the dull heat of that place that pressed on my brain. Still, I'll take back one thing I said. I'm not sure that I shan't forgive you after all, if I find next spring that that maze has been grubbed up.'

'Whether or no that's done, you shall have the plan, Lady Wardrop. I have made one, and no later than tonight I can trace you a copy.'

'Admirable. A pencil tracing will be all I want, with an indication of the scale. I can easily have it brought into line with the rest of my plates. Many, many thanks.'

'Very well, you shall have that tomorrow. I wish you could help me to a solution of my block-puzzle.'

'What, those stories in the summer-house? That *is* a puzzle. They are in no sort of order? Of course not. But the men who put them down must have had some directions – perhaps you'll find a paper about it among your uncle's things. If not, you'll have to call in somebody who's an expert in ciphers.'

'Advise me about something else, please,' said Humphreys. 'That bush-thing under the library window: you would have that away, wouldn't you?'

'Which? That? Oh, I think not,' said Lady Wardrop. 'I can't see it very well from this distance, but it's not unsightly.'

'Perhaps you're right. Only, looking out of my window, just above it, last night, I thought it took up too much room. It doesn't seem to, as one sees it from here, certainly.

'Very well, I'll leave it alone for a bit.'

Tea was the next business, soon after which Lady Wardrop drove off. But, halfway down the drive, she stopped the car and beckoned to Humphreys, who was still on the front-door steps.

He ran to glean her parting words, which were: 'It just occurs to me, it might be worth your while to look at the underside of those stones. They *must* have been numbered, mustn't they? *Good*-bye again.

'Home, please.'

The main occupation of this evening at any rate was settled. The tracing of the plan for Lady Wardrop and the careful collation of it with the original meant a couple of hours' work at least.

Accordingly, soon after nine Humphreys had his materials put out in the library and began. It was a still, stuffy evening. Windows had to stand open, and he had more than one grisly encounter with a bat. These unnerving episodes made him keep the tail of his eye on the window.

Once or twice it was a question whether there was – not a bat, but something more considerable – that had a mind to join him. How unpleasant it would be if someone had slipped noiselessly over the sill and was crouching on the floor!

The tracing of the plan was done. It remained to compare it with the original, and to see whether any paths had been wrongly closed or left open.

With one finger on each paper, he traced out the course that must be followed from the entrance. There were one or two slight mistakes, but here, near the centre, was a bad confusion, probably due to the entry of the Second or Third Bat. Before correcting the copy he followed out carefully the last turnings of the path on the original. These, at least, were right: they led without a hitch to the middle space.

Here was a feature which need not be repeated on the copy – an ugly black spot about the size of a shilling. Ink? No. It resembled a hole, but how should a hole be there?

He stared at it with tired eyes: the work of tracing had been very laborious, and he was drowsy and oppressed . . .

But surely this was a very odd hole. It seemed to go not only through
the paper, but through the table on which it lay. Yes, and through the floor
below that, down, and still down, even into infinite depths. He craned over
it, utterly bewildered.

Just as, when you were a child, you may have pored over a square inch
of counterpane until it became a landscape with wooded hills, and perhaps
even churches and houses, and you lost all thought of the true size, of yourself and it, so this hole seemed to Humphreys for the moment the only thing
in the world.

For some reason it was hateful to him from the first, but he had gazed at
it for some moments before any feeling of anxiety came upon him. And then
it did come, stronger and stronger – a horror lest something might emerge
from it, and a really agonising conviction that a terror was on its way, from
the sight of which he would not be able to escape.

Oh yes, far, far down there was a movement, and the movement was
upwards – towards the surface. Nearer and nearer it came, and it was of a
blackish-grey colour with more than one dark hole.

It took shape as a face – a human face – a *burnt* human face. And with
the odious writhings of a wasp creeping out of a rotten apple there clambered forth an appearance of a form, waving black arms prepared to clasp the
head that was bending over them.

With a convulsion of despair Humphreys threw himself back, struck his
head against a hanging lamp, and fell.

There was concussion of the brain, shock to the system, and a long confine-
ment to bed. The doctor was badly puzzled, not by the symptoms, but by
a request which Humphreys made to him as soon as he was able to say
anything.

'I wish you would open the ball in the maze.'

'Hardly room enough there, I should have thought,' was the best answer
he could summon up. 'But it's more in your way than mine – my dancing
days are over.'

At which Humphreys muttered and turned over to sleep, and the doctor intimated to the nurses that the patient was not out of the wood yet.

When he was better able to express his views, Humphreys made his meaning clear, and received a promise that the thing should be done at once.

He was so anxious to learn the result that the doctor, who seemed a little pensive next morning, saw that more harm than good would be done by saving up his report. 'Well,' he said, 'I am afraid the ball is done for. The metal must have worn thin, I suppose. Anyhow, it went all to bits with the first blow of the chisel.'

'Well? Go on, do!' said Humphreys impatiently.

'Oh! You want to know what we found in it, of course. Well, it was half-full of stuff like ashes.'

'Ashes? What did you make of them?'

'I haven't thoroughly examined them yet, there's hardly been time: but Cooper's made up his mind – I dare say from something I said – that it's a case of cremation . . .

'Now don't excite yourself, my good sir. Yes, I must allow I think he's probably right.'

The maze is gone, and Lady Wardrop has forgiven Humphreys. In fact, I believe he married her niece.

She was right, too, in her conjecture that the stones in the temple were numbered. There had been a numeral painted on the bottom of each. Some few of these had rubbed off, but enough remained to enable Humphreys to reconstruct the inscription. It ran thus:

PENETRANS AD INTERIORA MORTIS

Grateful as Humphreys was to the memory of his uncle, he could not quite forgive him for having burnt the journals and letters of the James Wilson who had gifted Wilsthorpe with the maze and the temple.

As to the circumstances of that ancestor's death and burial no tradition survived. But his will, which was almost the only record of him accessible, assigned an unusually generous legacy to a servant who bore an Italian name.

Mr. Cooper's view is that, humanly speaking, all these many solemn events have a meaning for us, if our limited intelligence permitted of our disintegrating it, while Mr. Calton has been reminded of an aunt now gone from us, who, about the year 1866, had been lost for upwards of an hour-and-a-half in the maze at Covent Gardens, or it might be Hampton Court.

One of the oddest things in the whole series of transactions is that the book which contained the Parable has entirely disappeared. Humphreys has never been able to find it since he copied out the passage to send to Lady Wardrop.

The Rose Garden

MR. AMD MRS. ANSTRUTHER were at breakfast in the parlour of West-field Hall, in the county of Essex. They were arranging plans for the day.

'George,' said Mrs. Anstruther, 'I think you had better take the car to Maldon and see if you can get any of those knitted things I was speaking about which would do for my stall at the bazaar.'

'Oh well, if you wish it, Mary, of course I can do that, but I had half-arranged to play a round with Geoffrey Williamson this morning. The bazaar isn't till Thursday of next week, is it?'

'What has that to do with it, George? I should have thought you would have guessed that if I can't get the things I want in Maldon I shall have to write to all manner of shops in town: and they are certain to send something quite unsuitable in price or quality the first time.'

'If you have actually made an appointment with Mr. Williamson, you had better keep it, but I must say I think you might have let me know.'

'Oh no, no, it wasn't really an appointment. I quite see what you mean. I'll go. And what shall you do yourself?'

'Why, when the work of the house is arranged for, I must see about laying out my new rose garden. By the way, before you start for Maldon I wish you would just take Collins to look at the place I fixed upon. You know it, of course.'

'Well, I'm not quite sure that I do, Mary. Is it at the upper end, towards the village?'

'Good gracious no, my dear George. I thought I had made that quite

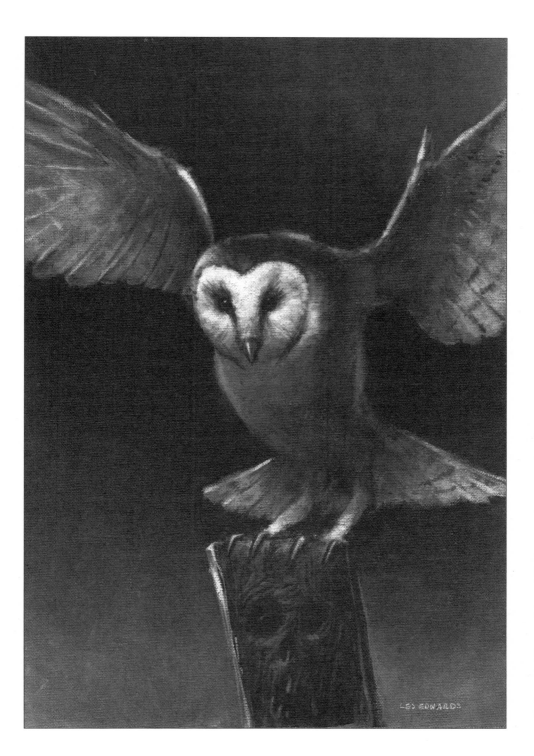

clear. No, it's that small clearing just off the shrubbery path that goes towards the church.'

'Oh yes, where we were saying there must have been a summer-house once: the place with the old seat and the posts. But do you think there's enough sun there?'

'My dear George, do allow me *some* common sense, and don't credit me with all your ideas about summer-houses. Yes, there will be plenty of sun when we have got rid of some of those box-bushes. I know what you are going to say, and I have as little wish as you to strip the place bare.

'All I want Collins to do is to clear away the old seats and the posts and things before I come out in an hour's time. And I hope you will manage to get off fairly soon. After luncheon I think I shall go on with my sketch of the church, and if you please you can go over to the links, or—'

'Ah, a good idea – very good! Yes, you finish that sketch, Mary, and I should be glad of a round.'

'I was going to say, you might call on the Bishop, but I suppose it is no use my making *any* suggestion. And now do be getting ready, or half the morning will be gone.'

Mr. Anstruther's face, which had shown symptoms of lengthening, shortened itself again, and he hurried from the room, and was soon heard giving orders in the passage. Mrs. Anstruther, a stately dame of some fifty summers, proceeded, after a second consideration of the morning's letters, to her housekeeping.

Within a few minutes Mr. Anstruther had discovered Collins in the green-house, and they were on their way to the site of the projected rose garden.

I do not know much about the conditions most suitable to these nurseries, but I am inclined to believe that Mrs. Anstruther, though in the habit of describing herself as 'a great gardener', had not been well advised in the selection of a spot for the purpose.

It was a small, dank clearing, bounded on one side by a path, and on the other by thick box-bushes, laurels, and other evergreens. The ground was almost bare of grass and dark of aspect. Remains of rustic seats and an old and corrugated oak post somewhere near the middle of the clearing had given rise to Mr. Anstruther's conjecture that a summer-house had once stood there.

Clearly Collins had not been put in possession of his mistress' intentions with regard to this plot of ground, and when he learnt them from Mr. Anstruther he displayed no enthusiasm.

'Of course I could clear them seats away soon enough,' he said. 'They aren't no ornament to the place, Mr. Anstruther, and rotten too. Look 'ere, sir' – and he broke off a large piece – 'rotten right through. Yes, clear them away, to be sure we can do that.'

'And the post,' said Mr. Anstruther, 'that's got to go too.'

Collins advanced, and shook the post with both hands. Then he rubbed his chin.

'That's firm in the ground, that post is,' he said. 'That's been there a number of years, Mr. Anstruther. I doubt I shan't get that up not quite so soon as what I can do with them seats.'

'But your mistress specially wishes it to be got out of the way in an hour's time,' said Mr. Anstruther.

Collins smiled and shook his head slowly. 'You'll excuse me, sir, but you feel of it for yourself. No, sir, no one can't do what's impossible to 'em, can they, sir? I could git that post up by after tea-time, sir, but that'll want a lot of digging.

'What you require, you see, sir, if you'll excuse me naming of it, you want the soil loosening round this post 'ere, and me and the boy we shall take a little time doing of that. But now, these 'ere seats,' said Collins, appearing to appropriate this portion of the scheme as due to his own resourcefulness, 'why, I can get the barrer round and 'ave them cleared away in, why less than an hour's time from now, if you'll permit of it. Only—'

'Only what, Collins?'

'Well now, it ain't for me to go against orders no more than what it is for you yourself – or anyone else' (this was added somewhat hurriedly), 'but if you'll pardon me, sir, this ain't the place I should have picked out for no rose garden myself. Why look at them box and laurestinus, 'ow they reg'lar preclude the light from—'

'Ah yes, but we've got to get rid of some of them, of course.'

'Oh, indeed, get rid of them! Yes, to be sure, but – I beg your pardon, Mr. Anstruther—'

'I'm sorry, Collins, but I must be getting on now. I hear the car at the door. Your mistress will explain exactly what she wishes. I'll tell her, then, that you can see your way to clearing away the seats at once, and the post this afternoon. Good morning.'

Collins was left rubbing his chin.

Mrs. Anstruther received the report with some discontent, but did not insist upon any change of plan.

By four o'clock that afternoon she had dismissed her husband to his golf, had dealt faithfully with Collins and with the other duties of the day, and, having sent a campstool and umbrella to the proper spot, had just settled down to her sketch of the church as seen from the shrubbery, when a maid came hurrying down the path to report that Miss Wilkins had called.

Miss Wilkins was one of the few remaining members of the family from whom the Anstruthers had bought the Westfield estate some few years back. She had been staying in the neighbourhood, and this was probably a farewell visit.

'Perhaps you could ask Miss Wilkins to join me here,' said Mrs. Anstruther, and soon Miss Wilkins, a person of mature years, approached.

'Yes, I'm leaving the Ashes tomorrow, and I shall be able to tell my brother how tremendously you have improved the place. Of course he can't help regretting the old house just a little – as I do myself – but the garden is really delightful now.'

'I am so glad you can say so. But you mustn't think we've finished our improvements. Let me show you where I mean to put a rose garden. It's close by here.'

The details of the project were laid before Miss Wilkins at some length, but her thoughts were evidently elsewhere.

'Yes, delightful,' she said at last rather absently. 'But do you know, Mrs. Anstruther, I'm afraid I was thinking of old times. I'm *very* glad to have seen just this spot again before you altered it. Frank and I had quite a romance about this place.'

'Yes?' said Mrs. Anstruther smilingly. 'Do tell me what it was. Something quaint and charming, I'm sure.'

'Not so very charming, but it has always seemed to me curious. Neither of us would ever be here alone when we were children, and I'm not sure that I should care about it now in certain moods. It is one of those things that can hardly be put into words – by me at least – and that sound rather foolish if they are not properly expressed. I can tell you after a fashion what it was that gave us – well, almost a horror of the place when we were alone.

'It was towards the evening of one very hot autumn day, when Frank had disappeared mysteriously about the grounds, and I was looking for him to fetch him to tea, and going down this path I suddenly saw him, not hiding in the bushes, as I rather expected, but sitting on the bench in the old summer-house – there was a wooden summer-house here, you know – up in the corner, asleep, but with such a dreadful look on his face that I really thought he must be ill or even dead.

'I rushed at him and shook him, and told him to wake up; and wake up he did, with a scream. I assure you the poor boy seemed almost beside himself with fright. He hurried me away to the house, and was in a terrible state all that night, hardly sleeping. Someone had to sit up with him, as far as I remember.

'He was better very soon, but for days I couldn't get him to say why he had been in such a condition. It came out at last that he had really been asleep and had had a very odd disjointed sort of dream. He never *saw* much of what was around him, but he *felt* the scenes most vividly.

'First he made out that he was standing in a large room with a number of people in it, and that someone was opposite to him who was "very powerful", and he was being asked questions which he felt to be very important, and, whenever he answered them, someone – either the person opposite to him, or someone else in the room – seemed to be, as he said, making something up against him.

'All the voices sounded to him very distant, but he remembered bits of the things that were said: "Where were you on the 19th of October?" and "Is this your handwriting?" and so on.

'I can see now, of course, that he was dreaming of some trial. But we were never allowed to see the papers, and it was odd that a boy of eight should have such a vivid idea of what went on in a court. All the time he felt, he said, the most intense anxiety and oppression and hopelessness (though I don't suppose he used such words as that to me).

'Then, after that, there was an interval in which he remembered being dreadfully restless and miserable, and then there came another sort of picture, when he was aware that he had come out of doors on a dark raw morning with a little snow about.

'It was in a street, or at any rate among houses, and he felt that there were numbers and numbers of people there too, and that he was taken up some creaking wooden steps and stood on a sort of platform, but the only thing he could actually see was a small fire burning somewhere near him.

'Someone who had been holding his arm left hold of it and went towards this fire, and then he said the fright he was in was worse than at any other part of his dream, and if I had not wakened him up he didn't know what would have become of him.

'A curious dream for a child to have, wasn't it? Well, so much for that. It must have been later in the year that Frank and I were here, and I was sitting in the arbour just about sunset. I noticed the sun was going down, and told Frank to run in and see if tea was ready while I finished a chapter in the book I was reading.

'Frank was away longer than I expected, and the light was going so fast that I had to bend over my book to make it out. All at once I became conscious that someone was whispering to me inside the arbour. The only words I could distinguish, or thought I could, were something like "Pull, pull. I'll push, you pull."

'I started up in something of a fright. The voice – it was little more than a whisper – sounded so hoarse and angry, and yet as if it came from a long, long way off – just as it had done in Frank's dream. But, though I was startled, I had enough courage to look round and try to make out where the sound came from.

'And – this sounds very foolish, I know, but still it is the fact – I made sure that it was strongest when I put my ear to an old post which was part of the end of the seat. I was so certain of this that I remember making some marks on the post – as deep as I could with the scissors out of my work-basket. I don't know why.

'I wonder, by the way, whether that isn't the very post itself . . . Well, yes, it might be: there *are* marks and scratches on it – but one can't be sure. Anyhow, it was just like that post you have there. My father got to know that both of us had had a fright in the arbour, and he went down there himself one evening after dinner, and the arbour was pulled down at very short notice.

'I recollect hearing my father talking about it to an old man who used to do odd jobs in the place, and the old man saying, "Don't you fear for that, sir: he's fast enough in there without no one don't take and let him out." But when I asked who it was, I could get no satisfactory answer. Possibly my father or mother might have told me more about it when I grew up, but, as you know, they both died when we were still quite children.

'I must say it has always seemed very odd to me, and I've often asked the older people in the village whether they knew of anything strange. But either they knew nothing or they wouldn't tell me.

'Dear, dear, how I have been boring you with my childish remembrances! But indeed that arbour did absorb our thoughts quite remarkably for a time. You can fancy, can't you, the kind of stories that we made up for ourselves.

'Well, dear Mrs. Anstruther, I must be leaving you now. We shall meet in town this winter, I hope, shan't we?' etc., etc.

The seats and the post were cleared away and uprooted respectively by that evening. Late summer weather is proverbially treacherous, and during dinner-time Mrs. Collins sent up to ask for a little brandy, because her husband had took a nasty chill and she was afraid he would not be able to do much next day.

Mrs. Anstruther's morning reflections were not wholly placid. She was sure some roughs had got into the plantation during the night. 'And another thing, George: the moment that Collins is about again, you must tell him to do something about the owls. I never heard anything like them, and I'm positive one came and perched somewhere just outside our window.

'If it had come in I should have been out of my wits: it must have been a very large bird, from its voice. Didn't you hear it? No, of course not, you were sound asleep as usual. Still, I must say, George, you don't look as if your night had done you much good.'

'My dear, I feel as if another of the same would turn me silly. You have no idea of the dreams I had. I couldn't speak of them when I woke up, and if this room wasn't so bright and sunny I shouldn't care to think of them even now.'

'Well, really, George, that isn't very common with you, I must say. You must have – no, you only had what I had yesterday – unless you had tea at that wretched club-house. Did you?'

'No, no; nothing but a cup of tea and some bread and butter. I should really like to know how I came to put my dream together – as I suppose one does put one's dreams together from a lot of little things one has been seeing or reading. Look here, Mary, it was like this – if I shan't be boring you—'

'I *wish* to hear what it was, George. I will tell you when I have had enough.'

'All right. I must tell you that it wasn't like other nightmares in one way, because I didn't really see anyone who spoke to me or touched me, and yet I was most fearfully impressed with the reality of it all.

'First I was sitting, no, moving about, in an old-fashioned sort of panelled room. I remember there was a fireplace and a lot of burnt papers in it, and I was in a great state of anxiety about something. There was someone else – a servant, I suppose, because I remember saying to him, "Horses, as quick as you can", and then waiting a bit. And next I heard several people coming upstairs and a noise like spurs on a boarded floor, and then the door opened and whatever it was that I was expecting happened.'

'Yes, but what was that?'

'You see, I couldn't tell: it was the sort of shock that upsets you in a dream. You either wake up or else everything goes black. That was what happened to me.

'Then I was in a big dark-walled room, panelled, I think, like the other, and a number of people, and I was evidently—'

'Standing your trial, I suppose, George.'

'Goodness! Yes, Mary, I was. But did you dream that too? How very odd!'

'No, no. I didn't get enough sleep for that. Go on, George, and I will tell you afterwards.'

'Yes. Well, I *was* being tried, for my life, I've no doubt, from the state I was in. I had no one speaking for me, and somewhere there was a most fearful fellow on the bench, I should have said, only that he seemed to be pitching into me most unfairly, and twisting everything I said, and asking most abominable questions.'

'What about?'

'Why, dates when I was at particular places, and letters I was supposed to have written, and why I had destroyed some papers. And I recollect his laughing at answers I made in a way that quite daunted me. It doesn't sound much, but I can tell you, Mary, it was really appalling at the time. I am quite certain there was such a man once, and a most horrible villain he must have been. The things he said—'

'Thank you, I have no wish to hear them. I can go to the links any day myself. How did it end?'

'Oh, against me. *He* saw to that. I do wish, Mary, I could give you a notion of the strain that came after that, and seemed to me to last for days: waiting and waiting, and sometimes writing things I knew to be enormously important to me, and waiting for answers and none coming, and after that I came out—'

'Ah!'

'What makes you say that? Do you know what sort of thing I saw?'

'Was it a dark cold day, and snow in the streets, and a fire burning somewhere near you?'

'By George, it was! You *have* had the same nightmare! Really not? Well, it is the oddest thing! Yes. I've no doubt it was an execution for high treason. I know I was laid on straw and jolted along most wretchedly, and then had to go up some steps, and someone was holding my arm, and I remember seeing a bit of a ladder and hearing a sound of a lot of people. I really don't think I could bear now to go into a crowd of people and hear the noise they make talking. However, mercifully, I didn't get to the real business. The dream passed off with a sort of thunder inside my head. But, Mary—'

'I know what you are going to ask. I suppose this is an instance of a kind of thought-reading. Miss Wilkins called yesterday and told me of a dream her brother had as a child when they lived here, and something did no doubt make me think of that when I was awake last night listening to those horrible owls and those men talking and laughing in the shrubbery (by the way, I wish you would see if they have done any damage, and speak to the police about it).

'And so, I suppose, from my brain it must have got into yours while you were asleep. Curious, no doubt, and I am sorry it gave you such a bad night. You had better be as much in the fresh air as you can today.'

'Oh, it's all right now. But I think I *will* go over to the Lodge and see if I can get a game with any of them. And you?'

'I have enough to do for this morning; and this afternoon, if I am not interrupted, there is my drawing.'

'To be sure – I want to see that finished very much.'

No damage was discoverable in the shrubbery. Mr. Anstruther surveyed with faint interest the site of the rose garden, where the uprooted post still lay, and the hole it had occupied remained unfilled.

Collins, upon inquiry made, proved to be better, but quite unable to come to his work. He expressed, by the mouth of his wife, a hope that he hadn't done nothing wrong clearing away them things.

Mrs. Collins added that there was a lot of talking people in Westfield, and the hold ones was the worst: seemed to think everything of them having been in the parish longer than what other people had. But as to what they said no more could then be ascertained than that it had quite upset Collins, and was a lot of nonsense.

Recruited by lunch and a brief period of slumber, Mrs. Anstruther settled herself comfortably upon her sketching chair in the path leading through the shrubbery to the side-gate of the churchyard. Trees and buildings were among her favourite subjects, and here she had good studies of both.

She worked hard, and the drawing was becoming a really pleasant thing to look upon by the time that the wooded hills to the west had shut off the sun. Still she would have persevered, but the light changed rapidly, and it became obvious that the last touches must be added on the morrow.

She rose and turned towards the house, pausing for a time to take delight in the limpid green western sky. Then she passed on between the dark box-bushes, and, at a point just before the path debouched on the lawn, she stopped once again and considered the quiet evening landscape, and made a mental note that that must be the tower of one of the Roothing churches that one caught on the skyline.

Then a bird (perhaps) rustled in the box-bush on her left, and she turned and started at seeing what at first she took to be a Fifth of November mask peeping out among the branches. She looked closer.

It was not a mask. It was a face – large, smooth, and pink. She remembers the minute drops of perspiration which were starting from its forehead. She remembers how the jaws were clean-shaven and the eyes shut. She remembers also, and with an accuracy which makes the thought intolerable to her, how the mouth was open and a single tooth appeared below the upper lip. As she looked the face receded into the darkness of the bush.

The shelter of the house was gained and the door shut before she collapsed.

Mr. and Mrs. Anstruther had been for a week or more recruiting at Brighton before they received a circular from the Essex Archæological Society, and a query as to whether they possessed certain historical portraits which it was desired to include in the forthcoming work on Essex Portraits, to be published under the Society's auspices.

There was an accompanying letter from the Secretary which contained the following passage:

```
We are specially anxious to know whether you possess
the original of the engraving of which I enclose a
photograph. It represents
    Sir ———, Lord Chief Justice under Charles II, who,
as you doubtless know, retired after his disgrace to
Westfield, and is supposed to have died there of remorse.
    It may interest you to hear that a curious entry has
recently been found in the registers, not of Westfield
but of Priors Roothing, to the effect that the parish
was so much troubled after his death that the rector of
Westfield summoned the parsons of all the Roothings to
come and lay him; which they did.
    The entry ends by saying: 'The stake is in a field
adjoining to the churchyard of Westfield, on the west
side.' Perhaps you can let us know if any tradition to
this effect is current in your parish.
```

The incidents which the 'enclosed photograph' recalled were productive of a severe shock to Mrs. Anstruther. It was decided that she must spend the winter abroad.

Mr. Anstruther, when he went down to Westfield to make the necessary arrangements, not unnaturally told his story to the rector (an old gentleman), who showed little surprise.

'Really I had managed to piece out for myself very much what must have happened, partly from old people's talk and partly from what I saw in your grounds. Of course we have suffered to some extent also.

'Yes, it was bad at first: like owls, as you say, and men talking sometimes. One night it was in this garden, and at other times about several of the cottages. But lately there has been very little. I think it will die out.

'There is nothing in our registers except the entry of the burial, and what I for a long time took to be the family motto. But last time I looked at it I noticed that it was added in a later hand and had the initials of one of our rectors quite late in the 17th century, A.C. – Augustine Crompton.

'Here it is, you see – *quieta non movere*. I suppose— Well, it is rather hard to say exactly what I do suppose.'

A School Story

Two men in a smoking-room were talking of their private-school days.

'At *our* school,' said A., 'we had a ghost's footmark on the staircase.'

'What was it like?'

'Oh, very unconvincing. Just the shape of a shoe, with a square toe, if I remember right. The staircase was a stone one. I never heard any story about the thing. That seems odd, when you come to think of it. Why didn't somebody invent one, I wonder?'

'You never can tell with little boys. They have a mythology of their own. There's a subject for you, by the way – "The Folklore of Private Schools".'

'Yes. The crop is rather scanty, though. I imagine, if you were to investigate the cycle of ghost stories, for instance, which the boys at private schools tell each other, they would all turn out to be highly-compressed versions of stories out of books.'

'Nowadays the *Strand* and *Pearson's*, and so on, would be extensively drawn upon.'

'No doubt: they weren't born or thought of in *my* time. Let's see. I wonder if I can remember the staple ones that I was told. First, there was the house with a room in which a series of people insisted on passing a night; and each of them in the morning was found kneeling in a corner, and had just time to say, "I've seen it", and died.'

'Wasn't that the house in Berkeley Square?'

'I dare say it was. Then there was the man who heard a noise in the passage at night, opened his door, and saw someone crawling towards him on all fours with his eye hanging out on his cheek.

'There was besides, let me think— Yes! the room where a man was found dead in bed with a horseshoe mark on his forehead, and the floor under the bed was covered with marks of horseshoes also. I don't know why. Also there was the lady who, on locking her bedroom door in a strange house, heard a thin voice among the bed-curtains say, "Now we're shut in for the night".

'None of those had any explanation or sequel. I wonder if they go on still, those stories.'

'Oh, likely enough – with additions from the magazines, as I said. You never heard, did you, of a real ghost at a private school? I thought not, nobody has that ever I came across.'

'From the way in which you said that, I gather that *you* have.'

'I really don't know, but this is what was in my mind. It happened at my private school thirty odd years ago, and I haven't any explanation of it.

'The school I mean was near London. It was established in a large and fairly old house – a great white building with very fine grounds about it. There were large cedars in the garden, as there are in so many of the older gardens in the Thames valley, and ancient elms in the three or four fields which we used for our games. I think probably it was quite an attractive place, but boys seldom allow that their schools possess any tolerable features.

'I came to the school in a September, soon after the year 1870. And among the boys who arrived on the same day was one whom I took to: a Highland boy, whom I will call McLeod. I needn't spend time in describing him: the main thing is that I got to know him very well. He was not an exceptional boy in any way – not particularly good at books or games – but he suited me.

'The school was a large one: there must have been from 120 to 130 boys there as a rule, and so a considerable staff of masters was required, and there were rather frequent changes among them.

'One term – perhaps it was my third or fourth – a new master made his appearance. His name was Sampson. He was a tallish, stoutish, pale, black-bearded man. I think we liked him. He had travelled a good deal, and had stories which amused us on our school walks, so that there was some competition among us to get within earshot of him.

'I remember too – dear me, I have hardly thought of it since then – that he had a charm on his watch-chain that attracted my attention one day, and he let me examine it. It was, I now suppose, a gold Byzantine coin. There was an effigy of some absurd emperor on one side; the other side had been worn practically smooth, and he had had cut on it – rather barbarously – his own initials, G.W.S., and a date, 24 July, 1865. Yes, I can see it now: he told me he had picked it up in Constantinople. It was about the size of a florin, perhaps rather smaller.

'Well, the first odd thing that happened was this. Sampson was doing Latin grammar with us. One of his favourite methods – perhaps it is rather a good one – was to make us construct sentences out of our own heads to illustrate the rules he was trying to make us learn. Of course that is a thing which gives a silly boy a chance of being impertinent: there are lots of school stories in which that happens – or anyhow there might be. But Sampson was too good a disciplinarian for us to think of trying that on with him.

'Now, on this occasion he was telling us how to express *remembering* in Latin, and he ordered us each to make a sentence bringing in the verb *memini*, "I remember".

'Well, most of us made up some ordinary sentence such as "I remember my father", or "He remembers his book", or something equally uninteresting. And I dare say a good many put down *memino librum meum*, and so forth. But the boy I mentioned – McLeod – was evidently thinking of something more elaborate than that.

'The rest of us wanted to have our sentences passed, and get on to something else, so some kicked him under the desk, and I, who was next to him, poked him and whispered to him to look sharp. But he didn't seem to attend.

'I looked at his paper and saw he had put down nothing at all. So I jogged him again harder than before and upbraided him sharply for keeping us all waiting. That did have some effect. He started and seemed to wake up, and then very quickly he scribbled about a couple of lines on his paper, and showed it up with the rest.

'As it was the last, or nearly the last, to come in, and as Sampson had a good deal to say to the boys who had written *meminiscimus patri meo* and the rest of it, it turned out that the clock struck twelve before he had got to McLeod, and McLeod had to wait afterwards to have his sentence corrected.

'There was nothing much going on outside when I got out, so I waited for him to come. He came very slowly when he did arrive, and I guessed there had been some sort of trouble.

'"Well," I said, "what did you get?"

'"Oh, I don't know," said McLeod, "nothing much. But I think Sampson's rather sick with me."

'"Why, did you show him up some rot?"

'"No fear," he said. "It was all right as far as I could see. It was like this: *Memento* – that's right enough for remember, and it takes a genitive – *memento putei inter quatuor taxos.*"

'"What silly rot!" I said. "What made you shove that down? What does it mean?"

'"That's the funny part," said McLeod. "I'm not quite sure what it does mean. All I know is, it just came into my head and I corked it down. I know what I *think* it means, because just before I wrote it down I had a sort of picture of it in my head.

'"I believe it means 'Remember the well among the four—' What are those dark sort of trees that have red berries on them?"

'"Mountain ashes, I s'pose you mean."

'"I never heard of them," said McLeod. "No, *I'll* tell you – yews."

'"Well, and what did Sampson say?"

'"Why, he was jolly odd about it. When he read it he got up and went to the mantelpiece and stopped quite a long time without saying anything, with his back to me. And then he said, without turning round, and rather quiet, 'What do you suppose that means?'

'"I told him what I thought, only I couldn't remember the name of the silly tree. And then he wanted to know why I put it down, and I had to say something or other. And after that he left off talking about it, and asked me how long I'd been here, and where my people lived, and things like that. And then I came away, but he wasn't looking a bit well."

'I don't remember any more that was said by either of us about this. Next day McLeod took to his bed with a chill or something of the kind, and it was a week or more before he was in school again. And as much as a month went by without anything happening that was noticeable.

'Whether or not Mr. Sampson was really startled, as McLeod had thought, he didn't show it. I am pretty sure, of course, now, that there was something very curious in his past history, but I'm not going to pretend that we boys were sharp enough to guess any such thing.

'There was one other incident of the same kind as the last which I told you. Several times since that day we had had to make up examples in school to illustrate different rules, but there had never been any row except when we did them wrong. At last there came a day when we were going through those dismal things which people call Conditional Sentences, and we were told to make a conditional sentence, expressing a future consequence. We did it, right or wrong, and showed up our bits of paper, and Sampson began looking through them.

'All at once he got up, made some odd sort of noise in his throat, and rushed out by a door that was just by his desk. We sat there for a minute or two, and then – I suppose it was incorrect – but we went up, I and one or two others, to look at the papers on his desk.

'Of course I thought someone must have put down some nonsense or other, and Sampson had gone off to report him. All the same, I noticed that he hadn't taken any of the papers with him when he ran out.

'Well, the top paper on the desk was written in red ink – which no one used – and it wasn't in anyone's hand who was in the class. They all looked at it – McLeod and all – and took their dying oaths that it wasn't theirs.

'Then I thought of counting the bits of paper.

'And of this I made quite certain: that there were seventeen bits of paper on the desk, and sixteen boys in the form. Well, I bagged the extra paper, and kept it, and I believe I have it now.

'And now you will want to know what was written on it. It was simple enough, and harmless enough, I should have said: *Si tu non veneris ad me, ego veniam ad te,* which means, I suppose, "If you don't come to me, I'll come to you".'

'Could you show me the paper?' interrupted the listener.

'Yes, I could. But there's another odd thing about it. That same afternoon I took it out of my locker – I know for certain it was the same bit, for I made a finger-mark on it – and no single trace of writing of any kind was there on it.

'I kept it, as I said, and since that time I have tried various experiments to see whether sympathetic ink had been used, but absolutely without result.

'So much for that. After about half-an-hour Sampson looked in again: said he had felt very unwell, and told us we might go. He came rather gingerly to his desk, and gave just one look at the uppermost paper, and I suppose he thought he must have been dreaming. Anyhow, he asked no questions.

'That day was a half-holiday, and next day Sampson was in school again, much as usual. That night the third and last incident in my story happened.

'We – McLeod and I – slept in a dormitory at right angles to the main building. Sampson slept in the main building on the first floor. There was a very bright full moon. At an hour which I can't tell exactly, but some time between one and two, I was woken up by somebody shaking me. It was McLeod, and a nice state of mind he seemed to be in.

'"Come," he said. "Come! There's a burglar getting in through Sampson's window."

'As soon as I could speak, I said, "Well, why not call out and wake everybody up?"

'"No, no," he said. "I'm not sure who it is. Don't make a row: come and look."

'Naturally I came and looked, and naturally there was no one there. I was cross enough, and should have called McLeod plenty of names, only – I couldn't tell why – it seemed to me that there *was* something wrong – something that made me very glad I wasn't alone to face it.

'We were still at the window looking out, and as soon as I could, I asked him what he had heard or seen.

'"I didn't *hear* anything at all," he said, "but about five minutes before I woke you, I found myself looking out of this window here, and there was a man sitting or kneeling on Sampson's window-sill, and looking in, and I thought he was beckoning."

'"What sort of man?"

'McLeod wriggled. "I don't know," he said, "but I can tell you one thing – he was beastly thin, and he looked as if he was wet all over. And," he said, looking round and whispering as if he hardly liked to hear himself, "I'm not at all sure that he was alive."

'We went on talking in whispers some time longer, and eventually crept back to bed. No one else in the room woke or stirred the whole time. I believe we did sleep a bit afterwards, but we were very cheap next day.

'And next day Mr. Sampson was gone: not to be found; and I believe no trace of him has ever come to light since.

'In thinking it over, one of the oddest things about it all has seemed to me to be the fact that neither McLeod nor I ever mentioned what we had seen to any third person whatever. Of course no questions were asked on the subject, and if they had been, I am inclined to believe that we could not have made any answer: we seemed unable to speak about it.

'That is my story,' said the narrator. 'The only approach to a ghost story connected with a school that I know, but still, I think, an approach to such a thing.'

The sequel to this may perhaps be reckoned highly conventional; but a sequel there is, and so it must be produced.

There had been more than one listener to the story, and, in the latter part of that same year, or of the next, one such listener was staying at a country house in Ireland.

One evening his host was turning over a drawer full of odds and ends in the smoking-room. Suddenly he put his hand upon a little box. 'Now,' he said, 'you know about old things. Tell me what that is.'

My friend opened the little box, and found in it a thin gold chain with an object attached to it. He glanced at the object and then took off his spectacles to examine it more narrowly. 'What's the history of this?' he asked.

'Odd enough,' was the answer. 'You know the yew thicket in the shrubbery: well, a year or two back we were cleaning out the old well that used to be in the clearing here, and what do you suppose we found?'

'Is it possible that you found a body?' said the visitor, with an odd feeling of nervousness.

'We did that. But what's more, in every sense of the word, we found two.'

'Good Heavens! Two? Was there anything to show how they got there? Was this thing found with them?'

'It was. Amongst the rags of the clothes that were on one of the bodies. A bad business, whatever the story of it may have been. One body had the arms tight round the other. They must have been there thirty years or more

– long enough before we came to this place. You may judge we filled the well up fast enough. Do you make anything of what's cut on that gold coin you have there?'

'I think I can,' said my friend, holding it to the light (but he read it without much difficulty). 'It seems to be G.W.S., 24 July, 1865.'

The Tractate Middoth

TOWARDS THE END of an autumn afternoon an elderly man with a thin face and grey Piccadilly weepers pushed open the swing-door leading into the vestibule of a certain famous library, and addressing himself to an attendant, stated that he believed he was entitled to use the library, and inquired if he might take a book out.

Yes, if he were on the list of those to whom that privilege was given. He produced his card – *Mr. John Eldred* – and, the register being consulted, a favourable answer was given.

'Now, another point,' said he. 'It is a long time since I was here, and I do not know my way about your building. Besides, it is near closing-time, and it is bad for me to hurry up and down stairs. I have here the title of the book I want: is there anyone at liberty who could go and find it for me?'

After a moment's thought the doorkeeper beckoned to a young man who was passing. 'Mr. Garrett,' he said, 'have you a minute to assist this gentleman?'

'With pleasure,' was Mr. Garrett's answer. The slip with the title was handed to him. 'I think I can put my hand on this; it happens to be in the class I inspected last quarter, but I'll just look it up in the catalogue to make sure. I suppose it is that particular edition that you require, sir?'

'Yes, if you please; that, and no other,' said Mr. Eldred. 'I am exceedingly obliged to you.'

'Don't mention it I beg, sir,' said Mr. Garrett, and hurried off. 'I thought so,' he said to himself, when his finger, travelling down the pages of the catalogue, stopped at a particular entry. 'Talmud: Tractate Middoth, with the commentary of Nachmanides, Amsterdam, 1707. 11.3.34. Hebrew class, of course. Not a very difficult job this.'

Mr. Eldred, accommodated with a chair in the vestibule, awaited anxiously the return of his messenger – and his disappointment at seeing an empty-handed Mr. Garrett running down the staircase was very evident.

'I'm sorry to disappoint you, sir,' said the young man, 'but the book is out.'

'Oh dear!' said Mr. Eldred, 'is that so? You are sure there can be no mistake?'

'I don't think there is much chance of it, sir: but it's possible, if you like to wait a minute, that you might meet the very gentleman that's got it. He must be leaving the library soon, and I *think* I saw him take that particular book out of the shelf.'

'Indeed! You didn't recognise him, I suppose? Would it be one of the professors or one of the students?'

'I don't think so: certainly not a professor. I should have known him; but the light isn't very good in that part of the library at this time of day, and I didn't see his face. I should have said he was a shortish old gentleman, perhaps a clergyman, in a cloak. If you could wait, I can easily find out whether he wants the book very particularly.'

'No, no,' said Mr. Eldred, 'I won't – I can't wait now, thank you – no. I must be off. But I'll call again tomorrow if I may, and perhaps you could find out who has it.'

'Certainly, sir, and I'll have the book ready for you if we—'

But Mr. Eldred was already off, and hurrying more than one would have thought wholesome for him.

Garrett had a few moments to spare; and, thought he, 'I'll go back to that case and see if I can find the old man. Most likely he could put off using the book for a few days. I dare say the other one doesn't want to keep it for long.' So off with him to the Hebrew class.

But when he got there it was unoccupied, and the volume marked 11.3.34 was in its place on the shelf. It was vexatious to Garrett's self-respect to have disappointed an inquirer with so little reason. And he would have liked, had it not been against library rules, to take the book down to the vestibule then and there, so that it might be ready for Mr. Eldred when he called. However, next morning he would be on the look-out for him, and he begged the door-keeper to send and let him know when the moment came.

As a matter of fact, he was himself in the vestibule when Mr. Eldred arrived, very soon after the library opened and when hardly anyone besides the staff were in the building.

'I'm very sorry,' he said; 'it's not often that I make such a stupid mistake, but I did feel sure that the old gentleman I saw took out that very book and kept it in his hand without opening it, just as people do, you know, sir, when they mean to take a book out of the library and not merely refer to it. But, however, I'll run up now at once and get it for you this time.'

And here intervened a pause. Mr. Eldred paced the entry, read all the notices, consulted his watch, sat and gazed up the staircase, did all that a very impatient man could, until some twenty minutes had run out. At last he addressed himself to the doorkeeper and inquired if it was a very long way to that part of the library to which Mr. Garrett had gone.

'Well, I was thinking it was funny, sir: he's a quick man as a rule, but to be sure he might have been sent for by the librarian, but even so I think he'd have mentioned to him that you was waiting. I'll just speak him up on the toob and see.'

And to the tube he addressed himself. As he absorbed the reply to his question his face changed, and he made one or two supplementary inquir-ies which were shortly answered. Then he came forward to his counter and spoke in a lower tone.

'I'm sorry to hear, sir, that something seems to have 'appened a little awkward. Mr. Garrett has been took poorly, it appears, and the librarian sent him 'ome in a cab the other way. Something of an attack, by what I can hear.'

'What, really? Do you mean that someone has injured him?'

'No, sir, not violence 'ere, but, as I should judge, attacked with an attack, what you might term it, of illness. Not a strong constitootion, Mr. Garrett. But as to your book, sir, perhaps you might be able to find it for yourself. It's too bad you should be disappointed this way twice over—'

'Er – well, but I'm so sorry that Mr. Garrett should have been taken ill in this way while he was obliging me. I think I must leave the book, and call and inquire after him. You can give me his address, I suppose.'

That was easily done. Mr. Garrett, it appeared, lodged in rooms not far from the station.

'And one other question. Did you happen to notice if an old gentleman, perhaps a clergyman, in a – yes – in a black cloak, left the library after I did yesterday? I think he may have been a – I think, that is, that he may be staying – or rather that I may have known him.'

'Not in a black cloak, sir. No. There were only two gentlemen left later than what you done, sir, both of them youngish men. There was Mr. Carter took out a music-book and one of the prefessors with a couple o' novels. That's the lot, sir; and then I went off to me tea, and glad to get it. Thank you, sir, much obliged.'

Mr. Eldred, still a prey to anxiety, betook himself in a cab to Mr. Garrett's address, but the young man was not yet in a condition to receive visitors. He was better, but his landlady considered that he must have had a severe shock. She thought most likely from what the doctor said that he would be able to see Mr. Eldred tomorrow.

Mr. Eldred returned to his hotel at dusk and spent, I fear, but a dull evening.

On the next day he was able to see Mr. Garrett. When in health Mr. Garrett was a cheerful and pleasant-looking young man. Now he was a very white and shaky being, propped up in an armchair by the fire, and inclined to shiver and keep an eye on the door. If, however, there were visitors whom he was not prepared to welcome, Mr. Eldred was not among them.

'It really is I who owe you an apology, and I was despairing of being able to pay it, for I didn't know your address. But I am very glad you have called. I do dislike and regret giving all this trouble, but you know I could not have foreseen this – this attack which I had.'

'Of course not; but now, I am something of a doctor. You'll excuse my asking; you have had, I am sure, good advice. Was it a fall you had?'

'No. I did fall on the floor – but not from any height. It was, really, a shock.'

'You mean something startled you. Was it anything you thought you saw?'

'Not much *thinking* in the case, I'm afraid. Yes, it was something I saw. You remember when you called the first time at the library?'

'Yes, of course. Well, now, let me beg you not to try to describe it – it will not be good for you to recall it, I'm sure.'

'But indeed it would be a relief to me to tell anyone like yourself: you might be able to explain it away. It was just when I was going into the class where your book is—'

'Indeed, Mr. Garrett, I insist. Besides, my watch tells me I have but very little time left in which to get my things together and take the train. No – not another word – it would be more distressing to you than you imagine, perhaps.

'Now there is just one thing I want to say. I feel that I am really indirectly responsible for this illness of yours, and I think I ought to defray the expense which it has – eh?'

But this offer was quite distinctly declined. Mr. Eldred, not pressing it, left almost at once. Not, however, before Mr. Garrett had insisted upon his taking a note of the class-mark of the Tractate Middoth, which, as he said, Mr. Eldred could at leisure get for himself.

But Mr. Eldred did not reappear at the library.

William Garrett had another visitor that day in the person of a contemporary and colleague from the library, one George Earle.

Earle had been one of those who found Garrett lying insensible on the floor just inside the 'class' or cubicle (opening upon the central alley of a spacious gallery) in which the Hebrew books were placed, and Earle had naturally been very anxious about his friend's condition. So as soon as library hours were over he appeared at the lodgings.

'Well,' he said (after other conversation), 'I've no notion what it was that put you wrong, but I've got the idea that there's something wrong in the atmosphere of the library.

'I know this, that just before we found you I was coming along the gallery with Davis, and I said to him, "Did ever you know such a musty smell anywhere as there is about here? It can't be wholesome." Well now, if one goes on living a long time with a smell of that kind (I tell you it was worse than I ever knew it) it must get into the system and break out some time, don't you think?'

Garrett shook his head. 'That's all very well about the smell – but it isn't always there, though I've noticed it the last day or two – a sort of unnaturally strong smell of dust. But no – that's not what did for me. It was something I *saw*. And I want to tell you about it.

'I went into that Hebrew class to get a book for a man that was inquiring for it down below. Now that same book I'd made a mistake about the day before. I'd been for it, for the same man, and made sure that I saw an old parson in a cloak taking it out.

'I told my man it was out. Off he went, to call again next day. I went back to see if I could get it out of the parson: no parson there, and the book on the shelf.

'Well, yesterday, as I say, I went again. This time, if you please – ten o'clock in the morning, remember, and as much light as ever you get in those classes, and there was my parson again, back to me, looking at the books on the shelf I wanted. His hat was on the table, and he had a bald head. I waited a second or two looking at him rather particularly.

'I tell you, he had a very nasty bald head. It looked to me dry, and it looked dusty, and the streaks of hair across it were much less like hair than cobwebs. Well, I made a bit of a noise on purpose, coughed and moved my feet. He turned round and let me see his face – which I hadn't seen before. I tell you again, I'm not mistaken.

'Though, for one reason or another I didn't take in the lower part of his face, I did see the upper part; and it was perfectly dry, and the eyes were very deep-sunk. And over them, from the eyebrows to the cheek-bone, there were *cobwebs* – thick.

'Now that closed me up, as they say, and I can't tell you anything more.'

What explanations were furnished by Earle of this phenomenon it does not very much concern us to inquire. At all events they did not convince Garrett that he had not seen what he had seen.

Before William Garrett returned to work at the library, the librarian insisted upon his taking a week's rest and change of air. Within a few days' time, therefore, he was at the station with his bag, looking for a desirable smoking compartment in which to travel to Burnstow-on-Sea, which he had not previously visited.

One compartment and one only seemed to be suitable. But, just as he approached it, he saw, standing in front of the door, a figure so like one bound up with recent unpleasant associations that, with a sickening qualm, and hardly knowing what he did, he tore open the door of the next compartment and pulled himself into it as quickly as if death were at his heels.

The train moved off, and he must have turned quite faint, for he was next conscious of a smelling-bottle being put to his nose. His physician was a nice-looking old lady, who, with her daughter, was the only passenger in the carriage.

But for this incident it is not very likely that he would have made any overtures to his fellow travellers. As it was, thanks and inquiries and general conversation supervened inevitably, and Garrett found himself provided before the journey's end not only with a physician, but with a landlady: for Mrs. Simpson had apartments to let at Burnstow, which seemed in all ways suitable.

The place was empty at that season, so that Garrett was thrown a good deal into the society of the mother and daughter. He found them very acceptable company. On the third evening of his stay he was on such terms with them as to be asked to spend the evening in their private sitting-room.

During their talk it transpired that Garrett's work lay in a library.

'Ah, libraries are fine places,' said Mrs. Simpson, putting down her work with a sigh. 'But for all that, books have played me a sad turn, or rather *a* book has.'

'Well, books give me my living, Mrs. Simpson, and I should be sorry to say a word against them: I don't like to hear that they have been bad for you.'

'Perhaps Mr. Garrett could help us to solve our puzzle, mother,' said Miss Simpson.

'I don't want to set Mr. Garrett off on a hunt that might waste a lifetime, my dear, nor yet to trouble him with our private affairs.'

'But if you think it in the least likely that I could be of use, I do beg you to tell me what the puzzle is, Mrs. Simpson. If it is finding out anything about a book, you see, I am in rather a good position to do it.'

'Yes, I do see that, but the worst of it is that we don't know the name of the book.'

'Nor what it is about?'

'No, nor that either.'

'Except that we don't think it's in English, mother – and that is not much of a clue.'

'Well, Mr. Garrett,' said Mrs. Simpson, who had not yet resumed her work, and was looking at the fire thoughtfully, 'I shall tell you the story. You will please keep it to yourself, if you don't mind? Thank you.

'Now it is just this. I had an old uncle, a Dr. Rant. Perhaps you may have heard of him? Not that he was a distinguished man, but from the odd way he chose to be buried.'

'I rather think I have seen the name in some guidebook.'

'That would be it,' said Miss Simpson. 'He left directions – horrid old man! – that he was to be put, sitting at a table in his ordinary clothes, in a brick room that he'd had made underground in a field near his house. Of course the country people say he's been seen about there in his old black cloak.'

'Well, dear, I don't know much about such things,' Mrs. Simpson went on, 'but anyhow he is dead, these twenty years and more. He was a clergyman, though I'm sure I can't imagine how he got to be one. But he did no duty for the last part of his life, which I think was a good thing.

'And he lived on his own property: a very nice estate not a great way from here. He had no wife or family; only one niece, who was myself, and one nephew, and he had no particular liking for either of us – nor for anyone else, as far as that goes. If anything, he liked my cousin better than he did me – for John was much more like him in his temper, and, I'm afraid I must say, his very mean sharp ways. It might have been different if I had not married; but I did, and that he very much resented.

'Very well: here he was with this estate and a good deal of money, as it turned out, of which he had the absolute disposal, and it was understood that we – my cousin and I – would share it equally at his death.

'In a certain winter, over twenty years back, as I said, he was taken ill, and I was sent for to nurse him. My husband was alive then, but the old man would not hear of *his* coming. As I drove up to the house I saw my cousin John driving away from it in an open fly and looking, I noticed, in very good spirits. I went up and did what I could for my uncle, but I was very soon sure that this would be his last illness; and he was convinced of it too.

'During the day before he died he got me to sit by him all the time, and I could see there was something, and probably something unpleasant, that he was saving up to tell me, and putting it off as long as he felt he could afford the strength – I'm afraid purposely in order to keep me on the stretch. But, at last, out it came.

'"Mary," he said, "Mary, I've made my will in John's favour: he has everything, Mary."

'Well, of course that came as a bitter shock to me, for we – my husband and I – were not rich people, and if he could have managed to live a little easier than he was obliged to do, I felt it might be the prolonging of his life. But I said little or nothing to my uncle, except that he had a right to do what he pleased. Partly because I couldn't think of anything to say, and partly because I was sure there was more to come: and so there was.

'"But, Mary," he said, "I'm not very fond of John, and I've made another will in *your* favour. *You* can have everything. Only you've got to find the will, you see: and I don't mean to tell you where it is." Then he chuckled to himself, and I waited, for again I was sure he hadn't finished.

'"That's a good girl," he said after a time, "you wait, and I'll tell you as much as I told John. But just let me remind you, you can't go into court with what I'm saying to you, for *you* won't be able to produce any collateral evidence beyond your own word, and John's a man that can do a little hard swearing if necessary.

'"Very well then, that's understood. Now, I had the fancy that I wouldn't write this will quite in the common way, so I wrote it in a book, Mary, a printed book. And there's several thousand books in this house. But there! You needn't trouble yourself with them, for it isn't one of them. It's in safe keeping elsewhere: in a place where John can go and find it any day, if he only knew, and you can't.

'"A good will it is: properly signed and witnessed, but I don't think you'll find the witnesses in a hurry."

'Still I said nothing. If I had moved at all I must have taken hold of the old wretch and shaken him. He lay there laughing to himself, and at last he said:

'"Well, well, you've taken it very quietly, and as I want to start you both on equal terms, and John has a bit of a purchase in being able to go where the book is, I'll tell you just two other things which I didn't tell him. The will's in English, but you won't know that if ever you see it. That's one thing, and another is that when I'm gone you'll find an envelope in my desk directed to you, and inside it something that would help you to find it, if only you have the wits to use it."

'In a few hours from that he was gone, and though I made an appeal to John Eldred about it—'

'John Eldred? I beg your pardon, Mrs. Simpson – I think I've seen a Mr. John Eldred. What is he like to look at?'

'It must be ten years since I saw him: he would be a thin elderly man now, and unless he has shaved them off, he has that sort of whiskers which people used to call Dundreary or Piccadilly something.'

'—Weepers. Yes, that *is* the man.'

'Where did you come across him, Mr. Garrett?'

'I don't know if I could tell you,' said Garrett mendaciously, 'in some public place. But you hadn't finished.'

'Really I had nothing much to add, only that John Eldred, of course, paid no attention whatever to my letters, and has enjoyed the estate ever since, while my daughter and I have had to take to the lodging-house business here, which I must say has not turned out by any means so unpleasant as I feared it might.'

'But about the envelope.'

'To be sure! Why, the puzzle turns on that. Give Mr. Garrett the paper out of my desk.'

It was a small slip, with nothing whatever on it but five numerals, not divided or punctuated in any way: *11334*.

Mr. Garrett pondered, but there was a light in his eye. Suddenly he 'made a face', and then asked, 'Do you suppose that Mr. Eldred can have any more clue than you have to the title of the book?'

'I have sometimes thought he must,' said Mrs. Simpson, 'and in this way: that my uncle must have made the will not very long before he died (that, I think, he said himself), and got rid of the book immediately afterwards. But all his books were very carefully catalogued: and John has the catalogue. And John was most particular that no books whatever should be sold out of the house.

'And I'm told that he is always journeying about to booksellers and libraries; so I fancy that he must have found out just which books are missing from my uncle's library of those which are entered in the catalogue, and must be hunting for them.'

'Just so, just so,' said Mr. Garrett, and relapsed into thought.

No later than next day he received a letter which, as he told Mrs. Simpson with great regret, made it absolutely necessary for him to cut short his stay at Burnstow.

Sorry as he was to leave them (and they were at least as sorry to part with him), he had begun to feel that a crisis, all-important to Mrs. (and shall we add, Miss?) Simpson, was very possibly supervening.

In the train Garrett was uneasy and excited. He racked his brains to think whether the press mark of the book which Mr. Eldred had been inquiring after was one in any way corresponding to the numbers on Mrs. Simpson's little bit of paper. But he found to his dismay that the shock of the previous week had really so upset him that he could neither remember any vestige of the title or nature of the book, or even of the locality to which he had gone to seek it. And yet all other parts of library topography and work were clear as ever in his mind.

And another thing – he stamped with annoyance as he thought of it – he had at first hesitated, and then had forgotten, to ask Mrs. Simpson for the name of the place where Eldred lived. That, however, he could write about.

At least he had his clue in the figures on the paper. If they referred to a press mark in his library, they were only susceptible of a limited number of interpretations. They might be divided into 1.13.34, 11.33.4, or 11.3.34. He could try all these in the space of a few minutes, and if any one were missing he had every means of tracing it.

He got very quickly to work, though a few minutes had to be spent in explaining his early return to his landlady and his colleagues. 1.13.34. was in place and contained no extraneous writing. As he drew near to Class II in the same gallery, its association struck him like a chill. But he *must* go on. After a cursory glance at 11.33.4 (which first confronted him, and was a perfectly new book) he ran his eye along the line of quartos which fills 11.3. The gap he feared was there: 34 was out. A moment was spent in making sure that it had not been misplaced, and then he was off to the vestibule.

'Has 11.3.34 gone out? Do you recollect noticing that number?'

'Notice the number? What do you take me for, Mr. Garrett? There, take and look over the tickets for yourself, if you've got a free day before you.'

'Well then, has a Mr. Eldred called again? – The old gentleman who came the day I was taken ill. Come! You'd remember him.'

'What do you suppose? Of course I recollect of him. No, he haven't been in again, not since you went off for your 'oliday. And yet I seem to – there now. Roberts'll know. Roberts, do you recollect of the name of Heldred?'

'Not arf,' said Roberts. 'You mean the man that sent a bob over the price for the parcel, and I wish they all did.'

'Do you mean to say you've been sending books to Mr. Eldred? Come, do speak up! Have you?'

'Well now, Mr. Garrett, if a gentleman sends the ticket all wrote correct and the secketry says this book may go and the box ready addressed sent with the note, and a sum of money sufficient to deefray the railway charges, what would be *your* action in the matter, Mr. Garrett, if I may take the liberty to ask such a question?

'Would you or would you not have taken the trouble to oblige, or would you have chucked the 'ole thing under the counter and—'

'You were perfectly right, of course, Hodgson – perfectly right: only, would you kindly oblige me by showing me the ticket Mr. Eldred sent, and letting me know his address?'

'To be sure, Mr. Garrett; so long as I'm not 'ectored about and informed that I don't know my duty, I'm willing to oblige in every way feasible to my power. There is the ticket on the file. J. Eldred, 11.3.34. Title of work: T-a-l-m – well, there, you can make what you like of it – not a novel, I should 'azard the guess. And here is Mr. Heldred's note applying for the book in question, which I see he terms it a track.'

'Thanks, thanks: but the address? There's none on the note.'

'Ah, indeed. Well, now . . . stay now, Mr. Garrett, I 'ave it. Why, that note come inside of the parcel, which was directed very thoughtful to save all trouble, ready to be sent back with the book inside. And if I *have* made any mistake in this 'ole transaction, it lays just in the one point that I neglected to enter the address in my little book here what I keep.

'Not but what I dare say there was good reasons for me not entering of it: but there, I haven't the time, neither have you, I dare say, to go into 'em just now. And – no, Mr. Garrett, I do *not* carry it in my 'ed, else what would be the use of me keeping this little book here – just a ordinary common notebook, you see, which I make a practice of entering all such names and addresses in it as I see fit to do?'

'Admirable arrangement, to be sure – but – all right, thank you. When did the parcel go off?'

'Half-past ten, this morning.'

'Oh, good; and it's just one now.'

Garrett went upstairs in deep thought. How was he to get the address? A telegram to Mrs. Simpson: he might miss a train by waiting for the answer. Yes, there was one other way. She had said that Eldred lived on his uncle's estate. If this were so, he might find that place entered in the donation-book. That he could run through quickly, now that he knew the title of the book.

The register was soon before him, and, knowing that the old man had died more than twenty years ago, he gave him a good margin, and turned back to 1870. There was but one entry possible. 1875, August 14th. *Talmud: Tractatus Middoth cum comm. R. Nachmanidæ*. Amstelod. 1707. Given by J. Rant, D.D., of Bretfield Manor.

A gazetteer showed Bretfield to be three miles from a small station on the main line. Now to ask the doorkeeper whether he recollected if the name on the parcel had been anything like Bretfield.

'No, nothing like. It was, now you mention it, Mr. Garrett, either Bredfield or Britfield, but nothing like that other name what you coated.'

So far well. Next, a timetable. A train could be got in twenty minutes – taking two hours over the journey. The only chance, but one not to be missed. And the train was taken.

If he had been fidgety on the journey up, he was almost distracted on the journey down. If he found Eldred, what could he say? That it had been discovered that the book was a rarity and must be recalled? An obvious untruth. Or that it was believed to contain important manuscript notes? Eldred would of course show him the book, from which the leaf would already have been removed.

He might, perhaps, find traces of the removal – a torn edge of a fly-leaf probably – and who could disprove what Eldred was certain to say, that he too had noticed and regretted the mutilation? Altogether the chase seemed very hopeless. The one chance was this. The book had left the library at 10:30: it might not have been put into the first possible train, at 11:20. Granted that, then he might be lucky enough to arrive simultaneously with it and patch up some story which would induce Eldred to give it up.

It was drawing towards evening when he got out upon the platform of his station, and, like most country stations, this one seemed unnaturally quiet. He waited about till the one or two passengers who got out with him had drifted off, and then inquired of the station-master whether Mr. Eldred was in the neighbourhood.

'Yes, and pretty near too, I believe. I fancy he means calling here for a parcel he expects. Called for it once today already, didn't he, Bob?' (to the porter).

'Yes, sir, he did. And appeared to think it was all along of me that it didn't come by the two o'clock. Anyhow, I've got it for him now,' and the porter flourished a square parcel, which – a glance assured Garrett – contained all that was of any importance to him at that particular moment.

'Bretfield, sir? Yes – three miles just about. Short cut across these three fields brings it down by half-a-mile. There: there's Mr. Eldred's trap.'

A dog-cart drove up with two men in it, of whom Garrett, gazing back as he crossed the little station yard, easily recognised one. The fact that Eldred was driving was slightly in his favour – for most likely he would not open the parcel in the presence of his servant. On the other hand, he would get home quickly, and unless Garrett were there within a very few minutes of his arrival, all would be over. He must hurry; and that he did.

His short cut took him along one side of a triangle, while the cart had two sides to traverse. And it was delayed a little at the station, so that Garrett was in the third of the three fields when he heard the wheels fairly near. He had made the best progress possible, but the pace at which the cart was coming made him despair. At this rate it *must* reach home ten minutes before him, and ten minutes would more than suffice for the fulfilment of Mr. Eldred's project.

It was just at this time that the luck fairly turned. The evening was still, and sounds came clearly. Seldom has any sound given greater relief than that which he now heard: that of the cart pulling up. A few words were exchanged, and it drove on. Garrett, halting in the utmost anxiety, was able to see as it drove past the stile (near which he now stood) that it contained only the servant and not Eldred. Further, he made out that Eldred was following on foot.

From behind the tall hedge by the stile leading into the road he watched the thin wiry figure pass quickly by with the parcel beneath its arm, and feeling in its pockets. Just as he passed the stile something fell out of a pocket upon the grass, but with so little sound that Eldred was not conscious of it. In a moment more it was safe for Garrett to cross the stile into the road and pick up – a box of matches.

Eldred went on, and, as he went, his arms made hasty movements, difficult to interpret in the shadow of the trees that overhung the road. But, as Garrett followed cautiously, he found at various points the key to them – a piece of string, and then the wrapper of the parcel – meant to be thrown over the hedge, but sticking in it.

Now Eldred was walking slower, and it could just be made out that he had opened the book and was turning over the leaves. He stopped, evidently troubled by the failing light. Garrett slipped into a gate-opening, but still watched.

Eldred, hastily looking around, sat down on a felled tree-trunk by the roadside and held the open book up close to his eyes. Suddenly he laid it, still open, on his knee, and felt in all his pockets: clearly in vain, and clearly to his annoyance. 'You would be glad of your matches now,' thought Garrett. Then he took hold of a leaf, and was carefully tearing it out, when two things happened.

First, something black seemed to drop upon the white leaf and run down it, and then as Eldred started and was turning to look behind him, a little dark form appeared to rise out of the shadow behind the tree-trunk and from it two arms enclosing a mass of blackness came before Eldred's face and covered his head and neck. His legs and arms were wildly flourished, but no sound came. Then, there was no more movement. Eldred was alone. He had fallen back into the grass behind the tree-trunk. The book was cast into the roadway.

Garrett, his anger and suspicion gone for the moment at the sight of this horrid struggle, rushed up with loud cries of 'Help!' and so too, to his enormous relief, did a labourer who had just emerged from a field opposite. Together they bent over and supported Eldred, but to no purpose. The conclusion that he was dead was inevitable.

'Poor gentleman!' said Garrett to the labourer, when they had laid him down, 'what happened to him, do you think?'

'I wasn't two hundred yards away,' said the man, 'when I see Squire Eldred setting reading in his book, and to my thinking he was took with one of these fits – face seemed to go all over black.'

'Just so,' said Garrett. 'You didn't see anyone near him? It couldn't have been an assault?'

'Not possible – no one couldn't have got away without you or me seeing them.'

'So I thought. Well, we must get some help, and the doctor and the policeman; and perhaps I had better give them this book.'

It was obviously a case for an inquest, and obvious also that Garrett must stay at Bretfield and give his evidence.

The medical inspection showed that, though some black dust was found on the face and in the mouth of the deceased, the cause of death was a shock to a weak heart, and not asphyxiation. The fateful book was produced, a respectable quarto printed wholly in Hebrew, and not of an aspect likely to excite even the most sensitive.

'You say, Mr. Garrett, that the deceased gentleman appeared at the moment before his attack to be tearing a leaf out of this book?'

'Yes; I think one of the fly-leaves.'

'There is here a fly-leaf partially torn through. It has Hebrew writing on it. Will you kindly inspect it?'

'There are three names in English, sir, also, and a date. But I am sorry to say I cannot read Hebrew writing.'

'Thank you. The names have the appearance of being signatures. They are John Rant, Walter Gibson, and James Frost, and the date is 20 July, 1875. Does anyone here know any of these names?'

The Rector, who was present, volunteered a statement that the uncle of the deceased, from whom he inherited, had been named Rant.

The book being handed to him, he shook a puzzled head. 'This is not like any Hebrew I ever learnt.'

'You are sure that it is Hebrew?'

'What? Yes – I suppose . . . No – my dear sir, you are perfectly right – that is, your suggestion is exactly to the point. Of course – it is not Hebrew at all. It is English, and it is a will.'

It did not take many minutes to show that here was indeed a will of Dr. John Rant, bequeathing the whole of the property lately held by John Eldred to Mrs. Mary Simpson. Clearly the discovery of such a document would amply justify Mr. Eldred's agitation. As to the partial tearing of the leaf, the coroner pointed out that no useful purpose could be attained by speculations whose correctness it would never be possible to establish.

The Tractate Middoth was naturally taken in charge by the coroner for further investigation, and Mr. Garrett explained privately to him the history of it, and the position of events so far as he knew or guessed them.

He returned to his work next day, and on his walk to the station passed the scene of Mr. Eldred's catastrophe. He could hardly leave it without another look, though the recollection of what he had seen there made him shiver, even on that bright morning.

He walked round, with some misgivings, behind the felled tree. Something dark that still lay there made him start back for a moment: but it hardly stirred. Looking closer, he saw that it was a thick black mass of cobwebs; and, as he stirred it gingerly with his stick, several large spiders ran out of it into the grass.

There is no great difficulty in imagining the steps by which William Garrett, from being an assistant in a great library, attained to his present position of prospective owner of Bretfield Manor, now in the occupation of his mother-in-law, Mrs. Mary Simpson.

The Story of a Disappearance and an Appearance

THE LETTERS WHICH I now publish were sent to me recently by a person who knows me to be interested in ghost stories. There is no doubt about their authenticity. The paper on which they are written, the ink, and the whole external aspect put their date beyond the reach of question.

The only point which they do not make clear is the identity of the writer. He signs with initials only, and as none of the envelopes of the letters are preserved, the surname of his correspondent – obviously a married brother – is as obscure as his own. No further preliminary explanation is needed, I think. Luckily the first letter supplies all that could be expected.

Letter I

GREAT CHRISHALL,
Dec. 22, 1837.

MY DEAR ROBERT,

It is with great regret for the enjoyment I am losing, and for a reason which you will deplore equally with myself, that I write to inform you that I am unable to join your circle for this Christmas. But you will agree with me that it is unavoidable when I say that I have within these few hours received a letter from Mrs.

Hunt at B——, to the effect that our Uncle Henry has suddenly
and mysteriously disappeared, and begging me to go down there
immediately and join the search that is being made for him.

Little as I, or you either, I think, have ever seen of Uncle, I
naturally feel that this is not a request that can be regarded lightly,
and accordingly I propose to go to B—— by this afternoon's mail,
reaching it late in the evening. I shall not go to the Rectory, but
put up at the King's Head, and to which you may address letters.
I enclose a small draft, which you will please make use of for the
benefit of the young people.

I shall write you daily (supposing me to be detained more than a
single day) what goes on, and you may be sure, should the business
be cleared up in time to permit of my coming to the Manor after all,
I shall present myself.

I have but a few minutes at disposal.
With cordial greetings to you all, and many regrets, believe me, your
affectionate Bro.,

W.R.

Letter II

KING'S HEAD,
Dec. 23, '37.

MY DEAR ROBERT,
In the first place, there is as yet no news of Uncle H., and I think
you may finally dismiss any idea – I won't say hope – that I might
after all 'turn up' for Xmas. However, my thoughts will be with you,
and you have my best wishes for a really festive day. Mind that none
of my nephews or nieces expend any fraction of their guineas on
presents for me.

Since I got here I have been blaming myself for taking this
affair of Uncle H. too easily. From what people here say, I gather
that there is very little hope that he can still be alive; but whether it
is accident or design that carried him off I cannot judge.

The facts are these. On Friday the 19th, he went as usual shortly before five o'clock to read evening prayers at the Church; and when they were over the clerk brought him a message, in response to which he set off to pay a visit to a sick person at an outlying cottage the better part of two miles away.

He paid the visit, and started on his return journey at about half-past six. This is the last that is known of him.

The people here are very much grieved at his loss; he had been here many years, as you know, and though, as you also know, he was not the most genial of men, and had more than a little of the martinet in his composition, he seems to have been active in good works, and unsparing of trouble to himself.

Poor Mrs. Hunt, who has been his housekeeper ever since she left Woodley, is quite overcome: it seems like the end of the world to her. I am glad that I did not entertain the idea of taking quarters at the Rectory; and I have declined several kindly offers of hospitality from people in the place, preferring as I do to be independent, and finding myself very comfortable here.

You will, of course, wish to know what has been done in the way of inquiry and search. First, nothing was to be expected from investigation at the Rectory; and to be brief, nothing has transpired. I asked Mrs. Hunt — as others had done before — whether there was either any unfavourable symptom in her master such as might portend a sudden stroke, or attack of illness, or whether he had ever had reason to apprehend any such thing: but both she, and also his medical man, were clear that this was not the case. He was quite in his usual health.

In the second place, naturally, ponds and streams have been dragged, and fields in the neighbourhood which he is known to have visited last, have been searched — without result. I have myself talked to the parish clerk and — more important — have been to the house where he paid his visit.

There can be no question of any foul play on these people's part. The one man in the house is ill in bed and very weak: the wife and the children of course could do nothing themselves, nor is there the shadow of a probability that they or any of them should have agreed to decoy poor Uncle H. out in order that he might be attacked on the way back.

They had told what they knew to several other inquirers already, but the woman repeated it to me. The Rector was looking just as usual: he wasn't very long with the sick man – 'He ain't,' she said, 'like some what has a gift in prayer; but there, if we was all that way, 'owever would the chapel people get their living?'

He left some money when he went away, and one of the children saw him cross the stile into the next field. He was dressed as he always was: wore his bands – I gather he is nearly the last man remaining who does so – at any rate in this district.

You see I am putting down everything. The fact is that I have nothing else to do, having brought no business papers with me; and, moreover, it serves to clear my own mind, and may suggest points which have been overlooked. So I shall continue to write all that passes, even to conversations if need be – you may read or not as you please, but pray keep the letters. I have another reason for writing so fully, but it is not a very tangible one.

You may ask if I have myself made any search in the fields near the cottage. Something – a good deal – has been done by others, as I mentioned; but I hope to go over the ground tomorrow. Bow Street has now been informed, and will send down by tonight's coach, but I do not think they will make much of the job. There is no snow, which might have helped us. The fields are all grass.

Of course I was on the qui vive for any indication today both going and returning; but there was a thick mist on the way back, and I was not in trim for wandering about unknown pastures, especially on an evening when bushes looked like men, and a cow lowing in the distance might have been the last trump. I assure you, if Uncle Henry had stepped out from among the trees in a little copse which borders the path at one place, carrying his head under his arm, I should have been very little more uncomfortable than I was.

To tell you the truth, I was rather expecting something of the *kind. But I must drop my pen for the moment: Mr. Lucas, the curate, is announced.*

Later. Mr. Lucas has been, and gone, and there is not much beyond the decencies of ordinary sentiment to be got from him. I can see that he has given up any idea that the Rector can be alive, and that, so far as he can be, he is truly sorry. I can also discern that even in a more emotional person than Mr. Lucas, Uncle Henry was not likely to inspire strong attachment.

Besides Mr. Lucas, I have had another visitor in the shape of my Boniface – mine host of the 'King's Head' – who came to see whether I had everything I wished, and who really requires the pen of a Boz to do him justice. He was very solemn and weighty at first.

'Well, sir,' he said, 'I suppose we must bow our 'ead beneath the blow, as my poor wife had used to say. So far as I can gather there's been neither hide nor yet hair of our late respected incumbent scented out as yet; not that he was what the Scripture terms a hairy man in any sense of the word.'

I said – as well as I could – that I supposed not, but could not help adding that I had heard he was sometimes a little difficult to deal with. Mr. Bowman looked at me sharply for a moment, and then passed in a flash from solemn sympathy to impassioned declamation.

'When I think,' he said, 'of the language that man see fit to employ to me in this here parlour over no more a matter than a cask of beer – such a thing as I told him might happen any day of the week to a man with a family – though as it turned out he was quite under a mistake, and that I knew at the time, only I was that shocked to hear him I couldn't lay my tongue to the right expression.'

He stopped abruptly and eyed me with some embarrassment. I only said, 'Dear me, I'm sorry to hear you had any little differences: I suppose my uncle will be a good deal missed in the parish?'

Mr. Bowman drew a long breath. 'Ah, yes!' he said. 'Your uncle! You'll understand me when I say that for the moment it had slipped my remembrance that he was a relative; and natural enough, I must say, as it should, for as to you bearing any resemblance to – to him, the notion of any such a thing is clean ridiculous.

'All the same, 'ad I 'ave bore it in my mind, you'll be among the first to feel, I'm sure, as I should have abstained my lips, or rather I should not have abstained my lips with no such reflections.'

I assured him that I quite understood, and was going to have asked him some further questions, but he was called away to see after some business. By the way, you need not take it into your head that he has anything to fear from the inquiry into poor Uncle Henry's disappearance – though, no doubt, in the watches of the night it will occur to him that I think he has, and I may expect explanations tomorrow. I must close this letter: it has to go by the late coach.

Letter III

Dec. 25, '37.

MY DEAR ROBERT,

This is a curious letter to be writing on Christmas Day, and yet after all there is nothing much in it. Or there may be – you shall be the judge. At least, nothing decisive. The Bow Street men practically say that they have no clue. The length of time and the weather conditions have made all tracks so faint as to be quite useless: nothing that belonged to the dead man – I'm afraid no other word will do – has been picked up.

As I expected, Mr. Bowman was uneasy in his mind this morning; quite early I heard him holding forth in a very distinct voice – purposely so, I thought – to the Bow Street officers in the bar, as to the loss that the town had sustained in their Rector, and as to the necessity of leaving no stone unturned (he was very great on this phrase) in order to come at the truth. I suspect him of being an orator of repute at convivial meetings.

When I was at breakfast he came to wait on me, and took an opportunity when handing a muffin to say in a low tone, 'I 'ope, sir,

you reconise as my feelings towards your relative is not actuated
by any taint of what you may call melignity – you can leave the
room, Eliza, I will see the gentleman 'as all he requires with my own
hands – I ask your pardon, sir, but you must be well aware a man
is not always master of himself: and when that man has been 'urt in
his mind by the application of expressions which I will go so far as
to say 'ad not ought to have been made use of (his voice was rising
all this time and his face growing redder); no, sir.

'And 'ere, if you will permit of it, I should like to explain to you
in a very few words the exact state of the bone of contention. This
cask – I might more truly call it a firkin – of beer –'

I felt it was time to interpose, and said that I did not see that
it would help us very much to go into that matter in detail. Mr.
Bowman acquiesced, and resumed more calmly: 'Well, sir, I bow
to your ruling, and as you say, be that here or be it there, it don't
contribute a great deal, perhaps, to the present question.

'All I wish you to understand is that I am as prepared as you are
yourself to lend every hand to the business we have afore us, and – as
I took the opportunity to say as much to the Orficers not three-
quarters of an hour ago – to leave no stone unturned as may throw
even a spark of light on this painful matter.'

In fact, Mr. Bowman did accompany us on our exploration, but
though I am sure his genuine wish was to be helpful, I am afraid he
did not contribute to the serious side of it. He appeared to be under
the impression that we were likely to meet either Uncle Henry or the
person responsible for his disappearance, walking about the fields,
and did a great deal of shading his eyes with his hand and calling
our attention, by pointing with his stick, to distant cattle and
labourers.

He held several long conversations with old women whom we met,
and was very strict and severe in his manner, but on each occasion
returned to our party saying, 'Well, I find she don't seem to 'ave no
connexion with this sad affair. I think you may take it from me,
sir, as there's little or no light to be looked for from that quarter; not
without she's keeping somethink back intentional.'

We gained no appreciable result, as I told you at starting; the Bow Street men have left the town, whether for London or not I am not sure.

This evening I had company in the shape of a bagman, a smartish fellow. He knew what was going forward, but though he has been on the roads for some days about here, he had nothing to tell of suspicious characters – tramps, wandering sailors or gypsies.

He was very full of a capital Punch and Judy Show he had seen this same day at W——, and asked if it had been here yet, and advised me by no means to miss it if it does come. The best Punch and the best Toby dog, he said, he had ever come across. Toby dogs, you know, are the last new thing in the shows. I have only seen one myself, but before long all the men will have them.

Now why, you will want to know, do I trouble to write all this to you? I am obliged to do it, because it has something to do with another absurd trifle (as you will inevitably say), which in my present state of rather unquiet fancy – nothing more, perhaps – I have to put down. It is a dream, sir, which I am going to record, and I must say it is one of the oddest I have had. Is there anything in it beyond what the bagman's talk and Uncle Henry's disappearance could have suggested? You, I repeat, shall judge: I am not in a sufficiently cool and judicial frame to do so.

It began with what I can only describe as a pulling-aside of curtains: and I found myself seated in a place – I don't know whether indoors or out. There were people – only a few – on either side of me, but I did not recognise them, or indeed think much about them. They never spoke, but, so far as I remember, were all grave and pale-faced and looked fixedly before them. Facing me there was a Punch and Judy Show, perhaps rather larger than the ordinary ones, painted with black figures on a reddish-yellow ground. Behind it and on each side was only darkness, but in front there was a sufficiency of light.

I was 'strung up' to a high degree of expectation and looked every moment to hear the pan-pipes and the Roo-too-too-it. Instead of that there came suddenly an enormous – I can use no other word

— an enormous single toll of a bell, I don't know from how far off — somewhere behind. The little curtain flew up and the drama began.

I believe someone once tried to re-write Punch as a serious tragedy; but whoever he may have been, this performance would have suited him exactly. There was something Satanic about the hero. He varied his methods of attack: for some of his victims he lay in wait, and to see his horrible face — it was yellowish-white, I may remark — peering round the wings made me think of the Vampyre in Fuseli's foul sketch. To others he was polite and carneying — particularly to the unfortunate alien who can only say Shallabalah — though what Punch said I never could catch. But with all of them I came to dread the moment of death. The crack of the stick on their skulls, which in the ordinary way delights me, had here a crushing sound as if the bone was giving way, and the victims quivered and kicked as they lay.

The baby — it sounds more ridiculous as I go on — the baby, I am sure, was alive. Punch wrung its neck, and if the choke or squeak which it gave were not real, I know nothing of reality.

The stage got perceptibly darker as each crime was consummated, and at last there was one murder which was done quite in the dark, so that I could see nothing of the victim, and took some time to effect. It was accompanied by hard breathing and horrid muffled sounds, and after it Punch came and sat on the foot-board and fanned himself and looked at his shoes, which were bloody, and hung his head on one side, and sniggered in so deadly a fashion that I saw some of those beside me cover their faces, and I would gladly have done the same.

But in the meantime the scene behind Punch was clearing, and showed, not the usual house front, but something more ambitious — a grove of trees and the gentle slope of a hill, with a very natural — in fact, I should say a real — moon shining on it. Over this there rose slowly an object which I soon perceived to be a human figure with something peculiar about the head — what, I was unable at first to see.

It did not stand on its feet, but began creeping or dragging itself across the middle distance towards Punch, who still sat back to it;

and by this time, I may remark (though it did not occur to me at the moment) that all pretence of this being a puppet show had vanished. Punch was still Punch, it is true, but, like the others, was in some sense a live creature, and both moved themselves at their own will.

When I next glanced at him he was sitting in malignant reflection; but in another instant something seemed to attract his attention, and he first sat up sharply and then turned round, and evidently caught sight of the person that was approaching him and was in fact now very near. Then, indeed, did he show unmistakable signs of terror: catching up his stick, he rushed towards the wood, only just eluding the arm of his pursuer, which was suddenly flung out to intercept him.

It was with a revulsion which I cannot easily express that I now saw more or less clearly what this pursuer was like. He was a sturdy figure clad in black, and, as I thought, wearing bands: his head was covered with a whitish bag.

The chase which now began lasted I do not know how long, now among the trees, now along the slope of the field, sometimes both figures disappearing wholly for a few seconds, and only some uncertain sounds letting one know that they were still afoot. At length there came a moment when Punch, evidently exhausted, staggered in from the left and threw himself down among the trees. His pursuer was not long after him, and came looking uncertainly from side to side. Then, catching sight of the figure on the ground, he too threw himself down – his back was turned to the audience – with a swift motion twitched the covering from his head, and thrust his face into that of Punch. Everything on the instant grew dark.

There was one long, loud, shuddering scream, and I awoke to find myself looking straight into the face of – what in all the world do you think? but – a large owl, which was seated on my window-sill immediately opposite my bed-foot, holding up its wings like two shrouded arms. I caught the fierce glance of its yellow eyes, and then it was gone. I heard the single enormous bell again – very likely, as you are saying to yourself, the church clock; but I do not think so – and then I was broad awake.

All this, I may say, happened within the last half-hour. There was no probability of my getting to sleep again, so I got up, put on clothes enough to keep me warm, and am writing this rigmarole in the first hours of Christmas Day. Have I left out anything? Yes. There was no Toby dog, and the names over the front of the Punch and Judy booth were Kidman and Gallop, which were certainly not what the bagman told me to look out for.

By this time, I feel a little more as if I could sleep, so this shall be sealed and wafered.

Letter IV

Dec. 26, '37.

MY DEAR ROBERT,

All is over. The body has been found.

I do not make excuses for not having sent off my news by last night's mail, for the simple reason that I was incapable of putting pen to paper. The events that attended the discovery bewildered me so completely that I needed what I could get of a night's rest to enable me to face the situation at all. Now I can give you my journal of the day, certainly the strangest Christmas Day that ever I spent or am likely to spend.

The first incident was not very serious. Mr. Bowman had, I think, been keeping Christmas Eve, and was a little inclined to be captious: at least, he was not on foot very early, and to judge from what I could hear, neither men nor maids could do anything to please him. The latter were certainly reduced to tears; nor am I sure that Mr. Bowman succeeded in preserving a manly composure.

At any rate, when I came downstairs, it was in a broken voice that he wished me the compliments of the season, and a little later on when he paid his visit of ceremony at breakfast, he was far from cheerful, even Byronic, I might almost say, in his outlook on life.

'I don't know,' he said, 'if you think with me, sir; but every Christmas as comes round the world seems a hollerer thing to me.

Why, take an example now from what lays under my own eye. There's my servant Eliza – been with me now for going on fifteen years. I thought I could have placed my confidence in Eliza, and yet this very morning – Christmas morning too, of all the blessed days in the year – with the bells a-ringing and – and – all like that – I say, this very morning, had it not have been for Providence watching over us all, that girl would have put – indeed I may go so far to say, 'ad put the cheese on your breakfast-table –'

He saw I was about to speak, and waved his hand at me. 'It's all very well for you to say, "Yes, Mr. Bowman, but you took away the cheese and locked it up in the cupboard," which I did, and have the key here, or if not the actual key, one very much about the same size. That's true enough, sir, but what do you think is the effect of that action on me? Why, it's no exaggeration for me to say that the ground is cut from under my feet. And yet when I said as much to Eliza, not nasty, mind you, but just firm-like, what was my return? "Oh," she says, "well," she says, "there wasn't no bones broke, I suppose."

'Well, sir, it 'urt me, that's all I can say: it 'urt me, and I don't like to think of it now.'

There was an ominous pause here, in which I ventured to say something like, 'Yes, very trying,' and then asked at what hour the church service was to be.

'Eleven o'clock,' Mr. Bowman said with a heavy sigh. 'Ah, you won't have no such discourse from poor Mr. Lucas as what you would have done from our late Rector. Him and me may have had our little differences, and did do, more's the pity.'

I could see that a powerful effort was needed to keep him off the vexed question of the cask of beer, but he made it. 'But I will say this, that a better preacher, nor yet one to stand faster by his rights or what he considered to be his rights – however, that's not the question now – I for one, never set under. Some might say, "Was he a eloquent man?" and to that my answer would be: "Well, there you've a better right per'aps to speak of your own uncle than what I have." Others might ask, "Did he keep a hold of his congregation?"

and there again I should reply, "That depends." But as I say – yes, Eliza, my girl, I'm coming – eleven o'clock, sir, and you inquire for the King's Head pew.'

I believe Eliza had been very near the door, and shall consider it in my vail.

The next episode was church: I felt Mr. Lucas had a difficult task in doing justice to Christmas sentiments, and also to the feeling of disquiet and regret which, whatever Mr. Bowman might say, was clearly prevalent. I do not think he rose to the occasion. I was uncomfortable.

The organ wolved – you know what I mean: the wind died – twice in the Christmas Hymn, and the tenor bell, I suppose owing to some negligence on the part of the ringers, kept sounding faintly about once in a minute during the sermon. The clerk sent up a man to see to it, but he seemed unable to do much. I was glad when it was over.

There was an odd incident, too, before the service. I went in rather early, and came upon two men carrying the parish bier back to its place under the tower. From what I overheard them saying, it appeared that it had been put out by mistake, by someone who was not there. I also saw the clerk busy folding up a moth-eaten velvet pall – not a sight for Christmas Day.

I dined soon after this, and then, feeling disinclined to go out, took my seat by the fire in the parlour, with the last number of Pickwick, which I had been saving up for some days. I thought I could be sure of keeping awake over this, but I turned out as bad as our friend Smith. I suppose it was half-past two when I was roused by a piercing whistle and laughing and talking voices outside in the market-place.

It was a Punch and Judy – I had no doubt the one that my bagman had seen at W——. I was half-delighted, half-not – the latter because my unpleasant dream came back to me so vividly; but, anyhow, I determined to see it through, and I sent Eliza out with a crown-piece to the performers and a request that they would face my window if they could manage it.

The show was a very smart new one. The names of the

proprietors, I need hardly tell you, were Italian, Foresta and Calpigi. The Toby dog was there, as I had been led to expect. All B—— turned out, but did not obstruct my view, for I was at the large first-floor window and not ten yards away.

The play began on the stroke of a quarter to three by the church clock. Certainly it was very good; and I was soon relieved to find that the disgust my dream had given me for Punch's onslaughts on his ill-starred visitors was only transient. I laughed at the demise of the Turncock, the Foreigner, the Beadle, and even the baby. The only drawback was the Toby dog's developing a tendency to howl in the wrong place. Something had occurred, I suppose, to upset him, and something considerable: for, I forget exactly at what point, he gave a most lamentable cry, leapt off the foot-board, and shot away across the market-place and down a side street.

There was a stage-wait, but only a brief one. I suppose the men decided that it was no good going after him, and that he was likely to turn up again at night.

We went on. Punch dealt faithfully with Judy, and in fact with all comers; and then came the moment when the gallows was erected, and the great scene with Mr. Ketch was to be enacted. It was now that something happened of which I can certainly not yet see the import fully.

You have witnessed an execution, and know what the criminal's head looks like with the cap on. If you are like me, you never wish to think of it again, and I do not willingly remind you of it. It was just such a head as that, that I, from my somewhat higher post, saw in the inside of the show-box; but at first the audience did not see it. I expected it to emerge into their view, but instead of that there slowly rose for a few seconds an uncovered face, with an expression of terror upon it, of which I have never imagined the like.

It seemed as if the man, whoever he was, was being forcibly lifted, with his arms somehow pinioned or held back, towards the little gibbet on the stage. I could just see the nightcapped head behind him. Then there was a cry and a crash. The whole show-box fell over backwards; kicking legs were seen among the ruins, and then two figures — as some said; I can only answer for one — were visible running at top speed across the square and disappearing in a lane which leads to the fields.

Of course everybody gave chase. I followed, but the pace was killing; and very few were in, literally, at the death.

It happened in a chalk pit: the man went over the edge quite blindly and broke his neck. They searched everywhere for the other, until it occurred to me to ask whether he had ever left the market-place. At first everyone was sure that he had. But when we came to look, he was there, under the show-box, dead too.

But in the chalk pit it was that poor Uncle Henry's body was found, with a sack over the head, the throat horribly mangled. It was a peaked corner of the sack sticking out of the soil that attracted attention. I cannot bring myself to write in greater detail.
I forgot to say the men's real names were Kidman and Gallop. I feel sure I have heard them, but no one here seems to know anything about them.

I am coming to you as soon as I can after the funeral. I must tell you when we meet what I think of it all.

An Episode of Cathedral History

THERE WAS ONCE a learned gentleman who was deputed to examine and report upon the archives of the Cathedral of Southminster. The examination of these records demanded a very considerable expenditure of time – hence it became advisable for him to engage lodgings in the city, for though the Cathedral body were profuse in their offers of hospitality, Mr. Lake felt that he would prefer to be master of his day. This was recognised as reasonable.

The Dean eventually wrote advising Mr. Lake, if he were not already suited, to communicate with Mr. Worby, the principal Verger, who occupied a house convenient to the church and was prepared to take in a quiet lodger for three or four weeks.

Such an arrangement was precisely what Mr. Lake desired. Terms were easily agreed upon, and early in December, like another Mr. Datchery (as he remarked to himself), the investigator found himself in the occupation of a very comfortable room in an ancient and 'cathedraly' house.

One so familiar with the customs of Cathedral churches, and treated with such obvious consideration by the Dean and Chapter of this Cathedral in particular, could not fail to command the respect of the Head Verger. Mr. Worby even acquiesced in certain modifications of statements he had been accustomed to offer for years to parties of visitors. Mr. Lake, on his part, found the Verger a very cheery companion, and took advantage of any occasion that presented itself for enjoying his conversation when the day's work was over.

One evening, about nine o'clock, Mr. Worby knocked at his lodger's door. 'I've occasion,' he said, 'to go across to the Cathedral, Mr. Lake, and I think I made you a promise when I did so next I would give you the opportunity to see what it looks like at night time. It's quite fine and dry outside, if you care to come.'

'To be sure I will; very much obliged to you, Mr. Worby, for thinking of it, but let me get my coat.'

'Here it is, sir, and I've another lantern here that you'll find advisable for the steps, as there's no moon.'

'Anyone might think we were Jasper and Durdles, over again, mightn't they?' said Lake, as they crossed the close, for he had ascertained that the Verger had read *Edwin Drood*.

'Well, so they might,' said Mr. Worby, with a short laugh, 'though I don t know whether we ought to take it as a compliment. Odd ways, I often think, they had at that Cathedral, don't it seem so to you, sir? Full choral matins at seven o'clock in the morning all the year round. Wouldn't suit our boys' voices nowadays, and I think there's one of two of the men would be applying for a rise if the Chapter was to bring it in – particular the alltoes.'

They were now at the south-west door. As Mr. Worby was unlocking it, Lake said, 'Did you ever find anybody locked in here by accident?'

'Twice I did. One was a drunk sailor; however he got in I don't know. I s'pose he went to sleep in the service, but by the time I got to him he was praying fit to bring the roof in. Lor'! What a noise that man did make! Said it was the first time he'd been inside a church for ten years, and blest if ever he'd try it again. The other was an old sheep: them boys it was, up to their games. That was the last time they tried it on, though.

'There, sit, now you see what we look like – our late Dean used now and again to bring parties in, but he preferred a moonlight night, and there was a piece of verse he'd coat to 'em, relating to a Scotch cathedral, I understand, but I don't know. I almost think the effect's better when it's all dark-like. Seems to add to the size and heighth.

'Now if you won't mind stopping somewhere in the nave while I go up into the choir where my business lays, you'll see what I mean.'

Accordingly Lake waited, leaning against a pillar, and watched the light wavering along the length of the church, and up the steps into the choir, until it was intercepted by some screen or other furniture, which only allowed the reflection to be seen on the piers and roof.

Not many minutes had passed before Worby reappeared at the door of the choir and by waving his lantern signalled to Lake to rejoin him.

'I suppose it *is* Worby, and not a substitute,' thought Lake to himself, as he walked up the nave.

There was, in fact, nothing untoward. Worby showed him the papers which he had come to fetch out of the Dean's stall, and asked him what he thought of the spectacle. Lake agreed that it was well worth seeing. 'I suppose,' he said, as they walked towards the altar-steps together, 'that you're too much used to going about here at night to feel nervous – but you must get a start every now and then, don't you, when a book falls down or a door swings to?'

'No, Mr. Lake, I can't say I think much about noises, not nowadays: I'm much more afraid of finding an escape of gas or a burst in the stove pipes than anything else. Still there have been times, years ago.

'Did you notice that plain altar-tomb there – 15th century we say it is, I don't know if you agree to that? Well, if you didn't look at it, just come back and give it a glance, if you'd be so good.'

It was on the north side of the choir, and rather awkwardly placed: only about three feet from the enclosing stone screen. Quite plain, as the Verger had said, but for some ordinary stone panelling. A metal cross of some size on the northern side (that next to the screen) was the solitary feature of any interest.

Lake agreed that it was not earlier than the Perpendicular period, 'But,' he said, 'unless it's the tomb of some remarkable person, you'll forgive me for saying that I don't think it's particularly noteworthy.'

'Well, I can't say as it is the tomb of anybody noted in 'istory,' said Worby, who had a dry smile on his face, 'for we don't own any record whatsoever of who it was put up to. For all that, if you've half-an-hour to spare, sir, when we get back to the house, Mr. Lake, I could tell you a tale about that tomb. I won't begin on it now; it strikes cold here, and we don't want to be dawdling about all night.'

'Of course I should like to hear it immensely.'

'Very well, sir, you shall. Now if I might put a question to you,' he went on, as they passed down the choir aisle, 'in our little local guide – and not only there, but in the little book on our Cathedral in the series – you'll find it stated that this portion of the building was erected previous to the 12th century. Now of course I should be glad enough to take that view, but – mind the step, sir – but, I put it to you: does the lay of the stone 'ere in this portion of the wall (which he tapped with his key), does it to your eye carry the flavour of what you might call Saxon masonry?

'No, I thought not, no more it does to me. Now, if you'll believe me, I've said as much to those men – one's the librarian of our Free Libry here, and the other came down from London on purpose – fifty times, if I have once, but I might just as well have talked to that bit of stonework. But there it is, I suppose every one's got their opinions.'

The discussion of this peculiar trait of human nature occupied Mr. Worby almost up to the moment when he and Lake re-entered the former's house. The condition of the fire in Lake's sitting-room led to a suggestion from Mr. Worby that they should finish the evening in his own parlour.

We find them accordingly settled there some short time afterwards.

Mr. Worby made his story a long one, and I will not undertake to tell it wholly in his own words, or in his own order. Lake committed the substance of it to paper immediately after hearing it, together with some few passages of the narrative which had fixed themselves *verbatim* in his mind. I shall probably find it expedient to condense Lake's record to some extent.

Mr. Worby was born, it appeared, about the year 1828. His father before him had been connected with the Cathedral, and likewise his grandfather. One or both had been choristers, and in later life both had done work as mason and carpenter respectively about the fabric. Worby himself, though possessed, as he frankly acknowledged, of an indifferent voice, had been drafted into the choir at about ten years of age.

It was in 1840 that the wave of the Gothic revival smote the Cathedral of Southminster. 'There was a lot of lovely stuff went then, sir,' said Worby, with a sigh. 'My father couldn't hardly believe it when he got his orders to clear out the choir. There was a new dean just come in – Dean Burscough it was – and my father had been 'prenticed to a good firm of joiners in the city, and knew what good work was when he saw it.

'Crool it was, he used to say: all that beautiful wainscot oak, as good as the day it was put up, and garlands-like of foliage and fruit, and lovely old gilding work on the coats of arms and the organ pipes. All went to the timber yard – every bit except some little pieces worked up in the Lady Chapel, and 'ere in this overmantel.

'Well – I may be mistook, but I say our choir never looked as well since. Still there was a lot found out about the history of the church, and no doubt but what it did stand in need of repair. There was very few winters passed but what we'd lose a pinnacle.'

Mr. Lake expressed his concurrence with Worby's views of restoration, but owns to a fear about this point lest the story proper should never be reached. Possibly this was perceptible in his manner.

Worby hastened to reassure him, 'Not but what I could carry on about that topic for hours at a time, and do do when I see my opportunity.

'But Dean Burscough he was very set on the Gothic period, and nothing would serve him but everything must be made agreeable to that. And one morning after service he appointed for my father to meet him in the choir, and he came back after he'd taken off his robes in the vestry, and he'd got a roll of paper with him, and the verger that was then brought in a table, and they begun spreading it out on the table with prayer books to keep it down, and my father helped 'em, and he saw it was a picture of the inside of a choir in a Cathedral; and the Dean – he was a quick-spoken gentleman – he says, "Well, Worby, what do you think of that?"

'"Why," says my father, "I don't think I 'ave the pleasure of knowing that view. Would that be Hereford Cathedral, Mr. Dean?"

'"No, Worby," says the Dean, "that's Southminster Cathedral as we hope to see it before many years."

'"Indeed, sir," says my father, and that was all he did say – leastways to the Dean – but he used to tell me he felt really faint in himself when he looked round our choir as I can remember it, comfortable, and furnished-like, and then see this nasty little dry picter, as he called it, drawn out by some London architect.

'Well, there I am again. But you'll see what I mean if you look at this old view.'

Worby reached down a framed print from the wall. 'Well, the long and the short of it was that the Dean he handed over to my father a copy of an order of the Chapter that he was to clear out every bit of the choir – make a clean sweep – ready for the new work that was being designed up in town, and he was to put it in hand as soon as ever he could get the breakers together.

'Now then, sir, if you look at that view, You'll see where the pulpit used to stand – that's what I want you to notice, if you please.'

It was, indeed, easily seen; an unusually large structure of timber with a domed sounding-board, standing at the east end of the stalls on the north side of the choir, facing the bishop's throne.

Worby proceeded to explain that during the alterations, services were held in the nave, the member of the choir being thereby disappointed of an anticipated holiday, and the organist in particular incurring the suspicion of having wilfully damaged the mechanism of the temporary organ that was hired at considerable expense from London.

The work of demolition began with the choir screen and organ loft, and proceeded gradually east-wards, disclosing, as Worby said, many interesting features of older work.

While this was going on, the members of the Chapter were, naturally, in and about the choir a great deal, and it soon became apparent to the elder Worby – who could not help overhearing some of their talk – that, on the part of the senior Canons especially, there must have been a good deal of disagreement before the policy now being carried out had been adopted.

Some were of opinion that they should catch their deaths of cold in the return-stalls, unprotected by a screen from the draughts in the nave; others objected to being exposed to the view of persons in the choir aisles, espe-cially, they said, during the sermons, when they found it helpful to listen in a posture which was liable to misconstruction.

The strongest opposition, however, came from the oldest of the body, who up to the last moment objected to the removal of the pulpit. 'You ought not to touch it, Mr. Dean,' he said with great emphasis one morning, when the two were standing before it. 'You don't know what mischief you may do.'

'Mischief? It's not a work of any particular merit, Canon.'

'Don't call me Canon,' said the old man with great asperity, 'that is, for thirty years I've been known as Dr. Ayloff, and I shall be obliged, Mr. Dean, if you would kindly humour me in that matter. And as to the pulpit (which

I've preached from for thirty years, though I don't insist on that), all I'll say is, I *know* you're doing wrong in moving it.'

'But what sense could there be, my dear Doctor, in leaving it where it is, when we're fitting up the rest of the choir in a totally different *style*? What reason could be given – apart from the look of the thing?'

'Reason! Reason!' said old Dr. Ayloff. 'If you young men – if I may say so without any disrespect, Mr. Dean – if you'd only listen to reason a little, and not be always asking for it, we should get on better. But there, I've said my say.'

The old gentleman hobbled off, and as it proved, never entered the Cathedral again.

The season – it was a hot summer – turned sickly on a sudden, Dr. Ayloff was one of the first to go, with some affection of the muscles of the thorax, which took him painfully at night. And at many services the number of choir-men and boys was very thin.

Meanwhile the pulpit had been done away with. In fact, the sounding-board (part of which still exists as a table in a summer-house in the palace garden) was taken down within an hour or two of Dr. Ayloff's protest. The removal of the base – not effected without considerable trouble – disclosed to view, greatly to the exultation of the restoring party, an altar-tomb – the tomb, of course, to which Worby had attracted Lake's attention that same evening.

Much fruitless research was expended in attempts to identify the occupant; from that day to this he has never had a name put to him. The structure had been most carefully boxed in under the pulpit-base, so that such slight ornament as it possessed was not defaced. Only on the north side of it there was what looked like an injury – a gap between two of the slabs composing the side. It might be two or three inches across.

Palmer, the mason, was directed to fill it up in a week's time, when he came to do some other small jobs near that part of the choir.

The season was undoubtedly a very trying one. Whether the church was built on a site that had once been a marsh, as was suggested, or for whatever reason, the residents in its immediate neighbourhood had, many of them, but little enjoyment of the exquisite sunny days and the calm nights of August and September.

To several of the older people – Dr. Ayloff, among others, as we have seen – the summer proved downright fatal, but even among the younger, few escaped either a sojourn in bed for a matter of weeks, or at the least, a brooding sense of oppression, accompanied by hateful nightmares.

Gradually there formulated itself a suspicion – which grew into a conviction – that the alterations in the Cathedral had something to say in the matter. The widow of a former old verger, a pensioner of the Chapter of Southminster, was visited by dreams, which she retailed to her friends, of a shape that slipped out of the little door of the south transept as the dark fell in, and flitted – taking a fresh direction every night – about the Close, disappearing for a while in house after house, and finally emerging again when the night sky was paling.

She could see nothing of it, she said, but that it was a moving form – only she had an impression that when it returned to the church, as it seemed to do in the end of the dream, it turned its head. And then, she could not tell why, but she thought it had red eyes.

Worby remembered hearing the old lady tell this dream at a tea-party in the house of the chapter clerk. Its recurrence might, perhaps, he said, be taken as a symptom of approaching illness. At any rate before the end of September the old lady was in her grave.

The interest excited by the restoration of this great church was not confined to its own county. One day that summer an F.S.A., of some celebrity, visited the place. His business was to write an account of the discoveries that had been made, for the Society of Antiquaries, and his wife, who accompanied him, was to make a series of illustrative drawings for his report.

In the morning she employed herself in making a general sketch of the choir; in the afternoon she devoted herself to details. She first drew the newly-exposed altar-tomb, and when that was finished, she called her husband's attention to a beautiful piece of diaper-ornament on the screen just behind it, which had, like the tomb itself, been completely concealed by the pulpit.

Of course, he said, an illustration of that must be made. So she seated herself on the tomb and began a careful drawing which occupied her till dusk.

Her husband had by this time finished his work of measuring and description, and they agreed that it was time to be getting back to their hotel. 'You may as well brush my skirt, Frank,' said the, lady, 'it must have got covered with dust, I'm sure.'

He obeyed dutifully. But, after a moment, he said, 'I don't know whether you value this dress particularly, my dear, but I'm inclined to think it's seen its best days. There's a great bit of it gone.'

'Gone? Where?' said she.

'I don't know where it's gone, but it's off at the bottom edge behind here.'

She pulled it hastily into sight, and was horrified to find a jagged tear extending some way into the substance of the stuff, very much, she said, as if a dog had rent it away. The dress was, in any case, hopelessly spoilt, to her great vexation, and though they looked everywhere, the missing piece could not be found.

There were many ways, they concluded, in which the injury might have come about, for the choir was full of old bits of woodwork with nails sticking out of them. Finally, they could only suppose that one of these had caused the mischief, and that the workmen, who had been about all day, had carried off the particular piece with the fragment of dress still attached to it.

It was about this time, Worby thought, that his little dog began to wear an anxious expression when the hour for it to be put into the shed in the back yard approached. (For his mother had ordained that it must not sleep in the house.)

One evening, he said, when he was just going to pick it up and carry it out, it looked at him 'like a Christian, and waved its 'and, I was going to say – well, you know 'ow they do carry on sometimes, and the end of it was I put it under my coat, and 'uddled it upstairs – and I'm afraid I as good as deceived my poor mother on the subject. After that the dog acted very artful with 'iding itself under the bed for half-an-hour or more before bedtime came, and we worked it so as my mother never found out what we'd done.'

Of course Worby was glad of its company anyhow, but more particularly when the nuisance that is still remembered in Southminster as 'the crying' set in.

'Night after night,' said Worby, 'that dog seemed to know it was coming – he'd creep out, he would, and snuggle into the bed and cuddle right up to me shivering, and when the crying come he'd be like a wild thing, shoving his head under my arm, and I was fully near as bad.

'Six or seven times we'd hear it, not more, and when he'd dror out his 'ed again I'd know it was over for that night. What was it like, sir? Well, I never heard but one thing that seemed to hit it off.

'I happened to be playing about in the Close, and there was two of the Canons met and said "Good morning" one to another.

'"Sleep well last night?" says one – it was Mr. Henslow that one, and Mr. Lyall was the other.

'"Can't say I did," says Mr. Lyall, "rather too much of Isaiah xxxiv. 14 for me."

'"Xxxiv. 14," says Mr. Henslow, "what's that?"

'"You call yourself a Bible reader!" says Mr. Lyall. (Mr. Henslow, you must know, he was one of what used to be termed Simeon's lot – pretty much what we should call the Evangelical party.) "You go and look it up."

'I wanted to know what he was getting at myself, and so off I ran home and got out my own Bible, and there it was: "the satyr shall cry to his fellow." Well, I thought, is that what we've been listening to these past nights? And I tell you it made me look over my shoulder a time or two.

'Of course I'd asked my father and mother about what it could be before that, but they both said it was most likely cats, but they spoke very short, and I could see they was troubled. My word! That was a noise – 'ungry-like, as if it was calling after someone that wouldn't come. If ever you felt you wanted company, it would be when you was waiting for it to begin again.

'I believe two or three nights there was men put on to watch in different parts of the Close, but they all used to get together in one corner, the nearest they could to the High Street, and nothing came of it.

'Well, the next thing was this. Me and another of the boys – he's in business in the city now as a grocer, like his father before him – we'd gone up in the choir after morning service was over, and we heard old Palmer the mason bellowing to some of his men. So we went up nearer, because we knew he was a rusty old chap and there might be some fun going.

'It appears Palmer 'd told this man to stop up the chink in that old tomb. Well, there was this man keeping on saying he'd done it the best he could, and there was Palmer carrying on like all possessed about it.

'"Call that making a job of it?" he says. "If you had your rights you'd get the sack for this. What do you suppose I pay you your wages for? What do you suppose I'm going to say to the Dean and Chapter when they come round, as come they may do any time, and see where you've been bungling about covering the 'ole place with mess and plaster and Lord knows what?"

"'Well, master, I done the best I could," says the man. "I don't know no more than what you do 'ow it come to fall out this way. I tamped it right in the 'ole," he says, "and how it's fell out," he says, "I never see."

"'Fell out?" says old Palmer, "why it's nowhere near the place. Blowed out, you mean," and he picked up a bit of plaster, and so did I, that was laying up against the screen, three or four feet off, and not dry yet. And old Palmer he looked at it curious-like, and then he turned round on me and he says, "Now then, you boys, have you been up to some of your games here?"

"'No," I says, "I haven't, Mr. Palmer. There's none of us been about here till just this minute."

'And while I was talking the other boy, Evans, he got looking in through the chink, and I heard him draw in his breath, and he came away sharp and up to us, and says he, "I believe there's something in there. I saw something shiny."

"'What! I dare say!" says old Palmer. "Well, I ain't got time to stop about there. You, William, you go off and get some more stuff and make a job of it this time; if not, there'll be trouble in my yard," he says.

'So the man he went off, and Palmer too, and us boys stopped behind, and I says to Evans, "Did you really see anything in there?"

"'Yes," he says, "I did indeed."

'So then I says, "Let's shove something in and stir it up."

'And we tried several of the bits of wood that was laying about, but they were all too big. Then Evans he had a sheet of music he'd brought with him, an anthem or a service, I forget which it was now, and he rolled it up small and shoved it in the chink. Two or three times he did it, and nothing happened.

"'Give it me, boy," I said, and I had a try.

'No, nothing happened. Then, I don't know why I thought of it, I'm sure, but I stooped down just opposite the chink and put my two fingers in my mouth and whistled – you know the way – and at that I seemed to think I heard something stirring, and I says to Evans, "Come away," I says. "I don't like this."

'"Oh, rot," he says, "give me that roll," and he took it and shoved it in. And I don't think ever I see anyone go so pale as he did.

'"I say, Worby," he says, "it's caught, or else someone's got hold of it."

'"Pull it out or leave it," I says. "Come and let's get off."

'So he gave a good pull, and it came away. Leastways most of it did, but the end was gone. Torn off it was, and Evans looked at it for a second and then he gave a sort of a croak and let it drop, and we both made off out of there as quick as ever we could.

'When we got outside Evans says to me, "Did you see the end of that paper?"

'"No," I says, "only it was torn."

'"Yes, it was," he says, "but it was wet too, and black!"

'Well, partly because of the fright we had, and partly because that music was wanted in a day or two, and we knew there'd be a set-out about it with the organist, we didn't say nothing to anyone else, and I suppose the workmen they swept up the bit that was left along with the rest of the rubbish.

'But Evans, if you were to ask him this very day about it, he'd stick to it he saw that paper wet and black at the end where it was torn.'

After that the boys gave the choir a wide berth, so that Worby was not sure what was the result of the mason's renewed mending of the tomb. Only he made out from fragments of conversation dropped by the workmen passing through the choir that some difficulty had been met with, and that the governor – Mr. Palmer to wit – had tried his own hand at the job.

A little later, he happened to see Mr. Palmer himself knocking at the door of the Deanery and being admitted by the butler. A day or so after that, he gathered from a remark his father let fall at breakfast that something a little out of the common was to be done in the Cathedral after morning service on the morrow.

'And I'd just as soon it was today,' his father added. 'I don't see the use of running risks.'

'"Father," I says, "what are you going to do in the Cathedral tomorrow?"

'And he turned on me as savage as I ever see him – he was a wonderful good-tempered man as a general thing, my poor father was. "My lad," he says, "I'll trouble you not to go picking up your elders' and betters' talk – it's not manners and it's not straight. What I'm going to do or not going to do in the Cathedral tomorrow is none of your business, and if I catch sight of you hanging about the place tomorrow after your work's done, I'll send you home with a flea in your ear. Now you mind that."

'Of course I said I was very sorry and that, and equally of course I went off and laid my plans with Evans. We knew there was a stair up in the corner of the transept which you can get up to the triforium, and in them days the door to it was pretty well always open, and even if it wasn't we knew the key usually laid under a bit of matting hard by.

'So we made up our minds we'd be putting away music and that, next morning while the rest of the boys was clearing off, and then slip up the stairs and watch from the triforium if there was any signs of work going on.

'Well, that same night I dropped off asleep as sound as a boy does, and all of a sudden the dog woke me up, coming into the bed, and thought I, now we're going to get it sharp, for he seemed more frightened than usual.

'After about five minutes sure enough came this cry. I can't give you no idea what it was like; and so near too – nearer than I'd heard it yet – and a funny thing, Mr. Lake, you know what a place this Close is for an echo, and particular if you stand this side of it. Well, this crying never made no sign of an echo at all. But, as I said, it was dreadful near this night; and on the top of the start I got with hearing it, I got another fright – for I heard something rustling outside in the passage.

'Now to be sure I thought I was done; but I noticed the dog seemed to perk up a bit, and next there was someone whispered outside the door, and I very near laughed out loud, for I knew it was my father and mother that had got out of bed with the noise.

'"Whatever is it?" says my mother.

'"Hush! I don't know," says my father, excited-like, "don't disturb the boy. I hope he didn't hear nothing."

'So, me knowing they were just outside, it made me bolder, and I slipped out of bed across to my little window – giving on the Close – but the dog he bored right down to the bottom of the bed – and I looked out.

'First go off I couldn't see anything. Then right down in the shadow under a buttress I made out what I shall always say was two spots of red – a dull red it was — nothing like a lamp or a fire, but just so as you could pick 'em out of the black shadow. I hadn't but just sighted 'em when it seemed we wasn't the only people that had been disturbed, because I see a window in a house on the left-hand side become lighted up, and the light moving.

'I just turned my head to make sure of it, and then looked back into the shadow for those two red things, and they were gone, and for all I peered about and stared, there was not a sign more of them.

'Then come my last fright that night – something come against my bare leg – but that was all right: that was my little dog had come out of bed, and prancing about making a great to-do, only holding his tongue, and me seeing he was quite in spirits again, I took him back to bed and we slept the night out!

'Next morning I made out to tell my mother I'd had the dog in my room, and I was surprised, after all she'd said about it before, how quiet she took it. "Did you?" she says. "Well, by good rights you ought to go without your break-fast for doing such a thing behind my back, but I don't know as there's any great harm done, only another time you ask my permission, do you hear?"

'A bit after that I said something to my father about having heard the cats again. "*Cats?*" he says; and he looked over at my poor mother, and she coughed and he says, "Oh! Ah! Yes, cats. I believe I heard 'em myself."

'That was a funny morning altogether: nothing seemed to go right. The organist he stopped in bed, and the minor Canon he forgot it was the 19th day and waited for the *Venite*; and after a bit the deputy he set off playing the chant for evensong, which was a minor; and then the Decani boys were laughing so much they couldn't sing, and when it came to the anthem the solo boy he got took with the giggles, and made out his nose was bleeding, and shoved the book at me what hadn't practised the verse and wasn't much of a singer if I had known it. Well, things was rougher, you see, fifty years ago, and I got a nip from the counter-tenor behind me that I remembered.

'So we got through somehow, and neither the men nor the boys weren't by way of waiting to see whether the Canon in residence – Mr. Henslow it was – would come to the vestries and fine 'em, but I don't believe he did. For one thing I fancy he'd read the wrong lesson for the first time in his life, and knew it.

'Anyhow, Evans and me didn't find no difficulty in slipping up the stairs as I told you, and when we got up we laid ourselves down flat on our stom-achs where we could just stretch our heads out over the old tomb, and we hadn't but just done so when we heard the verger that was then, first shutting the iron porch-gates and locking the south-west door, and then the transept door, so we knew there was something up, and they meant to keep the public out for a bit.

'Next thing was, the Dean and the Canon come in by their door on the north, and then I see my father, and old Palmer, and a couple of their best men, and Palmer stood a talking for a bit with the Dean in the middle of the choir. He had a coil of rope and the men had crows. All of 'em looked a bit nervous.

'So there they stood talking, and at last I heard the Dean say, "Well, I've no time to waste, Palmer. If you think this'll satisfy Southminster people, I'll permit it to be done. But I must say this, that never in the whole course of my life have I heard such arrant nonsense from a practical man as I have from you. Don't you agree with me, Henslow?"

'As far as I could hear Mr. Henslow said something like "Oh well! We're told, aren't we, Mr. Dean, not to judge others?"

'And the Dean he gave a kind of sniff, and walked straight up to the tomb, and took his stand behind it with his back to the screen, and the others they come edging up rather gingerly. Henslow, he stopped on the south side and scratched on his chin, he did.

'Then the Dean spoke up: "Palmer," he says, "which can you do easiest, get the slab off the top, or shift one of the side slabs?"

'Old Palmer and his men they pottered about a bit looking round the edge of the top slab and sounding the sides on the south and east and west and everywhere but the north. Henslow said something about it being better to have a try at the south side, because there was more light and more room to move about in.

'Then my father who'd been watching of them, went round to the north side, and knelt down and felt of the slab by the chink, and he got up and dusted his knees and says to the Dean: "Beg pardon, Mr. Dean, but I think if Mr. Palmer'll try this here slab he'll find it'll come out easy enough. Seems to me one of the men could prise it out with his crow by means of this chink."

'"Ah! Thank you, Worby," says the Dean. "That's a good suggestion. Palmer, let one of your men do that, will you?"

'So the man come round, and put his bar in and bore on it, and just that minute when they were all bending over, and we boys got our heads well over the edge of the triforium, there come a most fearful crash down at the west end of the choir, as if a whole stick of big timber had fallen down a flight of stairs.

'Well, you can't expect me to tell you everything that happened all in a minute. Of course there was a terrible commotion. I heard the slab fall out, and the crowbar on the floor, and I heard the Dean say, "Good God!"

'When I looked down again I saw the Dean tumbled over on the floor, the men was making off down the choir, Henslow was just going to help the Dean up, Palmer was going to stop the men (as he said afterwards) and my father was sitting on the altar step with his face in his hands.

'The Dean he was very cross. "I wish to goodness you'd look where you're coming to, Henslow," he says. "Why you should all take to your heels when a stick of wood tumbles down I cannot imagine." And all Henslow could do, explaining he was right away on the other side of the tomb, would not satisfy him.

'Then Palmer came back and reported there was nothing to account for this noise and nothing seemingly fallen down, and when the Dean finished feeling of himself they gathered round – except my father, he sat where he was – and someone lighted up a bit of candle and they looked into the tomb.

'"Nothing there," says the Dean, "what did I tell you? Stay! Here's something. What's this? A bit of music paper, and a piece of torn stuff – part of a dress it looks like. Both quite modern – no interest whatever. Another time perhaps you'll take the advice of an educated man" – or something like that, and off he went, limping a bit, and out through the north door, only as he went he called back angry to Palmer for leaving the door standing open.

'Palmer called out "Very sorry, sir," but he shrugged his shoulders.

'And Henslow says, "I fancy Mr. Dean's mistaken. I closed the door behind me, but he's a little upset."

'Then Palmer says, "Why, where's Worby?' and they saw him sitting on the step and went up to him. He was recovering himself, it seemed, and wiping his forehead, and Palmer helped him up on to his legs, as I was glad to see.

'They were too far off for me to hear what they said, but my father pointed to the north door in the aisle, and Palmer and Henslow both of them looked very surprised and scared.

'After a bit, my father and Henslow went out of the church, and the others made what haste they could to put the slab back and plaster it in. And about as the clock struck twelve the Cathedral was opened again and us boys made the best of our way home.

'I was in a great taking to know what it was had given my poor father such a turn, and when I got in and found him sitting in his chair taking a glass of spirits, and my mother standing looking anxious at him, I couldn't keep from bursting out and making confession where I'd been.

'But he didn't seem to take on, not in the way of losing his temper. "You was there, was you? Well, did you see it?"

'"I see everything, father," I said, "except when the noise came."

'"Did you see what it was knocked the Dean over?" he says, "that what come out of the monument? You didn't? Well, that's a mercy."

'"Why, what was it, father?" I said.

'"Come, you must have seen it," he says. "*Didn't* you see? A thing like a man, all over hair, and two great eyes to it?"

'Well, that was all I could get out of him that time, and later on he seemed as if he was ashamed of being so frightened, and he used to put me off when I asked him about it.

'But years after, when I was got to be a grown man, we had more talk now and again on the matter, and he always said the same thing. "Black it was," he'd say, "and a mass of hair, and two legs, and the light caught on its eyes."

'Well, that's the tale of that tomb, Mr. Lake. It's one we don't tell to our visitors, and I should be obliged to you not to make any use of it till I'm out of the way. I doubt Mr. Evans'll feel the same as I do, if you ask him.'

This proved to be the case. But over twenty years have passed by, and the grass is growing over both Worby and Evans, so Mr. Lake felt no difficulty about communicating his notes – taken in 1890 – to me.

He accompanied them with a sketch of the tomb and a copy of the short inscription on the metal cross which was affixed at the expense of Dr. Lyall to the centre of the northern side. It was from the Vulgate of Isaiah xxxiv., and consisted merely of the three words—

IBI CUBAVIT LAMIA.

The Diary of Mr. Poynter

THE SALE-ROOM of an old and famous firm of book auctioneers in London is, of course, a great meeting-place for collectors, librarians, dealers. Not only when an auction is in progress, but perhaps even more notably when books that are coming on for sale are upon view.

It was in such a sale-room that the remarkable series of events began which were detailed to me not many months ago by the person whom they principally affected – namely, Mr. James Denton, M.A., F.S.A., etc., etc., some time of Trinity Hall, now, or lately, of Rendcomb Manor in the county of Warwick.

He, on a certain spring day in a recent year, was in London for a few days upon business connected principally with the furnishing of the house which he had just finished building at Rendcomb.

It may be a disappointment to you to learn that Rendcomb Manor was new; that I cannot help. There had, no doubt, been an old house; but it was not remarkable for beauty or interest. Even had it been, neither beauty nor interest would have enabled it to resist the disastrous fire which about a couple of years before the date of my story had razed it to the ground.

I am glad to say that all that was most valuable in it had been saved, and that it was fully insured. So that it was with a comparatively light heart that Mr. Denton was able to face the task of building a new and consider-ably more convenient dwelling for himself and his aunt who constituted his whole *ménage*.

Being in London, with time on his hands, and not far from the sale-room at which I have obscurely hinted, Mr. Denton thought that he would spend an hour there upon the chance of finding, among that portion of the famous Thomas collection of MSS., which he knew to be then on view, something bearing upon the history or topography of his part of Warwickshire.

He turned in accordingly, purchased a catalogue and ascended to the sale-room, where, as usual, the books were disposed in cases and some laid out upon the long tables.

At the shelves, or sitting about at the tables, were figures, many of whom were familiar to him. He exchanged nods and greetings with several, and then settled down to examine his catalogue and note likely items. He had made good progress through about two hundred of the five hundred lots – every now and then rising to take a volume from the shelf and give it a cursory glance – when a hand was laid on his shoulder, and he looked up.

His interrupter was one of those intelligent men with a pointed beard and a flannel shirt, of whom the last quarter of the 19th century was, it seems to me, very prolific.

It is no part of my plan to repeat the whole conversation which ensued between the two. I must content myself with stating that it largely referred to common acquaintances, e.g., to the nephew of Mr. Denton's friend who had recently married and settled in Chelsea, to the sister-in-law of Mr. Denton's friend who had been seriously indisposed, but was now better, and to a piece of china which Mr. Denton's friend had purchased some months before at a price much below its true value.

From which you will rightly infer that the conversation was rather in the nature of a monologue.

In due time, however, the friend bethought himself that Mr. Denton was there for a purpose, and said he, 'What are you looking out for in particular? I don't think there's much in this lot.'

'Why, I thought there might be some Warwickshire collections, but I don't see anything under Warwick in the catalogue.'

'No, apparently not,' said the friend. 'All the same, I believe I noticed something like a Warwickshire diary. What was the name again? Drayton? Potter? Painter – either a P or a D, I feel sure.'

He turned over the leaves quickly. 'Yes, here it is. Poynter. Lot 486. That might interest you. There are the books, I think: out on the table. Some one has been looking at them. Well, I must be getting on. Goodbye – you'll look us up, won't you? Couldn't you come this afternoon? We've got a little music about four. Well, then, when you're next in town.' He went off.

Mr. Denton looked at his watch and found to his confusion that he could spare no more than a moment before retrieving his luggage and going for the train. The moment was just enough to show him that there were four largish volumes of the diary – that it concerned the years about 1710, and that there seemed to be a good many insertions in it of various kinds.

It seemed quite worth while to leave a commission of five and twenty pounds for it, and this he was able to do, for his usual agent entered the room as he was on the point of leaving it.

That evening he rejoined his aunt at their temporary abode, which was a small dower-house not many hundred yards from the Manor.

On the following morning the two resumed a discussion that had now lasted for some weeks as to the equipment of the new house.

Mr. Denton laid before his relative a statement of the results of his visit to town – particulars of carpets, of chairs, of wardrobes, and of bedroom china.

'Yes, dear,' said his aunt, 'but I don't see any chintzes here. Did you go to ——?'

Mr. Denton stamped on the floor (where else, indeed, could he have stamped?). 'Oh dear, oh dear,' he said, 'the one thing I missed. I *am* sorry. The fact is I was on my way there and I happened to be passing Robins's.'

His aunt threw up her hands. 'Robins's! Then the next thing will be another parcel of horrible old books at some outrageous price. I do think, James, when I am taking all this trouble for you, you might contrive to remember the one or two things which I specially begged you to see after.

'It's not as if I was asking it for myself. I don't know whether you think I get any pleasure out of it, but if so I can assure you it's very much the reverse. The thought and worry and trouble I have over it you have no idea of, and *you* have simply to go to the shops and order the things.'

Mr. Denton interposed a moan of penitence. 'Oh, aunt—'

'Yes, that's all very well, dear, and I don't want to speak sharply, but you *must* know how very annoying it is: particularly as it delays the whole of our business for I can't tell how long. Here is Wednesday – the Simpsons come tomorrow, and you can't leave them. Then on Saturday we have friends, as you know, coming for tennis. Yes, indeed, you spoke of asking them yourself, but, of course, I had to write the notes, and it is ridiculous, James, to look like that. We must occasionally be civil to our neighbours – you wouldn't like to have it said we were perfect bears.

'What was I saying? Well, anyhow it comes to this, that it must be Thursday in next week at least, before you can go to town again, and until we have decided upon the chintzes it is impossible to settle upon one single other thing.'

Mr. Denton ventured to suggest that as the paint and wallpapers had been dealt with, this was too severe a view. But this his aunt was not prepared to admit at the moment. Nor, indeed, was there any proposition he could have advanced which she would have found herself able to accept.

However, as the day went on, she receded a little from this position: examined with lessening disfavour the samples and price lists submitted by her nephew, and even in some cases gave a qualified approval to his choice.

As for him, he was naturally somewhat dashed by the consciousness of duty unfulfilled, but more so by the prospect of a lawn-tennis party, which, though an inevitable evil in August, he had thought there was no occasion to fear in May.

But he was to some extent cheered by the arrival on the Friday morning of an intimation that he had secured at the price of £12 10*s.* the four volumes of Poynter's manuscript diary, and still more by the arrival on the next morning of the diary itself.

The necessity of taking Mr. and Mrs. Simpson for a drive in the car on Saturday morning and of attending to his neighbours and guests that afternoon prevented him from doing more than open the parcel until the party had retired to bed on the Saturday night.

It was then that he made certain of the fact, which he had before only suspected, that he had indeed acquired the diary of Mr. William Poynter, Squire of Acrington (about four miles from his own parish) – that same Poynter who was for a time a member of the circle of Oxford antiquaries, the centre of which was Thomas Hearne, and with whom Hearne seems ultimately to have quarrelled – a not uncommon episode in the career of that excellent man.

As is the case with Hearne's own collections, the diary of Poynter contained a good many notes from printed books, descriptions of coins and other antiquities that had been brought to his notice, and drafts of letters on these subjects, besides the chronicle of everyday events.

The description in the sale-catalogue had given Mr. Denton no idea of the amount of interest which seemed to lie in the book, and he sat up reading in the first of the four volumes until a reprehensibly late hour.

On the Sunday morning, after church, his aunt came into the study and was diverted from what she had been going to say to him by the sight of the four brown leather quartos on the table.

'What are these?' she said suspiciously. 'New, aren't they? Oh! Are these the things that made you forget my chintzes? I thought so. Disgusting. What did you give for them, I should like to know? Over Ten Pounds? James, it is really sinful.

'Well, if you have money to throw away on this kind of thing, there *can* be no reason why you should not subscribe – and subscribe handsomely – to my anti-Vivisection League. There is not, indeed, James, and I shall be very seriously annoyed if—.

'Who did you say wrote them? Old Mr. Poynter, of Acrington? Well, of course, there is some interest in getting together old papers about this neighbourhood. But Ten Pounds!'

She picked up one of the volumes – not that which her nephew had been reading – and opened it at random, dashing it to the floor the next instant with a cry of disgust as an earwig fell from between the pages.

Mr. Denton picked it up with a smothered expletive and said, 'Poor book! I think you're rather hard on Mr. Poynter.'

'Was I, my dear? I beg his pardon, but you know I cannot abide those horrid creatures. Let me see if I've done any mischief.'

'No, I think all's well. But look here what you've opened him on.'

'Dear me, yes, to be sure! How very interesting. Do unpin it, James, and let me look at it.'

It was a piece of patterned stuff about the size of the quarto page, to which it was fastened by an old-fashioned pin. James detached it and handed it to his aunt, carefully replacing the pin in the paper.

Now, I do not know exactly what the fabric was, but it had a design printed upon it, which completely fascinated Miss Denton.

She went into raptures over it, held it against the wall, made James do the same, that she might retire to contemplate it from a distance. Then pored over it at close quarters, and ended her examination by expressing in the warmest terms her appreciation of the taste of the ancient Mr. Poynter who had had the happy idea of preserving this sample in his diary.

'It is a most charming pattern,' she said, 'and remarkable too. Look, James, how delightfully the lines ripple. It reminds one of hair, very much, doesn't it. And then these knots of ribbon at intervals. They give just the relief of colour that is wanted. I wonder—'

'I was going to say,' said James with deference, 'I wonder if it would cost much to have it copied for our curtains.'

'Copied? How could you have it copied, James?'

'Well, I don't know the details, but I suppose that is a printed pattern, and that you could have a block cut from it in wood or metal.'

'Now, really, that is a capital idea, James. I am almost inclined to be glad that you were so – that you forgot the chintzes on Monday. At any rate, I'll promise to forgive and forget if you get this *lovely* old thing copied. No one will have anything in the least like it, and mind, James, we won't allow it to be sold.

'Now I *must* go, and I've totally forgotten what it was I came in to say. Never mind, it'll keep.'

After his aunt had gone James Denton devoted a few minutes to examining the pattern more closely than he had yet had a chance of doing.

He was puzzled to think why it should have struck Miss Benton so forcibly. It seemed to him not specially remarkable or pretty. No doubt it was suitable enough for a curtain pattern: it ran in vertical bands, and there was some indication that these were intended to converge at the top. She was right, too, in thinking that these main bands resembled rippling – almost curling – tresses of hair.

Well, the main thing was to find out by means of trade directories, or otherwise, what firm would undertake the reproduction of an old pattern of this kind.

Not to delay the reader over this portion of the story, a list of likely names was made out, and Mr. Denton fixed a day for calling on them, or some of them, with his sample.

The first two visits which he paid were unsuccessful, but there is luck in odd numbers. The firm in Bermondsey which was third on his list was accustomed to handling this line. The evidence they were able to produce justified their being entrusted with the job.

'Our Mr. Cattell' took a fervent personal interest in it.

'It's 'eartrending, isn't it, sir,' he said, 'to picture the quantity of reelly lovely medeevial stuff of this kind that lays well-nigh unnoticed in many of our residential country 'ouses. Much of it in peril, I take it, of being cast aside as so much rubbish.

'What is it Shakespeare says – unconsidered trifles. Ah, I often say he 'as a word for us all, sir. I say Shakespeare, but I'm well aware all don't 'old with me there – I 'ad something of an upset the other day when a gentleman came in – a titled man, too, he was, and I think he told me he'd wrote on the topic, and I 'appened to cite out something about 'Ercules and the painted cloth. Dear me, you never see such a pother.

'But as to this, what you've kindly confided to us, it's a piece of work we shall take a reel enthusiasm in achieving it out to the very best of our ability.

'What man 'as done, as I was observing only a few weeks back to another esteemed client, man can do, and in three to four weeks' time, all being well, we shall 'ope to lay before you evidence to that effect, sir.

'Take the address, Mr. 'Iggins, if you please.'

Such was the general drift of Mr. Cattell's observations on the occasion of his first interview with Mr. Denton.

About a month later, being advised that some samples were ready for his inspection, Mr. Denton met him again, and had, it seems, reason to be satisfied with the faithfulness of the reproduction of the design.

It had been finished off at the top in accordance with the indication I mentioned, so that the vertical bands joined. But something still needed to be done in the way of matching the colour of the original. Mr. Cattell had suggestions of a technical kind to offer, with which I need not trouble you. He had also views as to the general desirability of the pattern which were vaguely adverse.

'You say you don't wish this to be supplied excepting to personal friends equipped with a authorisation from yourself, sir. It shall be done. I quite understand your wish to keep it exclusive – lends it a catchit, does it not, to the suite? What's every man's, it's been said, is no man's.'

'Do you think it would be popular if it were generally obtainable?' asked Mr. Denton.

'I 'ardly think it, sir,' said Cattell, pensively clasping his beard. 'I 'ardly think it. Not popular. It wasn't popular with the man that cut the block, was it, Mr. 'Iggins?'

'Did he find it a difficult job?'

'He'd no call to do so, sir. But the fact is that the artistic temperament – and our men are artists, sir, every man of them – true artists as much as many that the world styles by that term – it's apt to take some strange 'ardly accountable likes or dislikes, and here was an example.

'The twice or thrice that I went to inspect his progress: language I could understand, for that's 'abitual to him, but reel distaste for what I should call a dainty enough thing, I did not, nor am I now able to fathom. It seemed,' said Mr. Cattell, looking narrowly upon Mr. Denton, 'as if the man scented something almost Hevil in the design.'

'Indeed? Did he tell you so? I can't say I see anything sinister in it myself.'

'Neether can I, sir. In fact I said as much. "Come, Gatwick," I said, "what's to do here? What's the reason of your prejudice – for I can call it no more than that?" But, no! No explanation was forthcoming. And I was merely reduced, as I am now, to a shrug of the shoulders, and a *cui bono*. However, here it is,' and with that the technical side of the question came to the front again.

The matching of the colours for the background, the hem, and the knots of ribbon was by far the longest part of the business, and necessitated many sendings to and fro of the original pattern and of new samples. During part of August and September, too, the Dentons were away from the Manor.

So that it was not until October was well in that a sufficient quantity of the stuff had been manufactured to furnish curtains for the three or four bedrooms which were to be fitted up with it.

On the feast of Simon and Jude the aunt and nephew returned from a short visit to find all completed, and their satisfaction at the general effect was great. The new curtains, in particular, agreed to admiration with their surroundings.

When Mr. Denton was dressing for dinner, and took stock of his room, in which there was a large amount of the chintz displayed, he congratulated himself over and over again on the luck which had first made him forget his aunt's commission and had then put into his hands this extremely effective means of remedying his mistake.

The pattern was, as he said at dinner, so restful and yet so far from being dull.

And Miss Denton – who, by the way, had none of the stuff in her own room – was much disposed to agree with him.

At breakfast next morning he was induced to qualify his satisfaction to some extent – but very slightly. 'There is one thing I rather regret,' he said, 'that we allowed them to join up the vertical bands of the pattern at the top. I think it would have been better to leave that alone.'

'Oh?' said his aunt interrogatively.

'Yes. As I was reading in bed last night they kept catching my eye rather. That is, I found myself looking across at them every now and then. There was an effect as if someone kept peeping out between the curtains in one place or another, where there was no edge, and I think that was due to the joining up of the bands at the top. The only other thing that troubled me was the wind.'

'Why, I thought it was a perfectly still night.'

'Perhaps it was only on my side of the house, but there was enough to sway my curtains and rustle them more than I wanted.'

That night a bachelor friend of James Denton's came to stay, and was lodged in a room on the same floor as his host, but at the end of a long passage, halfway down which was a red baize door, put there to cut off the draught and intercept noise.

The party of three had separated. Miss Denton a good first, the two men at about eleven.

James Denton, not yet inclined for bed, sat him down in an armchair and read for a time. Then he dozed, and then he woke, and bethought himself that his brown spaniel, which ordinarily slept in his room, had not come upstairs with him.

Then he thought he was mistaken: for happening to move his hand which hung down over the arm of the chair within a few inches of the floor, he felt on the back of it just the slightest touch of a surface of hair, and stretching it out in that direction he stroked and patted a rounded something. But the feel of it, and still more the fact that instead of a responsive movement, absolute stillness greeted his touch, made him look over the arm.

What he had been touching rose to meet him. It was in the attitude of one that had crept along the floor on its belly, and it was, so far as could be collected, a human figure. But of the face which was now rising to within a few inches of his own no feature was discernible, only hair.

Shapeless as it was, there was about it so horrible an air of menace that as he bounded from his chair and rushed from the room he heard himself moaning with fear: and doubtless he did right to fly.

As he dashed into the baize door that cut the passage in two, and – forgetting that it opened towards him – beat against it with all the force in him, he felt a soft ineffectual tearing at his back which, all the same, seemed to be growing in power, as if the hand, or whatever worse than a hand was there, were becoming more material as the pursuer's rage was more concentrated.

Then he remembered the trick of the door – he got it open – he shut it behind him – he gained his friend's room, and that is all we need know.

It seems curious that, during all the time that had elapsed since the purchase of Poynter's diary, James Denton should not have sought an explanation of the presence of the pattern that had been pinned into it.

Well, he had read the diary through without finding it mentioned, and had concluded that there was nothing to be said. But, on leaving Rendcomb Manor (he did not know whether for good), as he naturally insisted upon doing on the day after experiencing the horror I have tried to put into words, he took the diary with him. And at his seaside lodgings he examined more narrowly the portion whence the pattern had been taken.

What he remembered having suspected about it turned out to be correct. Two or three leaves were pasted together, but written upon, as was patent when they were held up to the light. They yielded easily to steaming, for the paste had lost much of its strength, and they contained something relevant to the pattern.

The entry was made in 1707.

Old Mr. Casbury, of Acrington, told me this day much of young Sir Everard Charlett, whom he remember'd Commoner of University College, and thought was of the same Family as Dr. Arthur Charlett, now master of ye Coll.

This Charlett was a personable young gent., but a loose atheistical companion, and a great Lifter, as they then call'd the hard drinkers, and for what I know do so now. He was noted, and subject to severall censures at different times for his extravagancies: and if the full history of his debaucheries had bin known, no doubt would have been expell'd ye Coll., supposing that no interest had been imploy'd on his behalf, of which Mr. Casbury had some suspicion.

He was a very beautiful person, and constantly wore his own Hair, which was very abundant, from which, and his loose way of living, the cant name for him was Absalom, and he was accustom'd to say that indeed he believ'd he had shortened old David's days, meaning his father, Sir Job Charlett, an old worthy cavalier. Note that Mr. Casbury said that he remembers not the year of Sir Everard Charlett's death, but it was 1692 or 3. He died suddenly in October. [Several lines describing his unpleasant habits and reputed delinquencies are omitted.]

Having seen him in such topping spirits the night before, Mr. Casbury was amaz'd when he learn'd the death. He was found in the town ditch, the hair as was said pluck'd clean off his head. Most bells in Oxford rung out for him, being a nobleman, and he was buried next night in St. Peter's in the East.

But two years after, being to be moved to his country estate by his successor, it was said the coffin, breaking by mischance, proved quite full of Hair: which sounds fabulous, but yet I believe precedents are upon record, as in Dr. Plot's History of Staffordshire.

His chambers being afterwards stripp'd, Mr. Casbury came by part of the hangings of it, which 'twas said this Charlett had design'd expressly for a memorial of his Hair, giving the Fellow that drew it a lock to work by, and the piece which I have fasten'd in here was parcel of the same, which Mr. Casbury gave to me.

He said he believ'd there was a subtlety in the drawing, but had never discover'd it himself, nor much liked to pore upon it.

The money spent upon the curtains might as well have been thrown into the fire, as they were.

Mr. Cattell's comment upon what he heard of the story took the form of a quotation from Shakespeare. You may guess it without difficulty. It began with the words 'There are more things'.

The Residence at Whitminster

DR. ASHTON – Thomas Ashton, Doctor of Divinity – sat in his study, habited in a dressing-gown, and with a silk cap on his shaven head – his wig being for the time taken off and placed on its block on a side table.

He was a man of some fifty-five years, strongly made, of a sanguine complexion, an angry eye, and a long upper lip. Face and eye were lighted up at the moment when I picture him by the level ray of an afternoon sun that shone in upon him through a tall sash window, giving, on the west.

The room into which it shone was also tall, lined with bookcases, and, where the wall showed between them, panelled.

On the table near the doctor's elbow was a green cloth, and upon it what he would have called a silver standish – a tray with inkstands – quill pens, a calf-bound book or two, some papers, a churchwarden pipe and brass tobacco-box, a flask cased in plaited straw, and a liqueur glass.

The year was 1730, the month December, the hour somewhat past three in the afternoon.

I have described in these lines pretty much all that a superficial observer would have noted when he looked into the room. What met Dr. Ashton's eye when he looked out of it, sitting in his leather armchair?

Little more than the tops of the shrubs and fruit-trees of his garden could be seen from that point, but the red-brick wall of it was visible in almost all the length of its western side. In the middle of that was a gate – a double gate of rather elaborate iron scrollwork, which allowed something of a view beyond.

Through it he could see that the ground sloped away almost at once to a bottom, along which a stream must run, and rose steeply from it on the other side, up to a field that was park-like in character, and thickly studded with oaks, now, of course, leafless.

They did not stand so thick together but that some glimpse of sky and horizon could be seen between their stems. The sky was now golden and the horizon, a horizon of distant woods, it seemed, was purple.

But all that Dr. Ashton could find to say, after contemplating this prospect for many minutes, was: 'Abominable!'

A listener would have been aware, immediately upon this, of the sound of footsteps coming somewhat hurriedly in the direction of the study. By the resonance he could have told that they were traversing a much larger room.

Dr. Ashton turned round in his chair as the door opened, and looked expectant. The incomer was a lady – a stout lady in the dress of the time; though I have made some attempt at indicating the doctor's costume, I will not enterprise that of his wife – for it was Mrs. Ashton who now entered.

She had an anxious, even a sorely distracted, look, and it was in a very disturbed voice that she almost whispered to Dr. Ashton, putting her head close to his, 'He's in a very sad way, love, worse, I'm afraid.'

'Tt-tt, is he really?' and he leaned back and looked in her face.

She nodded.

Two solemn bells, high up, and not far away, rang out the half-hour at this moment. Mrs. Ashton started. 'Oh, do you think you can give order that the minster clock be stopped chiming tonight? 'Tis just over his chamber, and will keep him from sleeping, and to sleep is the only chance for him, that's certain.'

'Why, to be sure, if there were need, real need, it could be done, but not upon any light occasion. This Frank, now, do you assure me that his recovery stands upon it?' said Dr. Ashton. His voice was loud and rather hard.

'I do verily believe it,' said his wife.

'Then, if it must be, bid Molly run across to Simpkins and say on my authority that he is to stop the clock chimes at sunset. And – yes – she is after that to say to my lord Saul that I wish to see him presently in this room.'

Mrs. Ashton hurried off.

Before any other visitor enters, it will be well to explain the situation.

Dr. Ashton was the holder, among other preferments, of a prebend in the rich collegiate church of Whitminster, one of the foundations which, though not a cathedral, survived Dissolution and Reformation, and retained its constitution and endowments for a hundred years after the time of which I write.

The great church, the residences of the dean and the two prebendaries, the choir and its appurtenances, were all intact and in working order. A dean who flourished soon after 1500 had been a great builder, and had erected a spacious quadrangle of red brick adjoining the church for the residence of the officials.

Some of these persons were no longer required: their offices had dwindled down to mere titles, borne by clergy or lawyers in the town and neighbourhood. And so the houses that had been meant to accommodate eight or ten people were now shared among three – the dean and the two prebendaries.

Dr. Ashton's included what had been the common parlour and the dining-hall of the whole body. It occupied a whole side of the court, and at one end had a private door into the minster. The other end, as we have seen, looked out over the country.

So much for the house. As for the inmates, Dr. Ashton was a wealthy man and childless, and he had adopted, or rather undertaken to bring up, the orphan son of his wife's sister.

Frank Sydall was the lad's name: he had been a good many months in the house. Then one day came a letter from an Irish peer, the Earl of Kildonan (who had known Dr. Ashton at college), putting it to the doctor whether he would consider taking into his family the Viscount Saul, the Earl's heir, and acting in some sort as his tutor.

Lord Kildonan was shortly to take up a post in the Lisbon Embassy, and the boy was unfit to make the voyage. 'Not that he is sickly,' the Earl wrote, 'though you'll find him whimsical, or of late I've thought him so, and to confirm this, 'twas only today his old nurse came expressly to tell me he was possess'd. But let that pass.

'I'll warrant you can find a spell to make all straight. Your arm was stout enough in old days, and I give you plenary authority to use it as you see fit. The truth is, he has here no boys of his age or quality to consort with, and is given to moping about in our raths and graveyards; and he brings home romances that fright my servants out of their wits. So there are you and your lady forewarned.'

It was perhaps with half an eye open to the possibility of an Irish bishopric (at which another sentence in the Earl's letter seemed to hint) that Dr. Ashton accepted the charge of my Lord Viscount Saul and of the 200 guineas a year that were to come with him.

So he came, one night in September. When he got out of the chaise that brought him, he went first and spoke to the postboy and gave him some money, and patted the neck of his horse.

Whether he made some movement that scared it or not, there was very nearly a nasty accident: for the beast started violently, and the postilion being unready was thrown and lost his fee, as he found afterwards, and the chaise lost some paint on the gateposts, and the wheel went over the man's foot who was taking out the baggage.

When Lord Saul came up the steps into the light of the lamp in the porch to be greeted by Dr. Ashton, he was seen to be a thin youth of, say, sixteen years old, with straight black hair and the pale colouring that is common to such a figure.

He took the accident and commotion calmly enough, and expressed a proper anxiety for the people who had been, or might have been, hurt. His voice was smooth and pleasant, and without any trace, curiously, of an Irish brogue.

Frank Sydall was a younger boy, perhaps of eleven or twelve, but Lord Saul did not for that reject his company. Frank was able to teach him various games he had not known in Ireland, and he was apt at learning them. Apt, too, at his books, though he had had little or no regular teaching at home.

It was not long before he was making a shift to puzzle out the inscriptions on the tombs in the minster, and he would often put a question to the doctor about the old books in the library that required some thought to answer.

It is to be supposed that he made himself very agreeable to the servants, for within ten days of his coming they were almost falling over each other in their efforts to oblige him. At the same time, Mrs. Ashton was rather put to it to find new maidservants; for there were several changes, and some of the families in the town from which she had been accustomed to draw seemed to have no one available. She was forced to go farther afield than was usual.

These generalities I gather from the doctor's notes in his diary and from letters. They are generalities, and we should like, in view of what has to be told, something sharper and more detailed.

We get it in entries which begin late in the year, and, I think, were posted up all together after the final incident. But they cover so few days in all that there is no need to doubt that the writer could remember the course of things accurately.

On a Friday morning it was that a fox, or perhaps a cat, made away with Mrs. Ashton's most prized black cockerel, a bird without a single white feather on its body. Her husband had told her often enough that it would make a suitable sacrifice to Æsculapius. That had discomfited her much, and now she would hardly be consoled.

The boys looked everywhere for traces of it. Lord Saul brought in a few feathers, which seemed to have been partially burnt on the garden rubbish-heap. It was on the same day that Dr. Ashton, looking out of an upper window, saw the two boys playing in the corner of the garden at a game he did not understand.

Frank was looking earnestly at something in the palm of his hand. Saul stood behind him and seemed to be listening. After some minutes he very gently laid his hand on Frank's head, and almost instantly thereupon, Frank suddenly dropped whatever it was that he was holding, clapped his hands to his eyes, and sank down on the grass.

Saul, whose face expressed great anger, hastily picked the object up, of which it could only be seen that it was glittering, put it in his pocket, and turned away, leaving Frank huddled up on the grass.

Dr. Ashton rapped on the window to attract their attention, and Saul looked up as if in alarm, and then springing to Frank, pulled him up by the arm and led him away.

When they came in to dinner, Saul explained that they had been acting a part of the tragedy of Radamistus, in which the heroine reads the future fate of her father's kingdom by means of a glass ball held in her hand, and is overcome by the terrible events she has seen.

During this explanation Frank said nothing, only looked rather bewilderedly at Saul. He must, Mrs. Ashton thought, have contracted a chill from the wet of the grass, for that evening he was certainly feverish and disordered;

and the disorder was of the mind as well as the body, for he seemed to have something he wished to say to Mrs. Ashton, only a press of household affairs prevented her from paying attention to him.

And when she went, according to her habit, to see that the light in the boys' chamber had been taken away, and to bid them good night, he seemed to be sleeping, though his face was unnaturally flushed, to her thinking. Lord Saul, however, was pale and quiet, and smiling in his slumber.

Next morning it happened that Dr. Ashton was occupied in church and other business, and unable to take the boys' lessons. He therefore set them tasks to be written and brought to him. Three times, if not oftener, Frank knocked at the study door, and each time the doctor chanced to be engaged with some visitor, and sent the boy off rather roughly, which he later regretted.

Two clergymen were at dinner this day, and both remarked – being fathers of families – that the lad seemed sickening for a fever, in which they were too near the truth, and it had been better if he had been put to bed forthwith – for a couple of hours later in the afternoon he came running into the house, crying out in a way that was really terrifying, and rushing to Mrs. Ashton, clung about her, begging her to protect him, and saying, 'Keep them off! Keep them off!' without intermission.

And it was now evident that some sickness had taken strong hold of him.

He was therefore got to bed in another chamber from that in which he commonly lay, and the physician brought to him: who pronounced the disorder to be grave and affecting the lad's brain, and prognosticated a fatal end to it if strict quiet were not observed, and those sedative remedies used which he should prescribe.

We are now come by another way to the point we had reached before. The minster clock has been stopped from striking, and Lord Saul is on the threshold of the study.

'What account can you give of this poor lad's state?' was Dr. Ashton's first question.

'Why, sir, little more than you know already, I fancy. I must blame myself, though, for giving him a fright yesterday when we were acting that silly play you saw. I fear I made him take it more to heart than I meant.'

'How so?'

'Well, by telling him foolish tales I had picked up in Ireland of what we call the second sight.'

'*Second* sight! What kind of sight might that be?'

'Why, you know our ignorant people pretend that some are able to foresee what is to come – sometimes in a glass, or in the air, maybe, and at Kildonan we had an old woman that pretended to such a power.

'And I dare say I coloured the matter more highly than I should: but I never dreamed Frank would take it so near as he did.'

'You were wrong, my lord, very wrong, in meddling with such superstitious matters at all, and you should have considered whose house you were in, and how little becoming such actions are to my character and person or to your own.

'But pray how came it that you, acting, as you say, a play, should fall upon any thing that could so alarm Frank?'

'That is what I can hardly tell, sir. He passed all in a moment from rant about battles and lovers and Cleodora and Antigenes to something I could not follow at all, and then dropped down as you saw.'

'Yes. Was that at the moment when you laid your hand on the top of his head?'

Lord Saul gave a quick look at his questioner – quick and spiteful – and for the first time seemed unready with an answer. 'About that time it may have been,' he said. 'I have tried to recollect myself, but I am not sure. There was, at any rate, no significance in what I did then.'

'Ah!' said Dr. Ashton, 'well, my lord, I should do wrong were I not to tell you that this fright of my poor nephew may have very ill consequences to him. The doctor speaks very despondingly of his state.'

Lord Saul pressed his hands together and looked earnestly upon Dr. Ashton.

'I am willing to believe you had no bad intention, as assuredly you could have no reason to bear the poor boy malice. But I cannot wholly free you from blame in the affair.'

As he spoke, the hurrying steps were heard again, and Mrs. Ashton came quickly into the room, carrying a candle, for the evening had by this time closed in.

She was greatly agitated. 'O come!' she cried, 'come directly. I'm sure he is going.'

'Going? Frank? Is it possible? Already?' With some such incoherent words the doctor caught up a book of prayers from the table and ran out after his wife.

Lord Saul stopped for a moment where he was. Molly, the maid, saw him bend over and put both hands to his face. If it were the last words she had to speak, she said afterwards, he was striving to keep back a fit of laughing. Then he went out softly, following the others.

Mrs. Ashton was sadly right in her forecast. I have no inclination to imagine the last scene in detail. What Dr. Ashton records is, or may be taken to be, important to the story.

They asked Frank if he would like to see his companion, Lord Saul, once again. The boy was quite collected, it appears, in these moments.

'No,' he said, 'I do not want to see him. But you should tell him I am afraid he will be very cold.'

'What do you mean, my dear?' said Mrs. Ashton.

'Only that,' said Frank. 'But say to him besides that I am free of them now, but he should take care. And I am sorry about your black cockerel, Aunt Ashton. But he said we must use it so, if we were to see all that could be seen.'

Not many minutes after, he was gone.

Both the Ashtons were grieved, she naturally most. But the doctor, though not an emotional man, felt the pathos of the early death. And, besides, there was the growing suspicion that all had not been told him by Saul, and that there was something here which was out of his beaten track.

When he left the chamber of death, it was to walk across the quadrangle of the residence to the sexton's house. A passing bell, the greatest of the minster bells, must be rung, a grave must be dug in the minster yard, and there was now no need to silence the chiming of the minster clock.

As he came slowly back in the dark, he thought he must see Lord Saul again. That matter of the black cockerel – trifling as it might seem – would have to be cleared up. It might be merely a fancy of the sick boy, but if not, was there not a witch-trial he had read, in which some grim little rite of sacrifice had played a part? Yes, he must see Saul.

I rather guess these thoughts of his than find written authority for them. That there was another interview is certain; certain also that Saul would (or, as he said, could) throw no light on Frank's words: though the message, or some part of it, appeared to affect him horribly. But there is no record of the talk in detail.

It is only said that Saul sat all that evening in the study, and when he bid good night, which he did most reluctantly, asked for the doctor's prayers.

The month of January was near its end when Lord Kildonan, in the Embassy at Lisbon, received a letter that for once gravely disturbed that vain man and neglectful father.

Saul was dead.

The scene at Frank's burial had been very distressing. The day was awful in blackness and wind: the bearers, staggering blindly along under the flapping black pall, found it a hard job, when they emerged from the porch of the minster, to make their way to the grave.

Mrs. Ashton was in her room – women did not then go to their kinsfolk's funerals – but Saul was there, draped in the mourning cloak of the time, and his face was white and fixed as that of one dead, except when, as was noticed three or four times, he suddenly turned his head to the left and looked over his shoulder. It was then alive with a terrible expression of listening fear.

No one saw him go away, and no one could find him that evening.

All night the gale buffeted the high windows of the church, and howled over the upland and roared through the woodland. It was useless to search in the open: no voice of shouting or cry for help could possibly be heard. All that Dr. Ashton could do was to warn the people about the college, and the town constables, and to sit up, on the alert for any news, and this he did.

News came early next morning, brought by the sexton, whose business it was to open the church for early prayers at seven, and who sent the maid rushing upstairs with wild eyes and flying hair to summon her master.

The two men dashed across to the south door of the minster, there to find Lord Saul clinging desperately to the great ring of the door, his head sunk between his shoulders, his stockings in rags, his shoes gone, his legs torn and bloody.

This was what had to be told to Lord Kildonan, and this really ends the first part of the story.

The tomb of Frank Sydall and of the Lord Viscount Saul – only child and heir to William Earl of Kildonan – is one: a stone altar tomb in Whitminster churchyard.

Dr. Ashton lived on for over thirty years in his prebendal house, I do not know how quietly, but without visible disturbance.

His successor preferred a house he already owned in the town, and left that of the senior prebendary vacant. Between them these two men saw the 18th century out and the 19th in; for Mr. Hindes, the successor of Ashton, became prebendary at nine-and-twenty and died at nine-and-eighty.

So that it was not till 1823 or 1824 that anyone succeeded to the post who intended to make the house his home.

The man who did so was Dr. Henry Oldys, whose name may be known to some of my readers as that of the author of a row of volumes labelled *Oldys's Works*, which occupy a place that must be honoured, since it is so rarely touched, upon the shelves of many a substantial library.

Dr. Oldys, his niece, and his servants took some months to transfer furniture and books from his Dorsetshire parsonage to the quadrangle of Whitminster, and to get everything into place. But eventually the work was done, and the house (which, though untenanted, had always been kept sound and weather-tight) woke up, and like Monte Cristo's mansion at Auteuil, lived, sang, and bloomed once more.

On a certain morning in June it looked especially fair, as Dr. Oldys strolled in his garden before breakfast and gazed over the red roof at the minster tower with its four gold vanes, backed by a very blue sky, and very white little clouds.

'Mary,' he said, as he seated himself at the breakfast-table and laid down something hard and shiny on the cloth, 'here's a find which the boy made just now. You'll be sharper than I if you can guess what it's meant for.'

It was a round and perfectly smooth tablet – as much as an inch thick – of what seemed clear glass.

'It is rather attractive, at all events,' said Mary. She was a fair woman, with light hair and large eyes, rather a devotee of literature.

'Yes,' said her uncle, 'I thought you'd be pleased with it. I presume it came from the house. It turned up in the rubbish-heap in the corner.'

'I'm not sure that I do like it, after all,' said Mary, some minutes later.

'Why in the world not, my dear?'

'I don't know, I'm sure. Perhaps it's only fancy.'

'Yes, only fancy and romance, of course. What's that book, now – the name of that book, I mean, that you had your head in all yesterday?'

'*The Talisman*, Uncle. Oh, if this should turn out to be a talisman, how enchanting it would be!'

'Yes, *The Talisman*. Ah, well, you're welcome to it, whatever it is. I must be off about my business. Is all well in the house? Does it suit you? Any complaints from the servants' hall?'

'No, indeed, nothing could be more charming. The only *soupçon* of a complaint besides the lock of the linen closet, which I told you of, is that Mrs. Maple says she cannot get rid of the sawflies out of that room you pass through at the other end of the hall.'

'By the way, are you sure you like your bedroom? It is a long way off from anyone else, you know.'

'Like it? To be sure I do. The farther off from you, my dear, the better. There, don't think it necessary to beat me: accept my apologies.'

'But what are sawflies? Will they eat my coats? If not, they may have the room to themselves for what I care. We are not likely to be using it.'

'No, of course not. Well, what she calls sawflies are those reddish things like a daddy-long-legs, but smaller,[†] and there are a great many of them perching about that room, certainly. I don't like them, but I don't fancy they are mischievous.'

'There seem to be several things you don't like this fine morning,' said her uncle, as he closed the door.

Miss Oldys remained in her chair looking at the tablet, which she was holding in the palm of her hand. The smile that had been on her face faded slowly from it and gave place to an expression of curiosity and almost strained attention.

Her reverie was broken by the entrance of Mrs. Maple, and her invariable opening, 'Oh, Miss, could I speak to you a minute?'

---

† Apparently the ichneumon fly (*Ophion obscurum*), and not the true sawfly, is meant.

A letter from Miss Oldys to a friend in Lichfield, begun a day or two before, is the next source for this story. It is not devoid of traces of the influence of that leader of female thought in her day, Miss Anna Seward, known to some as the Swan of Lichfield.

*My sweetest Emily will be rejoiced to hear that we are at length –
my beloved uncle and myself settled in the house that now calls us
master – nay, master and mistress – as in past ages it has called
so many others. Here we taste a mingling of modern elegance and
hoary antiquity, such as has never ere now graced life for either
of us.*

*The town, small as it is, affords us some reflection, pale indeed,
but veritable, of the sweets of polite intercourse: the adjacent country
numbers amid the occupants of its scattered mansions some whose
polish is annually refreshed by contact with metropolitan splendour,
and others whose robust and homely geniality is, at times, and by
way of contrast, not less cheering and acceptable.*

*Tired of the parlours and drawing-rooms of our friends, we have
ready to hand a refuge from the clash of wits or the small talk of the
day amid the solemn beauties of our venerable minster, whose silver
chimes daily 'knoll us to prayer', and in the shady walks of whose
tranquil graveyard we muse with softened heart, and ever and anon
with moistened eye, upon the memorials of the young, the beautiful,
the aged, the wise, and the good.*

Here there is an abrupt break both in the writing and the style.

*But my dearest Emily, I can no longer write with the care which you
deserve, and in which we both take pleasure. What I have to tell you
is wholly foreign to what has gone before.*

*This morning my uncle brought in to breakfast an object which
had been found in the garden. It was a glass or crystal tablet of this
shape* [a little sketch is given], *which he handed to me, and which,
after he left the room, remained on the table by me.*

I gazed at it, I know not why, for some minutes, till called away by the day's duties; and you will smile incredulously when I say that I seemed to myself to begin to descry reflected in it objects and scenes which were not in the room where I was.

You will not, however, think it strange that after such an experience I took the first opportunity to seclude myself in my room with what I now half-believed to be a talisman of mickle might. I was not disappointed.

I assure you, Emily, by that memory which is dearest to both of us, that what I went through this afternoon transcends the limits of what I had before deemed credible. In brief, what I saw, seated in my bedroom, in the broad daylight of summer, and looking into the crystal depth of that small round tablet, was this.

First, a prospect, strange to me, of an enclosure of rough and hillocky grass, with a grey stone ruin in the midst, and a wall of rough stones about it. In this stood an old, and very ugly, woman in a red cloak and ragged skirt, talking to a boy dressed in the fashion of maybe a hundred years ago. She put something which glittered into his hand, and he something into hers, which I saw to be money, for a single coin fell from her trembling hand into the grass.

The scene passed. I should have remarked, by the way, that on the rough walls of the enclosure I could distinguish bones, and even a skull, lying in a disorderly fashion.

Next, I was looking upon two boys: one the figure of the former vision, the other younger. They were in a plot of garden, walled round, and this garden, in spite of the difference in arrangement, and the small size of the trees, I could clearly recognise as being that upon which I now look from my window.

The boys were engaged in some curious play, it seemed. Something was smouldering on the ground. The elder placed his hands upon it, and then raised them in what I took to be an attitude of prayer. And I saw, and started at seeing, that on them, were deep stains of blood. The sky above was overcast.

The same boy now turned his face towards the wall of the garden, and beckoned with both his raised hands, and as he did so I was conscious that some moving objects were becoming visible over the top of the wall — whether heads or other parts of some animal or human forms I could not tell.

Upon the instant the elder boy turned sharply, seized the arm of the younger (who all this time had been poring over what lay on the ground), and both hurried off. I then saw blood upon the grass, a little pile of bricks, and what I thought were black feathers scattered about.

That scene closed, and the next was so dark that perhaps the full meaning of it escaped me. But what I seemed to see was a form, at first crouching low among trees or bushes that were being threshed by a violent wind, then running very swiftly, and constantly turning a pale face to look behind him, as if he feared a pursuer: and, indeed, pursuers were following hard after him.

Their shapes were but dimly seen, their number — three or four, perhaps — only guessed. I suppose they were on the whole more like dogs than anything else, but dogs such as we have seen they assuredly were not. Could I have closed my eyes to this horror, I would have done so at once, but I was helpless.

The last I saw was the victim darting beneath an arch and clutching at some object to which he clung. And those that were pursuing him overtook him, and I seemed to hear the echo of a cry of despair. It may be that I became unconscious: certainly I had the sensation of awaking to the light of day after an interval of darkness.

Such, in literal truth, Emily, was my vision — I can call it by no other name — of this afternoon. Tell me, have I not been the unwilling witness of some episode of a tragedy connected with this very house?'

The letter is continued next day.

The tale of yesterday was not completed when I laid down my pen. I said nothing of my experiences to my uncle — you know, yourself, how little his robust common sense would be prepared to allow of them, and how in his eyes the specific remedy would be a black draught or a glass of port.

After a silent evening, then – silent, not sullen – I retired to rest. Judge of my terror, when, not yet in bed, I heard what I can only describe as a distant bellow, and knew it for my uncle's voice, though never in my hearing so exerted before.

His sleeping-room is at the farther extremity of this large house, and to gain access to it one must traverse an antique hall some eighty feet long, a lofty panelled chamber, and two unoccupied bedrooms.

In the second of these – a room almost devoid of furniture – I found him, in the dark, his candle lying smashed on the floor. As I ran in, bearing a light, he clasped me in arms that trembled for the first time since I have known him, thanked God, and hurried me out of the room. He would say nothing of what had alarmed him.

'Tomorrow, tomorrow,' was all I could get from him.

A bed was hastily improvised for him in the room next to my own. I doubt if his night was more restful than mine. I could only get to sleep in the small hours, when daylight was already strong, and then my dreams were of the grimmest – particularly one which stamped itself on my brain, and which I must set down on the chance of dispersing the impression it has made.

It was that I came up to my room with a heavy foreboding of evil oppressing me, and went with a hesitation and reluctance I could not explain to my chest of drawers. I opened the top drawer, in which was nothing but ribbons and handkerchiefs, and then the second, where was as little to alarm, and then, O heavens, the third and last: and there was a mass of linen neatly folded, upon which, as I looked with a curiosity that began to be tinged with horror, I perceived a movement in it, and a pink hand was thrust out of the folds and began to grope feebly in the air.

I could bear it no more, and rushed from the room, clapping the door after me, and strove with all my force to lock it. But the key would not turn in the wards, and from within the room came a sound of rustling and bumping, drawing nearer and nearer to the door. Why I did not flee down the stairs I know not. I continued grasping the handle, and mercifully, as the door was plucked from my hand with an irresistible force, I awoke.

You may not think this very alarming, but I assure you it was so to me.

At breakfast today my uncle was very uncommunicative, and I think ashamed of the fright he had given us. But afterwards he inquired of me whether Mr. Spearman was still in town, adding that he thought that was a young man who had some sense left in his head.

I think you know, my dear Emily, that I am not inclined to disagree with him there, and also that I was not unlikely to be able to answer his question. To Mr. Spearman he accordingly went, and I have not seen him since.

I must send this strange budget of news to you now, or it may have to wait over more than one post.

The reader will not be far out if he guesses that Miss Mary and Mr. Spearman made a match of it not very long after this month of June. Mr. Spearman was a young spark, who had a good property in the neighbourhood of Whitminster, and not unfrequently about this time spent a few days at the King's Head, ostensibly on business.

But he must have had some leisure, for his diary is copious, especially for the days of which I am telling the story. It is probable to me that he wrote this episode as fully as he could at the bidding of Miss Mary.

Uncle Oldys (how I hope I may have the right to call him so before long!) called this morning. After throwing out a good many short remarks on indifferent topics, he said, 'I wish, Spearman, you'd listen to an odd story and keep a close tongue about it just for a bit, till I get more light on it.'

'To be sure,' said I, 'you may count on me.'

'I don't know what to make of it,' he said. 'You know my bedroom. It is well away from everyone else's, and I pass through the great hall and two or three other rooms to get to it.'

'Is it at the end next the minster, then?' I asked.

'Yes, it is. Well, now, yesterday morning my Mary told me that the room next before it was infested with some sort of fly that the

housekeeper couldn't get rid of. That may be the explanation, or it may not. What do you think?'

'Why,' said I, 'you've not yet told me what has to be explained.'

'True enough, I don't believe I have; but by the by, what are these sawflies? What's the size of them?'

I began to wonder if he was touched in the head.

'What I call a sawfly,' I said very patiently, 'is a red animal, like a daddy-long-legs, but not so big, perhaps an inch long, perhaps less. It is very hard in the body, and to me' – I was going to say 'particularly offensive' – but he broke in.

'Come, come; an inch or less. That won't do.'

'I can only tell you,' I said, 'what I know. Would it not be better if you told me from first to last what it is that has puzzled you, and then I may be able to give you some kind of an opinion.'

He gazed at me meditatively. 'Perhaps it would,' he said. 'I told Mary only today that I thought you had some vestiges of sense in your head.' (I bowed my acknowledgements.) 'The thing is, I've an odd kind of shyness about talking of it. Nothing of the sort has happened to me before.

'Well, about eleven o'clock last night, or after, I took my candle and set out for my room. I had a book in my other hand – I always read something for a few minutes before I drop off to sleep. A dangerous habit: I don't recommend it, but I know how to manage my light and my bed curtains.

'Now then, first, as I stepped out of my study into the great hall that's next to it, and shut the door, my candle went out. I supposed I had clapped the door behind me too quick, and made a draught, and I was annoyed, for I'd no tinder-box nearer than my bedroom. But I knew my way well enough, and went on.

'The next thing was that my book was struck out of my hand in the dark. If I said twitched out of my hand it would better express the sensation. It fell on the floor. I picked it up, and went on, more annoyed than before, and a little startled.

'But as you know, that hall has many windows without curtains, and in summer nights like these it's easy to see not only where the

furniture is, but whether there's anyone or anything moving: and there was no one – nothing of the kind.

'So on I went through the hall and through the audit chamber next to it, which also has big windows, and then into the bedrooms which lead to my own, where the curtains were drawn, and I had to go slower because of steps here and there.

'It was in the second of those rooms that I nearly got my quietus. The moment I opened the door of it I felt there was something wrong.

'I thought twice, I confess, whether I shouldn't turn back and find another way there is to my room rather than go through that one. Then I was ashamed of myself, and thought what people call better of it, though I don't know about "better" in this case.

'If I was to describe my experience exactly, I should say this: there was a dry, light, rustling sound all over the room as I went in, and then (you remember it was perfectly dark) something seemed to rush at me, and there was – I don't know how to put it – a sensation of long thin arms, or legs, or feelers, all about my face, and neck, and body.

'Very little strength in them, there seemed to be, but, Spearman, I don't think I was ever more horrified or disgusted in all my life, that I remember: and it does take something to put me out.

'I roared out as loud as I could, and flung away my candle at random, and, knowing I was near the window, I tore at the curtain and somehow let in enough light to be able to see something waving which I knew was an insect's leg, by the shape of it: but, Lord, what a size! Why, the beast must have been as tall as I am.

'And now you tell me sawflies are an inch long or less. What do you make of it, Spearman?'

'For goodness' sake finish your story first, I said. 'I never heard anything like it.'

'Oh,' said he, 'there's no more to tell. Mary ran in with a light, and there was nothing there. I didn't tell her what was the matter. I changed my room for last night, and I expect for good.'

'Have you searched this odd room of yours?' I said. 'What do you keep in it?'

'We don't use it,' he answered. 'There's an old press there, and some other furniture.'

'And the press?' said I.

'I don't know. I never saw it opened, but I do know that it's locked.'

'Well, I should have it looked into, and, if you had time, I own to having some curiosity the see the palace myself.'

'I didn't exactly like to ask you, but that's rather what I hoped you'd say. Name your time and I'll take you there.'

'No time like the present,' I said at once, for I saw he would never settle down to anything while this affair was in suspense.

He got up with great alacrity, and looked at me, I am tempted to think, with marked approval. 'Come along,' was all he said, however, and was pretty silent all the way to his house.

My Mary (as he calls her in public, and I in private) was summoned, and we proceeded to the room.

The Doctor had gone so far as to tell her that he had had something of a fright there last night, of what nature he had not yet divulged. But now he pointed out and described, very briefly, the incidents of his progress.

When we were near the important spot, he pulled up, and allowed me to pass on. 'There's the room,' he said. 'Go in, Spearman, and tell us what you find.'

Whatever I might have felt at midnight, noonday I was sure would keep back anything sinister, and I flung the door open with an air and stepped in.

It was a well-lighted room, with its large window on the right, though not, I thought, a very airy one. The principal piece of furniture was the gaunt old press of dark wood. There was, too, a four-post bedstead, a mere skeleton which could hide nothing, and there was a chest of drawers.

On the window-sill and the floor near it were the dead bodies of many hundred sawflies, and one torpid one which I had some satisfaction in killing.

I tried the door of the press, but could not open it. The drawers, too, were locked. Somewhere, I was conscious, there was a faint

rustling sound, but I could not locate it, and when I made my report
to those outside, I said nothing of it. But, I said, clearly the next
thing was to see what was in those locked receptacles.

Uncle Oldys turned to Mary. 'Mrs. Maple,' he said, and Mary
ran off – no one, I am sure, steps like her — and soon came back at
a soberer pace, with an elderly lady of discreet aspect.

'Have you the keys of these things, Mrs. Maple?' said Uncle
Oldys. His simple words let loose a torrent (not violent, but copious)
of speech. Had she been a shade or two higher in the social scale,
Mrs. Maple might have stood as the model for Miss Bates.

'Oh, Doctor, and Miss, and you too, sir,' she said, acknowledging
my presence with a bend, 'them keys! Who was that again that
come when first we took over things in this house – a gentleman in
business it was, and I gave him his luncheon in the small parlour on
account of us not having everything as we should like to see it in the
large one – chicken, and apple-pie, and a glass of madeira – dear,
dear, you'll say I'm running on, Miss Mary; but I only mention it
to bring back my recollection. And there it comes – Gardner, just
the same as it did last week with the artichokes and the text of
the sermon.

'Now that Mr. Gardner, every key I got from him were labelled
to itself, and each and every one was a key of some door or another
in this house, and sometimes two. And when I say door, my meaning
is door of a room, not like such a press as this is. Yes, Miss Mary, I
know full well, and I'm just making it clear to your uncle and you
too, sir.

'But now there was a box which this same gentleman he give over
into my charge, and thinking no harm after he was gone I took the
liberty, knowing it was your uncle's property, to rattle it: and unless
I'm most surprisingly deceived, in that box there was keys, but what
keys, that, Doctor, is known Elsewhere, for open the box, no that I
would not do.'

I wondered that Uncle Oldys remained as quiet as he did under
this address. Mary, I knew, was amused by it, and he probably had
been taught by experience that it was useless to break in upon it.

At any rate he did not, but merely said at the end, 'Have you that box handy, Mrs. Maple? If so, you might bring it here.'

Mrs. Maple pointed her finger at him, either in accusation or in gloomy triumph. 'There,' she said, 'was I to choose out the very words out of your mouth, Doctor, them would be the ones. And if I've took it to my own rebuke one half-a-dozen times, it's been nearer fifty.

'Laid awake I have in my bed, sat down in my chair I have, the same you and Miss Mary gave me the day I was twenty year in your service, and no person could desire a better — yes, Miss Mary, but it is the truth, and well we know who it is would have it different if he could. "All very well," says I to myself, "but pray, when the Doctor calls you to account for that box, what are you going to say?"

'No, Doctor, if you was some masters I've heard of and I was some servants I could name, I should have an easy task before me, but things being, humanly speaking, what they are, the one course open to me is just to say to you that without Miss Mary comes to my room and helps me to my recollection, which her wits may manage what's slipped beyond mine, no such box as that, small though it be, will cross your eyes thus many a day to come.'

'Why, dear Mrs. Maple, why didn't you tell me before that you wanted me to help you to find it?' said my Mary. 'No, never mind telling me why it was: let us come at once and look for it.'

They hastened off together. I could hear Mrs. Maple beginning an explanation which, I doubt not, lasted into the farthest recesses of the housekeeper's department. Uncle Oldys and I were left alone.

'A valuable servant,' he said, nodding towards the door. 'Nothing goes wrong under her: the speeches are seldom over three minutes.'

'How will Miss Oldys manage to make her remember about the box?' I asked.

'Mary? Oh, she'll make her sit down and ask her about her aunt's last illness, or who gave her the china dog on the mantelpiece — something quite off the point. Then, as Maple says, one thing brings up another, and the right one will come round sooner than you could suppose. There! I believe I hear them coming back already.'

*It was indeed so, and Mrs. Maple was hurrying on ahead of
Mary with the box in her outstretched hand, and a beaming face.
'What was it,' she cried as she drew near, 'what was it as I said,
before ever I come out of Dorsetshire to this place? Not that I'm a
Dorset woman myself, nor had need to be. "Safe bind, safe find," and
there it was in the place where I'd put it — what? — two months back,
I dare say.'*

*She handed it to Uncle Oldys, and he and I examined it with
some interest, so that I ceased to pay attention to Mrs. Ann Maple
for the moment, though I know that she went on to expound exactly
where the box had been, and in what way Mary had helped to refresh
her memory on the subject.*

*It was an oldish box, tied with pink tape and sealed, and
on the lid was pasted a label inscribed in old ink,* The Senior
Prebendary's House, Whitminster. *On being opened it was
found to contain two keys of moderate size, and a paper, on which,
in the same hand as the label, was* Keys of the Press and Box of
Drawers standing in the disused Chamber.

Also this: The Effects in this Press and Box are held by
me, and to be held by my successors in the Residence, in
trust for the noble Family of Kildonan, if claim be made by
any survivor of it. I having made all the Enquiry possible
to myself am of the opinion that that noble House is wholly
extinct: the last Earl having been, as is notorious, cast away
at sea, and his only Child and Heire deceas'd in my House
(the Papers as to which melancholy Casualty were by me
repos'd in the same Press in this year of our Lord 1753, 21
March). I am further of opinion that unless grave discomfort
arise, such persons, not being of the Family of Kildonan, as
shall become possess'd of these keys, will be well advised
to leave matters as they are: which opinion I do not express
without weighty and sufficient reason; and am Happy to
have my judgement confirm'd by the other Members of this
College and Church who are conversant with the Events
referr'd to in this Paper.

—Tho. Ashton, *S.T.P., Præb. senr.* Will. Blake, *S.T.P., Decanus.* Hen. Goodman, *S.T.B., Præb. junr.*

'Ah!' *said Uncle Oldys, 'grave discomfort! So he thought there might be something. I suspect it was that young man,' he went on, pointing with the key to the line about the 'only Child and Heire'. 'Eh, Mary? The viscounty of Kildonan was Saul.'*

'How do you know that, Uncle?' *said Mary.*

'Oh, why not? It's all in Debrett — two little fat books. But I meant the tomb by the lime walk. He's there. What's the story, I wonder? Do you know it, Mrs. Maple? And, by the way, look at your sawflies by the window there.'*

Mrs. Maple, thus confronted with two subjects at once, was a little put to it to do justice to both. It was no doubt rash in Uncle Oldys to give her the opportunity. I could only guess that he had some slight hesitation about using the key he held in his hand.

'Oh them flies, how bad they was, Doctor and Miss, this three or four days. And you, too, sir, you wouldn't guess, none of you! And how they come, too!*

'First we took the room in hand, the shutters was up, and had been, I dare say, years upon years, and not a fly to be seen. Then we got the shutter bars down with a deal of trouble and left it so for the day, and next day I sent Susan in with the broom to sweep about, and not two minutes hadn't passed when out she come into the hall like a blind thing, and we had regular to beat them off her. Why, her cap and her hair, you couldn't see the colour of it, I do assure you, and all clustering round her eyes, too.*

'Fortunate enough she's not a girl with fancies, else if it had been me, why only the tickling of the nasty things would have drove me out of my wits. And now there they lay like so many dead things. Well, they was lively enough on the Monday, and now here's Thursday; is it, or no, Friday. Only to come near the door and you'd hear them pattering up against it, and once you opened it, dash at you, they would, as if they'd eat you.*

'I couldn't help thinking to myself, "If you was bats, where should we be this night?" Nor you can't cresh 'em, not like a usual* *kind of a fly. Well, there's something to be thankful for, if we could but learn by it.*

'And then this tomb, too,' she said, hastening on to her second point to elude any chance of interruption, 'of them two poor young lads. I say poor, and yet when I recollect myself, I was at tea with Mrs. Simpkins, the sexton's wife, before you come, Doctor and Miss Mary, and that's a family has been in the place, what? I dare say a hundred years in that very house, and could put their hand on any tomb or yet grave in all the yard and give you name and age.

'And his account of that young man, Mr. Simpkins, I mean to say — well!' She compressed her lips and nodded several times.

'Tell us, Mrs. Maple,' said Mary.

'Go on,' said Uncle Oldys. 'What about him?' said I.

'Never was such a thing seen in this place, not since Queen Mary's times and the Pope and all,' said Mrs. Maple. 'Why, do you know he lived in this very house, him and them that was with him, and for all I can tell in this identical room' (she shifted her feet uneasily on the floor).

'Who was with him? Do you mean the people of the house?' said Uncle Oldys suspiciously.

'Not to call people, Doctor, dear no,' was the answer. 'More what he brought with him from Ireland, I believe it was. No, the people in the house was the last to hear anything of his goings-on. But in the town not a family but knew how he stopped out at night: and them that was with him, why, they were such as would strip the skin from the child in its grave. And a withered heart makes an ugly thin ghost, says Mr. Simpkins.

'But they turned on him at the last, he says, and there's the mark still to be seen on the minster door where they run him down. And that's no more than the truth, for I got him to show it to myself, and that's what he said. A lord he was, with a Bible name of a wicked king, whatever his godfathers could have been thinking of.'

'Saul was the name,' said Uncle Oldys.

'To be sure it was Saul, Doctor, and thank you. And now isn't it King Saul that we read of raising up the dead ghost that was

slumbering in its tomb till he disturbed it, and isn't that a strange thing, this young lord to have such a name, and Mr. Simpkins' grandfather to see him out of his window of a dark night going about from one grave to another in the yard with a candle, and them that was with him following through the grass at his heels.

'And one night him to come right up to old Mr. Simpkins' window that gives on the yard and press his face up against it to find out if there was anyone in the room that could see him. And only just time there was for old Mr. Simpkins to drop down like, quiet, just under the window and hold his breath, and not stir till he heard him stepping away again, and this rustling-like in the grass after him as he went, and then when he looked out of his window in the morning there was treadings in the grass and a dead man's bone.

'Oh, he was a cruel child for certain, but he had to pay in the end, and after.'

'After?' said Uncle Oldys, with a frown.

'Oh yes, Doctor, night after night in old Mr. Simpkins' time, and his son, that's our Mr. Simpkins' father, yes, and our own Mr. Simpkins too. Up against that same window, particular when they've had a fire of a chilly evening, with his face right on the panes, and his hands fluttering out, and his mouth open and shut, open and shut, for a minute or more, and then gone off in the dark yard.

'But open the window at such times, no, that they dare not do, though they could find it in their heart to pity the poor thing, that pinched up with the cold, and seemingly fading away to a nothink as the years passed on. Well, indeed, I believe it is no more than the truth what our Mr. Simpkins says on his own grandfather's word, "A withered heart makes an ugly thin ghost".'

'I dare say,' said Uncle Oldys suddenly — so suddenly that Mrs. Maple stopped short. 'Thank you. Come away, all of you.'

'Why, Uncle,' said Mary, 'are you not going to open the press after all?'

Uncle Oldys blushed, actually blushed. 'My dear,' he said, 'you are at liberty to call me a coward, or applaud me as a prudent man, whichever you please. But I am neither going to open that press nor that chest of drawers myself, nor am I going to hand over the keys to you or to any other person.

'Mrs. Maple, will you kindly see about getting a man or two to move those pieces of furniture into the garret?'

'And when they do it, Mrs. Maple,' said Mary, who seemed to me — I did not then know why — more relieved than disappointed by her uncle's decision, 'I have something that I want put with the rest; only quite a small packet.'

We left that curious room not unwillingly, I think. Uncle Oldys's orders were carried out that same day.

'And so,' [concludes Mr. Spearman] 'Whitminster has a Bluebeard's chamber, and, I am rather inclined to suspect, a Jack-in-the-box, awaiting some future occupant of the residence of the senior prebendary.'

Two Doctors

IT IS A VERY COMMON THING, in my experience, to find papers shut up in old books; but one of the rarest things to come across any such that are at all interesting. Still it does happen, and one should never destroy them unlooked at.

Now it was a practice of mine before the war occasionally to buy old ledgers of which the paper was good, and which possessed a good many blank leaves, and to extract these and use them for my own notes and writings. One such I purchased for a small sum in 1911.

It was tightly clasped, and its boards were warped by having for years been obliged to embrace a number of extraneous sheets. Three-quarters of this inserted matter had lost all vestige of importance for any living human being: one bundle had not. That it belonged to a lawyer is certain, for it is endorsed: *The strangest case I have yet met*, and bears initials, and an address in Gray's Inn. It is only materials for a case, and consists of statements by possible witnesses. The man who would have been the defendant or prisoner seems never to have appeared.

The *dossier* is not complete, but, such as it is, it furnishes a riddle in which the supernatural appears to play a part. You must see what you can make of it.

The following is the setting and the tale as I elicit it.

The scene is Islington in 1718, and the time the month of June: a countrified place, therefore, and a pleasant season.

Dr. Abell was walking in his garden one afternoon waiting for his horse to be brought round that he might set out on his visits for the day. To him entered his confidential servant, Luke Jennett, who had been with him twenty years.

'I said I wished to speak to him, and what I had to say might take some quarter of an hour. He accordingly bade me go into his study, which was a room opening on the terrace path where he was walking, and came in himself and sat down.

'I told him that, much against my will, I must look out for another place. He inquired what was my reason, in consideration I had been so long with him. I said if he would excuse me he would do me a great kindness, because (this appears to have been common form even in 1718) I was one that always liked to have everything pleasant about me.

'As well as I can remember, he said that was his case likewise, but he would wish to know why I should change my mind after so many years, and, says he, "You know there can be no talk of a remembrance of you in my will if you leave my service now." I said I had made my reckoning of that.

'"Then," says he, "you must have some complaint to make, and if I could I would willingly set it right." And at that I told him, not seeing how I could keep it back, the matter of my former affidavit and of the bedstaff in the dispensing-room, and said that a house where such things happened was no place for me.

'At which he, looking very black upon me, said no more, but called me fool, and said he would pay what was owing me in the morning. And so, his horse being waiting, went out. So for that night I lodged with my sister's husband near Battle Bridge and came early next morning to my late master, who then made a great matter that I had not lain in his house and stopped a crown out of my wages owing.

'After that I took service here and there, not for long at a time, and saw no more of him till I came to be Dr. Quinn's man at Dodds Hall in Islington.'

There is one very obscure part in this statement – namely, the reference to the former affidavit and the matter of the bedstaff. The former affidavit is not in the bundle of papers. It is to be feared that it was taken out to be read because of its special oddity, and not put back. Of what nature the story was may be guessed later, but as yet no clue has been put into our hands.

The Rector of Islington, Jonathan Pratt, is the next to step forward. He furnishes particulars of the standing and reputation of Dr. Abell and Dr. Quinn, both of whom lived and practised in his parish.

'It is not to be supposed,' he says, 'that a physician should be a regular attendant at morning and evening prayers, or at the Wednesday lectures, but within the measure of their ability I would say that both these persons fulfilled their obligations as loyal members of the Church of England.

'At the same time (as you desire my private mind) I must say, in the language of the schools, *distinguo*. Dr. A. was to me a source of perplexity, Dr. Q. to my eye a plain, honest believer, not inquiring over closely into points of belief, but squaring his practice to what lights he had.

'The other interested himself in questions to which Providence, as I hold, designs no answer to be given us in this state. He would ask me, for example, what place I believed those beings now to hold in the scheme of creation which by some are thought neither to have stood fast when the rebel angels fell, nor to have joined with them to the full pitch of their transgression.

'As was suitable, my first answer to him was a question: What warrant he had for supposing any such beings to exist? For that there was none in Scripture I took it he was aware. It appeared – for as I am on the subject, the whole tale may be given – that he grounded himself on such passages as that of the satyr which Jerome tells us conversed with Antony; but thought too that some parts of Scripture might be cited in support.

'"And besides," said he, "you know 'tis the universal belief among those that spend their days and nights abroad, and I would add that if your calling took you so continuously as it does me about the country lanes by night, you might not be so surprised as I see you to be by my suggestion."

'You are then of John Milton's mind,' I said, 'and hold that "Millions of spiritual creatures walk the earth | Unseen, both when we wake and when we sleep".'

'"I do not know," he said, "why Milton should take upon himself to say 'unseen'; though to be sure he was blind when he wrote that. But for the rest, why, yes, I think he was in the right."

'"Well," I said, "though not so often as you, I am not seldom called abroad pretty late. But I have no mind of meeting a satyr in our Islington lanes in all the years I have been here. And if you have had the better luck, I am sure the Royal Society would be glad to know of it."

'I am reminded of these trifling expressions because Dr. A. took them so ill, stamping out of the room in a huff with some such word as that these high and dry parsons had no eyes but for a prayer-book or a pint of wine.

'But this was not the only time that our conversation took a remarkable turn. There was an evening when he came in, at first seeming gay and in good spirits, but afterwards as he sat and smoked by the fire falling into a musing way. Out of which to rouse him I said pleasantly that I supposed he had had no meetings of late with his odd friends.

'A question which did effectually arouse him, for he looked most wildly, and as if scared, upon me, and said, "*You* were never there? I did not see you. Who brought you?" And then in a more collected tone, "What was this about a meeting? I believe I must have been in a doze." To which I answered that I was thinking of fauns and centaurs in the dark lane, and not of a witches' Sabbath; but it seemed he took it differently.

'"Well," said he, "I can plead guilty to neither; but I find you very much more of a sceptic than becomes your cloth. If you care to know about the dark lane you might do worse than ask my housekeeper that lived at the other end of it when she was a child."

'"Yes," said I, "and the old women in the almshouse and the children in the kennel. If I were you, I would send to your brother Quinn for a bolus to clear your brain."

'"Damn Quinn," says he. "Talk no more of him: he has embezzled four of my best patients this month. I believe it is that cursed man of his, Jennett, that used to be with me, his tongue is never still – it should be nailed to the pillory if he had his deserts."

'This, I may say, was the only time of his showing me that he had any grudge against either Dr. Quinn or Jennett, and as was my business, I did my best to persuade him he was mistaken in them. Yet it could not be denied that some respectable families in the parish had given him the cold shoulder, and for no reason that they were willing to allege.

'The end was that he said he had not done so ill at Islington but that he could afford to live at ease elsewhere when he chose, and anyhow he bore Dr. Quinn no malice.

'I think I now remember what observation of mine drew him into the train of thought which he next pursued. It was, I believe, my mentioning some juggling tricks which my brother in the East Indies had seen at the court of the Rajah of Mysore.

'"A convenient thing enough," said Dr. Abell to me, "if by some arrangement a man could get the power of communicating motion and energy to inanimate objects."

'"As if the axe should move itself against him that lifts it – something of that kind?"

'"Well, I don't know that that was in my mind so much. But if you could summon such a volume from your shelf or even order it to open at the right page."

'He was sitting by the fire – it was a cold evening – and stretched out his hand that way, and just then the fire-irons, or at least the poker, fell over towards him with a great clatter, and I did not hear what else he said. But I told him that I could not easily conceive of an arrangement, as he called it, of such a kind that would not include as one of its conditions a heavier payment than any Christian would care to make; to which he assented.

'"But," he said, "I have no doubt these bargains can be made very tempting, very persuasive. Still, you would not favour them, eh, Doctor? No, I suppose not."

'This is as much as I know of Dr. Abell's mind, and the feeling between these men. Dr. Quinn, as I said, was a plain, honest creature, and a man to whom I would have gone – indeed I have before now gone to him – for advice on matters of business. He was, however, every now and again, and particularly of late, not exempt from troublesome fancies.

'There was certainly a time when he was so much harassed by his dreams that he could not keep them to himself, but would tell them to his acquaintances and among them to me. I was at supper at his house, and he was not inclined to let me leave him at my usual time.

'"If you go," he said, "there will be nothing for it but I must go to bed and dream of the chrysalis."

'"You might be worse off," said I.

'"I do not think it," he said, and he shook himself like a man who is displeased with the complexion of his thoughts.

'"I only meant," said I, "that a chrysalis is an innocent thing."

'"This one is not," he said, "and I do not care to think of it."

'However, sooner than lose my company he was fain to tell me (for I pressed him) that this was a dream which had come to him several times of late, and even more than once in a night.

'It was to this effect, that he seemed to himself to wake under an extreme compulsion to rise and go out of doors. So he would dress himself and go down to his garden door. By the door there stood a spade which he must take, and go out into the garden, and at a particular place in the shrubbery, somewhat clear, and upon which the moon shone (for there was always in his dream a full moon), he would feel himself forced to dig.

'And after some time the spade would uncover something light-coloured, which he would perceive to be a stuff, linen or woollen, and this he must clear with his hands. It was always the same: of the size of a man and shaped like the chrysalis of a moth, with the folds showing a promise of an opening at one end.

'He could not describe how gladly he would have left all at this stage and run to the house, but he must not escape so easily.

'So with many groans, and knowing only too well what to expect, he parted these folds of stuff, or, as it sometimes seemed to be, membrane, and disclosed a head covered with a smooth pink skin, which breaking as the creature stirred, showed him his own face in a state of death.

'The telling of this so much disturbed him that I was forced out of mere compassion to sit with him the greater part of the night and talk with him upon indifferent subjects.

'He said that upon every recurrence of this dream he woke and found himself, as it were, fighting for his breath.'

Another extract from Luke Jennett's long continuous statement comes in at this point.

'I never told tales of my master, Dr. Abell, to anybody in the neighbourhood. When I was in another service I remember to have spoken to my fellow-servants about the matter of the bedstaff, but I am sure I never said either I or he were the persons concerned, and it met with so little credit that I was affronted and thought best to keep it to myself.

'And when I came back to Islington and found Dr. Abell still there, who I was told had left the parish, I was clear that it behoved me to use great discretion, for indeed I was afraid of the man, and it is certain I was no party to spreading any ill report of him.

'My master, Dr. Quinn, was a very just, honest man, and no maker of mischief. I am sure he never stirred a finger nor said a word by way of inducement to a soul to make them leave going to Dr. Abell and come to him. Nay, he would hardly be persuaded to attend them that came, until he was convinced that if he did not they would send into the town for a physician rather than do as they had hitherto done.

'I believe it may be proved that Dr. Abell came into my master's house more than once. We had a new chambermaid out of Hertfordshire, and she asked me who was the gentleman that was looking after the master, that is Dr. Quinn, when he was out, and seemed so disappointed that he was out.

'She said whoever he was he knew the way of the house well, running at once into the study and then into the dispensing-room, and last into the bedchamber. I made her tell me what he was like, and what she said was suitable enough to Dr. Abell; but besides she told me she saw the same man at church, and someone told her that was the Doctor.

'It was just after this that my master began to have his bad nights, and complained to me and other persons, and in particular what discomfort he suffered from his pillow and bedclothes. He said he must buy some to suit him, and should do his own marketing. And accordingly brought home a parcel which he said was of the right quality, but where he bought it we had then no knowledge, only they were marked in thread with a coronet and a bird.

'The women said they were of a sort not commonly met with and very fine, and my master said they were the comfortablest he ever used, and he slept now both soft and deep. Also the feather pillows were the best sorted and his head would sink into them as if they were a cloud: which I have myself remarked several times when I came to wake him of a morning, his face being almost hid by the pillow closing over it.

'I had never any communication with Dr. Abell after I came back to Islington, but one day when he passed me in the street and asked me whether I was not looking for another service, to which I answered I was very well suited where I was, but he said I was a tickleminded fellow and he doubted not he should soon hear I was on the world again, which indeed proved true.'

Dr. Pratt is next taken up where he left off.

'On the 16th I was called up out of my bed soon after it was light – that is about five – with a message that Dr. Quinn was dead or dying. Making my way to his house I found there was no doubt which was the truth. All the persons in the house except the one that let me in were already in his chamber and standing about his bed, but none touching him.

'He was stretched in the midst of the bed, on his back, without any disorder, and indeed had the appearance of one ready laid out for burial. His hands, I think, were even crossed on his breast. The only thing not usual was that nothing was to be seen of his face, the two ends of the pillow or bolster appearing to be closed quite over it.

'These I immediately pulled apart, at the same time rebuking those present, and especially the man, for not at once coming to the assistance of his master. He, however, only looked at me and shook his head, having evidently no more hope than myself that there was anything but a corpse before us.

'Indeed it was plain to anyone possessed of the least experience that he was not only dead, but had died of suffocation. Nor could it be conceived that his death was accidentally caused by the mere folding of the pillow over his face. How should he not, feeling the oppression, have lifted his hands to put it away? Whereas not a fold of the sheet which was closely gathered about him, as I now observed, was disordered. The next thing was to procure a physician.

'I had bethought me of this on leaving my house, and sent on the messenger who had come to me to Dr. Abell. But I now heard that he was away from home, and the nearest surgeon was got, who, however, could tell no more, at least without opening the body, than we already knew.

'As to any person entering the room with evil purpose (which was the next point to be cleared), it was visible that the bolts of the door were burst from their stanchions, and the stanchions broken away from the door-post by main force. And there was a sufficient body of witness, the smith among them, to testify that this had been done but a few minutes before I came.

'The chamber being, moreover, at the top of the house, the window was neither easy of access nor did it show any sign of an exit made that way, either by marks upon the sill or footprints below upon soft mould.'

The surgeon's evidence forms of course part of the report of the inquest, but since it has nothing but remarks upon the healthy state of the larger organs and the coagulation of blood in various parts of the body, it need not be reproduced.

The verdict was 'Death by the visitation of God'.

Annexed to the other papers is one which I was at first inclined to suppose had made its way among them by mistake. Upon further consideration I think I can divine a reason for its presence.

It relates to the rifling of a mausoleum in Middlesex which stood in a park (now broken up), the property of a noble family which I will not name. The outrage was not that of an ordinary resurrection man. The object, it seemed likely, was theft.

The account is blunt and terrible. I shall not quote it. A dealer in the North of London suffered heavy penalties as a receiver of stolen goods in connection with the affair.

The Uncommon Prayer-book

I

MR. DAVIDSON WAS SPENDING the first week in January alone in a country town. A combination of circumstances had driven him to that drastic course: his nearest relations were enjoying winter sports abroad, and the friends who had been kindly anxious to replace them had an infectious complaint in the house.

Doubtless he might have found someone else to take pity on him. 'But,' he reflected, 'most of them have made up their parties, and after all it is only for three or four days at most that I have to fend for myself, and it will be just as well if I can get a move on with my introduction to the Leventhorp Papers.

'I might use the time by going down as near as I can to Gaulsford and making acquaintance with the neighbourhood. I ought to see the remains of the Leventhorp house, and the tombs in the church.'

The first day after his arrival at the Swan Hotel at Longbridge was so stormy that he got no farther than the tobacconist's. The next, comparatively bright, he used for his visit to Gaulsford, which interested him more than a little, but had no ulterior consequences. The third, which was really a pearl of a day for early January, was too fine to be spent indoors.

He gathered from the landlord that a favourite practice of visitors in the summer was to take a morning train to a couple of stations westward and walk back down the valley of the Tent, through Stanford St. Thomas and Stanford Magdalene, both of which were accounted highly picturesque villages.

He closed with this plan, and we now find him seated in a third-class carriage at 9:45 a.m., on his way to Kingsbourne Junction, and studying the map of the district.

One old man was his only fellow-traveller, a piping old man, who seemed inclined for conversation. So Mr. Davidson, after going through the necessary versicles and responses about the weather, inquired whether he was going far.

'No, sir, not far, not this morning, sir,' said the old man. 'I ain't only goin' so far as what they call Kingsbourne Junction. There isn't but two stations betwixt here and there. Yes, they calls it Kingsbourne Junction.'

'I'm going there, too,' said Mr. Davidson.

'Oh indeed, sir! Do you know that part?'

'No, I'm only going for the sake of taking a walk back to Longbridge, and seeing a bit of the country.'

'Oh indeed, sir! Well, 'tis a beautiful day for a gentleman as enjoys a bit of a walk.'

'Yes, to be sure. Have you got far to go when you get to Kingsbourne?'

'No, sir, I ain't got far to go, once I get to Kingsbourne Junction. I'm agoin' to see my daughter, sir. She live at Brockstone. That's about two mile across the fields from what they call Kingsbourne Junction, that is. You've got that marked down on your map, I expect, sir.'

'I expect I have. Let me see, Brockstone, did you say? Here's Kingsbourne, yes. And which way is Brockstone toward the Stanfords? Ah, I see it: Brockstone Court, in a park. I don't see the village, though.'

'No, sir, you wouldn't see no village of Brockstone. There ain't only the Court and the Chapel at Brockstone.'

'Chapel? Oh yes, that's marked here too. The Chapel – close by the Court, it seems to be. Does it belong to the Court?'

'Yes, sir, that's close up to the Court, only a step. Yes, that belong to the Court. My daughter, you see, sir, she's the keeper's wife now, and she live at the Court and look after things now the family's away.'

'No one living there now, then?'

'No, sir, not for a number of years. The old gentleman he lived there when

I was a lad, and the lady she lived on after him to very near upon ninety years of age. And then she died, and them that have it now, they've got this other place, in Warwickshire I believe it is, and they don't do nothin' about lettin' the Court out. But Colonel Wildman he have the shooting, and young Mr. Clark, he's the agent, he come over once in so many weeks to see to things, and my daughter's husband he's the keeper.'

'And who uses the Chapel? Just the people round about, I suppose.'

'Oh no, no one don't use the Chapel. Why, there ain't no one to go. All the people about, they go to Stanford St. Thomas Church. But my son-in-law he go to Kingsbourne Church now, because the gentleman at Stanford he have this Gregory singin', and my son-in-law he don't like that. He say he can hear the old donkey brayin' any day of the week, and he like something a little cheerful on the Sunday.'

The old man drew his hand across his mouth and laughed. 'That's what my son-in-law say; he say he can hear the old donkey,' etc., *da capo*.

Mr. Davidson also laughed as honestly as he could, thinking meanwhile that Brockstone Court and Chapel would probably be worth including in his walk, for the map showed that from Brockstone he could strike the Tent Valley quite as easily as by following the main Kingsbourne–Longbridge road.

So, when the mirth excited by the remembrance of the son-in-law's *bon mot* had died down, he returned to the charge, and ascertained that both the Court and the Chapel were of the class known as 'old-fashioned places,' and that the old man would be very willing to take him thither, and his daughter would be happy to show him whatever she could.

'But that ain't a lot, sir, not as if the family was livin' there; all the lookin'-glasses is covered up, and the paintin's, and the curtains and carpets folded away. Not but what I dare say she could show you a pair just to look at, because she go over them to see as the morth shouldn't get into 'em.'

'I shan't mind about that, thank you. If she can show me the inside of the Chapel, that's what I'd like best to see.'

'Oh, she can show you that right enough, sir. She have the key of the door, you see, and most weeks she go in and dust about. That's a nice Chapel, that is. My son-in-law he say he'll be bound they didn't have none of this Gregory singin' there. Dear! I can't help but smile when I think of him sayin'

that about th' old donkey. "I can hear him bray," he say, "any day of the week".
And so he can, sir. That's true, anyway.'

The walk across the fields from Kingsbourne to Brockstone was very
pleasant. It lay for the most part on the top of the country, and commanded
wide views over a succession of ridges, plough and pasture, or covered with
dark-blue woods – all ending, more or less abruptly, on the right, in head-
lands that overlooked the wide valley of a great western river.

The last field they crossed was bounded by a close copse, and no sooner
were they in it than the path turned downwards very sharply, and it became
evident that Brockstone was neatly fitted into a sudden and very narrow
valley.

It was not long before they had glimpses of groups of smokeless stone
chimneys, and stone-tiled roofs, close beneath their feet. And not many minutes after that, they were wiping their shoes at the back door of Brockstone
Court, while the keeper's dogs barked very loudly in unseen places, and Mrs.
Porter in quick succession screamed at them to be quiet, greeted her father,
and begged both her visitors to step in.

II

It was not to be expected that Mr. Davidson should escape being taken
through the principal rooms of the Court, in spite of the fact that the house
was entirely out of commission.

Pictures, carpets, curtains, furniture, were all covered up or put away, as
old Mr. Avery had said, and the admiration which our friend was very ready
to bestow had to be lavished on the proportions of the rooms, and on the
one painted ceiling, upon which an artist who had fled from London in the
plague-year had depicted the Triumph of Loyalty and Defeat of Sedition.
In this Mr. Davidson could show an unfeigned interest. The portraits of
Cromwell, Ireton, Bradshaw, Peters, and the rest, writhing in carefully-
devised torments, were evidently the part of the design to which most pains
had been devoted.

'That were the old Lady Sadleir had that paintin' done, same as the one
what put up the Chapel. They say she were the first that went up to London
to dance on Oliver Cromwell's grave.' So said Mr. Avery, and continued

musingly, 'Well, I suppose she got some satisfaction to her mind, but I don't know as I should want to pay the fare to London and back just for that. And my son-in-law, he say the same; he say he don't know as he should have cared to pay all that money only for that.

'I was tellin' the gentleman as we come along in the train, Mary, what your 'Arry says about this Gregory singin' down at Stanford here. We 'ad a bit of a laugh over that, sir, didn't us?'

'Yes, to be sure we did. Ha! Ha!' Once again Mr. Davidson strove to do justice to the pleasantry of the keeper. 'But,' he said, 'if Mrs. Porter can show me the Chapel, I think it should be now, for the days aren't long, and I want to get back to Longbridge before it falls quite dark.'

Even if Brockstone Court has not been illustrated in *Rural Life* (and I think it has not) I do not propose to point out its excellences here, but of the Chapel a word must be said.

It stands about a hundred yards from the house, and has its own little graveyard and trees about it. It is a stone building about seventy feet long, and in the Gothic style, as that style was understood in the middle of the 17th century. On the whole it resembles some of the Oxford college chapels as much as anything, save that it has a distinct chancel, like a parish church, and a fanciful domed bell-turret at the south-west angle.

When the west door was thrown open, Mr. Davidson could not repress an exclamation of pleased surprise at the completeness and richness of the interior. Screen-work, pulpit, seating, and glass – all were of the same period. And as he advanced into the nave and sighted the organ-case with its gold embossed pipes in the western gallery, his cup of satisfaction was filled. The glass in the nave windows was chiefly armorial. In the chancel were figure-subjects, of the kind that may be seen at Abbey Dore, of Lord Scudamore's work.

But this is not an archaeological review.

While Mr. Davidson was still busy examining the remains of the organ (attributed to one of the Dallams, I believe) old Mr. Avery had stumped up into the chancel and was lifting the dust-cloths from the blue velvet cushions of the stall-desks. Evidently it was here that the family sat.

Mr. Davidson heard him say in a rather hushed tone of surprise, 'Why, Mary, here's all the books open agin!'

The reply was in a voice that sounded peevish rather than surprised. 'Tt-tt-tt, well, there, I never!'

Mrs. Porter went over to where her father was standing, and they continued talking in a lower key. Mr. Davidson saw plainly that something not quite in the common run was under discussion, so he came down the gallery stairs and joined them.

There was no sign of disorder in the chancel any more than in the rest of the Chapel, which was beautifully clean. But the eight folio prayer-books on the cushions of the stall-desks were indubitably open.

Mrs. Porter was inclined to be fretful over it. 'Whoever can it be as does it?' she said. 'For there's no key but mine, nor yet door but the one we come in by, and the winders is barred, every one of 'em. I don't like it, father, that I don't.'

'What is it, Mrs. Porter? Anything wrong?' said Mr. Davidson.

'No, sir, nothing reely wrong, only these books. Every time, pretty near, that I come in to do up the place, I shuts 'em and spreads the cloths over 'em to keep off the dust, ever since Mr. Clark spoke about it when I first come.

'And yet there they are again, and always the same page – and as I says, whoever it can be as does it with the door and winders shut. And as I says, it makes anyone feel queer comin' in here alone as I 'ave to do, not as I'm given that way myself, not to be frightened easy, I mean to say. And there's not a rat in the place – not as no rat wouldn't trouble to do a thing like that, do you think, sir?'

'Hardly, I should say, but it sounds very queer. Are they always open at the same place, did you say?'

'Always the same place, sir, one of the psalms it is, and I didn't particular notice it the first time or two, till I see a little red line of printing, and it's always caught my eye since.'

Mr. Davidson walked along the stalls and looked at the open books. Sure enough, they all stood at the same page: Psalm cix., and at the head of it, just between the number and the *Dens laudum*, was a rubric: *For the 25th day of April*.

Without pretending to minute knowledge of the history of the Book of Common Prayer, he knew enough to be sure that this was a very odd and wholly unauthorised addition to its text, and though he remembered that

April 25 is St. Mark's Day, he could not imagine what appropriateness this very savage psalm could have to that festival.

With slight misgivings he ventured to turn over the leaves to examine the title-page, and knowing the need for particular accuracy in these matters, he devoted some ten minutes to making a line-for-line transcript of it. The date was 1653. The printer called himself Anthony Cadman. He turned to the list of Proper Psalms for certain days. Yes, added to it was that same inexplicable entry: *For the 25th day of April: the 109th Psalm.*

An expert would no doubt have thought of many other points to inquire into, but this antiquary, as I have said, was no expert. He took stock, however, of the binding – a handsome one of tooled blue leather, bearing the arms that figured in several of the nave windows in various combinations.

'How often,' he said at last to Mrs. Porter, 'have you found these books lying open like this?'

'Reely I couldn't say, sir, but it's a great many times now. Do you recollect, father, me telling you about it the first time I noticed it?'

'That I do, my dear. You was in a rare taking, and I don't so much wonder at it. That was five year ago I was paying you a visit at Michaelmas time, and you come in at tea-time, and says you, "Father, there's the books layin' open under the cloths agin". And I didn't know what my daughter was speakin' about, you see, sir, and I says, "Books?" just like that, I says. And then it all came out.

'But as Harry says – that's my son-in-law, sir – "whoever it can be," he says, "as does it, because there ain't only the one door, and we keeps the key locked up," he says, "and the winders is barred, every one on 'em. Well," he says, "I lay once I could catch 'em at it they wouldn't do it a second time," he says.

'And no more they wouldn't, I don't believe, sir. Well that was five year ago, and it's been happenin' constant ever since by your account, my dear. Young Mr. Clark he don't seem to think much to it. But then he don't live here, you see, and 'tisn't his business to come and clean up here of a dark afternoon, is it?'

'I suppose you never notice anything else odd when you are at work here, Mrs. Porter?' said Mr. Davidson.

'No, sir, I do not,' said Mrs. Porter, 'and it's a funny thing to me I don't, with the feeling I have as there's someone settin' here – no, it's the other side, just within the screen – and lookin' at me all the time I'm dustin' in the gallery and pews. But I never yet see nothin' worse than myself, as the sayin' goes, and I kindly hope I never may.'

III

In the conversation that followed (there was not much of it), nothing was added to the statement of the case.

Having parted on good terms with Mr. Avery and his daughter, Mr. Davidson addressed himself to his eight-mile walk. The little valley of Brockstone soon led him down into the broader one of the Tent, and on to Stanford St. Thomas, where he found refreshment.

We need not accompany him all the way to Longbridge. But as he was changing his socks before dinner, he suddenly paused and said half-aloud, 'By Jove, that is a rum thing!'

It had not occurred to him before how strange it was that any edition of the prayer-book should have been issued in 1653, seven years before the Restoration, five years before Cromwell's death, and when the use of the book, let alone the printing of it, was penal.

He must have been a bold man who put his name and a date on that title-page. Only, Mr. Davidson reflected, it probably was not his name at all, for the ways of printers in difficult times were devious.

As he was in the front hall of the Swan that evening, making some investigations about trains, a small motor stopped in front of the door, and out of it came a small man in a fur coat, who stood on the steps and gave directions in a rather yapping foreign accent to his chauffeur.

When he came into the hotel, he was seen to be black-haired and pale-faced, with a little pointed beard, and gold pince-nez. Altogether, very neatly turned out.

He went to his room, and Mr. Davidson saw no more of him till dinner-time. As they were the only two dining that night, it was not difficult for the newcomer to find an excuse for falling into talk. He was evidently wishing to make out what brought Mr. Davidson into that neighbourhood at that season.

'Can you tell me how far it is from here to Arlingworth?' was one of his early questions, and it was one which threw some light on his own plans. For Mr. Davidson recollected having seen at the station an advertisement of a sale at Arlingworth Hall, comprising old furniture, pictures and books. This, then, was a London dealer.

'No,' he said, 'I've never been there. I believe it lies out by Kingsbourne – it can't be less than twelve miles. I see there's a sale there shortly.'

The other looked at him inquisitively, and he laughed. 'No,' he said, as if answering a question, 'you needn't be afraid of my competing. I'm leaving this place tomorrow.'

This cleared the air, and the dealer, whose name was Homberger, admitted that he was interested in books, and thought there might be in these old country-house libraries something to repay a journey. 'For,' said he, 'we English have always this marvellous talent for accumulating rarities in the most unexpected places, ain't it?'

And in the course of the evening he was most interesting on the subject of finds made by himself and others. 'I shall take the occasion after this sale to look round the district a bit. Perhaps you could inform me of some likely spots, Mr. Davidson?'

But Davidson, though he had seen some very tempting locked-up bookcases at Brockstone Court, kept his counsel. He did not really like Mr. Homberger.

Next day, as he sat in the train, a little ray of light came to illuminate one of yesterday's puzzles. He happened to take out an almanac-diary that he had bought for the new year, and it occurred to him to look at the remarkable events for April 25.

There it was: *St. Mark. Oliver Cromwell born, 1599.*

That, coupled with the painted ceiling, seemed to explain a good deal. The figure of old Lady Sadleir became more substantial to his imagination, as of one in whom love for Church and King had gradually given place to intense hate of the power that had silenced the one and slaughtered the other.

What curious evil service was that which she and a few like her had been wont to celebrate year by year in that remote valley? And how in the world had she managed to elude authority?

And again, did not this persistent opening of the books agree oddly with the other traits of her portrait known to him? It would be interesting for anyone who chanced to be near Brockstone on the 25th of April to look in at the chapel and see if anything exceptional happened.

When he came to think of it, there seemed to be no reason why he should not be that person himself. He, and if possible, some congenial friend. He resolved that so it should be.

Knowing that he knew really nothing about the printing of prayer-books, he realised that he must make it his business to get the best light on the matter without divulging his reasons.

I may say at once that his search was entirely fruitless. One writer of the early part of the 19th century, a writer of rather windy and rhapsodical chat about books, professed to have heard of a special anti-Cromwellian issue of the prayer-book in the very midst of the Commonwealth period.

But he did not claim to have seen a copy, and no one had believed him. Looking into this matter, Mr. Davidson found that the statement was based on letters from a correspondent who had lived near Longbridge, so he was inclined to think that the Brockstone prayer-books were at the bottom of it, and had excited a momentary interest.

Months went on, and St. Mark's Day came near. Nothing interfered with Mr. Davidson's plans of visiting Brockstone, or with those of the friend whom he had persuaded to go with him, and to whom alone he had confided the puzzle.

The same 9:45 train which had taken him in January took them now to Kingsbourne. The same field-path led them to Brockstone.

But today they stopped more than once to pick a cowslip. The distant woods and ploughed uplands were of another colour, and in the copse there was, as Mrs. Porter said, 'a regular charm of birds. Why you couldn't hardly collect your mind sometimes with it.'

She recognised Mr. Davidson at once, and was very ready to do the honours of the Chapel. The new visitor, Mr. Witham, was as much struck by the completeness of it as Mr. Davidson had been. 'There can't be such another in England,' he said.

'Books open again, Mrs. Porter?' said Davidson, as they walked up to the chancel.

'Dear, yes, I expect so, sir,' said Mrs. Porter, as she drew off the cloths. 'Well, there!' she exclaimed the next moment, 'if they ain't shut! That's the first time ever I've found 'em so.

'But it's not for want of care on my part, I do assure you, gentlemen, if they wasn't, for I felt the cloths the last thing before I shut up last week, when the gentleman had done photografting the heast winder, and every one was shut, and where there was ribbons left, I tied 'em.

'Now I think of it, I don't remember ever to 'ave done that before, and per'aps, whoever it is, it just made the difference to 'em. Well, it only shows, don't it? If at first you don't succeed, try, try, try again.'

Meanwhile the two men had been examining the books, and now Davidson spoke.

'I'm sorry to say I'm afraid there's something wrong here, Mrs. Porter. These are not the same books.'

It would make too long a business to detail all Mrs. Porter's outcries, and the questionings that followed. The upshot was this. Early in January the gentleman had come to see over the Chapel, and thought a great deal of it, and said he must come back in the spring weather and take some photografts.

And only a week ago he had drove up in his motoring car, and a very 'eavy box with the slides in it, and she had locked him in because he said something about a long explosion, and she was afraid of some damage happening. And he says, no, not explosion, but it appeared the lantern what they take the slides with worked very slow.

And so he was in there the best part of an hour and she come and let him out, and he drove off with his box and all and gave her his visiting-card, and oh, dear, dear, to think of such a thing! He must have changed the books and took the old ones away with him in his box.

'What sort of man was he?'

'Oh, dear, he was a small-made gentleman, if you can call him so after the way he've behaved, with black hair, that is if it was hair, and gold eye-glasses, if they was gold.

'Reely, one don't know what to believe. Sometimes I doubt he weren't a reel Englishman at all, and yet he seemed to know the language, and had the name on his visiting-card like anybody else might.'

'Just so. Might we see the card? Yes. T.W. Henderson, and an address somewhere near Bristol.

'Well, Mrs. Porter, it's quite plain this Mr. Henderson, as he calls himself, has walked off with your eight prayer-books and put eight others about the same size in place of them.

'Now listen to me. I suppose you must tell your husband about this, but neither you nor he must say one word about it to anyone else. If you'll give me the address of the agent – Mr. Clark, isn't it? – I will write to him and tell him exactly what has happened, and that it really is no fault of yours.

'But, you understand, we must keep it very quiet. And why? Because this man who has stolen the books will of course try to sell them one at a time – for I may tell you they are worth a good deal of money – and the only way we can bring it home to him is by keeping a sharp look out and saying nothing.'

By dint of repeating the same advice in various forms, they succeeded in impressing Mrs. Porter with the real need for silence, and were forced to make a concession only in the case of Mr. Avery, who was expected on a visit shortly.

'But you may be safe with father, sir,' said Mrs. Porter. 'Father ain't a talkin' man.'

It was not quite Mr. Davidson's experience of him. Still, there were no neighbours at Brockstone, and even Mr. Avery must be aware that gossip with anybody on such a subject would be likely to end in the Porters having to look out for another situation.

A last question was whether Mr. Henderson, so-called, had anyone with him.

'No, sir, not when he come he hadn't. He was working his own motoring car himself, and what luggage he had, let me see: there was his lantern and this box of slides inside the carriage, which I helped him into the Chapel and out of it myself with it, if only I'd knowed!

'And as he drove away under the big yew tree by the monument, I see the long white bundle laying on the top of the coach, what I didn't notice when he drove up. But he set in front, sir, and only the boxes inside behind him. And do you reely think, sir, as his name weren't Henderson at all?

'Oh dear me, what a dreadful thing! Why, fancy what trouble it might bring to a innocent person that might never have set foot in the place but for that!'

They left Mrs. Porter in tears. On the way home there was much discussion as to the best means of keeping watch upon possible sales.

What Henderson/Homberger (for there could be no real doubt of the identity) had done was, obviously, to bring down the requisite number of folio prayer-books – disused copies from college chapels and the like, bought ostensibly for the sake of the bindings, which were superficially like enough to the old ones – and to substitute them at his leisure for the genuine articles.

A week had now passed without any public notice being taken of the theft. He would take a little time himself to find out about the rarity of the books, and would ultimately, no doubt, 'place' them cautiously.

Between them, Davidson and Witham were in a position to know a good deal of what was passing in the book-world, and they could map out the ground pretty completely.

A weak point with them at the moment was that neither of them knew under what other name or names Henderson/Homberger carried on business. But there are ways of solving these problems.

And yet all this planning proved unnecessary.

IV

We are transported to a London office on this same 25th of April. We find there, within closed doors, late in the day, two police inspectors, a commissionaire and a youthful clerk. The two latter, both rather pale and agitated in appearance, are sitting on chairs and being questioned.

'How long do you say you've been in this Mr. Poschwitz's employment? Six months? And what was his business? Attended sales in various parts and brought home parcels of books. Did he keep a shop anywhere? No? Disposed of 'em here and there, and sometimes to private collectors. Right.

'Now then, when did he go out last? Rather better than a week ago? Tell you where he was going? No? Said he was going to start next day from his private residence, and shouldn't be at the office – that's here, eh? – before two days. You was to attend as usual.

'Where is his private residence? Oh, that's the address, Norwood way. I see. Any family? Not in this country?

'Now, then, what account do you give of what's happened since he came back? Came back on the Tuesday, did he? And this is the Saturday. Bring any books? One package. Where is it? In the safe? You got the key? No, to be sure, it's open, of course. How did he seem when he got back – cheerful? Well, but how do you mean – curious? Thought he might be in for an illness. He said that, did he? Odd smell got in his nose, couldn't get rid of it. Told you to let him know who wanted to see him before you let 'em in? That wasn't usual with him?

'Much the same all Wednesday, Thursday, Friday. Out a good deal. Said he was going to the British Museum. Often went there to make inquiries in the way of his business. Walked up and down a lot in the office when he was in.

'Anyone call in on those days? Mostly when he was out. Anyone find him in? Oh, Mr. Collinson? Who's Mr. Collinson? An old customer. Know his address? All right, give it us afterwards.

'Well, now, what about this morning? You left Mr. Poschwitz's here at twelve and went home. Anybody see you? Commissionaire, you did? Remained at home till summoned here. Very well.

'Now, Commissionaire: we have your name – Watkins. eh? Very well, make your statement. Don't go too quick, so as we can get it down.'

'I was on duty 'ere later than usual, Mr. Potwitch 'aving asked me to remain on, and ordered his lunching to be sent in, which come as ordered. I was in the lobby from eleven-thirty on, and see Mr. Bligh [the clerk] leave at about twelve. After that no one come in at all except Mr. Potwitch's lunching come at one o'clock and the man left in five minutes' time.

'Towards the afternoon I became tired of waitin' and I come upstairs to this first floor. The outer door what lead to the orfice stood open, and I come up to the plate-glass door here.

'Mr. Potwitch he was standing behind the table smoking a cigar, and he laid it down on the mantelpiece and felt in his trouser pockets and took out a key and went across to the safe. And I knocked on the glass, thinkin' to see if he wanted me to come and take away his tray, but he didn't take no notice, bein' engaged with the safe door. Then he got it open and stooped down and seemed to be lifting up a package off of the floor of the safe.

'And then, sir, I see what looked to be like a great roll of old shabby white flannel, about four to five feet high, fall for'ards out of the inside of the safe right against Mr. Potwitch's shoulder as he was stooping over.

'And Mr. Porwitch, he raised himself up as it were, resting his hands on the package, and give a exclamation. And I can't hardly expect you should take what I says, but as true as I stand here I see this roll had a kind of a face in the upper end of it, sir. You can't be more surprised than what I was, I can assure you, and I've seen a lot in me time.

'Yes, I can describe it if you wish it, sir. It was very much the same as this wall here in colour [the wall had an earth-coloured distemper] and it had a bit of a band tied round underneath. And the eyes, well they was dry-like, and much as if there was two big spiders' bodies in the holes.

'Hair? No, I don't know as there was much hair to be seen. The flannel-stuff was over the top of the 'ead. I'm very sure it warn't what it should have been. No, I only see it in a flash, but I took it in like a photograft – wish I hadn't.

'Yes, sir, it fell right over on to Mr. Potwitch's shoulder, and this face hid in his neck – yes, sir, about where the injury was – more like a ferret going for a rabbit than anythink else. And he rolled over, and of course I tried to get in at the door. But as you know, sir, it were locked on the inside, and all I could do, I rung up everyone, and the surgeon come, and the police and you gentlemen, and you know as much as what I do.

'If you won't be requirin' me any more today I'd be glad to be getting off home. It's shook me up more than I thought for.'

'Well,' said one of the inspectors, when they were left alone.

And 'Well?' said the other inspector. And, after a pause, 'What's the surgeon's report again? You've got it there. Yes. Effect on the blood like the worst kind of snake-bite. Death almost instantaneous.

'I'm glad of that, for his sake. He was a nasty sight. No case for detaining this man Watkins, anyway. We know all about him. And what about this safe, now? We'd better go over it again. And, by the way, we haven't opened that package he was busy with when he died.'

'Well, handle it careful,' said the other. 'There might be this snake in it, for what you know. Get a light into the corners of the place, too. Well, there's room for a shortish person to stand up in, but what about ventilation?'

'Perhaps,' said the other slowly, as he explored the safe with an electric torch, 'perhaps they didn't require much of that. My word! It strikes warm coming out of that place! Like a vault, it is.

'But here, what's this bank-like of dust all spread out into the room? That must have come there since the door was opened. It would sweep it all away if you moved it – see? Now what do you make of that?'

'Make of it? About as much as I make of anything else in this case. One of London's mysteries this is going to be, by what I can see. And I don't believe a photographer's box full of large-size old-fashioned prayer-books is going to take us much further. For that's just what your package is.'

It was a natural but hasty utterance. The preceding narrative shows that there was, in fact, plenty of material for constructing a case. And when once Messrs. Davidson and Witham had brought their end to Scotland Yard, the join-up was soon made, and the circle completed.

To the relief of Mrs. Porter, the owners of Brockstone decided not to replace the books in the Chapel. They repose, I believe, in a safe-deposit in town.

The police have their own methods of keeping certain matters out of the newspapers. Otherwise it can hardly be supposed that Watkins' evidence about Mr. Poschwitz's death could have failed to furnish a good many head-lines of a startling character to the press.

The Five Jars

BEING MORE OR LESS OF A FAIRY TALE
CONTAINED IN A LETTER TO A YOUNG PERSON

I: The Discovery

My dear Jane,

You remember that you were puzzled when I told you I had heard something from the owls – or if not puzzled (for I know you have some experience of these things), you were at any rate anxious to know exactly how it happened. Perhaps the time has now come for you to be told.

It was really luck, and not any skill of mine, that put me in the way of it; luck, and also being ready to believe more than I could see. I have promised not to put down on paper the name of the wood where it happened: that can keep till we meet; but all the rest I can tell exactly as it came about.

It is a wood with a stream at the edge of it; the water is brown and clear. On the other side of it are flat meadows, and beyond these a hillside quite covered with an oak wood. The stream has alder-trees along it, and is pretty well shaded over; the sun hits it in places and makes flecks of light through the leaves.

The day I am thinking of was a very hot one in early September. I had come across the meadows with some idea of sitting by the stream and reading. The only change in my plans that I made was that instead of sitting down I lay down, and instead of reading I went to sleep.

You know how sometimes – but very, very seldom – you see something in a dream which you are quite sure is real. So it was with me this time. I did not dream any story or see any people; I only dreamt of a plant. In the dream no one told me anything about it. I just saw it growing under a tree: a small bit of the tree root came into the picture, an old gnarled root covered with moss, and with three sorts of eyes in it, round holes trimmed with moss – you know the kind.

The plant was not one I should have thought much about, though certainly it was not one that I knew: it had no flowers or berries, and grew quite squat in the ground; more like a yellow aconite without the flower than anything else. It seemed to consist of a ring of six leaves spread out pretty flat with nine points on each leaf. As I say, I saw this quite clearly, and remembered it because six times nine makes fifty-four, which happens to be a number which I had a particular reason for remembering at that moment.

Well, there was no more in the dream than that: but, such as it was, it fixed itself in my mind like a photograph, and I was sure that if ever I saw that tree root and that plant, I should know them again. And, though I neither saw nor heard anything more of them than I have told you, it was borne in upon my mind that the plant *was* worth finding.

When I woke up I still lay, feeling very lazy, on the grass with my head within a foot or two of the edge of the stream and listened to its noise, until in five or six minutes – whether I began to doze off again or not does not much matter – the water-sound became like words, and said, '*Trickle-up, trickle-up*', an immense number of times.

It pleased me, for though in poetry we hear a deal about babbling brooks, and though I am particularly fond of the noise they make, I never was able before to pretend that I could hear any words.

And when I did finally get up and shake myself awake I thought I would anyhow pay so much attention to what the water said as to stroll up the stream instead of down.

So I did: it took me through the flat meadows, but still along the edge of the wood, and still every now and then I heard the same peculiar noise which sounded like *Trickle-up*.

Not so very long after, I came to a place where another stream ran out of the wood into the one I had been following, and just below the place where the two joined there was – not a bridge, but a pole across, and another pole to serve as a rail, by which you could cross, without trouble.

I did cross, not thinking much about it, but with some idea of looking at this new little stream, which went at a very quick pace and seemed to promise small rapids and waterfalls a little higher up.

Now when I got to the edge of it, there was no mistake: it was saying '*Trickle-up*', or even '*Track-up*', much plainer than the old one. I stepped across it and went a few yards up the old stream. Before the new one joined it, it was saying nothing of the kind. I went back to the new one: it was talking as plain as print.

Of course there were no two words about what must be done now. Here was something quite new, and even if I missed my tea, it had got to be looked into. So I went up the new stream into the wood.

Though I was well on the look-out for unusual things – in particular the plant, which I could not help thinking about – I cannot say there was anything peculiar about the stream or the plants or the insects or the trees (except the words which the water kept saying) so long as I was in the flat part of the wood.

But soon I came to a steepish bank – the land began to slope up suddenly and the rapids and waterfalls of the brook were very gay and interesting. Then, besides *Track-up*, which was now its word always instead of *Trickle*, I heard every now and then *All right*, which was encouraging and exciting. Still, there was nothing out of the way to be seen, look as I might.

The climb up the slope or bank was fairly long. At the top was a kind of terrace, pretty level and with large old trees growing upon it, mainly oaks. Behind there was a further slope up and still more woodland: but that does not matter now.

For the present I was at the end of my wanderings. There was no more stream, and I had found what of all natural things I think pleases me best, a real spring of water quite untouched.

Five or six oaks grew in something like a semicircle, and in the middle of the flat ground in front of them was an almost perfectly round pool, not more than four or five feet across. The bottom of it in the middle was pale sand which was continually rising up in little egg-shaped mounds and falling down again. It was the clearest and strongest spring of the kind I had ever seen, and I could have watched it for hours.

I did sit down by it and watch it for some time without thinking of anything but the luck I had had to find it. But then I began to wonder if it would say anything. Naturally I could not expect it to say '*Track-up*' any more, for here I was at the end of it. So I listened with some curiosity.

It hardly made so much noise as the stream: the pool was deeper. But I thought it must say something, and I put my head down as close as I could to the surface of the water. If I am not mistaken (and as things turned out I am sure I was right) the words were: *Gather gather, pick pick*, or *quick quick*.

Now I had not been thinking about the plant for a little time; but, as you may suppose, this brought it back to my mind and I got up and began to look about at the roots of the old oaks which grew just round the spring. No, none of the roots on this side which faced towards the water were like that which I had seen – still, the feeling was strong upon me that this, if any, was the kind of place, and even the very place, where the plant must be.

So I walked to the back of the trees, being careful to go from right to left, according to the course of the sun.

Well, I was not mistaken. At the back of the middlemost oak-tree there were the roots I had dreamt of with the moss and the holes like eyes, and between them was the plant. I think the only thing which was new to me in the look of it was that it was so extraordinarily *green*. It seemed to have in it all the greenness that was possible or that would be wanted for a whole field of grass.

I had some scruples about touching it. In fact, I actually went back to the spring and listened, to make sure that it was still saying the same thing. Yes, it was: '*Gather gather, pick*'. But there was something else every now and then which I could *not* for the life of me make out at first.

I lay down, put my hand round my ear and held my breath. It might have been *bark tree* or *dark tree* or *cask free*. I got impatient at last and said:

'Well, I'm very sorry, but do what I will I *cannot* make out what you are trying to say.'

Instantly a little spurt of water hit me on the ear, and I heard, as clear as possible, what it was: '*Ask tree.*'

I got up at once. 'I *beg* your pardon,' I said, 'of course. Thank you very much.'

And the water went on saying '*Gather gather, all right, dip dip*'.

After thinking how best to greet it, I went back to the oak, stood in front of it and said (of course baring my head):

'Oak, I humbly desire your good leave to gather the green plant which grows between your roots. If an acorn falls into this my right hand' (which I held out) 'I will count it that you answer yes – and give you thanks.'

The acorn fell straight into the palm of my hand. I said, 'I thank you, Oak: good growth to you. I will lay this your acorn in the place whence I gather the plant.'

Then very carefully I took hold of the stalk of the plant (which was very short, for, as I said, it grew rather flat on the ground) and pulled, and to my surprise it came up as easily as a mushroom. It had a clean round bulb without any rootlets and left a smooth neat hole in the ground, in which, according to promise, I laid the acorn, and covered it in with earth. I think it very likely that it will turn into a second plant.

Then I remembered the last word of the spring and went back to dip the plant in it. I had a shock when I did so, and it was lucky I was holding it firm, for when it touched the water it struggled in my hand like a fish or a newt and almost slipped out.

I dipped it three times and thought I felt it growing smaller in my hand: and indeed when I looked at it I found it had shut up its leaves and curled them in quite close, so that the whole thing was little more than a bulb. As I looked at it I thought the water changed its note and said:

'*That'll do, that'll do.*'

I thought it was time to thank the spring for all it had done for me, though, as you may suppose, I did not yet know in the least what was to be done with the plant, or what use it was going to be.

So I went over and said in the politest words I could how much I was obliged, and if there was anything I had or could do which would be agreeable, how glad I should be. Then I listened carefully, for it seemed by this time quite natural that I should get some sort of answer. It came.

There was a sudden change in the sound, and the water said clearly and rapidly, '*Silver silver silver silver*'.

I felt in my pocket. Luckily I had several shillings, sixpences and half-crowns. I thought the best way was to offer them all, so I put them in the palm of my right hand and held it under the water, open, just over the dancing sand.

For a few seconds the water ran over the silver without doing anything: only the coins seemed to grow very bright and clean. Then one of the shillings was very neatly and smoothly slid off, and then another and a sixpence.

I waited, but no more happened, and the water seemed to draw itself down and away from my hand, and to say '*All right*'. So I got up.

The three coins lay on the bottom of the pool looking brighter than even the newest I have ever seen, and gradually as they lay there they began to appear larger. The shillings looked like half-crowns and the sixpence like a shilling. I thought for a moment that it was because water magnifies, but I soon saw that this could not be the reason, for they went on growing larger, and of course thinner, until they finally spread into a kind of silver film all over the bottom of the pool; and as they did so the water began to take on a musical sound, much like the singing that comes when you wet your finger and draw it round the edge of a finger glass at dessert (which some people's idea of table manners allows them to do).

It was a pretty sight and sound, and I listened and looked for a long time.

But all this time what had become of the plant? Why, when I gave the silver to the spring I had wrapped the plant carefully in a silk handkerchief and put it safe in my breast pocket. I took the handkerchief out now, and for a moment I was afraid the plant was gone; but it was not. It had shrunk to a very small whity-green ball. Now what was to be done with it, or rather what could it do?

It was plain to me that it must have a strange and valuable property or virtue, since I had been put on its track in such a remarkable way. I thought I could not do better than ask the spring.

I said, 'O Spring of water, have I your good leave to ask what I should do with this precious plant to put it to the best use?'

The silver lining of the spring made its words much easier to catch when it said anything – for I should tell you that for the most part now it did not speak, or not in any language that I could understand, but rather sang – and it now said, '*Swallow swallow, drink, swallow*'.

Prompt obedience, dear Jane, has always been my motto, as it is doubtless yours, and I at once laid myself down, drank a mouthful of water from the spring, and put the little bulb in my mouth. It instantly grew soft and slipped down my throat. How prosaic! I have no idea what it tasted like.

And again I addressed the spring: 'Is there anything more for me to do?'

'No no, no no, you'll see, you'll see – good-bye, good-bye,' was the answer which came at once.

Accordingly I once more thanked the spring, wished it clear water, no mud, no tramplings of cattle, and bade it farewell. But, I said, I should hope to visit it again.

Then I turned away and looked about me, wondering whether, now that I had swallowed the mysterious plant, I should see anything different. The only thing I noticed was due, I suppose, not to the plant, but to the spring; but it was odd enough.

All the trees hard by were crowded with little birds of all kinds sitting in rows on the branches as they do on telegraph wires. I have no doubt they were listening to the silver bell in the spring. They were quite still, and did not take any notice when I began to walk away.

I said, you will remember, that the ground I was on was a sort of flat terrace at the top of a steep slope. Now at one end this terrace just went down into the wood, but at the other end there was a little mound or hillock with thick underwood behind it. I felt a curiosity, an inclination, to walk that way: I have very little doubt that the plant was at the bottom of it.

As I walked I looked at the ground, and noticed a curious thing: the roots of the plants and grasses seemed to show more than I was accustomed to see them.

It was not a great way to the hillock. When I got to it I wondered why I had gone, for there was nothing odd about it. Still I stepped on to the top, and then I did see something, namely, a square flat stone just in front of my feet.

I poked at it with my walking-stick, but somehow I did not seem to touch it, nor was there any scraping noise. This was funny. I tried again, and now I saw that my stick was not touching it at all; there was something in between. I felt with my hands, and they met with what seemed like grass and earth, certainly not like stone.

Then I understood. The plant was the one which makes you able to see what is under the ground!

I need not tell you all I thought, or how surprising and delightful it was. The first thing was to get at the flat stone and find out what was underneath it.

Accordingly, what with a knife and what with my fingers, I soon had it uncovered: it was four or five inches under the surface. There were no marks on it; it measured more than a foot each way. I lifted it.

It was the cover of a sort of box with bottom and sides each made of a slab just like the lid. In this box was another, made of some dark metal, which I took to be lead. I pulled it out and found that the lid of the box was all of one piece with the rest, like a sardine tin. Evidently I could not open it there and then. It was rather heavy, but I did not care, and I managed without too much inconvenience to carry it home to the place I was lodging in. Of course I put back the stone neatly and covered it up with earth and grass again.

I was late for tea, but I had found what was better than tea.

II: The First Jar

That night I waited till the moon was up before trying to open the box. I do not well know why, but it seemed the right thing, and I followed my instinct, feeling that it might be the plant that made me think as I did.

I drew up the blind and laid the box on a table near the window, where the moon shone full on it, and waited to see if anything else occurred to me. Suddenly I heard a sort of metallic snap. I went and looked at the box. Nothing appeared on the side nearest to me – but when I turned it round I saw that all along the side which the moon had shone upon there was a line along the metal. I turned another side to the moonlight, and another snap came in two or three minutes. Of course I went on.

When the moon had made a groove on all four sides, I tried the lid. It would not come off yet, so there was nothing to be done but continue the process. Three times I did it: every side I turned to the moon thrice, and when that was done the lid was free. I lifted it, and what did I see in the box? All this writing would be very little use if I did not tell you, so it must be done.

There were five compartments in the box: in each of them was a little jar or vase of glass with a round body, a narrow neck, and spreading out a little at the top. The top of each was covered with a plate of metal and on each plate was a word or two in capital letters.

On the one in the middle there were the words *unge oculos*, the other jars had one word apiece, *aures, linguam, frontem, pectus*.

Now, years ago, I took great pains to learn the Latin language, and on many occasions I have found it *most useful*, whatever you may see to the contrary in the newspaper: but seldom or never have I found it more useful than now.

I saw at once that the words meant *anoint the eyes, the ears, the tongue, the forehead, the chest*. What would be the result of my doing this, of course I knew no more than you: but I was pretty sure that it would not do to try them all at once, and another thing I felt, that it would be better to wait till next day before trying any of them.

It was past midnight now, so I went to bed: but first I locked up the box in a cupboard, for I did not want anyone to see it as yet.

Next day I woke bright and early, looked at my watch, found there was no need to think about getting up yet, and, like a wise creature, went to sleep again. I mention this, not merely by way of being jocose, but because after I went to sleep I had a dream which most likely came from the plant and certainly had to do with the box.

I seemed to see a room, or to be in a room about which I only noticed that the floor was paved with mosaic in a pattern mostly red and white, that there were no pictures on the walls and no fireplace, no sashes or indeed panes in the window, and the moon was shining in very bright.

There was a table and a chest. Then I saw an old man, rather badly shaved and bald, in a Roman dress, white for the most part, with a purple stripe somewhere, and sandals. He looked by no means a wicked or designing old man. I was glad of that.

He opened the chest, took out my box, and placed it carefully on the table in the moonlight. Then he went to a part of the room I could not see, and I heard a sound of water being poured into a metal basin, and he came into sight again, wiping his hands on a white towel.

He opened the box, took out a little silver spoon and one of the jars, took off the lid and dipped the spoon in the jar and touched first his right eye and then his left with it. Then he put the jar and the spoon back, laid the lid on the box and put it back in the chest. After that he went to the window and stood there looking out, and seemed to be very much amused with what he saw. That was all.

'Hints for me,' I remember thinking. 'Perhaps it will be best not to touch the box before the moon is up tonight, and always with washed hands.'

I suppose I woke up immediately, for it was all very fresh in my mind when I did.

It was something of a disappointment to have to put off my experiments till the night came round. But it was all for the best, for letters came by the post which I had to attend to: in fact, I was obliged to go to the town a little way off to see someone and to send telegrams and so on.

I was a little doubtful about the seeing things underground, but I soon found that unless I – so to say – turned on the tap, and specially wished and tried to use the power, it did not interfere with my ordinary seeing. When I did, it seemed to come forward from the back of my eyes, and was stronger than the day before. I could see rabbits in their burrows and followed the roots of one oak-tree very deep down.

Once it threatened to be awkward, when I stooped to pick up a silver coin in the street, and grazed my knuckle against a paving stone, under which, of course, it was.

So much for that. By the way, I had taken a look at the box after breakfast, I found (not very much to my surprise) that the lid was as tight on it as when I found it first.

After dinner that evening I put out the light – the moon being now bright – placed the box on the table, washed my hands, opened it and, shutting my eyes, put my hand on one of the jars at random and took it out. As I had rather expected, I heard a little rattle as I did so, and feeling in the compartment, I found a little, a very little, spoon. All was well.

Now to see which jar chance or the plant had chosen for my first experiment. I took it to the window: it was the one marked *aures* – ears – and the spoon had on the handle a letter A.

I opened the jar. The lid fitted close but not over tightly. I put in the spoon as the old man had done, as near as I could remember. It brought out a very small drop of thick stuff with which I touched first my right ear and then my left. When I had done so I looked at the spoon. It was perfectly dry.

I put it and the jar back, closed the box, locked it up, and, not knowing in the least what to expect, went to the open window and put my head out.

For some little time I heard nothing. That was to be expected, and I was not in the least inclined to distrust the jar. Then I was rewarded: a bat flew by, and I, who have not heard a bat even squeak these twenty years, now heard this one say in a whistling angry tone, 'Would you, would you, *I've* got you – no, drat, drat.'

It was not a very exciting remark, but it was enough to show me that a whole new world (as the books say) was open to me.

This, of course, was only a beginning. There were some plants and flowering shrubs under the window, and though I could see nothing, I began to hear voices – two voices – talking among them. They sounded young: of course they were anyhow very small, but they seemed to belong to young creatures of their kind.

'Hullo, I say, what have you got there? Do let's look; you might as well.'

Then a pause – another voice: 'I believe it's a bad one.'

Number one: 'Taste it.'

Number two, after another pause, with a slight sound (very diminutive) of spitting: 'Heugh! Bad! I should rather think it was. Maggot!'

Number one (after laughing rather longer than I thought kind): 'Look here – don't chuck it away – let's give it to the old man. Here – shove the piece in again and rub it over – here he is!' (Very demurely): 'O sir, we've got such a nice-looking—' (*I could not catch what it was*) 'here; we thought you might perhaps like it, sir. Would you, sir? . . . Oh no, thank you, sir, we've had plenty, sir, but this was the biggest we found.'

A third voice said something; it was a deeper one and less easy to hear.

Number two: 'Bitten, sir? Oh no, I don't think so. Do you ——?' (*a name which I did not make out*).

Number one: 'Why, how could it be?'

Number three again – angry, I thought.

Number two (rather anxiously): 'But, sir, really, sir, I don't much like

367

them ... Must I really, sir? ... O *sir*, it's got a maggot in it, and I believe they're poison.' (*Smack, smack, smack, smack.*)

Two voices, very lamentable: 'O *sir*, sir, please sir!'

A considerable pause, and sniffing. Then *Number two*, in a broken voice: 'You silly fool, why did you go laughing like that right under his snout? You might have known he'd cog it.' ('Cog.' I had not heard the word since 1876.) 'There'll be an awful row tomorrow. Look here, I shall go to bed.'

The voices died away; I thought *Number one* seemed to be apologising.

That was all I heard *that* night. After eleven o'clock things seemed to get very still, and I began to feel just a little apprehensive lest something of a less innocent kind should come along.

So I went to bed.

III: The Second Jar

Next day, I must say, was very amusing. I spent the whole of it in the fields just strolling about and sitting down, as the fancy took me, listening to what went on in the trees and hedges.

I will not write down yet the kind of thing I heard, for it was only the beginning. I had not yet found out the way of using the new power to the very best advantage. I felt the want of being able to put in a remark or a question of my own every now and then. But I was pretty sure that the jar which had *linguam* on it would manage that.

Very nearly all the talking I heard was done by the birds and animals – especially the birds; but perhaps half a dozen times, as I sat under a tree or walked along the road, I was aware of voices which sounded exactly like those of people (some grown-up and some children) passing by or coming towards me and talking to each other as they went along.

Needless to say, there was nothing to be *seen*: no movement of the grass and no track on the dusty road, even when I could tell exactly where the people who owned the voices must be. It interested me more than anything else to guess what sort of creatures they were, and I determined that the next jar I tried should be the Eye one.

Once, I must tell you, I ventured to say 'Good afternoon' when I heard a couple of these voices within a yard of me. I think the owners must nearly have had a fit. They stopped dead: one of them gave a sort of cry of surprise, and then, I believe, they ran or flew away. I felt a little breath of wind on my face, and heard no more.

It wasn't (as I know now) that they couldn't see me: but they felt much as you would if a tree or a cow were to say 'Good afternoon' to you.

When I was at supper that evening, the cat came in, as she usually did, to see what was going. I had always been accustomed to think that cats talk when they mew, dogs when they bark, and so on. It is not so at all.

Their talking is almost all done (except when they are in a great state of mind) in a tone which you cannot possibly hear without help. Mewing is for the most part only shouting without saying any words. Purring is, as we often say, singing.

Well, this cat was an ordinary nice creature, tabby, and in she came, and sat watching me while I had soup. To all appearance she was as innocent as a lamb – but no matter for that. What she was saying was something of this kind:

'Get on with it, do: shove it down, lap it up! Who cares about soup? Get to business. I know there's fish coming.'

When the fish actually came, there was a great deal of good feeling shown at first. 'Oh, *how* much we have to be thankful for, all of us, have we not? Fish, fish: what a thought! Dear, kind, generous people all around us, all striving to supply us with what is best and pleasantest for us.'

Then there was a silence for a short time, then in a somewhat different tone I heard: 'Ah dear! The longer I live, the wiser I find it is not to expect too much consideration from others! Self-love! How few, how terribly few, are really free from it! The nature that knows how to take a hint, how rare it is!'

Another short silence, and then: 'There you go – another great bit. I wonder you don't choke or burst! Disgusting! A good scratch all down your horrible fat cheek is what you want, and I know some cats that would give it you. No more notion how to behave than a cockroach.'

About this time I rang the bell and the fish was taken away. The cat went too, circling round the maid with trusting and childlike glances, and I heard her saying in the former tone:

'Well, I daresay after all there are *some* kind hearts in the world, some that can feel for a poor weary creature, and know what a deal of strength and nourishment even the least bit of fish can give—' And I lost the rest.

When the time came and the box was open once more, I duly anointed my eyes and went to the window. I knew something of what I might expect to see, but I had not realised at all how much of it there would be.

In the first place there were a great many buildings, in fact a regular village, all about the little lawn on which my window looked. They were, of course, not big; perhaps three feet high was the largest size. The roofs seemed to be of tiles, the walls were white, the windows were brightly lighted, and I could see people moving about inside.

But there were plenty of people outside, too – people about six inches high – walking about, standing about, talking, running, playing some game which might have been hockey. These were on levelled spaces, for the grass, neatly kept as it was, would have come half-way up their legs; and there were some driving along smooth tracks in carriages drawn by horses of the right size, which were really the most charming little animals I ever saw.

You may suppose that I should not soon have got tired of watching them and listening to the little treble buzz of voices that went on, but I was interrupted.

Just in front of me I heard what I can only call a snigger. I looked down, and saw four heads supported by four pairs of elbows leaning on the window-sill and looking up at me. They belonged to four boys who were standing on the twigs of a bush that grew up against the wall, and who seemed to be very much amused. Every now and again one of them nudged another and pointed towards me; and then, for some unexplained reason, they sniggered again. I felt my ears growing warm and red.

'Well, young gentlemen,' I said, 'you seem to be enjoying yourselves.'

No answer.

'I appear to be so fortunate as to afford you some gratification,' I went on, in my sarcastic manner. 'Perhaps you would do me the honour of stepping into my poor apartment?'

Again no answer, but more undisguised amusement. I was thinking out a really withering remark, when one of them said:

'Do look at his nose. I wonder if they know how ridiculous they are. I *should* like to talk to one of them for five minutes.'

'Well,' I said, 'that can be managed very easily, and I assure you I should be equally glad of the opportunity. *My* remarks would deal with the subject of good manners.'

Another one spoke this time, but did not answer me. 'Oh, I don't know,' he said, 'I expect they're pretty stupid. They look it – at least this one does.'

'Can they talk?' said the third. 'I've never heard 'em.'

'No, but you can see them moving their jaws and mouths and things. This one did just now.'

I saw how it was now, and, becoming cooler, I recognised that these youths were behaving very much as I might have done myself in the presence of someone who I was sure could neither see nor hear me. I even smiled. One of them pointed at me at once:

'Thought of a joke, I s'pose. Don't keep it all to yourself, old chap.'

At this moment the fourth, who had not said anything so far, but seemed to have been listening, piped up: 'I say! I believe I know what it is that makes that hammering noise: it's something he has got in his clothes.'

I could not resist this. 'Right again,' I said; 'it's my watch, and you're very welcome to look at it.' And I took it out and put it on the window-sill.

An awful horror and surprise came into their faces. In a second they had dived down like so many ducks. In another second I saw them walking across the grass, and each of them threw his arms round the waist or the neck of one of the elder people who were walking about among the houses. The person so attacked pulled himself up and listened attentively to what the boy was saying. The particular one I was watching looked towards my window and then burst out laughing, slapped the boy on the back, and resumed his walk. The boy went slowly off towards one of the houses.

One or two of the other 'men' came and stood nearer to the window, looking up. I thought I would venture a bow, and made one rather ceremoniously. It did not produce much effect, and I could not at the moment think of anything I could do that would show them quite clearly that I saw them.

They went on looking at me quietly enough, and then I heard a deep low bell, seemingly very far off, toll five times. They heard it too, turned sharply round and walked off to the houses. Soon after that the lights in the windows died down and everything became very still. I looked at my watch. It was ten o'clock.

I waited for a while to see if anything would happen, but there was nothing; so I got some books out (which took a few minutes) and before I settled down to them I thought I would just take one more look out of the window.

Where were all the little houses? At the first glance I thought they had vanished, but it was not exactly so. I found I could still see the chimneys above the grass, but as I looked they too disappeared. It was done very neatly: there was no hole, the turf closed in upon the roofs as they sank down, just as if it was of india-rubber. There was not a trace left of houses or roads or playgrounds or anything.

I was strongly tempted to go out and walk over the site of the village, but I did not. For one thing I was afraid I might disturb the people of the house, and besides there was a mist coming up over the meadows which sloped away outside the garden. So I stopped where I was.

But what a very odd mist, I began to think. It was not coming in all in one piece as it should. It was more in patches or even pillars of a smoky grey which moved at different rates, some of them occasionally standing still, others even seeming to go to and fro.

And now I began to hear something like a hollow whispering coming from their direction. It was not conversation, for it went on quite continuously in the same tone: it sounded more as if something was being recited. I did not like it.

Then I saw what I liked less. Seven of these pillars of mist, each about the size of a man, were standing in a row just outside the garden fence, and in each I thought I saw two dull red eyes; and the hollow whispering grew louder.

Just then I heard a noise behind me in the room, as if the fire-irons had suddenly fallen down. So they had: and the reason why they had was that an old horseshoe which was on the mantelpiece had, for no reason that I could see, tumbled over and knocked them. Something I had heard came into my mind. I took the horseshoe and laid it on the window-sill.

The pillars of mist swayed and quivered as if a sudden gust of wind had struck them, and seemed all at once to go farther off; and the hollow murmur was no longer to be heard.

I shut the window and went to bed.

But, the last thing, I looked out once again. The meadow was clear of mist and bright beneath the light of the moon.

As I lay in bed I thought and thought over what I had seen last. I was quite sure that the pillars of mist concealed some beings who wished me no good: but why should they have any spite against me? I was also sure that they wanted to get into the house: but again, why? You may think I was slow in the wits, but I must confess that some few minutes passed before I guessed.

Of course they wanted to get hold of the box with the five jars.

The thought disturbed me so much that I got up, lighted a candle, and went to the cupboard to see if all was safe. Yes, the box was there, but the cupboard door, which I knew I had locked, was unfastened, and when I had to turn the key it became plain that the lock was hampered and useless.

How could this have come about? Earlier in the evening it had been perfectly right, and nobody had been in the room since I locked it last.

Whoever had done it, they had made the cupboard no safe place for the box. I took it into the bedroom and after a minute's thought cleared out a space in a suitcase which I had brought with me, locked it in that, and put the key on the ring of my watch-chain. Watch and all went under my pillow, and once more I got into bed.

IV: The Small People

You will have made sure that the next jar I meant to try was the one for the tongue, in hopes that it would help me to speak to some of the creatures. Though I looked forward to the experiment very much, and felt somewhat restless until I had made it, I did get a good deal of amusement out of what I saw and heard the next day.

The small people were not to be seen – at least not in the morning. No, I am wrong: I found a bunch of three of them – young ones – asleep in a hollow tree. They woke up and looked at me without much interest, and when I was withdrawing my head they blew kisses to me. I am afraid there is no doubt they did so in derision.

But there were others. I passed a cottage garden in which a little dog was barking most furiously. It seemed to be barking at a clothes-line, on which, with a lot of other things, was a print dress with rather a staring pattern of flowers. The dress caught my eye, and so did something red at the top which stuck up above the line. I gave it another glance, and really I had a most dreadful shock. It was a face.

I gazed at it in horror, and was just gathering my wits to run and call for help or something, when I saw that it was laughing. Then I realised that it could not be an ordinary person, hanging as it was on a thin bit of cord and blowing to and fro in the breeze. I went nearer, staring at it with all my eyes, and made out that it was the face of an old woman, very cheerful and ruddy, and, as I said, laughing and swinging to and fro.

Suddenly she seemed to catch my eye and to see that I saw her, and in a flash she was off the line and round the corner of the house, nearly tumbling over the dog as she went. It rushed after her, still very angry, but soon came trotting back, rather out of breath, and *that* incident was over.

I walked on. Among the village people I met, there were one or two whom I didn't think I had seen before – elderly, bright-eyed people they were – who seemed very much surprised when I said 'Good morning' to them, and stopped still, looking after me, when I passed on.

At last, some little way outside the village, I saw in the distance the same bright-coloured dress that had been on the clothes-line. The person who wore it was going slowly, and looking in the grass and hedges, and sometimes stooping to pick a plant, as it seemed. I quickened my pace and came up with her, and when I was just behind her, I cleared my throat rather loudly and said, 'Fine day,' or words to that effect.

You should have seen her jump! I was well paid for the fright she had given me just before. However, the startled look cleared away from her face, and she drew herself up and looked at me very calmly.

'Yes,' she said, 'it's a fine day.' Then she actually blushed and went on: 'I think I ought to beg your pardon for giving you such a turn just now.'

'Well,' I said, 'I certainly was a good deal startled, but no harm was done. The dog took it more to heart than I did.'

She gave a short laugh. 'Yes,' she said. 'I hardly know why I was behaving like that. I suppose we all of us feel skittish at times.' She paused and said with some little hesitation, 'You have them, I suppose?' and at the same time she rapidly touched her ears, eyes and mouth with her forefinger.

I looked at her in some doubt, for I thought, might not she be one of the unknown who wished to get hold of the Five Jars? But her eye was honest, and my instinct was to trust her: so I nodded, and put my finger on my lips.

'Of course,' she said. 'Well, you are the first since I was a little thing, and that's fourteen hundred years ago.' (You may think I opened my eyes.) 'Yes, Vitalis was the last, and he lived in the villa – they called it so – down by the stream. You'll find the place some of these days if you look. I heard talk yesterday that someone had got them, and I'm told the mist was about last night. Perhaps you saw it?'

'Yes,' I said, 'I did, and I guessed what it meant.' And I told her all that had happened, and ended by asking if she could kindly advise me what to do.

She thought for a moment, and then handed me a little bunch of the leaves she held in her hand. 'Four-leaved clover,' she said. 'I know nothing better. Lay it on the box itself. You'll hear of them again, be sure.'

'Who are *they*?' I asked in a whisper.

She shook her head. 'Not allowed,' was all she would say. 'I must be going.' And she was gone, sure enough.

You might suppose (as I did, when I came to think of it) that my new sight ought to have been able to see what became of her. I think it would, if she had gone straight away from me; but what I believe she did was to dart round behind me and then go away in a straight line, so that I was left looking in front of me while she was travelling away behind me like a bullet from a gun. You need practice with these things, and I had only been at it a couple of days.

I turned and walked rather quickly homewards, for I thought it would be wise to protect my box as soon as possible now that I had the means. I think it was fortunate that I did.

As I opened the garden gate I saw an old woman coming down the path – an old woman very unlike the last. 'Old' was not the word for her face: she might have been born before the history-books begin. As to her expression, if ever you saw a snake with red rims to its eyes and the expression of a parrot, you might have some idea of it.

She was hobbling along with a stick, in quite the proper manner, but I felt certain that all that was put on, and that she could have glided as swift as an adder if she pleased.

I confess I was afraid of her. I had a feeling that she knew everything and hated everybody.

'And what,' I suddenly thought, 'has she been up to? If she has got at the box, where am I? And more than that, what mischief will she and her company work among the small people and the birds and beasts?' There would be no mercy for them; a glance at her eye told me that.

It was an immense relief to see that she could not possibly have got the box about her, and another relief when my eye travelled to the door of the house and I saw no fewer than three horseshoes nailed above it. I smiled to myself. Oh, how angry she looked!

But she had to act her part, and with feeble curtseys and in a very small hoarse trembling voice she wished me a good day (though I noticed her pointing to the ground with her thumb as she said the words) and would be very obliged if I could tell her the right time.

I was going to pull out my watch (and if I had, she would have seen a certain key we know of), when something said suddenly and clearly to my brain, 'Look out', and by good luck I heard a clock inside the house strike one before I could answer.

'Just struck one,' was my reply accordingly, and I said it as innocently as I could.

She drew her breath in hard and quivered all over, and her mouth remained open like a cat's when it is using its worst expressions, and when she eventually thanked me I leave it to you to imagine how gracefully she did it.

Well, she had no more cards to play at the moment, and no excuse for remaining. I stood my ground and watched her out of the gate. A path led down the meadow, and, much against her will no doubt, she had to keep up the pretence and toil painfully along it until she reached another hedge and could reckon on being out of my sight. After that I neither saw nor expected to see anything more of her.

I went up to my room and found all safe, and laid the four-leaved clover on the box.

At luncheon I took occasion to find out from the maid, without asking her in so many words, whether the old woman had been visible to her; evidently she had not. Evidently also, the evil creatures were really on the track of the Five Jars, knew that I had them, and had a very fair idea of where they were kept.

However, if the maid had not seen her, the cat had, and murmured a good deal to herself, and was in a rather nervous state. She sat, with her ears turned different ways, on the window-sill, looking out, and twitching her back uncomfortably, like an old lady who feels a draught.

When I was available, she came and sat on my knee (a very uncommon attention on her part) with an air half of wishing to be protected and half of undertaking to protect me.

'If there is fish tonight,' I said, 'you shall have some.' But I was not yet in a position to make myself understood.

'Pussy's been sleepin' on your box all the afternoon, sir,' said the maid when I came in to tea. 'I couldn't get her to come off. And when I did turn her out of the room, I do believe she climbed up and got in again by the winder.'

'I don't mind at all,' I said. 'Let her be there if she likes.'

And indeed I felt quite grateful to the cat. I don't know that she could have done much if there had been any attempt on the box, but I was sure her intentions were good.

There was fish that evening, and she had a good deal of it. She did not say much that I could follow, but chiefly sang songs without words.

Not to go over the preliminaries again, I did, when the proper time came, touch my tongue with the contents of the third jar. I found that it worked in this way: I could not hear what I was saying myself, when I was talking to an animal: I only *thought* the remark very clearly, and then I felt my tongue and lips moving in an odd fashion, which I can't describe.

But with the small people in human shape it was different. I spoke in the ordinary way to them, and though I dare say my voice went up an octave or two, I can't say I perceived it.

The village was there again tonight, and the life going on in it seemed much the same. I was set upon making acquaintance in a natural sort of way with the people, and as it would not do to run any risk of startling them, I just took my place near the window and made some pretence of playing Patience. I thought it likely that some of the young people would come and watch me, in spite of the fright they had had the night before.

And it was not long before I heard a rustling in the shrubs under the window and voices saying:

'Is he in there? Can you see? Oh, I say, *do* look out: you all but had me over that time!'

They were suddenly quiet after this, and apparently one must have, very cautiously, climbed up and looked into the room. When he got down again there was a great fuss.

'No, is he really?'

'What d'you say he was doing?'

'What sort of charm?'

'I say, d'you think we'd better get down?'

'No, but what is he really doing?'

'Laying out rows of flat things on the table, with marks on them.'

'I don't believe it.'

'Well, you go and look yourself.'

'All right, I shall.'

'Yes, but, I say, do look out: suppose you get shut in and we're late for the bell?'

'Why, you fool, I shan't go into the room, only stop on the window-sill.'

'Well, I don't know, but I do believe he saw us last night, and my father said he thought so too.'

'Oh, well, he can't move very quick, anyway, and he's some way off the window. *I* shall go up.'

I managed, without altering my position too much, to keep my eye on the window-sill, and, sure enough, in a second or two a small round head came into sight. I went on with my game.

At first I could see that the watcher was ready to duck down at the slightest provocation, but as I took no sort of notice, he gained confidence, leant his elbows on the sill, and then actually pulled himself up and sat down on it. He bent over and whispered to the others below, and it was not long before I saw a whole row of heads filling up the window-sill from end to end. There must have been a dozen of them.

I thought the time was come, and without moving, and in as careless a tone as I could, I said:

'Come in, gentlemen, come in; don't be shy.'

There was a rustle, and two or three heads disappeared, but nobody said anything.

'Come in, if you like,' I said again; 'you can hear the bell quite well from here, and I shan't shut the window.'

'Promise!' said the one who was sitting on the sill.

'I promise, honour bright,' I said, whereupon he made the plunge. First he dropped on to the seat of a chair by the window, and from that to the floor. Then he wandered about the room, keeping at a distance from me at first, and, I have no doubt, watching very anxiously to see whether I had any intention of pouncing on him.

The others followed, first one by one and then two or three at a time. Some remained sitting on the window-sill, but most plucked up courage to get down on to the floor and explore. I had now my first good chance of seeing what they were like.

They all wore the same fashion of clothes – a tunic and close-fitting hose and flat caps – seemingly very much what a boy would have worn in Queen Elizabeth's time. The colours were sober – dark blue, dark red, grey, brown – and each one's clothes were of one colour all through. They had some white linen underneath; it showed a little at the neck.

There were both fair and dark among them: all were clean and passably good-looking, one or two certainly handsome.

The firstcomer was ruddy and auburn-haired and evidently a leader. They called him Wag.

I heard whispers from corners of the room, and appeals to Wag to explain what this and that unfamiliar object was, and noticed that he was never at a loss for an answer of some kind, correct or not.

The fireplace, which had its summer dressing, was, it appeared, a rock garden; an old letter lying on the floor was a charm ('Better not touch it'); the waste-paper basket (not unnaturally) a prison; the pattern on the carpet was – 'Oh, you wouldn't understand it if I was to tell you.'

Soon a voice – Wag's voice – came from somewhere near my foot.

'I say, could I get up on the top?'

I offered to lift him, but he declined rather hastily and said my leg would be all right if I didn't mind putting it out a bit sloping: and he then ran up it on all fours – he was quite a perceptible weight – and got on to the table from my knee without any difficulty.

Once there, there was a great deal to interest him – books, papers, ink, pens, pipes, matches and cards. He was full of questions about them, and his being so much at his ease encouraged the others to follow him, so that before very long the whole lot were perambulating the table and making me very nervous lest they should fall off, while Wag was standing close up to me and putting me through a catechism.

'What do you have such *little* spears for?' he wanted to know, brandishing a pen at me. 'Is that blood on the end? Whose blood? Well then, what do you do with it? Let's see – only that?' (when I wrote a word or two). 'Well, you can tell me about it another time. Now I want to know what these clubs in the chest are.'

I said, 'We make fire with them; if you like I'll show you – but it makes a little noise.'

'Go on,' said Wag; and I struck a match, rather expecting a stampede. But no, they were quite unmoved, and Wag said, 'Beastly row and smell – why don't you do the ordinary way?'

He brushed the palm of his left hand along the tips of the fingers on his right hand, put them to his lips and then to his eyes, and behold! His eyes began to glow from behind with a light which would have been quite bright enough for him to read by.

'Quite simple,' he said. 'Don't you know it?'

Then he did the same thing in reverse order, touching eyes, lips and hand, and the light was gone.

I didn't like to confess that this was beyond me.

'Yes, that's all very well,' I said, 'but how do you manage about your houses? I am sure I saw lights in the windows.'

'Course,' he said, 'put as many as you want.' And he ran round the table dabbing his hand here and there on the cloth, or on anything that lay on it, and at every place a little round bud or drop of very bright but also soft light came out. 'See?' he said, and darted round again, passing his hands over the lights and touching his lips; and they were gone.

He came back and said, 'It's a *much* better way; it is *really*,' as if it were only my native stupidity that prevented me from using it myself.

A smaller one, who looked to me rather a quieter sort than Wag, had come up and was standing by him. He now said in a low voice:

'P'raps they can't.'

It seemed a new idea to Wag: he made his eyes very round. 'Can't? Oh, rot! It's quite simple.'

The other shook his head and pointed to my hand which rested on the table. Wag looked at it too, and then at my face.

'Could I see it spread out?' he said.

'Yes, if you'll promise not to spoil it.'

He laughed slightly, and then both he and the other – whom he called Slim – bent over and looked closely at the tips of my fingers.

'Other side, please,' he said after a time, and they subjected my nails to a like examination.

The others, who had been at the remoter parts of the table, wandered up and looked over their shoulders. After tapping my nails and lifting up one or more fingers, Wag stood upright and said:

'Well, I s'pose it's true, and you can't. I thought your sort could do anything.'

'I thought much the same about you,' I said in self-defence. 'I always thought you could fly, but you—'

'So we can,' said Wag very sharply, and his face grew red.

'Oh,' I said, 'then why haven't you been doing it tonight?'

He kicked one foot with the other and looked quickly at Slim. The rest said nothing and edged away, humming to themselves.

'Well, we *can* fly perfectly well, only—'

'Only not tonight, I suppose,' said I, rather unkindly.

'No, *not* tonight,' said Wag. 'And you needn't laugh, either – we'll soon show you.'

'That *will* be nice,' I said. 'And when will you show me?'

'Let's see' (he turned to Slim), 'two nights more, isn't it? All right then (to me), in two nights more you'll see.'

Just then a moth which flew in caused a welcome diversion – for I could see that somehow I had touched on a sore subject, and that he was feeling awkward – and he first jumped at it and then ran after it. Slim lingered.

I raised my eyebrows and pointed at Wag. Slim nodded.

'The fact is,' he said in a low voice, 'he got us into rather a row yesterday and we're all stopped flying for three nights.'

'Oh,' said I. 'I *see*: you must tell him I am very sorry for being so stupid. May I ask who stopped you?'

'Oh, just the old man, not the owls.'

'You do go to the owls for something, then?' I asked, trying to appear intelligent.

'Yes, history and geography.'

'To be sure,' I said. 'Of course they've seen a lot, haven't they?'

'So they say,' said Slim, 'but—'

Just then the low toll of the bell was wafted through the window and there was an instant scurry to the edge of the table, then to the seat of the chair, and up to the window-sill; small arms waved caps at me, the shrubs rustled, and I was left alone.

V: Danger to the Jars

Now my ears and eyes and tongue had been dealt with, and what remained were the forehead and the chest. I could not guess what would come of treating these with the ointment, but I thought I would try the forehead first.

There was still a day or two when the moon would be bright enough for the trial. I hoped that perhaps the effect of these two last jars might be to make me able to go on with my experiences – to keep in touch with the new people I had come across – during the time when she – the moon, I mean – was out of sight.

I had one anxiety. The precious box must be guarded from those who were after it. About this I had a conviction, that if I could keep them off until I had used each of the five jars, the box and I would be safe.

Why I felt sure of this I could not say, but my experience had led me to trust these beliefs that came into my head, and I meant to trust this one. It would be best, I thought, if I did not go far from the house – perhaps even if I did not leave it at all till the time of danger was past.

Several things happened in the course of the morning which confirmed me in my belief.

I took up a position at the table by the window of my sitting-room. I had put the box in my suitcase, which I had locked, and I now laid it beside me where I could keep an eye upon it.

The view from my window showed me, first, the garden of the cottage, with its lawn and little flower-beds, its hedge and back gate, and beyond that a path leading down across a field. More fields, I knew, came after that one, and sloped pretty sharply down to a stream in the valley, which I could not see. But I could see the steep slope of fields, partly pasture, and then clothed with green woods towards the top. There were no other houses in sight. The road was behind me, passing the front of the cottage, and my bedroom looked out that way.

I had some writing and reading to do, and I had not long finished breakfast before I settled down to it, and heard the maid 'doing out' the bedroom as usual, accompanied every now and then by a slight mew from the cat, who (also as usual) was watching her at work.

These mews meant nothing in particular, I may say; they were only intended to be met by an encouraging remark, such as 'There you are, then, pussy,' or 'Don't get in my way, now,' or 'All in good time.'

Finally I heard 'Come along then, and let's see what we've got for you downstairs,' and the door was shut. I mention this because of what happened about a quarter of an hour later.

There was suddenly a fearful crash in the bedroom, a fall, a breaking of glass and crockery and snapping of wood, and then, fainter, sobbings and moans of pain. I started up.

'Goodness!' I thought, 'she must have been dusting that heavy shelf high up on the wall with all the china on it, and the whole thing has given way. She must be badly hurt! But why doesn't her mistress come rushing upstairs? And what was that rasping noise just beside me?'

I looked at my suitcase, which lay on the table just inside the open window. Across the new smooth top of it there were three deep scratches running towards the window, which had not been there before.

I moved it to the other side of me and sat down. There had been an attempt to decoy me out of the room, and it had failed. Certainly there would be more.

I waited; but everything was quiet in the house: no more noise from the bedroom and no one moving about, upstairs or downstairs; nothing but the pump clanking in the scullery. I turned to my work again.

Half an hour must have gone by, and, though on the look-out, I was not fidgety. Then I was aware of a confused noise from the field outside.

'Help! Help! Keep off, you brute! Help, you there!' as well as I could make out, again and again.

Towards the far end of the field, which was a pretty large one, a poor old man was trying to get to a gate in the hedge at a staggering run, and striking now and then with his stick at a great deer-hound which was leaping up at him with hollow barks. It seemed as if nothing but the promptest dash to the spot could save him; it seemed, too, as if he had caught sight of me at the window, for he beckoned.

How strange the cries sounded! It was as if someone was shouting into an empty jug. My field-glasses were by me on the table, and I thought I would take just *one* look before I rushed out. I am glad I did; for, do you know, when I had the glasses focused on the dog and the man, all that I could see was a sort of fuzz of dancing vapour, much as if the shimmering air that you see on the heath on a hot day had been gathered up and rolled into a shape.

'Ha! Ha!' I said, as I put down the glasses; and something in the air, about four yards off, made a sharp hissing sound. No doubt there were words, but I could not distinguish them.

A second attempt had failed; you may be sure I was well on the alert for the next.

I put away my books now, and sat looking out of the window, and wondering as I watched whether there was anything out of the common to be noticed. For one thing, I thought there were more little birds about than I expected. At first I did not see them, for they were not hopping about on the lawn; but as I stared at the hedge of the garden, and at that of the field, I became aware that these were full of life.

On almost every twig that could hold a bird in shelter – not on the top of the hedges – a bird was sitting, quite still, and they were all looking towards the window, as if they were expecting something to happen there. Occasionally one would flutter its wings a little and turn its head towards its neighbour; but this was all they did.

I picked up my glasses and began to study the bottom of the hedges and the bushes, where there was some quantity of dead leaves, and here, too, I could see that there were spectators. A small bright eye or a bit of a nose was visible almost wherever I looked; in short, the mice, and, I don't doubt, some of the rats, hedgehogs, and toads as well, were collected there and were as intently on the watch as the birds.

'What a chance for the cat, if only she knew!'

I put my head cautiously out of the window, and looking down on the sill of the window below, I could see her head, with the ears pushed forward; she was looking earnestly at the hedge, but she did not move. Only, at the slight noise I made, she turned her face upwards and crowed to me in a modest but encouraging manner.

Time passed on. Luncheon was laid – on another table – and was over, before anything else happened.

The next thing was that I heard the maid saying sharply:

'What business 'ave you got going round to the back? We don't want none of your rubbish here.'

A hoarse voice answered inaudibly.

Maid: 'No, nor the gentleman don't want none of your stuff neither; and how do you know there's a gentleman here at all I should like to know? What? Don't mean no offence? I dare say. That's more than I know. Well, that's the last word I've got to say.'

In a minute more there was a knock at my door, and at the same time a step on the gravel path under my window, and a loud hiss from the cat. As I said 'Come in' to the knock, I hastily looked out of the window, but saw nothing.

It was the maid who had knocked. She had come to ask if there was anything I should like from the village, or anything I should want before tea-time, because the mistress was going out, and wanted her to go over and fetch something from the shop.

I said there was nothing except the letters and perhaps a small parcel from the post office.

She lingered a moment before going, and finally said:

'You'll excuse me naming it, sir, but there seems to be some funny people about the roads today, if you'd please to be what I mean to say a bit on the look-out, if you're not a-going out yourself.'

'Certainly,' I said. 'No, I don't mean to go out. By the way, who was it came to the door just now?'

'Oh, it was one of these 'awking men, not one I've seen before, and he must be a stranger in this part, I think, because he began going round to the garden door, only I stopped him. He'd got these cheap rubbishing 'atpins and what not; leastways, if you understand me, what I thought to myself I shouldn't like to be seen with 'em, whatever others might.'

'Yes, I see,' I answered. And she went, and I turned to my books once more.

Within a very few minutes I began to suspect that I was getting sleepy. Yes, it was undoubtedly so. What with the warmth of the day, and lunch, and not having been out . . .

There was a curious smell in the room, too, not exactly nasty, like something burning.

What did it remind me of? Wood smoke from a cottage fire, that one smells on an autumn evening as one comes bicycling down the hill into a village? Not quite so nice as that; something more like a chemist's shop. I wondered: and as I wondered, my eyes closed and my head went forward.

A sharp pain on the back of my hand, and a crash of glass!

Up I jumped, and which of three or four things I realised first I don't know now.

But I did realise in a second or two that my hand was bleeding from a scratch all down the back of it, that a pane of the window was broken and that the whole window was darkened with little birds that were bumping their chests against it; that the cat was on the table gazing into my face with intense expression, that a little smoke was drifting into the room, and that my suitcase was on the point of slipping out over the window-sill.

A despairing dash at it I made, and managed to clutch it; but for the life of me I could not pull it back. I could see no string or cord, much less any hand that was dragging at it. I hardly dared to take my hand from it to catch up something and hack at the thief I could not see. Besides, there was nothing within reach.

Then I remembered the knife in my pocket. Could I get it out and open it without losing hold?

'They hate steel,' I thought.

Somehow – frantically holding on with one hand – I got out the knife, and opened it, goodness knows how, for it was horribly small and stiff, with my teeth, and sheared and stabbed indiscriminately all round the farther end of the suitcase. Thank goodness, the strain relaxed.

I got the thing inside the window, dropped it, and stood on it, craning over the garden path and round the corner of the house. Of course there was nothing to be seen.

The birds were gone.

The cat was still on the table saying 'O you owl! O you owl!'

The sole and only clue to what had been happening was a small earthenware saucer that lay on the path immediately below the window, with a little heap of ashes in it, from which a thin column of smoke was coming straight up and curling over when it reached the window level. That, I could not doubt, was the cause of my sudden sleepiness.

I dropped a large book straight on to it, and had the satisfaction of hearing it crush to bits and of seeing the smoke go four ways along the ground and vanish.

I was perfectly awake now. I looked at the cat, and showed her the back of my hand. She sat quite still and said:

'Well, what did you expect? I had to do something. I'll lick it if you like, but I'd rather not. No particular ill-feeling, you understand; all the same a hundred years hence.'

I was not in a position to answer her, so I shook my head at her, wound up my hand in a handkerchief, and then stroked her. She took it agreeably, jumped off the table, and requested to be let out.

So the third attack had failed.

I sat down and looked out. The hedges were empty; not a bird, not a mouse was left. I took this to mean that the dangerous time was past, and great was the relief. Soon I heard the maid come back from her errands in the village, then the mistress's chaise, then the clock striking five. I felt it would be all right for me to go out after tea.

And so I did; first, however, concealing the suitcase in my bedroom – not that I supposed hiding it would be of much use – and piling upon it poker, tongs, knife, horseshoe, and anything else I could find which I thought would keep off trespassers.

I had, by the way, to explain to the maid that a bird had flown against the window and broken it, and when she said 'Stupid, tiresome little things they are,' I am afraid I did not contradict her.

I went out by way of the garden and crossed the field, near the middle of which stands a large old oak. I went up to this, for no particular reason, and stood gazing at the trunk. As I did so I became aware that my eyes were beginning to 'see through', and behold! A family of owls was inside.

As it was near evening, they were getting wakeful, stirring, smacking their beaks and opening their wings a little from time to time. At last one of them said:

'Time's nearly up. Out and about! Out and about!'

'Anyone outside?' said another.

'No harm there,' said the first.

This short way of talking, I believe, was due to the owls not being properly awake and consequently sulky. As they brightened up and got their eyes open, they began to be more easy in manner.

'Oop! Oop! Oop! I've had a very good day of it. You have, too, I hope?'

'Sound as a rock, I thank you, except when they were carrying on at the cottage.'

'Oh goodness! I forgot! They didn't bring it off, I hope.'

'Not they; the watch was too well set, but it was wanted. I had a leaf about it a few minutes after, and it seems they got him asleep.'

'Well! I never heard anyone bring a leaf.'

'I dare say not, but I was expecting it; pigeon dropped it. There it is, on that child's back.'

I saw the hen-owl stoop and examine a dead chestnut leaf which lay, as the other had said, on an owlet's back.

'Fa-a-ther!' said this owlet suddenly, in a shrill voice, 'mayn't I go out tonight?'

But all that Father did was to clasp its head in his claw and push it to and fro several times. When he let go, the owlet made no sound, but crept away and hid its face in a corner, and heaved as if with sobs. Father closed his eyes slowly and opened them slowly – amused, I thought. The mother had been reading the leaf all the time.

'Dear me! *Very* interesting!' she said. 'I suppose now the worst of it is over.'

'All's quiet for tonight, anyhow,' said Father, 'but I wish he could see someone about tomorrow; that's their last chance, and they *may*—' He ruffled up his feathers, lifted first one foot and then the other. 'The awkward-ness is,' he went on, 'if I say too much and they do get the jars, there's one risk; and if there's no warning and they get them, there's another risk.'

'But if there *is* a warning and they *don't* get them,' said she, very sensibly.

'Well, to be sure, that would be better, even though we don't know much about him.'

'But where do you suppose he is, and whom ought he to see?' (It was just what I wanted to know, and I thanked her.)

'Why, as to the first, I suspect he's outside; there is someone there, and why they should stop there all this time unless they're listening, I don't know.'

'Good gracious! Listening to our private conversation! And me with my feathers all anyhow!' She began to peck at herself vigorously; but this was straying from the point, and annoyed me. However, Father went slowly on:

'As to that, I don't much care whether he's listening or not. As to whom he ought to see, that's rather more difficult. If he's got as far as talking to any of the Right People (he said this as if they had capital letters), they'd know, of course; and some of them down about the village, they'd know; and the Old Mother knows, and—'

'What about the boys?' said she, pausing in the middle of her toilet and poking her head up at him. He wholly disdained to answer, and merely butted at her with his head, so that she slipped down off her ledge several inches, with a great scrabbling. 'Oh, *don't*!' she said peevishly, as she climbed back. 'I'm all untidy again.'

'Well then, don't ask such ridiculous questions. I shall buffle you with both wings next time. And now, as soon as the coast is clear, I shall be out and about.'

I took the hint and moved off, for I had learnt as much perhaps as I could expect, even if all was not yet plain; and before I had gone many paces I was aware of the pair both sailing smoothly off in the opposite direction.

I was 'seeing through' a good deal that evening; it is surprising what a lot of coppers people drop, even on a field path; surprising, too, in how many places there lie, unsuspected, bones of men. Some things I saw which were ugly and sad, like that, but more that were amusing and even exciting.

There is one spot I could show where four gold cups stand round what was once a book, but the book is no more than earth now. That, however, I did not see on this particular evening.

What I remember best is a family of young rabbits huddled round their parents in a burrow, and the mother telling a story: 'And so then he went a little farther and found a dandelion, and stopped and sat up and began to eat it. And when he had eaten two large leaves and one little one, he saw a fly on it – no, two flies; and then he thought he had had enough of that dandelion, and he went a little farther and found another dandelion . . .'

And so it went on interminably, and entirely stupid, like everything else I ever heard a rabbit say, for they have forgotten all about their ancestor, Brer Rabbit. However, the children were absorbed in the story, so much so that they never heard a stoat making its way down the burrow.

But I heard it, and by stamping and driving my stick in I was able to make it turn tail and go off, cursing. All stoats, weasels, ferrets, polecats, are of the wrong people, as you may imagine, and so are most rats and bats.

At last I left off seeing through, by trying not to do so, and went back to the house, where I found all safe and quiet.

I ought to say that I had not as yet tried speaking to any animal, even to the cat when she scratched me, but I thought I would try it now.

So when she came in at dinner-time and circled about, with what I may call pious aspirations about fish and other such things, I summoned up my courage and said (using my voice in the way I described, or rather did not describe, before):

'I used to be told, "If you are hungry, you can eat dry bread".'

She was certainly horribly startled. At first I thought she would have dashed up the chimney or out of the window; but she recovered pretty quickly and sat down, still looking at me with intense surprise.

'I suppose I might have guessed,' she said. 'But dear! What a turn you did give me! I feel quite faint. And gracious! What a day it has been! When I found you dozing off like a great— Well, no one wants to be rude, do they? But I can tell you I had more than half a mind to go at your face.'

'I am glad you didn't,' I said. 'And really, you know, it wasn't my fault: it was that stuff they were burning on the path.'

'I know that well enough,' she said. 'But to come back to the point, all this anxiety has made me as empty in myself as a clean saucer.'

'Just what I was saying. If you are hungry, you can—'

'Say that again, say it just once more,' she said, and her eyes grew narrow as she said it, 'and I shall—'

'What shall you do?' I asked, for she stopped suddenly.

She calmed herself. 'Oh, you know how it is when one's been all excited-like and worked up; we all say more than we mean. But that about dry bread! Well, there! I simply can't bear it. It's a wicked, cruel untruth, that's what it is. And besides, you *can't* be going to eat all the whole of what she's put down for you.'

Excitement was coming on again, and she ended with a loud ill-tempered mew.

Well, I gave her what she seemed to want, and shortly after, worn out doubtless with the fatigues of the day, she went to sleep on a chair, not even caring to follow the maid downstairs when things were cleared away.

VI: The Cat, Wag, Slim and Others

I got out my precious casket. I sat by the window and watched. The moon shone out, the lid of the box loosened in due course, and I touched my fore-head with the ointment. But neither at once nor for some little time after did I notice any fresh power coming to me.

With the moon, up came also the little town, and no sooner were the doors of the houses level with the grass than the boys were out of them and running in some numbers towards my window; in fact, some slipped out of their own windows, not waiting for the doors to be available.

Wag was the first. Slim, more sedate, came among the crowd that followed. These were still the only two who felt no hesitation about talking to me. The others were all fully occupied in exploring the room.

'Tomorrow,' I said (after some sort of how-do-you-do's had been exchanged), 'you'll be flying all over the place, I suppose.'

'Yes,' said Wag, shortly. 'But I want to know – I say, Slim, what was it we wanted first?'

'Wasn't there a message from your father?' said Slim.

'Oh, yes, of course. "If they're about the house," he said, "give them horseshoes; if there's a bat-ball, squirt at it": he thinks there's a squirt in the tool-house – Oh, there's the cat; I must—' After delivering all this in one sentence, he rushed to the edge of the table and took a kind of header into the midst of the unfortunate animal, who, however, only moaned or crowed without waking, and turned partly over on her back.

Slim remained sitting on a book and gazing soberly at me.

'Well,' I said, 'it's very kind of Wag's father to send me a message, but I must say I can't make much of it.'

Slim nodded. 'So he said, and he said you'd see when the time came. Of course I don't know, myself: I've never seen a bat-ball. Wag says he has, but you never know with Wag.'

'Well, I must do the best I can, I suppose. But look here, Slim, I wish you could tell me one or two things. What *are* you? What do they call you?'

'They call me Slim: and the whole of us they call the Right People,' said Slim; 'but it's no good asking us much, because we don't know, and besides, it isn't good for us.'

'How do you mean?'

'Why, you see, our job is to keep the little things right, and if we do more than that, or if we try to find out much more, then we burst.'

'And is that the end of you?'

'Oh, no!' he said cheerfully, 'but that's one of the things it's no good asking.'

'And if you don't do your job, what then?'

'Oh, then they get smaller and have no sense.' (He said *they*, not *we*, I noticed.)

'I see. Well now, you go to school, don't you?' He nodded. 'What for? Isn't that likely to be bad for you?' (I hardly liked to say 'make you burst'.)

'No,' he said. 'You see, it's to learn our job. We have to be told what used to go on, so as we can put things right, or keep them right. And the owls, you see, they remember a long way back, but they don't know any more than we do about the swell things.'

I was very shy about putting the next question I had in mind, but I felt I must. 'Now do you know how old you are, or how long it takes you to grow up, or how – how long you go on when you *are* grown up!'

He pressed his hands to his head, and I was dreadfully afraid for the moment that it might be swelling and would burst; but it was not so bad as that. After a few seconds he looked up and said:

'I think it's seven times seven moons since I went to school and seven times seven times seven moons before I grow up; and the rest is no good asking. But it's all right,' upon which he smiled.

And this, I may say, was the most part of what I ventured to ask any of them about themselves. But at other times I gathered that as long as they 'did their job' nothing could injure them. And they were regularly measured – all of them – to see if they were getting smaller, and a careful record kept. But if anyone lost as much as a quarter of his height, he was doomed, and he crept off out of the settlement.

Whether such a one ever came back I could not be sure; most of the failures (and they were not common) went and lived in hollow trees or by brooks, and were happy enough, but in a feeble way, not remembering much, nor able to make anything. And it was supposed that very slowly they shrunk to the size of a pin's point, and probably to nothing. All the same, it was believed that they *could* recover.

Many other things that *you* would have asked, I did not, being anxious to avoid giving trouble.

But this time, anyhow, I felt I had catechised Slim long enough, so I broke off and said:

'What can Wag be doing all this while?'

'There's no knowing,' said Slim. 'But he's very quiet for him; either he's doing something awful, or he's asleep.'

'I saw him with the cat last,' I said. 'You might go and look at her.'

He walked to the edge of the table, and said, 'Why, he *is* asleep!' And so he was, with his head on the cat's chest, under her chin, which she had turned up; and she had put her front paws together over the top of his head.

As for the others, I descried them sitting in a circle in a corner of the room, also very quiet. (I imagine they were a little afraid of doing much without Wag, and also of waking him.) But I could not make out what they were doing, so I asked Slim.

'Racing earwigs, I should think,' he said, with something of contempt.

'Well, I hope they won't leave them about when they go. I don't like earwigs.'

'Who does?' he said. 'But they'll take them away all right; they're prize ones, some of them.'

I went over and looked at the racing for a little. The course was neatly marked out with small lights sprouting out of the boards, and the circle was at the winning-post, the starters being at the other end, some six feet away.

I watched one heat. The earwigs seemed to me neither very speedy nor very intelligent, and all except one were apt to stop in mid-course and engage in personal encounters with each other.

I was beginning to wonder how long this would go on, when Wag woke up. Like most of us, he was not willing to allow that he had been asleep.

'I thought I'd just lie down a bit,' he said, 'and then I didn't want to bustle your cat, so I stopped there. And now I want to know – Slim, I say, what was it you were asking me?'

'Me asking you? I don't know.'

'Oh, yes, you do. What he was doing the other time before we came in.'

'I didn't ask you that, you asked me.'

'Well, it doesn't matter who asked.' (Turning to me): 'What *were* you doing?'

'I don't know,' I said. 'Was it these things I was using' (taking up a pack of cards), 'or something like this?' (I held up a book.)

'Yes, that one. What were you doing with it? What's it for?'

'We call it reading a book,' and I tried to explain what the idea was, and read out a few lines. It happened to be *Pickwick*. They were absorbed.

Slim said, half to himself, 'Something like a glass,' which I thought quite meaningless at the time. Then I showed them a picture in another book. That they made out very quickly.

'But when's it going to move on?' said Slim.

'Never,' I said. 'Ours stop just like that always. Do yours move on?'

'Of course they do – look here.' He lay down on the tablecloth and pressed his forehead on it, but evidently could make nothing of it. 'It's all rough,' he said. I gave him a sheet of paper. 'That's better,' and he lay down again in the same posture for a few seconds. Then he got up and began rubbing the paper all over with the palms of his hands. As he did so a coloured picture came out pretty quickly, and when it was finished he drew aside to let me see, and said, somewhat bashfully, 'I don't think I've got it *quite* right, but I meant it for what happened the other evening.'

He had certainly not got it right as far as I was concerned. It was a view of the window of the house, seen from outside by moonlight, and there was a back view of a row of figures with their elbows on the sill. So far, so good; but inside the open window was standing a figure which was plainly – much too plainly, I thought – meant for me: far too short and fat, far too red-faced, and with an owlish expression which I am sure I never wear.

This person was now seen to move his hand – a very poor hand, with only about three fingers – to his side, and pull, apparently, out of his body, a round object more or less like a watch (at any rate it was white on one side with black marks, and yellow on the other) and lay it down in front of him. At this the figures at the window-sill threw up their arms in all directions and fell or slid down like so many dolls. Then the picture began to get fainter, and disappeared from the paper.

Slim looked at me expectantly.

'Well,' I said, 'it's very interesting to see how you do it, but is that the best likeness of me that you can make?'

'What's wrong with it?' said he. 'Isn't it handsome enough or something?'

I heard Wag throw himself down on the table, and, looking at him, I saw that he had got both hands pressed over his mouth.

'May I ask what the joke is?' I said rather dryly (for it is surprising how touchy one can be over one's personal appearance, even at my time of life).

He looked up for an instant at me, and then gasped and hid his face again. Slim went up to him and kicked him in the ribs.

'Where's your manners?' he said in a loud whisper. Wag rolled over and sat up, wiping his eyes.

'I'm very sorry,' he said. 'I'm sure I don't know what I was laughing for.' Slim whistled. 'Well,' said Wag, 'what *was* I?'

'Him, of course, and you know perfectly well!'

'Oh, was I? Well, perhaps you'll tell me what there is to laugh at about him?' said Wag, rather basely, I thought. So, as Slim put his finger to his lip and looked unhappy, I interrupted.

'Get up a minute, Wag,' I said. 'I want to see something.'

'What?' said he, jumping up at once.

'Stand back to back with Slim, if you don't mind. That's it. Dear me! I thought you were taller than that – you looked to me taller last night. My mistake, I dare say. All right, thanks.'

But there they stood, gazing at each other with horror, and I felt I had been trifling with a most serious subject, so I laughed and said, 'Don't disturb yourselves. I was only chaffing you, Wag, because you seemed to be doing something of the kind to me.'

Slim understood, and heaved a sigh of relief. Wag sat down on a book and looked reproachfully upon me. Neither said a word. I was very much ashamed, and begged their pardon as nicely as I knew how. Luckily Wag was soon convinced that I was not in earnest, and he recovered his spirits directly.

'All *right*,' he said, nodding at me. 'Did I hear you say you didn't like earwigs? That's worth remembering, Slim.'

This reduced me at once. I tried to point out that he had begun it, and that it would be a mean revenge, and very hard on the earwigs, if he filled my room with them, for I should be obliged to kill all I could.

'Why,' he said, 'they needn't be real earwigs; my own tickle every bit as much as real ones.'

This was no better for me, and I tried to make more appeals to his better feelings. He did not seem to be listening very attentively, though his eyes were fixed on me.

'What's that on your neck?' he said suddenly, and at the same moment I felt a procession of legs walking over my skin. I brushed at it hastily, and something seemed to fall on the table.

'No, the other side I mean,' said he, and again I felt the same horrid tickling and went through the same exercises, with a face, I've no doubt, contorted with terror. Anyhow, it seemed to amuse them very much. Wag, in fact, was quite unable to speak, and could only point.

It was dull of me not to have realised at once that these were 'his' earwigs and not real ones. But now I did, and though I still felt the tickling, I did not move, but sat down and gazed severely at him.

Soon he got the better of his mirth and said, 'I think we are quits now.' Then, with sudden alarm, 'I say, what's become of the others? The bell hasn't gone, has it?'

'How should I know?' I said. 'If you hadn't been making all this disturb-ance, perhaps we might have heard it.'

He took a flying leap – an extraordinary feat it was – from the edge of the table to a chair in the window, scrambled up to the sill, and gazed out. 'It's all right,' he said, in a faint voice of infinite relief; let himself down limply to the floor, and climbed slowly up my leg to his former place.

'Well,' I said, 'the bell hasn't gone, it seems, but where are the rest? I've hardly seen anything of them.'

'Oh, *you* go and find 'em, Slim; I'm worn out with all these frights.'

Slim went to the farther end of the table, prospected, and returned. He reported them 'all right, but they're having rather a slow time of it, I think.'

I, too, got up, walked round, and looked. They were seated in a solemn circle on the floor round the cat, who was now curled up and fast asleep on a round footstool. Not a word was being said by anybody. I thought I had better address them, so I said:

'Gentlemen, I'm afraid I've been very inattentive to you this evening. Isn't there anything I can do to amuse you? Won't you come up on the table? You're welcome to walk up my leg if you find that convenient.'

I was almost sorry I had spoken the moment after, for they made but one rush at my legs as I stood by the table, and the sensation was rather like that, I imagine, of a swarm of rats climbing up one's trousers.

However, it was over in a few seconds, and all of them – over a dozen – were with Wag and Slim on the table, except one, who, whether by mistake or on purpose, went on climbing me by way of my waistcoat buttons, rather deliberately, until he reached my shoulder.

I didn't object, of course, but I turned round (which made him catch at my ear) and went back to my chair, seated in which I felt rather as if I was presiding at a meeting. The one on my shoulder sat down and, I thought, folded his arms and looked at his friends with some triumph. Wag evidently took this to be a liberty.

'My word!' he said. 'What do you mean by it, Wisp? Come off it!'

Wisp was a little daunted, as I judged by his fidgeting somewhat, but put a bold face on it and said, 'Why should I come off?'

I put in a word: 'I don't mind his being here.'

'I dare say not; that's not the point,' said Wag. 'Are you coming down?'

'No,' said Wisp, 'not for you.' But his tone was rather blustering than brave.

'Very well, don't then,' said Wag; and I expected him to run up and pull Wisp down by the legs, but he didn't do that. He took something out of the breast of his tunic, put it in his mouth, lay down on his stomach, and, with his eyes on Wisp, puffed out his cheeks.

Two or three seconds passed, during which I felt Wisp shifting about on his perch, and breathing quickly. Then he gave a sharp shriek, which went right through my head, slipped rapidly down my chest and legs and on to the floor, where he continued to squeal and to run about like a mad thing, to the great amusement of everyone on the table.

Then I saw what was the matter. All round his head were a multitude of little sparks, which flew about him like a swarm of bees, every now and then settling and coming off again, and, I suppose, burning him every time. If he beat them off, they attacked his hands, so he was in a bad way.

After watching him for about a minute from the edge of the table, Wag called out:

'Do you apologise?'

'Yes!' he screamed.

'All right,' said Wag. 'Stand still! Stand still, you bat! How can I get 'em back if you don't?'

Wag was back to me and I couldn't see what he did, but Wisp sat down on the carpet free of sparks, and wiped his face and neck with his handkerchief for some time, while the rest gradually recovered from their laughter.

'You can come up again now,' said Wag. And so he did, though he was slow and shy about it.

'Why didn't he send sparks at Wag?' said I to Slim.

'He hasn't got 'em to send,' was the answer. 'It's only the Captain of the moon.'

'Well now, what about a little peace and quiet?' I said. 'And, you know, I've never been introduced to you all properly. Wouldn't it be a good idea to do that, before the bell goes?'

'Very well,' said Wag. 'We'll *do* it properly. You bring 'em up one at a time, Slim, and' (to me) 'you put your sun-hand out on the table.'

(*I*: 'Sun-hand?'

Wag: 'Yes, sun-hand. Don't you know?' He held up his right hand, then his left: 'Sun-hand, Moon-hand, Day-hand, Night-hand, Star-hand, Cloud-hand, and so on.'

I: 'Thank you.')

This was done, and meanwhile Slim formed the troop into a queue and beckoned them up one by one. Wag stood on a book on the right and proclaimed the name of each. First he had made me arrange my right hand edgeways on the table, with the forefinger out. Then 'Gold!' said Wag. Gold stepped forward and made a lovely bow, which I returned with an inclination of my head, then took as much of my forefinger top joint in his right hand as he could manage, bent over it and shook it or tried to, and then took up a position on the left and watched the next comer.

The ceremony was the same for everyone, but not all the bows were equally elegant; some of the boys were jocular, and shook my finger with both hands and a great display of effort. These were frowned upon by Wag.

The names (I need not set them all down now) were all of the same kind as you have heard: there was Red, Wise, Dart, Sprat, and so on. After Wisp, who came last and was rather humble, Wag called out Slim, and, after him, descended and presented himself in the same form.

'And now,' he said, 'perhaps you'll tell us *your* name.'

I did so (one is always a little shamefaced about it, I don't know why) in full. He whistled.

'Too much,' he said. 'What's the easiest you can do?'

After some thought I said, 'What about M or N?'

'Much better! If M's all right for you, it'll do for us.' So M was agreed upon.

I was still rather afraid that the rank and file had been passing a dull evening and would not come again, and I tried to express as much to them. But they said:

'Dull? Oh no, M; why we've found out all sorts of things!'

'Really? What sort of things?'

'Well, inside the wall in that corner there's the biggest spider I've ever seen, for one thing.'

'Good gracious!' I said. 'I hate 'em. I hope it can't get out?'

'It would have tonight if we hadn't stopped up the hole. Something's been helping it to gnaw through.'

'Has it?' said Wag. 'My word! That looks bad. What was it made the hole?' Some called out, 'A bat,' and some 'A rat.'

'It doesn't matter much for that,' said Slim, 'so long as it's safe now. Where is it?'

'Gone down to the bottom and saying awful things,' Red answered.

'Well, I *am* obliged to you,' I said. 'Anything else?'

'There's a lot of this stuff under the floor,' said Dart, pointing with his foot at a half-crown which lay on the table.

'Is there? Whereabouts?' said I. 'Oh, but I was forgetting; I can look after that myself.'

'Yes, of course you can,' they said; 'and lots of things happened here before you came. We were watching. The old man and the woman, they were the worst, weren't they, Red?'

'Do you mean you've been here before?' I asked.

'No, no, but tonight we were looking at them, like we do at school.'

This was beyond me, and I thought it would be of no use to ask for more explanations. Besides, just at this moment we heard the bell. They all clambered down either me or the chairs or the tablecloth.

Slim lingered a moment to say, 'You'll look out, won't you?' and then followed the rest on to the window-sill, where, taking the time from Captain Wag, they all stood in a row, bowed with their caps *off*, straightened up again, each sang one note, which combined into a wonderful chord, faced round and disappeared.

I followed them to the window and saw the inhabitants of the house separating and going to their homes with the young ones capering round them. One or two of the elders – Wag's father in particular – looked up at me, paused in their walk, and bowed gravely, which courtesy I returned.

I went on gazing until the lawn was a blank once more, and then, closing and fastening the sitting-room window, I betook myself to the bedroom.

VII: The Bat-Ball

It had certainly been an eventful day and evening, and I felt that my adventures could not be quite at an end yet, for I had still to find out what new power or sense the Fourth Jar had brought me.

I stood and thought, and tried quite vainly to detect some difference in myself. And then I went to the window and drew the curtain aside and looked out on the road, and within a few minutes I began to understand.

There came walking rapidly along the road a young man, and he turned in at the garden gate and came straight up the path to the house door. I began to be surprised, not at his coming, for it was not so very late, but at the look of him.

He was young, as I said, rather red-faced, but not bad-looking; of the class of a farmer, I thought. He wore biggish brown whiskers – which is not common nowadays – and his hair was rather long at the back – which also is not common with young men who want to look smart – but his hat, and his clothes generally, were the really odd part of him.

The hat was a sort of low top-hat, with a curved brim; it spread out at the top and it was brushed rough instead of smooth. His coat was a blue swallow-tail with brass buttons. He had a broad tie wound round and round his neck, and a Gladstone collar. His trousers were tight all the way down and had straps under his feet. To put it in the dullest, shortest way, he was 'dressed in the fashion of eighty or ninety years ago', as we read in the ghost stories.

Evidently he knew his way about very well. He came straight up to the front door and, as far as I could tell, into the house, but I did not hear the door open or shut or any steps on the stairs. He must, I thought, be in my landlady's parlour downstairs.

I turned away from the window, and there was the next surprise. It was as if there was no wall between me and the sitting-room. I saw straight into it. There was a fire in the grate, and by it were sitting face to face an old man and an old woman. I thought at once of what one of the boys had said, and I looked curiously at them.

They were, you would have said, as fine specimens of an old-fashioned yeoman and his wife as anyone could wish to see. The man was hale and red-faced, with grey whiskers, smiling as he sat bolt upright in his armchair. The old lady was rosy and smiling too, with a smart silk dress and a smart cap, and tidy ringlets on each side of her face – a regular picture of wholesome old age; and yet I hated them both.

The young man, their son, I suppose, was in the room standing at the door with his hat in his hand, looking timidly at them. The old man turned half round in his chair, looked at him, turned down the corners of his mouth, looked across at the old lady, and they both smiled as if they were amused.

The son came farther into the room, put his hat down, leaned with both hands on the table, and began to speak (though nothing could be heard) with an earnestness that was painful to see, because I could be certain his pleading would be of no use. Sometimes he spread out his hands and shook them, every now and again he brushed his eyes. He was very much moved, and so was I, merely watching him.

The old people were not. They leaned forward a little in their chairs and sometimes smiled at each other – again as if they were amused.

At last he had done, and stood with his hands before him, quivering all over. His father and mother leaned back in their chairs and looked at each other. I think they said not a single word. The son caught up his hat, turned round, and went quickly out of the room. Then the old man threw back his head and laughed, and the old lady laughed too, not so boisterously.

I turned back to the window. It was as I expected. Outside the garden gate, in the road, a young slight girl in a large poke-bonnet and shawl and rather short-skirted dress was waiting, in great anxiety, as I could see by the way she held to the railings. Her face I could not see.

The young man came out. She clasped her hands, he shook his head; they went off together slowly up the road, he with bowed shoulders, supporting her, she, I dare say, crying. Again I looked round to the sitting-room. The wall hid it now.

It sounds a dull ordinary scene enough, but I can assure you it was horribly disturbing to watch, and the cruel calm way in which the father and mother, who looked so nice and worthy and were so abominable, treated their son, was like nothing I had ever seen.

Of course I know now what the effect of the Fourth Jar was: it made me able to see what had happened in any place. I did not yet know how far back the memories would go, or whether I was obliged to see them if I did not want to. But it was clear to me that the boys were sometimes taught in this way. 'We were watching them like we do at school,' one of them said, and though the grammar was poor, the meaning was plain, and I would ask Slim about it when we next met.

Meanwhile I must say I hoped the gift would not go on working instead of letting me go to sleep. It did not.

Next day I met my landlady employing herself in the garden, and asked her about the people who had formerly lived in the house.

'Oh yes,' said she. 'I can tell you about them, for my father he remembered old Mr. and Mrs. Eld quite well when he was a slip of a lad. They wasn't liked in the place, neither of them, partly through bein' so hard-like to their work-people, and partly from them treating their only son so bad – I mean to say turning him right off because he married without asking permission.

'Well, no doubt, that's what he shouldn't have done, but my father said it was a very nice respectable young girl he married, and it do seem hard for them never to say a word of kindness all those years and leave every penny away from the young people.

'What become of them, do you say, sir? Why, I believe they emigrated away to the United States of America and never was heard of again, but the old people they lived on here, and I never heard but what they was easy in their minds right up to the day of their death. Nice-looking old people they was too, my father used to say; seemed as if butter wouldn't melt in their mouths, as the saying is.

'Now I don't know when I've thought of them last, but I recollect my father speaking of them as well, and the way they're spoke of on their stone that lays just to the right-hand side as you go up the churchyard path – well, you'd think there never was such people. But I believe that was put up by them that got the property; now what was that name again?'

But about that time I thought I must be getting on. I also thought (as before) that it would be well for me not to go very far away from the house.

As I strolled up the road I pondered over the message which Wag's father had been so good as to send me. 'If they're about the house, give them horseshoes; if there's a bat-ball, squirt at it. I think there's a squirt in the tool-house.' All very well, no doubt. I had one horseshoe, but that was not much, and I could explore the tool-house and borrow the garden squirt. But more horseshoes?

At that moment I heard a squeak and a rustle in the hedge, and could not help poking my stick into it to see what had made the noise. The stick clinked against something with its iron ferrule. An old horseshoe! – evidently shown to me on purpose by a friendly creature.

I picked it up, and, not to make a long story of it, I was helped by much the same devices to increase my collection to four. And now I felt it would be wise to turn back.

As I turned into the back garden and came in sight of the little potting-shed or tool-house or whatever it was, I started. Someone was just coming out of it. I gave a loud cough. The party turned round hastily; it was an old man in a sleeved waistcoat, made up, I thought, to look like an 'odd man'. He touched his hat civilly enough, and showed no surprise; but, oh, horror! He held in his hand the garden squirt.

'Morning,' I said; 'going to do a bit of watering?'

He grinned. 'Just stepped up to borrer this off the lady; there's a lot of fly gets on the plants this weather.'

'I dare say there is. By the way, what a lot of horseshoes you people leave about. How many do you think I picked up this morning just along the road? Look here!' and I held one out to him, and his hand came slowly out to meet it, as though he could not keep it back.

His face wrinkled up into a horrible scowl, and what he was going to say I don't know, but just then his hand clutched the horseshoe and he gave a shout of pain, dropped the squirt and the horseshoe, whipped round as quick as any young man could, and was off round the corner of the shed before I had really taken in what was happening.

Before I tried to see what had become of him, I snatched up the squirt and the horseshoe, and almost dropped them again. Both were pretty hot – the squirt much the hotter of the two; but both of them cooled down in a few seconds. By that time my old man was completely out of sight.

And I should not wonder if he was away some time; for perhaps you know, and perhaps you don't know, the effect of an old horseshoe on that sort of people. Not only is it of iron, which they can't abide, but when they see or, still more, touch the shoe, they have to go over all the ground that the shoe went over since it was last in the blacksmith's hands. Only I doubt if the same shoe will work for more than one witch or wizard. Anyway, I put that one aside when I went indoors.

And then I sat and wondered what would come next, and how I could best prepare for it. It occurred to me that it would do no harm to put one of the shoes where it couldn't be seen at once, and it also struck me that under the rug just inside the bedroom door would not be a bad place. So there I put it, and then fell to smoking and reading.

A knock at the door.

'Come in,' said I, a little curious. But no, it was only the maid. As she passed me (which she did quickly) I heard her mutter something about ''ankerchieves for the wash,' and I thought there was something not quite usual about the voice. So I looked round. She was back to me, but the dress and the height and the hair was what I was accustomed to see.

Into the bedroom she hurried, and the next thing was a scream like that of at least two cats in agony! I could just see her leap into the air, come down again on the rug, scream again, and then bundle, hopping, limping – I don't know what – out of the room and down the stairs.

I did catch sight of her feet, though. They were bare, they were greenish, and they were webbed, and I think there were some large white blisters on the soles of them.

You would have thought that the commotion would have brought the household about my ears; but it did not, and I can only suppose that they heard no more of it than they did of the things which the birds and so on say to each other.

'Next, please!' said I, as I lighted a pipe; but if you will believe it, there was no next. Lunch, the afternoon, tea, all passed by, and I was completely undisturbed. 'They must be saving up for the bat-ball,' I thought. 'What in the world can it be?'

As candle-time came on, and the moon began to make herself felt, I took up my old position at the window, with the garden squirt at hand and two full jugs of water on the floor – plenty more to be got from the bathroom if wanted.

The leaden box of the Five Jars was in the right place for the moonbeams to fall on it . . . But no moonbeams would touch it tonight! Why was this? There were no clouds. Yet, between the orb of the moon and my box, there was some obstruction.

High up in the sky was a dancing film, thick enough to cast a shadow on the area of the window; and ever, as the moon rode higher in the heavens, this obstruction became more solid. It seemed gradually to get its bearings and settle into the place where it would shut off the light from the box most completely.

I began to guess. It was the bat-ball: neither more nor less than a dense cloud of bats, gradually forming itself into a solid ball, and coming lower, and nearer to my window. Soon they were only about thirty feet off, and I felt that the moment was come.

I have never much liked bats or desired their company, and now, as I studied them through the glass, and saw their horrid little wicked faces and winking wings, I felt justified in trying to make things as unpleasant for them as I could.

I charged the squirt and let fly, and again, and again, as quick as I could fill it. The water spread a bit before it reached the ball, but not too much to spoil the effect; and the effect was almost alarming. Some hundreds of bats all shrieking out at once, and shrieking with rage and fear (not merely from the excitement of chasing flies, as they generally do). Dozens of them dropping away, with wings too soaked to fly, some on to the grass, where they hopped and fluttered and rolled in ecstasies of passion, some into bushes, one or two plumb on to the path, where they lay motionless; that was the first tableau.

Then came a new feature. From both sides there darted into the heart of the ball two squadrons of figures flying at great speed (though without wings) and perfectly horizontal, with arms joined and straight out in front of them, and almost at the same instant seven or eight more plunged into the ball from above, as if taking headers. The boys were out.

I stopped squirting, for I did not know whether the water would fell them as it felled the bats; but a shrill cry rose from below:

'Go on, M! Go on, M!'

So I aimed again, and it was time, for a knot of bats just then detached itself from the main body and flew full-face towards me. My shot caught the middle one on the snout, and as I swung the squirt to left and right, it disabled four or five others, and discouraged the rest.

Meanwhile the ball was cloven again and again by the arms of the flying squadrons, which shot through it from side to side and from top to bottom (though never, as appeared later, quite through the middle), and though it kept closing up again, it was plainly growing smaller as more and more of the bats outside, which were exposed to the squirt, dropped away.

I suddenly felt something alight on my shoulder, and a voice said in my ear, 'Wag says if you *could* throw a shoe into the middle now, he believes it would finish them. Can you?' It was, I think, Dart who had been sent with the message.

'Horseshoes, I suppose he means,' I said. 'I'll try.'

'Wait till we're out of the way,' said Dart, and was off.

In a moment more I heard – not what I was rather expecting, a horn of Elf-land, but two strokes on the bell. I saw the figures of the boys shoot up and away to left and right, leaving the bat-ball clear, and the bats shrieked aloud, I dare say in triumph at the enemy's retreat.

There were two horseshoes left. I had no idea how they would fly, and I had not much confidence in my power of aiming; but it must be tried, and I threw them edgeways, like quoits. The first skimmed the top of the ball, the second went straight through the middle.

Something which the bats in the very centre were holding – something soft – was pierced by it, and burst. I think it must have been a globe of jelly-like stuff in a thin skin. The contents spurted out on to some of the bats, and seemed to scald the fur off them in an instant and singe up all the membranes of their wings. They fell down at once, with broken screams. The rest darted off in every direction, and the ball was gone.

'Now don't be long,' said a voice from the window-sill.

I thought I knew what was meant, and looked to the leaden casket.

As if to make up for lost time, the moonbeam had already made an opening all round the part on which it shone, and I had but to turn the other side towards it – not even very slowly – to get the whole lid free.

After cleansing my hands in the water, I made trial of the Fifth Jar, and, as I replaced it, a chorus of applause and cheering came up from below.

The Jars were mine.

VIII: Wag at Home

There was no scrambling up to the window-sill this time. My visitors shot in like so many arrows, and 'brought up' on their hands on the tablecloth, or lit on their feet on the top rail of a chair-back or on my shoulder, as the fancy took them.

It would be tedious to go through all the congratulations and thanks which I offered, and indeed received, for it was important to them that the Jars should not get into wrong hands.

'Father says,' said Wag, who was sitting on a book, as usual— 'Oh, what fun it is to be able to fly again!' And he darted straight and level and butted head first into the back of – Sprat, was it? – who was standing near the edge of the table. Sprat was merely propelled into the air a foot or two off, and remained standing, but, of course, turned round and told Wag what he thought of him.

Wag returned contentedly to his book. 'Father says,' he resumed, 'he hopes you'll come and see us now. He says you did all right, and he's very glad the stuff got spilt, because they'll take moons and moons to get as much of it together again. He says they meant to squirt some of it on you when they got near enough, and while you were trying to get it off they'd have got hold of—' He pointed to the box of jars; there was a shyness about mentioning it.

'Your father's very kind,' I said, 'and I hope you'll thank him from me; but I don't quite see how I'm to get into your house.'

'Fancy you not knowing that!' said Wag. 'I'll tell him you'll come.' And he was out of the window. As usual, I had recourse to Slim.

'Why, you did put some on your chest, didn't you?' was Slim's question.

'Yes, but nothing came of it.'

'Well, I believe you can go pretty well anywhere with that, if you think you can.'

'Can I fly, then?'

'No, I should say not. I mean, if you couldn't fly before, you can't now.'

'How do you fly? I don't see any wings.'

'No, we never have wings, and I'm rather glad we don't; the things that have them are always going wrong somehow. We just work it in the proper way with our backs, and there you are; like this.' He made a slight movement of his shoulders, and was standing in the air an inch off the table. 'You never tried that, I suppose?' he went on.

'No,' I said, 'only in dreams,' which evidently meant nothing to him.

'Well now,' I said, 'do you tell me that if I went to Wag's house now, I could get inside it? Look at the size I am!'

'It doesn't look as if you could,' he agreed, 'but my father said just the same as Wag's father about it.'

Here Wag shot on to my shoulder. 'Are you coming?'

'Yes, if I knew how.'

'Well, come and try, anyhow.'

'Very well, as you please; anything to oblige.'

I picked up a hat and went downstairs. All the rest followed, if you can call it following, when there was at least as much flying up steps and in and out of banisters as going down. When we were out on the path, Wag said with more seriousness than usual:

'Now you do mean to come into our house, don't you?'

'Certainly I do, if you wish me to.'

'Then that's all right. This way. There's Father.'

We were on the grass now, and very long it was, and nice and wet I thought I should be with all the dew. As I looked up to see the elder Wag I very nearly fell over a large log which it was very careless of anyone to have left about.

But here was Mr. Wag within a yard of me, and to my extreme surprise he was quite a sizeable man of middle height, with a sensible, good-humoured face, in which I could see a strong likeness to his son.

We both bowed, and then shook hands, and Mr. Wag was very complimentary and pleasant about the occurrences of the evening.

'We've pretty well got the mess cleared up, you see. Yes, don't be alarmed,' he went on, and took hold of my elbow, for he had, no doubt, seen a bewildered look in my eyes.

The fact was, as I suppose you have made out, not that he had grown to my size, but that I had come down to his. 'Things right themselves; you'll have no difficulty about getting back when the time comes. But come in, won't you?'

You will expect me to describe the house and the furniture. I shall not, further than to say that it seemed to me to be of a piece with the fashion in which the boys were dressed; that is, it was like my idea of a good citizen's house in Queen Elizabeth's time; and I shall not describe Mrs. Wag's costume. She did not wear a ruff, anyhow.

Wag, who had been darting about in the air while we walked to his home, followed us in on foot. He now reached up to my shoulder. Slim, who came in too, was shorter.

'Haven't you got any sisters?' I took occasion to say to Wag.

'Of course,' said he. 'Don't you see 'em? Oh! I forgot. Come out, you sillies!'

Upon which there came forward three nice little girls, each of whom was putting away something into a kind of locket which she wore round her neck.

No, it is no use asking me what *their* dresses were like; none at all. All I know is that they curtsied to me very nicely, and that when we all sat down the youngest came and put herself on my knee as if it was a matter of course.

'Why didn't I see you before?' I asked her.

'I suppose because the flowers were in our hair.'

'Show him what you mean, my dear,' said her father. 'He doesn't know our ways yet.'

Accordingly she opened her locket and took out of it a small blue flower, looking as if it was made of enamel, and stuck it in her hair over her forehead. As she did so she vanished, but I could still feel the weight of her on my knee. When she took it out again (as no doubt she did) she became visible, put it back in the locket, and smiled agreeably at me.

Naturally, I had a good many questions to ask about this, but you will hardly expect me to put them all down. Becoming invisible in this way was a privilege which the girls always had till they were grown up, and I suppose I may say 'came out'.

Of course, if they presumed on it, the lockets were taken away for the time being – just in the same way as the boys were sometimes stopped from flying, as we have seen. But their own families could always see them, or at any rate the flowers in their hair, and they could always see each other.

But dear me! How much am I to tell of the conversation of that evening? One part at least: I remembered to ask about the pictures of the things that had happened in former times in places where I chanced to be. Was I obliged to see them, whether they were pleasant or horrible?

'Oh no,' they said. If you shut your eyes from below – that meant pushing up the lower eyelids – you would be rid of them; and you would only begin seeing them, either if you wanted to, or else if you left your mind quite blank, and were thinking of nothing in particular. Then they would begin to come, and there was no knowing how old they might be; that depended on how angry or excited or happy or sad the people had been to whom they happened.

And that reminds me of another thing. Wag had got rather fidgety while we were talking, and was flying up to the ceiling and down again, and walking on his hands, and so forth, when his mother said:

'Dear, do be quiet. Why don't you take a glass and amuse yourself with it? Here's the key of the cupboard.'

She threw it to him and he caught it and ran to a tall bureau opposite and unlocked it. After humming and flitting about in front of it for a little time, he pulled a thing like a slate off a shelf where there were a large number of them.

'What have you got?' said his mother.

'The one I didn't get to the end of yesterday, about the dragon.'

'Oh, that's a very good one,' said she. 'I used to be very fond of that.'

'I liked it awfully as far as I got,' he said, and was betaking himself to a settle on the other side of the room when I asked if I might see it, and he brought it to me.

It was just like a small looking-glass in a frame, and the frame had one or two buttons or little knobs on it. Wag put it into my hand and then got behind me and put his chin on my shoulder.

'That's where I'd got to,' he said. 'He's just going out through the forest.'

I thought at the first glance that I was looking at a very good copy of a picture. It was a knight on horseback, in plate-armour, and the armour looked as if it had really seen service. The horse was a massive white beast, rather of the cart-horse type, but not so 'hairy in the hoof'. The background was a wood, chiefly of oak-trees; but the undergrowth was wonderfully painted. I felt that if I looked into it I should see every blade of grass and every bramble-leaf.

'Ready?' said Wag, and reached over and moved one of the knobs. The knight shook his rein, and the horse began to move at a foot-pace.

'Well, but he can't *hear* anything, Wag,' said his father.

'I thought you wanted to be quiet,' said Wag, 'but we'll have it aloud if you like.'

He slid aside another knob, and I began to hear the tread of the horse and the creaking of the saddle and the chink of the armour, as well as a rising breeze which now came sighing through the wood. Like a cinema, you will say, of course. Well, it was; but there was colour and sound, and you could hold it in your hand, and it wasn't a photograph, but the live thing which you could stop at pleasure, and look into every detail of it.

Well, I went on reading, as you may say, this glass. In a theatre, you know, if you saw a knight riding through a forest, the effect would be managed by making the scenery slide backwards past him; and in a cinema it could all be shortened up by increasing the pace or leaving out part of the film. Here it was not like that; we seemed to be keeping pace and going along with the knight.

Presently he began to sing. He had a loud voice and uttered his words crisply, so that I had no difficulty in making out the song. It was about a lady who was very proud and haughty to him and would have nothing to say to his suit, and it declared that the only thing left for him was to lay himself down under a tree. But he seemed quite cheerful about it, and indeed neither his complexion nor the glance of his eye gave any sign that he was suffering the pangs of hopeless love.

Suddenly his horse stopped short and snorted uneasily. The knight left off singing in the middle of a verse, looked earnestly into the wood at the back of the picture, and then out towards us, and then behind him. He patted his horse's neck, and then, humming to himself, put on his gauntlets, which were hanging at his saddle bow, managed somehow to latch or bolt the fastenings of them, slipped down his visor, and took the hilt of his sword in one hand and the sheath in the other and loosened the blade in the sheath.

He had hardly done this when the horse shied violently and reared. And out of the thicket on the near side of the road (I suppose) something shot up in front of him on the saddle. We all drew in our breath.

'Don't be frightened, dear,' said Mrs. Wag to the youngest girl, who had given a sort of jump. 'He's quite safe this time.'

I must say it did not look like it. The beast that had leapt on to the saddle was tearing with its claws, drawing back its head and driving it forward again with horrid force against the visor, and was at such close quarters that the knight could not possibly either draw or use his sword.

It was a horrible beast, too; evidently a young dragon. As it sat on the saddle-bow, its head was just about on a level with the knight's. It had four short legs with long toes and claws. It clung to the saddle with the hind feet and tore with the fore feet, as I said. Its head was rather long, and had two pointed ears and two small sharp horns. Besides, it had bat wings, with which it buffeted the knight, but its tail was short. I don't know whether it had been bitten or cut off in some previous fight. It was all of a mustard-yellow colour.

The knight was for the moment having a bad time of it, for the horse was plunging and the dragon doing its very worst. The crisis was not long, though. The knight took hold of the right wing with both hands and tore the membrane upwards to the root, like parchment. It bled yellow blood, and the dragon gave a grating scream. Then he clutched it hard by the neck and managed to wrench it away from its hold on the saddle; and when it was in the air, he whirled its body, heavy as it was, first over his back and then forwards again, and its neck-bone, I suppose, broke, for it was quite limp when he cast it down.

He looked down at it for a little, and seeing it stir, he got off, with the rein over his arm, drew his sword, cut the head off, and kicked it away some yards. The next thing he did was to push up his visor, look upward, mutter something I could not well hear, and cross himself; after which he said aloud, 'Where man finds one of a brood, he may look for more,' mounted, turned his horse's head and galloped off the way he had come.

We had not followed him far through the wood when—

'Bother!' said Wag, 'there's the bell,' and he reached over and slid back the knobs in the frame, and the knight stopped.

I was full of questions, but there was no time to put them. Good-nights had to be said quickly, and Father Wag saw me out of the front door.

I set out on what seemed a considerable walk across the rough grass towards the enormous building in which I lived. I suppose I did not really take many minutes about getting to the path; and as I stepped on to it – rather carefully, for it was a longish way down – why, without any shock or any odd feeling, I was my own size again. And I went to bed pondering much upon the events of the day.

* * *

Well, I began this communication by saying that I was going to explain to you how it was that I 'heard something from the owls', and I think I have explained how it is that I am able to say that I have done so. Exactly what it was that you and I were talking about when I mentioned the owls, I dare say neither of us remembers.

As you can see, I have had more exciting experiences than merely conversing with them – interesting, and, I think, unusual as that is. I have not, of course, told you nearly all there is to tell, but perhaps I have said enough for the present. More, if you should wish it, another time.

As to present conditions. Today there is a slight coolness between Wisp and the cat. He made his way into a mouse-hole which she was watching, and enticed her close up to it by scratchings and other sounds, and then, when she came quite near (taking great trouble, of course, to make no noise whatever), he put his head out and blew in her face, which affronted her very much. However, I believe I have persuaded her that he meant no harm.

The room is rather full of them tonight. Wag and most of the rest are rehearsing a play which they mean to present before I go. Slim, who happens not to be wanted for a time, is manœuvring on the table, facing me, and is trying to produce a portrait of me which shall be a little less libellous than his first effort.

He has just now shown me the final production, with which he is greatly pleased. I am not.

Farewell. I am, with the usual expressions of regard,

Yours,

M (or N).

The Haunted Dolls' House

'I SUPPOSE YOU GET stuff of that kind through your hands pretty often?' said Mr. Dillet, as he pointed with his stick to an object which shall be described when the time comes. And when he said it, he lied in his throat, and knew that he lied.

Not once in twenty years – perhaps not once in a lifetime – could Mr. Chittenden, skilled as he was in ferreting out the forgotten treasures of half-a-dozen counties, expect to handle such a specimen.

It was collectors' palaver, and Mr. Chittenden recognised it as such.

'Stuff of that kind, Mr. Dillet! It's a museum piece, that is.'

'Well, I suppose there are museums that'll take anything.'

'I've seen one, not as good as that, years back,' said Mr. Chittenden thoughtfully. 'But that's not likely to come into the market, and I'm told they 'ave some fine ones of the period over the water. No, I'm only telling you the truth, Mr. Dillet, when I was to say that if you was to place an unlimited order with me for the very best that could be got – and you know I 'ave facilities for getting to know of such things, and a reputation to maintain – well, all I can say is, I should lead you straight up to that one and say, "I can't do no better for you than that, sir".'

'Hear, hear!' said Mr. Dillet, applauding ironically with the end of his stick on the floor of the shop. 'How much are you sticking the innocent American buyer for it, eh?'

'Oh, I shan't be over hard on the buyer, American or otherwise. You see, it stands this way, Mr. Dillet – if I knew just a bit more about the pedigree—'

415

'Or just a bit less,' Mr. Dillet put in.

'Ha, ha! You will have your joke, sir. No, but as I was saying, if I knew just a little more than what I do about the piece – though anyone can see for themselves it's a genuine thing, every last corner of it, and there's not been one of my men allowed to so much as touch it since it came into the shop – there'd be another figure in the price I'm asking.'

'And what's that: five and twenty?'

'Multiply that by three and you've got it, sir. Seventy-five's my price.'

'And fifty's mine,' said Mr. Dillet.

The point of agreement was, of course, somewhere between the two, it does not matter exactly where – I think sixty guineas. But half-an-hour later the object was being packed, and within an hour Mr. Dillet had called for it in his car and driven away.

Mr. Chittenden, holding the cheque in his hand, saw him off from the door with smiles, and returned, still smiling, into the parlour where his wife was making the tea. He stopped at the door.

'It's gone,' he said.

'Thank God for that!' said Mrs. Chittenden, putting down the teapot. 'Mr. Dillet, was it?'

'Yes, it was.'

'Well, I'd sooner it was him than another.'

'Oh, I don't know; he ain't a bad feller, my dear.'

'Maybe not, but in my opinion he'd be none the worse for a bit of a shake up.'

'Well, if that's your opinion, it's my opinion he's put himself into the way of getting one. Anyhow, we shan't have no more of it, and that's something to be thankful for.'

And so Mr. and Mrs. Chittenden sat down to tea.

And what of Mr. Dillet and his new acquisition? What it was, the title of this story will have told you. What it was like, I shall have to indicate as well as I can.

There was only just enough room for it in the car, and Mr. Dillet had to sit with the driver. He had also to go slow, for though the rooms of the Dolls' House had all been stuffed carefully with soft cotton wool, jolting was to be avoided, in view of the immense number of small objects which thronged them. And the ten-mile drive was an anxious time for him, in spite of all the precautions he insisted upon.

At last his front door was reached, and Collins, the butler, came out.

'Look here, Collins, you must help me with this thing – it's a delicate job. We must get it out upright, see? It's full of little things that mustn't be displaced more than we can help.

'Let's see, where shall we have it? (After a pause for consideration.) Really, I think I shall have to put it in my own room, to begin with at any rate. On the big table – that's it.'

It was conveyed – with much talking – to Mr. Dillet's spacious room on the first floor, looking out on the drive.

The sheeting was unwound from it, and the front thrown open, and for the next hour or two Mr. Dillet was fully occupied in extracting the padding and setting in order the contents of the rooms.

When this thoroughly congenial task was finished, I must say that it would have been difficult to find a more perfect and attractive specimen of a Dolls' House in Strawberry Hill Gothic than that which now stood on Mr. Dillet's large kneehole table, lighted up by the evening sun which came slanting through three tall slash-windows.

It was quite six feet long, including the Chapel or Oratory which flanked the front on the left as you faced it, and the stable on the right. The main block of the house was, as I have said, in the Gothic manner: that is to say, the windows had pointed arches and were surmounted by what are called ogival hoods, with crockets and finials such as we see on the canopies of tombs built into church walls. At the angles were absurd turrets covered with arched panels. The Chapel had pinnacles and buttresses, and a bell in the turret and coloured glass in the windows.

When the front of the house was open you saw four large rooms, bed-room, dining-room, drawing-room and kitchen, each with its appropriate furniture in a very complete state.

The stable on the right was in two storeys, with its proper complement of horses, coaches and grooms, and with its clock and Gothic cupola for the clock bell.

Pages, of course, might be written on the outfit of the mansion – how many frying-pans, how many gilt chairs, what pictures, carpets, chandeliers, four-posters, table linen, glass, crockery and plate it possessed; but all this must be left to the imagination.

I will only say that the base or plinth on which the house stood (for it was fitted with one of some depth which allowed of a flight of steps to the front door and a terrace, partly balustraded) contained a shallow drawer or drawers in which were neatly stored sets of embroidered curtains, changes of raiment for the inmates, and, in short, all the materials for an infinite series of variations and refittings of the most absorbing and delightful kind.

'Quintessence of Horace Walpole, that's what it is: he must have had something to do with the making of it.' Such was Mr. Dillet's murmured reflection as he knelt before it in a reverent ecstasy. 'Simply wonderful! This is my day and no mistake. Five hundred pounds coming in this morning for that cabinet which I never cared about, and now this tumbling into my hands for a tenth, at the very most, of what it would fetch in town. Well, well! It almost makes one afraid something'll happen to counter it. Let's have a look at the population, anyhow.'

Accordingly, he set them before him in a row. Again, here is an opportunity, which some would snatch at, of making an inventory of costume: I am incapable of it.

There were a gentleman and lady, in blue satin and brocade respectively. There were two children, a boy and a girl. There was a cook, a nurse, a footman, and there were the stable servants, two postilions, a coachman, two grooms.

'Anyone else? Yes, possibly.'

The curtains of the four-poster in the bedroom were closely drawn round all four sides of it, and he put his finger in between them and felt in the bed. He drew the finger back hastily, for it almost seemed to him as if something had – not stirred, perhaps, but yielded – in an odd live way as he pressed it.

Then he put back the curtains, which ran on rods in the proper manner, and extracted from the bed a white-haired old gentleman in a long linen night-dress and cap, and laid him down by the rest. The tale was complete.

Dinner-time was now near, so Mr. Dillet spent but five minutes in putting the lady and children into the drawing-room, the gentleman into the dining-room, the servants into the kitchen and stables, and the old man back into his bed.

He retired into his dressing-room next door, and we see and hear no more of him until something like eleven o'clock at night.

His whim was to sleep surrounded by some of the gems of his collection. The big room in which we have seen him contained his bed, bath, wardrobe, and all the appliances of dressing were in a commodious room adjoining. But his four-poster, which itself was a valued treasure, stood in the large room where he sometimes wrote, and often sat, and even received visitors. Tonight he repaired to it in a highly complacent frame of mind.

There was no striking clock within earshot – none on the staircase, none in the stable, none in the distant church tower. Yet it is indubitable that Mr. Dillet was started out of a very pleasant slumber by a bell tolling One.

He was so much startled that he did not merely lie breathless with wide-open eyes, but actually sat up in his bed.

He never asked himself, till the morning hours, how it was that, though there was no light at all in the room, the Dolls' House on the kneehole table stood out with complete clearness. But it was so.

The effect was that of a bright harvest moon shining full on the front of a big white stone mansion – a quarter of a mile away it might be, and yet every detail was photographically sharp. There were trees about it, too – trees rising behind the chapel and the house. He seemed to be conscious of the scent of a cool still September night.

He thought he could hear an occasional stamp and clink from the stables, as of horses stirring. And with another shock he realised that, above the house, he was looking, not at the wall of his room with its pictures, but into the profound blue of a night sky.

There were lights, more than one, in the windows, and he quickly saw that this was no four-roomed house with a movable front, but one of many rooms and staircases – a real house, but seen as if through the wrong end of a telescope.

'You mean to show me something,' he muttered to himself, and he gazed earnestly on the lighted windows. They would in real life have been shut-tered or curtained, no doubt, he thought; but, as it was, there was nothing to intercept his view of what was being transacted inside the rooms.

Two rooms were lighted – one on the ground floor to the right of the door, one upstairs, on the left – the first brightly enough, the other rather dimly. The lower room was the dining-room: a table was laid, but the meal was over, and only wine and glasses were left on the table.

The man of the blue satin and the woman of the brocade were alone in the room, and they were talking very earnestly, seated close together at the table, their elbows on it; every now and again stopping to listen, as it seemed.

Once *he* rose, came to the window and opened it and put his head out and his hand to his ear. There was a lighted taper in a silver candlestick on a sideboard. When the man left the window he seemed to leave the room also; and the lady, taper in hand, remained standing and listening.

The expression on her face was that of one striving her utmost to keep down a fear that threatened to master her – and succeeding. It was a hateful face, too: broad, flat and sly.

Now the man came back and she took some small thing from him and hurried out of the room. He, too, disappeared, but only for a moment or two. The front door slowly opened and he stepped out and stood on the top of the *perron*, looking this way and that; then turned towards the upper window that was lighted, and shook his fist.

It was time to look at that upper window. Through it was seen a four-post bed; a nurse or other servant in an arm-chair, evidently sound asleep; in the bed an old man lying: awake, and, one would say, anxious, from the way in which he shifted about and moved his fingers, beating tunes on the coverlet.

Beyond the bed a door opened. Light was seen on the ceiling, and the lady came in. She set down her candle on a table, came to the fireside and roused the nurse. In her hand she had an old-fashioned wine bottle, ready uncorked.

The nurse took it, poured some of the contents into a little silver sauce-pan, added some spice and sugar from casters on the table, and set it to warm on the fire.

Meanwhile the old man in the bed beckoned feebly to the lady, who came to him, smiling, took his wrist as if to feel his pulse, and bit her lip as if in consternation. He looked at her anxiously, and then pointed to the window, and spoke. She nodded, and did as the man below had done: opened the casement and listened – perhaps rather ostentatiously – then drew in her head and shook it, looking at the old man, who seemed to sigh.

By this time the posset on the fire was steaming, and the nurse poured it into a small two-handled silver bowl and brought it to the bedside.

The old man seemed disinclined for it and was waving it away, but the lady and the nurse together bent over him and evidently pressed it upon him. He must have yielded, for they supported him into a sitting position, and put it to his lips. He drank most of it, in several draughts, and they laid him down.

The lady left the room, smiling good night to him, and took the bowl, the bottle and the silver saucepan with her. The nurse returned to the chair, and there was an interval of complete quiet.

Suddenly the old man started up in his bed – and he must have uttered some cry, for the nurse started out of her chair and made but one step of it to the bedside.

He was a sad and terrible sight – flushed in the face, almost to blackness, the eyes glaring whitely, both hands clutching at his heart, foam at his lips. For a moment the nurse left him, ran to the door, flung it wide open, and, one supposes, screamed aloud for help, then darted back to the bed and seemed to try feverishly to soothe him – to lay him down – anything.

But as the lady, her husband, and several servants, rushed into the room with horrified faces, the old man collapsed under the nurse's hands and lay back, and his features, contorted with agony and rage, relaxed slowly into calm.

A few moments later, lights showed out to the left of the house, and a coach with flambeaux drove up to the door. A white-wigged man in black got nimbly out and ran up the steps, carrying a small leather trunk-shaped box. He was met in the doorway by the man and his wife, she with her handkerchief clutched between her hands, he with a tragic face, but retaining his self-control.

They led the newcomer into the dining-room, where he set his box of papers on the table, and, turning to them, listened with a face of consternation at what they had to tell. He nodded his head again and again, threw out his hands slightly, declined, it seemed, offers of refreshment and lodging for the night, and within a few minutes came slowly down the steps, entering the coach and driving off the way he had come.

As the man in blue watched him from the top of the steps, a smile not pleasant to see stole slowly over his fat white face.

Darkness fell over the whole scene as the lights of the coach disappeared.

But Mr. Dillet remained sitting up in the bed. He had rightly guessed that there would be a sequel.

The house front glimmered out again before long. But now there was a difference. The lights were in other windows, one at the top of the house, the other illuminating the range of coloured windows of the chapel.

How he saw through these is not quite obvious, but he did.

The interior was as carefully furnished as the rest of the establishment, with its minute red cushions on the desks, its Gothic stall-canopies, and its western gallery and pinnacled organ with gold pipes. On the centre of the black and white pavement was a bier: four tall candles burned at the corners. On the bier was a coffin covered with a pall of black velvet.

As he looked the folds of the pall stirred. It seemed to rise at one end: it slid downwards, it fell away, exposing the black coffin with its silver handles and name-plate. One of the tall candlesticks swayed and toppled over. Ask no more, but turn, as Mr. Dillet hastily did, and look in at the lighted window at the top of the house, where a boy and girl lay in two truckle-beds, and a four-poster for the nurse rose above them.

The nurse was not visible for the moment; but the father and mother were there, dressed now in mourning, but with very little sign of mourning in their demeanour. Indeed, they were laughing and talking with a good deal of animation, sometimes to each other, and sometimes throwing a remark to one or other of the children, and again laughing at the answers.

Then the father was seen to go on tiptoe out of the room, taking with him as he went a white garment that hung on a peg near the door. He shut the door after him.

A minute or two later it was slowly opened again, and a muffled head poked round it. A bent form of sinister shape stepped across to the truckle-beds, and suddenly stopped, threw up its arms and revealed, of course, the father, laughing.

The children were in agonies of terror, the boy with the bedclothes over his head, the girl throwing herself out of bed into her mother's arms. Attempts at consolation followed – the parents took the children on their laps, patted them, picked up the white gown and showed there was no harm in it, and so forth; and at last putting the children back into bed, left the room with encouraging waves of the hand.

As they left it, the nurse came in, and soon the light died down.

Still Mr. Dillet watched immovable.

A new sort of light – not of lamp or candle – a pale ugly light, began to dawn around the door-case at the back of the room. The door was opening again. The seer does not like to dwell upon what he saw entering the room: he says it might be described as a frog – the size of a man – but it had scanty white hair about its head. It was busy about the truckle-beds, but not for long. The sound of cries – faint, as if coming out of a vast distance – but, even so, infinitely appalling, reached the ear.

There were signs of a hideous commotion all over the house: lights moved along and up, and doors opened and shut, and running figures passed within the windows. The clock in the stable turret tolled one, and darkness fell again.

It was only dispelled once more, to show the house-front. At the bottom of the steps dark figures were drawn up in two lines, holding flaming torches. More dark figures came down the steps, bearing, first one, then another small coffin. And the lines of torch-bearers with the coffins between them moved silently onward to the left.

The hours of night passed on – never so slowly, Mr. Dillet thought. Gradually he sank down from sitting to lying in his bed – but he did not close an eye, and early next morning he sent for the doctor.

The doctor found him in a disquieting state of nerves, and recommended sea-air. To a quiet place on the East Coast he accordingly repaired by easy stages in his car.

One of the first people he met on the sea front was Mr. Chittenden, who, it appeared, had likewise been advised to take his wife away for a bit of a change.

Mr. Chittenden looked somewhat askance upon him when they met, and not without cause.

'Well, I don't wonder at you being a bit upset, Mr. Dillet. What? Yes, well, I might say 'orrible upset, to be sure, seeing what me and my poor wife went through ourselves.

'But I put it to you, Mr. Dillet, one of two things: was I going to scrap a lovely piece like that on the one 'and, or was I going to tell customers: "I'm selling you a regular picture-palace-dramar in reel life of the olden time, billed to perform regular at one o'clock a.m."?

'Why, what would you 'ave said yourself? And next thing you know, two Justices of the Peace in the back parlour, and pore Mr. and Mrs. Chittenden off in a spring cart to the County Asylum and everyone in the street saying, "Ah, I thought it 'ud come to that. Look at the way the man drank!" – and me next door, or next door but one, to a total abstainer, as you know. Well, there was my position.

'What? Me 'ave it back in the shop? Well, what do you think? No, but I'll tell you what I will do. You shall have your money back, bar the ten pound I paid for it, and you make what you can.'

Later in the day, in what is offensively called the 'smoke-room' of the hotel, a murmured conversation between the two went on for some time.

'How much do you really know about that thing, and where it came from?'

'Honest, Mr. Dillet, I don't know the 'ouse. Of course, it came out of the lumber room of a country 'ouse – that anyone could guess. But I'll go as far as say this, that I believe it's not a hundred miles from this place. Which direction and how far I've no notion. I'm only judging by guess-work.

'The man as I actually paid the cheque to ain't one of my regular men, and I've lost sight of him; but I 'ave the idea that this part of the country was his beat, and that's every word I can tell you.

'But now, Mr. Dillet, there's one thing that rather physicks me. That old chap – I suppose you saw him drive up to the door – I thought so. Now, would he have been the medical man, do you take it? My wife would have it so, but I stuck to it that was the lawyer, because he had papers with him, and one he took out was folded up.'

'I agree,' said Mr. Dillet. 'Thinking it over, I came to the conclusion that was the old man's will, ready to be signed.'

'Just what I thought,' said Mr. Chittenden, 'and I took it that will would have cut out the young people, eh? Well, well! It's been a lesson to me, I know that. I shan't buy no more dolls' houses, nor waste no more money on the pictures – and as to this business of poisonin' grandpa, well, if I know myself, I never 'ad much of a turn for that. Live and let live: that's bin my motto throughout life, and I ain't found it a bad one.'

Filled with these elevated sentiments, Mr. Chittenden retired to his lodgings.

Mr. Dillet next day repaired to the local Institute, where he hoped to find some clue to the riddle that absorbed him. He gazed in despair at a long file of the Canterbury and York Society's publications of the Parish Registers of the District. No print resembling the house of his nightmare was among those that hung on the staircase and in the passages.

Disconsolate, he found himself at last in a derelict room, staring at a dusty model of a church in a dusty glass case: *Model of St. Stephen's Church, Coxham. Presented by J. Merewether, Esq., of Ilbridge House, 1877. The work of his ancestor James Merewether, d. 1786.* There was something in the fashion of it that reminded him dimly of his horror.

He retraced his steps to a wall map he had noticed, and made out that Ilbridge House was in Coxham Parish. Coxham was, as it happened, one of the parishes of which he had retained the name when he glanced over the file of printed registers, and it was not long before he found in them the record of the burial of Roger Milford, aged 76, on the 11th of September, 1757, and of Roger and Elizabeth Merewether, aged 9 and 7, on the 19th of the same month.

It seemed worthwhile to follow up this clue, frail as it was, and in the afternoon he drove out to Coxham.

The east-end of the north aisle of the church is a Milford chapel, and on its north wall are tablets to the same persons: Roger, the elder, it seems, was distinguished by all the qualities which adorn *the Father, the Magistrate and the Man.* The memorial was erected by his attached daughter Elizabeth, *who did not long survive the loss of a parent ever solicitous for her welfare, and of two amiable children.* The last sentence was plainly an addition to the original inscription.

A yet later slab told of James Merewether, husband of Elizabeth, *who in the dawn of life practised, not without success, those arts which, had he continued their exercise, might in the opinion of the most competent judges have earned for him the name of the British Vitruvius: but who, overwhelmed by the visitation which deprived him of an affectionate partner and a blooming offspring, passed his Prime and Age in a secluded yet elegant Retirement: his grateful Nephew and Heir indulges a pious sorrow by this too brief recital of his excellences.*

The children were more simply commemorated. Both died on the night of the 12th of September.

Mr. Dillet felt sure that in Ilbridge House he had found the scene of his drama. In some old sketchbook, possibly in some old print, he may yet find convincing evidence that he is right.

But the Ilbridge House of today is not that which he sought: it is an Elizabethan erection of the forties, in red brick with stone quoins and dressings. A quarter of a mile from it, in a low part of the park, backed by ancient, stag-horned, ivy-strangled trees and thick undergrowth, are marks of a terraced platform overgrown with rough grass. A few stone balusters lie here and there, and a heap or two, covered with nettles and ivy, of wrought stones with badly-carved crockets. This, someone told Mr. Dillet, was the site of an older house.

As he drove out of the village, the hall clock struck four, and Mr. Dillet started up and clapped his hands to his ears. It was not the first time he had heard that bell.

Awaiting an offer from the other side of the Atlantic, the dolls' house still reposes, carefully sheeted, in a loft over Mr. Dillet's stables, whither Collins conveyed it on the day when Mr. Dillet started for the sea coast.

[It will be said, perhaps, and not unjustly, that this is no more than a variation on a former story of mine called 'The Mezzotint'. I can only hope that there is enough of variation in the setting to make the repetition of the *motif* tolerable.]

A Neighbour's Landmark

THOSE WHO SPEND the greater part of their time in reading or writing books are, of course, apt to take rather particular notice of accumulations of books when they come across them.

They will not pass a stall, a shop, or even a bedroom-shelf without reading some title, and if they find themselves in an unfamiliar library, no host need trouble himself further about their entertainment.

The putting of dispersed sets of volumes together, or the turning right way up of those which the dusting housemaid has left in an apoplectic condition, appeals to them as one of the lesser Works of Mercy.

Happy in these employments, and in occasionally opening an 18th-century octavo, to see 'what it is all about', and to conclude after five minutes that it deserves the seclusion it now enjoys, I had reached the middle of a wet August afternoon at Betton Court—

'You begin in a deeply Victorian manner,' I said. 'Is this to continue?'

'Remember, if you please,' said my friend, looking at me over his spectacles, 'that I am a Victorian by birth and education, and that the Victorian tree may not unreasonably be expected to bear Victorian fruit.

'Further, remember that an immense quantity of clever and thoughtful Rubbish is now being written about the Victorian age. Now,' he went on, laying his papers on his knee, 'that article, "The Stricken Years", in *The Times Literary Supplement* the other day – able? Of course it is able, but, oh! – my soul and body – do just hand it over here, will you? It's on the table by you.'

'I thought you were to read me something you had written,' I said, with-out moving, 'but, of course—'

'Yes, I know,' he said. 'Very well, then, I'll do that first. But I *should* like to show you afterwards what I mean. However—' And he lifted the sheets of paper and adjusted his spectacles.

—at Betton Court, where, generations back, two country-house libraries had been fused together, and no descendant of either stock had ever faced the task of picking them over or getting rid of duplicates.

Now I am not setting out to tell of rarities I may have discovered, of Shakespeare quartos bound up in volumes of political tracts, or anything of that kind, but of an experience which befell me in the course of my search – an experience which I cannot either explain away or fit into the scheme of my ordinary life.

It was, I said, a wet August afternoon, rather windy, rather warm. Outside the window great trees were stirring and weeping. Between them were stretches of green and yellow country (for the Court stands high on a hillside), and blue hills far off, veiled with rain. Up above was a very restless and hopeless movement of low clouds travelling north-west.

I had suspended my work – if you call it work – for some minutes to stand at the window and look at these things, and at the greenhouse roof on the right with the water sliding off it, and the Church tower that rose behind that. It was all in favour of my going steadily on – no likelihood of a clearing up for hours to come.

I, therefore, returned to the shelves, lifted out a set of eight or nine volumes, lettered 'Tracts', and conveyed them to the table for closer examination.

They were for the most part of the reign of Anne. There was a good deal of *The Late Peace*, *The Late War*, *The Conduct of the Allies*. There were also *Letters to a Convocation Man*; *Sermons Preached at St. Michael's, Queenhithe*; *Enquiries into a Late Charge of the Rt. Rev. the Lord Bishop of Winchester* (or more probably Winton) *to His Clergy* – things all very lively once, and indeed still keeping so much of their old sting that I was tempted to betake myself into an armchair in the window, and give them more time than I had intended.

Besides, I was somewhat tired by the day. The Church clock struck four, and it really was four, for in 1889 there was no saving of daylight.

So I settled myself. And first I glanced over some of the War pamphlets, and pleased myself by trying to pick out Swift by his style from among the undistinguished. But the War pamphlets needed more knowledge of the geography of the Low Countries than I had.

I turned to the Church, and read several pages of what the Dean of Canterbury said to the Society for Promoting Christian Knowledge on the occasion of their anniversary meeting in 1711.

When I turned over to a Letter from a Beneficed Clergyman in the Country to the Bishop of C——r, I was becoming languid, and I gazed for some moments at the following sentence without surprise:

This Abuse (for I think myself justified in calling it by that name) is one which I am persuaded Your Lordship would (if 'twere known to you) exert your utmost efforts to do away. But I am also persuaded that you know no more of its existence than (in the words of the Country Song)

*'That which walks in Betton Wood
Knows why it walks or why it cries.'*

Then indeed I did sit up in my chair, and run my finger along the lines to make sure that I had read them right.

There was no mistake.

Nothing more was to be gathered from the rest of the pamphlet. The next paragraph definitely changed the subject: 'But I have said enough upon this *Topick*' were its opening words.

So discreet, too, was the namelessness of the Beneficed Clergyman that he refrained even from initials, and had his letter printed in London.

The riddle was of a kind that might faintly interest anyone. To me, who have dabbled a good deal in works of folklore, it was really exciting. I was set upon solving it – on finding out, I mean, what story lay behind it. And, at least, I felt myself lucky in one point, that, whereas I might have come on the paragraph in some College Library far away, here I was at Betton, on the very scene of action.

The Church clock struck five, and a single stroke on a gong followed. This, I knew, meant tea. I heaved myself out of the deep chair, and obeyed the summons.

My host and I were alone at the Court. He came in soon, wet from a round of landlord's errands, and with pieces of local news which had to be passed on before I could make an opportunity of asking whether there was a particular place in the parish that was still known as Betton Wood.

'Betton Wood,' he said, 'was a short mile away, just on the crest of Betton Hill, and my father stubbed up the last bit of it when it paid better to grow corn than scrub oaks.

'Why do you want to know about Betton Wood?'

'Because,' I said, 'in an old pamphlet I was reading just now, there are two lines of a country song which mention it, and they sound as if there was a story belonging to them. Someone says that someone else knows no more of whatever it may be:

> "Than that which walks in Betton Wood
> Knows why it walks or why it cries".'

'Goodness,' said Philipson, 'I wonder whether that was why . . . I must ask old Mitchell.' He muttered something else to himself, and took some more tea, thoughtfully.

'Whether that was why—?' I said.

'Yes, I was going to say, whether that was why my father had the Wood stubbed up. I said just now it was to get more plough-land, but I don't really know if it was.

'I don't believe he ever broke it up: it's rough pasture at this moment. But there's one old chap at least who'd remember something of it – old Mitchell.' He looked at his watch. 'Blest if I don't go down there and ask him. I don't think I'll take you,' he went on. 'He's not so likely to tell anything he thinks is odd if there's a stranger by.'

'Well, mind you remember every single thing he does tell. As for me, if it clears up, I shall go out, and if it doesn't, I shall go on with the books.'

It did clear up, sufficiently at least to make me think it worthwhile to walk up the nearest hill and look over the country. I did not know the lie of the land. It was the first visit I had paid to Philipson, and this was the first day of it.

So I went down the garden and through the wet shrubberies with a very open mind, and offered no resistance to the indistinct impulse – was it, however, so very indistinct? – which kept urging me to bear to the left whenever there was a forking of the path.

The result was that after ten minutes or more of dark going between dripping rows of box and laurel and privet, I was confronted by a stone arch in the Gothic style set in the stone wall which encircled the whole demesne.

The door was fastened by a spring-lock, and I took the precaution of leaving this on the jar as I passed out into the road. That road I crossed, and entered a narrow lane between hedges which led upward. And that lane I pursued at a leisurely pace for as much as half-a-mile, and went on to the field to which it led.

I was now on a good point of vantage for taking in the situation of the Court, the village, and the environment, and I leant upon a gate and gazed westward and downward.

I think we must all know the landscapes – are they by Birket Foster, or somewhat earlier? – which, in the form of woodcuts, decorate the volumes of poetry that lay on the drawing-room tables of our fathers and grandfathers – volumes in 'Art Cloth, embossed bindings': that strikes me as being the right phrase.

I confess myself an admirer of them, and especially of those which show the peasant leaning over a gate in a hedge and surveying, at the bottom of a downward slope, the village church spire – embosomed amid venerable trees, and a fertile plain intersected by hedgerows, and bounded by distant hills, behind which the orb of day is sinking (or it may be rising) amid level clouds illumined by his dying (or nascent) ray.

The expressions employed here are those which seem appropriate to the pictures I have in mind. And were there opportunity, I would try to work in the Vale, the Grove, the Cot, and the Flood.

Anyhow, they are beautiful to me, these landscapes, and it was just such a one that I was now surveying. It might have come straight out of *Gems of Sacred Song, Selected by a Lady* and given as a birthday present to Eleanor Philipson in 1852 by her attached friend Millicent Graves.

All at once I turned as if I had been stung. There thrilled into my right ear and pierced my head a note of incredible sharpness, like the shriek of a bat, only ten times intensified – the kind of thing that makes one wonder if something has not given way in one's brain.

I held my breath, and covered my ear, and shivered. Something in the circulation. Another minute or two, I thought, and I return home. But I must fix the view a little more firmly in my mind.

Only, when I turned to it again, the taste was gone out of it.

The sun was down behind the hill, and the light was off the fields, and when the clock bell in the Church tower struck seven, I thought no longer of kind mellow evening hours of rest, and scents of flowers and woods on evening air; and of how someone on a farm a mile or two off would be saying 'How clear Betton bell sounds tonight after the rain!'.

But instead images came to me of dusty beams and creeping spiders and savage owls up in the tower, and forgotten graves and their ugly contents below, and of flying Time and all it had taken out of my life. And just then into my left ear – close as if lips had been put within an inch of my head, the frightful scream came thrilling again.

There was no mistake possible now. It *was* from outside. 'With no language but a cry' was the thought that flashed into my mind.

Hideous it was beyond anything I had heard or have heard since, but I could read no emotion in it, and doubted if I could read any intelligence. All its effect was to take away every vestige, every possibility, of enjoyment, and make this no place to stay in one moment more.

Of course there was nothing to be seen: but I was convinced that, if I waited, the thing would pass me again on its aimless, endless beat, and I could not bear the notion of a third repetition.

I hurried back to the lane and down the hill. But when I came to the arch in the wall I stopped. Could I be sure of my way among those dank alleys, which would be danker and darker now! No, I confessed to myself that I was afraid: so jarred were all my nerves with the cry on the hill that I really felt I could not afford to be startled even by a little bird in a bush, or a rabbit.

I followed the road which followed the wall, and I was not sorry when I came to the gate and the lodge, and descried Philipson coming up towards it from the direction of the village.

'And where have you been?' said he.

'I took that lane that goes up the hill opposite the stone arch in the wall.'

'Oh! Did you? Then you've been very near where Betton Wood used to be: at least, if you followed it up to the top, and out into the field.'

And if the reader will believe it, that was the first time that I put two and two together.

Did I at once tell Philipson what had happened to me? I did not. I have not had other experiences of the kind which are called super-natural, or -normal, or -physical, but, though I knew very well I must speak of this one before long, I was not at all anxious to do so. And I think I have read that this is a common case.

So all I said was: 'Did you see the old man you meant to?'

'Old Mitchell? Yes, I did. And got something of a story out of him. I'll keep it till after dinner. It really is rather odd.'

So when we were settled after dinner he began to report, faithfully, as he said, the dialogue that had taken place.

Mitchell, not far off eighty years old, was in his elbow-chair. The married daughter with whom he lived was in and out preparing for tea.

After the usual salutations: 'Mitchell, I want you to tell me something about the Wood.'

'What Wood's that, Master Reginald?'

'Betton Wood. Do you remember it?'

Mitchell slowly raised his hand and pointed an accusing forefinger. 'It were your father done away with Betton Wood, Master Reginald, I can tell you that much.'

'Well, I know it was, Mitchell. You needn't look at me as if it were my fault.'

'Your fault? No, I says it were your father done it, before your time.'

'Yes, and I dare say if the truth was known, it was your father that advised him to do it, and I want to know why.'

Mitchell seemed a little amused. 'Well,' he said, 'my father were wood-man to your father and your grandfather before him, and if he didn't know what belonged to his business, he'd oughter done. And if he did give advice that way, I suppose he might have had his reasons, mightn't he now?'

'Of course he might, and I want you to tell me what they were.'

'Well now, Master Reginald, whatever makes you think as I know what his reasons might 'a been I don't know how many year ago?'

'Well, to be sure, it is a long time, and you might easily have forgotten, if ever you knew. I suppose the only thing is for me to go and ask old Ellis what he can recollect about it.'

That had the effect I hoped for.

'Old Ellis!' he growled. 'First time ever I hear anyone say old Ellis were any use for any purpose. I should 'a thought you know'd better than that yourself, Master Reginald. What do you suppose old Ellis can tell you better'n what I can about Betton Wood, and what call have he got to be put afore me, I should like to know.

'His father warn't woodman on the place: he were ploughman – that's what he was, and so anyone could tell you what knows. Anyone could tell you that, I says.'

'Just so, Mitchell, but if you know all about Betton Wood and won't tell me, why, I must do the next best I can, and try and get it out of somebody else. And old Ellis has been on the place very nearly as long as you have.'

'That he ain't, not by eighteen months! Who says I wouldn't tell you nothing about the Wood? I ain't no objection. Only it's a funny kind of a tale, and 'taint right to my thinkin' it should be all about the parish.

'You, Lizzie, do you keep in your kitchen a bit. Me and Master Reginald wants to have a word or two private.

'But one thing I'd like to know, Master Reginald, what come to put you upon asking about it today?'

'Oh! Well, I happened to hear of an old saying about something that walks in Betton Wood. And I wondered if that had anything to do with its being cleared away, that's all.'

'Well, you was in the right, Master Reginald, however you come to hear of it, and I believe I can tell you the rights of it better than anyone in this parish, let alone old Ellis.

'You see it came about this way: that the shortest road to Allen's Farm laid through the Wood, and when we was little my poor mother she used to go so many times in the week to the farm to fetch a quart of milk, because Mr. Allen what had the farm then under your father, he was a good man, and anyone that had a young family to bring up, he was willing to allow 'em so much in the week.

'But never you mind about that now. And my poor mother she never liked to go through the Wood, because there was a lot of talk in the place, and sayings like what you spoke about just now.

'But every now and again, when she happened to be late with her work, she'd have to take the short road through the Wood, and as sure as ever she did, she'd come home in a rare state.

'I remember her and my father talking about it, and he'd say, "Well, but it can't do you no harm, Emma," and she'd say, "Oh! But you haven't an idear of it, George. Why, it went right through my head," she says, "and I came over all bewildered-like, and as if I didn't know where I was.

'"You see, George," she says, "it ain't as if you was about there in the dusk. You always goes there in the daytime, now don't you?" and he says: "Why, to be sure I do: do you take me for a fool?" And so they'd go on.

'And time passed by, and I think it wore her out, because, you understand, it warn't no use to go for the milk not till the afternoon, and she wouldn't never send none of us children instead, for fear we should get a fright. Nor she wouldn't tell us about it herself. "No," she says, "it's bad enough for me. I don't want no one else to go through it, nor yet hear talk about it."

'But one time I recollect she says, "Well, first it's a rustling-like all along in the bushes, coming very quick, either towards me or after me according to the time, and then there comes this scream as appears to pierce right through from the one ear to the other, and the later I am coming through, the more like I am to hear it twice over. But thanks be, I never yet heard it the three times."

'And then I asked her, and I says: "Why, that seems like someone walking to and fro all the time, don't it?" and she says, "Yes, it do, and whatever it is she wants, I can't think." And I says, "Is it a woman, mother?" and she says, "Yes, I've heard it is a woman."

'Anyway, the end of it was my father he spoke to your father, and told him the Wood was a bad wood. "There's never a bit of game in it, and there's never a bird's nest there," he says, "and it ain't no manner of use to you."

'And after a lot of talk, your father he come and see my mother about it, and he see she warn't one of these silly women as gets nervish about nothink

435

at all, and he made up his mind there was somethink in it, and after that he asked about in the neighbourhood, and I believe he made out somethink, and wrote it down in a paper what very like you've got up at the Court, Master Reginald.

'And then he gave the order, and the Wood was stubbed up. They done all the work in the daytime, I recollect, and was never there after three o'clock.'

'Didn't they find anything to explain it, Mitchell? No bones or anything of that kind?'

'Nothink at all, Master Reginald, only the mark of a hedge and ditch along the middle, much about where the quickset hedge run now. And with all the work they done, if there had been anyone put away there, they was bound to find 'em.

'But I don't know whether it done much good, after all. People here don't seem to like the place no better than they did afore.'

'That's about what I got out of Mitchell,' said Philipson, 'and as far as any explanation goes, it leaves us very much where we were. I must see if I can't find that paper.'

'Why didn't your father ever tell you about the business?' I said.

'He died before I went to school, you know, and I imagine he didn't want to frighten us children by any such story. I can remember being shaken and slapped by my nurse for running up that lane towards the Wood when we were coming back rather late one winter afternoon. But in the daytime no one interfered with our going into the Wood if we wanted to – only we never did want.'

'Hm!' I said, and then, 'Do you think you'll be able to find that paper that your father wrote?'

'Yes,' he said, 'I do. I expect it's no farther away than that cupboard behind you. There's a bundle or two of things specially put aside, most of which I've looked through at various times, and I know there's one envelope labelled "Betton Wood". But as there was no Betton Wood any more, I never thought it would be worthwhile to open it, and I never have. We'll do it now, though.'

'Before you do,' I said (I was still reluctant, but I thought this was perhaps the moment for my disclosure), 'I'd better tell you I think Mitchell was right when he doubted if clearing away the Wood had put things straight.'

And I gave the account you have heard already. I need not say Philipson was interested.

'Still there?' he said. 'It's amazing. Look here, will you come out there with me now, and see what happens?'

'I will do no such thing,' I said, 'and if you knew the feeling, you'd be glad to walk ten miles in the opposite direction. Don't talk of it. Open your envelope, and let's hear what your father made out.'

He did so, and read me the three or four pages of jottings which it contained.

At the top was written a motto from Scott's *Glenfinlas*, which seemed to me well-chosen:

Where walks, they say, the shrieking ghost.

Then there were notes of his talk with Mitchell's mother, from which I extract only this much: 'I asked her if she never thought she saw anything to account for the sounds she heard. She told me, no more than once, on the darkest evening she ever came through the Wood: and then she seemed forced to look behind her as the rustling came in the bushes, and she thought she saw something all in tatters with the two arms held out in front of it coming on very fast, and at that she ran for the stile, and tore her gown all to finders getting over it.'

Then he had gone to two other people whom he found very shy of talking. They seemed to think, among other things, that it reflected discredit on the parish.

However, one, Mrs. Emma Frost, was prevailed upon to repeat what her mother had told her. 'They say it was a lady of title that married twice over, and her first husband went by the name of Brown, or it might have been Bryan ("Yes, there were Bryans at the Court before it came into our family," Philipson put in), and she removed her neighbour's landmark: leastways she took in a fair piece of the best pasture in Betton parish what belonged by rights to two children as hadn't no one to speak for them, and they say years after she went from bad to worse, and made out false papers to gain thousands of pounds up in London, and at last they was proved in law to be false, and she would have been tried and put to death very like, only she escaped away for the time.

'But no one can't avoid the curse that's laid on them that removes the landmark, and so we take it she can't leave Betton before someone take and put it right again.'

At the end of the paper there was a note to this effect: 'I regret that I cannot find any clue to previous owners of the fields adjoining the Wood. I do not hesitate to say that if I could discover their representatives, I should do my best to indemnify them for the wrong done to them in years now long past. For it is undeniable that the Wood is very curiously disturbed in the manner described by the people of the place.

'In my present ignorance alike of the extent of the land wrongly appropriated, and of the rightful owners, I am reduced to keeping a separate note of the profits derived from this part of the estate, and my custom has been to apply the sum that would represent the annual yield of about five acres to the common benefit of the parish and to charitable uses. And I hope that those who succeed me may see fit to continue this practice.'

So much for the elder Mr. Philipson's paper. To those who, like myself, are readers of the State Trials it will have gone far to illuminate the situation.

They will remember how between the years 1678 and 1684 the Lady Ivy, formerly Theodosia Bryan, was alternately Plaintiff and Defendant in a series of trials in which she was trying to establish a claim against the Dean and Chapter of St. Paul's for a considerable and very valuable tract of land in Shadwell.

How in the last of those trials, presided over by L.C.J. Jeffreys, it was proved up to the hilt that the deeds upon which she based her claim were forgeries executed under her orders. And how, after an information for perjury and forgery was issued against her, she disappeared completely – so completely, indeed, that no expert has ever been able to tell me what became of her.

Does not the story I have told suggest that she may still be heard of on the scene of one of her earlier and more successful exploits?

* * *

'That,' said my friend, as he folded up his papers, 'is a very faithful record of my one extraordinary experience. And now—'

But I had so many questions to ask him, as for instance, whether his friend had found the proper owner of the land, whether he had done anything about the hedge, whether the sounds were ever heard now, what was the exact title and date of his pamphlet, etc., etc., that bed-time came and passed, without his having an opportunity to revert to the *Literary Supplement* of *The Times*.

[Thanks to the researches of Sir John Fox, in his book on *The Lady Ivie's Trial* (Oxford, 1929), we now know that my heroine died in her bed in 1695, having – heaven knows how – been acquitted of the forgery, for which she had undoubtedly been responsible.]

After Dark in the Playing Fields

THE HOUR WAS LATE and the night was fair. I had halted not far from Sheeps' Bridge and was thinking about the stillness, only broken by the sound of the weir, when a loud tremulous hoot just above me made me jump.

It is always annoying to be startled; but I have a kindness for owls. This one was evidently very near; I looked about for it. There it was, sitting plumply on a branch about twelve feet up.

I pointed my stick at it and said, 'Was that you?'

'Drop it,' said the owl. 'I know it ain't only a stick, but I don't like it. Yes, of course it was me – who do you suppose it would be if it warn't?'

We will take as read the sentences about my surprise. I lowered the stick.

'Well,' said the owl, 'what about it? If you will come out here of a Midsummer evening like what this is, what do you expect?'

'I beg your pardon,' I said, 'I should have remembered. May I say that I think myself very lucky to have met you tonight? I hope you have time for a little talk?'

'Well,' said the owl ungraciously, 'I don't know as it matters so particular tonight. I've had me supper as it happens, and if you ain't too long over it – ah-h-h!'

Suddenly it broke into a loud scream, flapped its wings furiously, bent forward and clutched its perch tightly, continuing to scream. Plainly something was pulling hard at it from behind. The strain relaxed abruptly, the owl nearly fell over, and then whipped round, ruffling up all over, and made a vicious dab at something unseen by me.

'Oh, I *am* sorry,' said a small clear voice in a solicitous tone. 'I made sure it was loose. I do hope I didn't hurt you.'

'Didn't 'urt me?' said the owl bitterly. 'Of course you 'urt me, and well you know it, you young infidel. That feather was no more loose than – oh, if I could git at you! Now I shouldn't wonder but what you've throwed me all out of balance. Why can't you let a person set quiet for two minutes at a time without you must come creepin' up and – well, you've done it this time, anyway. I shall go straight to 'eadquarters and' – (finding it was now addressing the empty air) – 'why, where have you got to now? Oh, it is too bad, that it is!'

'Dear me!' I said, 'I'm afraid this isn't the first time you've been annoyed in this way. May I ask exactly what happened?'

'Yes, you may ask,' said the owl, still looking narrowly about as it spoke, 'but it 'ud take me till the latter end of next week to tell you. Fancy coming and pulling out anyone's tail feather! 'Urt me something crool, it did. And what for, I should like to know? Answer me that! Where's the *reason* of it?'

All that occurred to me was to murmur, 'The clamorous owl that nightly hoots and wonders at our quaint spirits.'

I hardly thought the point would be taken, but the owl said sharply: 'What's that? Yes, you needn't to repeat it. I 'eard. And I'll tell you what's at the bottom of it, and you mark my words.' It bent towards me and whispered, with many nods of its round head: 'Pride! stand-offish-ness! that's what it is! *Come not near our fairy queen*' (this in a tone of bitter contempt). 'Oh, dear no! we ain't good enough for the likes of them. Us that's been noted time out of mind for the best singers in the Fields – now, ain't that so?'

'Well,' I said, doubtfully enough, 'I like to hear you very much, but, you know, some people think a lot of the thrushes and nightingales and so on; you must have heard of that, haven't you? And then, perhaps – of course I don't know – perhaps your style of singing isn't exactly what they think suitable to accompany their dancing, eh?'

'I should kindly 'ope not,' said the owl, drawing itself up. 'Our family's never give in to dancing, nor never won't neither. Why, what ever are you thinkin' of!' it went on with rising temper. 'A pretty thing it would be for me to set there hiccuppin' at them' – it stopped and looked cautiously all round it and up and down and then continued in a louder voice – 'them little ladies and gentlemen. If it ain't sootable for them, I'm very sure it ain't sootable for me. And' (temper rising again) 'if they expect me never to say a word just because they're dancin' and carryin' on with their foolishness, they're very much mistook, and so I tell 'em.'

From what had passed before I was afraid this was an imprudent line to take, and I was right. Hardly had the owl given its last emphatic nod when four small slim forms dropped from a bough above, and in a twinkling some sort of grass rope was thrown round the body of the unhappy bird, and it was borne off through the air, loudly protesting, in the direction of Fellows' Pond.

Splashes and gurgles and shrieks of unfeeling laughter were heard as I hurried up. Something darted away over my head, and as I stood peering over the bank of the pond, which was all in commotion, a very angry and dishevelled owl scrambled heavily up the bank, and stopping near my feet shook itself and flapped and hissed for several minutes without saying anything I should care to repeat.

Glaring at me, it eventually said – and the grim suppressed rage in its voice was such that I hastily drew back a step or two – ''Ear that? Said they was very sorry, but they'd mistook me for a duck. Oh, if it ain't enough to make anyone go reg'lar distracted in their mind and tear everythink to flinders for miles round.'

So carried away was it by passion, that it began the process at once by rooting up a large beakful of grass, which alas! got into its throat; and the choking that resulted made me really afraid that it would break a vessel. But the paroxysm was mastered, and the owl sat up, winking and breathless but intact.

Some expression of sympathy seemed to be required; yet I was chary of offering it, for in its present state of mind I felt that the bird might interpret the best-meant phrase as a fresh insult. So we stood looking at each other without speech for a very awkward minute, and then came a diversion.

First the thin voice of the pavilion clock, then the deeper sound from the Castle quadrangle, then Lupton's Tower, drowning the Curfew Tower by its nearness.

'What's that?' said the owl, suddenly and hoarsely.

'Midnight, I should think,' said I, and had recourse to my watch.

'Midnight?' cried the owl, evidently much startled, 'and me too wet to fly a yard! Here, you pick me up and put me in the tree; don't, I'll climb up your leg, and you won't ask me to do that twice. Quick now!'

I obeyed. 'Which tree do you want?'

'Why, my tree, to be sure! Over there!' It nodded towards the Wall.

'All right. Bad-calx tree do you mean?' I said, beginning to run in that direction.

''Ow should I know what silly names you call it? The one what 'as like a door in it. Go faster! They'll be coming in another minute.'

'Who? What's the matter?' I asked as I ran, clutching the wet creature, and much afraid of stumbling and coming over with it in the long grass.

'*You'll* see fast enough,' said this selfish bird. 'You just let me git on the tree, *I* shall be all right.'

And I suppose it was, for it scrabbled very quickly up the trunk with its wings spread and disappeared in a hollow without a word of thanks.

I looked round, not very comfortably. The Curfew Tower was still playing St. David's tune and the little chime that follows, for the third and last time, but the other bells had finished what they had to say, and now there was silence, and again the 'restless changing weir' was the only thing that broke – no, that emphasised it.

Why had the owl been so anxious to get into hiding? That of course was what now exercised me. Whatever and whoever was coming, I was sure that this was no time for me to cross the open field – I should do best to dissemble my presence by staying on the darker side of the tree. And that is what I did.

All this took place some years ago, before summertime came in. I do sometimes go into the Playing Fields at night still, but I come in before true midnight. And I find I do not like a crowd after dark – for example at the Fourth of June fireworks.

You see – no, you do not, but I see – such curious faces; and the people to whom they belong flit about so oddly, often at your elbow when you least expect it, and looking close into your face, as if they were searching for someone – who may be thankful, I think, if they do not find him.

'Where do they come from?' Why, some, I think, out of the water, and some out of the ground. They look like that. But I am sure it is best to take no notice of them, and not to touch them.

Yes, I certainly prefer the daylight population of the Playing Fields to that which comes there after dark.

There Was a Man Dwelt by a Churchyard

THIS, YOU KNOW, is the beginning of the story about sprites and goblins which Mamilius, the best child in Shakespeare, was telling to his mother the queen, and the court ladies, when the king came in with his guards and hurried her off to prison. There is no more of the story. Mamilius died soon after without having a chance of finishing it.

Now what was it going to have been? Shakespeare knew, no doubt, and I will be bold to say that I do. It was not going to be a new story: it was to be one which you have most likely heard, and even told. Everybody may set it in what frame he likes best.

This is mine:

There was a man dwelt by a churchyard. His house had a lower storey of stone and an upper one of timber. The front windows looked out on the street and the back ones on the churchyard.

It had once belonged to the parish priest, but (this was in Queen Elizabeth's days) the priest was a married man and wanted more room. Besides, his wife disliked seeing the churchyard at night out of her bedroom window. She said she saw – but never mind what she said.

Anyhow, she gave her husband no peace till he agreed to move into a larger house in the village street, and the old one was taken by John Poole, who was a widower, and lived there alone. He was an elderly man who kept very much to himself, and people said he was something of a miser.

445

It was very likely true: he was morbid in other ways, certainly. In those days it was common to bury people at night and by torchlight. And it was noticed that whenever a funeral was toward, John Poole was always at his window, either on the ground floor or upstairs, according as he could get the better view from one or the other.

There came a night when an old woman was to be buried. She was fairly well to do, but she was not liked in the place. The usual thing was said of her, that she was no Christian, and that on such nights as Midsummer Eve and All Hallows, she was not to be found in her house. She was red-eyed and dreadful to look at, and no beggar ever knocked at her door. Yet when she died she left a purse of money to the Church.

There was no storm on the night of her burial: it was fair and calm. But there was some difficulty about getting bearers, and men to carry the torches, in spite of the fact that she had left larger fees than common for such as did that work.

She was buried in woollen, without a coffin. No one was there but those who were actually needed – and John Poole, watching from his window. Just before the grave was filled in, the parson stooped down and cast something upon the body – something that clinked – and in a low voice he said words that sounded like 'Thy money perish with thee'. Then he walked quickly away, and so did the other men, leaving only one torch-bearer to light the sexton and his boy while they shovelled the earth in.

They made no very neat job of it, and next day, which was a Sunday, the churchgoers were rather sharp with the sexton, saying it was the untidiest grave in the yard. And indeed, when he came to look at it himself, he thought it was worse than he had left it.

Meanwhile John Poole went about with a curious air, half-exulting, as it were, and half-nervous. More than once he spent an evening at the inn, which was clean contrary to his usual habit, and to those who fell into talk with him there he hinted that he had come into a little bit of money and was looking out for a somewhat better house.

'Well, I don't wonder,' said the smith one night, 'I shouldn't care for that place of yours. I should be fancying things all night.'

The landlord asked him what sort of things.

'Well, maybe somebody climbing up to the chamber window, or the like

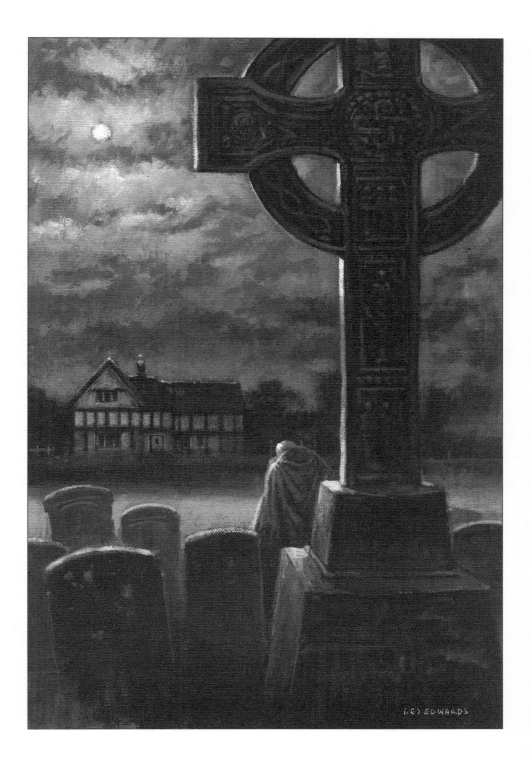

LES EDWARDS

of that,' said the smith. 'I don't know – old mother Wilkins that was buried a week ago today, eh?'

'Come, I think you might consider of a person's feelings,' said the landlord. 'It ain't so pleasant for Master Poole, is it now?'

'Master Poole don't mind,' said the smith. 'He's been there long enough to know. I only says it wouldn't be my choice. What with the passing bell, and the torches when there's a burial, and all them graves laying so quiet when there's no one about. Only they say there's lights – don't you never see no lights, Master Poole?'

'No, I don't never see no lights,' said Master Poole sulkily, and called for another drink, and went home late.

That night, as he lay in his bed upstairs, a moaning wind began to play about the house, and he could not go to sleep. He got up and crossed the room to a little cupboard in the wall. He took out of it something that clinked, and put it in the breast of his bedgown. Then he went to the window and looked out into the churchyard.

Have you ever seen an old brass in a church with a figure of a person in a shroud? It is bunched together at the top of the head in a curious way. Something like that was sticking up out of the earth in a spot of the churchyard which John Poole knew very well. He darted into his bed and lay there very still indeed.

Presently something made a very faint rattling at the casement. With a dreadful reluctance John Poole turned his eyes that way. Alas! Between him and the moonlight was the black outline of the curious bunched head ... Then there was a figure in the room. Dry earth rattled on the floor. A low cracked voice said 'Where is it?' and steps went hither and thither, faltering steps as of one walking with difficulty. It could be seen now and again, peering into corners, stooping to look under chairs; finally it could be heard fumbling at the doors of the cupboard in the wall, throwing them open.

There was a scratching of long nails on the empty shelves. The figure whipped round, stood for an instant at the side of the bed, raised its arms, and with a hoarse scream of *'You've got it!'* —

At this point HRH Prince Mamilius (who would, I think, have made the story a good deal shorter than this) flung himself with a loud yell upon the youngest of the court ladies present, who responded with an equally piercing cry.

He was instantly seized upon by HM Queen Hermione, who, repressing an inclination to laugh, shook and slapped him very severely. Much flushed, and rather inclined to cry, he was about to be sent to bed. But, on the intercession of his victim, who had now recovered from the shock, he was eventually permitted to remain until his usual hour for retiring; by which time he too had so far recovered as to assert, in bidding goodnight to the company, that he knew another story quite three times as dreadful as that one, and would tell it on the first opportunity that offered.

A View From a Hill

HOW PLEASANT IT CAN BE, alone in a first-class railway carriage, on the first day of a holiday that is to be fairly long, to dawdle through a bit of English country that is unfamiliar, stopping at every station.

You have a map open on your knee, and you pick out the villages that lie to right and left by their church towers. You marvel at the complete still-ness that attends your stoppage at the stations, broken only by a footstep crunching the gravel. Yet perhaps that is best experienced after sundown, and the traveller I have in mind was making his leisurely progress on a sunny afternoon in the latter half of June.

He was in the depths of the country. I need not particularise further than to say that if you divided the map of England into four quarters, he would have been found in the south-western of them.

He was a man of academic pursuits, and his term was just over. He was on his way to meet a new friend, older than himself. The two of them had met first on an official inquiry in town, had found that they had many tastes and habits in common, liked each other, and the result was an invitation from Squire Richards to Mr. Fanshawe which was now taking effect.

The journey ended about five o'clock. Fanshawe was told by a cheerful country porter that the car from the Hall had been up to the station and left a message that something had to be fetched from half-a-mile farther on, and would the gentleman please to wait a few minutes till it came back?

'But I see,' continued the porter, 'as you've got your bysticle, and very like you'd find it pleasanter to ride up to the 'All yourself. Straight up the road 'ere, and then first turn to the left – it ain't above two mile – and I'll see as your things is put in the car for you.

'You'll excuse me mentioning it, only I thought it were a nice evening for a ride. Yes, sir, very seasonable weather for the haymakers: let me see, I have your bike ticket. Thank you, sir; much obliged. You can't miss your road, etc., etc.'

The two miles to the Hall were just what was needed, after the day in the train, to dispel somnolence and impart a wish for tea. The Hall, when sighted, also promised just what was needed in the way of a quiet resting-place after days of sitting on committees and college-meetings.

It was neither excitingly old nor depressingly new. Plastered walls, sash-windows, old trees, smooth lawns, were the features which Fanshawe noticed as he came up the drive. Squire Richards, a burly man of sixty odd, was awaiting him in the porch with evident pleasure.

'Tea first,' he said, 'or would you like a longer drink? No? All right, tea's ready in the garden. Come along, they'll put your machine away. I always have tea under the lime-tree by the stream on a day like this.'

Nor could you ask for a better place. Midsummer afternoon, shade and scent of a vast lime-tree, cool, swirling water within five yards. It was long before either of them suggested a move.

But about six, Mr. Richards sat up, knocked out his pipe, and said: 'Look here, it's cool enough now to think of a stroll, if you're inclined? All right: then what I suggest is that we walk up the park and get on to the hillside, where we can look over the country. We'll have a map, and I'll show you where things are; and you can go off on your machine, or we can take the car, according as you want exercise or not. If you're ready, we can start now and be back well before eight, taking it very easy.'

'I'm ready. I should like my stick, though, and have you got any field-glasses? I lent mine to a man a week ago, and he's gone off Lord knows where and taken them with him.'

Mr. Richards pondered. 'Yes,' he said, 'I have, but they're not things I use myself, and I don't know whether the ones I have will suit you. They're old-fashioned, and about twice as heavy as they make 'em now. You're welcome to have them, but I won't carry them. By the way, what do you want to drink after dinner?'

Protestations that anything would do were overruled, and a satisfactory settlement was reached on the way to the front hall, where Mr. Fanshawe found his stick, and Mr. Richards, after thoughtful pinching of his lower lip, resorted to a drawer in the hall-table, extracted a key, crossed to a cupboard in the panelling, opened it, took a box from the shelf, and put it on the table.

'The glasses are in there,' he said, 'and there's some dodge of opening it, but I've forgotten what it is. You try.'

Mr. Fanshawe accordingly tried. There was no keyhole, and the box was solid, heavy and smooth: it seemed obvious that some part of it would have to be pressed before anything could happen.

'The corners,' said he to himself, 'are the likely places; and infernally sharp corners they are too,' he added, as he put his thumb in his mouth after exerting force on a lower corner.

'What's the matter?' said the Squire.

'Why, your disgusting Borgia box has scratched me, drat it,' said Fanshawe.

The Squire chuckled unfeelingly. 'Well, you've got it open, anyway,' he said.

'So I have! Well, I don't begrudge a drop of blood in a good cause, and here are the glasses. They *are* pretty heavy, as you said, but I think I'm equal to carrying them.'

'Ready?' said the Squire. 'Come on then; we go out by the garden.'

So they did, and passed out into the park, which sloped decidedly upwards to the hill which, as Fanshawe had seen from the train, dominated the country. It was a spur of a larger range that lay behind.

On the way, the Squire, who was great on earthworks, pointed out various spots where he detected or imagined traces of war-ditches and the like. 'And here,' he said, stopping on a more or less level plot with a ring of large trees, 'is Baxter's Roman villa.'

'Baxter?' said Mr. Fanshawe.

'I forgot; you don't know about him. He was the old chap I got those glasses from. I believe he made them. He was an old watch-maker down in the village, a great antiquary. My father gave him leave to grub about where he liked; and when he made a find he used to lend him a man or two to help him with the digging. He got a surprising lot of things together, and when he died – I dare say it's ten or fifteen years ago – I bought the whole lot and gave them to the town museum. We'll run in one of these days, and look over them.

'The glasses came to me with the rest, but of course I kept them. If you look at them, you'll see they're more or less amateur work – the body of them. Naturally the lenses weren't his making.'

'Yes, I see they are just the sort of thing that a clever workman in a different line of business might turn out. But I don't see why he made them so heavy. And did Baxter actually find a Roman villa here?'

'Yes, there's a pavement turfed over, where we're standing: it was too rough and plain to be worth taking up, but of course there are drawings of it. And the small things and pottery that turned up were quite good of their kind. An ingenious chap, old Baxter: he seemed to have a quite out-of-the-way instinct for these things. He was invaluable to our archæologists.

'He used to shut up his shop for days at a time, and wander off over the district, marking down places, where he scented anything, on the ordnance map; and he kept a book with fuller notes of the places. Since his death, a good many of them have been sampled, and there's always been something to justify him.'

'What a good man!' said Mr. Fanshawe.

'Good?' said the Squire, pulling up brusquely.

'I meant useful to have about the place,' said Mr. Fanshawe. 'But was he a villain?'

'I don't know about that either,' said the Squire; 'but all I can say is, if he was good, he wasn't lucky. And he wasn't liked – I didn't like him,' he added, after a moment.

'Oh?' said Fanshawe interrogatively.

'No, I didn't; but that's enough about Baxter. Besides, this is the stiffest bit, and I don't want to talk and walk as well.'

Indeed it was hot, climbing a slippery grass slope that evening.

'I told you I should take you the short way,' panted the Squire, 'and I wish I hadn't. However, a bath won't do us any harm when we get back. Here we are, and there's the seat.'

A small clump of old Scotch firs crowned the top of the hill. And, at the edge of it, commanding the cream of the view, was a wide and solid seat, on which the two disposed themselves, and wiped their brows, and regained breath.

'Now, then,' said the Squire, as soon as he was in a condition to talk connectedly, 'this is where your glasses come in. But you'd better take a general look round first. My word! I've never seen the view look better.'

Writing as I am now with a winter wind flapping against dark windows and a rushing, tumbling sea within a hundred yards, I find it hard to summon up the feelings and words which will put my reader in possession of the June evening and the lovely English landscape of which the Squire was speaking.

Across a broad level plain they looked upon ranges of great hills, whose uplands – some green, some furred with woods – caught the light of a sun, westering but not yet low. And all the plain was fertile, though the river which traversed it was nowhere seen. There were copses, green wheat, hedges and pasture-land: the little compact white moving cloud marked the evening train. Then the eye picked out red farms and grey houses, and nearer home scattered cottages, and then the Hall, nestled under the hill. The smoke of chimneys was very blue and straight. There was a smell of hay in the air: there were wild roses on bushes hard by. It was the acme of summer.

After some minutes of silent contemplation, the Squire began to point out the leading features, the hills and valleys, and told where the towns and villages lay.

'Now,' he said, 'with the glasses you'll be able to pick out Fulnaker Abbey. Take a line across that big green field, then over the wood beyond it, then over the farm on the knoll.'

'Yes, yes,' said Fanshawe. 'I've got it. What a fine tower!'

'You must have got the wrong direction,' said the Squire. 'There's not much of a tower about there that I remember, unless it's Oldbourne Church that you've got hold of. And if you call that a fine tower, you're easily pleased.'

'Well, I do call it a fine tower,' said Fanshawe, the glasses still at his eyes, 'whether it's Oldbourne or any other. And it must belong to a largish church; it looks to me like a central tower – four big pinnacles at the corners, and four smaller ones between. I must certainly go over there. How far is it?'

'Oldbourne's about nine miles, or less,' said the Squire. 'It's a long time since I've been there, but I don't remember thinking much of it. Now I'll show you another thing.'

Fanshawe had lowered the glasses, and was still gazing in the Oldbourne direction. 'No,' he said, 'I can't make out anything with the naked eye. What was it you were going to show me?'

'A good deal more to the left – it oughtn't to be difficult to find. Do you see a rather sudden knob of a hill with a thick wood on top of it? It's in a dead line with that single tree on the top of the big ridge.'

'I do,' said Fanshawe, 'and I believe I could tell you without much difficulty what it's called.'

'Could you now?' said the Squire. 'Say on.'

'Why, Gallows Hill,' was the answer.

'How did you guess that?'

'Well, if you don't want it guessed, you shouldn't put up a dummy gibbet and a man hanging on it.'

'What's that?' said the Squire abruptly. 'There's nothing on that hill but wood.'

'On the contrary,' said Fanshawe, 'there's a largish expanse of grass on the top and your dummy gibbet in the middle; and I thought there was something on it when I looked first. But I see there's nothing – or is there? I can't be sure.'

'Nonsense, nonsense, Fanshawe, there's no such thing as a dummy gibbet, or any other sort, on that hill. And it's thick wood – a fairly young plantation. I was in it myself not a year ago. Hand me the glasses, though I don't suppose I can see anything.' After a pause: 'No, I thought not: they won't show a thing.'

Meanwhile Fanshawe was scanning the hill – it might be only two or three miles away. 'Well, it's very odd,' he said, 'it does look exactly like a wood without the glass.' He took it again. 'That is one of the oddest effects. The gibbet is perfectly plain, and the grass field, and there even seem to be people on it, and carts, or a cart, with men in it. And yet when I take the glass away, there's nothing. It must be something in the way this afternoon light falls: I shall come up earlier in the day when the sun's full on it.'

'Did you say you saw people and a cart on that hill?' said the Squire incredulously. 'What should they be doing there at this time of day, even if the trees have been felled? Do talk sense – look again.'

'Well, I certainly thought I saw them. Yes, I should say there were a few, just clearing off. And now – by Jove, it does look like something hanging on the gibbet. But these glasses are so beastly heavy I can't hold them steady for long. Anyhow, you can take it from me there's no wood. And if you'll show me the road on the map, I'll go there tomorrow.'

The Squire remained brooding for some little time. At last he rose and said, 'Well, I suppose that will be the best way to settle it. And now we'd better be getting back. Bath and dinner is my idea.' And on the way back he was not very communicative.

They returned through the garden, and went into the front hall to leave sticks, etc., in their due place. And here they found the aged butler Patten evidently in a state of some anxiety. 'Beg pardon, Master Henry,' he began at once, 'but someone's been up to mischief here, I'm much afraid.' He pointed to the open box which had contained the glasses.

'Nothing worse than that, Patten?' said the Squire. 'Mayn't I take out my own glasses and lend them to a friend? Bought with my own money, you recollect? At old Baxter's sale, eh?'

Patten bowed, unconvinced. 'Oh, very well, Master Henry, as long as you know who it was. Only I thought proper to name it, for I didn't think that box'd been off its shelf since you first put it there. And, if you'll excuse me, after what happened . . .' The voice was lowered, and the rest was not audible to Fanshawe. The Squire replied with a few words and a gruff laugh, and called on Fanshawe to come and be shown his room.

And I do not think that anything else happened that night which bears on my story.

Except, perhaps, the sensation which invaded Fanshawe in the small hours that something had been let out which ought not to have been let out. It came into his dreams.

He was walking in a garden which he seemed half to know, and stopped in front of a rockery made of old wrought stones, pieces of window tracery from a church, and even bits of figures. One of these moved his curiosity: it seemed to be a sculptured capital with scenes carved on it. He felt he must pull it out, and worked away, and, with an ease that surprised him, moved the stones that obscured it aside, and pulled out the block. As he did so, a tin label fell down by his feet with a little clatter. He picked it up and read on it: *On no account move this stone. Yours sincerely, J. Patten.*

As often happens in dreams, he felt that this injunction was of extreme importance; and with an anxiety that amounted to anguish he looked to see if the stone had really been shifted. Indeed it had. In fact, he could not see it anywhere. The removal had disclosed the mouth of a burrow, and he bent down to look into it.

Something stirred in the blackness, and then, to his intense horror, a hand emerged – a clean right hand in a neat cuff and coat-sleeve, just in the attitude of a hand that means to shake yours. He wondered whether it would not be rude to let it alone.

But, as he looked at it, it began to grow hairy and dirty and thin, and also to change its pose and stretch out as if to take hold of his leg. At that he dropped all thought of politeness, decided to run, screamed and woke himself up.

This was the dream he remembered. But it seemed to him (as, again, it often does) that there had been others of the same import before, but not so insistent. He lay awake for some little time, fixing the details of the last dream in his mind, and wondering in particular what the figures had been which he had seen or half-seen on the carved capital. Something quite incongruous, he felt sure; but that was the most he could recall.

Whether because of the dream, or because it was the first day of his holiday, he did not get up very early; nor did he at once plunge into the exploration of the country.

He spent a morning, half-lazy, half-instructive, in looking over the volumes of the County Archæological Society's transactions, in which were many contributions from Mr. Baxter on finds of flint implements, Roman sites, ruins of monastic establishments – in fact, most departments of archæology. They were written in an odd, pompous, only half-educated style. If the man had had more early schooling, thought Fanshawe, he would have been a very distinguished antiquary. Or he might have been (he thus qualified his opinion a little later), but for a certain love of opposition and controversy, and, yes, a patronising tone as of one possessing superior knowledge, which left an unpleasant taste.

He might have been a very respectable artist. There was an imaginary restoration and elevation of a priory church which was very well conceived. A fine pinnacled central tower was a conspicuous feature of this – it reminded Fanshawe of that which he had seen from the hill, and which the Squire had told him must be Oldbourne. But it was not Oldbourne; it was Fulnaker Priory.

'Oh, well,' he said to himself, 'I suppose Oldbourne Church may have been built by Fulnaker monks, and Baxter has copied Oldbourne tower. Anything about it in the letterpress? Ah, I see it was published after his death – found among his papers.'

After lunch the Squire asked Fanshawe what he meant to do.

'Well,' said Fanshawe, 'I think I shall go out on my bike about four as far as Oldbourne and back by Gallows Hill. That ought to be a round of about fifteen miles, oughtn't it?'

'About that,' said the Squire, 'and you'll pass Lambsfield and Wanstone, both of which are worth looking at. There's a little glass at Lambsfield and the stone at Wanstone.'

'Good,' said Fanshawe, 'I'll get tea somewhere, and may I take the glasses? I'll strap them on my bike, on the carrier.'

'Of course, if you like,' said the Squire. 'I really ought to have some better ones. If I go into the town today, I'll see if I can pick up some.'

'Why should you trouble to do that if you can't use them yourself?' said Fanshawe.

'Oh, I don't know; one ought to have a decent pair. And – well, old Patten doesn't think those are fit to use.'

'Is he a judge?'

'He's got some tale. I don't know: something about old Baxter. I've promised to let him tell me about it. It seems very much on his mind since last night.'

'Why that? Did he have a nightmare like me?'

'He had something. He was looking an old man this morning, and he said he hadn't closed an eye.'

'Well, let him save up his tale till I come back.'

'Very well, I will if I can. Look here, are you going to be late? If you get a puncture eight miles off and have to walk home, what then? I don't trust these bicycles. I shall tell them to give us cold things to eat.'

'I shan't mind that, whether I'm late or early. But I've got things to mend punctures with. And now I'm off.'

It was just as well that the Squire had made that arrangement about a cold supper, Fanshawe thought, and not for the first time, as he wheeled his bicycle up the drive about nine o'clock.

So also the Squire thought and said, several times, as he met him in the hall, rather pleased at the confirmation of his want of faith in bicycles than sympathetic with his hot, weary, thirsty, and indeed haggard, friend. In fact, the kindest thing he found to say was: 'You'll want a long drink tonight? Cider-cup do? All right. Hear that, Patten? Cider-cup, iced, lots of it.' Then to Fanshawe, 'Don't be all night over your bath.'

By half-past nine they were at dinner, and Fanshawe was reporting progress, if progress it might be called.

'I got to Lambsfield very smoothly, and saw the glass. It is very interesting stuff, but there's a lot of lettering I couldn't read.'

'Not with glasses?' said the Squire.

'Those glasses of yours are no manner of use inside a church – or inside anywhere, I suppose, for that matter. But the only places I took 'em into were churches.'

'H'm! Well, go on,' said the Squire.

'However, I took some sort of a photograph of the window, and I dare say an enlargement would show what I want. Then Wanstone. I should think that stone was a very out-of-the-way thing, only I don't know about that class of antiquities. Has anybody opened the mound it stands on?'

'Baxter wanted to, but the farmer wouldn't let him.'

'Oh, well, I should think it would be worth doing. Anyhow, the next thing was Fulnaker and Oldbourne. You know, it's very odd about that tower I saw from the hill. Oldbourne Church is nothing like it, and of course there's nothing over thirty feet high at Fulnaker, though you can see it had a central tower.

'I didn't tell you, did I? That Baxter's fancy drawing of Fulnaker shows a tower exactly like the one I saw.'

'So you thought, I dare say,' put in the Squire.

'No, it wasn't a case of thinking. The picture actually *reminded* me of what I'd seen, and I made sure it was Oldbourne, well before I looked at the title.'

'Well, Baxter had a very fair idea of architecture. I dare say what's left made it easy for him to draw the right sort of tower.'

'That may be it, of course, but I'm doubtful if even a professional could have got it so exactly right. There's absolutely nothing left at Fulnaker but the bases of the piers which supported it. However, that isn't the oddest thing.'

'What about Gallows Hill?' said the Squire. 'Here, Patten, listen to this. I told you what Mr. Fanshawe said he saw from the hill.'

'Yes, Master Henry, you did. And I can't say I was so much surprised, considering.'

'All right, all right. You keep that till afterwards. We want to hear what Mr. Fanshawe saw today. Go on, Fanshawe. You turned to come back by Ackford and Thorfield, I suppose?'

'Yes, and I looked into both the churches. Then I got to the turning which goes to the top of Gallows Hill. I saw that if I wheeled my machine over the field at the top of the hill I could join the home road on this side. It was about half-past six when I got to the top of the hill, and there was a gate on my right, where it ought to be, leading into the belt of plantation.'

'You hear that, Patten? A belt, he says.'

'So I thought it was – a belt. But it wasn't. You were quite right, and I was hopelessly wrong. I *cannot* understand it. The whole top is planted quite thick.

'Well, I went on into this wood, wheeling and dragging my bike, expecting every minute to come to a clearing, and then my misfortunes began. Thorns, I suppose. First I realised that the front tyre was slack, then the back. I couldn't stop to do more than try to find the punctures and mark them; but even that was hopeless. So I ploughed on, and the farther I went, the less I liked the place.'

'Not much poaching in that cover, eh, Patten?' said the Squire.

'No, indeed, Master Henry. There's very few cares to go—'

'No, I know. Never mind that now. Go on, Fanshawe.'

'I don't blame anybody for not caring to go there. I know I had all the fancies one least likes: steps crackling over twigs behind me, indistinct people stepping behind trees in front of me, yes, and even a hand laid on my shoulder. I pulled up very sharp at that and looked round, but there really was no branch or bush that could have done it. Then, when I was just about at the middle of the plot, I was convinced that there was someone looking down on me from above – and not with any pleasant intent.

'I stopped again, or at least slackened my pace, to look up. And as I did, down I came, and barked my shins abominably on, what do you think? A block of stone with a big square hole in the top of it. And within a few paces there were two others just like it. The three were set in a triangle. Now, do you make out what they were put there for?'

'I think I can,' said the Squire, who was now very grave and absorbed in the story. 'Sit down, Patten.'

It was time, for the old man was supporting himself by one hand, and leaning heavily on it. He dropped into a chair, and said in a very tremulous voice, 'You didn't go between them stones, did you, sir?'

'I did *not*,' said Fanshawe, emphatically. 'I dare say I was an ass, but as soon as it dawned on me where I was, I just shouldered my machine and did my best to run. It seemed to me as if I was in an unholy evil sort of graveyard, and I was most profoundly thankful that it was one of the longest days and still sunlight.

'Well, I had a horrid run, even if it was only a few hundred yards. Everything caught on everything: handles and spokes and carrier and pedals – caught in them viciously, or I fancied so. I fell over at least five times. At last I saw the hedge, and I couldn't trouble to hunt for the gate.'

'There *is* no gate on my side,' the Squire interpolated.

'Just as well I didn't waste time, then. I dropped the machine over somehow and went into the road pretty near head-first; some branch or something got my ankle at the last moment. Anyhow, there I was out of the wood, and seldom more thankful or more generally sore.

'Then came the job of mending my punctures. I had a good outfit and I'm not at all bad at the business; but this was an absolutely hopeless case. It was seven when I got out of the wood, and I spent fifty minutes over one tyre. As fast as I found a hole and put on a patch, and blew it up, it went flat again. So I made up my mind to walk. That hill isn't three miles away, is it?'

'Not more across country, but nearer six by road.'

'I thought it must be. I thought I couldn't have taken well over the hour over less than five miles, even leading a bike. Well, there's my story. Where's yours and Patten's?'

'Mine? I've no story,' said the Squire. 'But you weren't very far out when you thought you were in a graveyard. There must be a good few of them up there, Patten, don't you think? They left 'em there when they fell to bits, I fancy.'

Patten nodded, too much interested to speak.

'Don't,' said Fanshawe.

'Now then, Patten,' said the Squire, 'you've heard what sort of a time Mr. Fanshawe's been having. What do you make of it? Anything to do with Mr. Baxter? Fill yourself a glass of port, and tell us.'

'Ah, that done me good, Master Henry,' said Patten, after absorbing what was before him. 'If you really wish to know what were in my thoughts, my answer would be clear in the affirmative. Yes,' he went on, warming to his work, 'I should say as Mr. Fanshawe's experience of today were very largely doo to the person you named.

'And I think, Master Henry, as I have some title to speak, in view of me 'aving been many years on speaking terms with him, and swore in to be jury on the Coroner's inquest near this time ten years ago, you being then, if you carry your mind back, Master Henry, travelling abroad, and no one 'ere to represent the family.'

'Inquest?' said Fanshawe. 'An inquest on Mr. Baxter, was there?'

'Yes, sir, on – on that very person. The facts as led up to that occurrence was these. The deceased was, as you may have gathered, a very peculiar individual in 'is 'abits – in my idear, at least, but all must speak as they find. He lived very much to himself, without neither chick nor child, as the saying is. And how he passed away his time was what very few could orfer a guess at.'

'He lived unknown, and few could know when Baxter ceased to be,' said the Squire to his pipe.

'I beg pardon, Master Henry, I was just coming to that. But when I say how he passed away his time – to be sure we know 'ow intent he was in rummaging and ransacking out all the 'istry of the neighbourhood and the number of things he'd managed to collect together – well, it was spoke of for miles round as Baxter's Museum, and many a time when he might be in the mood, and I might have an hour to spare, have he showed me his pieces of pots and what not, going back by his account to the times of the ancient Romans. However, you know more about that than what I do, Master Henry.

'Only what I was a-going to say was this: as know what he might and interesting as he might be in his talk, there was something about the man – well, for one thing, no one ever remember to see him in church nor yet chapel at service-time. And that made talk. Our rector he never come in the house but once. "Never ask me what the man said" – that was all anybody could ever get out of *him*. Then how did he spend his nights, particularly about this season of the year?

'Time and again the labouring men'd meet him coming back as they went out to their work, and he'd pass 'em by without a word, looking, they says, like someone straight out of the asylum. They see the whites of his eyes all round. He'd have a fish-basket with him, that they noticed, and he always come the same road. And the talk got to be that he'd made himself some business, and that not the best kind – well, not so far from where you was at seven o'clock this evening, sir.

'Well, now, after such a night as that, Mr. Baxter he'd shut up the shop, and the old lady that did for him had orders not to come in. And knowing what she did about his language, she took care to obey them orders.

'But one day it so happened, about three o'clock in the afternoon, the house being shut up as I said, there come a most fearful to-do inside, and smoke out of the windows, and Baxter crying out seemingly in an agony. So the man as lived next door he run round to the back premises and burst the door in, and several others come too.

'Well, he tell me he never in all his life smelt such a fearful – well, odour, as what there was in that kitchen-place. It seem as if Baxter had been boiling something in a pot and overset it on his leg. There he laid on the floor, trying to keep back the cries, but it was more than he could manage, and when he seen the people come in – oh, he was in a nice condition. If his tongue warn't blistered worse than his leg it warn't his fault.

'Well, they picked him up, and got him into a chair, and run for the medical man, and one of 'em was going to pick up the pot, and Baxter, he screams out to let it alone. So he did, but he couldn't see as there was any-thing in the pot but a few old brown bones.

'Then they says "Dr. Lawrence'll be here in a minute, Mr. Baxter; he'll soon put you to rights." And then he was off again. He must be got up to his room, he couldn't have the doctor come in there and see all that mess – they must throw a cloth over it – anything – the tablecloth out of the parlour. Well, so they did. But that must have been poisonous stuff in that pot, for it was pretty near on two months afore Baxter were about agin.

'Beg pardon, Master Henry, was you going to say something?'

'Yes, I was,' said the Squire. 'I wonder you haven't told me all this before. However, I was going to say I remember old Lawrence telling me he'd attended Baxter. He was a queer card, he said. Lawrence was up in the bedroom one day, and picked up a little mask covered with black velvet, and put it on in fun and went to look at himself in the glass. He hadn't time for a proper look, for old Baxter shouted out to him from the bed: "Put it down, you fool! Do you want to look through a dead man's eyes?" And it startled him so that he did put it down, and then he asked Baxter what he meant. And Baxter insisted on him handing it over, and said the man he bought it from was dead, or some such nonsense.

'But Lawrence felt it as he handed it over, and he declared he was sure it was made out of the front of a skull. He bought a distilling apparatus at Baxter's sale, he told me, but he could never use it: it seemed to taint everything, however much he cleaned it. But go on, Patten.'

'Yes, Master Henry, I'm nearly done now, and time, too, for I don't know what they'll think about me in the servants' 'all. Well, this business of the scalding was some few years before Mr. Baxter was took, and he got about again, and went on just as he'd used. And one of the last jobs he done was finishing up them actual glasses what you took out last night.

'You see he'd made the body of them some long time, and got the pieces of glass for them, but there was somethink wanted to finish 'em, whatever it was, I don't know, but I picked up the frame one day, and I says: "Mr. Baxter, why don't you make a job of this?"

'And he says, "Ah, when I've done that, you'll hear news, you will: there's going to be no such pair of glasses as mine when they're filled and sealed," and there he stopped.

'And I says: "Why, Mr. Baxter, you talk as if they was wine bottles: filled and sealed – why, where's the necessity for that?"

'"Did I say filled and sealed?" he says. "O, well, I was suiting my conversation to my company."

'Well, then come round this time of year, and one fine evening, I was passing his shop on my way home, and he was standing on the step, very pleased with hisself, and he says: "All right and tight now: my best bit of work's finished, and I'll be out with 'em tomorrow."

'"What, finished them glasses?" I says, "might I have a look at them?"

'"No, no," he says, "I've put 'em to bed for tonight, and when I do show 'em you, you'll have to pay for peepin', so I tell you." And that, gentlemen, were the last words I heard that man say.

'That were the 17th of June, and just a week after, there was a funny thing happened, and it was doo to that as we brought in "unsound mind" at the inquest, for barring that, no one as knew Baxter in business could anyways have laid that against him.

'But George Williams, as lived in the next house, and do now, he was woke up that same night with a stumbling and tumbling about in Mr. Baxter's premises, and he got out o' bed, and went to the front window on the street to see if there was any rough customers about. And it being a very light night, he could make sure as there was not.

'Then he stood and listened, and he hear Mr. Baxter coming down his front stair one step after another very slow, and he got the idear as it was like someone bein' pushed or pulled down and holdin' on to everythin' he could. Next thing he hear the street door come open, and out come Mr. Baxter into the street in his day-clothes, 'at and all, with his arms straight down by his sides, and talking to hisself, and shakin' his head from one side to the other, and walking in that peculiar way that he appeared to be going as it were against his own will.

'George Williams put up the window, and hear him say: "O mercy, gentlemen!" and then he shut up sudden as if, he said, someone clapped his hand over his mouth, and Mr. Baxter threw his head back, and his hat fell off. And Williams see his face looking something pitiful, so as he couldn't keep from calling out to him: "Why, Mr. Baxter, ain't you well?" and he was goin' to offer to fetch Dr. Lawrence to him, only he heard the answer: "'Tis best you mind your own business. Put in your head". But whether it were Mr. Baxter said it so hoarse-like and faint, he never could be sure.

'Still there weren't no one but him in the street, and yet Williams was that upset by the way he spoke that he shrank back from the window and went and sat on the bed. And he heard Mr. Baxter's step go on and up the road, and after a minute or more he couldn't help but look out once more and he see him going along the same curious way as before. And one thing he recollected was that Mr. Baxter never stopped to pick up his 'at when it fell off, and yet there it was on his head.

'Well, Master Henry, that was the last anybody see of Mr. Baxter, least-ways for a week or more. There was a lot of people said he was called off on business, or made off because he'd got into some scrape, but he was well known for miles round, and none of the railway people nor the public-house people hadn't seen him.

'And then ponds was looked into and nothink found; and at last one evening Fakes the keeper come down from over the hill to the village, and he says he seen the Gallows Hill planting black with birds, and that were a funny thing, because he never see no sign of a creature there in his time. So they looked at each other a bit, and first one says: "I'm game to go up," and another says: "So am I, if you are," and half-a-dozen of 'em set out in the evening time, and took Dr. Lawrence with them, and you know, Master Henry, there he was between them three stones with his neck broke.'

Useless to imagine the talk which this story set going. It is not remembered. But before Patten left them, he said to Fanshawe: 'Excuse me, sir, but did I understand as you took out them glasses with you today? I thought you did; and might I ask, did you make use of them at all?'

'Yes. Only to look at something in a church.'

'Oh, indeed, you took 'em into the church, did you, sir?'

'Yes, I did; it was Lambsfield church. By the way, I left them strapped on to my bicycle, I'm afraid, in the stable-yard.'

'No matter for that, sir. I can bring them in the first thing tomorrow, and perhaps you'll be so good as to look at 'em then.'

Accordingly, before breakfast, after a tranquil and well-earned sleep, Fanshawe took the glasses into the garden and directed them to a distant hill. He lowered them instantly, and looked at top and bottom, worked the screws, tried them again and yet again, shrugged his shoulders and replaced them on the hall-table.

'Patten,' he said, 'they're absolutely useless. I can't see a thing: it's as if someone had stuck a black wafer over the lens.'

'Spoilt my glasses, have you?' said the Squire. 'Thank you: the only ones I've got.'

'You try them yourself,' said Fanshawe, 'I've done nothing to them.'

So after breakfast the Squire took them out to the terrace and stood on the steps. After a few ineffectual attempts, 'Lord, how heavy they are!' he said impatiently, and in the same instant dropped them on to the stones, and the lens splintered and the barrel cracked. A little pool of liquid formed on the stone slab. It was inky black, and the odour that rose from it is not to be described.

'Filled and sealed, eh?' said the Squire. 'If I could bring myself to touch it, I dare say we should find the seal. So that's what came of his boiling and distilling, is it? Old Ghoul!'

'What in the world do you mean?'

'Don't you see, my good man? Remember what he said to the doctor about looking through dead men's eyes? Well, this was another way of it. But they didn't like having their bones boiled, I take it, and the end of it was they carried him off whither he would not. Well, I'll get a spade, and we'll bury this thing decently.'

As they smoothed the turf over it, the Squire, handing the spade to Patten, who had been a reverential spectator, remarked to Fanshawe: 'It's almost a pity you took that thing into the church: you might have seen more than you did. Baxter had them for a week, I make out, but I don't see that he did much in the time.'

'I'm not sure,' said Fanshawe, 'there is that picture of Fulnaker Priory Church.'

A Warning to the Curious

THE PLACE ON THE EAST COAST which the reader is asked to consider is Seaburgh. It is not very different now from what I remember it to have been when I was a child. Marshes intersected by dykes to the south, recalling the early chapters of *Great Expectations*; flat fields to the north, merging into heath; heath, fir woods, and, above all, gorse, inland. A long sea-front and a street: behind that a spacious church of flint, with a broad, solid western tower and a peal of six bells.

How well I remember their sound on a hot Sunday in August, as our party went slowly up the white, dusty slope of road towards them, for the church stands at the top of a short, steep incline. They rang with a flat clacking sort of sound on those hot days, but when the air was softer they were mellower too.

The railway ran down to its little terminus farther along the same road. There was a gay white windmill just before you came to the station, and another down near the shingle at the south end the town, and yet others on higher ground to the north.

There were cottages of bright red brick with slate roofs . . . but why do I encumber you with these commonplace details? The fact is that they come crowding to the point of the pencil when it begins to write of Seaburgh. I should like to be sure that I had allowed the right ones to get on to the paper. But I forgot. I have not quite done with the word-painting business yet.

Walk away from the sea and the town, pass the station, and turn up the road on the right. It is a sandy road, parallel with the railway, and if you

LES EDWARDS

follow it, it climbs to somewhat higher ground. On your left (you are now going northward) is heath, on your right (the side towards the sea) is a belt of old firs, wind-beaten, thick at the top, with the slope that old seaside trees have. Seen on the skyline from the train they would tell you in an instant, if you did not know it, that you were approaching a windy coast.

Well, at the top of my little hill, a line of these firs strikes out and runs towards the sea, for there is a ridge that goes that way. And the ridge ends in a rather well-defined mound commanding the level fields of rough grass, and a little knot of fir trees crowns it. And here you may sit on a hot spring day, very well content to look at blue sea, white windmills, red cottages, bright green grass, church tower, and distant Martello tower on the south.

As I have said, I began to know Seaburgh as a child; but a gap of a good many years separates my early knowledge from that which is more recent. Still it keeps its place in my affections, and any tales of it that I pick up have an interest for me.

One such tale is this: it came to me in a place very remote from Seaburgh, and quite accidentally, from a man whom I had been able to oblige – enough in his opinion to justify his making me his confidant to this extent.

I know all that country more or less (he said). I used to go to Seaburgh pretty regularly for golf in the spring. I generally put up at the Bear, with a friend – Henry Long it was, you knew him perhaps – ('Slightly,' I said) and we used to take a sitting-room and be very happy there. Since he died I haven't cared to go there. And I don't know that I should anyhow after the particular thing that happened on our last visit.

It was in April, 19—, we were there, and by some chance we were almost the only people in the hotel. So the ordinary public rooms were practically empty, and we were the more surprised when, after dinner, our sitting-room door opened, and a young man put his head in.

We were aware of this young man. He was rather a rabbity anæmic subject – light hair and light eyes – but not unpleasing. So when he said: 'I beg your pardon, is this a private room?' we did not growl and say: 'Yes, it is,' but Long said, or I did – no matter which: 'Please come in.' 'Oh, may I?' he said, and seemed relieved. Of course it was obvious that he wanted company; and as he was a reasonable kind of person – not the sort to bestow his whole family history on you – we urged him to make himself at home.

'I dare say you find the other rooms rather bleak,' I said.

Yes, he did; but it was really too good of us, and so on. That being got over, he made some pretence of reading a book. Long was playing Patience, I was writing. It became plain to me after a few minutes that this visitor of ours was in rather a state of fidgets or nerves, which communicated itself to me, and so I put away my writing and turned to at engaging him in talk.

After some remarks, which I forget, he became rather confidential.

'You'll think it very odd of me' (this was the sort of way he began), 'but the fact is I've had something of a shock.'

Well, I recommended a drink of some cheering kind, and we had it. The waiter coming in made an interruption (and I thought our young man seemed very jumpy when the door opened), but after a while he got back to his woes again.

There was nobody he knew in the place, and he did happen to know who we both were (it turned out there was some common acquaintance in town), and really he did want a word of advice, if we didn't mind.

Of course we both said: 'By all means,' or 'Not at all,' and Long put away his cards. And we settled down to hear what his difficulty was.

'It began,' he said, 'more than a week ago, when I bicycled over to Froston, only about five or six miles, to see the church. I'm very much interested in architecture, and it's got one of those pretty porches with niches and shields.

'I took a photograph of it, and then an old man who was tidying up in the churchyard came and asked if I'd care to look into the church. I said yes, and he produced a key and let me in.

'There wasn't much inside, but I told him it was a nice little church, and he kept it very clean, "but," I said, "the porch is the best part of it".

'We were just outside the porch then, and he said, "Ah, yes, that is a nice porch. And do you know, sir, what's the meanin' of that coat of arms there?"

'It was the one with the three crowns, and though I'm not much of a herald, I was able to say yes, I thought it was the old arms of the kingdom of East Anglia.

'"That's right, sir," he said, "and do you know the meanin' of them three crowns that's on it?"

471

'I said I'd no doubt it was known, but I couldn't recollect to have heard it myself.

'"Well, then," he said, "for all you're a scholard, I can tell you something you don't know. Them's the three 'oly crowns what was buried in the ground near by the coast to keep the Germans from landing – ah, I can see you don't believe that. But I tell you, if it hadn't have been for one of them 'oly crowns bein' there still, them Germans would a landed here time and again, they would. Landed with their ships, and killed man, woman and child in their beds. Now then, that's the truth what I'm telling you, that is. And if you don't believe me, you ast the rector. There he comes: you ast him, I says."

'I looked round, and there was the rector, a nice-looking old man, coming up the path. And before I could begin assuring my old man, who was getting quite excited, that I didn't disbelieve him, the rector struck in, and said: "What's all this about, John? Good day to you, sir. Have you been looking at our little church?"

'So then there was a little talk which allowed the old man to calm down, and then the rector asked him again what was the matter.

'"Oh," he said, "it warn't nothink, only I was telling this gentleman he'd ought to ast you about them 'oly crowns."

'"Ah, yes, to be sure," said the rector, "that's a very curious matter, isn't it? But I don't know whether the gentleman is interested in our old stories, eh?"

'"Oh, he'll be interested fast enough," says the old man, "he'll put his confidence in what you tells him, sir. Why, you known William Ager yourself, father and son too."

'Then I put in a word to say how much I should like to hear all about it, and before many minutes I was walking up the village street with the rector, who had one or two words to say to parishioners, and then to the rectory, where he took me into his study.

'He had made out, on the way, that I really was capable of taking an intelligent interest in a piece of folklore, and not quite the ordinary tripper. So he was very willing to talk, and it is rather surprising to me that the particular legend he told me has not made its way into print before.

'His account of it was this: "There has always been a belief in these parts in the three holy crowns. The old people say they were buried in different places near the coast to keep off the Danes or the French or the Germans. And they say that one of the three was dug up a long time ago, and another has disappeared by the encroaching of the sea, and one's still left doing its work, keeping off invaders.

"'Well, now, if you have read the ordinary guides and histories of this county, you will remember perhaps that in 1687 a crown, which was said to be the crown of Redwald, King of the East Angles, was dug up at Rendlesham, and alas! alas! melted down before it was even properly described or drawn. Well, Rendlesham isn't on the coast, but it isn't so very far inland, and it's on a very important line of access. And I believe that is the crown which the people mean when they say that one has been dug up.

"'Then on the south you don't want me to tell you where there was a Saxon royal palace which is now under the sea, eh? Well, there was the second crown, I take it. And up beyond these two, they say, lies the third."

"'Do they say where it is?" of course I asked.

'He said, "Yes, indeed, they do, but they don't tell," and his manner did not encourage me to put the obvious question.

'Instead of that I waited a moment, and said: "What did the old man mean when he said you knew William Ager, as if that had something to do with the crowns?"

"'To be sure," he said, "now that's another curious story. These Agers – it's a very old name in these parts, but I can't find that they were ever people of quality or big owners – these Agers say, or said, that their branch of the family were the guardians of the last crown.

"'A certain old Nathaniel Ager was the first one I knew – I was born and brought up quite near here – and he, I believe, camped out at the place during the whole of the war of 1870. William, his son, did the same, I know, during the South African War. And young William, *his* son, who has only died fairly recently, took lodgings at the cottage nearest the spot, and I've no doubt hastened his end, for he was a consumptive, by exposure and night watching.

"'And he was the last of that branch. It was a dreadful grief to him to think that he was the last, but he could do nothing, the only relations at all near to him were in the colonies. I wrote letters for him to them imploring them to come over on business very important to the family, but there has been no answer.

'"So the last of the holy crowns, if it's there, has no guardian now."

'That was what the rector told me, and you can fancy how interesting I found it. The only thing I could think of when I left him was how to hit upon the spot where the crown was supposed to be. I wish I'd left it alone.

'But there was a sort of fate in it, for as I bicycled back past the church-yard wall my eye caught a fairly new gravestone, and on it was the name of William Ager. Of course I got off and read it. It said: *of this parish, died at Seaburgh, 19—, aged 28.* There it was, you see. A little judicious questioning in the right place, and I should at least find the cottage nearest the spot.

'Only I didn't quite know what was the right place to begin my question-ing at. Again there was fate: it took me to the curiosity-shop down that way – you know – and I turned over some old books, and, if you please, one was a prayer-book of 1740 odd, in a rather handsome binding – I'll just go and get it, it's in my room.'

He left us in a state of some surprise, but we had hardly time to exchange any remarks when he was back, panting, and handed us the book opened at the fly-leaf, on which was, in a straggly hand:

Nathaniel Ager is my name and England is my nation,
Seaburgh is my dwelling-place and Christ is my Salvation,
When I am dead and in my Grave, and all my bones are rotton,
I hope the lord will think on me when I am quite forgotton.

This poem was dated 1754, and there were many more entries of Agers, Nathaniel, Frederick, William, and so on, ending with William, 19—.

'You see,' he said, 'anybody would call it the greatest bit of luck. *I* did, but I don't now. Of course I asked the shopman about William Ager, and of course he happened to remember that he lodged in a cottage in the North Field and died there.

'This was just chalking the road for me. I knew which the cottage must be: there is only one sizeable one about there. The next thing was to scrape some sort of acquaintance with the people, and I took a walk that way at once. A dog did the business for me: he made at me so fiercely that they had to run out and beat him off, and then naturally begged my pardon, and we got into talk.

'I had only to bring up Ager's name, and pretend I knew, or thought I knew something of him, and then the woman said how sad it was him dying so young, and she was sure it came of him spending the night out of doors in the cold weather.

'Then I had to say: "Did he go out on the sea at night?" and she said: "Oh, no, it was on the hillock yonder with the trees on it." And there I was.

'I know something about digging in these barrows: I've opened many of them in the down country. But that was with owner's leave, and in broad daylight and with men to help.

'I had to prospect very carefully here before I put a spade in. I couldn't trench across the mound, and with those old firs growing there I knew there would be awkward tree roots. Still the soil was very light and sandy and easy, and there was a rabbit hole or so that might be developed into a sort of tunnel.

'The going out and coming back at odd hours to the hotel was going to be the awkward part. When I made up my mind about the way to excavate I told the people that I was called away for a night, and I spent it out there. I made my tunnel – I won't bore you with the details of how I supported it and filled it in when I'd done, but the main thing is that I got the crown.'

Naturally we both broke out into exclamations of surprise and interest. I for one had long known about the finding of the crown at Rendlesham and had often lamented its fate. No one has ever seen an Anglo-Saxon crown – at least no one had. But our man gazed at us with a rueful eye.

'Yes,' he said, 'and the worst of it is I don't know how to put it back.'

'Put it back?' we cried out. 'Why, my dear sir, you've made one of the most exciting finds ever heard of in this country. Of course it ought to go to the Jewel House at the Tower. What's your difficulty? If you're thinking about the owner of the land, and treasure-trove, and all that, we can certainly help you through. Nobody's going to make a fuss about technicalities in a case of this kind.'

Probably more was said, but all he did was to put his face in his hands, and mutter: 'I don't know how to put it back.'

At last Long said: 'You'll forgive me, I hope, if I seem impertinent, but are you *quite* sure you've got it?'

I was wanting to ask much the same question myself, for of course the story did seem a lunatic's dream when one thought over it. But I hadn't quite dared to say what might hurt the poor young man's feelings.

However, he took it quite calmly – really, with the calm of despair, you might say. He sat up and said: 'Oh, yes, there's no doubt of that: I have it here, in my room, locked up in my bag. You can come and look at it if you like. I won't offer to bring it here.'

We were not likely to let the chance slip. We went with him – his room was only a few doors off. The boots was just collecting shoes in the passage, or so we thought. Afterwards we were not sure.

Our visitor – his name was Paxton – was in a worse state of shivers than before, and went hurriedly into the room, and beckoned us after him, turned on the light, and shut the door carefully. Then he unlocked his kit-bag, and produced a bundle of clean pocket-handkerchiefs in which something was wrapped, laid it on the bed, and undid it.

I can now say I *have* seen an actual Anglo-Saxon crown. It was of silver – as the Rendlesham one is always said to have been – it was set with some gems, mostly antique intaglios and cameos, and was of rather plain, almost rough workmanship. In fact, it was like those you see on the coins and in the manuscripts.

I found no reason to think it was later than the 9th century. I was intensely interested, of course, and I wanted to turn it over in my hands, but Paxton prevented me.

'Don't *you* touch it,' he said, 'I'll do that.' And with a sigh that was, I declare to you, dreadful to hear, he took it up and turned it about so that we could see every part of it. 'Seen enough?' he said at last, and we nodded. He wrapped it up and locked it in his bag, and stood looking at us dumbly.

'Come back to our room,' Long said, 'and tell us what the trouble is.'

He thanked us, and said: 'Will you go first and see if – if the coast is clear?'

That wasn't very intelligible, for our proceedings hadn't been, after all, very suspicious, and the hotel, as I said, was practically empty. However, we were beginning to have inklings of – we didn't know what, and anyhow nerves are infectious.

So we did go, first peering out as we opened the door, and fancying (I found we both had the fancy) that a shadow, or more than a shadow – but it made no sound – passed from before us to one side as we came out into the passage.

'It's all right,' we whispered to Paxton – whispering seemed the proper tone – and we went, with him between us, back to our sitting-room. I was preparing, when we got there, to be ecstatic about the unique interest of what we had seen, but when I looked at Paxton I saw that would be terribly out of place, and I left it to him to begin.

'What *is* to be done?' was his opening.

Long thought it right (as he explained to me afterwards) to be obtuse, and said: 'Why not find out who the owner of the land is, and inform—'

'Oh, no, no!' Paxton broke in impatiently, 'I beg your pardon. You've been very kind, but don't you see it's *got* to go back, and I daren't be there at night, and daytime's impossible. Perhaps, though, you don't see – well, then, the truth is that I've never been alone since I touched it.'

I was beginning some fairly stupid comment, but Long caught my eye, and I stopped.

Long said: 'I think I do see, perhaps. But wouldn't it be – a relief – to tell us a little more clearly what the situation is?'

Then it all came out. Paxton looked over his shoulder and beckoned to us to come nearer to him, and began speaking in a low voice. We listened most intently, of course, and compared notes afterwards, and I wrote down our version, so I am confident I have what he told us almost word for word.

He said: 'It began when I was first prospecting, and put me off again and again. There was always somebody – a man – standing by one of the firs. This was in daylight, you know. He was never in front of me. I always saw him with the tail of my eye on the left or the right, and he was never there when I looked straight for him.

'I would lie down for quite a long time and take careful observations, and make sure there was no one, and then when I got up and began prospecting again, there he was.

'And he began to give me hints, besides. For wherever I put that prayer-book – short of locking it up, which I did at last – when I came back to my room it was always out on my table open at the flyleaf where the names are, and one of my razors across it to keep it open. I'm sure he just can't open my bag, or something more would have happened.

'You see, he's light and weak, but all the same I daren't face him. Well, then, when I was making the tunnel, of course it was worse, and if I hadn't been so keen I should have dropped the whole thing and run. It was like someone scraping at my back all the time. I thought for a long time it was only soil dropping on me, but as I got nearer the – the crown, it was unmistakable. And when I actually laid it bare and got my fingers into the ring of it and pulled it out, there came a sort of cry behind me – oh, I can't tell you how desolate it was! And horribly threatening too. It spoilt all my pleasure in my find – cut it off that moment. And if I hadn't been the wretched fool I am, I should have put the thing back and left it.

'But I didn't. The rest of the time was just awful. I had hours to get through before I could decently come back to the hotel. First I spent time filling up my tunnel and covering my tracks, and all the while he was there trying to thwart me. Sometimes, you know, you see him, and sometimes you don't, just as he pleases, I think – he's there, but he has some power over your eyes.

'Well, I wasn't off the spot very long before sunrise, and then I had to get to the junction for Seaburgh, and take a train back. And though it was daylight fairly soon, I don't know if that made it much better. There were always hedges, or gorse-bushes, or park fences along the road – some sort of cover, I mean – and I was never easy for a second.

'And then when I began to meet people going to work, they always looked behind me very strangely. It might have been that they were surprised at seeing anyone so early, but I didn't think it was only that, and I don't now – they didn't look exactly at me. And the porter at the train was like that too. And the guard held open the door after I'd got into the carriage – just as he would if there was somebody else coming, you know.

'Oh, you may be very sure it isn't my fancy,' he said with a dull sort of laugh. Then he went on: 'And even if I do get it put back, he won't forgive me. I can tell that. And I was so happy a fortnight ago.' He dropped into a chair, and I believe he began to cry.

We didn't know what to say, but we felt we must come to the rescue somehow, and so – it really seemed the only thing – we said if he was so set on putting the crown back in its place, we would help him.

And I must say that after what we had heard it did seem the right thing. If these horrid consequences had come on this poor man, might there not really be something in the original idea of the crown having some curious power bound up with it, to guard the coast? At least, that was my feeling, and I think it was Long's too.

Our offer was very welcome to Paxton, anyhow. When could we do it? It was nearing half-past ten. Could we contrive to make a late walk plausible to the hotel people that very night? We looked out of the window: there was a brilliant full moon – the Paschal moon.

Long undertook to tackle the boots and propitiate him. He was to say that we should not be much over the hour, and if we did find it so pleasant that we stopped out a bit longer we would see that he didn't lose by sitting up.

Well, we were pretty regular customers of the hotel, and did not give much trouble, and were considered by the servants to be not under the mark in the way of tips. And so the boots *was* propitiated, and let us out on to the sea-front, and remained, as we heard later, looking after us.

Paxton had a large coat over his arm, under which was the wrapped-up crown.

So we were off on this strange errand before we had time to think how very much out of the way it was. I have told this part quite shortly on purpose, for it really does represent the haste with which we settled our plan and took action.

'The shortest way is up the hill and through the churchyard,' Paxton said, as we stood a moment before the hotel looking up and down the front.

There was nobody about – nobody at all. Seaburgh out of the season is an early, quiet place.

'We can't go along the dyke by the cottage, because of the dog,' Paxton also said, when I pointed to what I thought a shorter way along the front and across two fields.

The reason he gave was good enough. We went up the road to the church, and turned in at the churchyard gate. I confess to having thought that there might be some lying there who might be conscious of our business. But if it was so, they were also conscious that one who was on their side, so to say, had us under surveillance, and we saw no sign of them. But under observation we felt we were, as I have never felt it at another time.

Specially was it so when we passed out of the churchyard into a narrow path with close high hedges, through which we hurried as Christian did through that Valley, and so got out into open fields. Then along hedges, though I would sooner have been in the open, where I could see if anyone was visible behind me. Over a gate or two, and then a swerve to the left, taking us up on to the ridge which ended in that mound.

As we neared it, Henry Long felt, and I felt too, that there were what I can only call dim presences waiting for us, as well as a far more actual one attending us.

Of Paxton's agitation all this time I can give you no adequate picture. He breathed like a hunted beast, and we could not either of us look at his face. How he would manage when we got to the very place we had not troubled to think – he had seemed so sure that that would not be difficult.

Nor was it. I never saw anything like the dash with which he flung himself at a particular spot in the side of the mound, and tore at it, so that in a very few minutes the greater part of his body was out of sight. We stood holding the coat and that bundle of handkerchiefs, and looking, very fearfully, I must admit, about us.

There was nothing to be seen: a line of dark firs behind us made one skyline, more trees and the church tower half-a-mile off on the right, cottages and a windmill on the horizon on the left, calm sea dead in front, faint barking of a dog at a cottage on a gleaming dyke between us and it; full moon making that path we know across the sea; the eternal whisper of the Scotch firs just above us, and of the sea in front.

Yet, in all this quiet, an acute, an acrid consciousness of a restrained hostility very near us, like a dog on a leash that might be let go at any moment.

Paxton pulled himself out of the hole, and stretched a hand back to us. 'Give it to me,' he whispered, 'unwrapped.'

We pulled off the handkerchiefs, and he took the crown. The moonlight just fell on it as he snatched it.

We had not ourselves touched that bit of metal, and I have thought since that it was just as well.

In another moment Paxton was out of the hole again and busy shovelling back the soil with hands that were already bleeding. He would have none of our help, though. It was much the longest part of the job to get the place to look undisturbed. Yet – I don't know how – he made a wonderful success of it.

At last he was satisfied and we turned back.

We were a couple of hundred yards from the hill when Long suddenly said to him: 'I say, you've left your coat there. That won't do. See?'

And I certainly did see it – the long dark overcoat lying where the tunnel had been.

Paxton had not stopped, however. He only shook his head, and held up the coat on his arm. And when we joined him, he said, without any excitement, but as if nothing mattered any more: 'That wasn't my coat.'

And, indeed, when we looked back again, that dark thing was not to be seen.

Well, we got out on to the road, and came rapidly back that way. It was well before twelve when we got in, trying to put a good face on it, and saying – Long and I – what a lovely night it was for a walk. The boots was on the look-out for us, and we made remarks like that for his edification as we entered the hotel.

He gave another look up and down the sea-front before he locked the front door, and said: 'You didn't meet many people about, I s'pose, sir?'

'No, indeed, not a soul,' I said, at which I remember Paxton looked oddly at me.

'Only I thought I see someone turn up the station road after you gentlemen,' said the boots. 'Still, you was three together, and I don't suppose he meant mischief.'

I didn't know what to say.

Long merely said 'Good night,' and we went off upstairs, promising to turn out all lights, and to go to bed in a few minutes.

Back in our room, we did our very best to make Paxton take a cheerful view. 'There's the crown safe back,' we said; 'very likely you'd have done better not to touch it' (and he heavily assented to that), 'but no real harm has been done, and we shall never give this away to anyone who would be so mad as to go near it.

'Besides, don't you feel better yourself? I don't mind confessing,' I said, 'that on the way there I was very much inclined to take your view about – well, about being followed. But going back, it wasn't at all the same thing, was it?'

No, it wouldn't do: '*You've* nothing to trouble yourselves about,' he said, 'but I'm not forgiven. I've got to pay for that miserable sacrilege still. I know what you are going to say. The Church might help. Yes, but it's the body that has to suffer.

'It's true I'm not feeling that he's waiting outside for me just now. But—' Then he stopped. Then he turned to thanking us, and we put him off as soon as we could.

And naturally we pressed him to use our sitting-room next day, and said we should be glad to go out with him. Or did he play golf, perhaps? Yes, he did, but he didn't think he should care about that tomorrow.

Well, we recommended him to get up late and sit in our room in the morning while we were playing, and we would have a walk later in the day. He was very submissive and *piano* about it all – ready to do just what we thought best, but clearly quite certain in his own mind that what was coming could not be averted or palliated.

You'll wonder why we didn't insist on accompanying him to his home and seeing him safe into the care of brothers or someone. The fact was he had nobody. He had had a flat in town, but lately he had made up his mind to settle for a time in Sweden, and he had dismantled his flat and shipped off his belongings, and was whiling away a fortnight or three weeks before he made a start.

Anyhow, we didn't see what we could do better than sleep on it – or not sleep very much, as was my case – and see what we felt like tomorrow morning.

We felt very different, Long and I, on as beautiful an April morning as you could desire. And Paxton also looked very different when we saw him at breakfast.

'The first approach to a decent night I seem ever to have had,' was what he said. But he was going to do as we had settled – stay in probably all the morning, and come out with us later.

We went to the links. We met some other men and played with them in the morning, and had lunch there rather early, so as not to be late back. All the same, the snares of death overtook him.

Whether it could have been prevented, I don't know. I think he would have been got at somehow, do what we might. Anyhow, this is what happened.

We went straight up to our room. Paxton was there, reading quite peaceably.

'Ready to come out shortly?' said Long, 'say in half-an-hour's time?'

'Certainly,' he said, and I said we would change first, and perhaps have baths, and call for him in half-an-hour.

I had my bath first, and went and lay down on my bed, and slept for about ten minutes. We came out of our rooms at the same time, and went together to the sitting-room.

Paxton wasn't there – only his book.

Nor was he in his room, nor in the downstair rooms.

We shouted for him.

A servant came out and said: 'Why, I thought you gentlemen was gone out already, and so did the other gentleman. He heard you a-calling from the path there, and run out in a hurry, and I looked out of the coffee-room window, but I didn't see you. 'Owever, he run off down the beach that way.'

Without a word we ran that way too – it was the opposite direction to that of last night's expedition.

It wasn't quite four o'clock, and the day was fair, though not so fair as it had been, so that was really no reason, you'd say, for anxiety. With people about, surely a man couldn't come to much harm.

But something in our look as we ran out must have struck the servant, for she came out on the steps, and pointed, and said, 'Yes, that's the way he went.'

We ran on as far as the top of the shingle bank, and there pulled up. There was a choice of ways: past the houses on the sea-front, or along the sand at the bottom of the beach, which, the tide being now out, was fairly broad. Or of course we might keep along the shingle between these two tracks and have some view of both of them, only that was heavy going.

We chose the sand, for that was the loneliest, and someone *might* come to harm there without being seen from the public path.

Long said he saw Paxton some distance ahead, running and waving his stick, as if he wanted to signal to people who were on ahead of him. I couldn't be sure: one of these sea-mists was coming up very quickly from the south. There was someone, that's all I could say.

And there were tracks on the sand as of someone running who wore shoes; and there were other tracks made before those – for the shoes sometimes trod in them and interfered with them – of someone not in shoes.

Oh, of course, it's only my word you've got to take for all this: Long's dead, we'd no time or means to make sketches or take casts, and the next tide washed everything away. All we could do was to notice these marks as we hurried on. But there they were over and over again, and we had no doubt whatever that what we saw was the track of a bare foot, and one that showed more bones than flesh.

The notion of Paxton running after – after anything like this, and supposing it to be the friends he was looking for, was very dreadful to us.

You can guess what we fancied: how the thing he was following might stop suddenly and turn round on him, and what sort of face it would show, half-seen at first in the mist – which all the while was getting thicker and thicker.

And as I ran on wondering how the poor wretch could have been lured into mistaking that other thing for us, I remembered his saying, 'He has some power over your eyes'. And then I wondered what the end would be, for I had no hope now that the end could be averted, and – well, there is no need to tell all the dismal and horrid thoughts that flitted through my head as we ran on into the mist.

It was uncanny, too, that the sun should still be bright in the sky and we could see nothing. We could only tell that we were now past the houses and had reached that gap there is between them and the old Martello tower.

When you are past the tower, you know, there is nothing but shingle for a long way – not a house, not a human creature, just that spit of land, or rather shingle, with the river on your right and the sea on your left.

But just before that, just by the Martello tower, you remember there is the old battery, close to the sea. I believe there are only a few blocks of concrete left now – the rest has all been washed away, but at this time there was a lot more, though the place was a ruin.

Well, when we got there, we clambered to the top as quick as we could to take breath and look over the shingle in front if by chance the mist would let us see anything. But a moment's rest we must have. We had run a mile at least.

Nothing whatever was visible ahead of us, and we were just turning by common consent to get down and run hopelessly on, when we heard what I can only call a laugh. And if you can understand what I mean by a breathless, a lungless laugh, you have it. But I don't suppose you can.

It came from below, and swerved away into the mist. That was enough. We bent over the wall.

Paxton was there at the bottom.

You don't need to be told that he was dead. His tracks showed that he had run along the side of the battery, had turned sharp round the corner of it, and, small doubt of it, must have dashed straight into the open arms of someone who was waiting there.

His mouth was full of sand and stones, and his teeth and jaws were broken to bits. I only glanced once at his face.

At the same moment, just as we were scrambling down from the battery to get to the body, we heard a shout, and saw a man running down the bank of the Martello tower.

He was the caretaker stationed there, and his keen old eyes had managed to descry through the mist that something was wrong. He had seen Paxton fall, and had seen us a moment after, running up – fortunate this, for otherwise we could hardly have escaped suspicion of being concerned in the dreadful business.

Had he, we asked, caught sight of anybody attacking our friend?

He could not be sure.

We sent him off for help, and stayed by the dead man till they came with the stretcher.

It was then that we traced out how he had come, on the narrow fringe of sand under the battery wall. The rest was shingle, and it was hopelessly impossible to tell whither the other had gone.

What were we to say at the inquest?

It was a duty, we felt, not to give up, there and then, the secret of the crown, to be published in every paper.

I don't know how much you would have told, but what we did agree upon was this: to say that we had only made acquaintance with Paxton the day before, and that he had told us he was under some apprehension of danger at the hands of a man called William Ager.

Also that we had seen some other tracks besides Paxton's when we followed him along the beach. But of course by that time everything was gone from the sands.

No one had any knowledge, fortunately, of any William Ager living in the district. The evidence of the man at the Martello tower freed us from all suspicion. All that could be done was to return a verdict of wilful murder by some person or persons unknown.

Paxton was so totally without connections that all the inquiries that were subsequently made ended in a No Thoroughfare.

And I have never been at Seaburgh, or even near it, since.

An Evening's Entertainment

NOTHING IS MORE COMMON FORM in old-fashioned books than the description of the winter fireside, where the aged grandam narrates to the circle of children that hangs on her lips story after story of ghosts and fairies, and inspires her audience with a pleasing terror. But we are never allowed to know what the stories were. We hear, indeed, of sheeted spectres with saucer eyes, and – still more intriguing – of 'Rawhead and Bloody Bones' (an expression which the *Oxford Dictionary* traces back to 1550), but the context of these striking images eludes us.

Here, then, is a problem which has long obsessed me; but I see no means of solving it finally. The aged grandams are gone, and the collectors of folklore began their work in England too late to save most of the actual stories which the grandams told. Yet such things do not easily die quite out, and imagination, working on scattered hints, may be able to devise a picture of an evening's entertainment, such an one as Mrs. Marcet's *Evening Conversations*, Mr. Joyce's *Dialogues on Chemistry* and somebody else's *Philosophy in Sport Made Science in Earnest* aimed at extinguishing by substituting for Error and Superstition the light of Utility and Truth; in some such terms as these:

Charles: I think, papa, that I now understand the properties of the lever, which you so kindly explained to me on Saturday; but I have been very much puzzled since then in thinking about the pendulum, and have wondered why it is that, when you stop it, the clock does not go on any more.

Papa: (You young sinner, have you been meddling with the clock in the

487

hall? Come here to me! *No, this must be a gloss that has somehow crept into the text.*) Well, my boy, though I do not wholly approve of your conducting without my supervision experiments which may possibly impair the usefulness of a valuable scientific instrument, I will do my best to explain the principles of the pendulum to you. Fetch me a piece of stout whipcord from the drawer in my study, and ask cook to be so good as to lend you one of the weights which she uses in her kitchen.

And so we are off.

How different the scene in a household to which the beams of Science have not yet penetrated! The Squire, exhausted by a long day after the partridges, and replete with food and drink, is snoring on one side of the fireplace. His old mother sits opposite to him knitting, and the children (Charles and Fanny, not Harry and Lucy: they would never have stood it) are gathered about her knee.

Grandmother: Now, my dears, you must be very good and quiet, or you'll wake your father, and you know what'll happen then.

Charles: Yes, I know: he'll be woundy cross-tempered and send us off to bed.

Grandmother (stops knitting and speaks with severity): What's that? Fie upon you, Charles! That's not a way to speak. Now I *was* going to have told you a story, but if you use such-like words, I shan't. (*Suppressed outcry:* 'Oh, granny!') Hush! Hush! Now I believe you have woke your father!

Squire (thickly): Look here, mother, if you can't keep them brats quiet—

Grandmother: Yes, John, yes! It's too bad. I've been telling them if it happens again, off to bed they shall go.

Squire relapses.

Grandmother: There, now, you see, children, what did I tell you? You *must* be good and sit still. And I'll tell you what: tomorrow you shall go a-blackberrying, and if you bring home a nice basketful, I'll make you some jam.

Charles: Oh yes, granny, do! And I know where the best blackberries are: I saw 'em today.

Grandmother: And where's that, Charles?

Charles: Why, in the little lane that goes up past Collins' cottage.

Grandmother (laying down her knitting): Charles! Whatever you do, don't you dare to pick one single blackberry in that lane. Don't you *know*

– but there, how should you – what was I thinking of? Well, anyway, you mind what I say—

Charles and Fanny: But why, granny? Why shouldn't we pick 'em there?

Grandmother: Hush! Hush! Very well then, I'll tell you all about it, only you mustn't interrupt. Now let me see. When I was quite a little girl that lane had a bad name, though it seems people don't remember about it now.

And one day – dear me, just as it might be tonight – I told my poor mother when I came home to my supper – a summer evening it was – I told her where I'd been for my walk, and how I'd come back down that lane, and I asked her how it was that there were currant and gooseberry bushes growing in a little patch at the top of the lane.

And oh, dear me, such a taking as she was in! She shook me and she slapped me, and says she, 'You naughty, naughty child, haven't I forbid you twenty times over to set foot in that lane? And here you go dawdling down it at night-time,' and so forth, and when she'd finished I was almost too much taken aback to say anything. But I did make her believe that was the first I'd ever heard of it; and that was no more than the truth.

And then, to be sure, she was sorry she'd been so short with me, and to make up she told me the whole story after my supper. And since then I've often heard the same from the old people in the place, and had my own reasons besides for thinking there was something in it.

Now, up at the far end of that lane – let me see, is it on the right- or the left-hand side as you go up? – the left-hand side – you'll find a little patch of bushes and rough ground in the field, and something like a broken old hedge round about, and you'll notice there's some old gooseberry and currant bushes growing among it – or there used to be, for it's years now since I've been up that way.

Well, that means there was a cottage stood there, of course; and in that cottage, before I was born or thought of, there lived a man named Davis. I've heard that he wasn't born in the parish, and it's true there's nobody of that name been living about here since I've known the place. But however that may be, this Mr. Davis lived very much to himself and very seldom went to the public-house, and he didn't work for any of the farmers, having as it seemed enough money of his own to get along.

But he'd go to the town on market-days and take up his letters at the post-

489

house where the mails called. And one day he came back from market, and brought a young man with him; and this young man and he lived together for some long time, and went about together, and whether he just did the work of the house for Mr. Davis, or whether Mr. Davis was his teacher in some way, nobody seemed to know.

I've heard he was a pale, ugly young fellow and hadn't much to say for himself. Well, now, what did those two men do with themselves? Of course I can't tell you half the foolish things that the people got into their heads, and we know, don't we, that you mustn't speak evil when you aren't sure it's true, even when people are dead and gone.

But as I said, those two were always about together, late and early, up on the downland and below in the woods – and there was one walk in particular that they'd take regularly once a month, to the place where you've seen that old figure cut out in the hillside. And it was noticed that in the summer-time when they took that walk, they'd camp out all night, either there or somewhere near by.

I remember once my father – that's your great-grandfather – told me he had spoken to Mr. Davis about it (for it's his land he lived on) and asked him why he was so fond of going there, but he only said: 'Oh, it's a wonderful old place, sir, and I've always been fond of the old-fashioned things, and when him (that was his man he meant) and me are together there, it seems to bring back the old times so plain.'

And my father said, 'Well,' he said, 'it may suit *you*, but *I* shouldn't like a lonely place like that in the middle of the night.'

And Mr. Davis smiled, and the young man, who'd been listening, said, 'Oh, we don't want for company at such times,' and my father said he couldn't help thinking Mr. Davis made some kind of sign, and the young man went on quick, as if to mend his words, and said, 'That's to say, Mr. Davis and me's company enough for each other, ain't we, master?'

'And then there's a beautiful air there of a summer night, and you can see all the country round under the moon, and it looks so different, seemingly, to what it do in the daytime. Why, all them harrows on the down—'

And then Mr. Davis cut in, seeming to be out of temper with the lad, and said, 'Ah yes, they're old-fashioned places, ain't they, sir? Now, what would you think was the purpose of them?'

And my father said (now, dear me, it seems funny, doesn't it, that I should recollect all this: but it took my fancy at the time, and though it's dull perhaps for you, I can't help finishing it out now), well, he said, 'Why, I've heard, Mr. Davis, that they're all graves, and I know, when I've had occasion to plough up one, there's always been some old bones and pots turned up.

'But whose graves they are, I don't know – people say the ancient Romans were all about this country at one time, but whether they buried their people like that I can't tell.'

And Mr. Davis shook his head, thinking, and said, 'Ah, to be sure: well they look to me to be older-like than the ancient Romans, and dressed different – that's to say, according to the pictures the Romans was in armour, and you didn't never find no armour, did you, sir, by what you said?'

And my father was rather surprised and said, 'I don't know that I mentioned anything about armour, but it's true I don't remember to have found any. But you talk as if you'd seen 'em, Mr. Davis.'

And they both of them laughed, Mr. Davis and the young man, and Mr. Davis said, 'Seen 'em, sir? that would be a difficult matter after all these years. Not but what I should like well enough to know more about them old times and people, and what they worshipped and all.'

And my father said, 'Worshipped? Well, I dare say they worshipped the old man on the hill.'

'Ah, indeed!' Mr. Davis said. 'Well, I shouldn't wonder.'

And my father went on and told them what he'd heard and read about the heathens and their sacrifices: what you'll learn some day for yourself, Charles, when you go to school and begin your Latin. And they seemed to be very much interested, both of them. But my father said he couldn't help thinking the most of what he was saying was no news to them.

That was the only time he ever had much talk with Mr. Davis, and it stuck in his mind, particularly, he said, the young man's word about *not wanting for company*: because in those days there was a lot of talk in the villages round about – why, but for my father interfering, the people here would have ducked an old lady for a witch.

Charles: What does that mean, granny, ducked an old lady for a witch? Are there witches here now?

Grandmother: No, no, dear! Why, what ever made me stray off like that? No, no, that's quite another affair.

What I was going to say was that the people in other places round about believed that some sort of meetings went on a night-time on that hill where the man is, and that those who went there were up to no good.

But don't you interrupt me now, for it's getting late.

Well, I suppose it was a matter of three years that Mr. Davis and this young man went on living together; and then all of a sudden, a dreadful thing happened. I don't know if I ought to tell you. (*Outcries of* 'Oh yes! yes, granny, you must,' etc.)

Well, then, you must promise not to get frightened and go screaming out in the middle of the night. ('No, no, we won't, of course not!')

One morning very early towards the turn of the year, I think it was in September, one of the woodmen had to go up to his work at the top of the long covert just as it was getting light.

And just where there were some few big oaks in a sort of clearing deep in the wood he saw at a distance a white thing that looked like a man through the mist, and he was in two minds about going on, but go on he did, and made out as he came near that it *was* a man: dressed in a sort of white gown he was, and hanging by his neck to the limb of the biggest oak, quite, quite dead. And near his feet there lay on the ground a hatchet all in a gore of blood.

Well, what a terrible sight that was for anyone to come upon in that lonely place! This poor man was nearly out of his wits: he dropped everything he was carrying and ran as hard as ever he could straight down to the Parsonage, and woke them up and told them what he'd seen.

And old Mr. White, who was the parson then, sent him off to get two or three of the best men, the blacksmith and the church-wardens and what not, while he dressed himself, and all of them went up to this dreadful place with a horse to lay the poor body on and take it to the house.

When they got there, everything was just as the woodman had said: but it was a terrible shock to them all to see how the corpse was dressed, specially to old Mr. White, for it seemed to him to be like a mockery of the church surplice that was on it, only, he told my father, not the same in the fashion of it.

And when they came to take down the body from the oak tree they found there was a chain of some metal round the neck and a little ornament like a wheel hanging to it on the front, and it was very old looking, they said.

Now in the meantime they had sent off a boy to run to Mr. Davis' house and see whether he was at home; for of course they couldn't but have their suspicions. And Mr. White said they must send too to the constable of the next parish, and get a message to another magistrate (he was a magistrate himself), and so there was running hither and thither.

But my father as it happened was away from home that night, otherwise they would have fetched him first. So then they laid the body across the horse, and they say it was all they could manage to keep the beast from bolting away from the time they were in sight of the tree, for it seemed to be mad with fright.

However, they managed to bind the eyes and lead it down through the wood and back into the village street. And there, just by the big tree where the stocks are, they found a lot of women gathered together, and this boy whom they'd sent to Mr. Davis' house lying in the middle, as white as paper, and not a word could they get out of him, good or bad.

So they saw there was something worse yet to come, and they made the best of their way up the lane to Mr. Davis' house. And when they got near that, the horse they were leading seemed to go mad again with fear, and reared up and screamed, and struck out with its forefeet and the man that was leading it was as near as possible being killed, and the dead body fell off its back.

So Mr. White bid them get the horse away as quick as might be, and they carried the body straight into the living-room, for the door stood open. And then they saw what is was that had given the poor boy such a fright, and they guessed why the horse went mad, for you know horses can't bear the smell of dead blood.

There was a long table in the room, more than the length of a man, and on it there lay the body of Mr. Davis. The eyes were bound over with a linen band and the arms were tied across the back, and the feet were bound together with another band. But the fearful thing was that the breast being quite bare, the bone of it was split through from the top downwards with an axe!

Oh, it was a terrible sight. Not one there but turned faint and ill with it, and had to go out into the fresh air. Even Mr. White, who was what you might call a hard nature of a man, was quite overcome and said a prayer for strength in the garden.

At last they laid out the other body as best they could in the room, and searched about to see if they could find out how such a frightful thing had come to pass. And in the cupboards they found a quantity of herbs and jars with liquors, and it came out, when people that understood such matters had looked into it, that some of these liquors were drinks to put a person asleep.

And they had little doubt that that wicked young man had put some of this into Mr. Davis' drink, and then used him as he did, and, after that, the sense of his sin had come upon him and he had cast himself away.

Well now, you couldn't understand all the law business that had to be done by the coroner and the magistrates, but there was a great coming and going of people over it for the next day or two, and then the people of the parish got together and agreed that they couldn't bear the thought of those two being buried in the churchyard alongside of Christian people.

For I must tell you there were papers and writings found in the drawers and cupboards that Mr. White and some other clergymen looked into. And they put their names to a paper that said these men were guilty, by their own allowing, of the dreadful sin of idolatry, and they feared there were some in the neighbouring places that were not free from that wickedness, and called upon them to repent, lest the same fearful thing that was come to these men should befall them also. And then they burnt those writings.

So then, Mr. White was of the same mind as the parishioners, and late one evening twelve men that were chosen went with him to that evil house, and with them they took two biers made very roughly for the purpose and two pieces of black cloth. And down at the cross-road, where you take the turn for Bascombe and Wilcombe, there were other men waiting with torches, and a pit dug. And a great crowd of people gathered together from all round about.

And the men that went to the cottage went in with their hats on their heads, and four of them took the two bodies and laid them on the biers and covered them over with the black cloths, and no one said a word. But they bore them down the lane, and they were cast into the pit and covered over with stones and earth, and then Mr. White spoke to the people that were gathered together.

My father was there, for he had come back when he heard the news, and he said he never should forget the strangeness of the sight, with the torches burning and those two black things huddled together in the pit, and not a sound from any of the people, except it might be a child or a woman whimpering with the fright.

And so, when Mr. White had finished speaking, they all turned away and left them lying there.

They say horses don't like the spot even now, and I've heard there was something of a mist or a light hung about for a long time after, but I don't know the truth of that.

But this I do know, that next day my father's business took him past the opening of the lane, and he saw three or four little knots of people standing at different places along it, seemingly in a state of mind about something. And he rode up to them, and asked what was the matter. And they ran up to him and said, 'Oh, Squire, it's the blood! Look at the blood!' and kept on like that.

So he got off his horse and they showed him. And there, in four places, I think it was, he saw great patches in the road, of blood. But he could hardly see it was blood, for almost every spot of it was covered with great black flies, that never changed their place or moved. And that blood was what had fallen out of Mr. Davis' body as they bore it down the lane.

Well, my father couldn't bear to do more than just take in the nasty sight so as to be sure of it, and then he said to one of those men that was there, 'Do you make haste and fetch a basket or a barrow full of clean earth out of the churchyard and spread it over these places, and I'll wait here till you come back.'

And very soon he came back, and the old man that was sexton with him, with a shovel and the earth in a hand-barrow. And they set it down at the first of the places and made ready to cast the earth upon it – and as soon as ever they did that, what do you think? The flies that were on it rose up in the air in a kind of a solid cloud and moved off up the lane towards the house.

And the sexton (he was parish clerk as well) stopped and looked at them and said to my father, 'Lord of flies, sir,' and no more would he say.

And just the same it was at the other places, every one of them.

Charles: But what did he mean, granny?

Grandmother: Well, dear, you remember to ask Mr. Lucas when you go to him for your lesson tomorrow. I can't stop now to talk about it – it's long past bedtime for you already.

The next thing was, my father made up his mind no one was going to live in that cottage again, or yet use any of the things that were in it. So, though it was one of the best in the place, he sent round word to the people that it was to be done away with, and anyone that wished could bring a faggot to the burning of it. And that's what was done.

They built a pile of wood in the living-room and loosened the thatch so as the fire could take good hold, and then set it alight. And as there was no brick, only the chimney-stack and the oven, it wasn't long before it was all gone.

I seem to remember seeing the chimney when I was a little girl, but that fell down of itself at last.

Now this that I've got to is the last bit of all.

You may be sure that for a long time the people said Mr. Davis and that young man were seen about, the one of them in the wood and both of them where the house had been, or passing together down the lane, particularly in the spring of the year and at autumn-time.

I can't speak to that, though if we were sure there are such things as ghosts, it would seem likely that people like that wouldn't rest quiet.

But I can tell you this, that one evening in the month of March, just before your grandfather and I were married, we'd been taking a long walk in the woods together and picking flowers and talking as young people will that are courting, and so much taken up with each other that we never took any particular notice where we were going.

And on a sudden I cried out, and your grandfather asked what was the matter. The matter was that I'd felt a sharp prick on the back of my hand, and I snatched it to me and saw a black thing on it, and struck it with the other hand and killed it.

And I showed it him, and he was a man who took notice of all such things, and he said, 'Well, I've never seen ought like that fly before,' and though to my own eye it didn't seem very much out of the common, I've no doubt he was right.

And then we looked about us, and lo and behold if we weren't in the very lane, just in front of the place where that house had stood, and, as they told me after, just where the men set down the biers a minute when they bore them out of the garden gate.

You may be sure we made haste away from there – at least, I made your grandfather come away quick, for I was wholly upset at finding myself there – but he would have lingered about out of curiosity if I'd have let him. Whether there was anything about there more than we could see I shall never be sure.

Perhaps it was partly the venom of that horrid fly's bite that was working in me that made me feel so strange. For, dear me, how that poor arm and hand of mine did swell up, to be sure! I'm afraid to tell you how large it was round! And the pain of it, too!

Nothing my mother could put on it had any power over it at all, and it wasn't till she was persuaded by our old nurse to get the wise man over at Bascombe to come and look at it, that I got any peace at all. But he seemed to know all about it, and said I wasn't the first that had been taken that way.

'When the sun's gathering his strength,' he said, 'and when he's in the height of it, and when he's beginning to lose his hold, and when he's in his weakness, them that haunts about that lane had best to take heed to themselves.'

But what it was he bound on my arm and what he said over it, he wouldn't tell us. After that I soon got well again, but since then I've heard often enough of people suffering much the same as I did. Only of late years it doesn't seem to happen but very seldom, and maybe things like that do die out in the course of time.

But that's the reason, Charles, why I say to you that I won't have you gathering me blackberries, no, nor eating them either, in that lane. And now you know all about it, I don't fancy you'll want to yourself.

There! Off to bed you go this minute.

What's that, Fanny? A light in your room? The idea of such a thing! You get yourself undressed at once and say your prayers, and perhaps if your father doesn't want me when he wakes up, I'll come and say goodnight to you.

And you, Charles, if I hear anything of you frightening your little sister on the way up to your bed, I shall tell your father that very moment, and you know what happened to you the last time.

The door closes, and granny, after listening intently for a minute or two, resumes her knitting. The Squire still slumbers.

Wailing Well

IN THE YEAR 19— there were two members of the Troop of Scouts attached to a famous school, named respectively Arthur Wilcox and Stanley Judkins. They were the same age, boarded in the same house, were in the same division, and naturally were members of the same patrol. They were so much alike in appearance as to cause anxiety and trouble, and even irritation, to the masters who came in contact with them. But oh how different were they in their inward man, or boy!

It was to Arthur Wilcox that the Head Master said, looking up with a smile as the boy entered chambers, 'Why, Wilcox, there will be a deficit in the prize fund if you stay here much longer! Here, take this handsomely bound copy of the *Life and Works of Bishop Ken*, and with it my hearty congratulations to yourself and your excellent parents.'

It was Wilcox again, whom the Provost noticed as he passed through the playing fields, and, pausing for a moment, observed to the Vice-Provost, 'That lad has a remarkable brow!'

'Indeed, yes,' said the Vice-Provost. 'It denotes either genius or water on the brain.'

As a Scout, Wilcox secured every badge and distinction for which he competed. The Cookery Badge, the Map-making Badge, the Life-saving Badge, the Badge for picking up bits of newspaper, the Badge for not slamming the door when leaving pupil-room, and many others.

Of the Life-saving Badge I may have a word to say when we come to treat of Stanley Judkins.

You cannot be surprised to hear that Mr. Hope Jones added a special verse to each of his songs, in commendation of Arthur Wilcox, or that the Lower Master burst into tears when handing him the Good Conduct Medal in its handsome claret-coloured case: the medal which had been unanimously voted to him by the whole of Third Form.

Unanimously, did I say? I am wrong. There was one dissentient, Judkins *mi.*, who said that he had excellent reasons for acting as he did. He shared, it seems, a room with his major.

You cannot, again, wonder that in after years Arthur Wilcox was the first, and so far the only boy, to become Captain of both the School and of the Oppidans, or that the strain of carrying out the duties of both positions, coupled with the ordinary work of the school, was so severe that a complete rest for six months, followed by a voyage round the world, was pronounced an absolute necessity by the family doctor.

It would be a pleasant task to trace the steps by which he attained the giddy eminence he now occupies; but for the moment enough of Arthur Wilcox. Time presses, and we must turn to a very different matter: the career of Stanley Judkins – Judkins *ma.*

Stanley Judkins, like Arthur Wilcox, attracted the attention of the authorities – but in quite another fashion. It was to him that the Lower Master said, with no cheerful smile, 'What, again, Judkins? A very little persistence in this course of conduct, my boy, and you will have cause to regret that you ever entered this academy. There, take that, and that, and think yourself very lucky you don't get that and that!'

It was Judkins, again, whom the Provost had cause to notice as he passed through the playing fields, when a cricket ball struck him with considerable force on the ankle, and a voice from a short way off cried, 'Thank you, cut-over!'

'I think,' said the Provost, pausing for a moment to rub his ankle, 'that that boy had better fetch his cricket ball for himself!'

'Indeed, yes,' said the Vice-Provost, 'and if he comes within reach, I will do my best to fetch him something else.'

As a Scout, Stanley Judkins secured no badge save those which he was able to abstract from members of other patrols. In the cookery competition he was detected trying to introduce squibs into the Dutch oven of the next-door competitors. In the tailoring competition he succeeded in sewing two boys together very firmly, with disastrous effect when they tried to get up. For the Tidiness Badge he was disqualified, because, in the Midsummer schooltime, which chanced to be hot, he could not be dissuaded from sitting with his fingers in the ink: as he said, for coolness' sake. For one piece of paper which he picked up, he must have dropped at least six banana skins or orange peels. Aged women seeing him approaching would beg him with tears in their eyes not to carry their pails of water across the road. They knew too well what the result would inevitably be.

But it was in the life-saving competition that Stanley Judkins' conduct was most blameable and had the most far-reaching effects. The practice, as you know, was to throw a selected lower boy, of suitable dimensions, fully dressed, with his hands and feet tied together, into the deepest part of Cuckoo Weir, and to time the Scout whose turn it was to rescue him.

On every occasion when he was entered for this competition Stanley Judkins was seized, at the critical moment, with a severe fit of cramp, which caused him to roll on the ground and utter alarming cries. This naturally distracted the attention of those present from the boy in the water, and had it not been for the presence of Arthur Wilcox the death-roll would have been a heavy one.

As it was, the Lower Master found it necessary to take a firm line and say that the competition must be discontinued. It was in vain that Mr. Beasley Robinson represented to him that in five competitions only four lower boys had actually succumbed. The Lower Master said that he would be the last to interfere in any way with the work of the Scouts; but that three of these boys had been valued members of his choir, and both he and Dr. Ley felt that the inconvenience caused by the losses outweighed the advantages of the competitions.

Besides, the correspondence with the parents of these boys had become annoying, and even distressing: they were no longer satisfied with the printed form which he was in the habit of sending out, and more than one of them had actually visited Eton and taken up much of his valuable time with complaints.

So the life-saving competition is now a thing of the past.

In short, Stanley Judkins was no credit to the Scouts, and, there was talk on more than one occasion of informing him that his services were no longer required. This course was strongly advocated by Mr. Lambart: but in the end milder counsels prevailed, and it was decided to give him another chance.

So it is that we find him at the beginning of the Midsummer Holidays of 19— at the Scouts' camp in the beautiful district of W (or X) in the county of D (or Y).

It was a lovely morning, and Stanley Judkins and one or two of his friends – for he still had friends – lay basking on the top of the down. Stanley was lying on his stomach with his chin propped on his hands, staring into the distance.

'I wonder what that place is,' he said.

'Which place?' said one of the others.

'That sort of clump in the middle of the field down there.'

'Oh, ah! How should I know what it is?'

'What do you want to know for?' said another.

'I don't know: I like the look of it. What's it called? Nobody got a map?' said Stanley. 'Call yourselves Scouts!'

'Here's a map all right,' said Wilfred Pipsqueak, ever resourceful, 'and there's the place marked on it. But it's inside the red ring. We can't go there.'

'Who cares about a red ring?' said Stanley. 'But it's got no name on your silly map.'

'Well, you can ask this old chap what it's called if you're so keen to find out.'

'This old chap' was an old shepherd who had come up and was standing behind them.

'Good morning, young gents,' he said, 'you've got a fine day for your doin's, ain't you?'

'Yes, thank you,' said Algernon de Montmorency, with native politeness. 'Can you tell us what that clump over there's called? And what's that thing inside it?'

'Course I can tell you,' said the shepherd. 'That's Wailin' Well, that is. But you ain't got no call to worry about that.'

'Is it a well in there?' said Algernon. 'Who uses it?'

The shepherd laughed. 'Bless you,' he said, 'there ain't from a man to a sheep in these parts uses Wailin' Well, nor haven't done all the years I've lived here.'

'Well, there'll be a record broken today, then,' said Stanley Judkins, 'because I shall go and get some water out of it for tea!'

'Sakes alive, young gentleman!' said the shepherd in a startled voice, 'don't you get to talkin' that way! Why, ain't your masters give you notice not to go by there? They'd ought to have done.'

'Yes, they have,' said Wilfred Pipsqueak.

'Shut up, you ass!' said Stanley Judkins. 'What's the matter with it? Isn't the water good? Anyhow, if it was boiled, it would be all right.'

'I don't know as there's anything much wrong with the water,' said the shepherd. 'All I know is, my old dog wouldn't go through that field, let alone me or anyone else that's got a morsel of brains in their heads.'

'More fool them,' said Stanley Judkins, at once rudely and ungrammatically. 'Who ever took any harm going there?' he added.

'Three women and a man,' said the shepherd gravely. 'Now just you listen to me. I know these 'ere parts and you don't, and I can tell you this much: for these ten years last past there ain't been a sheep fed in that field, nor a crop raised off of it – and it's good land, too. You can pretty well see from here what a state it's got into with brambles and suckers and trash of all kinds. *You've* got a glass, young gentleman,' he said to Wilfred Pipsqueak, 'you can tell with that anyway.'

'Yes,' said Wilfred, 'but I see there's tracks in it. Someone must go through it sometimes.'

'Tracks!' said the shepherd. 'I believe you! Four tracks: three women and a man.'

'What d'you mean, three women and a man?' said Stanley, turning over for the first time and looking at the shepherd (he had been talking with his back to him till this moment: he was an ill-mannered boy).

'Mean? Why, what I says: three women and a man.'

'Who are they?' asked Algernon. 'Why do they go there?'

'There's some p'r'aps could tell you who they *was*,' said the shepherd, 'but it was afore my time they come by their end. And why they goes there still is more than the children of men can tell: except I've heard they was all bad 'uns when they was alive.'

'By George, what a rum thing!' Algernon and Wilfred muttered; but Stanley was scornful and bitter.

'Why, you don't mean they're deaders? What rot! You must be a lot of fools to believe that. Who's ever seen them, I'd like to know?'

'*I've* seen 'em, young gentleman!' said the shepherd, 'seen 'em from near by on that bit of down: and my old dog, if he could speak, he'd tell you he've seen 'em, same time.

'About four o'clock of the day it was, much such a day as this. I see 'em, each one of 'em, come peerin' out of the bushes and stand up, and work their way slow by them tracks towards the trees in the middle where the well is.'

'And what were they like? Do tell us!' said Algernon and Wilfred eagerly.

'Rags and bones, young gentlemen: all four of 'em: flutterin' rags and whity bones. It seemed to me as if I could hear 'em clackin' as they got along. Very slow they went, and lookin' from side to side.'

'What were their faces like? Could you see?'

'They hadn't much to call faces,' said the shepherd, 'but I could seem to see as they had teeth.'

'Lor'!' said Wilfred, 'and what did they do when they got to the trees?'

'I can't tell you that, sir,' said the shepherd. 'I wasn't for stayin' in that place, and if I had been, I was bound to look to my old dog: he'd gone! Such a thing he never done before as leave me. But gone he had, and when I came up with him in the end, he was in that state he didn't know me, and was fit to fly at my throat. But I kep' talkin' to him, and after a bit he remembered my voice and came creepin' up like a child askin' pardon. I never want to see him like that again, nor yet no other dog.'

The dog, who had come up and was making friends all round, looked up at his master, and expressed agreement with what he was saying very fully.

The boys pondered for some moments on what they had heard: after which Wilfred said: 'And why's it called Wailing Well?'

'If you was round here at dusk of a winter's evening, you wouldn't want to ask why,' was all the shepherd said.

'Well, I don't believe a word of it,' said Stanley Judkins, 'and I'll go there next chance I get: blowed if I don't!'

'Then you won't be ruled by me?' said the shepherd. 'Nor yet by your masters as warned you off? Come now, young gentleman, you don't want for sense, I should say. What should I want tellin' you a pack of lies? It ain't sixpence to me anyone goin' in that field: but I wouldn't like to see a young chap snuffed out like in his prime.'

'I expect it's a lot more than sixpence to you,' said Stanley. 'I expect you've got a whisky still or something in there, and want to keep other people away. Rot I call it. Come on back, you boys.'

So they turned away. The two others said, 'Good evening' and 'Thank you' to the shepherd, but Stanley said nothing.

The shepherd shrugged his shoulders and stood where he was, looking after them rather sadly.

On the way back to the camp there was great argument about it all, and Stanley was told as plainly as he could be told all the sorts of fools he would be if he went to the Wailing Well.

That evening, among other notices, Mr. Beasley Robinson asked if all maps had got the red ring marked on them. 'Be particular,' he said, 'not to trespass inside it.'

Several voices – among them the sulky one of Stanley Judkins – said, 'Why not, sir?'

'Because not,' said Mr. Beasley Robinson, 'and if that isn't enough for you, I can't help it.' He turned and spoke to Mr. Lambart in a low voice, and then said, 'I'll tell you this much: we've been asked to warn Scouts off that field. It's very good of the people to let us camp here at all, and the least we can do is to oblige them – I'm sure you'll agree to that.'

Everybody said, 'Yes, sir!' except Stanley Judkins, who was heard to mutter, 'Oblige them be blowed!'

Early in the afternoon of the next day, the following dialogue was heard:

'Wilcox, is all your tent there?'

'No, sir, Judkins isn't!'

'That boy is *the* most infernal nuisance ever invented! Where do you suppose he is?'

'I haven't an idea, sir.'

'Does anybody else know?'

'Sir, I shouldn't wonder if he'd gone to the Wailing Well.'

'Who's that? Pipsqueak? What's the Wailing Well?'

'Sir, it's that place in the field by – well, sir, it's in a clump of trees in a rough field.'

'D'you mean inside the red ring? Good heavens! What makes you think he's gone there?'

'Why, he was terribly keen to know about it yesterday, and we were talking to a shepherd man, and he told us a lot about it and advised us not to go there. But Judkins didn't believe him, and said he meant to go.'

'Young ass!' said Mr. Hope Jones, 'did he take anything with him?'

'Yes, I think he took some rope and a can. We did tell him he'd be a fool to go.'

'Little brute! What the deuce does he mean by pinching stores like that! Well, come along, you three, we must see after him. Why can't people keep the simplest orders? What was it the man told you? No, don't wait, let's have it as we go along.'

And off they started – Algernon and Wilfred talking rapidly and the other two listening with growing concern. At last they reached that spur of down overlooking the field of which the shepherd had spoken the day before. It commanded the place completely: the well inside the clump of bent and gnarled Scotch firs was plainly visible, and so were the four tracks winding about among the thorns and rough growth.

It was a wonderful day of shimmering heat. The sea looked like a floor of metal. There was no breath of wind. They were all exhausted when they got to the top, and flung themselves down on the hot grass.

'Nothing to be seen of him yet,' said Mr. Hope Jones, 'but we must stop here a bit. You're done up – not to speak of me. Keep a sharp look-out,' he went on after a moment, 'I thought I saw the bushes stir.'

'Yes,' said Wilcox, 'so did I. Look . . . no, that can't be him. It's somebody though, putting their head up, isn't it?'

'I thought it was, but I'm not sure.'

Silence for a moment. Then:

'That's him, sure enough,' said Wilcox, 'getting over the hedge on the far side. Don't you see? With a shiny thing. That's the can you said he had.'

'Yes, it's him, and he's making straight for the trees,' said Wilfred.

At this moment Algernon, who had been staring with all his might, broke into a scream.

'What's that on the track? On all fours – O, it's the woman. O, don't let me look at her! Don't let it happen!' And he rolled over, clutching at the grass and trying to bury his head in it.

'Stop that!' said Mr. Hope Jones loudly – but it was no use. 'Look here,' he said, 'I must go down there. You stop here, Wilfred, and look after that boy. Wilcox, you run as hard as you can to the camp and get some help.'

They ran off, both of them. Wilfred was left alone with Algernon, and did his best to calm him, but indeed he was not much happier himself. From time to time he glanced down the hill and into the field. He saw Mr. Hope Jones drawing nearer at a swift pace, and then, to his great surprise, he saw him stop, look up and round about him, and turn quickly off at an angle! What could be the reason?

He looked at the field, and there he saw a terrible figure – something in ragged black – with whitish patches breaking out of it: the head, perched on a long thin neck, half-hidden by a shapeless sort of blackened sun-bonnet. The creature was waving thin arms in the direction of the rescuer who was approaching, as if to ward him off: and between the two figures the air seemed to shake and shimmer as he had never seen it. And as he looked, he began himself to feel something of a waviness and confusion in his brain, which made him guess what might be the effect on someone within closer range of the influence.

He looked away hastily, to see Stanley Judkins making his way pretty quickly towards the clump, and in proper Scout fashion: evidently picking his steps with care to avoid treading on snapping sticks or being caught by arms of brambles. Evidently, though he saw nothing, he suspected some sort of ambush, and was trying to go noiselessly.

Wilfred saw all that, and he saw more, too. With a sudden and dreadful sinking at the heart, he caught sight of someone among the trees, waiting: and again of someone – another of the hideous black figures – working slowly along the track from another side of the field, looking from side to side, as the shepherd had described it.

Worst of all, he saw a fourth – unmistakably a man this time – rising out of the bushes a few yards behind the wretched Stanley, and painfully, as it seemed, crawling into the track. On all sides the miserable victim was cut off.

Wilfred was at his wits' end. He rushed at Algernon and shook him. 'Get up,' he said. 'Yell! Yell as loud as you can. Oh, if we'd got a whistle!'

Algernon pulled himself together. 'There's one,' he said, 'Wilcox's: he must have dropped it.'

So one whistled, the other screamed. In the still air the sound carried. Stanley heard; he stopped; he turned round; and then indeed a cry was heard more piercing and dreadful than any that the boys on the hill could raise.

It was too late.

The crouched figure behind Stanley sprang at him and caught him about the waist. The dreadful one that was standing waving her arms waved them again, but in exultation. The one that was lurking among the trees shuffled forward, and she too stretched out her arms as if to clutch at something coming her way; and the other, farthest off, quickened her pace and came on, nodding gleefully.

The boys took it all in in an instant of terrible silence, and hardly could they breathe as they watched the horrid struggle between the man and his victim. Stanley struck with his can, the only weapon he had. The rim of a broken black hat fell off the creature's head and showed a white skull with stains that might be wisps of hair.

By this time one of the women had reached the pair, and was pulling at the rope that was coiled about Stanley's neck. Between them they over-powered him in a moment. The awful screaming ceased, and then the three passed within the circle of the clump of firs.

Yet for a moment it seemed as if rescue might come. Mr. Hope Jones, striding quickly along, suddenly stopped, turned, seemed to rub his eyes, and then started running *towards* the field. More: the boys glanced behind them, and saw not only a troop of figures from the camp coming over the top of the next down, but the shepherd running up the slope of their own hill. They beckoned, they shouted, they ran a few yards towards him and then back again. He mended his pace.

Once more the boys looked towards the field. There was nothing. Or, was there something among the trees? Why was there a mist about the trees? Mr. Hope Jones had scrambled over the hedge, and was plunging through the bushes.

The shepherd stood beside them, panting. They ran to him and clung to his arms. 'They've got him! In the trees!' was as much as they could say, over and over again.

'What? Do you tell me he's gone in there after all I said to him yesterday? Poor young thing! Poor young thing!' He would have said more, but other voices broke in. The rescuers from the camp had arrived. A few hasty words, and all were dashing down the hill.

They had just entered the field when they met Mr. Hope Jones. Over his shoulder hung the corpse of Stanley Judkins. He had cut it from the branch to which he found it hanging, waving to and fro. There was not a drop of blood in the body.

On the following day Mr. Hope Jones sallied forth with an axe and with the expressed intention of cutting down every tree in the clump, and of burning every bush in the field. He returned with a nasty cut in his leg and a broken axe-helve. Not a spark of fire could he light, and on no single tree could he make the least impression.

I have heard that the present population of the Wailing Well field consists of three women, a man, and a boy.

The shock experienced by Algernon de Montmorency and Wilfred Pipsqueak was severe. Both of them left the camp at once. And the occurrence undoubtedly cast a gloom – if but a passing one – on those who remained. One of the first to recover his spirits was Judkins *mi*.

Such, gentlemen, is the story of the career of Stanley Judkins, and of a portion of the career of Arthur Wilcox. It has, I believe, never been told before. If it has a moral, that moral is, I trust, obvious. If it has none, I do not well know how to help it.

Rats

'AND IF YOU WAS TO WALK through the bedrooms now, you'd see the ragged, mouldy bedclothes a-heaving and a-heaving like seas.'

'And a-heaving and a-heaving with what?' he says.

'Why, with the rats under 'em.'

But was it with the rats?

I ask, because in another case it was not.

I cannot put a date to the story, but I was young when I heard it, and the teller was old. It is an ill-proportioned tale, but that is my fault, not his.

It happened in Suffolk, near the coast. In a place where the road makes a sudden dip and then a sudden rise. As you go northward, at the top of that rise, stands a house on the left of the road.

It is a tall red-brick house, narrow for its height. Perhaps it was built around 1770. The top of the front has a low triangular pediment with a round window in the centre. Behind it are stables and offices, and such garden as it has is behind them.

Scraggy Scotch firs are near it; an expanse of gorse-covered land stretches away from it. It commands a view of the distant sea from the upper windows of the front.

A sign on a post stands before the door; or did so stand, for though it was an inn of repute once, I believe it is so no longer.

To this inn came my acquaintance, Mr. Thomson, when he was a young man, on a fine spring day, coming from the University of Cambridge, and

LES EDWARDS

desirous of solitude in tolerable quarters and time for reading.

These he found, for the landlord and his wife had been in service and could make a visitor comfortable, and there was no one else staying at the inn.

He had a large room on the first floor commanding the road and the view, and if it faced east, why, that could not be helped. The house was well built and warm.

He spent very tranquil and uneventful days: work all the morning, and afternoon perambulation of the country round, a little conversation with country company or the people of the inn in the evening over the then fashionable drink of brandy and water, a little more reading and writing, and bed.

And he would have been content that this should continue for the full month he had at disposal, so well was his work progressing, and so fine was the April of that year – which I have reason to believe was that which Orlando Whistlecraft chronicles in his weather record as the 'Charming Year'.

One of his walks took him along the northern road, which stands high and traverses a wide common, called a heath.

On the bright afternoon when he first chose this direction his eye caught a white object some hundreds of yards to the left of the road, and he felt it necessary to make sure what this might be.

It was not long before he was standing by it, and found himself looking at a square block of white stone fashioned somewhat like the base of a pillar, with a square hole in the upper surface. Just such another you may see this day on Thetford Heath.

After taking stock of it he contemplated for a few minutes the view, which offered a church tower or two, some red roofs of cottages and windows winking in the sun, and the expanse of sea – also with an occasional wink and gleam upon it – and so pursued his way.

In the desultory evening talk in the bar, he asked why the white stone was there on the common.

'A old-fashioned thing, that is,' said the landlord (Mr. Betts). 'We was none of us alive when that was put there.'

'That's right,' said another.

'It stands pretty high,' said Mr. Thomson, 'I dare say a sea-mark was on it some time back.'

'Ah! Yes,' Mr. Betts agreed, I 'ave heard they could see it from the boats. But whatever there was, it's fell to bits this long time.'

'Good job too,' said a third. ''Twar'nt a lucky mark, by what the old men used to say. Not lucky for the fishin', I mean to say.'

'Why ever not?' said Thomson.

'Well, I never see it myself,' was the answer, 'but they 'ad some funny ideas, what I mean, peculiar, them old chaps, and I shouldn't wonder but what they made away with it theirselves.'

It was impossible to get anything clearer than this. The company, never very voluble, fell silent, and when next someone spoke it was of village affairs and crops. Mr. Betts was the speaker.

Not every day did Thomson consult his health by taking a county walk. One very fine afternoon found him busily writing at three o'clock. Then he stretched himself and rose, and walked out of his room into the passage.

Facing him was another room, then the stair-head, then two more rooms, one looking out to the back, and the other to the south.

At the south end of the passage was a window, to which he went, considering to himself that it was rather a shame to waste such a fine afternoon.

However, work was paramount just at the moment. He thought he would just take five minute off and go back to it, and those five minutes he would employ – the Bettses could not possibly object – to looking at the other rooms in the passage, which he had never seen.

Nobody at all, it seemed, was indoors. Probably, as it was market day, they were all gone to the town, except perhaps a maid in the bar. Very still the house was, and the sun shone really hot; early flies buzzed in the window-panes.

So he explored.

The room facing his was undistinguished except for an old print of Bury St. Edmunds. The two next him on his side of the passage were gay and clean, with one window apiece, whereas his had two. Remained the south-west room, opposite to the last which he had entered.

This was locked, but Thomson was in a mood of quite indefensible curiosity, and feeling confident that there could be no damaging secrets in a place so easily got at, he proceeded to fetch the key of his own room, and when that did not answer, to collect the keys of the other three.

One of them fitted, and he opened the door.

The room had two windows looking south and west, so it was as bright and the sun as hot upon it as it could be. Here there was no carpet, but bare boards; no pictures, no washing-stand, only a bed, in the farther corner: an iron bed, with mattress and bolster, covered with a bluish check counterpane.

As featureless a room as you can well imagine, and yet there was something that made Thomson close the door again very quickly and yet quietly behind him and lean against the window-sill in the passage, actually quivering all over.

It was this, that under the counterpane someone lay, and not only lay, but stirred. That it was some *one* and not some *thing* was certain, because the shape of a head was unmistakable on the bolster. And yet it was all covered, and no one lies with covered head but a dead person. And this was not dead, not truly dead, because it heaved and shivered.

If he had seen these things in dusk or by the light of a flickering candle, Thomson could have comforted himself and talked of fancy. On this bright day that was impossible.

What was to be done?

First, lock the door at all costs.

Very gingerly he approached it and bending down listened, holding his breath. Perhaps there might be a sound of heavy breathing, and a prosaic explanation. There was absolute silence.

But as, with a rather tremulous hand, he put the key into its hole and turned it, it rattled, and on the instant a stumbling padded tread was heard coming towards the door.

Thomson fled like a rabbit to his room and locked himself in.

Futile enough, he knew it was; would doors and locks be any obstacle to what he suspected? But it was all he could think of at the moment, and in fact nothing happened. Only there was a time of acute suspense – followed by a misery of doubt as to what to do.

The impulse, of course, was to slip away as soon as possible from a house which contained such an inmate. But only the day before he had said he should be staying for at least a week more, and how if he changed plans could he avoid the suspicion of having pried into places where he certainly had no business?

Moreover, either the Bettses knew all about the inmate, and yet did not leave the house, or knew nothing, which equally meant there was nothing to be afraid of, or knew just enough to make them shut up the room, but not enough to weigh on their spirits. In any of these cases it seemed that not much was to be feared, and certainly so far he had had no sort of ugly experience.

On the whole the line of least resistance was to stay.

Well, he stayed out his week. Nothing took him past that door, and, often as he would pause in a quiet hour of day or night in the passage and listen, and listen, no sound whatever issued from that direction.

You might have thought that Thomson would have made some attempt at ferreting out stories connected with the inn – hardly perhaps from Betts, but from the parson of the parish, or old people in the village; but no, the reticence which commonly falls on people who have had strange experiences, and believe in them, was upon him.

Nevertheless, as the end of his stay drew near, his yearning after some kind of explanation grew more and more acute.

On his solitary walks he persisted in planning out some way, the least obtrusive, of getting another daylight glimpse into that room, and eventually arrived at this scheme.

He would leave by an afternoon train – about four o'clock. When his fly was waiting, and his luggage on it, he would make one last expedition upstairs to look round his own room and see if anything was left unpacked, and then, with that key, which he had contrived to oil (as if that made any difference!), the door should once more be opened, for a moment, and shut.

So it worked out. The bill was paid, the consequent small talk gone through while the fly was loaded: 'Pleasant part of the country – been very comfortable, thanks to you and Mrs. Betts – hope to come back some time', on one side.

On the other: 'Very glad you've found satisfaction, sir, done our best – always glad to 'ave your good word – very much favoured we've been with the weather, to be sure.'

Then, 'I'll just take a look upstairs in case I've left a book or something out – no, don't trouble, I'll be back in a minute.'

And as noiselessly as possible he stole to the door and opened it.

The shattering of the illusion! Propped, or you might say sitting, on the edge of the bed was – nothing in the round world but a scarecrow!

A scarecrow out of the garden, of course, dumped into the deserted room . . . Yes, but here amusement ceased.

Have scarecrows bare bony feet? Do their heads loll on their shoulders? Have they iron collars and links of chain about their necks? Can they get up and move, if never so stiffly, across a floor, with wagging heads and arms close at their sides? And shiver?

The slam of the door, the dash to the stair-head, the leap downstairs, were followed by a faint.

Awakening, Thomson saw Betts standing over him with the brandy bottle and a very reproachful face. 'You shouldn't a done so, sir, really you shouldn't. It ain't a kind way to act by persons as done the best they could for you.'

Thomson heard words of this kind, but what he said in reply he did not know.

Mr. Betts, and perhaps even more Mrs. Betts, found it hard to accept his apologies and his assurances that he would say no word that could damage the good name of the house. However, they *were* accepted.

Since the train could not now be caught, it was arranged that Thomson should be driven to the town to sleep there.

Before he went the Bettses told him what little they knew. 'They say he was a landlord 'ere a long time back, and was in with the 'ighwaymen that 'ad their beat about the 'eath.

'That's how he come by his end: 'ung in chains, they say, up where you see that stone what the gallus stood in. Yes, the fishermen made away with that, I believe, because they see it out at sea and it kep' the fish off, according to their idea.

'Yes, we 'ad the account from the people that 'ad the 'ouse before we come. "You keep that room shut up," they says, "but don't move the bed out, and you'll find there won't be no trouble." And no more there 'as been. Not once he haven't come out into the 'ouse, though what he may do now there ain't no sayin'.

'Anyway, you're the first I know that's seen him since we've been 'ere. I never set eyes on him myself, nor don't want. And ever since we've made the servants rooms in the stablin', we ain't 'ad no difficulty that way.

'Only I do 'ope, sir, as you'll keep a close tongue, considerin' 'ow an 'ouse do get talked about': with more to this effect.

The promise of silence was kept for many years.

The occasion of my hearing the story at last was this: that when Mr. Thomson came to stay with my father it fell to me to show him to his room, and instead of letting me open the door for him he stepped forward and threw it open himself, and then for some moments stood in the doorway holding up his candle and looking narrowly into the interior.

Then he seemed to recollect himself and said: 'I beg your pardon. Very absurd, but I can't help doing that, for a particular reason.'

What that reason was I heard some days afterwards, and you have heard now.

The Experiment

A NEW YEAR'S EVE GHOST STORY
(Full Directions will be found at the End)

THE REVEREND DR. HALL was in his study making up the entries for the year in the parish register, it being his custom to note baptisms, weddings and burials in a paper book as they occurred, and in the last days of December to write them out fairly in the vellum book that was kept in the parish chest.

To him entered his housekeeper, in evident agitation. 'Oh, sir,' said she, 'whatever do you think? The poor Squire's gone!'

'The Squire? Squire Bowles? What are you talking about, woman? Why, only yesterday—'

'Yes, I know, sir, but it's the truth. Wickem, the clerk, just left word on his way down to toll the bell – you'll hear it yourself in a minute. There now, just listen.'

Sure enough the sound broke on the still night – not loud, for the Rectory did not immediately adjoin the churchyard.

Dr. Hall rose hastily.

'Terrible, terrible,' he said. 'I must see them at the Hall at once. He seemed so greatly better yesterday.' He paused. 'Did you hear any word of the sickness having come this way at all? There was nothing said in Norwich. It seems so sudden.'

'No, indeed, sir, no such thing. Just caught away with a choking in his

518

throat, Wickem says. It do make one feel – well, I'm sure I had to set down as much as a minute or more, I come over that queer when I heard the words – and by what I could understand they'll be asking for the burial very quick. There's some can't bear the thought of the cold corpse laying in the house, and—'

'Yes. Well, I must find out from Madam Bowles herself or Mr. Joseph. Get me my cloak, will you? Ah, and could you let Wickem know that I desire to see him when the tolling is over?'

He hurried off.

In an hour's time he was back and found Wickem waiting for him. 'There is work for you, Wickem,' he said, as he threw off his cloak, 'and not over-much time to do it in.'

'Yes, sir,' said Wickem, 'the vault to be opened to be sure—'

'No, no, that's not the message I have. The poor Squire, they tell me, charged them before now not to lay him in the chancel. It was to be an earth grave in the yard, on the north side.'

He stopped at an inarticulate exclamation from the clerk. 'Well?' he said.

'I ask pardon, sir,' said Wickem in a shocked voice, 'but did I understand you right? No vault, you say, and on the north side? Tt-tt-! Why the poor gentleman must a been wandering.'

'Yes, it does seem strange to me, too,' said Dr. Hall, 'but no, Mr. Joseph tells me it was his father's – I should say stepfather's – clear wish, expressed more than once, and when he was in good health. Clean earth and open air. You know, of course, the poor Squire had his fancies, though he never spoke of this one to me. And there's another thing, Wickem. No coffin.'

'Oh dear, dear, sir,' said Wickem, yet more shocked. 'Oh, but that'll make sad talk, that will, and what a disappointment for Wright, too! I know he'd looked out some beautiful wood for the Squire, and had it by him years past.'

'Well, well, perhaps the family will make it up to Wright in some way,' said the Rector, rather impatiently, 'but what you have to do is to get the grave dug and all things in a readiness – torches from Wright you must not forget – by ten o'clock tomorrow night. I don't doubt but there will be some-what coming to you for your pains and hurry.'

'Very well, sir, if those be the orders, I must do my best to carry them out. And should I call in on my way down and send the women up to the Hall to lay out the body, sir?'

'No. That, I think – I am sure – was not spoken of. Mr. Joseph will send, no doubt, if they are needed. No, you have enough without that. Goodnight, Wickem. I was making up the registers when this doleful news came. Little had I thought to add such an entry to them as I must now.'

All things had been done in decent order. The torchlighted cortège had passed from the Hall through the park, up the lime avenue to the top of the knoll on which the church stood. All the village had been there, and such neighbours as could be warned in the few hours available. There was no great surprise at the hurry.

Formalities of law there were none then, and no one blamed the stricken widow for hastening to lay her dead to rest. Nor did anyone look to see her following in the funeral train. Her son Joseph – only issue of her first marriage with a Calvert of Yorkshire – was the chief mourner.

There were, indeed, no kinsfolk on Squire Bowles's side who could have been bidden. The will, executed at the time of the Squire's second marriage, left everything to the widow.

And what was 'everything'? Land, house, furniture, pictures, plate were all obvious. But there should have been accumulations in coin, and beyond a few hundreds in the hands of agents – honest men and no embezzlers – cash there was none.

Yet Francis Bowles had for years received good rents and paid little out. Nor was he a reputed miser; he kept a good table, and money was always forthcoming for the moderate spendings of his wife and stepson. Joseph Calvert had been maintained ungrudgingly at school and college.

What, then, had he done with it all? No ransacking of the house brought any secret hoard to light; no servant, old or young, had any tale to tell of meeting the Squire in unexpected places at strange hours.

No, Madam Bowles and her son were fairly nonplussed. As they sat one evening in the parlour discussing the problem for the twentieth time:

'You have been at his books and papers, Joseph, again today, haven't you?'

'Yes, mother, and no forwarder.'

'What was it he would be writing at, and why was he always sending letters to Mr. Fowler at Gloucester?'

'Why, you know he had a maggot about the Middle State of the Soul. 'Twas over that he and that other were always busy. The last thing he wrote would be a letter that he never finished. I'll fetch it . . . Yes, the same song over again.

'"Honoured friend, I make some slow advance in our studies, but I know not well how far to trust our authors. Here is one lately come my way who will have it that for a time after death the soul is under control of certain spirits, as Raphael, and another whom I doubtfully read as Nares; but still so near to this state of life that on prayer to them he may be free to come and disclose matters to the living.

'"Come, indeed, he must, if he be rightly called, the manner of which is set forth in an experiment. But having come, and once opened his mouth, it may chance that his summoner shall see and hear more than of the hid treasure which it is likely he bargained for; since the experiment puts this in the forefront of things to be enquired.

'"But the eftest way is to send you the whole, which herewith I do; copied from a book of recipes which I had of good Bishop Moore."'

Here Joseph stopped, and made no comment, gazing on the paper. For more than a minute nothing was said, then Madam Bowles, drawing her needle through her work and looking at it, coughed and said, 'There was no more written?'

'No, nothing, mother.'

'No? Well, it is strange stuff. Did ever you meet this Mr. Fowler?'

'Yes, it might be once or twice, in Oxford, a civil gentleman enough.'

'Now I think of it,' said she, 'it would be but right to acquaint him with – with what has happened: they were close friends. Yes, Joseph, you should do that. You will know what should be said. And the letter is his, after all.'

'You are in the right, mother, and I'll not delay it.' And forthwith he sat down to write.

From Norfolk to Gloucester was no quick transit. But a letter went, and a larger packet came in answer; and there were more evening talks in the panelled parlour at the Hall.

At the close of one, these words were said: 'Tonight, then, if you are certain of yourself, go round by the field path. Ay, and here is a cloth will serve.'

'What cloth is that, mother? A napkin?'

'Yes, of a kind: what matter?' So he went out by the way of the garden, and she stood in the door, musing, with her hand on her mouth. Then the hand dropped and she said half-aloud: 'If only I had not been so hurried! But it was the face cloth, sure enough.'

It was a very dark night, and the spring wind blew loud over the black fields – loud enough to drown all sounds of shouting or calling. If calling there was, there was no voice, nor any that answered, nor any that regarded – yet.

Next morning, Joseph's mother was early in his chamber. 'Give me the cloth,' she said, 'the maids must not find it. And tell me, tell me, quick!'

Joseph, seated on the side of the bed with his head in his hands, looked up at her with bloodshot eyes. 'We have opened his mouth,' he said. 'Why in God's name did you leave his face bare?'

'How could I help it? You know how I was hurried that day? But do you mean you saw it?'

Joseph only groaned and sunk his head in his hands again. Then, in a low voice, 'He said you should see it, too.'

With a dreadful gasp she clutched at the bedpost and clung to it.

'Oh, but he's angry,' Joseph went on. 'He was only biding his time, I'm sure. The words were scarce out of my mouth when I heard like the snarl of a dog in under there.' He got up and paced the room. 'And what can we do? He's free! And I daren't meet him! I daren't take the drink and go where he is! I daren't lie here another night. Oh, why did you do it? We could have waited.'

'Hush,' said his mother. Her lips were dry. ''Twas you, you know it, as much as I. Besides, what use in talking? Listen to me: 'tis but six o'clock. There's money to cross the water: such as they can't follow. Yarmouth's not so far, and most night boats sail for Holland, I've heard. See you to the horses. I can be ready.'

Joseph stared at her. 'What will they say here?'

'What? Why, cannot you tell the parson we have wind of property lying in Amsterdam which we must claim or lose? Go, go; or if you are not man enough for that, lie here again tonight.'

He shivered and went.

That evening after dark a boatman lumbered into an inn on Yarmouth

Quay, where a man and a woman sat, with saddle-bags on the floor by them.

'Ready, are you, mistress and gentleman?' he said. 'She sails before the hour, and my other passenger he's waitin' on the quay. Be there all your baggage?' and he picked up the bags.

'Yes, we travel light,' said Joseph. 'And you have more company bound for Holland?'

'Just the one,' said the boatman, 'and he seem to travel lighter yet.'

'Do you know him?' said Madam Bowles. She laid her hand on Joseph's arm, and they both paused in the doorway.

'Why no, but for all he's hooded I'd know him again fast enough, he have such a cur'ous way of speakin', and I doubt you'll find he know you, by what he said. "Goo you and fetch 'em out," he say, "and I'll wait on 'em here," he say, and sure enough he's a-comin' this way now.'

Poisoning of a husband was petty treason then, and women guilty of it were strangled at the stake and burnt.

The Assize records of Norwich tell of a woman so dealt with and of her son hanged thereafter, convict on their own confession, made before the Rector of their parish, the name of which I withhold, for there is still hid treasure to be found there.

Bishop Moore's book of recipes is now in the University Library at Cambridge, marked Dd 11, 45, and on the leaf numbered 144 this is written:

An experiment most often proved true, to find out tresure hidden in the ground, theft, manslaughter, or anie other thynge. Go to the grave of a ded man, and three tymes call hym by his nam at the hed of the grave, and say. Thou, N., N., N., I coniure the, I require the, and I charge the, by thi Christendome that thou takest leave of the Lord Raffael and Nares and then askest leave this night to come and tell me trewlie of the tresure that lyith hid in such a place. Then take of the earth of the grave at the dead bodyes hed and knitt it in a lynnen clothe and put itt under thi right eare and sleape theruppon: and wheresoever thou lyest or slepest, that night he will com and tell thee trewlie in waking or sleping.

The Malice of Inanimate Objects

THE MALICE OF INANIMATE OBJECTS is a subject upon which an old friend of mine was fond of dilating, and not without justification.

In the lives of all of us, short or long, there have been days, dreadful days, on which we have had to acknowledge with gloomy resignation that our world has turned against us.

I do not mean the human world of our relations and friends: to enlarge on that is the province of nearly every modern novelist. In their books it is called 'Life' and an odd enough hash it is as they portray it.

No, it is the world of things that do not speak or work or hold congresses and conferences. It includes such beings as the collar stud, the inkstand, the fire, the razor, and, as age increases, the extra step on the staircase which leads you either to expect or not to expect it.

By these and such as these (for I have named but the merest fraction of them) the word is passed round, and the day of misery arranged.

Is the tale still remembered of how the Cock and Hen went to pay a visit to Squire Korbes? How on the journey they met with and picked up a number of associates, encouraging each with the announcement:

'To Squire Korbes we are going
For a visit is owing.'

Thus they secured the company of the Needle, the Egg, the Duck, the Cat, possibly – for memory is a little treacherous here – and finally the Millstone.

And when it was discovered that Squire Korbes was for the moment out, they took up positions in his mansion and awaited his return.

He did return, wearied no doubt by a day's work among his extensive properties. His nerves were first jarred by the raucous cry of the Cock. He threw himself into his armchair and was lacerated by the Needle. He went to the sink for a refreshing wash and was splashed all over by the Duck. Attempting to dry himself with the towel he broke the Egg upon his face.

He suffered other indignities from the Hen and her accomplices, which I cannot now recollect, and finally, maddened with pain and fear, rushed out by the back door and had his brains dashed out by the Millstone that had perched itself in the appropriate place.

'Truly,' in the concluding words of the story, 'this Squire Korbes must have been either a very wicked or a very unfortunate man.'

It is the latter alternative which I incline to accept.

There is nothing in the preliminaries to show that any slur rested on his name, or that his visitors had any injury to avenge. And will not this narrative serve as a striking example of that Malice of which I have taken upon me to treat?

It is, I know, the fact that Squire Korbes's visitors were not all of them, strictly speaking, inanimate. But are we sure that the perpetrators of this Malice are really inanimate either? There are tales which seem to justify a doubt.

Two men of mature years were seated in a pleasant garden after breakfast. One was reading the day's paper, the other sat with folded arms, plunged in thought, and on his face were a piece of sticking plaster and lines of care.

His companion lowered his paper. 'What,' said he, 'is the matter with you? The morning is bright, the birds are singing, I can hear no aeroplanes or motor bikes.'

'No,' replied Mr. Burton, 'it is nice enough, I agree, but I have a bad day before me. I cut myself shaving and spilt my tooth powder.'

'Ah,' said Mr. Manners, 'some people have all the luck,' and with this expression of sympathy he reverted to his paper. 'Hullo,' he exclaimed, after a moment, 'here's George Wilkins dead! You won't have any more bother with him, anyhow.'

'George Wilkins?' said Mr. Burton, more than a little excitedly, 'Why, I didn't even know he was ill.'

'No more he was, poor chap. Seems to have thrown up the sponge and put an end to himself. Yes,' he went on, 'it's some days back: this is the inquest. Seemed very much worried and depressed, they say. What about, I wonder? Could it have been that will you and he were having a row about?'

'Row?' said Mr. Burton angrily, 'there was no row. He hadn't a leg to stand on: he couldn't bring a scrap of evidence. No, it may have been half-a-dozen things, but Lord! I never imagined he'd take anything so hard as that.'

'I don't know,' said Mr. Manners, 'he was a man, I thought, who did take things hard: they rankled. Well, I'm sorry, though I never saw much of him. He must have gone through a lot to make him cut his throat. Not the way I should choose, by a long sight. Ugh! Lucky he hadn't a family, anyhow. Look here, what about a walk round before lunch? I've an errand in the village.'

Mr. Burton assented rather heavily. He was perhaps reluctant to give the inanimate objects of the district a chance of getting at him. If so, he was right.

He just escaped a nasty purl over the scraper at the top of the steps; a thorny branch swept off his hat and scratched his fingers, and as they climbed a grassy slope he fairly leapt into the air with a cry and came down flat on his face.

'What in the world?' said his friend coming up. 'A great string, of all things! What business – Oh, I see – belongs to that kite' (which lay on the grass a little farther up). 'Now if I can find out what little beast has left that kicking about, I'll let him have it – or rather I won't, for he shan't see his kite again. It's rather a good one, too.'

As they approached, a puff of wind raised the kite and it seemed to sit up on its end and look at them with two large round eyes painted red, and, below them, three large printed red letters: I.C.U.

Mr. Manners was amused and scanned the device with care. 'Ingenious,' he said, 'it's a bit off a poster, of course: I see! Full Particulars, the word was.'

Mr. Burton on the other hand was not amused, but thrust his stick through the kite.

Mr. Manners was inclined to regret this. 'I dare say it serves him right,' he said, 'but he'd taken a lot of trouble to make it.'

'Who had?' said Mr. Burton sharply. 'Oh, I see, you mean the boy.'

'Yes, to be sure, who else? But come on down now: I want to leave a message before lunch.'

As they turned a corner into the main street, a rather muffled and choky voice was heard to say, 'Look out! I'm coming.'

They both stopped as if they had been shot.

'Who was that?' said Manners. 'Blest if I didn't think I knew—' Then, with almost a yell of laughter he pointed with his stick.

A cage with a grey parrot in it was hanging in an open window across the way.

'I was startled, by George. It gave you a bit of a turn, too, didn't it?' Burton was inaudible. 'Well, I shan't be a minute: you can go and make friends with the bird.'

But when he rejoined Burton, that unfortunate was not, it seemed, in trim for talking with either birds or men. He was some way ahead and going rather quickly.

Manners paused for an instant at the parrot window and then hurried on laughing more than ever. 'Have a good talk with Polly?' said he, as he came up.

'No, of course not,' said Burton, testily. 'I didn't bother about the beastly thing.'

'Well, you wouldn't have got much out of her if you'd tried,' said Manners. 'I remembered after a bit: they've had her in the window for years. She's stuffed.'

Burton seemed about to make a remark, but suppressed it.

Decidedly this was not Burton's day out. He choked at lunch, he broke a pipe, he tripped in the carpet, he dropped his book in the pond in the garden.

Later on he had or professed to have a telephone call summoning him back to town next day and cutting short what should have been a week's visit. And so glum was he all the evening that Manners' disappointment in losing an ordinarily cheerful companion was not very sharp.

At breakfast Mr. Burton said little about his night. But he did intimate that he thought of looking in on his doctor. 'My hand's so shaky,' he said, 'I really daren't shave this morning.'

'Oh, I'm sorry,' said Mr. Manners, 'my man could have managed that for you. But they'll put you right in no time.'

Farewells were said.

By some means and for some reason Mr. Burton contrived to reserve a compartment to himself. (The train was not of the corridor type.) But these precautions avail little against the angry dead.

I will not put dots or stars, for I dislike them, but I will say that apparently someone tried to shave Mr. Burton in the train, and did not succeed overly well.

He was however satisfied with what he had done, if we may judge from the fact that on a once-white napkin spread on Mr. Burton's chest was an inscription in red letters:

GEO. W. FECI.

Do not these facts – if facts they are – bear out my suggestion that there is something not inanimate behind the Malice of Inanimate Objects?

Do they not further suggest that when this malice begins to show itself we should be very particular to examine and if possible rectify any obliquities in our recent conduct?

And do they not, finally, almost force upon us the conclusion that, like Squire Korbes, Mr. Burton must have been either a very wicked or a singularly unfortunate man?

A Vignette

You are asked to think of the spacious garden of a country rectory, adjacent to a park of many acres, and separated therefrom by a belt of trees of some age which we knew as the Plantation. It is but about thirty or forty yards broad. A close gate of split oak leads to it from the path encircling the garden, and when you enter it from that side you put your hand through a square hole cut in it and lift the hook to pass along to the iron gate which admits to the park from the Plantation.

It has further to be added that from some windows of the rectory, which stands on a somewhat lower level than the Plantation, parts of the path leading thereto, and the oak gate itself can be seen. Some of the trees, Scotch firs and others, which form a backing and a surrounding, are of considerable size, but there is nothing that diffuses a mysterious gloom or imparts a sinister flavour – nothing of melancholy or funereal associations.

The place is well clad, and there are secret nooks and retreats among the bushes, but there is neither offensive bleakness nor oppressive darkness. It is, indeed, a matter for some surprise when one thinks it over, that any cause for misgivings of a nervous sort have attached itself to so normal and cheerful a spot, the more so, since neither our childish mind when we lived there nor the more inquisitive years that came later ever nosed out any legend or reminiscence of old or recent unhappy things.

Yet to me they came, even to me, leading an exceptionally happy wholesome existence, and guarded – not strictly but as carefully as was any way necessary – from uncanny fancies and fear. Not that such guarding avails to close up all gates.

I should be puzzled to fix the date at which any sort of misgiving about the Plantation gate first visited me. Possibly it was in the years just before I went to school, possibly on one later summer afternoon of which I have a faint memory, when I was coming back after solitary roaming in the park, or, as I bethink me, from tea at the Hall: anyhow, alone, and fell in with one of the villagers also homeward bound just as I was about to turn off the road on to the track leading to the Plantation.

We broke off our talk with 'good nights', and when I looked back at him after a minute or so I was just a little surprised to see him standing still and looking after me. But no remark passed, and on I went.

By the time I was within the iron gate and outside the park, dusk had undoubtedly come on; but there was no lack yet of light, and I could not account to myself for the questionings which certainly did rise as to the presence of anyone else among the trees, questionings to which I could not very certainly say 'No', nor, I was glad to feel, 'Yes', because if there were anyone they could not well have any business there.

To be sure, it is difficult, in anything like a grove, to be quite certain that nobody is making a screen out of a tree trunk and keeping it between you and him as he moves round it and you walk on. All I can say is that if such a one was there he was no neighbour or acquaintance of mine, and there was some indication about him of being cloaked or hooded. But I think I may have moved at a rather quicker pace than before, and have been particular about shutting the gate.

I think, too, that after that evening something of what Hamlet calls a 'gain-giving' may have been present in my mind when I thought of the Plantation. I do seem to remember looking out of a window which gave in that direction, and questioning whether there was or was not any appearance of a moving form among the trees. If I did, and perhaps I did, hint a suspicion to the nurse the only answer to it will have been 'The hidea of such a thing!' and an injunction to make haste and get into my bed.

Whether it was on that night or a later one that I seem to see myself again in the small hours gazing out of the window across moonlit grass and hoping I was mistaken in fancying any movement in that half-hidden corner of the garden, I cannot now be sure. But it was certainly within a short while that I began to be visited by dreams which I would much rather not have had – which, in fact, I came to dread acutely; and the point round which they centred was the Plantation gate.

As years go on it but seldom happens that a dream is disturbing. Awkward it may be, as when, while I am drying myself after a bath, I open the bedroom door and step out on to a populous railway platform and have to invent rapid and flimsy excuses for the deplorable *déshabille*.

But such a vision is not alarming, though it may make one despair of ever holding up one's head again. But in the times of which I am thinking, it did happen, not often, but oftener than I liked, that the moment a dream set in I knew that it was going to turn out ill, and that there was nothing I could do to keep it on cheerful lines.

Ellis the gardener might be wholesomely employed with rake and spade as I watched at the window; other familiar figures might pass and repass on harmless errands; but I was not deceived. I could see that the time was coming when the gardener and the rest would be gathering up their properties and setting off on paths that led homeward or into some safe outer world, and the garden would be left – to itself, shall we say, or to denizens who did not desire quite ordinary company and were only waiting for the word 'all clear' to slip into their posts of vantage.

Now, too, was the moment near when the surroundings began to take on a threatening look; that the sunlight lost power and a quality of light replaced it which, though I did not know it at the time, my memory years after told me was the lifeless pallor of an eclipse. The effect of all this was to intensify the foreboding that had begun to possess me, and to make me look anxiously about, dreading that in some quarter my fear would take a visible shape.

I had not much doubt which way to look. Surely behind those bushes, among those trees, there was motion, yes, and surely – and more quickly than seemed possible – there was motion, not now among the trees, but on the very path towards the house. I was still at the window, and before I could adjust myself to the new fear there came the impression of a tread on the stairs and a hand on the door.

That was as far as the dream got, at first; and for me it was far enough. I had no notion what would have been the next development, more than that it was bound to be horrifying.

That is enough in all conscience about the beginning of my dreams. A beginning it was only, for something like it came again and again; how often I can't tell, but often enough to give me an acute distaste for being left alone in that region of the garden. I came to fancy that I could see in the behaviour of the village people whose work took them that way an anxiety to be past a certain point, and moreover a welcoming of company as they approached that corner of the park. But on this it will not do to lay overmuch stress, for, as I have said, I could never glean any kind of story bound up with the place.

However, the strong probability that there had been one once I cannot deny.

I must not by the way give the impression that the whole of the Plantation was haunted ground. There were trees there most admirably devised for climbing and reading in; there was a wall, along the top of which you could walk for many hundred yards and reach a frequented road, passing farmyard and familiar houses; and once in the park, which had its own delights of wood and water, you were well out of range of anything suspicious – or, if that is too much to say, of anything that suggested the Plantation gate.

But I am reminded, as I look on these pages, that so far we have had only preamble, and that there is very little in the way of actual incident to come, and that the criticism attributed to the devil when he sheared the sow is like to be justified. What, after all, was the outcome of the dreams to which without saying a word about them I was liable during a good space of time? Well, it presents itself to me thus.

One afternoon – the day being neither overcast nor threatening – I was at my window in the upper floor of the house. All the family were out. From some obscure shelf in a disused room I had worried out a book, not very recondite: it was, in fact, a bound volume of a magazine in which were contained parts of a novel. I know now what novel it was, but I did not then, and a sentence struck and arrested me.

Someone was walking at dusk up a solitary lane by an old mansion in Ireland, and being a man of imagination he was suddenly forcibly impressed by what he calls 'the aerial image of the old house, with its peculiar malign, scared, and skulking aspect' peering out of the shade of its neglected old trees.

The words were quite enough to set my own fancy on a bleak track. Inevitably I looked and looked with apprehension, to the Plantation gate. As was but right it was shut, and nobody was upon the path that led to it or from it. But as I said a while ago, there was in it a square hole giving access to the fastening; and through that hole, I could see – and it struck like a blow on the diaphragm – something white or partly white.

Now this I could not bear, and with an access of something like courage – only it was more like desperation, like determining that I must know the worst – I did steal down and, quite uselessly, of course, taking cover behind bushes as I went, I made progress until I was within range of the gate and the hole. Things were – alas! – worse than I had feared: through that hole a face was looking my way.

It was not monstrous, not pale, fleshless, spectral. Malevolent I thought and think it was; at any rate the eyes were large and open and fixed. It was pink and, I thought, hot, and just above the eyes the border of a white linen drapery hung down from the brows.

There is something horrifying in the sight of a face looking at one out of a frame as this did; more particularly if its gaze is unmistakably fixed upon you. Nor does it make the matter any better if the expression gives no clue to what is to come next.

I said just now that I took this face to be malevolent, and so I did, but not in regard of any positive dislike or fierceness which it expressed. It was, indeed, quite without emotion. I was only conscious that I could see the whites of the eyes all round the pupil, and that, we know, has a glamour of madness about it.

The immovable face was enough for me. I fled, but at what I thought must be a safe distance inside my own precincts I could not but halt and look back. There was no white thing framed in the hole of the gate, but there was a draped form shambling away among the trees.

Do not press me with questions as to how I bore myself when it became necessary to face my family again. That I was upset by something I had seen must have been pretty clear, but I am very sure that I fought off all attempts to describe it.

Why I make a lame effort to do it now I cannot very well explain: it undoubtedly has had some formidable power of clinging through many years to my imagination. I feel that even now I should be circumspect in passing that Plantation gate; and every now and again the query haunts me:

Are there here and there sequestered places which some curious creatures still frequent, whom once on a time anybody could see and speak to as they went about on their daily occasions, whereas now only at rare intervals in a series of years does one cross their paths and become aware of them? And perhaps that is just as well for the peace of mind of simple people.

The Bulbul and the Cuckoo

THERE WAS ONCE A BULBUL, and one day as he was flying about he saw a tree on which was a little fruit. The bulbul was much pleased, and said, 'I will sit here till this fruit is ripe and then I will eat it.'

So he deserted his nest and his wife and sat there for twelve years without eating anything, and every day he said, 'Tomorrow I will eat this fruit.'

During those twelve years a great many birds tried to sit on the tree and wished to build nests in it, but whenever they came the bulbul sent them away saying, 'This fruit is not good. Don't come here.'

One day a cuckoo came and said, 'Why do you send us away? Why should we not come and sit here too? All the trees here are not yours.'

'Never mind,' said the bulbul, 'I am going to sit here, and when this fruit is ripe, I shall eat it.'

Now the cuckoo knew that this tree was the cotton-tree, but the bulbul did not. First comes the bud, which the bulbul thought a fruit, then comes the flower; the flower becomes a big pod, the pod bursts, and all the cotton flies away.

The bulbul was delighted when he saw the beautiful red flower, which he still thought a fruit, and said, 'When it is ripe, it will be a delicious fruit.'

The flower became a pod, and the pod burst.

'What is all this that is flying about?' said the bulbul. 'The fruit must be ripe now.'

So he looked into the pod, and it was empty – all the cotton had fallen out.

Then the cuckoo came and said to the angry bulbul, 'You see, if you had allowed us to come and sit on the tree, you would have had something good to eat; but as you were selfish, and would not let any one share with you, God is angry and has punished you by giving you a hollow fruit.'

And the cuckoo called all the other birds and they came and mocked the bulbul. The bulbul got very angry, and all the birds went away.

After they had gone, the bulbul said to the tree, 'You are a bad tree. You are of use to no one. You give food to no one.'

The tree said, 'You are mistaken. God made me what I am. My flower is given to sheep to eat. My cotton makes pillows and mattresses for man.'

Since that day no bulbul goes near a cotton tree.

Stories I Have Tried to Write

I HAVE NEITHER much experience nor much perseverance in the writing of stories – I am thinking exclusively of ghost stories, for I have never cared to try any other kind – and it has amused me sometimes to think of the stories which have crossed my mind from time to time and never materialised properly.

Never properly: for some of them I have actually written down, and they repose in a drawer somewhere. To borrow Sir Walter Scott's most frequent quotation, 'Look on (them) again I dare not'. They are not good enough. Yet some of them had ideas in them which refused to blossom in the surroundings I had devised for them, but perhaps came up in other forms in stories that did get as far as print. Let me recall them for the benefit (so to style it) of someone else.

There was the story of a man travelling in a train in France. Facing him sat a typical Frenchwoman of mature years, with the usual moustache and a very confirmed countenance. He had nothing to read but an antiquated novel he had bought for the binding – *Madame de Lichtenstein* it was called.

Tired of looking out of the window and studying his *vis-à-vis*, he began drowsily turning the pages and paused at a conversation between two of the characters. They were discussing an acquaintance, a woman who lived in a largish house at Marcilly-le-Hayer. The house was described, and – here we are coming to a point – the mysterious disappearance of the woman's husband. Her name was mentioned, and my reader couldn't help thinking he knew it in some other connection.

Just then the train stopped at a country station, the traveller, with a start, woke up from a doze – the book open in his hand – the woman opposite him got out, and on the label of her bag he read the name that seemed to be in his novel.

Well, he went on to Troyes, and from there he made excursions, and one of these took him – at lunch-time – to – yes, to Marcilly-le-Hayer. The hotel in the Grand Place faced a three-gabled house of some pretensions. Out of it came a well-dressed woman, *whom he had seen before*. Conversation with the waiter. Yes, the lady was a widow, or so it was believed. At any rate nobody knew what had become of her husband. Here I think we broke down. Of course, there was no such conversation in the novel as the traveller thought he had read.

Then there was quite a long one about two undergraduates spending Christmas in a country house that belonged to one of them. An uncle, next heir to the estate, lived near. Plausible and learned Roman priest, living with the uncle, makes himself agreeable to the young men. Dark walks home at night after dining with the uncle. Curious disturbances as they pass through the shrubberies. Strange, shapeless tracks in the snow round the house, observed in the morning. Efforts to lure away the companion and isolate the proprietor and get him to come out after dark. Ultimate defeat and death of the priest, upon whom the Familiar, baulked of another victim, turns.

Also the story of two students of King's College, in the 16th century (who were, in fact, expelled thence for magical practices), and their nocturnal expedition to a witch at Fenstanton, and of how, at the turning to Lolworth, on the Huntingson road, they met a company leading an unwilling figure whom they seemed to know. And of how, on arriving at Fenstanton, they learned of the witch's death, and of what they saw seated upon her newly-dug grave.

These were some of the tales which got as far as the stage of being written down, at least in part. There were others that flitted across the mind from time to time, but never really took shape.

The man, for instance (naturally a man with *something* on his mind), who, sitting in his study one evening, was startled by a slight sound, turned hastily, and saw a certain dead face looking out from between the window curtains: a dead face, but with living eyes. He made a dash at the curtains and tore them apart. A pasteboard mask fell to the floor. But there was no one there, and the eyes of the mask were but eye-holes. What was to be done about that?

There is the touch on the shoulder that comes when you are walking quickly homewards in the dark hours, full of anticipation of the warm room and bright fire, and when you pull up, startled, what face or no-face do you see?

Similarly, when Mr. Badman had decided to settle the hash of Mr. Goodman and had picked out just the right thicket by the roadside from which to fire at him, how came it exactly that when Mr. Goodman and his unexpected friend actually did pass, they found Mr. Badman weltering in the road? He was able to tell them something of what he found waiting for him – even beckoning to him – in the thicket: enough to prevent them from looking into it themselves. There were possibilities here, but the labour of constructing the proper setting has been beyond me.

There were possibilities, too, in the Christmas cracker, if the right people pull it, and if the motto which they find inside has the right message on it. They will probably leave the party early, pleading indisposition; but very likely a *previous engagement of long standing* would be the more truthful excuse.

In parenthesis, many common objects may be made the vehicles of retribution, and where retribution is not called for, of malice. Be careful how you handle the packet you pick up in the carriage-drive, particularly if it contains nail parings and hair. Do not, in any case, bring it into the house. It may not be alone . . . (Dots are believed by many writers of our day to be a good substitute for effective writing. They are certainly an easy one. Let us have a few more . . . . . .)

Late on Monday night a toad came into my study. And, though nothing has so far seemed to link itself with this appearance, I feel that it may not be quite prudent to brood over topics which may open the interior eye to the presence of more formidable visitants.

Enough said.

A Night in King's College Chapel

'It is curious how few people ever notice the painted glass in our Chapel – comparatively few, that is. One has heard enthusiastic worshippers sometimes remark on the extreme excellence of the West window. But these are generally the ones who would like to see some handsome gas standards in place of all those guttering candles, and would like the service brightened up a little by some hearty congregational singing – "Hark, hark my soul" or "Dare to be a Daniel". No, our windows are a sealed book to most visitors; and did anyone say all residents? People complain that they are so hard to make anything of, and there is a certain amount of truth in this statement. Indeed the object of this paper is to throw some little light on the erudition of these masterpieces of mediaeval art. I must remind you that in the year 1754 . . .'

I had written so much of an article on the windows intended for the *Cambridge Review*, sitting in one of the stalls of the chapel after an afternoon service, and at that point I stopped for a little and, gradually succumbing to the associations of my place, fell into a doze. You will guess the next sentence and I will not therefore pain you with the repetition of it. I was awaked by the south door banging to, and discovered that I was locked in. Under the circumstances there is no chance of making yourself heard except by ringing the bell, and for the moment I was too surprised and lazy to do anything at all. There I sat. The moon was shining and I could see some of the figures in the windows, which pleased me, and I fixed my attention on that which represents Reuben looking at the empty well where he expected to find Joseph.

To my horror I saw him, distinctly, lower his arms (which had been raised over his head in surprise), retire to the edge of the well, and sit down on it. Then he yawned – I heard him – and began feeling about in his drapery. Then he began to say something in a somewhat metallic tone which became more natural as he went on.

'Well, I suppose that feller Joseph 'as took and gorn off on one of his larks. I thought he worn't in that pit. And now for a pipe.'

Yes – he said 'a pipe'. You may imagine my feelings when, apparently from the bosom of his red shirt, he produced an extraordinarily murky clay, filled it, struck a match on the stonework of the well and lit up, so that soon an odour as of the worst variety of shag stole over the sacred edifice. But Reuben was not destined to enjoy his evening smoke altogether undisturbed. Just opposite to him is a representation of the Manna falling – in the shape of large halfcrowns – and I was suddenly brought to a recollection of this by hearing a sharp rattling sound, and seeing Reuben start, draw up his leg and begin rubbing his shin, muttering execrations. Suddenly he put down his pipe on the edge of the well and advanced to the foreground in a sad state of anger.

'Moses,' he said, 'I've spoke about this time and again. If you can't keep them Children of Israel in better order I shall speak to the Guvnor to 'ave you took out of that and put in one of the broke windows. You knows right well it'll be done too. I will *not* 'ave them throwin' of their Manner at me and, to my thinking, you want all the Manners you can git yourself. You 'aven't got none to spare. I may be only a Type, but I ain't goin' to be put upon.'

There was a dead silence at this, followed by a whispering in the Manna window. Then Moses (as well as I could make out for he was on the same side as I) stepped forward and apologised, saying that his attention had been diverted for the moment, and promising that the offence should not be repeated. This explanation, which seemed to satisfy Reuben, was followed by a smart application of Moses' rod to the backs and shoulders of some of Reuben's descendants – he even sent across one of the 'Messengers' who occupy the middle lights to borrow the rod belonging to his double in the scene with the Golden Calf.

But you must not suppose that these were the only windows which assumed so new an aspect. There was a perfect buzz of conversation on all sides; voices male, female and animal. I noticed that all the New Testament lights remained dark and inanimate while the Types and Messengers and Pontius Pilate seemed to be lighted up from some internal source.

'Do get up,' said Naomi from her position at the East end, to her deceased husband. 'Who do you suppose is a going to set and cry over you all night as well as all day?' And Elimelech got up in a submissive manner and muttered something about going across to see Job.

Job's wife (who, you will remember, is scolding him, usually assisted by a hideous demon) was rather inclined to continue the process now, as I judged from her opening words: '. . . setting there as naked as Adam on that nasty filthy dunghill – in a perfect coat of dirt. You ought to be ashamed of yourself,' etc, etc. But here even the demon interposed and said he wasn't going to stand by and see the gentleman put upon. If Mr. Job didn't choose to stand up for himself, and a more affable gent he never see, then it was time his friends stood up for him. And as to sitting on dunghills and having no clothes to wear, well, all he should like to know was, who brought him to it?

A new element was here introduced into the discussion by the arrival of Eve, who had unfortunately overheard the remarks made by Mrs. Job on Adam's scanty attire, and now came rapidly up accompanied by the serpent, to inquire precisely what was meant to be conveyed by those words. Here were the materials for a very pretty quarrel, which in fact lasted a considerable time. But I was glad to notice that Job and Elimelech were able to slip off and join Adam in the Garden of Eden where, I concluded, they were having a quiet cigar.

The gentlemen who occupy the centre lights and hold long scrolls seemed to be forming themselves into a kind of servants' club in the West window, which, as being modern glass, had entirely disappeared. Some of them left their scrolls behind, but most took them with them, and left them about on the ground of the window. They were dreadfully mixed next day in some cases. One or two, I noticed, tied them round their necks in a bow, and these, from having been treated in this way persistently for three centuries, are almost entirely illegible now. The only ones who would not join the party were the four exactly similar figures of St. Luke, which hurried off at once to the broken windows at the West end and dragged out Enoch, who, between the fact that he is being translated and that he is also very much mutilated, is in no condition to be roughly handled. However, the St. Lukes were not inclined to think much of that.

'Come out,' they said. 'We'll have you right tonight, old man. You shall be thoroughly set to rights. Just drink off this electuary and we'll have you to pieces.'

'No, not the electuary yet,' said the second. 'The purge – you forget the purge. Galen saith, "let a purge precede every incision".'

'Purge quotha?' said the third. 'Galen? Drink your own filthy purge. His salt humours must be dispersed or we shall have trouble anon. Exhibit a solution of the dust from the altar, and frankincense and a fat chapel spider.'

Enoch groaned. 'I hate spiders,' he said, 'and the dust you gave me last night nearly made me burst, because it's a week-day and I can only cough when the organ's playing loud.'

Nobody paid any attention. The fourth St. Luke, who had said nothing, but had been slowly dancing round and round to himself, as it were, and trying the edge of his penknife on his thumb, now advanced, and said slowly, 'There's only a little ink on it. Come here. You've got a rush of blood to the head' (though as a fact, few people could have been paler than Enoch at this moment), 'and what you want is a good blood-letting: and by Theophilus you shall have it.' They closed in upon him and I heard a faint scream. I have since thought that every day I look at Enoch in his place, he seems more hopelessly confused, and should he be treated in this way for a much longer time, I fear he will be too far gone for the College ever to mend him.

Others of these distinguished personages had their troubles. Tobias' mother, a respectable old lady enough, was anxious to get over to the Shunammite to have a chat, but had several difficulties to contend with. First there was her own son's dog, a vicious little creature which kept barking and howling at her, to her extreme terror. Then she wasn't sure if 'that young man with the lions', (meaning presumably Daniel), 'was to be trusted': had he got the animals quite under his control, because she *had* heard of so many unfortunate accidents occurring in menageries and that, 'not but what he didn't keep no menagerie, far from it.'

These imputations Daniel indignantly repudiated, but there seemed some ground for them in as much as one of the curious breed of lions, which the two Daniels keep, had just made an ugly rush at King Darius, and this had so frightened the angel in the next window, who is carrying Habakkuk by the hair, that he let that unhappy seer fall right into the den, where the promptest action on the part of Daniel was required to avert destruction.

Besides the lion and the dog, Mrs. Tobit had another awkward neighbour in the shape of Jonah's whale, which (I heard her saying) was always flapping about the place, and splashing one's silk dress when one went out to tea with any lady, and 'what a blessing it would be if some people as give themselves airs about being prophets could keep themselves to themselves a trifle more.' An innuendo which so moved Jonah that he said, with some asperity, that he had yet to learn that a prophet, even though he might have only five chapters, wasn't a cut above an old woman out of the Apocrypha with half a dozen verses to bless herself with. Besides, wasn't it a trifle mean to complain of a harmless animal like that whale, which after all was very likely only an allegory? To which Mrs. Tobit, together with much other matter, retorted that if it was a whale it couldn't be an allegory. She hoped she'd learnt her geography better than that when she was a girl, and allegories didn't live at Ninevah but Egypt.

I saw and heard much more that night, but these were some of the more noteworthy incidents and, in selecting even these, I fear I have detained you too long.

[Earlier Fragment]

After this there was an interval of silence broken only by the quiet fall of the manna onto the top of the stalls – and I was able to look round and notice some of the changes that had taken place in the disposition of the windows since night had come on. Reuben was sitting on the edge of the well, peering curiously into its depths, and I heard him muttering. 'Well for three hundred years I've been put up here to look at this old hole and blowed if I won't find out whether there's something in it after all.' So saying he craned over further and further, till at last there came a sudden splash, and several shouts which roused the keenest interest in the other Old Testament characters, who rushed to the edge of their windows, though the New Testament ones succeeded pretty well in preserving the calm composure on which they prided themselves. Presently Reuben crawled out, very wet and draggled, into the middle light occupied by the messengers, who both protested loudly but vainly against the intrusion. Reuben not only refused to quit the usurped position but insisted on borrowing the messenger's cloak and scroll to dry himself with, remarking at the same time in sulky tones, 'Well, it says distinctly in Genesis that there was no water in the pit, and of course that was in summer, but they must mind and alter it in the Revised Version'. With which emendation he wrapped the cloak round the head of the shivering messenger, and retired to his place.

The Fenstanton Witch

I

NICHOLAS HARDMAN and Stephen Ashe were two Fellows of the King's College in Cambridge: they had come like all their contemporaries from the sister College at Eton where they had spent their lives from about the age of six to that of sixteen, and at the time when we encounter them, they were both men of about thirty years old. Hardman was the son of a Lincolnshire parson, living at Thorganby-on-the-Wolds, while Ashe's father was a yeoman-farmer of Ospringe in Kent.

Hardman was black, dour and saturnine with a rasping voice and a strong Lincolnshire accent which cannot be reproduced here. Ashe had the sturdy and somewhat slow intelligence of his Kentish ancestors; the phrase 'a good friend and a bad enemy' represents the opinion which the men of his year held of him. Both were in priests' orders, and each, we might suppose, looked forward in the fullness of time to occupying College livings, marrying and bringing up a son or two: one most likely to reproduce his father's career; another, perhaps, to go on the land and become a reputable farmer in a small way.

I say we might suppose their aspirations to have been of this nature: for such was the programme of a majority of Fellows of Colleges at that time. But there is an entry in the book called Harwood's *Alumni* which shows that they entertained ideas of a very different sort; and it has occurred to me that it may be worthwhile to tell the story of what they adventured and what came of it.

I have alluded more than once to 'their times' but I have not yet told you when they lived. Anne was filling the throne of England, Scotland, Ireland and France, and Dr. James Roderick was Provost of the College, having been elected by the Fellows in preference to Sir Isaac Newton, whom the Prince of Orange, King William the Third of blessed memory, would have intruded into that pasture. The Fellows of King's had vindicated their right of election and the Lower Master of Eton occupied the Lodge – he was known as one of the 'four Smoking Heads' – while Sir Isaac lived in the Observatory over Trinity Great Gate, and, according to popular legends, gently remonstrated with his dog Diamond, or cut holes in his door to admit his cat and kitten. The University was a happy, sleepy place in those days, one is apt to think; but after all, what with the Church in danger and the excitement of depriving Dr Richard Bentley, then Master of Trinity, of his degrees, there was probably no lack of sport to be had within the precincts. And certainly just outside them there was more than there is now. Snipe were shot on Parker's Piece, and the dreary expanse of undrained fen was the haunt of many a strange fowl, not to speak of other inhabitants of whom I may one day find an occasion to tell.

But it is time to leave generalities. The two sheep to whom we must return – and I am afraid they were black ones – were very close friends; but few men in the University, or indeed in the King's College itself, could boast of more than a speaking acquaintance with either. They occupied one room in the Old School of King's, north of the Chapel, which room was always locked when they were out. And these were not days when Fellows, nor still less Scholars, were in the habit of dropping into each other's abodes to partake of casual hospitality in the way of tobacco or whiskey and water. The common life, such as it was, was confined to Chapel, Hall and the Fellows' Parlour.

All that was known of Hardman and Ashe's way of employing 'their leisure' was that they went for long walks together and smoked apparently very bad tobacco when they came back.

It was a fine afternoon in October when these events began, or to speak more truly, came to a head, which served to show what manner of men were Nicholas Hardman and Stephen Ashe. Chapel service, we may be sure, was at three, and both of our friends were there, staring at each other from opposite stalls. The reedy and pedalless organ helped the rather infirm and jaded choir through a new verse anthem by Dr. Blow during which the snoring of Provost Roderick was not doubtfully heard. At near four, Dr. Tudway, the organist, played out the scant congregation with a march of his own composition. The choirmen hurried off to go through a similar performance at Trinity. The boys rushed off to whatever haunts in the town they had emerged from. The Provost strolled to his Lodge, then at the eastern end of the Chapel, and the Fellows and Scholars made their way across the strip of ground on the north side, holding on their caps – for a strong west wind was blowing the yellow leaves about – and so into the Old Court, and to dine in Hall. A coarse meal, I expect it was, and a silent one. The Vice Provost and three or four Seniors occupied one table on the dais; the Masters of Arts – among whom were Hardman and Ashe – filled a second along with the Fellow-Commoners; and the Bachelors and Undergraduate Fellows and Scholars, two more. There may have been fifty people in the room. Not much passed at dinner, which lasted about forty minutes; but afterwards the Fellows returned to the parlour and the Scholars to their rooms. With these last we are not concerned, but we may as well follow the Seniors. They are sitting at a large table, cloth-less, with some decanters of wine (I don't know whether port or claret: much depends upon the date of Lord Methuen's treaty with Portugal), and something like conversation has broken out.

'Where did ye ride today, Mr. Bates?' said Mr. Glynne.

'Only so far as Fenstanton.'

'Fenstanton. Ah – is that where the witch was ducked last week? Lord Blandford was riding by at the time' (this was the Duke of Marlboro's son and heir who died shortly afterwards and was now a Fellow-Commoner), 'and his Lordship made some hot-headed show at rescuing the old creature. Has there been any stir made? Dodgson of Magdalene has this living, but I doubt, if he hath not moved, no one will. 'Tis a lost place, Fenstanton, for all it be on the Huntingdon road.' Thus far Mr. Glynne, who had rather a knack of monopolising conversation.

'Well, to tell truth,' says Bates, 'I had not heard of the matter, but the bell was tolling for a burying as I rode through, and I happened to meet Dodgson coming from his beer and pipe, as I judge, to the churchyard. He did let fall something which could fit with what you say. Pray, did you hear the name, Glynne, Galpin or Gibson; some word with a "G" in it?'

'Gibson! Mother Gibson! That was the name for a guinea! So that ducking has finished the poor creature,' said good-natured Glynne. 'These fen-rustics are little but brutes. I vow the coroner should have sat, and there should have been a dozen strung up at the Assizes, and in any but Dodgson's parish there would have been. But Lord! the man thinks of nothing but his tithes and his beer.'

'Matthews had the parsonage before Dodgson,' said Bates, 'and in his time there were four attempts at swimming that old woman. Not a boy nor man in the parish, he told me, but was ready to swear she had signed herself away. But Matthews threatened to call in the sheriff, and he would have done it too, so they kept mum in his time.'

'For all that,' said Glynne, 'I remember his saying in this parlour that when he looked at her he was half in a mind to believe the tale. He pointed her out to me one day, and it is sure that she might have sat for a portrait of the Enemy as far as her eyes were concerned: they were as red as blood and the pupils like a goat's.' With which Mr. Glynne was silent and shuddered slightly.

'Did they bury her in the churchyard, Bates?' said Dr. Morell, the Vice Provost.

'Yes, Mr. Vice Provost. I noticed a grave dug on the north side, which I take it was for her.'

'All this talk about burying witches puts me in mind of William of Malmesbury's tale, that Dr. Gale printed not so long back.' This was from a new contributor to the conversation, Mr. Newborough, afterwards Head Master of Eton, who was more bookishly inclined than many of his compeers. 'Do you know it, Mr. Glynne? You should look at Malmesbury': and he proceeded to tell the story which Southey has put into rhyme under the name of the 'Old Woman of Berkeley'. After that came a short discussion of the Witch of Endor; then the conversation drifted to Dr. Hody's book on the Versions of the Bible, then by a not uncommon fate to Dr. Bentley's last enormities, and thence back to the familiar question of College livings and probable vacancies.

In the midst of this, Hardman and Ashe made their bow to the Vice Provost and went out. They had neither of them made any remark since dinner but Dr. Morell, an observant man, noticed that they had taken a very considerable interest in the early part of the conversation.

'Two dull dogs gone,' said Dr. Glynne, when the door closed behind them: 'I pity their wives if ever they marry and their parishes if ever they take 'em.'

'Quiet enough if they are dull,' said Newborough.

'I don't know that, Newborough,' said Morell. 'The man that has chambers under theirs doesn't always sleep best. What can keep those two men treading about the whole night, as I am told they do, and what have they on their minds that makes them sigh and moan like two sick owls, as Burton says? You know everyone in College, Glynne; tell us, pray, were you ever in Hardman's and Ashe's chambers?'

'Not I,' said Glynne. 'I knocked at their door one day, I recollect, last year. Such a clatter as they made before they opened it, I vow I never heard, but all I can tell of the matter is that Hardman was as pale as a ghost when he opened to me, and that the place smelt as sweet as a bonfire of old rags and bones. Hardman made shift to ask my business, and then shut the door in my face!'

'Well,' said the Vice Provost, 'he might have spared himself the question, Glynne. I never knew you have any business in this life yet. Never matter! 'Tis time to turn unto the coffeehouse, Gentlemen. I have told Dr. Cotes we should be there before eight, and the clocks are going the quarter now.'

The company adjourned therefore to a coffeehouse on the Market Place, and smoked clay pipes till ten with Dr. Roger Cotes and some other gentlemen from Trinity, Queens' and Bene't Colleges.

II

The curfew bell was ringing and it was a fine night when Hardman and Ashe, each with a packet and a stick, emerged from the gates of King's College and told the porter – a fuddling old ruffian, as were most College servants of that day – that they were not like to be returning that night. Neither said any word until they were clear of the town and on the Huntingdon road. Then said Nicholas Hardman, 'If all goes as it should tonight, Ashe, we shall know a matter worth knowing.'

'Yes, Nick, and there will be a matter worth having in one of these bundles,' said Ashe: 'I dare swear though that there will be some disappointment. Newborough's tale of the old witch set me a-thinking. You have the book upon you, Nick?'

'Book, what book? Dr. Gales' print of Malmesbury, I suppose? A fat folio of a stone weight. It is likely?'

'No, not Malmesbury. *Our* book, *the* book, I mean.'

'Call me fool if you like, Stephen, but don't ask such another question: have I come forth without my head? That is as likely as it would be for me to leave the book in my chambers. But why, pray, does that ass Newborough's old story set you thinking?'

'Why, only, that if the same gentry that came for their friend in that story were thinking of waiting upon *our* friend at Fenstanton tonight, it is like we may see trouble.'

Hardman gave a snort. 'And if they did, do you think a circle is broken so easily? Have I nothing here that avails to make them give back? Still, you are right in a way, Stephen, as you have been before. If we are later in the field than they, there may be trouble, even danger. But what we would have is not what they want. If we get the three locks of hair and the winding sheet, we are masters of the Elementals. The *others* want the soul.'

It was a thought that seemed to dash both of them for a moment, and they were silent. So the clouds flew across the moon, and the wind blew over the bare fields, and the bells of Cambridge came more faintly to the ear, as they walked quietly on towards the sleeping village of Fenstanton.

III

Those who remember the road between Cambridge and Fenstanton will bear me out when I say that it is eleven miles long, and presents few features of interest. There is an occasional wayside inn, a few farms lie a little off the road, and on a clear day we may see the lantern and western tower of Ely, and a good many nearer church towers. The church that lies nearest to the road is that of Lolworth, on the left hand, some five or six miles out. There was something doing at Lolworth when Hardman and Ashe passed it. The bell was going, and the windows lighted. Nocturnal funerals were almost the rule in Queen Anne's time for any one who claimed to be a magnate, so that it did not surprise the lookers-on when they saw two lines of torches working their way slowly through the trees near the church, and when they saw a figure in white flit out of the south porch to meet the *cortège*, they knew that it must be the parson. Yet a few moments, and the procession was in the church: then they walked on again, for they had paused a moment.

The turning out of the main road towards Lolworth church lay some little distance ahead, and down the lane were coming a group of figures at a great pace. They reached the road and turned down it towards the travellers: who were a little daunted thereby, because they did not wish to be recognised as Cambridge parsons at that hour of the night. There appeared to be seven people clustering round one in the midst, and their action and gait was like that of watchmen who had taken a prisoner. The party came on, and it seemed as if this conjecture might fit the situation, for the person in the midst was plainly reluctant, and as plainly was being hurried on by the rest. Hardman and Ashe drew toward the hedge to let these men pass, and their eyes were riveted upon the face of the captured man. It was not lightly to be forgotten, for it is not often that any one beholds the face of a man who has lost all hope, and yet has room in his brain for an unspeakable fear. This is the sight which those two ill-starred priests were now looking upon: and they saw moreover that, in spite of his terror and desperation, the captive could look nowhere save straight in front of him, for anything seemed tolerable rather than to see the faces of the seven who were about him. When they pictured the scene to themselves thereafter, they realised that his was the only face of which they had caught sight at all; nay, it even seemed to them that there was no other face for their eyes to catch.

The thing was passed; it passed quite silently, and for many moments these two men stayed breathless to within an ace of sudden flight or swooning. They knew that they had seen that which no mourner at that funeral had seen, and it was in their minds that it is not always well for those whose eyes are opened. It may happen to some to see the mountains full of bones and chariots of fire, but to others are shown very different sights from that. Yet the natures of both were so obstinate and dogged that neither would broach to the other the thought of returning, and giving up the dismal project they had in their minds. They went on.

Soon they sighted Fenstanton spire, and half a mile further they left the road and made their way across the fields to the side where the church-yard was accessible away from the street. It was not a difficult wall to climb, yet they were unnerved and took several minutes to get over it. Then they proceeded to go through the sinister rites and ceremonies which were to safeguard them against those powers with whom they supposed themselves to be leagued, for they are treacherous allies, as those tell us who claim to know the heart of the matter. On the north side of the dark church, even in its shadow, and not more than ten yards from a new-made grave – the only one on that side of the building – they picked out a space where the grass was shortest, and drew two large circles, one within the other. And in the space between the circles they marked out with some pains the sym-bols of the planets and a few Hebrew letters which were meant to indicate names of angels and of the Great Power, whose aid, by one of the strange contradictions of art magic, they promised themselves they would gain for the work they were at. When their defence was completed they stopped, and Ashe looked at his time-piece. The hour was something short of a quarter to twelve, so they must wait till the middle of night was reached.

And now – what was it that these two educated clergymen proposed to themselves? And how came it that they were on an enterprise which one associates, not always correctly, with the darkest mediaevalism and the most defective civilisation?

You have guessed that they were earnest and credulous students of art magic: how came such men to be in Cambridge in the reign of Queen Anne? I can only answer that in that day there were many such men in Germany, and that the instinct which prompts men to seek intercourse with the unseen peoples of the air is one that may come to the surface in any civilisation and in any century. Many have a sneaking idea that the intercourse has been sometimes gained, but that is little to the point.

That which Hardman and Ashe were determined upon was the obtaining of an ingredient for future spells, which should end in making them able to command the forces of nature to a degree which they believed many to have attained before them. They meant on this night – and they were confident of accomplishing it – to go through certain forms of words which would have power to make the corpse of the old woman buried that day to arise out of the grave and come to them, and give them – it is horrid to think of – the portion of the grave-clothes and the locks of hair of which Hardman spoke when they were on the road. Then should the body return to the earth as it was, and the soil be replaced above it. They were to go back to their College the next day; and in seven days' time, who so rich and powerful as Nicholas Hardman and Stephen Ashe, Esquires?

It was with a strange kind of exaltation that, as midnight came near, Hardman drew from his bosom a paper book, about a hundred years old, ill-written and full of diagrams like that which had just been drawn upon the ground, and within whose compass both of them were standing. He began to read, or intone, a Latin form of conjuration, a sinister kind of Church service, in which the most sacred of names were freely employed; and to this Ashe made the set appointed responses. The night had been disturbed through-out and windy, but no rain had fallen and the thin clouds kept covering the moon, which was by this time low and near the horizon. The wind rattled in the louvres of the tower, and every now and then swung the tongue of a bell so that it sounded in a dim and far off fashion. Nicholas Hardman read on, and read faster and louder, and Ashe responded at short intervals. They had now entered upon the 91st Psalm: *'Qui Habitat'*, 'Whoso dwelleth', and they were just promising themselves deliverance from the terror that walks in darkness when a blacker cloud than usual left the moon's face and Stephen Ashe fell like an ox at the feet of Hardman. For it seems that it had been determined that these fools should be answered according to their folly.

I have said that the miserable and criminous old woman whom the fen-men had killed was buried a bare ten yards away from the two conjurors: and their eyes were often fixed upon her grave as upon the point to which their spells were directed. Looking over at the grave, Hardman beheld crouched upon it a shape which there was small likelihood of his ever forgetting. It was the figure, one would say, at first sight, of an enormous bat, with folded wings and hints of head approaching the human form. In a short moment, Hardman caught sight of the folds of wrinkled skin or hide that hung down from the cheeks, of the wide ears which shone transparent in the moonlight, and of the two lines of dusky red fire which marked the almost closed eyes. And further, he declared afterwards, he saw the earth heap upon which this being was crouched stir and wave beneath it. Not long was he allowed to remain a spectator, for this terrific appearance rose to its height and for a minute seemed to look about as if for a victim whom it knew to be near. Hardman, almost at the pitch of despair, yet trusted dimly in his charmed circle. But the creature on a sudden turned full in his direction and stepped swift and straight towards him, not flinching for an instant at angelic names or planetary symbols. In another moment, its talons were raised toward his face, and he knew no more.

It was Ashe who helped him back to Cambridge in the morning of the next day: and it was Ashe also who, for the twenty years that he survived, sheltered him in the parsonage of Willoughton and ministered to him, himself a stricken man. But Hardman never saw light again.

The College at large never learned the rights of the story. Two days after the catastrophe, Mr. Glynne says to Mr. Morell, being Vice Provost, 'What did you do at the Seniors' Meeting this morning, Mr. Vice—?'

'Sealed the presentation to Weedon Lois, and received a declaration, Glynne.'

'A royal declaration, or what?'

'No, Glynne; Mr. Provost will tell you about it, maybe, if you ask him.'

So off goes Mr. Glynne to the Lodge. But Provost Roderick is pale, which is not natural to him, and not smoking, which is decidedly unnatural, and disturbed and uncommunicative. And Mr. Glynne can only learn that it is a matter which the Seniors have decided to keep private. During the next week, a barrowload of matters from one set of chambers in the King's College is wheeled off in the direction of Barton and does not come back: and most of the Seniors are very regular in their attendance in the Chapel for some months.

I cannot help connecting these events I have set down with that entry in the Protocollum book, which states that two gentlemen, being Fellows of the College, were permitted to register a solemn abjuration of all unlawful acts in the practising of which they had grievously transgressed: and that it was agreed that the Provost and Seniors shall exercise their utmost discretion to the end that this matter be kept strictly private to the Seniority.

John Humphreys

A YOUNG MAN is leaning over a gate that leads into a wood. The wood is on the top of a ridge. The man's back is turned to it, and he is looking at a wide and lovely view. The slope before him is fairly steep, and from its base spreads out a broad vale – perhaps the Vale Royal of England, perhaps another, for I must not be too precise in my indications. When I have said that my hero is gazing at a September sunset over an English river-valley, I have said nearly all that I am competent to put into words: my readers must fill in for themselves the details of the distant layers of moorland glorified in a golden mist, of smoke rising from unseen villages and great houses, and of a pinnacled tower here and there. And now that the scene is set, however sketchily, let the historic present be dropped.

The spectator did not soon tire of the view: few people would. But at length the sun sank in a limpid sky behind the wooded hills in the west, and he remembered that duty called him home. He scaled the gate and took his way down by a path through ancient pastures. He walked quickly, with his eyes for the most part of the time fixed on the ground before him and casting only an occasional glance ahead. A man or woman coming in his direction some two fields off was the only thing that diversified the familiar scene. Familiar it was, for he had been brought up in the manor house a mile or so away; a house which one or two unexpected deaths had thrown, with the surrounding estate, into his possession only a few months before. I do not think it necessary to set forth the genealogy nor to detail the accidents which had made him what he was: but briefly the situation was this, that

John Humphreys, an orphan and an only child, aged twenty-two, having just taken a very good degree at Cambridge, and intending to compete for a post in the Home Civil Service, was now a considerable landowner in a beautiful English county, and might expect to figure very respectably in the next issue of Burke's *Landed Gentry*.

He was not the athletic young giant of sixteen stone dear to some writers, nor the spectacled aesthete disliked by the majority: imagine him attractive, clever above the average, neither hating the conventionalities nor a slave to them, [anxious to do the best for his people and] thoroughly alive to the delights and the responsibilities of his position, and you have a notion of what he would have wished to be thought if he had reflected on that matter. He was not thinking about such things as he descended the slope, but rather about certain prosaic questions which he would have to discuss at length with his bailiff: and he also asked himself incidentally whether he knew or ought to know the person in black who was coming across the fields, and was by this time within a hundred yards of him. To that, however, he gave only a passing thought, and was just a little amused to see that if [after all] he had ventured on a greeting, it would have been addressed to a tall post newly covered with black and glistening tar which stood by the path on his left.

Two or three little bits of business – a word with the schoolmaster and another with the curate – made his walk home longer by twenty minutes than it need have been, and it was full dusk when he turned into his carriage-drive. But white paper shows up in the dusk and [my friend hated to see scraps of this sort lying about his grounds. Besides which] an envelope lying in the path did not escape my friend's notice. Even persons who are not offensively tidy dislike to have paper left lying about their premises. [*one-word space*] picked it up. It was unaddressed, but there seemed to be something in it. He put it in his pocket, and hurried on, anxious to get a letter off by the post which would leave in a quarter of an hour. All the whole of that time must be uninterrupted if the letter were to be finished and sent off: so that the sight of a clerical figure seemingly about to ring the front door bell was rather a vexation. It was a little unreasonable in the neighbouring clergy to select this time for paying their calls. Relief succeeded the next moment. No cleric was there: a pillar of the portico had made for itself a deceptive shadow. 'Coming events,' he thought (with little originality), 'cast their shadows before: probably tomorrow the place will be black with curates.'

The letter was despatched, and not long afterwards the bailiff, Mr. Runton, entered upon the scene; his business was long and he succeeded in making it appear highly intricate by starting in the middle and going alternately back to the beginning and forward to the end. So that by the time a policy was settled, Humphreys was more than ready for dinner.

In the course of dressing he turned out the pockets of the coat he had been wearing, with the view, I am afraid, of taking his pipe and tobacco downstairs with him: and among the letters which were gathering fluff and comminuted tobacco in these pockets he recognised the envelope which he had picked up in the drive that evening. It was closed but he could not feel much delicacy about opening it, since therein lay the only chance of returning it to its owner. The contents did not take him much further. Two or three pins, somewhat bent, a small ball of thread tightly rolled, a few withered leaves, and some brown dust: but no letter nor fragment of writing. He doubled up envelope and contents and threw them into the fender.

'Has anyone called here today? I didn't happen to look at the card tray in the hall,' he asked the footman as he entered the small room where he dined.

'Yes sir, there was a lady called to see the grounds.'

'Oh really? Who was that?'

'She didn't give no name, sir, and she 'adn't got a card, she said.'

'And didn't you know who she was? Where did she come from? Was she driving?'

'No sir, not driving, sir: she came on foot – a holdish lady, very respectable – quite the lady, sir. I don't know if I done wrong, sir, but I told her I didn't think there'd be any objection to her walking round the grounds, because I knew the men was about. I 'ope . . .'

'No, I daresay it's all right: and did she walk around the grounds?'

'Yes sir, she wasn't only about ten minutes to a quarter of an hour, and I see her go out again by the drive.'

'Well, I think another time it would be better if you asked anyone who came if they would kindly leave a card or write their names: keep a little book in the hall. I rather prefer to know who comes here.'

'Yes sir, very well, sir. I hope I didn't do wrong, but it was such a very respectable person – not like what'd be probable to do no mischief...'

'Oh no. I don't think any harm's done. I am quite willing that people should see the place; only, as I said, I rather like to know who they are.'

The problem of how to spend the evening alone in a large house was one which Humphreys had had some practice in solving of late. Neighbours were not many, and it happened that several of those families who would in the ordinary way have provided him with society were abroad. But he had just hit upon an employment which would dispose of his leisure for some days to come; and there were but a few days to be tided over before a friend of his own standing was to come for a long visit. This employment was the arranging of the library.

The manor house possessed something really deserving of the name of a library. It was a large room, specially built in the early years of the nineteenth century to contain books. The windows were on one side only, leaving the whole of the other long wall available for books and fireplaces, of which there were two. Projecting bookcases divided the room into three sections. The fittings were stately and solid. And the shelves held something like five and twenty thousand volumes, hardly a hundred of which were later than 1830. The good man who had brought the collection together had intended to digest it carefully into subjects, and had drawn up a plan of the classes. But he must have been cut off before he had had time to carry out his design; and his successors, though they kept the books as an appanage of a gentleman's establishment, had done very little more than put them on the shelves. By way of a catalogue there was a handsome series of volumes with gilt and lettered backs, and completely blank insides. Until quite lately the room had been lived in and kept warm, and though there was a musty flavour of unused paper, damp and mice had happily been kept aloof.

No one could have been better suited for the drudgery of getting the books into order than Humphreys, who was thoroughly fond of a library, and inquisitive about old things, if not deeply versed in them. He had determined to follow out the old collector's plan of arrangements, and had already spent two evenings in clearing out a division to contain the first class (which as usual was that of divinity). The ejected books were in rows on the floor, and he was gleaning the theology out of the other shelves and depositing it temporarily on long tables set out in the windows. He was getting them into sizes – folio, quarto, octavo and less – for such was the natural and also the ancestral plan – and [every now and then he would] at the same time taking rough notes of titles and dates upon a series of sheets of paper which lay ready. A long, interesting, tranquil process, and he felt at peace with everyone – except perhaps the untimely servant who was heading about with occasional knocks and raps in the passage. He could not be sure whether some of the noises were not knocks on the door, and in some irritation he eventually called out, 'Come in, do! Come in, if you want to!' Upon which the noise maker desisted and was heard no more. Humphreys pursued his work for another ten minutes, and then was shaken by a sudden sneeze. He was working in his shirtsleeves and the moment he was thus interrupted he felt that the room was colder than it had been. The reason was not far to seek; the door stood half open; a mistake easily rectified but one which he could not think he had made himself. Probably the footman had left the door on the latch when he had come to see to the fire and bring in the whisky.

It was now verging on eleven o'clock and Humphreys was conscious of approaching sleep – so he put his papers together and resolved to look through a book for a few minutes in his arm chair. He took a large one at random and settled himself with something to drink and something to smoke. But sleep was coming nearer and nearer, and even to open the book required something of an effort. When he did open it, he was disgusted to find that it was a volume of the projected Catalogue of the library, in which, as I said, not one word had been written, though the pages had been numbered. It was too much trouble to get another. He gradually but quickly allowed sleep to come as near as it would.

The next experience was that he was still in the big chair, and eagerly reading in the book. How was this? He had no time to think, but there was the printed page before him – curiously difficult to read – impossible somehow to glance ahead and take in the sense of the next lines, yet at the same time quite clear: and, though the type looked old – very old – the language was modern English. And as he read, the sentences seemed to fix themselves easily and certainly in his brain. It seemed to be partly a dialogue and partly his own thought, and partly something that he was seeing and doing.

'You will have to come with me.'

'Where to?' I said. He said, 'A long walk, hard work. It gets darker and I go. You go on. Rain always, and wind: darker still. Is it someone following? Not sure; don't quite like to stop. Nearly all dark now: one break lighter in the sky there on the left. Someone's head looking over a rock: gone now – moved down quickly. Must go on. Is that someone following? Wind too loud to hear. I don't like this. Shall I run? Shall I call out? *Who's there?* Something like shouting down the wind.'

'Don't!' I said. 'Don't! I know there's something I want to think of.'

'Yes, I daresay, but there's no time. If you could it might be better for you.'

'Listen, isn't that someone. Which way was I going? Let me remember. No time: if I stop to think they'll catch up. Don't let me lose my head. I'm getting frightened. Why did I come?'

'Yes, why indeed?' he said. 'But turn over and see who's after you.'

That was the last line on the page, and Humphreys felt a horror of turning over the leaf. Yet he could not by any means avoid it: it was inevitable, and with a sort of helpless moan he did turn over, and gazed heavily at a great face that was painted on the other side. I really do not know exactly what it was: but it was so terrible an image of corruption and malice and fear, peering out of a dark background, that it scared him clean out of sleep, and he flung the book away with a loud cry, and lay shivering in his chair. There was an oppression on his scalp and his forehead. It felt, he said, like a ragged hand – so much so that he durst not put up his own hand for fear of touching it. But he cowered his head down, and upon the movement it was gone.

He jumped up and for some time stood, back to the fire, warming himself and gazing over the brightly lit room, where, to be sure, there was nothing to cause him the least uneasiness. Then his eye fell on the accursed book which had given him the nightmare. He picked it up with no very friendly feelings, and it fell open at the leaf whose number he remembered too well. It was, of course, as blank as ever, though it did seem slightly discoloured. The sight of it brought the words of his dream back in a flash, and he determined to write them down as a good specimen of dream-literature. For a minute or two he had a difficulty in beginning; the first sentences were unwilling to come: then he happened to glance at the blank leaf of the open book, and from that moment he was certain of his ground. If a word ever failed him, he had but to look towards its probable position, and his brain at once supplied it. When it was done, he read it through. 'Yes,' he said, 'it seems to be mostly what someone else was trying to make me think – putting words into my mouth, and also answering for himself. I wonder what it was that I ought to have remembered: and where I was supposed to be?' [And by the way dare I turn over the page?]

Without much purpose, he turned over the leaf, and his heart gave a jump of fear, for the horror of the dream picture suddenly seized on him. It can only have been association. There was nothing but the slight discoloration which had been noticeable on the other side of the leaf.

There are few things more beautiful than a full September moon shining on the smooth lawns and dark trees of an English garden, and on the oak-grown slopes of an English park. The tide of the year's life is at the full – just past the full [and on the turn]: there is a lucid interval before death, before the great winds set in and the funereal pomp of the woods is put on. Humphreys felt something of the delight and the foreboding of the time when he threw open his bedroom window that night. Absolute stillness: everything might have been holding its breath and listening for the first whisper of a breeze from the distant sea. Only one prosaic thought crossed his mind as he gazed out – 'I'll have that tree down tomorrow: it spoils that lawn badly'. The tree he meant was a small Irish yew which stood very blackly in the near foreground. And with that he retired to bed, and spent, I fear, but a broken night of beginnings to set out on his 'long walk' and unavailing efforts to remember something which constantly just eluded him: while all the time he knew that if he could but secure it he would be safe and quiet.

After breakfast next morning Humphreys strolled round the garden [with his pipe] smoking: and, chancing to meet the head gardener, he remembered his unknown visitor of the day before, and asked if the men had noticed her.

'Yes, I think I did see the lady, Mr. [Humphreys 'Erbert] Humphreys, I *should* say, sir,' thus the gardener began [for he was afflicted with a propensity always to mention the name of the late deceased owner of the mansion]: 'she come – well, I was down at that bed [Mr. 'Erbert] what we 'ad the lobelias last year in it, if you recollect – no, to be sure you wasn't come among us, was you, Mr. – well there – Humphreys – you'll excuse me, and one of the lads 'elping me.

'And all in a minute someone passed by goin' along the walk towards the 'ouse, and I says, "William, do you know who that was?" "No," he says, "I don't, Mr. Barker." "Well," I says, "it's a funny thing to me as people should be coming round about 'ere as if the place belonged to 'em. You go and ask 'er, my lad, if she's any business 'ere. And mind you be'ave civil and touch your cap," I says for, mark you Mr. Humphreys, she was quite the lady in 'er [ways] appearance. And so the lad 'e went after 'er, and by what I could understand she was 'alfway up the drive goin' out when he see her, and not wishin' to keep me waitin' he come back: and reely that is the last Mr. ['Erb] – there again Mr. Humphreys . . .'

'I see, thanks,' put in Humphreys. 'I thought perhaps the lady might have been someone from the village whom you knew by sight.'

'No Sir, no, Mr. Humphreys, no one from the village, not that *I* know,' said Mr. Barker with ready zeal. 'Quite a visitor to this part I took her to be, sir.'

'Just so. Well, Mr. Barker, there's one little matter I wanted to mention – that little Irish yew just below my bedroom window. It rather spoils that bit of lawn, and it isn't much of a tree. I'd like you to make away with it altogether, please.'

Mr. Barker put his hand to his mouth as one who reflects. 'To be sure, sir,' he said. 'Well – there. If you don't mind the trouble, Mr. Humphreys, I should be very obliged to you just to step round and point it hout to me. Then there won't be no mistake about it. The reason why I hask you is because in the late Mr. 'Erbert's time there was one of these fancy maple trees we 'ad – I could show you the place now not an 'undred yards away – very well, another time, sir: any time I could point out the spot and welcome – and I recollect as well as possible 'im saying to me one morning . . .' The rest of the short journey was occupied with the recital of how the maple had been cut down and how subsequently Mr. Herbert had repudiated all knowledge of this matter and had spoken 'really very short' about it. 'And 'aving that in my view,' concluded

Mr. Barker, 'I like to avoid what mistakes I can do, and if you'll be so good as point me out the tree, Sir, I'll see to the matter at once.'

But there was no tree.

After some moments of silent astonishment – for he felt that he could not explain the situation to himself, and much less to Mr. Barker – Humphreys was fain to point out for destruction a perfectly inoffensive and rather handsome shrub which grew about forty yards off and palpably did not intrude on the lawn. And then had first to be told – what he knew already – that this was not an Irish yew, and next persuaded by much superfluous pleading, to spare it. ['Very well,' he said at last, 'perhaps you are the best judge.'] He returned to the library and to his morning's interview with the bailiff, feeling rather small.

The bailiff was not there but the curate had looked in. 'Were you reading this?' he said, after his business was settled. 'I found the book open on the table. These old preachers are very fine – Jeremy Taylor in particular. I don't know who this is: the first pages are gone and there's no title on the back.'

'No, I wasn't reading it,' said Humphreys, taking the little book from him. 'It must have blown open, I suppose. What is it? Oh, a Meditation on Death!'

'Well, just look at that page,' said the curate; 'full of imagination, isn't it?'

Humphreys read these sentences:

'And what when *your feet stumble upon the dark mountain*s as it is in *Jeremy*, when you go with *Job*, *whence you shall not return, into a land of darkness and the shadow of death, without any order and where the light is as darkness*: *ubi umbra mortis* saith *Hierome, et nullus ordo, sed sempiternus horror inhabitat*. Some, nay the most, and that warrantably, speak of fire and the company of tormented and tormentors: but here is figured no kind of light or society, what our ill dreams not seldom present, namely a solitude and yet no security. What purposeless journeyings, what unseen pursuings, what ambushes feared, what visages faintly seen and in part suspected, shall vex and scare poor souls nearly stript of their familiar raiment! Alone he shall find himself who but now talked with friends: houseless who lately sat.'

'Oh, some pages gone!' said Humphreys. 'Yes, it is imaginative; not very encouraging, though!', and he shuddered a little, for the words had brought back his dream.

'No, it isn't exactly,' the curate said slowly, looking at him. 'Perhaps it would have got more cheerful as it went on.'

'Perhaps it would,' answered Humphreys vaguely. 'Oh, by the way, Evans, couldn't you dine with me tonight? It would be kind.'

So that was settled. It was a relief to Humphreys, for the atmosphere of the house was becoming just a little oppressive to him, and he was not in the mood for another solitary evening. However, he would not have been condemned to solitude in any case, for later in the day a telegram arrived from George Rowland, the friend he was expecting, to ask if he might come that very afternoon [instead of two days later], and of course nothing could have been more welcome.

After luncheon, Humphreys was obliged to take the way he had gone the previous evening, through the fields and up the hill overlooking the valley. It is not clear how the thought came to him, but as he entered the field path, he found himself wondering why the post he had seen had been placed in the middle of one of the pastures – he remembered the spot exactly. The placing of the post may have been odd, but it was still odder to find that during the night it had been taken away so cleanly as to leave no mark. A labourer was not far off.

'Was there a black tarred post somewhere in this field by the path?' asked Humphreys.

No, that there wasn't, and as the man passed through the field twice a day or more, he could speak to it.

'Well, all right, thank you: my mistake,' said Humphreys and went on, wondering what further tricks his eyes proposed to play him. Two, no, three in one day so far, for he recollected the fancied figure in the porch: and on the top of that, the feeling that a hand was on his head the night before. Was he going to be a – well, a case for a brain specialist? There was nothing whatever in the history of his family to countenance such a fear, nor anything in his present physical condition. He felt as well, as unexcitable, as at any time of his life. No, it must be either an accumulation of coincidences or – what was that touching his arm? It might have been a branch, if he had not happened to be in the open field! Whatever it was, the effect was curious: it brought back the dream – he was beginning to think of it as the vision – of the evening before. The homely well known pasture seemed in a moment to widen into an illimitable grey expanse – an acute feeling of extreme loneliness and of being on a hopeless and aimless journey came over him and his whole being cried out for companionship and protection, and yet he felt that there was none, none whatever to be had: he was helpless in a world of hostile shadows. Nothing was interesting any more, nothing was or could be important, and for all that, there was an instant pressure of hurry and no time to stop and think. It was a bitterness of despair which could not, he said, be put into any human words, and he believes he sank down under it and cowered on the ground – fortunately not in sight of any passer-by – and here for how long he couldn't tell he wrestled for his life and his reason.

Of two things he felt convinced all the while: one was that this deadly fever came from someone outside himself, someone who was near to him then; the other that there was something which he ought to remember and could remember if the pressure [of dreadful images] on his brain would only relax for an instant! The only words he could summon were words of fear, that he had read that morning. They droned through his head incessantly, '*ubi umbra mortis et nullus ordo sed sempiternus horror inhabitat*'. Over and over again they came back and he felt himself being sucked away from the world of men, and indeed he does not see how he could have helped yielding to the strain that was on him, and giving up hope and reason if not life itself, had he not paused on the words *umbra mortis*. They brought to his mind in a moment the image of some lettering in a brass on a tomb – this is how he puts it – that he had been taken to see years before. '*Umbra mortis,*' he seemed to say to himself, 'to be sure, that was it – *etsi ambulavero.*' He raised his head and drew breath. 'Absurd,' he said again. 'Of course that was what I wanted. Dear me. Why couldn't I think of that before?' The strain was relaxed. He rose to his feet and looked about him: the field was its own familiar self again and the sun bright in the sky. An exaltation of spirit came upon him which he could hardly repress, and he does not know what surprises of laughter and singing he may have inflicted on casual hearers as he went home. [Upon his graver feelings there is no need to dwell]

The satisfaction he felt was complete and permanent: he [was sure now that even the bare unhoused spirit has nothing to fear] had a talisman now which could always [dispel the darkness] rout the influence that had been deliberately trying to kill his physical life and blind his mental eye. And soon he began to think what that influence could be. He had felt when he rose from the ground as if someone had hastily moved away, and that in anger. What more he thought, I do not think it necessary to set forth now.

[*new sheet*]

At eleven o'clock after a cheerful evening, the curate left Humphreys and his friend in the library and set off down the drive.

[*the rest of the sheet is blank*]

[*new sheet*]

It was a very cheerful trio that met at dinner. Humphreys was just in the mood to make an evening 'go'.

After the curate had left them, Rowland and Humphreys settled themselves in the library and the story we have heard came out.

'Well, of course,' Rowland said, 'if I hadn't seen something of you before you told me all this, I should have put it down to softening of the brain, but there isn't much wrong with you, John. What do you suppose is the reason for it yourself?'

'I can only be sure of one thing about it; that it comes from outside, and I'm rather driven to the supposition that somebody must be trying to frighten me out of my mind.'

'Oh *well*,' said Rowland, 'I can't see much in that idea. Who is there to do a thing like that, I mean? It's a very far-fetched way of managing the job.'

'Why, no doubt it would be simpler to take a shotgun, but if you come to think of it, this isn't such a very bad plan. If it succeeds no one can trace it to you, and if it doesn't, I suppose you're very much where you were. It isn't quite a new thing either; I was reading only the other day about a wizard sending a lot of spirits to plague a young woman.'

'Well, if you can find anybody whose interest it is to get you off the scenes and who practises secret arts, I'll accept your theory. Who's the heir-at-law?'

'Of this place? I don't know – nobody I ever saw. I can find out though. But, George, I doubt if you realise even now what a well-defined set of experiences it's been. First I see someone coming to meet me, and he turns out to be a post – and next day the post isn't there and never has been; then someone standing in the porch, and there's nobody there; then my dream in this room and the feeling a hand on my head – which I *know* wasn't only fancy; then seeing a tree out of the window where there wasn't one. Then next morning that funny little book turned up and set my thoughts going again. By the way, I was going to show it to you. It's on the table there – that little brown book – yes, that's it: it was page 69. You read it.'

[But it was not page] 'Are you sure you hadn't seen this before you fell asleep and had that dream?' said Rowland.

'Quite certain. I'd never opened the book before Evans showed it me today. And then there was that awful fright I had this afternoon in the field. All in twenty-four hours. And I tell you, if I hadn't got out of that sort of fit in the way I did, I'm quite sure I must have gone under altogether! No, it really is something altogether external to me. I'm not in the habit of think-ing about death and unhoused souls and those things.'

'It is odd, certainly,' said Rowland. 'Very odd. But, well, let's leave it at that for the present. I'm not sure what I think.'

They were in the library next day, Humphreys writing, Rowland exploring the shelves. Outside, the cheerful sound of the lawnmower made an agree-able accompaniment. Suddenly there was a pause in its whining, and voices were heard in eager conversation. ['Oh lor,' said a boy's voice a moment later, 'what ever is it] Rowland looked out and saw the two gardeners examining a small object which one of them was holding.

'Found something?' he called to them.

The head man looked up, touched his hat and advanced slowly to the window, still looking curiously at what he held.

'Good morning, sir,' he said. 'I just see this in the grass to one side of the mower. We should 'a broke it to pieces next turn.'

'What is it?' said Humphreys, who had come to the window.

'Well, Mr. Humphreys, that's the puzzle. Meself I should 'azzard the guess it was a child's plaything. Only for it bein' reely so very unsightly. But – well there – you take a look at it yourself, sir; that's the best plan. Then you'll be hable to form your own notion what it might be. Per'aps it's more of a fancy curio than anythink helse.'

With this verdict he handed the thing in. It was a small dirty tin box in which lay a very horrid little doll of black wax – roughly fashioned to look like a corpse. Round this was wound a strip of paper. They shook out the image and unwound the paper, and thereon was written:

'esto hic timor mortis'

[*about three or four lines left blank*]

was still waiting for an opinion. 'I suppose it is a fancy curio as you say. [said Humphreys when] I'll keep it and see if I can find an owner for it. Much obliged to you.' And as soon as the mowing machine had resumed work: 'Now then, George; doesn't this look like secret arts? What an infernal piece of spite. Did you ever hear of anything to touch it? I declare, if I can find who put that thing there, I'll . . .' He stamped about the room inarticulate with anger.

[I should say you had a very fair chance of finding who it was if you want to do that, Rowlands said.] 'Now come, Johnny, do you really believe that anyone can give you the jumps by leaving dolls about on the front lawn?'

'Well, I don't know,' said Humphreys, stopping. 'It's pretty plain at least that someone thought they could. Isn't it?'

'Yes, perhaps they did. But—

—and also that

[*manuscript ends*]

Marcilly-le-Hayer

THE OTHER STORY might perhaps be considered a variation on the same theme: no doubt it was suggested by an incident as the first. It was told as a personal experience of the narrator's. He said:

I was travelling [a good many years ago] in France and found myself at a place called Moulins. I went into a curiosity shop [in a street] not far off the Hotel de Ville to inquire the price of a drawing I had noticed in the window. The man asked more than I wanted to give so I began looking at other things. There were a few old books, all totally uninteresting to me; but, as it turned out, there was nothing else in the shop that I cared in the least to acquire and so by way of doing something to justify the trouble I had given, I bought five or six of the smallest of these books.

Next day I went by train to Troyes [Nevers] and when I was tired of looking out of the window I opened my handbag and took out at random one of my purchases. It was a [n odd] volume of an old novel called *Caroline de Lichtenfeld*: the sort of book that is rarely disturbed from any resting place it may have found, by me at any rate: for all I know it may be a standard work.

I began at the beginning and turned over forty [odd] pages or so: the story made very little progress. Then my eye was attracted by some building we were passing, and I studied the landscape for two or three miles. After that, I returned to my book and noted that I had reached page 43 and was in the middle of a dialogue which ran thus:

'*Où descendez-vous?*'

'À l'Hôtel des Ambassadeurs.'

'Bon,' dit-il, 'vous avez sans doute commandé une chambre?'

'Ah, non,' dis-je, 'je n'y avais pas même songé. Mais cela s'arrangera sans doute. La ville ne serait pas en fête ces jours-ci?'

Il haussa les épaules. 'Qui sait?' fit-il. 'Parlons d'autre chose: Vous la connaissez, je pense, la ville de [Nevers]?'

'Je n'ai fait que passer par là il y a dix ans.'

At this point I turned over the page and at the same time glanced up. My eye fell on my opposite neighbour who was an elderly lady, stout, and wearing a slight black moustache and a highly determined expression. She was not otherwise interesting. I resumed my reading: the words were curiously appropriate.

'Vous regardiez votre vis-à-vis,' continua-t-il.

'Eh oui! Qu'y a-t-il de singulier en cela.'

'En effet, très peu de chose, seulement, [vous la verrez égorgés ce soir] savez-vous où elle demeure?'

'[Monsieur! ne parlez pas de la sorte] Comment donc? – moi qui la vois pour la première fois.'

'Eh bien. Je vous le dirai. C'est à Marcilly-le-Hayer sur la place. La maison à trois pignons.'

'[Vraiment?] C'est [bien] possible: mais pour vrai vous dire elle me paraît pas bien intéressante.'

'A very long-winded dialogue this,' I thought, 'not much concentration about it'; and I turned over a leaf or two to see where we were getting to. I found that the personage who had volunteered the information about the woman in the book was now disgorging more – in fact was giving her whole biography. She had been a labourer's daughter in the village of Marcilly-le-Hayer. Her good looks had attracted the notice of a middle-aged man who owned a good deal of property in the place, a M. Giraud – Émile Giraud (a name which to me seemed unaccountably familiar). He was, said the book, a thoroughly reputable, honest, and amiable person: and his love for the girl – Eugeiné Dupont – was sincere. The match was of course an extremely advantageous one for her. She had no lover of her own rank whom she was in the least inclined to favour, and the marriage took place. [Eighteen months afterward] After nearly three years of what seemed to all their acquaintances a very happy married life, M. Giraud disappeared from Marcilly leaving absolutely no trace. [Like many country people of his class] He used to leave a not inconsiderable sum of ready money in the house towards the end of each week to pay his men. It was on a Friday that he was found to be missing, and the money was gone too. The widow was obliged to procure a further supply from the branch of the *Société Genérale* in the village. She felt the loss of her husband acutely and never married again.

'*Société Genérale*,' I said to myself: 'I didn't think that existed in the eighteenth century.'

But, said the book, in continuation, if any one were to go to Marcilly-le-Hayer and call at the house with the three gables, and ask [to see] the mistress, and ask her what she keeps under the pavement in the further corner of the stable, he would then find out whether she was interesting or not.

'It would be a very impertinent question to ask anyone,' I thought, and with that I put the book away, and took another.

The train to Troyes was very full, and I realized to my disgust, before my journey was over, that a large cattle-show was going on there. I had very great difficulty in finding any room at all: at last I was accommodated with a bed in a rather second rate establishment called the Hotel Terminus. The only part of this place which had any pretension to novelty was the name which was palimpsested over the door. I amused myself by deciphering the old sign, still partly visible underneath: it read 'Hotel des Ambassadeurs'.

After exploring Troyes, I found I had a day or two to spare, and I studied the map of the department. There I found, as you might find, the name of Marcilly-le-Hayer occupying a very prominent place in the midst of the uplands which no railway touches. I believe – I say I believe – that I had forgotten all about the story in my book in the days which had passed since I read it. But I now recollected it, and this, combined with the fact that there seemed to be some interesting buildings in and near Marcilly, determined me to go there. I bicycled thither – a laborious ride – and arrived late in the afternoon. There was an inn on the *Place* which was quite satisfactory and I had, of course, come prepared to spend a night there. Immediately opposite to the window of my room was a house with three gables.

In the evening, I had some talk with the people of the house, and asked if there were any interesting features in the town. I was told of a very fine carved chimney-piece 'chez Mme. Giraud'. And where did she live? I naturally asked (we were at the door of the inn). 'Straight opposite,' said my informants, pointing to the house with the three gables.

I pondered and pondered: but no light came. The persistence of names of [*unreadable word*] in a place like Marcilly must be a marked feature. One other question was inevitable. What, I asked, was Mme. Giraud's maiden name? 'Dupont, Monsieur. Eugeiné Dupont.'

When I got back to my luggage at Troyes, I looked again at the volume of *Caroline de Lichtenfeld*. It was a defective copy, pp 33-80 were absent – had evidently never been bound up in it. On the flyleaf in a feminine hand was the name: Émile Giraud.

The Game of Bear

TWO ELDERLY PERSONS sat reading and smoking in the library of a country house after tea on an afternoon in the Christmas holidays, and outside a number of the children of the house were playing about. They had turned out all the lights and were engaged in the dreadful game of 'Bear' which entails stealthy creepings up and down staircases and along passages, and being leapt upon from doorways with loud and hideous cries. Such a cry, and an answering scream of great poignancy, were heard just outside the library door. One of the two readers – an uncle of the young things who were disporting themselves there – leapt from his chair and dashed the door open. 'I will *not* have you doing that!' he shouted (and his voice was vibrant with real anger); 'do you hear? Stop it at once. I can't stand it. You – you – Why can't you find something else? What?... Well, I don't care, I can't put up with it... Yes, very well, go and do it somewhere where I can't hear it.' He subsided into a growl and came back to his chair; but his friend saw that his nerves were really on edge, and ventured something sympathetic. 'It's all very well,' said the uncle, 'but I can *not* bear that jumping out and screaming. Stupid of me to fly out like that, but I couldn't help it. It reminded me of all that business – *you* know.'

'Well,' said the friend after a short pause, 'I'm really not sure that I do. Oh!' he added, in a more concerned tone, 'unless you mean Purdue.' 'That's it,' said the uncle. There was another silence, and then the friend said, 'Really, I'm not sorry that happened just now, for I never did hear the rights of the Purdue business. Will you tell me exactly what happened?'

'I don't know,' said the uncle: 'I *really* don't know, if I ought. But I think I will. Not just now, though. I'll tell you what: if it's fine tomorrow we'll take a walk in the morning; and tonight I'll think over the whole affair and get it straight in my mind. I *have* often felt some-body besides me ought to know about it, and all his people are out of the way now.'

The next day *was* fine, and the two men walked out to a hill at no real distance, which was known as Windmill Hill. The mill that had topped it was gone but a bit of the brick foundation remained and afforded a seat from which a good stretch of pleasant wild country could be seen. Here then Mr. A and Mr. B sat down on the short, dry grass with their backs against the warm brick wall, and Mr. A produced a little bundle of folded paper and a pocket-book which he held up before Mr. B as an indication that he was prepared not only to tell the story to which he stood pledged, but to back it with documentary evidence.

'I brought you here,' he said, 'partly because you can see Purdue's place. There!' He pointed with his stick to a wooded slope which might be three or four miles off. In the wood was a large clearing and in the clearing stood a mansion of yellow stone with a portico, upon which, as it chanced, the sun was shining very brilliantly, so that the house stood out brightly against the background of dark trees.

'Where shall I begin?' said Mr. A.

'Why,' said Mr. B, 'I'll tell you exactly how little I know, and then you can judge. You and Purdue, you remember, were senior to me at school and at Cambridge. He went down after his three years; you stayed up for part of a fourth, and then I began to see more of you: before that, I was more with people of my own year, and, beyond a fair number of meetings with Purdue at breakfast and lunch and so on, I never saw much of him – not nearly as much as I should have liked, in fact. Then I remember your going to stay with him – there, I suppose' (pointing with his stick) – 'in the Easter Vac, and – well, that was the last of it.'

'Just so,' said Mr. A; 'I didn't come up again, and you and I practically didn't meet till a year or two back, did we? Though you were a better correspondent than any of my other Cambridge friends. Very well, then, there it is: I was never inclined to write the story down in a letter, and the long and short of it is that you have never heard it: but you do know what sort of man Purdue was, and how fond I was of him.

'When I stayed with him over there, the place was his only home, and yet it wasn't his. He was an orphan and practically adopted by his uncle and aunt who were quite old childless people. There had been another uncle who had married a village woman, and had one daughter. That couple were very odd squalid creatures, and died off, I think from drink, but the daughter survived and went on living in a cottage in the next parish. She wasn't left destitute by any means in the way of money; but she lived all by herself, and I think always with a sense of injury upon her that she wasn't noticed by the county families and such. The remaining uncle and aunt had been kind enough to her and at one time used to invite her over to their place, but she had a very difficult temper and was always on the look-out for slights and injuries, and at last they gave up the effort to be cordial, and saw no more of her. It wasn't to be expected after that that they would pass on the property to her (it was entirely at their disposition, to do what they liked with it) and no more they did. When they died it went to Purdue, about a year before his own death, that was.

'So there he was, settled, you would say, into a happy life: he'd been brought up in the country and knew all the neighbourhood, places and people, very well; and was interested in farming and forestry and prepared to make himself useful. That last visit I paid him was particularly delightful: he was on such excellent terms with everybody in the village. 'Master Henry' to all of them, and just as well liked by the neighbours in the larger houses. I think the only fly in the ointment was that woman Caroline Purdue. She took to attending our parish church and we used to find her in our pew every Sunday morning. She didn't say much to Henry, but all the service time she sat and looked at him through her veil. A short stout redfaced woman she was, with black hair and snappy black eyes. She used to wait in the church-yard till we had gone out and then set off on her three mile walk home. She gave me the creeps, I couldn't say why; I suppose there was a flavour of concentrated hostility about her.

'Henry was anxious of something of the same kind. His lawyer told me after his death that he had tried through them to get her to accept a handsome addition to her income and the gift of a suitable house wherever she liked in some other part of the county. They said she was as impracticable a woman as they had ever come across: she just sat and smiled broadly at them and said she was quite comfortable where she was, and didn't want to move out of reach of her cousin Henry. "But wouldn't it be more lively and amusing for you to be in some place where there's more to be seen – theatres, and that sort of thing?" No, oh no, she had plenty of things to occupy herself with: and – again – she didn't want to move out of reach of her cousin Henry.

'"But, but: your cousin Henry, you know; he's likely to be a busy man – travelling about a good deal, and occupied with his men friends: it isn't probable that he'll be able to see much of you." Oh, she was quite content to take her chance of that: they would often be meeting when he was riding about, and no doubt there would be times when he was alone at the Court, and she could look in on him. "Ah well, that's just the point. Are you sure that Mr. Purdue will welcome that?" "Yes, to be sure, why not?" "Well, we have reason to think that he doesn't wish it." Oh indeed! and pray had he commissioned these gentlemen to tell his own cousin that he had cast her off? A nice thing for a relative to hear, that her own flesh and blood preferred not to have anything to do with her. What had she done, she should like to know, to be treated in that way?

'There was more to the same effect, and the storm rose quickly, culminating in a short burst of tears, and a rapid stumping out of the room. The gentlemen who had been conducting the interview were left looking at each other and feeling they had not done much to advance their client's wishes. But at least Miss Purdue left off her attendance at our church, and, we gathered, did not favour any other place of worship in its stead.

'She was not more popular with the rest of the community than with Henry.

'How is the rest of this to be told? I have here some papers which bear on it, but they are fragmentary, of course. When Henry Purdue was alone in that big house he did what at other times was rather foreign to his habits – confided his feelings to paper. Here are some entries.'

'Letter from CP' (Caroline Purdue, of course). 'Infernal woman. May she come and see me and talk over this painful matter. No, she mayn't.'

[*manuscript ends*]

Speaker Lenthall's Tomb

I

FIFTY YEARS carries us back to the times of the Oxford Movement, the first rage of the Gothic Revival and the restorations of many of the finest churches in England, restorations whose results were often of the most deplorable kind. Pugin was at the head of the Gothicists; Wailes, Willement and Hardman were trying their prentice hands upon the rediscovery of the art of glass painting with very indifferent success; Newman had joined the Roman Church, and many other interesting names were in men's mouths, of which I could tell you more if I happened to know anything about them.

Among the many beautiful country towns in the southern shires, few are more complete or fascinating than the town of Burford in Oxon. It is very much out of the world; there is hardly a new house in it, and there are several exceptionally fine old ones, as well as a magnificent parish church. To Burford it was that Cromwell's Speaker, Lenthall, retired: there he built his beautiful home, now almost a ruin, and there he died and was buried. His house must be very shortly described. It is of stone, with a surprisingly rich front, and a chapel attached thereto by a covered walk, possessing one of the last rose windows ever made in England before this century. Texts are carved and painted on the walls, and there are indications that the fittings must at one time have been sumptuous. But the roof is gone and the place a shattered ruin.

But fifty years ago things were not quite so bad, though even then the chapel had been long disused. The house was inhabited, and was perfectly sound, and well-furnished, even to richness. It had passed away from the Lenthalls to the not less ancient and reputable line of the Claxtons, once considerable people in Suffolk; but they too had left off living there, and it was now held on lease by a rich clergyman, Mr. Cave, who had some sons and daughters, and in the evening of his days had retired from active duty and brought his family and his library to Burford where he found existence tolerable enough. A rich clergyman, said I, and one considerably learned in ancient matters, and with a strong turn for Gothic architecture as it was then understood.

What was more natural than that he should work upon the feelings of the rector – an old friend – and lead very handsomely a subscription list for the restoring of St. Mary's Church? He had been little more than a year in the place when the Movement was fairly started; and now we find Mr. Cave, young Mr. Cave, Miss Cave, Mr. Eldon the rector, and Mr. Green the architect, a disciple of Pugin's, conferring upon the necessary alterations, after dinner and a long day spent in and about the Church.

'The galleries and pews must go, Eldon; that is clear enough: the organ shifts into the north transept. The nave is reseated with pitch pine: the monuments ranged along the walls on each side. I do wish we could get rid of that hideous erection of Speaker Lenthall's. It fills up the whole of the north choir aisle, and we might have arranged such a pretty little morning chapel there for the daily service.'

The erection alluded to is indeed large, but of alabaster and other marbles, and we do not nowadays call it hideous. It is covered with emblematical statuettes of virtues and arts and is really extremely imposing.

'Yes, my dear Cave, that is a block, to be sure: miserable debased work, one wonders that in any age it could have been thought to possess the least merit.'

'Well, can nothing be done? Could you get a faculty or whatever it is to remove it?' said young Cave (aged some three and twenty and now at Trinity, Oxford).

'Ah, my dear sir, the faculty might be got easily enough,' said Mr. Green the architect. 'The only question is, are there surviving relatives of Speaker Lenthall's, and can their consent to the removal of the monument be obtained? If so, all is easy.'

'Really? Well, that sounds very promising. There can hardly be any Lenthalls left, I should think, eh, father?'

'Ask the rector, my boy; *I* should hardly imagine it, either?'

'Well, Harry, I think you may set your mind at ease on that point. We certainly have a Lenthall in Burford, but in Burford Almshouse. But she is nearer ninety than eighty and it has been ascertained, I believe with certainty, that she is the last of the name. One can hardly doubt that a five pound note would be more of an object to her than fifty Speaker's monuments.'

'You are clear, Green, that we must get her consent to the removal in due form?' said Mr. Cave. 'What I mean is that if there was likely to be any difficulty with her – if she is doting or obstinate or anything of that kind, – we might easily wait for the sand to run. It can't in nature be long before the poor old thing is out of the way.'

'Yes, Mr. Cave; if there are any survivors, their written consent must be obtained. The law is very clear on that point.'

'Well, Cave,' said the rector, 'I propose that Green and you and Harry and I go down in force tomorrow morning and call on Mrs. Elizabeth Lenthall with a document ready prepared, to which she can set her name. I fancy, do you know, that you might have some time to wait if you put off the matter till she is dead. She is as upright as a dart and certainly she has a will of her own. I don't think she is on speaking terms with any of her neighbours in the almshouses. There has been a terrible feud about the pump, I understand, though I don't know the rights of it. Green had better bring his drawings with him, hadn't he, so as to impress the old lady with the extent of the improvement which would result from the clearing away of her ancestor's tomb?'

'I think,' said the architect, 'if it would help matters at all, Mr. Eldon, I could easily work some of the statuettes into a reredos for the Chapel. And of course we would have a sketch of the monument done before it was taken down, and a slab laid in the floor. The Speaker's effigy could be kept in the vestry, could it not?'

'O yes, I think that could be managed easily enough. But really the whole thing is in such wretched taste that I would sooner make a clean sweep of it myself.'

'To be sure, so would I,' said Mr. Green. 'Perhaps my suggestions had better be reserved to form the basis of a compromise; if that proves necessary.'

'What sort of person was Lenthall, papa?' asked Miss Mary Cave. 'Was he a fine character at all?'

'Well no, my dear,' said her father. 'By all accounts he was something of a trimmer in his later days and a very hard customer in money matters. They say he did most bitterly repent his share in King Charles's death. But you should look him up in Clarendon. I'm afraid I am no authority on the Civil War period.'

'I suppose it's very bad taste on my part,' said the young lady after a moment, 'but I must say I always have admired that monument a good deal.'

'My dear! That gaudy half-classical nondescript erection! I always thought you had some sort of perception of what was good in art,' said her brother.

'Well, Harry, I said I supposed it was my bad taste and I daresay it is. But you must allow that the materials are really beautiful marbles, and the colouring and some of the modelling is very clever. Besides, I never could see the reason in refusing to admire a thing because it is not of a particular period or style. Surely there may be beautiful things made in more styles than one. I remember quite well when you used to admire St. Paul's tremendously, Harry, before you went to Oxford.'

'Yes, precisely: before I went to Oxford, and before I ever looked at a Gothic Church, and before I had made any attempt at educating my tastes and before two or three other things of equal importance, perhaps I did like St. Paul's. All I can say is I think differently now.'

'Well, perhaps in thirty or forty years you may be able to find room to admire St. Paul's as well as Gothic Churches. However, I must go – Goodnight, Harry.' And when she had said the other goodnights Miss Cave departed, Mr. Green's eyes following her with something of pity and amusement.

A declamation from Harry in the style peculiar to his University upon the wonderful character of female taste followed, which it is hardly necessary to transcribe: and soon after that the gentlemen dispersed also.

Next morning, they met again at Mr. Cave's house, and proceeded, with drawings and documents, in an imposing procession to the Burford Almshouses founded by Lenthall's daughter who had married a Claxton, in 1695. The houses are of the familiar type – a long row of cottages, one storey high, date and inscription in a pediment in the centre, a garden behind: her house and a share in the garden and pump belonging to each inmate. Mr. Green mourned melodiously over the design of the cottages and pointed out how far preferable to this would have been a Gothic *hospitium* with a chapel and statue of a patron saint.

'Well, Green,' said Mr. Cave, 'who knows but we may see that here yet: the endowment of this place is pretty good, and a few years' accumulation would go a long way towards supplying what you want. But that must wait until we have done with the Church.'

'Here is Mrs. Lenthall's house – the one at the end,' interposed the rector. 'Perhaps, as I be treasurer, pretty well, I had better begin the ball, Cave?'

The old lady was a fine and dignified object as she sat in her armchair by the fire, in the white cap and blue tippet which were *de rigueur* for the inheritrices of Dame Claxton's bounty. She rose on the entrance of the four gentlemen, and it was plain that the rector had not been exaggerating when he said that she was as upright as a dart. She had fine dark eyes, rather thick white eyebrows and strongly cut features. The only thing that singled out the functions of her parlour was a small oval portrait of Speaker Lenthall over the mantelpiece. It was by a good hand, and showed something of the strength of character and will which had reappeared in his descendant's face.

'We have come, Mrs. Lenthall,' said Mr. Green, 'upon a matter of business which we hope may turn out as well to your advantage as to that of the parish at large. I think you know Mr. Cave who lives at the Hall. This is his son whom I daresay you also know, and this is Mr. Green, the gentleman who has been good enough to undertake the important work of restoring our beautiful Parish Church to something of its ancient comeliness.'

'I am very happy, gentlemen, to see you,' said the old lady, in a strong and rather masculine voice. 'If you will be at the pains to find chairs for yourselves I shall be obliged to you: for I am rather past the age when bustling about suits me.'

There was a general murmur of 'Oh pray don't think of moving, Mrs. Lenthall,' and the four chairs were shuffled into position and occupied.

'The fact is, Mrs. Lenthall,' the rector went on, 'that we are in a difficulty as regards the large monument to Speaker Lenthall that stands in the chancel aisle of St. Mary's. It was no doubt considered a very beautiful structure in its day, and must have been a very costly one. But knowledge, we know, grows, and we have come to see in our more enlightened days that such memorials to the dead have much that is unsightly and unfitting about them.' Mrs. Lenthall fixed her eyes upon Mr. Eldon who coughed and went on.

'Now, Mr. Green has pointed out to us that were that monument removed from its position, we should be enabled to put up a most beautiful little chapel in which the beautiful liturgy of our Church might be daily said. And he has told us that in order to be able to obtain leave from our Bishop to destr . . . to remove the monument, we must first obtain the consent of the relations of the person who is buried there. I know, for you have often told me, that you are the last Lenthall now surviving – and I am sorry to think it . . .' Mrs. Lenthall bowed slightly. 'And we have made bold this morning to come and ask you if you would not be so kind as to put your name to this document which we have prepared, giving your consent to the dem . . . the alteration which we propose. Mr. Cave has been so good as to say that he will see that a sum of money shall be paid to you in consideration of your goodness, and I am confident that beyond that you will feel some satisfaction in having done a service to the parish in which you have been respected for so many years. Now, if you will just think it over quietly and look at this drawing which Mr. Green has prepared, showing the great advantage of the change, we shall be much indebted to you.'

Mrs. Lenthall examined the drawing for a minute or two. ''Tis your work then, young gentleman?' she suddenly said to the architect – so suddenly that he jumped.

'Yes, my good friend,' he said on recovering his presence of mind, 'and you see, do you not, what a handsome chapel for Matins will be the result of the destruction of that hideous pile that your ancestor erected.'

'That is sufficient, thank you kindly, young man,' said Mrs. Lenthall; 'it is no good trade to speak of the dead in that kind. Butcher Green's bills were paid regular by my grandmother, for I have them in the chest; and Lenthall's money went some way, I reckon, to prentice Butcher Green's great-grandson for a builder.'

There is no denying that Mr. Green was taken a good deal aback by this sally: he was of a burning red colour for some minutes, and no word escaped him. The two elder gentlemen were amused, if rather sorry for him. But Harry Cave who had rather taken up the architect was exceedingly angry.

'I really think you might keep a civil tongue in your head, my good woman,' he said viciously. 'We are only anxious to do our best for the Church, and you have a very plain question to answer – whether you object or do not object to Speaker Lenthall's tomb being destroyed.'

Mrs. Lenthall looked at him and smiled to herself; and then, turning to Mr. Cave, she said, 'Ah, sir, time flies, don't it! Master Harry's time for going to College will come soon enough, and maybe he'll turn out a sharp lad at his works yet. 'Tis not easy to tell with the young: but I warrant you he'll make a learner. But now, gentlemen, I have to answer you in regard of my great-grandfather's monument; and I would be glad not to send you away disappointed. Yet the matter is thus. I never will give my consent while I am a living woman to the touching of the Speaker's tomb in Burford Chancel. I have lived to hear it praised for a fine piece all my days, and I cannot tell but after I go, there will come those that will cry it up again. And, Rector, I say to you in all sadness, if there comes breaking down of Lenthall tombs when I am dead, Lenthalls will see to it and trouble will be heard. For the Speaker needs to rest quiet, and the Speaker was a strong man: and I am not very sure if Mr. Cave will not hear more of him than he thinks.'

Mr. Cave laughed quietly and said, 'Well, well, Mrs. Lenthall, I think I will take the risk of that.'

But Harry was still fuming, and not to be held in.

'All I can say is that you, Madam Lenthall, may be very proud of your ancestor the Speaker, but most of us would rather not have such an old ratter and trimmer in the family. And another thing I can tell you is that it will give me the greatest pleasure to knock that hideous tomb to bits as soon as – as I can do it.'

'Sit you there a moment, Master Harry,' said the old woman whom this speech seemed to have touched very nearly. 'You would say, as soon as I am in my grave, you will knock the Speaker's marble tomb to bits – the tomb that he had men from Italy to make, and paid them four hundred pounds for it – you that lives in his house and sleeps, I daresay, in his chamber. Well, you may begin it: I daresay you will. But you will not carry it through: not one of you will go through with the business; and you were well advised to look to yourself in the doing. Now, gentlemen, I will wish you a good morning, for I am not well in myself and such talk is not good for an old heart.'

The gentlemen took back their document and their drawings to the Lenthall house, and found themselves reduced to leave the Morning Chapel out of their programme for the present.

Miss Mary Cave paid a long visit to Miss Lenthall in the afternoon, and reported on her return that the old lady seemed very weak, and still much incensed against Harry; whom his sister took to task, but did not convince that he had been wanting in tact. This was on Thursday in March. On Saturday Mrs. Lenthall died; on Monday she was buried. Harry's spirits were only superficially damped, for he went back to Oxford for the Easter Term, and the plans for the Morning Chapel were completed by Mr. Green.

II

It is now the Long Vacation: the faculty for the removal of Lenthall's tomb has arrived. Harry is to superintend the destruction of that abomination of desolation. Miss Cave is still regretful and so are some of the inhabitants of Burford. Several farmers have driven their wives in to see the last of the monument, and Mr. Green has made a sketch of it, with a good deal of inaccuracy in detail, and has succeeded in making it appear as ugly and clumsy as he believed it to be. Enough.

The fated morning arrived. Harry and the workmen were round the monument, selecting the best point of attack: the headman suggested that the best way would be to get out one of the corner columns supporting the canopy; then the canopy would fall, and help to break up the effigy and the actual tomb below. So Harry was just loosening the base of the said column with the thin end of a mattock when smash! – down came the statuette of Envy which stood at the top of it, entwined with snakes, and took him on the shoulder in its descent. He could not get up and had to be helped. Evidently he was in a good deal of pain – collar bone broken and a cut on the head. No more mason's work for Harry just at present, was the doctor's verdict, and someone gave him an arm home. The masons meanwhile were examining the place whence the figure had fallen. It was a curious circumstance that it should have come down, for it was fixed on a strong iron dowel running up into it, and this did not seem to have rusted in the least. At any rate all the other figures were quite firm.

Harry Cave was so anxious to see the destruction of the tomb that the clerk of the works made no objection to putting it off for a week or two, as the men had plenty to do in other parts of the building. Harry spent a few days in bed and [an]other few in comparative quiet for him – interrupted by somewhat acrid disputes with his sister about the advisability of persisting in the design of the Morning Chapel. Pugin and Green were quoted on one side, and only Mrs. Lenthall and sentimental considerations on the other. Harry usually came off with flying colours, and these little battles aided him greatly in recovering his strength. It wanted now two days to the time when he had been told he might go to work again, and he was in great spirits at dinner and, I grieve to say, rather offensively exultant towards his sister. Bedtime arrived. Harry went to bed; but did not go to sleep very immediately after blowing out his candle. The room was rather light, only a blind being drawn over the window, and he was a little restless.

However, he turned his face to the wall, and composed himself by reflecting upon the improvements in ritual which he wished to see introduced at Burford. Suddenly he began to hear a faint sweeping or rustling noise approaching over the carpet. He turned half over – nothing to be seen – the room being, as I said, very fairly light by reason of the strong moonlight outside. It came to the side of the bed. Then a pause: next a very slight stretching of the bedclothes over his legs toward the outside of the bed, much as if a kitten had jumped up. Harry not much affected by this, but on the alert. The next phenomenon was the touch, on the bare back of his neck, of something bristly – so much so that it pricked the skin. He whipped over in the bed, thoroughly frightened, and had just time to see a very strange object against the white window blind before it disappeared. It was long and sharply crooked in the midst: he could only describe it by saying that it was like a very long finger covered thickly with short hairs. He was out of bed in a second, had a candle lighted, and searched the room thoroughly. The door was fastened and the window shut, and there was no sign of man or beast in any corner. For the rest of that night Harry read the *Tracts for the Times*.

He kept his experience to himself next day, feeling dimly that it was a point in favour of his sister's view of the question, he could hardly tell why, or how he came to connect it with Lenthall's tomb, but that he did so connect it, he couldn't deny.

He went down to the Church in the morning and had a talk with the mason about tomorrow's job. The mason showed him with pride the rope ready, attached to the pillar of the canopy, and pointed out that the fall of the heavy marble transoms would so effectually break up the Speaker that Miss Mary could construct a rockery from his remains. This was after Harry's own heart and he retailed it at luncheon. Mary was really very nearly in tears over the matter. Mr. Cave chaffed her good naturedly but was a little sorry himself. Mr. Green who arrived that day was suave and instructive but distinctly triumphant. Miss Cave spent the evening in cleaning up the portrait of Speaker Lenthall, which old Mrs. Lenthall had presented to her on the day when she had visited her for the last time. The gentlemen were in their rooms by eleven o'clock p.m.

It is very fortunate for Harry Cave that his father sat up late in his bedroom over a bundle of papers which had to be sorted. Otherwise he would not have heard a choking and crowing sound rising into a scream, which came from Harry's

[*page missing*]

bed clothes; and then straight upon that two sharp points had been plunged into his neck. He had cried out and clutched with his hands at the spot only to feel something hairy, which pricked his fingers and seemed to melt away under them: the room, searched as strictly as possible, yielded no evidence whatever.

But this adventure daunted him completely: it became clear that he was now as much frightened at the thought of destroying Lenthall's monument as he had been eager to do it. The scheme was dropped and Miss Cave triumphed. She bore it well. At the moment when Harry detailed to her the circumstances of his adventure she was engaged still in cleaning the lower half of the Lenthall portrait. Suddenly she started: 'What in the world is this on the table in the picture? Why, it's an enormous spider.' And so it was: painted there no doubt as the emblem of industry or avarice or both.

Merfield House

To William Chatteris Esq., Potton, Bedfordshire.

Sir,

It was in the month of March last that you put into my
hands a mass of papers and MSS belonging to the late
John Stedman of Merfield Hall, Beds, and requested me to
go through them and extract what I could relative to his
experiences in that house, of which he left you the heir,
and to the death of his friend Mr. Haydon there. I have
happily come upon a full narrative of those occurrences
in Mr. Stedman's own handwriting, signed by himself
and attested by his butler and housekeeper for the
time being, and not impossibly intended for the human
eye. I think the narrative will satisfy your curiosity
as far as is possible in a case where the attendant
circumstances are so mysterious. I enclose the MS
without further comment.

Yrs etc.

Henry Wiggins

John Stedman MS
First Sheet?

IN 1849 MY HALF BROTHER Charles Horsley, then a man of 37, came
into possession of Merfield Hall in the county of Bedfordshire. The Home
and Park and a sufficient income of some 3000£ a year were left to him by his
uncle, with whom he had always been a favourite. The two were much alike
in temperament: saturnine, cynical and secretive, and not a little inclined to
seclude themselves. I very well remember, when invited to spend Christmas
at Merfield as a boy (William having as usual preceded me by some days),
how for hours at a time I was left entirely alone to wander about the house
and grounds while uncle and nephew, closeted in the library, were elaborat-
ing their schemes – so at least I thought – to avenge themselves on a society
which despised them.

Before I relate the first incident which led me to view them and their
proceedings with something like terror, I must devote a few lines to describing the house as it was in my day. It dated from about 1690, and was a fine
solid building of red brick, 2 or 3 storied (whichever you call it) with a
pediment and round windows pierced in it, 2 wings projecting slightly. The
windows large with many panes and conspicuous white wooden framings;
a niche with scallopshell head in each wing; a tiled roof and good chimneys.
Within, a large hall, paved in squares of black and white marble. Fine staircases and many rooms, most of them, when I knew them first, unoccupied.
My uncle's room was in the left wing, towards the west, and Charles was
always put next door to him. I was as invariably banished to the East wing
and put in a room between two empty ones – one a disused bathroom with
the bath in it cobwebbed over – the other a bedroom with a few books.
The garden was pleasant with hedges of yew and hornbeam, and fair trees
– elm and lime. The Park had an elm avenue and an ornamental sheet of
water with a Fishing Temple – such as the last generation delighted in. The
county handbook said of this one that it had been built by the ingenious
Mr. Essex in the Gothick Taste and was much admired by all curiosi. As
far as I can recollect, some of its details were borrowed from Peterboro'
Cathedral and some from King's College Chapel in Cambridge, which the
architect was then engaged upon.

But to my stay. I was passing the library windows one morning on my way to the water to fish when I heard the two voices within laughing – a pleasurable laugh of anticipation. This was so unusual a thing that I could not for the life of me help stopping to try and catch a glimpse of the cause. I had only time to see my uncle and brother pushing away the heavy library table from its usual place in the middle of the room, when the latter caught sight of me standing outside. He came hastily to the window, and with an angry look at me drew down the blinds. I had expected as much for both were exceedingly jealous of an overlooking eye, and walked slowly on, puzzling over the laughter I had heard, when I heard behind me a peculiar shrill cry with a sort of dying sound to it as of a shout carried on a high blustering wind. I had never heard anything in the least like it, so fearfully lonely and desperate a tone was there in it, and I stopped in extreme fear. At the same time – I am sure of what I am saying – a sudden shade seemed to run over the whole landscape – it seemed to me like a shudder of all the Nature round me – and it went across to the South-West.

I was cold with terror and hardly knew what I did, but an instinct seemed to tell me to run to the library. I rushed to the window – which a few minutes before had been darkened to me. The blind was gone – torn down or pulled up, I knew not which – and I saw the two inside lying on the floor. As quickly as I could I got to the door, some of the servants following, but, though I am sure it was not locked, I felt for a moment some resistance from within to my efforts. At last, between us we got it open. It flew back – I had not thought I was pushing so hard – and after a moment's hesitation, whether it was timorousness or horror or something further that threw us back, we all rushed into the room.

My brother was already on his knees, white and shaking, and was trying to bring round my uncle who lay as he had fallen with his head against the wall, completely stunned. Suddenly, he too sat up and looked round at us, then, realising the situation and seeing the servants in the room, he staggered to his feet and would have us all be gone. I shall not set down here the terms of his command, but they were most urgent, and, seeing he was himself again, we had all nearly left the room when he called me back, and, clutching my arm: 'An experiment,' he said, speaking very fast and low; 'a scientific experiment, you know, went wrong, Johnny, and your brother

Charles and I might have been killed. Think of that! But all's right now and it's not worth making a fuss about. Don't get tattling with the servants about it and making mischief. Now go about your business; you needn't be afraid we shall try any more dangerous experiments.' And he smiled in a ghastly fashion, with a glance at Charles who was still shaking like an aspen and clutching the table.

[*manuscript ends*]

[*Second beginning*]

It was when I was an undergraduate at Cambridge that the only psychic experience of my life (for so out of deference to the taste of the day I must call it) befell me. I have been asked to detail it for the benefit of the Society, and I will proceed without further delay to do so.

I shall have to go some way back in order to give you the complete chain of events which led up to the main incident of my story. You probably know – in fact I am sure you know – something of the general outline. This much you have probably heard: that a house and park in Northamptonshire were left to me some time ago by a person quite unconnected with me or family, whom I had succeeded in obliging in some way; and that though a year and a half has elapsed since the bequest came to me, the place still remains unoccupied and, indeed, unless matters alter considerably, I see every likelihood of its remaining in that condition.

The old gentleman who left me the property in question was a Mr. William Stedman, well known in his day as a book collector and student. His hobby was the Elizabethan and Jacobean drama – in this department of literature he stood high: but beyond editing a book for the Roxburghe Club, of which he was a member, and writing frequently to *Notes and Queries*, he never produced anything, and his magnum opus, *Studies in English Drama*, lies still in MS among his papers at Merfield House. Of his early life I can tell little or nothing. He was a younger son, and had succeeded to the property on the death of his brother's wife, who followed her husband within a very short time. This couple, short as had been their tenure of Merfield, 7 years only, obviously had made a much greater impression on their neighbours in the village than the student recluse who succeeded them. He was 'close', said the bailiff who remembered them, and she was forward, and between them –

[*manuscript ends*]

Living Night

O William Frog, upon the log
How sweet your accents ring
An airy tune beneath the moon
Remote you sit and sing

All through the rushes, and in the bushes
Odd creatures slip in the dark
And dusky owls with feathery cowls
Go sweeping about the park

You hear on the breeze from behind the trees
The Ampton clock begin
And when it is still, how thin and shrill
The bell of the Hall chimes in

Then the horses stir and the sleepy cats purr
And something moves in the fern
And did you not see in the hollow oak tree
Two eyes begin to burn?

You heard a foot pass, it trailed over the grass
You shivered, it came so near
And was it the head of a man long dead
That raised itself out of the mere?

Then a call came clear from over the mere
And died in the night beyond
And the moor hens woke and you heard a croak
From the swan on the Judgement pond

Four black things with eyes of flame
In the hour before the dawn
And their dry throats cluck for they long to suck
The blood of a sleeping fawn

But all around from the trees and the ground
The elves and the owls creep on
And the black things shrink and we rather think
That their chance of a meal is gone

There blows a dull breath over Troston Heath
And cocks are crowing afar
And a pool of blood in the old Broom wood
Looks up at the morning star.

Some Remarks on Ghost Stories

VERY NEARLY ALL the ghost stories of old times claim to be true narratives of remarkable occurrences. At the outset I must make it clear that with these – be they ancient, mediaeval or post-mediaeval – I have nothing to do, any more than I have with those chronicled in our own days. I am concerned with a branch of fiction; not a large branch, if you look at the rest of the tree, but one which has been astonishingly fertile in the last thirty years. The avowedly fictitious ghost story is my subject, and that being understood I can proceed.

In the year 1854 George Borrow narrated to an audience of Welshmen, 'in the tavern of Gutter Vawr, in the county of Glamorgan', what he asserted to be 'decidedly the best ghost story in the world'. You may read this story either in English, in Knapp's notes to *Wild Wales*, or in Spanish, in a recent edition with excellent pictures (*Las Aventuras de Pánfilo*). The source is Lope de Vega's *El Peregrino en so patria* published in 1604. You will find it a remarkably interesting specimen of a tale of terror written in Shakespeare's lifetime, but I shall be surprised if you agree with Borrow's estimate of it. It is nothing but an account of a series of nightmares experienced by a wanderer who lodges for a night in a 'hospital', which had been deserted because of hauntings. The ghosts come in crowds and play tricks with the victim's bed. They quarrel over cards, they squirt water at the man, they throw torches about the room. Finally they steal his clothes and disappear; but next morning the clothes are where he put them when he went to bed. In fact they are rather goblins than ghosts.

Still, here you have a story written with the sole object of inspiring a pleasing terror in the reader; and as I think, that is the true aim of the ghost story.

As far as I know, nearly two hundred years pass before you find the literary ghost story attempted again. Ghosts of course figure on the stage, but we must leave them out of consideration. Ghosts are the subject of quasi-scientific research in this country at the hands of Glanville, Beaumont and others; but these collectors are out to prove theories of the future life and the spiritual world. Improving treatises, with illustrative instances, are written on the Continent, as by Lavater. All these, if they do afford what our ancestors called amusement (Dr Johnson decreed that *Coriolanius* was 'amusing'), do so by a side-wind. *The Castle of Otranto* is perhaps the progenitor of the ghost story as a literary genre, and I fear that it is merely amusing in the modern sense.

Then we come to Mrs. Radcliffe, whose ghosts are far better of their kind, but with exasperating timidity are all explained away; and to Monk Lewis, who in the book which gives him his nickname is odious and horrible without being impressive. But Monk Lewis was responsible for better things than he could produce himself. It was under his auspices that Scott's verse first saw the light: among the *Tales of Terror and Wonder* are not only some of his translations, but 'Glenfinlas' and the 'Eve of St John', which must always rank as fine ghost stories. The form into which he cast them was that of the ballads which he loved and collected, and we must not forget that the ballad is in the direct line of ancestry of the ghost story. Think of 'Clerk Saunders', 'Young Benjie', the 'Wife of Usher's Well'. I am tempted to enlarge on the *Tales of Terror*, for the most part supremely absurd, where Lewis holds the pen, and jigs along with such stanzas as:

> All present then uttered a terrified shout;
>> All turned with disgust from the scene.
> The worms they crept in, and the worms they crept out,
> And sported his eyes and his temples about,
>> While the spectre addressed Imogene.

But proportion must be observed.

If I were writing generally of horrific books which include supernatural appearances, I should be obliged to include Maturin's *Melmoth*, and doubtless imitations of it which I know nothing of. But *Melmoth* is a long – a cruelly long – book, and we must keep our eye on the short prose ghost story in the first place. If Scott is not the creator of this, it is to him that we owe two classical specimens – 'Wandering Willie's Tale' and the 'Tapestried Chamber'. The former we know is an episode in a novel; anyone who searches the novels of succeeding years will certainly find (as we, alas, find in *Pickwick* and *Nicholas Nickleby*!) stories of this type foisted in; and possibly some of them may be good enough to deserve reprinting.

But the real happy hunting ground, the proper habitat of our game is the magazine, the annual, the periodical publication destined to amuse the family circle. They came up thick and fast, the magazines, in the thirties and forties, and many died young. I do not, having myself sampled the task, envy the devoted one who sets out to examine the files, but it is not rash to promise him a measure of success. He will find ghost stories; but of what sort? Charles Dickens will tell us. In a paper from *Household Words*, which will be found among 'Christmas Stories' under the name of 'A Christmas Tree' (I reckon it among the best of Dickens's occasional writings), that great man takes occasion to run through the plots of the typical ghost stories of his time.

As he remarks, they are 'reducible to a very few general types and classes; for ghosts have little originality, and "walk" in a beaten track.' He gives us at some length the experience of the nobleman and the ghost of the beautiful young housekeeper who drowned herself in the park two hundred years before; and, more cursorily, the indelible bloodstain, the door that will not shut, the clock that strikes thirteen, the phantom coach, the compact to appear after death, the girl who meets her double, the cousin who is seen at the moment of his death far away in India, the maiden lady who 'really did see the Orphan Boy'. With such things as these we are still familiar. But we have rather forgotten – and I for my part have seldom met – those with which he ends his survey:

'Legion is the name of the German castles where we sit up alone to meet the spectre – where we are shown into a room made comparatively cheerful for our reception' (more detail, excellent of its kind, follows), 'and where, about the small hours of the night, we come into the knowledge of divers supernatural mysteries. Legion is the name of the haunted German students, in whose society we draw yet nearer to the fire, while the schoolboy in the corner opens his eyes wide and round, and flies off the footstool he has chosen for his seat, when the door accidentally blows open.'

As I have said, this German stratum of ghost stories is one of which I know little; but I am confident that the searcher of magazines will penetrate to it. Examples of the other types will accrue, especially when he reaches the era of Christmas Numbers, inaugurated by Dickens himself. His Christmas *Numbers* are not to be confused with his Christmas *Books*, though the latter led on to the former. Ghosts are not absent from these, but I do not call the *Christmas Carol* a ghost story proper; while I do assign that name to the stories of the Signalman and the Juryman (in 'Mugby Junction' and 'Dr Marigold').

These were written in 1865 and 1866, and nobody can deny that they conform to the modern idea of the ghost story. The setting and the personages are those of the writer's own day; they have nothing antique about them. Now this mode is not absolutely essential to success, but it is characteristic of the majority of successful stories: the belted knight who meets the spectre in the vaulted chamber and has to say 'By my halidom', or words to that effect, has little actuality about him. Anything, we feel, might have happened in the 15th century. No; the seer of ghosts must talk something like me, and be dressed, if not in my fashion, yet not too much like a man in a pageant, if he is to enlist my sympathy. Wardour Street has no business here.

If Dickens's ghost stories are good and of the right complexion, they are not the best that were written in his day. The palm must I think be assigned to J.S. Le Fanu, whose stories of 'The Watcher' (or 'The Familiar'), 'Mr Justice Harbottle', 'Carmilla', are unsurpassed, while 'Schalken the Painter', 'Squire Toby's Will', the haunted house in 'The House by the Churchyard', 'Dickon the Devil', 'Madam Crowl's Ghost', run them very close. Is it the blend of French and Irish in Le Fanu's descent and surroundings that gives him the knack of infusing ominousness into his atmosphere? He is anyhow an artist in words; who else could have hit on the epithets in this sentence: 'The aerial image of the old house for a moment stood before her, with its peculiar malign, scared and skulking aspect.' Other famous stories of Le Fanu there are which are not quite ghost stories – 'Green Tea' and 'The Room in the Dragon Volant'; and yet another, 'The Haunted Baronet', not famous, not even known but to a few, contains some admirable touches, but somehow lacks proportion. Upon mature consideration, I do not think that there are better ghost stories anywhere than the best of Le Fanu's; and among these I should give the first place to 'The Familiar' (alias 'The Watcher').

Other famous novelists of those days tried their hand – Bulwer Lytton for one. Nobody is permitted to write about ghost stories without mentioning 'The Haunters and the Haunted'. To my mind it is spoilt by the conclusion; the Cagliostro element (forgive an inaccuracy) is alien. It comes in with far better effect (though in a burlesque guise) in Thackeray's one attempt in this direction – 'The Notch in the Axe', in the 'Roundabout Papers'. This, to be sure, begins by being a skit partly on Dumas, partly on Lytton; but as Thackeray warmed to his work he got interested in the story and, as he says, was quite sorry to part with Pinto in the end. We have to reckon too with Wilkie Collins. 'The Haunted Hotel', a short novel, is by no means ineffective; grisly enough, almost, for the modern American taste.

Rhoda Broughton, Mrs. Riddell, Mrs. Henry Wood, Mrs. Oliphant – all these have some sufficiently absorbing stories to their credit. I own to reading not infrequently 'Featherston's Story' in the fifth series of 'Johnny Ludlow', to delighting in its domestic flavour and finding its ghost very convincing. (Johnny Ludlow, some young persons may not know, is by Mrs. Henry Wood.) The religious ghost story, as it may be called, was never done better than by Mrs. Oliphant in 'The Open Door' and 'A Beleaguered City'; though there is a competitor, and a strong one, in Le Fanu's 'Mysterious Lodger'.

Here I am conscious of a gap; my readers will have been conscious of many previous gaps. My memory does in fact slip on from Mrs. Oliphant to Marion Crawford and his horrid story of 'The Upper Berth', which (with the 'Screaming Skull' some distance behind) is the best in his collection of *Uncanny Tales*, and stands high among ghost stories in general.

That was I believe written in the late eighties. In the early nineties comes the deluge, the deluge of the illustrated monthly magazines, and it is no longer possible to keep pace with the output either of single stories or of volumes of collected ones. Never was the flow more copious than it is today, and it is only by chance that one comes across any given example. So nothing beyond scattering and general remarks can be offered. Some whole novels there have been which depend for all or part of their interest on ghostly matter. There is *Dracula*, which suffers by excess. (I fancy, by the way, that it must be based on a story in the fourth volume of Chambers's *Repository*, issued in the fifties.) There is 'Alice-for-Short',[†] in which I never cease to admire the skill with which the ghost is woven into the web of the tale. But that is a very rare feat.

Among the collections of short stories, E.F. Benson's three volumes rank high, though to my mind he sins occasionally by stepping over the line of legitimate horridness. He is however blameless in this aspect as compared with some Americans, who compile volumes called *Not At Night* and the like. These are merely nauseating, and it is very easy to be nauseating. I, *moi qui vous parle*, could undertake to make a reader physically sick, if I chose to think and write in terms of the Grand Guignol. The authors of the stories I have in mind tread, as they believe, in the steps of Edgar Allan Poe and Ambrose Bierce (himself sometimes unpardonable), but they do not possess the force of either.

Reticence may be an elderly doctrine to preach, yet from the artistic point of view I am sure it is a sound one. Reticence conduces to effect, blatancy ruins it, and there is much blatancy in a lot of recent stories. They drag in sex too, which is a fatal mistake; sex is tiresome enough in the novels; in a ghost story, or as the backbone of a ghost story, I have no patience with it.

At the same time don't let us be mild and drab. Malevolence and terror, the glare of evil faces, 'the stony grin of unearthly malice', pursuing forms in darkness, and 'long-drawn, distant screams', are all in place, and so is a modicum of blood, shed with deliberation and carefully husbanded; the weltering and wallowing that I too often encounter merely recall the methods of M.G. Lewis.

---

† by William Frend de Morgan (1907)

Clearly it is out of the question for me to begin upon a series of 'short notices' of recent collections; but an illustrative instance or two will be to the point. A.M. Burrage, in *Some Ghost Stories*, keeps on the right side of the line, and if about half of his ghosts are amiable, the rest have their terrors, and no mean ones. H.R. Wakefield, in *They Return at Evening* (a good title), gives us a mixed bag, from which I should remove one or two that leave a nasty taste. Among the residue are some admirable pieces, very inventive.

Going back a few years I light on Mrs. Everett's *The Death Mask*, of a rather quieter tone on the whole, but with some excellently conceived stories. Hugh Benson's *Light Invisible* and *Mirror of Shalott* are too ecclesiastical. K. and Hesketh Prichard's *Flaxman Low* is most ingenious and successful, but rather over-technically 'occult'. It seems impertinent to apply the same criticism to Algernon Blackwood, but *John Silence* is surely open to it. Mr. Elliott O'Donnell's multitudinous volumes I do not know whether to class as narratives of fact or exercises in fiction. I hope they may be of the latter sort, for life in a world managed by his gods and infested by his demons seems a risky business.

So I might go on through a long list of authors; but the remarks one can make in an article of this compass can hardly be illuminating. The reading of many ghost stories has shown me that the greatest successes have been scored by the authors who can make us envisage a definite time and place, and give us plenty of clear-cut and matter-of-fact detail, but who, when the climax is reached, allow us to be just a little in the dark as to the working of their machinery. We do not want to see the bones of their theory about the supernatural.

All this while I have confined myself almost entirely to the English ghost story. The fact is that either there are not many good stories by foreign writers, or (more probably) my ignorance has veiled them from me. But I should feel myself ungrateful if I did not pay a tribute to the supernatural tales of Erckmann-Chatrian. The blend of French with German in them, comparable to the French-Irish blend in Le Fanu, has produced some quite first-class romance of this kind. Among longer stories, *La Maison forestière* (and, if you will, *Hugues le loup*); among shorter ones *Le Blanc et le noir*, *Le Rêve du cousin Elof* and *L'Œil invisible* have for years delighted and alarmed me. It is high time that they were made more accessible than they are.

There need not be any peroration to a series of rather disjointed reflections. I will only ask the reader to believe that, though I have not hitherto mentioned it, I have read *The Turn of the Screw*.

Afterword

'THE STONY GRIN OF UNEARTHLY MALICE'
Stephen Jones

MONTAGUE RHODES JAMES was born in Goodnestone Parsonage in the village of Goodnestone, near Canterbury, Kent, on 1 August 1862, the fourth and youngest child of Mary Emily James (née Horton) and the Reverend Herbert James, a Church of England Perpetual Curate of an Evangelical persuasion.

At the age of three he moved with his family to the rectory in Great Livermere, Suffolk, a village just outside Bury St Edmunds (which would later serve as the inspiration for his final short story, 'A Vignette'). James' childhood interest in both the Suffolk countryside and ecclesiastical architecture would significantly shape the direction of his writings in his adult life.

He was educated at home until the age of eleven, after which, in September 1873, he was sent to Temple Grove Preparatory School in East Sheen (the setting for 'A School Story'). This is where he first met Arthur Christopher (A.C.) Benson; the two men were to remain lifelong friends as they followed almost identical academic paths.

In 1875, after having won a number of prizes for his Latin prose and verse, James was awarded a scholarship to Eton College, where he became one of the foremost scholars of his generation, distinguishing himself in Divinity, the Classics and French. After moving to King's College, Cambridge, he

605

decided not to follow the family tradition of joining either the clergy or military but to stay in academia, and his career progressed rapidly. 'Monty', as he was affectionately known to his many friends and admirers, served as Fellow, Dean and Tutor before, in May 1905, he became Provost of King's.

In September 1918 he accepted the Provostship of Eton, where he remained until his death.

'It is truly a pleasure,' he told a friend, 'the prospect of being knit up so closely with Eton, which of all places holds perhaps the first place in my affections.'

James was friendly and good-humoured by nature, with a 'genius for friendship' (according to the *Cambridge Review*), and in between his numerous commitments, he worked to remain in touch with old friends and former students alike. He also reportedly enjoyed such diversions as *Buffalo Bill's Wild West* show (which toured Great Britain and Europe in the early 1890s), Christmas pantomimes, detective novels and the works of P.G. Wodehouse.

His 'old and beloved' friend, the author and poet A.C. Benson, observed: 'He is one of the few people to whom I can say, and do say, exactly what I think and as I think it. He never misunderstands, is always amused, always appreciative.'

James' interest in the supernatural was evident while he was still a teenager. At the age of sixteen he was already entertaining fellow pupils with ghost stories ('in which capacity I am rather popular now,' he recorded in a letter), and a couple of years later he wrote in an 1880 issue of *The Eton Rambler*, edited by his friend Arthur Benson: 'Everyone can remember a time when he has carefully searched his curtains – and poked in the dark corners of his room before retiring to rest – with a sort of pleasurable uncertainty as to whether there might not be a saucer-eyed skeleton or a skinny-sheeted ghost in hiding somewhere. I invariably go through this ceremony myself.'

('I think it is rot,' is how James described this early article in a letter to his father, and he later dismissed his own work in the 'ephemeral' when he admitted: 'My own contributions to it I cannot now look at with patience.')

M.R. James did not start writing fiction until he was in his early thirties, when he originally conceived the idea of his now-celebrated 'antiquarian ghost stories' as Christmas entertainments, to be read aloud at gatherings of friends and fellow members of Cambridge's select Chit-Chat Club – whose number included future ghost-story authors Edward Frederic (E.F.) Benson and Robert Hugh (R.H.) Benson (Arthur's equally famous brothers), and Edmund Gill (E.G.) Swain.

'I have always thought that one very desirable quality in a ghost story is leisureliness,' wrote James. 'The ghost story is essentially a somewhat old-fashioned thing; that is one of the reasons why Christmas time, which appeals to old association in so many ways, is considered the proper season for ghost stories. And in so far as the ghost story *is* old-fashioned, it ought to move at a pace suitable to its age.'

After having been invited to write a story to read to the gathered assembly, James in fact concocted two tales – 'Canon Alberic's Scrap-book' (originally titled 'A Curious Book') and 'Lost Hearts' – which he first presented to an appreciative audience at the weekly meeting on 28 October 1893. He was asked to repeat his performance each year, ideally on Christmas Eve.

In his *A Memoir of Montague Rhodes James, with a List of His Writings* (1939), one of the author's closest friends, S.G. (Samuel Gurney 'Jimbo') Lubbock, gave a vivid description of these reading sessions:

'So the Ghost Stories began; and they were continued at the urgent request of a small party that was used to gather at King's just before Christmas. Some pressure was needed; and on the appointed evening the party met and waited till at last, about 11 p.m. as a rule, Monty appeared with the ink still wet on the last page. All lights except one were turned out and the story was read. Afterwards, when he was Provost, the same ritual was preserved; but by then the small party had grown . . .'

Oliffe Richmond, another listener at these gatherings, recalled: 'Monty emerged from the bedroom, manuscript in hand, at last, and blew out all the candles but one, by which he seated himself. He then began to read, with more confidence than anyone else could have mustered, his well-nigh illegible script in the dim light.'

As horror writer Ramsey Campbell noted in the Introduction to his Jamesian-inspired anthology *Meddling with Ghosts* (2001), 'In this James clearly meant to align himself with the tradition of the festive ghost story and indeed of oral storytelling . . . All this may suggest a certain cosiness, which would be confirmed by the standard view that the most important Jamesian attribute is his antiquarianism. Of course that is crucial to the verisimilitude of many of the stories, and many of them deal with scholars whose comfortable world is invaded by the malign supernatural.'

In his seminal essay 'Supernatural Horror in Literature', originally published in the first and only edition of W. Paul Cook's amateur publication *The Recluse* (1927), H.P. Lovecraft noted: 'The art of Dr. James is by no means haphazard, and in the preface to one of his collections he has formulated three very sound rules for macabre composition. A ghost story, he believes, should have a familiar setting in the modern period, in order to approach closely the reader's sphere of experience. Its spectral phenomena, moreover, should be malevolent rather than beneficent; since *fear* is the emotion primarily to be excited. And finally, the technical patois of "occultism" or pseudo-science ought carefully to be avoided; lest the charm of casual verisimilitude be smothered in unconvincing pedantry.

'Dr. James, practising what he preaches, approaches his themes in a light and often conversational way. Creating the illusion of every-day events, he introduces his abnormal phenomena cautiously and gradually; relieved at every turn by touches of homely and prosaic detail, and sometimes spiced with a snatch or two of antiquarian scholarship. Conscious of the close relation between present weirdness and accumulated tradition, he generally provides remote historical antecedents for his incidents; thus being able to utilise very aptly his exhaustive knowledge of the past, and his ready and convincing command of archaic diction and colouring. A favourite scene for a James tale is some centuried cathedral, which the author can describe with all the familiar minuteness of a specialist in that field.'

Following their reading to the Chit-Chat Club two years earlier, 'Canon Alberic's Scrap-book' was first published under the title 'The Scrap-book of Canon Alberic' in the March 1895 edition of the *National Review*. M.R. James' second story, 'Lost Hearts', appeared in the December issue of *Pall Mall Magazine* that same year.

In some ways like their author, many of James' protagonists are steeped in antiquarianism – scholarly men or studious clerics of limited worldly experience, absorbed in books and objects from the past.

'I attribute great importance to the setting of such a story,' wrote the author. 'I like, as I do in a detective novel, to make some sort of acquaintance with the actors. And, I would add, the more ordinary and normal both setting and actors are, the more effective will be the entangling of them in a dreadful situation, and the more ready will he who follows their adventures be to shake the head and murmur those words which I have long since registered as the proper ones for the reader of ghost stories, to wit, "If I'm not very careful, something like this may happen to me".'

'His main characters are almost always scholars, and almost always bachelors,' observed Geoff Ryman in *Horror: 100 Best Books* (1988). 'The world is seen through their eyes . . . The narrators of James' stories usually take no part in the action. They piece their stories together as historians would, through old documents or the evidence of friends.'

However, despite his somewhat pedantic approach to constructing a narrative, M.R. James is also justly credited as redefining the modern ghost story, throwing off the genre's Gothic trappings and bringing its spectres into the twentieth century.

While many of James' apparitions are revealed as merely a glimpse from the corner of the eye, they are still presented in a grisly and gruesome fashion that would have been unthinkable only a few years earlier.

'In inventing a new type of ghost, he has departed considerably from the conventional Gothic tradition,' continued Lovecraft, 'for where the older stock ghosts were pale and stately, and apprehended chiefly through the sense of sight, the average James ghost is lean, dwarfish, and hairy – a sluggish, hellish night-abomination midway betwixt beast and man – and usually *touched* before it is *seen*. Sometimes the spectre is of still more eccentric composition; a roll of flannel with spidery eyes, or an invisible entity

which moulds itself in bedding and shews *a face of crumpled linen*.'

'I say you must have horror and also malevolence,' James himself stated in a 1931 article for *The Evening News*, written to coincide with the publication of *The Collected Ghost Stories*. 'Not less necessary, however, is reticence.'

'M.R. James is thought of as a master of subtle suggestion,' explained Geoff Ryman. 'He almost never describes physical injury. But his terrors are described in great and very physical detail, and are the focus of the tales. The writing grows more specific when they appear – and there would be no story without them.'

As former British Poet Laureate Sir John Betjeman observed: 'M.R. James thought that his ghosts should be evil and only glimpsed. He was a master of the unexpected' – although James himself criticised his friend and contemporary E.F. Benson for sometimes 'stepping over the line of legitimate horridness' in his fiction.

In his Preface to *More Ghost Stories of an Antiquary*, the author expanded upon his thoughts about what a ghost should be: 'To be sure, I have my ideas as to how a ghost story ought to be laid out if it is to be effective. I think that, as a rule, the setting should be fairly familiar and the majority of the characters and their talk such as you may meet or hear any day. A ghost story of which the scene is laid in the twelfth or thirteenth century may succeed in being romantic or poetical: it will never put the reader into the position of saying to himself, "If I'm not very careful, something of this kind may happen to me!"

'Again, I feel that the technical terms of "occultism", if they are not very carefully handled, tend to put the mere ghost story (which is all that I am attempting) upon a quasi-scientific plane, and to call into play faculties quite other than the imaginative. I am well aware that mine is a nineteenth- (and not a twentieth-) century conception of this class of tale; but were not the prototypes of all the best ghost stories written in the sixties and seventies?

'However, I cannot claim to have been guided by any very strict rules. My stories have been produced (with one exception) at successive Christmas seasons. If they serve to amuse some readers at the Christmas-time that is coming – or at any time whatever – they will justify my action in publishing them.'

James' ghosts can also be insubstantial revenants, evoked through atmosphere, suggestion and imagination, leaving his reader to conjure up their own interpretation.

'Two ingredients most valuable in the concocting of a ghost story are, to me, the atmosphere and the nicely managed crescendo,' he explained in his Introduction to the 1924 anthology *Ghosts and Marvels*. 'Let us, then, be introduced to the actors in a placid way; let us see them going about their ordinary business, undisturbed by forebodings, pleased with their surroundings; and into this calm environment let the ominous thing put out its head, unobtrusively at first, and then more insistently, until it holds the stage.'

It also holds that most of the supernatural creatures that appear in his stories are inimical to those who come across them. 'Another requisite, in my opinion, is that the ghost should be malevolent or odious,' he continued. 'Amiable and helpful apparitions are all very well in fairy tales or in local legends, but I have no use for them in a fictitious ghost story.'

But although his ghosts were threatening apparitions, James urged others to follow his lead and employ restraint in their depiction of the supernatural. 'Reticence may be an elderly doctrine to preach,' he admitted in a 1929 article in *The Bookman Christmas Issue*, 'yet from the artistic point of view, I am sure it is a sound one. Reticence conduces to effect, blatancy ruins it, and there is much blatancy in a lot of recent stories... At the same time don't let us be mild and drab. Malevolence and terror, the glare of evil faces, "the stony grin of unearthly malice", pursuing forms in darkness, and "long-drawn, distant screams", are all in place, and so is a modicum of blood, shed with deliberation and carefully husbanded; the weltering and wallowing that I too often encounter merely recall the methods of M.G. Lewis.'

This advice is still as relevant to today's horror writers as it was more than eighty years ago, when James first made his pronouncement.

In the same article, James also complained: 'They drag in sex too, which is a fatal mistake; sex is tiresome enough in the novels; in a ghost story, or as the backbone of a ghost story, I have no patience with it.'

It is certainly a fact that women rarely feature in any meaningful way in M.R. James' stories and, as Nigel Kneale remarked in his Introduction to the Folio Society's edition of *Ghost Stories of M.R. James* (1973): 'In an age where every man is his own psychologist, M.R. James looks like rich and promising material.'

The American pulp writer and poet Clark Ashton Smith succinctly summed up the author's approach to the supernatural in his article, 'The Weird Works of M.R. James' in the February 1934 issue of *The Fantasy Fan*: 'Usually there is a more or less homely setting, often with a background of folklore and long-past happenings whose dim archaism provides a depth of shadow from which, as from a recessed cavern, the central horror emerges into the noontide of the present. Things and occurrences, sometimes with obvious off-hand relationship, are grouped cunningly, forcing the reader unaware to some frightful deduction; or there is an artful linkage of events seemingly harmless in themselves, that leave him confronted at a sudden turn with some ghoulish spectre or night-demon.

'The minutiæ of modern life, humour, character-drawing, scenic and archaeological description, are used as a foil to heighten the abnormal, but are never allowed to usurp a disproportionate interest. Always there is an element of supernatural menace, whose value is never impaired by scientific or spiritualistic explanation. Sometimes it is brought forth at the climax into full light; and sometimes, even then, it is merely half-revealed, is left undefined but perhaps all the more alarming. In any case, the presence of some unnatural but objective reality is assumed and established.'

James is also regarded as almost creating the 'cursed reliquary' story, in which an antiquarian or ecclesiastical object exerts a malevolent influence over the individual who discovers it.

'Many common objects may be made the vehicles of retribution,' he wrote, 'and where retribution is not called for, of malice. Be careful how you handle the packet you pick up in the carriage-drive, particularly if it contains nail-parings and hair. Do not, in any case, bring it into the house. It may not be alone...

'I am not conscious of other obligations to literature or local legend, written or oral, except in so far as I have tried to make my ghosts act in ways not inconsistent with the rules of folklore. As for the fragments of ostensible erudition which are scattered about my pages, hardly anything in them is not pure invention; there never was, naturally, any such book as that which I quote in "The Treasure of Abbot Thomas".'

As Clark Ashton Smith noted: 'Reading and re-reading these tales, one notes a predilection for certain milieus and motifs. Backgrounds of scholastic or ecclesiastic life are frequent and some of the best tales are laid in cathedral towns. In many of the supernatural entities, there recurs insistently the character of extreme and repulsive *hairiness*. Often the apparition is connected with, or evoked by, some material object, such as the bronze whistle from the ruins of a Templars' preceptory in "'*Oh, Whistle, and I'll Come to You, My Lad*'"; the old drawing of King Solomon and the night-demon in "*Canon Alberic's Scrap-book*"; the silver Anglo-Saxon crown from an immemorial barrow in "*A Warning to the Curious*"; and the strange curtain-pattern in "*The Diary of Mr. Poynter*" which had "a subtlety in its drawing".

James also readily admitted that he was often inspired by real locations for the settings for his stories: 'If anyone is curious about my local settings, let it be recorded that S. Bertrand de Comminges and Viborg are real places; that in "'Oh, Whistle, and I'll Come to You'", I had Felixstowe in mind; in "A School Story", Temple Grove, East Sheen; in "The Tractate Middoth", Cambridge University Library; in "Martin's Close", Sampford Courtenay in Devon; that the cathedrals of Barchester and Southminster were blends of Canterbury, Salisbury and Hereford; that Herefordshire was the imagined scene of "A View from a Hill", and Seaburgh in "A Warning to the Curious" is Aldeburgh in Suffolk.'

During his research of old texts, he also uncovered and transcribed various tales of hauntings and folklore in the British Museum. These were eventually published in their original Latin as 'Twelve Mediaeval Ghost Stories', with abundant footnotes by James, in the July 1922 edition of the *English Historical Review*, not receiving their first English-language publication until 1978, when they were presented in *The Man-Wolf and Other Horrors*, edited by Hugh Lamb.

The author's own belief in the supernatural was, at best, ambivalent. 'I answer that I am prepared to consider evidence and accept it if it satisfies me,' he wrote. During a debate on the existence of ghosts during his early years at Eton, James admitted that he 'could not but believe in anything and everything when in bed', and some years later he remarked to the Irish baronet [Sir John Randolph] Shane Leslie (recounted in the latter's 1955 *Ghost Book*), 'Some of these things are so, but we do not know the *rules*!'

In his 1926 memoir, *Eton and King's: Recollections, Mostly Trivial 1875–1925*, James also recalled: 'Ghosts and ghostly phenomena are rare in colleges and highly suspect when they do occur. Yet, on the staircase next to mine was a ghostly cry in the bedroom. Other professors knew of it, and knew whose voice it was believed to be – a man who died in 1878.'

He also revealed that at least one of his tales – possibly 'The Rose Garden', according to a later reminiscence by Montague Summers – was suggested by a vivid dream.

'Dr. James, for all his light touch, evokes fright and hideousness in their most shocking forms,' observed H.P. Lovecraft, whose own stories were also often inspired by dreams, 'and will certainly stand as one of the few really creative masters in his darksome province.'

'The goblins and phantoms devised by James are truly creative and are presented through images often so keen and vivid as to evoke an actual physical shock,' echoed Clark Ashton Smith. 'Sight, smell, hearing, taction, all are played upon with well-nigh surgical sureness, by impressions calculated to touch the shuddering quick of horror.'

M.R. James continued his Yuletide readings for many years, as his friend S.G. Lubbock recalled in his memoir: 'His reading of them aloud was – like his reading of the Bible – entirely untheatrical and immensely effective. In his later years, when the supply of new stories had ceased, he could generally be persuaded to read one of the old ones on Christmas night at King's, especially as it was youth, in the shape of some choral scholar, that would thrust a volume of them into his hand. He dined at King's on the Christmas night of 1934 and read us the Punch and Judy story ["The Story of a Disappearance and an Appearance"]; and that was the last.'

M.R. James' friends had been urging him for years to publish his ghost stories in book form and, although initially disinclined to the idea, he did eventually agree to have them collected in four hardcover editions, published by Edward Arnold of London.

The first, *Ghost-Stories of an Antiquary* (the title is hyphenated on the book's title-page but not the cover), contained eight stories and was published in November 1904 to some somewhat lukewarm reviews, although the reviewer for *The Guardian* was full in his

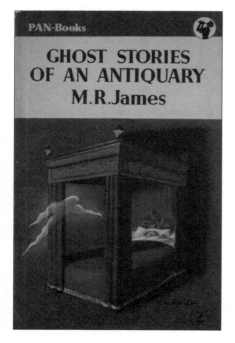

praise: 'In this book are no ordinary hauntings or common-place apparitions, but real, inexplicable, horrid Things belonging to another world, such as might have been summoned by mediaeval wizards to their own lasting undoing. We do not hesitate to say that these are among the best ghost stories we have ever read'.

'In this volume,' James later explained, '"Canon Alberic's Scrap-book" was written in 1894 [actually, more likely 1893] and printed soon after in the *National Review*; "Lost Hearts" appeared in the *Pall Mall Magazine*. Of the next five stories, most of which were read to friends at Christmas-time at King's College, Cambridge, I only recollect that I wrote "Number 13" in 1899, while "The Treasure of Abbot Thomas" was composed in summer 1904.'

The collection, which also included 'The Mezzotint', 'The Ash-tree', 'Count Magnus' and '"Oh, Whistle, and I'll Come to You, My Lad"', was reprinted the following year by Longmans Green in America.

'The stories themselves do not make any very exalted claim,' James wrote in his Preface. 'If any of them succeed in causing their readers to feel pleasantly uncomfortable when walking along a solitary road at nightfall, or sitting over a dying fire in the small hours, my purpose in writing them will have been attained.'

About one of the stories included in the book, H.P. Lovecraft wrote: '"Count Magnus" is assuredly one of the best, forming as it does a veritable Golconda of suspense and suggestion.'

James' friend, Eustace Talbot, told the author: 'You have succeeded in giving me two bad nights and one jumpy walk on a dark foggy evening in the country when every tree became possessed of horrible long arms and every step was dogged by hideous echoes about ten yards behind.'

Ghost-Stories of an Antiquary also featured four atmospheric illustrations by a close friend of the author, James McBryde. Ten years James' junior, McBryde had arrived in Cambridge from Shrewsbury in 1893 to read Natural Sciences and the already distinguished academic soon encouraged his new friend's habit of 'dropping in uninvited at a late hour of the evening, and joining a congregation which was usually to be found in the inner room.'

By 1904, McBryde had enrolled at the University's Slade, and was studying to become an artist. When it was suggested that he might illustrate James' first collection of ghost stories, even the author's interest in the project was rekindled, and he wrote to his young friend: 'They are at present in a very rough manuscript. Shall I have them typewritten or bring or send them as they are? Or do you remember any of them well enough to sketch out any ideas?'

McBryde's contributions to the book were his first professional commission, and he undertook it with gusto. In May 1904, he wrote to the author: 'I don't think I have ever done anything I liked better than illustrating your stories. To begin with I sat down and learned advanced perspective and the

laws of shadows . . . I have finished the Whistle ghost . . . I covered yards of paper to put in the moon shadows correctly and it is certainly the best thing I have ever drawn . . .'

Unfortunately, the artist never lived to see publication. James McBryde died at 9:30 a.m. on the morning of June 5th, a few days after undergoing an apparently routine operation to remove his appendix.

Only four illustrations had been completed, along with two unfinished drawings for 'Count Magnus' and a preliminary sketch for 'Number 13'. Another illustration for 'The Ash-tree' was planned but never started. However, when the publisher suggested that another artist should be brought in to finish the work, James firmly rejected the idea. Instead, he decided that the volume would stand as a tribute to its illustrator.

'I wrote these stories at long intervals, and most of them were read to patient friends,' James explained in his Preface to the book, 'usually at the season of Christmas. One of these friends offered to illustrate them, and it was agreed that, if he would do that, I would consider the question of publishing them.

'Four pictures he completed, which will be found in this volume, and then, very quickly and unexpectedly, he was taken away. This is the reason why the greater part of the stories are not provided with illustrations.

'Those who knew the artist will understand how much I wished to give a permanent form even to a fragment of his work; others will appreciate the fact that here a remembrance is made of one in whom many friendships centred.'

That same year, James McBryde's *The Story of a Troll-Hunt* was privately published – upon M.R. James' inducement – in a very limited subscription edition by the University Press, Cambridge, as a memorial to the artist. The illustrated comic fantasy, about three young men setting out to capture a living troll, was based on the bicycle holidays that McBryde, James and another young Cambridge friend, Will (W.J.) Stone, took around Denmark in 1899 and 1900. (These trips also supplied the background material for James' story 'Number 13'.)

McBryde and his wife Gwendolen had been married for just a year, and James agreed to become legal guardian to their daughter, Jane, who was born six months after her father's premature death. For the rest of his life, the author maintained a kindly and supportive correspondence with both Jane and her mother.

Jane McBryde was not the only child James wrote to; another of his young correspondents was Sibyl Cropper, whom he addressed as 'Dear Fellow-Scientist' or 'My Dear Apple Pie' in a series of fairy-tale epistles following a visit to her family's home in 1902. Thirty-seven years later, Miss Cropper collected and edited these letters, and they were published in the November 1939 issue of *Cornhill Magazine*.

Meanwhile, *Ghost-Stories of an Antiquary* went through eight printings that included McBryde's interior illustrations, before the book reverted to a cheaper format in the 1920s and '30s.

In his 'Supernatural Horror in Literature' essay, H.P. Lovecraft wrote:

'Gifted with an almost diabolic power of calling horror by gentle steps from the midst of prosaic daily life, is the scholarly Montague Rhodes James, Provost of Eton College, antiquary of note, and recognised authority on mediaeval manuscripts and cathedral history. Dr. James, long fond of telling spectral tales at Christmastide, has become by slow degrees a literary weird fictionist of the very first rank; and has developed a distinctive style and method likely to serve as models for an enduring line of disciples.'

Unfortunately, after receiving a copy of the amateur magazine that Lovecraft's piece originally appeared in, James declared himself not overly impressed with the American pulp author's tribute. 'In it is a disquisition of nearly 40 pages of double columns on Supernatural Horror in Literature by one H.P. Lovecraft,' he wrote to a correspondent, 'whose style is of the most offensive. He uses the word cosmic about 24 times.'

Some years later, Lovecraft's friend and contemporary, Clark Ashton Smith, wrote: 'James is perhaps unsurpassed in originality by any living writer: and he has made a salient contribution to the technique of the genre as well as to the enriching of its treasury of permanent masterpieces. His work is marked by rare intellectual skill and ingenuity, by power rising at times above the reaches of pure intellection, and by a sheer finesse of writing that will bear almost endless study.

'The peculiar genius of M.R. James, and his greatest power, lies in the convincing evocation of weird, malignant and preternatural phenomena such as I have instanced. It is safe to say that few writers, dead or living, have equalled him in this formidable necromancy and perhaps no one has excelled him.'

'The second volume, *More Ghost Stories*, appeared in 1911,' explained the author. 'Some years ago I promised to publish a second volume of ghost stories when a sufficient number of them

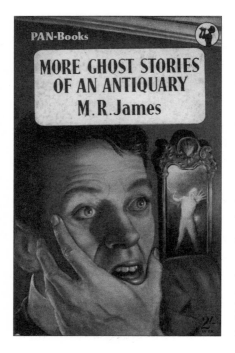

should have been accumulated. That time has arrived, and here is the volume. It is, perhaps, unnecessary to warn the critic that in evolving them I have not been possessed by that austere sense of the responsibility of authorship which is demanded of the writer of fiction in this generation; or that I have not sought to embody in them any well-considered scheme of "psychical" theory.

'The first six of the seven tales it contains were Christmas productions, the very first ("A School Story") having been made up for the benefit of the King's College Choir School. "The Stalls of Barchester Cathedral" was printed in the *Contemporary Review*; "Mr. Humphreys and His Inheritance" was written to fill up the volume.'

James' early title for 'The Stalls of Barchester Cathedral' had been 'The Cat of Death', while the other tales collected in the volume were 'The Rose Garden', 'The Tractate Middoth', 'Casting the Runes' and 'Martin's Close'.

Although the book's cover simply read *More Ghost Stories*, the title page carried the full designation of *More Ghost Stories of an Antiquary*.

This second collection did much to enhance James' reputation as a writer of supernatural fiction, and his celebrity admirers included Arthur Machen, Montague Summers, Thomas Hardy, A.E. Housman, Theodore Roosevelt and even the Prince of Wales.

'*A Thin Ghost and Others* was the third collection, containing five stories and published in 1919,' recalled James. 'In it, "An Episode of Cathedral History" and "The Story of a Disappearance and an Appearance" were contributed to the *Cambridge Review*.'

The book also featured 'The Residence at Whitminster', 'The Diary of Mr. Poynter' and 'Two Doctors'.

'I have had my doubts about the wisdom of publishing a third set of tales,' admitted the author in his Preface. 'Sequels are, not only proverbially but actually, very hazardous things.

'However, the tales make no pretence but to amuse, and my friends have not seldom asked for the publication. So not a great deal is risked, perhaps, and perhaps also some one's Christmas may be the cheerfuller for a story-book which, I think, only once mentions the war.'

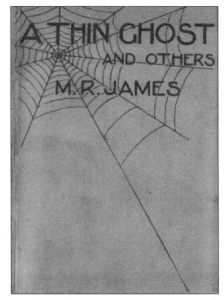

Despite the author's apparent reticence to see yet another collection of his works published, this third volume was issued by Longmans Green in America the same year.

James' single attempt at a longer work, the almost 25,000-word *The Five Jars*, was published by Edward Arnold in 1922, and has rarely been reprinted since then. Subtitled 'Being More or Less of a Fairy Tale Contained in a Letter to a Young Person', the story is about the discovery of a series of jars containing magic ointments that open up the senses to the hidden realms of animals and fairy-folk.

In a letter dated 1916, James first talked about his plans to write a story for Gwendolen McBryde's then eleven-year-old daughter, 'to explain to Jane what I have heard from the owls and other neighbours, and how it came about that I was able to do so.'

In the war between the powers of good and evil, the author was careful to include his beloved cats on the side of the 'Right People' while spiders – of which he had an almost pathological loathing – were one of the creatures aligned with the forces of darkness.

The Five Jars also shares certain characteristics with James' 1924 story 'After Dark in the Playing Fields', and some scholars have speculated that the shorter work may have had its origins in an abandoned attempt by the author to write a sequel to the novella.

When *The Five Jars* finally appeared in print, Jane McBryde was seventeen, and although her mother was inspired enough after reading the final draft to produce a series of illustrations for the book, the publisher decided to go with an artist named Gilbert James (no relation) instead. The author was reportedly not impressed with the other James' depictions, but that could have been because his friend had lost out on the commission.

Although the book never became an established children's classic – possibly because parents may have thought it was too dark for younger readers at the time

– *The Five Jars* did have its supporters, including *Peter Pan* author J.M. Barrie.

The novel was reprinted just a couple of times over a period of more than seventy years before Ash-Tree Press issued a hardcover printing with a new Introduction by Rosemary Pardoe in 1995. This edition was limited to around 300 numbered copies and two lettered copies in a deluxe binding.

James' fourth collection, *A Warning to the Curious and Other Ghost Stories*, was published in 1925 and went through four impressions between October and February the following year. As the author revealed, of the six stories contained in the book, 'The first, "The Haunted Dolls' House", was specially written for the library of Her Majesty the Queen's Dolls' House, and subsequently appeared in the *Empire Review*. "The Uncommon Prayer-book" saw the light in the *Atlantic Monthly*, the title-story in the *London Mercury*, and another, I think "A Neighbour's Landmark", in an ephemeral called *The Eton Chronic*.'

Also in the book were 'A View from a Hill', 'A Warning to the Curious' and 'An Evening's Entertainment'.

Seven years later, James revealed to Gwendolen McBryde that he was 'startled' to see 'A View from a Hill' reprinted in the February 1932 issue of *Pearson's Magazine*, apparently without his permission. 'The publisher "thought I wouldn't mind" and no more I do, particularly as they pay,' continued James, who revealed that he received half of the ten guineas fee. 'But I also noticed that they left out a number of sentences: and this I protest against. The publisher palliates his crime by saying he has sold about 3,000 copies of the number – which is doubtless a good result'.

In fact, once the matter was settled, *Pearson's Magazine* went on to also reprint James' stories "'Oh, Whistle, and I'll Come to You, My Lad'" and

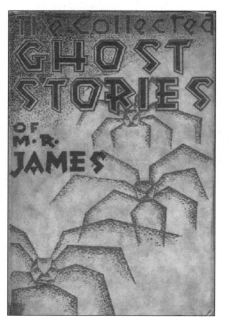

'Number 13' later that same year, after the author received a promise from the editor 'to leave out as little as he can in future'.

Another story, the grimly humorous 'Wailing Well', which James described as 'a story of a terrible nature', was written especially for the Eton College troop of Boy Scouts, and the author read it aloud around a campfire at Worbarrow Bay in Dorset, on 27 July 1927. It apparently led to several of the boys having 'a somewhat disturbed night'.

The story was privately published the following year by Robert Gathorne-Hardy and Kyrle Leng under the Mill House Press, Stanford Dingley imprint in a hardcover edition limited to just 157 copies, of which seven were signed by James that had the title page printed in blue and black.

The first omnibus edition of the author's short stories, *The Collected Ghost Stories of M.R. James*, appeared in both Britain and America 1931. As the author explained in his Preface: 'In accordance with a fashion which has recently become common, I am issuing my four volumes of ghost stories under one cover, and appending to them some matter of the same kind.

'I am told they have given

pleasure of a certain sort to my readers: if so, my whole object in writing them has been attained.'

The volume contained all the stories in James' first four collections (written, he later claimed, 'at fever heat' in his notoriously illegible hand-writing), and also added a number of other pieces: 'Not all of them strictly stories,' as the author helpfully pointed out. This additional material included 'There Was a Man Dwelt by a Churchyard', 'Rats', 'After Dark in the Playing Fields', 'Wailing Well' and the essay 'Stories I Have Tried to Write'. Except for 'Wailing Well' all of these had previously been first published in Eton 'ephemerals'.

However, although 'Rats' had originally been written for *At Random* ('Edited by present Etonians') in 1929, James was obviously so proud that the story had also appeared the same year in Lady Cynthia Asquith's anthology *Shudders: A Collection of New Nightmare Tales* that he couldn't help boasting about it to his readers.

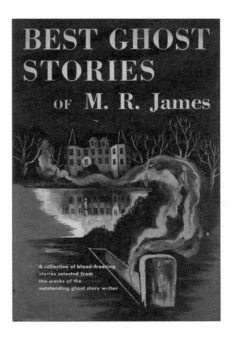

He additionally revealed in the same piece that 'a Norse version of four from my first volume, by Ragnhild Undset, was issued in 1919 under the title *Aander og Trolddom*'. He was perhaps unaware that a companion volume, *Abbedens skat*, published the same year by Cammermeyers Forlag, contained Undset's translations of the remaining four stories from *Ghost-Stories of an Antiquary*.

While reviewing the *Collected Ghost Stories* in 1934, Clark Ashton Smith summed up the author's œuvre: 'The personnel of James' *Pandemonium* is far from monotonous; one finds a satyr dwelling in a cathedral tomb; a carven cat-like monster that comes to life when touched by a murderer's hand; a mouldy smelling sack-like object in an unlit well, which suddenly puts its

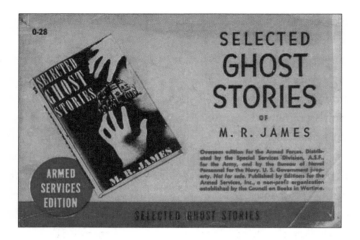

arms around the neck of a treasure-seeker; a cloaked and hooded shape with a tentacle in lieu of arms; a lean, hideously taloned terror, with a jaw "shallow as that of a beast"; dolls that repeat crime and tragedy; creatures that are dog-like but are not dogs; a saw fly tall as a man, met in a dim room full of rustling insects; and even a weak, ancient thing, which being wholly bodiless and insubstantial, makes for itself a body out of crumpled bed-linen.'

In a review of the book in the April 1931 *Spectator*, Peter Fleming described James as 'an acknowledged master of his craft: unrivalled at his best, for consistent merit never approached'.

James himself contributed an insightful Introduction to the 1924 anthology *Ghosts and Marvels: A Selection of Uncanny Tales from Daniel Defoe to Algernon Blackwood*, edited by V.H. (Vere Henry Gratz) Collins for the Oxford University Press/Humphrey Milford.

'Often have I been asked to formulate my views about ghost stories and tales of the marvellous, the mysterious, the supernatural,' he wrote. 'Never have I been able to find out whether I had any views that could be formulated. The truth is, I suspect, that the genre is too small and special to bear the imposition of far reaching principles. Widen the question, and ask what governs the construction of short stories in general, and a great deal might be said, and has been said. There are, of course, instances of whole novels in which the supernatural governs the plot; but among them are few successes. The ghost story is, at its best, only a particular sort of short story, and is subject to the same broad rules as the whole mass of them. Those rules, I imagine, no writer ever consciously follows. In fact, it is absurd to talk of them as rules; they are qualities which have been observed to accompany success.'

The author then went on to once again expound upon his ideas that the basis of a good ghost story relied on 'the atmosphere and the nicely managed crescendo', as well as the reader being 'introduced to the actors in a placid way'. He also reiterated his belief that, 'For the ghost story a slight haze of distance is desirable.'

However, he did qualify this latter comment: 'If a really remote date be chosen, there is more than one way of bringing the reader in contact with it. The finding of documents about it can be made plausible; or you may begin with your apparition and go back over the years to tell the cause of it; or (as in "Schalken the Painter") you may set the scene directly in the desired epoch, which I think is hardest to do with success. On the whole (though not a few instances might be quoted against me) I think that a setting so modern that the ordinary reader can judge of its naturalness for himself is preferable to anything antique. For some degree of actuality is the charm of the best ghost stories; not a very insistent actuality, but one strong enough to allow the reader to identify himself with the patient; while it is almost inevitable that the reader of an antique story should fall into the position of the mere spectator.'

James also championed the work of Irish writer J. (Joseph) Sheridan Le Fanu (1814–73), author of the above-mentioned story 'Schalken the Painter' and the classic vampire novella 'Carmilla', whom he described as standing 'absolutely in the first rank as a writer of ghost stories'.

He edited and provided the Introduction to Le Fanu's collection *Madame Crowl's Ghost and Other Tales of Mystery* (1923): 'Nobody sets the scene better than he,' enthused James, 'nobody touches in the effective detail more deftly.' Three years later he contributed an Introduction to a new edition of Le Fanu's novel *Uncle Silas*, in which he somewhat unconvincingly claimed to have exposed 'Conan Doyle's cribbing of the plot'.

James not only contributed an Introduction to Faber & Faber's *Hans Andersen: Forty Stories* in 1930, but he also supplied a new translation of the Danish writer's work because he was not happy with the previous attempts. The new edition featured twenty-four colour plates by Christine Jackson, and the *New Statesman* reviewer approved of the whole package, saying, 'We get possibly for the first time, a glimpse of the originals as they really are.'

Five years later, James' translation of Hans Christian Andersen's *The Little Mermaid* was issued in a separate edition by New York publisher Holiday House with illustrations by Pamela Bianco.

Not every story James set out to write reached completion, as the author explained in his essay 'Stories I Have Tried to Write', which was originally published in the 30 November 1929 edition of the small Eton magazine *The Touchstone*.

'It has amused me sometimes to think of the stories which have crossed my mind from time to time and never materialised properly,' he wrote. 'They are not good enough. Yet some of them had ideas in them which refused to blossom in the surroundings I had devised for them, but perhaps came up in other forms in stories that did get as far as print.'

The piece was subsequently reprinted in *The Collected Ghost Stories of M.R. James* and it has inspired numerous writers down the decades – including Sir Andrew Caldecott, Sheila Hodgson, David G. Rowlands, A.F. Kidd, C.E. Ward, Stephen Gresham, Rhys Hughes and Reggie Oliver, to name but a few – to try their own hand at completing these unfinished plot ideas.

Many more authors have been inspired to create their own ghost stories in the 'Jamesian tradition'. This has led to Ramsey Campbell – whose own 1989 story 'The Guide' was a tribute to the Jamesian method – to state that 'M.R. James is the most influential British writer of supernatural fiction', while author and editor Michael Cox speculated that 'it is probable that M.R. James has generated more imitators than any other English ghost story writer'.

James' own ghost stories were often rooted in his background as a scholar, and his life-long work was cataloguing the mediaeval manuscript libraries of the colleges in Cambridge. The first catalogue was published in 1895 and the last – more than 1,100 manuscripts later – in 1925.

He was also the author of such scholarly works as *The Wanderings and Homes of Manuscripts* (1919) and *The Apocalypse in Art* (1931), and the guidebooks *Abbeys* (1925) and *Suffolk and Norfolk: A Perambulation of the Two Counties with Notices of Their History and Their Ancient Buildings* (1930). He translated New Testament Apocrypha and also contributed to the *Encyclopædia Biblica: A Critical Dictionary of the Literary, Political and Religion History, the Archaeology, Geography and Natural History of the Bible* (1899–1903), edited by Thomas Kelly Cheyne and J. Sutherland Black.

James also took on the post of Director of the Fitzwilliam Museum at Cambridge between 1893–1908, and was responsible for acquiring many important antique manuscripts and works of art, including some notable portraits by the 16th-century Italian painter Titian (Tiziano Vecelli). In 1902 the abbey ruins at Bury St. Edmunds in West Suffolk were excavated after he found a fragment of ancient manuscript, which in turn led to the rediscovery of the graves of several 12th-century abbots.

Montague Rhodes James was awarded the British Commonwealth's prestigious Order of Merit in June 1930. He was a confirmed bachelor and never married, preferring his life of academia, and he died peacefully in his lodge on Friday, June 12th, 1936 at the age of 73. He was buried in Eton town cemetery three days later.

That same year, his final story appeared posthumously in the November issue of *The London Mercury and Bookman*, which had previously published 'A View from a Hill' (May, 1925) and 'A Warning to the Curious' (August,

M. R. JAMES (1862–1936) *late Provost of Eton College, must have been one of the most learned men who has ever written tales of the imagination's borderland. He edited and annotated numerous old texts, and it is possible that these labours helped to make him one of the greatest specialists on the uncanny. The title of his most famous collection, "Ghost Stories of an Antiquary," from which this tale is taken, is an apt one.*

1925). Although the author had indicated in his Preface to *The Collected Ghost Stories of M.R. James* that, when asked if he was going to write any more ghost stories, 'I fear I must answer, Probably not,' editor R.A. Scott-James explained to his readers how it had come about:

'A Vignette' is undoubtedly the last ghost story written by the late Dr. M.R. James, Provost of Eton, and probably his last piece of continuous writing intended for the press. It came into being in this way. Mr. Owen Hugh Smith was good enough to ask Dr. James to try to recapture the mood in which he wrote *Ghost-Stories of an Antiquary*, and to let me have something in similar vein for the Christmas number of *The London Mercury* (1935). The answer was that he would do his best. On December 12th of that year he sent off to me the MS, written in pencil, from The Lodge, Eton College, with the following letter:

I am ill satisfied with what I enclose. It comes late and is short and ill written. There have been a good many events conspiring to keep it back, besides a growing inability. So pray don't use it unless it has some quality I do not see in it.

I send it because I was enjoined to do something by Mr. Owen Smith.

It was then too late for our Christmas number, or, indeed, for the January number; so it was agreed that it should be held over till one of the closing months of this year.

At the moment of going to press, I see it announced that the original manuscripts of his ghost stories are to appear at Sotheby's sale on November 9th (written on foolscap paper). The original of 'A Vignette', of course, is not among them. Like the others, it is written on lined foolscap.

Five months after M.R. James' death, his library was sold through Sotheby's, the famous auction house in London. The sale included the original holographic manuscripts of fourteen of the author's stories, including 'The Ash-tree', 'Count Magnus', 'A Warning to the Curious' and 'Casting the Runes'.

According to a report in the *Daily Telegraph* the following morning, the sale of the manuscripts raised £140, with prices ranging from £5 10s for 'The Mezzotint' to £15 10s for '"Oh, Whistle, and I'll Come to You, My Lad"'. The total sale of the entire library – which included several rare volumes dating back to the 13th century – amounted to £794. The current whereabouts of several of James' original ghost story manuscripts, including some of those sold at auction in November 1936, is now a mystery.

A collection of the author's papers and surviving manuscripts are held at King's College Library in Cambridge. Much of this material was selected in November 1947 by the distinguished librarian A.N.L. Munby (author of the 1949 ghost story collection *The Alabaster Hand*, which was dedicated – in Latin – to M.R. James). Other material was added from the Sotheby's auction and as a gift from Jane McBryde, presented by Sir Shane Leslie.

Although he left behind a relatively small body of work, M.R. James' ghost stories have never been out of print, and many of his best-known tales have been adapted for television, the movies and radio.

The first televised version of James' work was Laurence Schwab's 'The Lost Will of Dr. Rant' (1951), an adaptation of 'The Tractate Middoth' by Doris Halman, which was part of the American NBC series *Lights Out*.

Leslie Nielsen played a Boston librarian who was asked to get an 'old and strangely curious book' by the querulous John Eldred (Russell Collins). Helped to recuperate by the owner (Pat Englund) of a failing boarding house after a terrifying encounter with a peculiarly *dusty* old man (Fred Ardath) amongst the stacks, he eventually discovered the secret of a long-lost inheritance written in Hebrew.

Now thought lost, the BBC's *Two Ghost Stories by M.R. James* (1954) featured 'The Mezzotint' and 'Canon Alberic's Scrap-book', both adapted and directed by Tony Richardson, and performed by Robert Farquharson and George Rose, respectively.

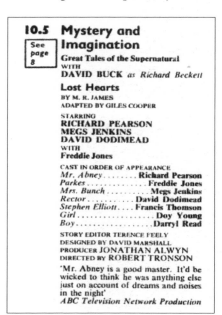

Broadcast in August 1961, Lewis Freedman directed 'Room 13', a version of James' 'Number 13' for the NBC series *Great Ghost Tales*. It starred William Redfield and Diana Van der Vlis.

Between 1966 and 1968, the Associated British Corporation series *Mystery and Imagination* aired four episodes based on the author's work. The first of these was 'The Tractate Middoth' (1966), directed by Kim Mills. Freddie Jones and Megs Jenkins appeared in Robert Tronson's memorable version of 'Lost Hearts' (1966), while another 'Room 13' (1966), directed by Patrick Dromgoole, featured Joss Ackland, David Battley, George Woodbridge and Tessa Wyatt. Finally, Robert Eddison portrayed Karswell in Alan Cooke's version of 'Casting the Runes' (1968), which also featured John Fraser and Gordon Jackson.

Although all these episodes are now considered lost, a short extract from the trailer for 'Casting the Runes' was recently rediscovered and issued as a DVD extra.

Perhaps the most famous television adaptation of James' work is *Whistle and I'll Come to You*, Jonathan Miller's somewhat idiosyncratic reinterpretation of "'Oh, Whistle, and I'll Come to You, My Lad'", first broadcast in June 1968 as part of the BBC's *Omnibus* series. Michael Hordern starred as a neurotic Professor Parkins, pursued down a wind-swept beach by a billowing white sheet.

Although not credited as such, 'The Cemetery' – the first segment of the Rod Serling-scripted pilot movie *Night Gallery* (1969) – was very obviously a direct steal of James' 'The Mezzotint'. Directed by Boris Sagal for NBC, a victim of Roddy McDowall's murderous black sheep of the family reached out from the grave to take his supernatural revenge through a painting that changed from moment to moment.

For fans of the author's work, however, the most definitive dramatisations of M.R. James' fiction continue to be the BBC's series of annual adaptations produced in the early 1970s under the umbrella title *A Ghost Story for Christmas*. Adapted and directed by Lawrence Gordon Clark, these hour-long dramas comprised 'Stalls of Barchester' (1971), 'A Warning to the Curious' (1972), 'Lost Hearts' (1973), 'The Treasure of Abbot Thomas' (1974) and 'The Ash-tree' (1975).

Each of these finely crafted shows featured a cast of solid character actors that included Robert Hardy, Clive Swift, Peter Vaughn, Michael Bryant, Edward Petherbridge and Barbara Ewing.

In 1976 Yorkshire Television broadcast a seventeen-minute adaptation of 'Mr. Humphreys and His Inheritance' for an episode of the schools'

programme *Music Scene*, about the use of
mood music in film. Scripted, produced
and directed by Tony Scull, it was filmed
on location in the maze at Roundhay
Park, Leeds, which was demolished later
that same year.

Even this short film for children
was better than the updated adaptation of 'Casting the Runes' for a 1979
episode of *ITV Playhouse*, directed by
Lawrence Gordon Clark and featuring
Jan Francis, Edward Petherbridge and
Iain Cuthbertson as Julian Karswell.

Actor Michael Bryant (who had
starred in the 1974 television production
of 'The Treasure of Abbot Thomas') read 'The Mezzotint', 'A School Story'
and 'The Diary of Mr. Poynter' for the BBC children's series *Spine Chillers*
in 1980.

Also presented as mostly readings, this time for adults, actor Robert
Powell narrated partially dramatised versions of 'The Mezzotint', 'The Ash-
tree', 'Wailing Well', '"Oh, Whistle, and I'll Come to You, My Lad"' and
'The Rose Garden' for the BBC 2 series *Classic Ghost Stories*, broadcast in
December 1986.

El Grabado (2000) was another version of 'The Mezzotint', made in
2000 by director Jorge Repolles for Spanish television. It featured Martín
García and Alex Hernández.

Iconic horror actor Christopher Lee portrayed James himself in half-hour
re-creations of the original Christmas readings of 'The Stalls of Barchester',
'The Ash-tree', 'Number 13' and 'A Warning to the Curious' for the BBC
Scotland series *M.R. James' Ghost Stories for Christmas* (2000).

'Unfortunately they were not his best stories, such as "Count Magnus",'
explained the actor, 'because the best are too long for TV. Nevertheless, the
shorter ones are well worth listening to.'

Lee himself had actually met the author in 1935, while he was a schoolboy
at Eton during James' last years as Provost. As he later recalled: 'The first

thing I saw was a mummy in a glass case. The second was a little old man in glasses with a skin like parchment. This was the Provost, M.R. James. I knew that he was a master of the macabre, and I knew *Ghost-Stories of an Antiquary* very well. And so did all my form mates.

'Of course, I heard all about the fact that he used to recite his ghost stories to groups of colleagues and occasionally boys on winter evenings, but I am afraid I was never lucky enough to be among those fortunate people – although apparently they were almost scared out of their wits by his masterful storytelling!'

In 2005, BBC Four briefly revived *A Ghost Story for Christmas* with a version of 'A View from a Hill' directed by Luke Watson and starring Mark Letheren as the owner of a pair of cursed binoculars. It was followed the next year by Pier Wilkie's forty-minute version of 'Number 13', in which Greg Wise's Professor Anderson discovered that his lodging house contained a ghostly room next to his own.

Originally broadcast by BBC 2 on Christmas Eve 2010, Andy de Emmony's misguided *Whistle and I'll Come to You* starred John Hurt and was billed as a 'modern reworking' of M.R. James' classic story. Unfortunately, scriptwriter Neil Cross seemed to mistakenly believe that he could improve upon the original, while the author's name was banished to the end credits.

Made by Anglia Television, Clive Dunn's documentary *A Pleasant Terror: The Life and Ghosts of M.R. James* (1995), co-written by the director and Michael Cox, featured dramatised extracts in which Michael Elwyn portrayed the author. Despite some unnecessary speculations about James' sexuality, the excellent hour-long documentary featured contributions from Christopher Lee, Ruth Rendell, Jonathan Miller, Daniel Easterman and Laurence Staig.

Peter Lawrence's *M.R. James: Supernatural Storyteller* (aka *M.R. James: The Corner of the Retina*, 2004) was a half-hour documentary produced by the BBC to introduce a series of repeats of the author's work. It featured numerous clips from the broadcaster's various adaptations of the author's stories, and Sir Christopher Frayling, Muriel Gray, Michael Cox, Ruth Rendell, Kim Newman and Lawrence Gordon Clark were amongst those who were interviewed.

The most memorable – and only credited – feature film adaptation of M.R. James' work is *Night of the Demon* (USA: *The Curse of the Demon*, 1957), directed by Jacques Tourneur. Based on 'Casting the Runes', Niall MacGinnis played the deceptively evil warlock Dr. Julian Karswell, who met his end at the claws of a fire-breathing demon (reportedly depicted on screen against the director's wishes).

Ramsey Campbell has described it as 'one of the most accomplished examples of British horror cinema'.

Campbell has also speculated that the scene in Hammer's *The Brides of Dracula* (1960), in which the padlocks drop one by one off a coffin before Andree Melly's fledgling vampire rises from it, were possibly inspired by a similar occurrence in 'Count Magnus'.

Michele Soavi's *La Chiesa* (*The Church*, 1989), co-scripted by Dario Argento, included several uncredited ideas from James' story 'The Treasure of Abbot Thomas', while Hideo Nakata's *Ring* (*Ringu*, 1997) also contained a number of Jamesian elements.

Sam Raimi's disappointing *Drag Me to Hell* (2009) reportedly started out as a remake of *Night of the Demon*, and a few elements of the original story were retained in the screenplay.

Co-writer and director Nick Murphy acknowledged that his 1920s-set supernatural drama *The Awakening* (2011) took its cues from some of the literature of that time, including the work of M.R. James.

There have also been a number of short films based on James' stories, including Patrick Amery's *Lost Hearts* (2007) and Stephen Gray's *Rats* (2010).

Given the author's propensity for reticence in his stories, it is no wonder that they have perhaps best been served by radio, where it is left up to the listener's imagination to conjure up the horrors only hinted at on the printed page.

The first known radio adaptation of James' work was *Madam, Will You Walk?*, a forty-minute version of 'Martin's Close', broadcast by the BBC on the Home Service in March 1938. Adapted by C. Whitaker-Wilson and produced by John Cheatle, the cast included A. Bromley-Davenport, Franklyn Bellamy, Gladys Young and the scriptwriter himself. Under its original title, 'Martin's Close' was also presented as an abridged reading by John Gloag on the same wireless service in April 1940.

The first American radio adaptation of M.R. James was William N. Robson's 'Casting the Runes', broadcast as the thirteenth episode of the CBS series *Escape* in November 1947. The show featured John MacIntyre as Edward Dunning and Bill Conrad as Karswell.

In February 1949, the BBC broadcast a dramatisation of "'Oh, Whistle, and I'll Come to You, My Lad'" as part of its *Man in Black* series on the Light Programme, and there were reportedly dramatisations of both 'Casting the Runes' and 'The Uncommon Prayer-book' on the Home Service in the early 1950s.

Around 1956, "'Oh, Whistle, and I'll Come to You, My Lad'" was produced for, of all things, *Children's Hour*, and radio's Man in Black himself, Valentine Dyall, read an adaptation of 'A Neighbour's Landmark' a year or two later on air.

'The Tractate Middoth' was atmospherically re-titled *A Mass of Cobwebs* when it was adapted by Brian Batchelor for an April 1959 broadcast on the BBC's Light Programme.

In the early 1960s, Erik Bauersfeld's *Black Mass* series, which ran on stations KPFK/KPFA in Berkeley, California, broadcast adaptations of both 'The Ash-tree' and 'An Evening's Entertainment'.

The well-known English stage actor-manager Sir Donald Wolfit appeared in a Home Service dramatisation of 'Martin's Close' in August 1963. Four months later, the same station broadcast a half-hour version of Michael and Mollie Hardwick's adaptation of "'Oh, Whistle, and I'll Come to You, My Lad'", which featured Michael Hordern as Perkins, a role he would recreate in Jonathan Miller's controversial television production five years later.

Between 1982 and 1988, Hordern also narrated a series of audio cassettes released by Decca Records under the Argo label that featured unabridged versions of James' stories.

'Count Magnus' was dramatised by the New York City Board of Education's radio station WNYE-FM in the mid-1960s as part of its *Tales of Mystery and Imagination* series, and Bernard Cribbins read 'Lost Hearts' on BBC Radio 3 in December 1971.

An updated version of 'Casting the Runes' formed the basis of 'This Will Kill You', originally broadcast in 1974 as part of the *CBS Radio Mystery Theater*, hosted by actor E.G. Marshall. 'The Mezzotint' was re-titled 'The Figure in the Moonlight' for the same show four years later.

In December 1975, Peter Barkworth read an abridgement of 'Number 13' on BBC Radio 4's *Story Time: Ghost Trilogy*, and *The Ghosts of M.R. James*, broadcast on Boxing Day 1977, featured a talk on the author by Michell Raper along with readings from 'Wailing Well', 'Lost Hearts', '"Oh, Whistle, and I'll Come to You, My Lad"' and 'Rats' by Gerald Cross, Norman Shelley and Kenneth Fortescue.

Robert Trotter read '"Oh, Whistle, and I'll Come to You, My Lad"' on the same station in December 1980, while readings of 'Rats' by Richard Hurndal and 'The Haunted Dolls' House' by David Ashford were featured on Radio 4's *Morning Story* slot in the early 1980s.

Conrad Phillips, Peter Copley and Kim Hartman starred in yet another version of 'Casting the Runes', written by Gregory Evans and re-titled 'The Hex', which was broadcast in January 1981 as an episode of Radio 4's *Afternoon Play*.

James Aubrey read 'Rats' on the same station in June 1986, while *The Late Book: Ghost Stories* was a series of fifteen-minute readings of M.R. James stories that ran on Radio 4 between 1997 and 1998. Abridged and produced by Paul Kent and narrated by Benjamin Whitrow, the titles adapted were 'Canon Alberic's Scrapbook' [sic], 'Lost Hearts', 'A School Story', 'The Haunted Dolls' House' and the ever-popular 'Rats'.

BBC Radio 4's *Woman's Hour* featured nine classic ghost stories dramatised by Robin Brooks in fifteen-minute slots and broadcast in December 2000. The two M.R. James stories included were 'Casting the Runes' and 'Count Magnus'.

Derek Jacobi took the role of James himself as he introduced Chris Harrald's fifteen-minute adaptations of '"Oh, Whistle, and I'll Come to You, My Lad"', 'The Tractate Middoth', 'Lost Hearts', 'The Rose Garden' and

'Number 13' on Radio 4's *M.R. James at Christmas* in 2007.

In October 2009, the BBC's digital station Radio 7 featured Robin Bailey reading 'The Mezzotint' as part of its *Classic Tales of Horror* series, originally released on audio CD, while Alex Jennings read an abridged version of 'A Warning to the Curious' on BBC Radio 3's *Twenty Minutes* in June 2011.

Between 1976 and 1992, BBC Radio 4 broadcast seven plays written by Sheila Hodgson which featured M.R. James as a character. David March portrayed the author in the first six, while Michael Williams took over the role for the final one. An eighth play was broadcast by Ireland's Raidió Telefís Éireann in 1994, with Aiden Grennell playing the part of James. Several of the plays were based on plots described in 'Stories I Have Tried to Write', and the prose versions were collected in Hodgson's *The Fellow Travellers and Other Ghost Stories*, published by Ash-Tree Press in 1998.

Over 2006 and 2007, the Cambridge-based Nunkie Theatre Company's one-man show, *A Pleasing Terror: Two Ghost Stories by M.R. James*, toured the UK and Ireland and featured Robert Lloyd Parry's acclaimed portrayal of M.R. James. The initial stage play adapted 'Canon Alberic's Scrap-book' and 'The Mezzotint', and was followed in 2007 by *Oh, Whistle . . .* ('"Oh, Whistle, and I'll Come to You, My Lad"' and 'The Ash-tree') and in 2009 by *A Warning to the Curious* (the title story and 'Lost Hearts').

Parry recreated his award-winning role for special performances at the 2007 World Fantasy Convention in Saratoga Springs, New York; the 2009 H.P. Lovecraft Film Festival in Portland, Oregon, and the 2010 World Horror Convention in Brighton, England, as well as for various audio books and DVD recordings.

Although James McBryde remains perhaps the best-known artist to have illustrated James' stories, he is far from the only one. There have been many interpretations over the years in books and magazines, and some of the most memorable depictions of the author's work include Clive Upton's illustration accompanying 'The Mezzotint' in the anthology *The Mammoth Book of Thrillers, Ghosts and Mysteries* (1936) and Ernest Wallcousins' scene from "'Oh, Whistle, and I'll Come to You, My Lad'", which was used as the frontispiece for the 1947 edition of *The Collected Ghost Stories of M.R. James*.

Charles Keeping produced nine lithographs for the Folio Society's 1973 collection *Ghost Stories of M.R. James*, selected by Nigel Kneale.

M.R. James' amusing

THE MEZZOTINT 341

. . . Seated on a chair opposite, gazing at it with undisguised horror.

The next moment he was half way through the window backwards.

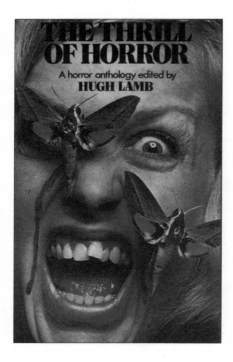

autobiography, *Eton and King's: Recollections, Mostly Trivial 1875–1925* was published by Williams & Norgate in 1926, but there was more to be found in American history professor Richard William Pfaff's privately-funded biography *Montague Rhodes James* (1980) and Michael Cox's complimentary study, *M.R. James: An Informal Portrait* (1983).

In 1956, Gwendolen McBryde – the widow of the illustrator of *Ghost-Stories of an Antiquary* – edited *Montague Rhodes James: Letters to a Friend*, in which she collected approximately 300 letters that she and her daughter had received from the author between December 1904 and December 1935.

As unlikely as it may seem today, James' final story, 'A Vignette', from the November 1936 issue of *The London Mercury and Bookman*, had languished in obscurity until editor Richard Dalby rediscovered it for his 1971 anthology *The Sorceress in Stained Glass and Other Ghost Stories*. Even more remarkably, there were more rediscoveries to come.

'The Experiment: A New Year's Eve Ghost Story' was originally published in the 31 December 1931 edition of the *Morning Post*. Once again, probably because it was published too late to be included in *The Collected Ghost Stories of M.R. James*, it remained mostly forgotten until anthologist Hugh Lamb reprinted it in *The Thrill of Horror* (1975).

'And to close this anthology of rare tales,' wrote Lamb in his introduction to the tale, 'I am extremely proud to present a story by the great M.R. James, not included in his collected volume, as far as I can ascertain never before published in book form and certainly forgotten for over forty years . . . Though I would be the first to acknowledge that it is by no means the best story James ever wrote, it still makes an important addition to the available works of the undisputed master of the ghost story.'

The tale was apparently written under some editorial constraints: 'The limits of space are tiresome,' complained James, 'and I don't know if they will take it – I'm not sure I would in their place'.

Even more obscure was 'The Malice of Inanimate Objects', which appeared in the first edition of a little Etonian magazine and then promptly disappeared for almost fifty years.

'In 1932 James compiled an incomplete list of his published writings on the back of an annotated Greek Testament whose interleaves served him as a rudimentary diary,' explained Michael Cox. 'During the preparation of my biography of James, I consulted the "diary" on several occasions and was puzzled by an item that seemed to indicate a connection with the ghost stories.

'The entry in question was "The Malice of Inanimate Objects"; there was a date – 1933 – and there were references to "Masquerade" and "Eton". Investigation revealed the existence of an Etonian ephemeral magazine called *The Masquerade*, the first number of which appeared in June 1933. There were two copies extant in the college library. On pages 29 through

32 was a short ghost story, "The Malice of Inanimate Objects" by M.R. James, who was then Provost of Eton.'

The story was finally reprinted in *Ghosts & Scholars* No.6 (1984) and received its first American publication the following year in the August edition of *Rod Serling's The Twilight Zone Magazine*.

'It is, to be sure,' continued Cox, 'far from being one of James' best stories, and shows every indication of having been written hastily, perhaps in response to a request for a tale from the editors of *The Masquerade*. But it is nonetheless an interesting addition to the corpus of perhaps the greatest modern ghost writer.'

Ghosts & Scholars was a small magazine that Rosemary Pardoe began publishing in 1979. Dedicated to M.R. James and stories in the Jamesian tradition, the irregular publication included non-fiction contributions from, amongst others, Mike Ashley, Hugh Lamb, Richard Dalby, A.F. Kidd, Christopher and Barbara Roden, and James himself.

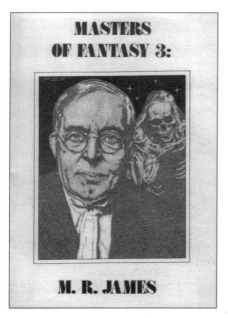

In 1987, Dalby edited *Masters of Fantasy 3: M.R. James* for a series of booklets produced by The British Fantasy Society. It not only included a biographical essay and a checklist of first editions by the editor, but Rosemary and Darroll

Pardoe contributed a guide to hotels the author stayed at, and there were reprints of James' 'A School Story' and his *Evening News* article 'Ghosts – Treat Them Gently!' – the first time that the latter had seen publication in fifty-six years!

That same year, Dalby and Rosemary Pardoe co-edited the illustrated hardcover anthology *Ghosts and Scholars: Ghost Stories in the Tradition of M.R. James.* Along with an Introduction by Michael Cox, the book also included 'Ghosts – Treat Them Gently!', twenty-three short stories, plus two of the better entries in a Christmas ghost story competition selected and judged by James himself on behalf of *The Spectator* magazine (27 December 1930).

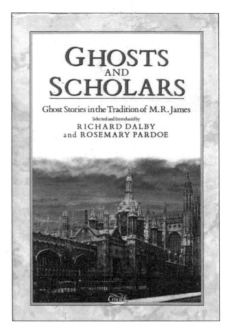

However, perhaps Rosemary Pardoe's most important contribution to the Jamesian canon was *The Fenstanton Witch and Others*, a fifty-three-page booklet of M.R. James material issued under her own Haunted Library imprint in 1999.

It contained revised versions of the titular short story draft (originally published in *Ghosts & Scholars* No.12 [1990]), 'Marcilly-le-Hayer' (*Ghosts & Scholars* No.22 [1996]), 'John Humphreys' (*Ghosts & Scholars* No.16 [1993]) and 'A Night in King's College Chapel',

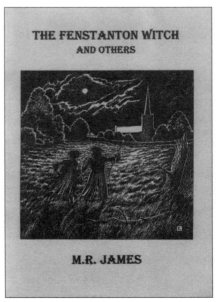

which was possibly written as early as 1892 and received its first publication in *Ghosts & Scholars* No.7 (1985).

The booklet also featured the first publication of the incomplete story drafts 'The Game of Bear', 'Speaker Lenthall's Tomb' (in a severely truncated version) and 'Merfield House', along with a reprint of 'The Malice of Inanimate Objects', the revised transcript of the original notes for a lecture James gave on 'The Novels and Stories of J. Sheridan Le Fanu' at the Royal Institution of Great Britain on 16 March 1923 (first published in *Ghosts & Scholars* No.7), a selection of letters written by the author to Sibyl Cropper and another, written in 1928, to Nicholas Llewelyn Davies (with notes by Jack Adrian).

After twenty-one years and thirty-three issues, Pardoe's *Ghosts & Scholars* changed its name to *The Ghosts & Scholars M.R. James Newsletter* in 2002, ceased publishing fiction and started producing both electronic and paper editions, but soon dropped the electronic version. A twice-yearly hard-copy edition continues to be published today, and the magazine has recently started including fiction again.

Issue No.20 (October 2011) included a previously unpublished supernatural poem by James, contained in a letter written to his family from Cyprus in January 1888. It was titled 'Living Night' for its appearance in the twice-yearly periodical.

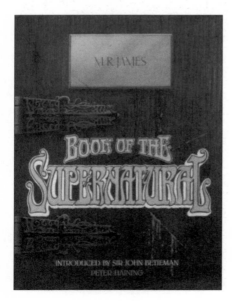

In 1979, respected British anthologist Peter Haining compiled *M.R. James – Book of the Supernatural*, which brought together various obscure pieces by and about the author (including the stories originally unearthed by Richard Dalby and Hugh Lamb), along with contributions by Joseph Sheridan Le Fanu and Erckmann-Chatrian. Sir John Betjeman supplied a brief Foreword, while Christopher Lee was represented by 'A Tribute to M.R.J.' The book was reprinted in America three years later under the title *M.R. James – The Book of Ghost Stories*.

The Ghost Story Press issued *Two Ghost Stories: A Centenary* in 1993, which included facsimile reproductions of the original manuscripts of 'Canon Alberic's Scrap-book' and 'Lost Hearts'. Limited to 200 numbered copies, the book was edited by Barbara and Christopher Roden, with an Introduction by Michael Cox and an Afterword by Rosemary Pardoe.

Selected by Ramsey Campbell and published by The British Library in 2001, *Meddling with Ghosts: Stories in the Tradition of M.R. James* was a tribute anthology containing stories by the author's precursors, contemporaries and successors, along with a useful Bibliography of 'The James Gang' by Rosemary Pardoe.

By far the most impressive volume ever produced of the author's work was *A Pleasing Terror: The Complete Supernatural Writings of M.R. James*, published by Canada's Ash-Tree Press the same year. Edited once again by the Rodens, this hefty (more than 650 pages) compilation contained annotated versions of all James' stories and fragments, plus various prefaces and articles. Steve Duffy contributed an Introduction, there was a memoir by S.G. Lubbock, along with a Select Bibliography and a checklist of James on

film, radio and television. Boasting thirty-three illustrations and cover art by Paul Lowe, the book was limited to just 1,000 copies and sold for $75.00. It quickly went out of print, and copies nowadays command £300 upwards.

In 2004, Rosemary Pardoe published *Occult Sciences*, which featured the first-ever publication of the text of a long talk given by James on 5 February 1881. *Tales from Lectoure* (2006), also from Pardoe, contained the first publication of an even longer talk given by the author on a strange series of 19th-century folk and supernatural tales from south-west France, and included James' translations of six of the stories.

Available as a print-on-demand volume from Hippocampus Press in 2007, *Warnings to the Curious: A Sheaf of Criticism on M.R. James* collected twenty-eight essays on the ghost story author, co-edited by S.T. Joshi and Rosemary Pardoe.

In 2012 – coincidentally the 150th anniversary of the author's birth – Britain's Royal Mail issued a commemorative M.R. James stamp as part of its 'Britons of Distinction' set, which also featured architects Sir Basil Spence and Augustus Pugin, composer Frederick Delius, textile designer Mary (May) Morris, inventor Thomas Newcomen, opera singer Kathleen Ferrier, mathematician and code-breaker Alan Turing, social reformer Joan Mary Fry, and World War II secret agent Odette Sansom Hallowes.

The First Class stamp featured a photo of the 'Cambridge academic and author of chilling ghost stories' from the collection of the National Portrait Gallery.

M.R. James' antiquarian ghost stories – despite their somewhat archaic language and dry protagonists – are as popular today as when they were first published, more than eighty years ago.

When asked about his approach to writing this kind of fiction, the author self-deprecatorily replied: 'There is no receipt for success in this form of fiction more than in any other. The public, as Dr. Johnson said, are the ultimate judges: if they are pleased, it is well; if not, it is no use to tell them why they ought to have been pleased.'

Given the enduring popularity of Dr. James' ghostly tales, I think that we can safely assume that the public is still very pleased indeed.

Stephen Jones
London, England
September, 2011

MONTAGUE RHODES JAMES (1862–1936) was Provost of King's College, Cambridge, and Eton. Most of his ghost stories were occasional pieces, written for friends or college magazines, and were collected in *Ghost-Stories of an Antiquary* (1904), *More Ghost Stories of an Antiquary* (1911), *A Thin Ghost and Others* (1919), and *A Warning to the Curious and Other Ghost Stories* (1925). Widely regarded as one of the finest authors of supernatural fiction in the English language, James is credited as the originator of the 'antiquarian ghost story', replacing the Gothic horrors of the previous century with more contemporary settings for his subtle hauntings. Many of his stories were originally written as Christmas entertainments and were read aloud by the author to selected gatherings of friends.

STEPHEN JONES is one of Britain's most acclaimed anthologists of horror and dark fantasy. He has more than 115 books to his credit and has won numerous awards. You can visit his website at *www.stephenjoneseditor.com*

LES EDWARDS is an award-winning artist who has established himself as a stalwart of the British fantasy, horror and science fiction illustration scene in a career spanning more than thirty-five years. You can visit his website at *www.lesedwards.com*